DAI-
SHO

ALSO BY MARC OLDEN

GIRI
POE MUST DIE
BOOK OF SHADOWS
GOSSIP

DAI-SHO

by

MARC OLDEN

ARBOR HOUSE

Acknowledgments

Diane Crafford, for her creative contributions; and Valentina Trepat-scheko, for fulfilling demanding typing requirements.

For my mother Courtenaye, with all my love

DAI-SHO. TWO SWORDS, ONE
LONG, THE OTHER SHORT,
CARRIED BY SAMURAI OF OLD
JAPAN. SOMETIMES TRANSLATED
AS A GREAT AND A SMALL.

BUT MY HEART'S LEANING WAS
FOR DEATH AND NIGHT AND
BLOOD.

Yukio Mishima
Confessions of a Mask

PROLOGUE

Karma: THE CONCEPT THAT
WHATEVER ONE DOES IN LIFE
BECOMES THE SEED WHICH
DETERMINES ONE'S DESTINY IN
THE NEXT LIFE. REBIRTH IS THE
ENDLESS RECREATION OF LIFE IN
OBEDIENCE TO MORAL
NECESSITY. WHENEVER A PERSON
DIES, THE KARMA IS LEFT. A NEW
LIFE MUST FOLLOW TO WORK
OUT THE RETRIBUTION
INVOLVED. IT IS A MATTER OF
ACTION AND REACTION. THE
PROCESS NEVER ENDS.

St. Elmo Nauman, Jr.
Dictionary of Asian Philosophies

Few men dared carry such a sword.

It had been forged by the legendary Muramasa, a brilliant but unstable swordsmith.

His blades, said to hunger after men's lives, were so bloodthirsty that they maddened their owners, compelling them to kill or commit suicide.

The way of the sword, kendo, was to protect the righteous and punish evil. But those who owned a sword of Muramasa were said to be unable to live without killing. A Muramasa blade, whispered the superstitious, could never rest peacefully in its scabbard.

IKUBA CASTLE
EDO, JAPAN
AUGUST, 1585, 2:00 A.M.

THE SAMURAI Gongoro Benkai walked to the castle window, stepped to his left and merged with the darkness before looking down on the walls rimming the moat. He did not hear the chirping of crickets that lived in chinks between the rough-hewn boulders forming the castle walls. His right hand dropped to the hilt of his Muramasa *katana*, his long sword. The silence could mean intruders.

He waited for geese and ducks that nested on the far side of the moat to cry out in alarm, but they remained silent. And the frogs continued to croak. Two signs that no intruder was attempting to cross the moat.

Benkai's long sword remained sheathed—a bared blade had the right to blood. Returning a sword unused to its scabbard insulted the weapon and branded the wearer as impulsive, unworthy to be a warrior. The sword was a divine symbol; long ago a god had dipped his sword in the ocean, held it up to the sun and the drops that fell from the blade became the islands of Japan.

Thus the sword was the warrior's link to a sacred tradition and a symbol of his royal ancestry. The sword was a samurai's soul.

As samurai, the ruling class, Benkai carried the *dai-sho*, the long and short swords, worn thrust through his sash, the cutting edges up and on the left side of his body. Both were in lacquered scabbards and tied to his sash by blue silk cords.

His skill as a fencer and the reach of the long sword made it a murderous weapon. Its hilt was covered in white enamel and gold, dotted with six emeralds and trimmed in red silk cord. The thirty-six-inch blade was slightly curved, with a razor-sharp cutting edge achieved by folding together and hammering twenty paper-thin layers of steel of varying hardness. The result was a sword both beautiful and well crafted, a sword that could slice through iron as though it were a melon. With it Benkai had killed more than sixty men.

At midnight a strong southern wind had sent a heavy rain horizontally against the castle and its stables, archery courts, shrines, barracks and pavilions. Two hours later the rain stopped and a humid darkness hid everything beyond the towering castle walls: the canals that drained low-lying marshes and rice fields; the thatched huts of the poor sprawled between the rice fields and the Sumida River; the luxury villas that rested on low hills ringed by pear, peach and cherry orchards.

Then the blind musician had come to the *dojo*, the fencing hall, with an urgent message for Benkai, who each night practiced one thousand cuts and two hundred fifty draws with the long sword. At the *dojo* entrance the musician dropped to his knees in fear, his head touching the mat. All samurai had the privilege of *kirisute gomen*, the right to kill any disrespectful commoner on the spot without fear of penalty.

"Honorable Lord Benkai, my mistress Saga asks please that you come to her quarters. Please at once. She knows of a plot by traitors here in the castle to murder our Lord Saburo. Mistress says that you alone can be trusted. You are the most faithful of any who served our beloved *daimyo*. Only you can prevent our merciful and gracious Lord Saburo from being murdered three days hence."

The blind musician did not see Benkai's eyes narrow into dark slits. If the musician spoke true, then Benkai's honor was at stake; honor demanded that a samurai serve his master with unswerving loyalty, whether in adversity or defeat. And loyalty had been known to continue past the grave. Because Benkai's loyalty matched his swordsmanship, Saburo had made him his bodyguard. Benkai was his lord's teeth and claws and the *daimyo* could not have chosen more wisely.

Gongoro Benkai was fifty, a bearded, squat, muscular man with dark hair worn samurai fashion, the back braided, then oiled and pulled forward in a queue across his shaven skull. Dark skinned and ugly, he was called Land Spider behind his back. His eyes had a wolflike brightness

12

that believers in black magic swore came from eating human flesh. He fenced with such fanatical skill that he was said to be the son of Shinigama, Lord of Death-desire and a fox, the animal capable of inducing demonic possession.

The most frightening rumor about Benkai, more frightening than his willingness to kill, credited the speed of his Muramasa blade to an *Iki-ryō*, an evil spirit created by Benkai's dark thoughts.

Shi-ryō, ghosts of the dead, those lost souls who haunted at night, were not as feared as an *Iki-ryō*, a ghost that sprang from the living and who could kill. Sinister and vile thoughts—anger, hatred, vengeance, bloodlust—were strong enough to send the *Iki-ryō* from a man's mind and into the world to destroy.

Benkai was icy nerved, with an assurance that came from self-knowledge. In combat he neither panicked nor showed mercy; he was what Lord Saburo called a tiger who had tasted blood and was therefore always dangerous. He also possessed the warrior's contempt for death.

At a time when all believed in demons, ghosts, goblins and spirits, only an invisible and deadly *Iki-ryō* could account for swordsmanship so beyond that of ordinary men. How else could the dreaded Land Spider fight and defeat as many as twelve attackers at once.

The crickets were silent.

An alert Benkai eyed the castle ramparts topped with pine trees and spears that allowed armed sentries to come and go without being visible. The massive walls were made of "hundred-man stones," named for the number of men needed to move each one, and were too thick for the crude cannon to penetrate. Benkai himself had chosen the expert archers stationed in the *yagura*, the corner towers, men rewarded with triple rice rations for any infiltrator killed between dusk and dawn.

The grounds within the walls were patrolled by armed guards and fighting dogs, mastiffs crossbred with bulldogs. Both drawbridges were made of iron and the moat was deep and wide.

Benkai's fingers toyed with the silken cord dangling from the hilt of his long sword. *Hai*, yes, a strong defense. Efficient. Impregnable. But most castles were not conquered from outside; they were betrayed from within, which explained the secret tunnel that led outside, if the *daimyo* was forced to abandon his fortress. A wise rat did not trust his life to only one hole.

Lord Takemori Saburo had need of such defenses, and of Benkai. By his treacherous conduct and vain posturing the *daimyo* had made an enemy of Toyotomi Hideyoshi, and a more dangerous enemy did not exist. Despite the presence of an emperor and royal court in Kyoto, the country was actually ruled by Hideyoshi. Until three years ago he had been a brilliant general under the shogun, the military dictator Oda Nobunaga. Aided by Hideyoshi's wisdom, Nobunaga had ended three hundred years of civil war by crushing the arrogant warlords and bringing most of Japan under his control.

After Nobunaga's assassination Hideyoshi, an ugly, dwarfish man of great cunning and charm, had vowed to surpass his dead master. "I shall make a single country out of China, Korea and Japan," he boasted. "It will be as easy as rolling up a straw mat and putting it under one's arm."

He began with Japan. Those he did not destroy, he won over with diplomacy. The Crowned Monkey, as he was called, was a born leader, gifted with the ability to win the confidence of others. Even those who had been prepared to fight Nobunaga to the death found themselves won over by the charismatic Hideyoshi. And as more of Japan came under his domination it became apparent that he had forever changed the way the country fought its wars.

He retained a huge army of spies and sent them to every Japanese province, village, valley, port and island. One group of agents sometimes observed another, and a detailed comparison was made of each report. Hideyoshi was the first to gather military intelligence far in advance of a planned campaign. He collected maps and information on rice harvests and fishing fleets, on troop movements and morale, on weather and military supplies, and he used the information unerringly. He also prepared psychological studies of warlords and their generals. A brave soldier and an excellent judge of men, Hideyoshi was gifted with two other valuable traits—patience and a superb sense of timing.

The Crowned Monkey was all that Lord Saburo was not, reason enough for the ruler of Ikuba Castle to hate him. The weak and sensual Saburo, who was forty, obese and completely hairless, outwardly pretended to be Hideyoshi's ally while plotting behind his back. Hideyoshi, meanwhile, pressured Saburo to join the growing number of lords who acknowledged him as Japan's sole ruler.

"The Monkey has asked me to tear down the walls of my castle, walls that have stood for over a hundred years," an angry Saburo protested to Benkai. "He claims it would be my gift to peace, that in the new Japan there is no need for such fortresses. Curse him! And in the same letter he dares raise the taxes and amount of tribute I must pay him. *Hai*, he plots my ruin. Yes, yes, my ruin."

Benkai nodded in silent agreement.

Saburo flicked his thick wrist, snapping open a large gold fan. Nervously fanning himself the bald *daimyo* rolled his eyes. "If I am cruel it is because I am forced to be. Hideyoshi, who does not even know his own father, presumes to elevate himself above me, *me*, whose ancestors are royalty descended from gods. Let this maggot-eating dwarf bow to me, not I to him."

He tapped Benkai on the chest with the fan. "He is a snake and if I...if we have our way, one day he will cease to hiss."

The two men were alone in the council room, yet Saburo looked around to make sure he wasn't being overheard. "I have talked to others, you know, and they too are desirous of removing the Monkey. The Monkey's appetite must be curbed. And soon. Yes, yes."

"With respect, honorable Lord," said Benkai, "Hideyoshi is too strong to face in open battle. He has many men and he has many lords on their knees to him. All have sworn to follow him unto death, as I have sworn to follow you."

"Yes, yes. Hideyoshi is the head and those who follow him are the body. But you see, Benkai, when the head is removed the body is useless."

Saburo brought the gold fan to his mouth and giggled coquettishly behind it. "*Ninja*. Yes, yes. *Ninja*."

Ninja. Clans of spies and assassins employed by rival warlords during the ceaseless power struggles that had torn Japan apart for hundreds of years. Men and women dressed in black, physically fit, and skilled in the martial arts. Masters of espionage, killing, blackmail. Masters of disguise, capable of assuming a thousand different faces.

The name meant "stealers in"; their trade, *ninjitsu*, was the art of stealth or invisibility. Both terms were a tribute to their training, which allowed *ninja* to perform feats perceived as supernatural by the frightened and ignorant.

The different *ninja* networks offered their services to the *daimyos* and military chieftains; it was the Koga clan, a network powerful enough to rule its own province, that Saburo, on behalf of himself and two other warlords, had petitioned to murder Hideyoshi.

"Our Monkey has been quite busy," said Saburo. "Let death bring him rest and eternal sleep."

"*Hai*." Again Benkai bowed his head in agreement. It was not for him to question his liege lord. Nor did he give any thought to the fact that three hundred years of brutal power struggles were coming to an end because of men like Nobunaga and Hideyoshi. Benkai had received rice, land, horses and servants from the *daimyo*, and he served him because he had vowed to do so, whether right or wrong.

Hideyoshi was a great lord, with qualities that Benkai admired. But he was Saburo's enemy, thus making him Benkai's enemy as well. Karma had ordained that Benkai serve Saburo, not Hideyoshi, and karma offered no escape. A man had to drink the wine in his glass.

*　*　*

THE crickets were silent.

Benkai turned from the window to look at the woman who sat on the floor, stirring the tea brewing in a pot over a hibachi with a bamboo whisk. She lived in lavish quarters decorated with exquisite wooden sculptures, wind chimes, painted folding screens and lacquered redwood chests. Here, as in the *daimyo's* quarters on the floor above, the straw mats were changed daily. Such luxury was not to Benkai's taste; he was a simple man who preferred plain things.

The woman was Saga, a seventeen-year-old concubine given to Saburo two years ago by one of the lords with whom he now plotted to kill Hideyoshi. She was elegant and exotic, a small woman with fashionably blackened teeth, shaved eyebrows and fragile combs of engraved oyster shells fastened in cocoons of black hair. Benkai found her insolent and too sure of herself. She neither wavered nor hesitated in her actions and either loved or hated, with no middle course.

Benkai looked down as Saga, kneeling on a straw mat, poured the green tea into drinking bowls. With extraordinary grace she bowed her head, picked up his tea bowl in her hands and extended both arms toward him. Her face, with its white lead makeup and small rouged mouth, was expressionless.

Benkai knelt opposite her, resting on his heels, palms down on his thighs. After long seconds he took the tea from her but did not drink.

He said, "I have decided. It is better that you write down the names of the men you accuse as traitors and sign it. I will see that it reaches my Lord Saburo."

"*Hai.*" She bowed, then rose to her feet in a rustle of silk and walked to a folding screen painted with golden herons and silver hawks. She disappeared behind it, then emerged seconds later holding her writing box. Kneeling opposite the samurai she opened the box, prepared the inkstone and ground the ink.

She selected a new brush and a sheet of yellow paper. "The men I shall list are important. They stand between me and my Lord Saburo. Each is a man of authority and position. They are pleased that he has found a new favorite."

Benkai almost permitted himself a smile. Tonight Saburo was taking

16

his pleasure with Hayama, a beautiful twelve-year-old boy, a gifted actor, singer and dancer. Benkai, among other warriors, fancied the boy and would have enjoyed him had not the *daimyo* claimed him first.

"How came you by the names of these men?"

"When you stepped to the window, I was about to—"

"I am here now. Proceed."

"Less than an hour ago my slave Ichiro overheard men talking in the stable where he sleeps. Certain men hiding there from the rain were careless with their words. Ichiro listened. He listened well."

"He cannot see. He makes music and he grovels."

Saga held his gaze. "He hears with the ears of a hawk, my lord. And he can only come to me. A slave cannot approach the *daimyo.*"

"You can approach him."

She lowered her head. "I no longer please him. To him I am a jealous woman, nothing more. And would not such a woman do anything to be received back into her lord's favor? Is it not wiser for you to approach him?"

"Such a woman," said Benkai, "might even lie."

Saga's smile had an edge to it. "*Hai*, such a woman might prove deceitful. But I shall prepare the list and hand it to you. Let our Lord Saburo be the judge of my loyalty. Even to speak to you of this places my life at risk. If these men learn you and I have met, I am undone."

Sighing, she laid down her brush, picked up her tea bowl and brought it to her mouth. She sipped, then eyed him across the bowl, waiting for him to drink.

Benkai brought his bowl to his lips. Saga held her breath, her eyes suddenly widening. The samurai tasted the tea and frowned.

Suddenly his head snapped toward the painted screen Saga had walked behind to get her writing box. Mosquitoes swarmed in front of the screen. Mosquitoes drawn by the presence of someone hidden behind the screen.

And the surface of the tea was cloudy. *Poison.*

Instantly Benkai hurled the tea bowl aside.

A trap.

Saga scrambled to her feet. The smile on her face was now cruel and triumphant. Reaching into a sleeve of her kimono, she took out a *tessen*, a war fan. A flick of her wrist and the fan opened, the light from a paper lantern reflected from its iron ribs and cutting edges.

There was pride in her voice. "It is too late. You will never reach him in time. Never."

Benkai now knew who she was. *Kunoichi*, a female *ninja*. And he knew why the crickets were silent.

To know and to act were one and the same. In one move Benkai was on his feet, the long sword quickly out of its scabbard and held overhead in a two-handed grip.

Two strides brought him to the screen where the sword, its blade a bluish-white sheen of steel, sped downward to splinter the bamboo and rice paper and cleave the skull of a crouching *ninja*. As the dead man tumbled forward Benkai pivoted left, his bloodied sword biting into a masked charging *ninja* wielding a *bo*, a hardwood staff. The stricken *ninja* stared down at the wet crimson line now dividing his body. Then as the *bo* slipped from his fingers, he dropped screaming to his knees and tried to push the streaming gray mass of his intestines back inside his body.

Three more *ninja* leaped through the open window and dropped noise-lessly to the mat-covered floor. Benkai, the rage to kill roaring in his blood, hurried to meet them, short sword now in his left hand, long sword in his right. The first *ninja*, lean and swift, squatted on his heels and swept his *shinobi-zue*, his bamboo staff, in front of him, keeping it close to the ground. From inside the staff uncoiled a six-foot-long chain with a steel weight at the end. Before the weight could wrap itself around his ankles, Benkai leaped high and to the left, letting the chain pass beneath him. A single thrust and the point of his short sword was deep into the chain wielder's throat.

One backstroke of the long sword and a *ninja* poised to hurl a *shuriken*, a flat, star-shaped knife, had both arms severed at the elbows.

The third *ninja*, sword in hand, charged with his arms extended, blade aimed at Benkai's heart. Using his long sword Benkai parried the attack, knocking it aside so strongly that the *ninja* was off balance, his left side defenseless. A vicious thrust and the samurai's short sword was buried to the hilt in the *ninja's* unprotected armpit.

Benkai whirled around and in that instant his skull almost shattered with pain. He willed himself to stand, to continue fighting, drawing on an inner fury, a maniacal strength that allowed his mind and body to accept the pain caused by the arrow embedded in his left eye.

The way of the warrior was death. Only by concentrating on this idea day and night could a samurai discharge his duties and maintain the dignity that was part of his honor. A samurai's life belonged to his master. To lay it down without regret or hesitation was the warrior's glory.

Half-blind, Benkai inhaled through his nose, then let the air out through his mouth. It was the rasp of a wounded, cornered but still dangerous animal. Across the room the *ninja* who had fired the arrow quickly notched another to the *hankyu*, the half-bow that could be con-cealed on the body. Bringing the bow up, he pulled back the string and released a second arrow. Benkai, his beard bright with his own blood,

18

brought up the long sword and scornfully flicked his wrist, knocking the arrow aside. For the moment, death must keep its distance.

Four *ninja* remained. Benkai saw the open space in the floor where they had hid. He saw Saga, standing among them, whisper to the leader and point her war fan at Benkai.

Shouts rose from the courtyard, the ramparts, from a tea pavilion near the north drawbridge. The castle had been betrayed by Saga, who had gained Lord Saburo's confidence in bed, and by false friends, who cared nothing for loyalty and honor. Before he died Benkai would drink of the black wine; he would have his revenge on the traitors. Retribution was sacred. Until Benkai returned evil for evil there would be no freedom for him in this world or the next.

Saga aimed her chin at the bodyguard. "Kill him! He must not reach Saburo!"

The *ninja* edged closer, emboldened, yet nervously intimidated by the arrow in Benkai's eye. No ordinary man could suffer such a wound and still stand. An ordinary man would be lying on the floor in agony, or already dead. But Benkai remained on his feet, sword at the ready.

Saga's voice was a low hiss. "He bleeds. He is no demon; he is an ordinary man. Kill him and you will be rewarded. I swear this."

Her words gave them courage; they fanned out, attempting to surround Benkai. He looked at their weapons with contempt. A hand sickle, hardwood staffs, weighted chains, climbing spikes, swords, a blowgun with poison darts. Weapons that could maim, blind, kill. But none that could equal Benkai's Muramasa blade.

There was no time to remove the arrow or stop the bleeding. Saburo was in grave danger, perhaps even dead. Honor demanded that Benkai hasten to the *daimyo*, or see the gods and his ancestors turn their faces from him. Better to be reborn five hundred times without his hands than to suffer eternal shame.

He had to fight his way to Saburo or die trying.

With the blood-coated arrow jutting from his eye like a wooden horn, a screaming Benkai leaped at a *ninja*.

*　　*　　*

A *week before the attack on Ikuba Castle the Koga* ninja *had infiltrated Edo disguised as horse traders, Buddhist monks, beggars and rich farmers. They concealed themselves in homes and businesses owned by Hideyoshi's agents, who gave them*

19

reports on Saburo, the castle, its troop strength and the weather. To prepare for the night raid the ninja spent the final twenty-four hours in total darkness. On a Friday midnight, with the southern rain as cover, the attack began.

First, the moat. After poisoning the geese and ducks, black-costumed ninja entered the water, submerged and breathed through bamboo tubes as they swam to the base of the castle's sixty-foot wall. Hidden by darkness and the heavy downpour they began the dangerous climb to the top. Each man bore, besides his weapons, the weight of metal spikes on his hands and feet, the better to grip the rain-wet stone. Strength, stamina and agility made the ninja a superb athlete and flawless killing machine, as well as a resourceful secret agent.

The Koga ninja knew about the corridors in Ikuba Castle called "nightingale floors," intricately sprung floors that "sang" or "squeaked" when anyone walked on them, reducing an assassin's chance of approaching the daimyo's quarters unawares. They also knew that one could cross these floors soundlessly if shown how. They knew, too, of castle corridors deliberately leading to dead ends, of rooms with trapdoors that opened onto bamboo spikes, of rooms rigged to drop nets down on an infiltrator.

And they knew about Saburo's secret tunnel.

East of Ikuba Castle, in a small wooden building that was a Buddhist shrine, four ninja stripped nude and rubbed oil over their bodies. Then they walked to an opening in the floor, where the leader stepped onto a ladder and descended into a tunnel. They carried no weapons, lanterns or torches. The last man closed a trapdoor over his head, leaving behind a dozen ninja standing in the light of a single oil lamp.

In a corner of the bare shrine lay two robed monks, the leather thongs that had strangled them still around their throats. A signal from one ninja and the monks were stripped. Minutes later two ninja wearing the Buddhists' robes, their faces hidden deep in the saffron hoods, sat near an open window and fingered lacquered beads. From a distance the shrine appeared peaceful, its caretakers silently meditating to the sound of the heavy downpour on the tiled roof.

20

Within the tunnel that was Saburo's secret escape route the four naked ninja ran over volcanic ash and mud, each step taking them west toward Ikuba Castle. Although the ninja had excellent night vision they trailed one hand along the dampened earth wall for direction and balance. Each had stuffed a cotton rag in his mouth to muffle his breathing.

Somewhere between the shrine and the castle, according to espionage reports, half a dozen guards were on tunnel duty. In the darkness, where it was impossible to distinguish friend from foe, the ninja using bare-hands would kill anyone wearing clothes.

They would change into the uniforms of dead guards and wait to be linked up with the ninja back at the shrine. Then the attacking force would make its way into the castle to kill Saburo and Benkai. Saburo, believing he was protected by his bodyguard's Iki-ryō, had boasted that not even the gods could make their way past Benkai's sword.

In the tunnel, the four naked ninja lay stomach down on the ground and listened. Ahead of them a spear brushed against a shield. There was the creak of leather armor and someone complained about the soldiers' poor rice ration. A sixteen-year-old guard, on tunnel duty for the first time, was teased by his sergeant about his lack of beard. Six voices were heard from ten feet away in a low-ceilinged, earthen room lit only by a pine torch stuck in a mud wall. This was the beginning of the secret tunnel, the entrance into Ikuba Castle.

The beardless guard dropped his sword and was severely tongue-lashed by his sergeant. Another guard used his knife to sharpen the tip of his spear. Weapons made noise, especially in the confined space of a tunnel, and the guards' weapons had become a disadvantage. It was the responsibility of the ninja leader to give his men the final advantage.

He removed the wet rag from his mouth, raised himself into a runner's crouch and looked over his shoulder to make sure his men were still lying down. Then without a word he raced forward with extraordinary speed, his muscled body glistening with oil and sweat. In seconds he was past the relaxed guards and reaching for the torch. He tore it from the wall, hurled it

*far back into the tunnel and over his prone men, throwing the
earthen room into darkness.*

*The young guard screamed in agony and then the scream
abruptly died.*

*　　*　　*

IT was a gray and muggy dawn over Ikuba Castle. On the horizon a
rising sun outlined the top of blue hills and the muddy Sumida River,
now rain swollen and overflowing its banks. On all sides of the castle
rice fields, roads, marshes and plains were black with Hideyoshi's cavalry
and foot soldiers, an army made confident by an unbroken string of
victories. Like the Koga *ninja*, the Crowned Monkey had used rain and
darkness as cover to "steal in." Ikuba Castle was surrounded, its garrison
outnumbered and cut off from any escape.

In Lord Saburo's quarters Benkai, the arrow still in his eye, watched
his *daimyo* prepare for *seppuku*, the cutting of the stomach, the ritual
suicide that was at the heart of the samurai's discipline. A frightened
Saburo stepped onto a thick red rug enclosed on three sides by a white
screen and dropped clumsily to his knees, his trembling hands fumbling
with his kimono. Benkai waited until Saburo had bared his chest before
nodding to one of the four guards in the richly ornamented rooms.
Stepping forward, the guard squatted behind Saburo and removed the
daimyo's sandals. A man about to commit *seppuku* sometimes let his
sandals fall off, due to nerves. This gave him an undignified appearance,
something to be avoided.

Benkai's own appearance was harrowing. There was the arrow, and
the blood on his face and chest, and there was Saga's head, tied to his
sash by her black hair. And there was the Muramasa. He had cleaned it
with white tissue paper and now it was held in his right hand, dangling
at his side, menacing in its sinister beauty. The guards had just witnessed
the Muramasa chop down half a dozen *ninja* sneaking out of the secret
tunnel, slashing and cutting until the infiltrators were driven back.

On the other side of the barred tunnel door the *ninja* taunted and
threatened Saburo. Benkai knew they would eventually find another way
to break through. This time, however, there would be no Saga to open
the door for them.

The guards found Benkai more terrifying than the idea of death at the
hands of the *ninja* or Hideyoshi, and they obeyed his commands without

question. Fear had robbed them of all judgment; nothing mattered except to obey Benkai.

He told them that *seppuku* was the only way for Saburo to retain his honor and avoid the shame of capture and disgrace. Defeat was certain. The chain of destiny, with all its sorrows, was now wound tightly around the *daimyo*'s throat. Taken alive he faced crucifixion or a slow, tortuous death from his captors cutting into the nerve centers of his spinal cord.

"A samurai must choose between disgrace and glory," said Benkai. "*Seppuku* is the way to glory."

"*Hai*," shouted the guards.

Saburo's rooms gleamed with the lavish use of lacquer and gold. Gilded ceilings, luxuriant with sunken panels of painted waterfalls and seashores, looked down on intricate ivory carvings, bamboo and redwood furniture, porcelain pillows, teakwood chests of jewelry and cedarwood folding screens inlaid with mother-of-pearl. The air was sweet with the smell of burning incense and the perfume of fifty-foot-high wild camellias growing south of the castle wall.

Near the barred oak door to the *daimyo*'s quarters the air smelled of smoke from fires burning on all three castle floors. Smoke poured from the courtyard and from buildings throughout the compound. There was the stench of the dead *ninja* and the corpse of the boy Hayama, who had taken a blow from a hand scythe intended for Saburo. The *daimyo* wept for the dead boy, a sign of weakness in Benkai's eyes.

Benkai had decided that his master must die before his spirit weakened further, before the *ninja* could take him alive. He signaled to the four guards he had ordered to act as *kenshi*, official witnesses to Saburo's suicide.

Asano, oldest of the guards, lit two candles that had been placed in front of the white folding screen. Each candle was four feet high, was wrapped in white silk and rested on a bamboo stand. White was the color of purity and of death.

A second guard brought Saburo a *hachimaki*, a white headband that symbolized readiness for a great spiritual or physical effort. As Benkai wrapped a white silk cloth around the hilt of his sword, a guard brought Saburo a bowl of rice wine; the *daimyo* took four swallows. The word for four and death was the same, *shi*. A guard placed Saburo's trembling hands behind him, where they could not be seen.

The warning drums, conch shells and gongs that had attempted to rally the *daimyo*'s men were now silent. Suddenly there was a new sound that made Benkai turn from Saburo and stare at the window. Humming arrows. Shrieking like crazed birds, they soared high from somewhere

23

within Ikuba Castle, then floated against a gray sky before dropping among Hideyoshi's forces. The arrows carried messages, and Benkai knew what they were.

The *ninja* had Saburo trapped in his quarters. They had slain his three generals, leaving his troops demoralized and leaderless. Wearing the uniform of the *daimyo*'s men, the *ninja* had moved around the compound and killed at will. Some of the garrison, terrified and not knowing which of their own to trust, had locked themselves inside a barracks, refusing to fight.

"Beware the day when cowards act on what they believe," said a bitter Saburo.

Outside Saburo's quarters, on the other side of a tall oak door, the nightingale floors squeaked under the sandals of the cursing, shouting *ninja* attempting to break in. Benkai, whose indifference to the torment in his skull chilled the four guards, turned an ear toward the door. There was a sudden silence in the hall, then the sound of running men. The door shook from the thrust of a battering ram.

Saburo, kneeling, hugged himself and bit his lip hard enough to draw blood. Since it was no longer possible to live proudly, he must die proudly. Would his courage hold out long enough to do what must be done?

At a black-and-gold lacquered cabinet Asano removed a white wooden tray on which lay a long knife wrapped in white tissue paper. Forcing himself to stay calm he crossed the room to Saburo, bowed, then placed the tray on the floor at the *daimyo*'s knees. Asano's part was finished. He looked at Benkai and willed himself not to flinch.

Benkai was to be the *kaishaku*, the executioner and second. His skill with a sword would lessen Saburo's agony; *seppuku* was excruciatingly painful, the strongest test of a samurai's courage. The Japanese believed that the soul rested within the abdomen and to open it would reveal if the soul was clean or polluted. The stomach was the center of a samurai's will, the focus of his spirit, boldness, anger, kindness, all that he was and held sacred. Stomach cutting was an ordeal requiring such composure and dispassion that only the true *bushi*, the warrior, the most controlled and bravest of men, could accomplish it.

The battering ram again pounded the door as Benkai walked behind the white screen and knelt facing his master's left side, his left knee on the ground, his right knee raised. He held his sword high in both hands in accordance with Saburo's rank.

"My lord, do not turn around," whispered Benkai. "Please bring the tray to your forehead, then place it back on the floor. After that you may reach for the knife at a moment of your choosing."

This was a merciful lie. There was no time left. The door would give way any second and the *ninja* would do anything to capture Saburo alive, to stop him from dying at his own hand.

Benkai knew too that his master's self-control could break at any time and that he would disgrace himself. Let the way of the sword show compassion. Some might call it a violation of the rites of *seppuku*, but Benkai was determined that his master should receive this last kindness.

Saburo, his eyes bright with tears, leaned forward to pick up the tray. When his fingers touched it Benkai, who had been watching his every move, leaped to his feet, paused only a second, then brought the blade down upon the *daimyo*'s neck.

There was a thud as the head, completely severed from the body, fell to the rug. In the silence blood poured from the neck while the body remained kneeling. Benkai bowed low in respect, then wiped the blade clean with a piece of tissue paper from inside his kimono. After sheathing his sword he reached down and pulled out Saburo's feet, causing the body to fall forward. He took more clean paper and a small dagger from inside his kimono, walked over to Saburo's head and shoved the dagger deep into the left ear. Picking up the bald head—there was no topknot to grip—Benkai placed in on the clean paper laid over the palm of his left hand and held it up to the witnesses.

One guard averted his gaze, and another fouled himself and had to clutch the man beside him for support.

"Look at it!" commanded Benkai. After each man had stared at the severed head Benkai placed it by the *daimyo*'s shoulders. On the rug Saburo's blood was a widening dark stain.

The oak door shattered, but the bar and hinges held.

Taking the knife from the tray Benkai walked from behind the screen and knelt facing the damaged door. Behind him the guards watched as he removed his *dai-sho*, placing both swords to his right. Then, opening his kimono, he waited.

It was time for him to open the seat of his soul, to prove his honor before the dogs. It was time for him to join his master. When the gods saw Benkai's sincerity they would grant him what he wanted most— revenge on those who had betrayed Lord Saburo. Even if it meant being reborn a thousand times Benkai would return evil for evil, blood for blood.

The door gave way, tearing itself loose from the hinges and sending shards of wood flying into the room. Masked *ninja* ran forward, then stopped at the sight of the composed Benkai. Instantly they knew what he planned to do. The sight of the arrow in his eye kept them rooted in place.

Laying the knife aside Benkai gripped the arrow in both hands, breathed deeply and broke it off close to his forehead, leaving a piece still in his eye. Contemptuously he threw the blood-coated shaft aside. His face was knotted with pain, but he refused to cry out.

After breathing deeply he said, "I will show you how a true warrior dies. None of you will ever tell of how you carried my head back to Hideyoshi, the monkey whose dirt you eat. I could kill many of you easily, but my master is dead and so the taking of your lives is a meaningless task. It is as useless as building a house on quicksand. I die to join my master. I die so that the gods can see the courage and purity of my release from this body and grant me the right to punish those who have betrayed my master. I die willingly, at a time and place of my choosing."

Without hesitation he took Saburo's knife in both hands and plunged it deep into his left side. His body shook slightly, but he uttered no sound. He drew the knife slowly across his stomach to the right side. Then he turned it in the wound, and brought it slightly upward in the crosswise cut called *jumonji*. This was an indication of even greater courage.

Benkai paused, his forehead beaded with perspiration, his neck rigid with corded veins. With trembling hands he yanked the knife out, placed the blood red blade in his mouth and fell face down on the floor.

As the silent *ninja* stood in awe the skies blackened, darkening the room. Lightning flashed across the black sky and thunder rumbled, then boomed, echoing and reechoing. A sudden downpour pelted the castle and the land around it with sheets of chilled rain and hailstones. In the courtyard horses reared out of control, pawing the air with their hooves, terrifying their handlers.

When the earth shook, the *ninja* in Saburo's quarters screamed and turned to flee. *Earthquake.* It could kill in seconds. The land vibrated and swayed, then roared and dipped and murdered the things upon it. Within the compound Ikuba Castle, resting on a stone base, stood firm against the quake. But most of the other buildings collapsed into open fissures or were flattened. Here and throughout Edo, the quake killed men and animals and destroyed shops, roads, rice fields. Fires followed and so did plague and in two days Hideyoshi lost a third of his men and half of his supplies.

It was then that he rescinded his order for Benkai to be given a warrior's burial. Following his instincts and the advice of his chief astrologer and sages, he ordered the bodyguard cremated and the ashes scattered to the four winds. With that the rains stopped and Hideyoshi's troops ceased to die.

But before the year ended the *ninja* leaders who had taken part in the Ikuba Castle raid died violently and only with luck did Hideyoshi, the supreme spymaster, survive an attempted assassination.

A few years later he tried to conquer Korea and failed. He lost thousands of men in a long and dismal campaign that was the biggest disaster of his life. Aiding the Koreans were the Chinese and leading the Chinese, it is said, was Benkai.

With his Muramasa and the *Iki-ryō*.

ONE

ZANSHIN

A STRONG MENTAL
CONCENTRATION; A
DETERMINATION TO FIGHT
UNTIL THE END AND
WITHOUT CARELESSNESS.

1

HONG KONG, JUNE 1982

AT NOON in Aberdeen Harbor a gunshot signaled the start of the race. Eleven-year-old Todd Hansard, watching with his mother from the deck of a moored yacht, immediately felt a fear in his bowels.

The women around him paid little attention. They were wives of the businessmen meeting below in a conference room, whose entrance was guarded by two gigantic Japanese with oiled topknots that identified them as *sumotori*, former sumo wrestlers. Smaller Japanese with Ingram M-11s guarded the gangplank of the yacht, which was registered to a Tokyo conglomerate and called *Kitaro*. The guards eyed the boats docked on either side and the crowds milling on the pier. For them the excitement of a twenty-five-hundred-year-old race in memory of a Chinese ghost did not exist.

The race was Tuen Ng, the Dragon Boat Festival held each June in honor of Chu Yuan, an honest Chinese statesman who had drowned centuries ago to protest the corrupt government of his time. Competing in the all-day event were dragon boats, long, narrow war canoes with a dragon's head carved at the bow and its tail carved on the stern. Each craft carried a rowing team of twenty men sponsored by police, firemen, unions, journalists, racetracks and banks, both Chinese and European. The event, one of Hong Kong's most popular, was a tribute to the vain

31

attempts by sympathizers who had rushed to the river to save the doomed Chu.

On the *Kitaro* Todd Hansard breathed in the odor of sawdust and wood chips. The yacht was anchored on Apleichau, the tiny island that housed Hong Kong's great boat builders, and the wood smells came from their greatest and most traditional work—eighty-foot junks made from teak logs without blueprints, built entirely on instinct. Out of respect for Chu's ghost, construction in the shipyard had temporarily stopped. So fervently did the Chinese believe in ancestor worship, as well as in the occult and the supernatural, that once a year the bones of ancestors were removed from their graves and lovingly washed. Construction had also stopped for another reason. The Chinese were gamblers and the workmen wanted to watch the race, on which they had bet heavily.

In Aberdeen, a village on Hong Kong island's south coast facing Apleichau Island, crowds of Chinese and a sprinkling of Europeans watched the race from white beaches, rocky coves and from the tops of parked cars and buses. They cheered their favorites in Cantonese, Mandarin, Shanghainese and English, and threw silk-wrapped packets of rice into the water to feed Chu's ghost. Some carried caged birds, a colony status symbol. Others sported caps, T-shirts and paper pennants in the colors of their favorite team and carried joss sticks for luck.

Noodle and meatball vendors had set up stalls on both sides of the harbor. Aberdeen's famed floating restaurants refused to allow more people aboard their already densely packed decks. On thousands of sampans and junks bobbing in the bay, the Tanka, the boat people who lived and died on this floating slum, banged cymbals and gongs to drive away evil spirits.

Todd Hansard watched his mother and the Japanese, Chinese and European women around her fan themselves and chatter rapidly in Oriental dialects and English. He was the only child and the only male among these *tai-tais*, women who belonged to wealthy men. A couple of them had flirted with Todd, a gesture he found uncomfortable and embarrassing. The helicopter saved him from further attention. It rose from behind Aberdeen's glass-and-steel high-rises, then swooped over the *Kitaro*; it carried police identification. Seconds later it banked left, hovering over some sampans that had strayed into the racing lane. The Chinese pilot, in mirrored sunglasses and a cowboy hat, used a loud hailer to order the small one-oared boats back to their flotilla.

Todd cringed and placed both hands over his ears. *The drums.* The dragon boats carried them to time cadence for the oar strokes and now their pounding filled his head with a throbbing pain that seemed to have been with him forever. A sudden raw iciness, brought on by the din from cymbals and gongs, left him quivering.

The nightmares had started two months ago, terror fraught and harrowing, followed by apparitions and specters during the day and always the omens, chilling forecasts of something ill-starred and malignant.

He swayed and felt himself about to pass out. Gripping the railing he focused his gaze on the sun, giving himself up to its heat and blinding whiteness. *He must not close his eyes.* Sleep had become a dark suffering, a look into hell that hid the unfinished tasks of past lifetimes. He believed in karma and knew that life was the sum of all of one's lives prior to birth. But he did not know what his unfinished tasks were. He knew only that a bygone horror was reaching out for him, and he did not know why.

He spoke of it to no one, not even to his mother. How could he tell her that he was terrified by the evil in his dreams, yet drawn to it by a promise of power.

*　　*　　*

TODD HANSARD was the son of a Chinese mother and a white father. He was a tall, thin boy, with straight black hair and a sad-faced, sloe-eyed beauty that was almost feminine. His eyes were unusual—one was a startling blue, the other a deep violet. There were similar contrasts in his disposition and energy. His moods alternated between friendly and withdrawn, while his energy had recently gone from low level to hyperkinetic and overactive.

To determine his future Todd's mother had consulted astrologers, seers, numerologists and spiritual advisers, a decision that angered her husband. "Good God, woman," he said. "When are you going to learn what not to believe?"

He scoffed even more when one seer noted that Todd possessed psychic powers, a mystic otherworldliness that so frightened the sage that he cut short his interview with the boy and fled the Hansard home.

Until a year ago Todd had been bullied and beaten by Chinese youngsters his own age. The Chinese sense of superiority and contempt for *gweilos*, foreigners, had made the half-caste Todd a target until he discovered the martial arts. His first teachers were the Chinese servants at his parents' home on Victoria Peak, Hong Kong's most exclusive enclave. They taught him kung fu and how to use weapons. In the early morning they took him to the Botanical Gardens where, surrounded by stunted Chinese pines and forests of bamboo, he joined hundreds of Chinese who were practicing the slow, balletlike movements of *tai chi chuan*. This was the boxing exercise derived from the calisthenics of ancient Buddhist monks.

But for reasons Todd himself never understood he preferred Japanese fighting forms, especially kendo, which he practiced obsessively. He progressed quickly, showing such skill that his instructor refused all payment and began to teach Todd privately, an honor bestowed rarely and only then to a student with extraordinary potential.

His fights away from the *dojo*, the fencing hall, now took a different turn. One which occurred a month before the dragon-boat race brought a police inspector to the Hansard home, a nineteenth-century mansion with bay windows, Chinese blackwood furniture and a veranda shaded by hanging bamboo blinds. He spoke with Todd's mother, a tall and lovely Shanghai woman whose black hair reached down to the small of her back. Such beauty actually depressed the inspector; he knew he could never possess it.

"Broke the leader's hip and fractured his cheekbone, you see," he said. The inspector was Welsh and had trouble reading from his notepad. He refused to wear his glasses in front of Katharine Hansard. "Knocked a second youth unconscious and tore the ligaments in the right knee of a third."

He flipped the note pad closed and smiled. "Day's work for any man, I should say. And your son is how old?"

Katharine Hansard did not return his smile. "Eleven. Inspector, I don't understand why you've come here. You've said these boys were members of a street gang, thugs who attacked my son without provocation."

"Thugs with knives, if you will. Boy of yours gave 'em a good thumpin'. Used a broom handle, he did. Snatched the broom from some old lady as she was sweeping the sidewalk in front of her shop. Witnesses said your son fought like a wild man, like one possessed, you might say. Appears you have a miniature Jekyll-and-Hyde on your hands, Mrs. Hansard. From what I've been able to learn from school and from friends he's usually quite well behaved. Quite respectful. No trouble at all."

The inspector combed his thick, red mustache with manicured fingertips and thought of her writhing beneath him in bed. "We must ask ourselves why he's become the belligerent lad of late." He tapped the note pad in the breast pocket of his jacket. "Not the first time, you see. Past three months he's had more than his share of punch-ups. Recent pattern of sorts. He's—"

34

"He's half-white."

"I've noticed that, madam." Another smile. Ignored.

"That is the reason he's been beaten," she said.

"Not lately, he hasn't. Your boy's come out on top every time of late. Hurt the other lads quite severely in every instance."

She touched her black hair with a slim, golden hand. The gesture made the inspector's heart jump. "My son has never attacked anyone, inspector. You probably have that written somewhere in your notes. Todd fights only in self-defense."

"Agreed. What brings me here, however, is the severity of that defense. Your son inevitably comes down hard on his attackers and always with a weapon."

He saw it in her eyes, a quick hardening, a slight lifting of the head. Just like your bloody father, thought the inspector. And a right nasty piece of work he is.

The inspector corrected himself. "Let me amend my last statement, if I may. Your son's used his fists but seems to prefer a weapon. *Prefer* is the operative word here. A stick, the branch of a tree. A *shinai*, the bamboo sword used in kendo. Appears to be a right little demon on occasions. Especially when there's something in his hands to fight with. Peaceful enough when left alone, but the moment the black flag goes up, he bloody well loses control."

The words were barely out before he knew he had gone too far. Katharine Hansard rose from her chair. "The houseboy will see you to the door."

"Mrs. Hansard, I didn't mean—"

"If there's anything further you wish to discuss, please contact my husband. You know who he is, I'm sure. And you know where to reach him."

Angered at being reminded of how powerless he was compared to the Hansards, the inspector coughed into his fist and looked through a bay window at a white-jacketed Chinese servant using a long-handled net to scoop leaves from a swimming pool. With just one year to retirement a policeman did not need the Hansards for enemies. What was it his coal-miner father used to say? *If you can't impose your terms on life, you must accept the terms life imposes on you.* In any case, it could have been worse. Mrs. High-and-Mighty Hansard could have threatened him with her wog father. That slant-eyed bastard was one of the most dangerous men in Hong Kong and had been responsible for a few deaths in his time, policemen among them.

As for Mr. Hansard, he was definitely a man to be reckoned with. He was a banker, and bankers, not the governor or the Queen's representatives bloody well ruled Hong Kong. A word from Ian Hansard in certain quarters could be the inspector's ruin.

He took his bifocals from an inside pocket, perched them on the end of his nose and tilted his head back to look at Katharine Hansard. She was even more beautiful than he had imagined. And then he saw the look on her face. Hatred. Hatred aimed at him for having tried to harm her son.

The inspector cleared his throat. "It won't be necessary to contact your husband, Mrs. Hansard. The last thing I wish to do is to disturb a man in his position. As a matter of fact, I suppose you might bring charges against Todd's attackers, should you choose to do so." He hesitated long enough to assert his independence, then added, "After all, he was the injured party."

At the window Katharine Hansard watched the inspector's car pull out of the graveled driveway, then turned and walked upstairs to look in on Todd. A hand went to her mouth in shock as she watched the sleeping boy toss and turn and moan. Suddenly he shot up in bed, drenched in perspiration, his chest rising and falling with his frenzied breathing. Rushing across the room she dropped onto his bed and took him in her arms.

She asked him about his dreams, but all he could remember was fear.

✻   ✻   ✻

KATHARINE HANSARD at thirty no longer worked as a nurse but devoted herself to sculpting and to her son, whom she had practically raised alone. She had been born to wealth and power; her father was a Triad leader, a power in Hong Kong's underworld. She had married a wealthy Englishman, Ian Hansard, president of a Hong Kong bank with branches around the world. She lacked for nothing and yet the quiet, reserved Katharine Hansard had lived a life of great pain, which lately she had come to see was self-chosen.

In defiance of her father she had an affair with an American, Todd's father, whom she had not seen since the boy's birth. To give the child a name Katharine had married Ian Hansard, whom she did not love. He was a small, blond Englishman with the good looks of an aging choirboy and a burning determination to lead a remarkable life. Depressed by his father's failed dreams in Socialist England, the ambitious Hansard had emigrated to Hong Kong, where business was all that counted.

In an environment where principle and morality could be harmful, he avoided both and prospered. At thirty-five he was the youngest of the colony's major bankers and only occasionally showed a private displeasure at what he had become.

He was never close to Todd. The boy, after all, was not his son, and in any case Hansard had the English reluctance to showing affection. What did annoy him was the closeness between Katharine and the boy, especially when they spoke in Cantonese, a dialect he neither understood nor ever intended to learn. He had married his wife for her exotic beauty and the envy it inspired in other men; he had no tolerance toward rivals for that beauty. What belonged to Hansard was his and not to be shared, particularly in his own household. Besides, Todd, while respectful and well behaved at home, was too intelligent for Ian Hansard's liking.

"Chap's a real genius," Hansard had said to his wife. "I don't pretend to understand the workings of his mind but he's got a brain cell or two between his ears. Function of a genius, I'm told, is to furnish us cretins with ideas twenty years later. I'll say this about his sudden interest in things Japanese: one can't be inquisitive without being malicious, don't you think? Not that I'm saying the boy's bonkers, you understand."

Hansard had to be careful when he talked to Katharine about the boy. One wrong word and she could be as unforgiving as fire. Hansard decided to go after the Japanese, a much safer target.

"Mind you," he said, "the Japs are malicious enough in their oh so polite way. I could tell Todd a thing or two about the bloody Nips, doing business with them as I do. Ian Fabian Charles Hansard knows facts about the Japanese that would make very interesting reading, should ever I decide to put them down on paper. But some things are best left unsaid. One never regrets one's silence, only one's words." He looked at his wife and thought of her father, one more wily Oriental gentleman with secrets to keep.

*   *   *

ON the sun-washed deck of the *Kitaro* a white-uniformed crewman wheeled a trolley of steaming bamboo baskets to an empty table shaded by an oversized deck umbrella. The baskets contained hors d'oeuvres, steamed dumplings, minced pork, rice flour balls, custard tarts and red bean paste soup. A second trolley followed with bottles of cognac, champagne, club soda, ice buckets, cans of soft drinks and bowls of fresh fruit. Murmuring approval the perspiring women seated themselves around the table. Todd remained alone at the rail and ignored his mother's call to join her.

The drums. The cymbals and gongs.

He dropped to his knees, hands over his left eye. A sudden pain in his head gnawed at his brain with sharp animal teeth. He fell back to the deck and rolled from side to side in a futile attempt to shake it off. His shirt was damp with cold sweat; he was fast losing consciousness. Katharine Hansard called his name, but he was falling swiftly now, dropping into a red darkness and frozen mist. The last thing he remembered before passing out was the warmth of his own blood on his hands and face.

* * *

He was in Japan, inside a castle lit by paper lanterns and pine torches. The castle was under seige and ninja *had found a way inside. Now they edged closer to him, black-clad phantoms bringing silent death. He drew his* katana *and held it overhead with both hands, waiting. He too wore black, a kimono of black-and-gray silk, with a* mons, *his family crest, on the back and sleeves. But something was wrong. The pain. A hideous pain in his left eye. But he must not falter, he must not give in to it. Stand and fight.* Hai.

From other rooms came the sound of sword upon sword and the screams of wounded men. He smelled smoke and heard footsteps racing across the singing floors. Something was tied to his belt. The woman's head, its eyes closed as though in sleep, the lips parted as if to speak. When had he killed her and why? A new urgency seized him and he knew he must get to a room on the upper floor. He must cut his way through the ninja. *Someone on the next floor needed him, but who? He didn't know. He knew only that he must go forward, that he must kill.*

TODD opened his eyes. He lay on deck, bone tired, his shirt soaked in perspiration. There was a life preserver under his head and his mother knelt beside him, her hand on his forehead. His stepfather, the *tai-tais*, and a few Japanese crewmen looked down as a small Japanese in a business suit squatted to take Todd's pulse. He spoke to Todd in Japanese.

An annoyed Ian Hansard said, "Well for God's sake, Todd, answer the man. How many times does he have to repeat himself?"

The boy frowned.

"Minute ago you were chattering away like a bloody magpie," said Hansard. "First I knew of your being able to speak Japanese."

Dazed and weak, Todd tried to push himself off the deck and failed.

"Don't, don't know Japanese," he said. "Can't speak—"

Hansard rolled his eyes upward. "Lord help us. Todd, we distinctly heard you speak Japanese. There's no need to lie. We don't give a damn what language you babble in, just don't waste our time lying about it, that's all."

Hansard felt his wife's eyes burn into him, but he refused to look at her. Damn them both for pulling him from a meeting that meant millions to his bank. This time he was going to speak his mind and tell the world that dear little Todd was as mad as a hatter. Definitely in cloud-cuckoo-land, that boy. It wasn't Hansard's style to dust Todd's jacket, to beat him, but this playacting nonsense could not go unanswered. And if Katharine didn't like it, she could bugger off.

Hansard suddenly saw an advantage in Todd's dockside charade. It was just the excuse he needed to pack the little blighter off to school in England or Switzerland where if the teachers were cruel, it was only to be kind. And Hansard could get his own back for the letters his wife continued to write to Todd's natural father in America.

True, she hadn't seen the American since Todd's birth and she made no attempt to hide the letters, which she kept in her studio. Hansard had secretly read a few, and knew the two still shared a closeness he could only envy. His own infidelity did nothing to ease his jealousy. Hansard might own Katharine, but he could never possess her. And as Todd grew older the banker looked into his face for signs of the American: all he saw was a reminder that he himself was not loved by the wife with whom he was obsessed.

"Todd," Hansard said, "below deck I was told that you were half-blind or something. Instead I see you with two eyes in working order. Wouldn't you say an explanation is called for?"

Katharine Hansard brought her son's hand to her cheek. "He was bleeding. The doctor—"

Hansard shook his head. "Katharine, dear heart. Doctor Orito said there's nothing physically wrong with Todd and that includes his eyes. Both eyes. Need I say that the doctor is not on board to indulge anyone in their fantasies. Is Todd going to come down with the same sort of mysterious attack at the party we're having next week for the film people? Could prove embarrassing to both of us. Very, very embarrassing."

He brushed imaginary lint from his shirt, one of dozens made for him at a cost of one hundred pounds each at Turnbull and Asser in London. "Katharine, darling, when we return home you and I must have a little heart-to-heart about Todd's future. There are places that will discipline a boy in a manner to make him much the better for it. Now if you'll excuse me, there are people waiting downstairs."

He crossed the deck and stepped into a passageway leading below. He was not happy with the discomfort he sensed in his wife at the thought of Todd being sent away. But Hansard did feel better for it.

Doctor Orito snapped his black bag shut and spoke to Katharine Hansard in English. "Please, your son, he has illness recently?"

She did not take her eyes off the boy. "He has trouble sleeping, yes. And bad dreams. Very bad dreams."

"Has he taken medication of any kind, anything that perhaps might cause him to hallucinate?"

"No."

"I see. He has a most strong imagination. He speaks of *ninja* and castles and a battle in which he fought." Orito smiled. "Perhaps he heard a little Japanese somewhere and remembered it, but did not know he remembered it."

"He studies kendo with a Japanese teacher. But he has not studied the language."

"Mmmm, yes." Orito looked at Todd, who held his gaze. "Strange eyes, your son. Most strange. Please take him inside, away from the sun and the excitement of the race."

Todd had been holding Katharine's hand and when his grip relaxed she looked down to find his head in her lap. Their eyes met; she smiled and then his eyes closed and he slept. Not the sleep of rest, but of exhaustion. In sleep he looked more vulnerable than ever, and she wondered if she had enough strength to continue to bear his suffering.

When Orito saw her tears he knew there was nothing more he could say to her; tears softened stones and tamed tigers. He had looked into the boy's eyes and heard his words and in both had read pages of danger. But he could not talk to the mother now. Tomorrow was in the hands of the gods and while the worst was not always certain, it was often very likely. He left without warning Katharine, without telling her that soon, according to her son, the *ninja* would kill her and her husband.

2

IN MODERN Tokyo one still finds shrines to Inari, the rice god, and the mysterious white foxes that served as his messengers. Most of them are kept up by businessmen and industrialists who pray for a harvest of corporate profits and unlimited wealth instead of an abundant rice harvest. On the edge of the city, in overcrowded neighborhoods of cheap houses and wooden shacks now resting on ancient rice fields, a modern version of the *Ta-asobi* ritual, an ancient fertility rite, is played out.

Here on a dark, cold February night, in front of a timeworn Shinto shrine, old men in white kimonos shove four bamboo stakes into the ground and encircle them with a straw rope. This is now the sacred rice field and in its center stands a large drum. Spring will come soon and the gods will leave their mountain homes to live in the rice fields. Demonic spirits and goblins will attack them. The *Ta-asobi* rites are a help to the gods in this conflict.

Inside the holy enclosure the old men till the ground with imaginary hoes. Then, as one of them thumps the drum, the others dance and scrape bamboo sticks one against the other to pantomime driving away birds. A prayer is sung to accompany symbolic plowing and fertilizing. Finally, four small boys playing the role of *saotome*, girls who plant the rice seedlings, are led to the enclosure. As onlookers clap and shriek, the boys are tossed over the large drum. The rice has been planted.

This pantomine allows the Japanese to deal with man's two selves: flesh and spirit, body and soul, material and metaphysical. Life and death, god and man, good and evil, the old and the new. All form an uninterrupted cycle, an eternal play, with neither beginning nor end.

There is also the rice ritual observed once a year, in secret and alone by one man. It occurs in the heart of Tokyo, within sight of luxury hotels, blocks of high-rises and garish nightclubs. The man is the emperor, who tends a tiny rice field deep within the walled gardens of the historic Imperial Palace. No one is allowed to watch him, but what he does dramatizes the inseparable connection between Japan's frenzied present and her mystic and savage past.

*　*　*

SHORTLY after sunrise two men carrying the black leather cases of kendoists stepped from Ikuba Castle into the castle courtyard. One was Kon Kenpachi, Japan's most famous and controversial film director. Behind him was Zenzo Nosaka, a wealthy industrialist and a power among the *zaikai*, the country's big business interests. Both men wore summer kimonos and *geta*, Japanese clogs that clacked against the cobblestones as the two crossed the courtyard and stopped at a garden.

The garden's stark beauty came from polished black rocks arranged in a semicircle on sand that had been skillfully raked to express a calm lake. At its edge stood a small Shinto shrine made of green bamboo. Resting on the shrine's single shelf was a round polished mirror and a sword, symbols of the wisdom and courage of Amaterasu, the Sun Goddess from whom Japan's early rulers claimed descent. To keep out evil spirits a braided straw cord was strung across the shrine's entrance.

Kenpachi and Nosaka bowed their heads in silence, then walked on. The film director, anxious to begin their fencing match, led the way.

Ikuba Castle, which belonged to Kenpachi, rested on a hill between an expressway and a public park in Shinjuku, Tokyo's Greenwich Village. The district's elegant shops, first-run movie theaters, bath houses and jazz clubs drew artists, homosexuals, the young and the *yakuza*, gangsters, who helped shape Kenpachi's image of himself.

The castle moat had been filled in with grass hundreds of years ago. Reflecting Kenpachi's love of luxury the compound included a swimming pool, twin guest cottages and a movie theater seating seventy-five with

44

an elaborate film-cutting room. Three gardens ringed the three-story, white wooden castle building; one was designed around an ornamental pond spanned by a slender redwood bridge taken from Hideyoshi's four-hundred-year-old Osaka Castle. The stables, long gone, had been replaced by garages housing a British Morgan, a Mercedes, a 1929 Daimler, a Silver Cloud Rolls Royce, a Lincoln Continental and several motor-cycles.

Only two buildings remained from Lord Saburo's day—the castle, with its black-tiled, horned roofs and the *dojo*, the original fencing hall used by Benkai, Saburo's bodyguard.

At the *dojo* entrance Kenpachi stopped to look east at the sun-reddened Tokyo Tower in the heart of the city. Later in the day the tower, fifty-nine feet higher than the Eiffel Tower on which it was modeled, would be hidden by pollution so thick that at major street intersections, billboards would flash electronically computed pollution levels.

As a boy Kenpachi had been able to stand anywhere in Tokyo and see Mount Fuji many miles away. Then the air had been clean and clear. The land had been respected and loved. But that had all changed. Today the beauty of the sacred snowcapped mountain and the blue sky above it were hidden by smoke from thousands of factories and by exhaust fumes from millions of cars and trucks. Wild flowers and smaller, weaker animals were dying.

In recent years Kenpachi's anger had grown at a Japan made morally bankrupt by a westernization, by greedy Japanese and Western business-men, by the spread of American culture. He had come to hate modern Japan and those responsible for it. Months ago he had decided to deal with these people. His response had been that of a samurai, one of blood and death.

Kon Kenpachi stood five feet seven inches with straight black hair, brown eyes and a scar between his left ear and cheekbone that gave his full-lipped, sullen handsomeness a dangerous edge. He was thirty-eight, slim yet muscular, and flat waisted from years of body building, from practicing karate and kendo. In exercise he acted out the role of a samurai, a warrior standing alone against the erosion of Japan's traditional values based on Bushido, the code of honor, loyalty and courage. It was a pose born of a desire for glory.

The flamboyant Kenpachi added theatrical flourishes to the martial arts and Bushido; when he hosted a party or press conference he would wear a kimono, *dai-sho*, jeweled bracelets on both wrists and dark glasses.

Though married he did not hide his obsession for *onnagata*, the male actors who played women's roles in the kabuki theater. In reporting on a party where a drunken Kenpachi and his *onnagata* lover hacked poolside lounge chairs to bits with samurai swords, a critic wrote, "Aeschylus was correct. A prosperous fool is a grievous burden. If anyone can be said to be an ass in a lion's skin, it is our Mr. Dai-sho."

Dai-sho, in this case, was slang for bisexual.

Kenpachi the film director had won two Oscars, plus numerous festival awards in Asia, Europe and South America. His movies were intense and mesmerizing, violent and erotic, personal statements of a dark vision that had made him a cult figure from Tokyo to Beverly Hills. As man or director he was charismatic and arrogant, an intellectual with a touch of the hoodlum who shamelessly courted celebrity while living in eight-hundred-year-old Ikuba Castle in the manner of a feudal *daimyo*.

The versatile Kenpachi was also an actor, poet, playwright, artist and composer, and lived life as though it were a prize to be taken by winners. He lost himself in his work and in his pleasures. The perfect life, he knew, was not doing all you were able to do; it was doing all you would like to do. Now, at the peak of his powers, he was directing his first film with Hollywood backing and a Japanese and American cast, a film which he boasted would be his masterpiece. Only Kenpachi and a handful of trusted associates knew that this movie was also to be his last.

When it was completed Kenpachi planned to commit *seppuku*.

*　　*　　*

THREE months ago the American film proposal had been one of three Kenpachi was considering as his final work. That was when he had gone to the sumptuous mansion of Zenzo Nosaka, located near the Imperial Palace. Nosaka was eighty-two, in excellent physical and mental health, an elfin, gray little man with the cold looks of a pitiless cat. He had become the most ruthless and feared of the *zaikai* by identifying the enemies of his interests with the enemies of humanity.

Nosaka, a descendant of one of Hideyoshi's most important captains, was Kenpachi's longtime mentor. In the director's early years Nosaka had rescued him from degrading poverty and backed his films. When scandal had threatened Kenpachi it was Nosaka's money and power that had saved him from blackmail, prison and disgrace. The *zaikai* leader, an excellent kendoist and noted collector of samurai swords, had introduced Kenpachi to fencing and even now remained his toughest fencing opponent. In the tradition of older to younger samurai, Nosaka and Kenpachi had once been lovers.

Throughout his life Kenpachi's choice had always been danger. This recklessness had brought him wealth and fame and saved him from failure and shame. To experience the maximum danger, *seppuku*, was all that remained to him. For this he needed Nosaka's help, but it would do no good to flatter the old man. Flattery was for the weak and Nosaka was not weak. For Kenpachi's plan to work he would have to show Nosaka that there was something in it for him.

"I speak of my death first, Nosaka-san. It will be a grand one, with a grand purpose. I propose a suicide of *kanshi*, one of protest and censure. *Hai*, of condemnation. I condemn Japan for what she has become and I die to arouse her. I give my heart's blood to free her from America. Someone must shame our country into changing course. I will open my *hara* and shock Japan into returning to the glorious Imperial Nippon of the past."

He closed his eyes. "The sanctity of our royal family is worth dying for. Let my death return the emperor to what he once was, a divine symbol of authority, a god here on earth. Japan cannot be great so long as the emperor is seen as mortal. Glory, Nosaka-san. I say glory is to be achieved through blood and death."

Nosaka fingered a long string of tiny black pearls that dangled from his neck. Attached to the pearls was a gold-rimmed monocle, which he now inserted into the socket of his left eye. He studied Kenpachi for long, silent seconds. Nosaka, descendant of samurai, was never surprised by death. Death was the embrace, the eternal night, that could not be avoided.

There was no happier man than he who knew when to die. Was Kenpachi-san such a man?

The film director poured tea into a pair of bowls, then handed one to the old man who sat across from him on the floor in a room with walls covered with samurai swords and other medieval weapons. Nosaka had given him much and guided his professional and personal life. But he could not take away Kenpachi's regrets. Regret at not having been born a samurai. Regret at not having fought for Japan in the last great war.

Kenpachi worshipped the royal family while hating them for what they had become since the occupation. It was disgraceful that the crown prince, heir to the throne, had married a commoner. Loving and hating at the same time was a contradiction, but not in one with Kenpachi's passions.

Kenpachi's main passion was his belief which tied death to youth and beauty. He was obsessed with finding a way to preserve beauty in the face of *mujo*, impermanence and inevitable change. And against all odds he had found a solution; beauty could be sustained forever, but only by dying young when beauty was at its most alluring and seductive. From this point on he romanticized death, bloody death, in his life and work. For him the death of the young was the ultimate in beauty.

Kenpachi's vanity about his own beauty was an open secret. There was the intense daily exercise, the constant examination of face and form for the slighest flaw, the fierce rededication to discipline following each instance of debauchery. It was this beauty that had brought him into Nosaka's life and to the *zaikai* leader Kenpachi had been son, disciple, lover. Nosaka had never loved any man or woman as he had the sensuous Kenpachi. Only the two of them knew how much pain this desire had brought the businessman; it had almost become Nosaka's slavery.

Kenpachi knew that Nosaka, with the wisdom of a samurai, would one day prefer to see this beauty which had given him such acute pleasure preserved through *seppuku*. Better to remember what you once loved as timelessly beautiful than to see it wither and die.

And Nosaka knew that Kenpachi's failings, his destructive excesses and indulgences, would one day exact their toll; pain followed pleasure and every action had its reaction. Nosaka was that rare man, one who knew how to be old. Kenpachi wasn't.

It was time to give Nosaka a reason to join Kenpachi in his grand plan.

"Nosaka-san, I have learned that the American, Jude Golden, is dying. For this and other reasons which I will explain, I ask your help in bringing back to life the Blood Oath League."

A stunned Nosaka pulled sharply on the string of black pearls, sending them bouncing on the straw mat. To calm himself he looked at a wall where he had hung a collection of *tsubas*, sword guards, the thin metal disks that protected a sword user's hand. Excited, Kenpachi watched the old man's eyes glaze over, and knew what was happening. The years were falling away; Nosaka was young again, a junior officer in the Kempai Tai, the dreaded military police. It was the 1930s, Japan's most eventful and violent time. The country was a fascist state, controlled by a military elite openly seeking war with China and secretly preparing for war with Britain and America. The military also controlled the emperor, clung to a rigid foreign policy and dreamed of an empire stretching through Asia and across the Pacific.

Supporting this dream were men like Zenzo Nosaka, who formed secret organizations with the backing of wealthy industrialists and retired military officers. The White Tigers, the Black Dragon Society and the Blood Oath League were a few such groups, all of which worked outside of the official security agencies and were often more feared. They posed

48

as patriotic clubs, cultural societies and martial arts clubs and dealt in espionage, blackmail and murder. Their targets were union leaders, journalists, foreign diplomats, liberal politicians, businessmen.

Nosaka, an expert kendoist and judoka, helped found the Blood Oath League. Unlimited funds from right-wing businessmen and his own talent for leadership enabled him to recruit the best fighters from Tokyo's *dojos* and weld the Blood Oath League into one of Japan's most efficient terrorist and espionage units.

When the war ended, Nosaka's ties to the league and his brutality against allied prisoners of war while a Kempai Tai officer brought him a death sentence from an American war-crimes tribunal. Jude Golden led the American prosecution team that won the conviction. The sentence, however, was never carried out.

By means of the martial arts Nosaka managed to cheat the hangman who still took the lives of his close comrades. Judo and kendo had toughened his body and mind, leaving him with an iron will, so that while others cringed before the conquerors or emerged from the war as broken men, he survived beatings, solitary confinement and attempts to starve him into submission.

Trial and imprisonment, however, had been a loss of face. The man Nosaka held most responsible for this and never forgave was Jude Golden.

The Blood Oath League. Neither time nor distance could erode such a memory.

When Nosaka looked at Kenpachi once more the old man's face was a stern mask. The film director grew uneasy; he feared, needed and loved the *zaikai* leader at once. Nosaka's gaze made Kanpachi feel as feeble and as deceitful as a woman. Kenpachi leaned forward and began to pick up Nosaka's pearls.

"What do you fear?" asked the old man.

"I wish to wipe away the shame the Americans have brought upon you, Nosaka-san. I—"

"I find it quite easy to deceive people who believe they are deceiving me. You have had my help and my affection over the years and though I sometimes find your self-love flagrant and notable, I will not turn my face from you. However, do not seek to manipulate me."

"Forgive me, Nosaka-san," whispered Kenpachi, his eyes cast down. "I do speak the truth about Jude Golden, but you are right about me, as always. I greatly fear old age, disease, decay. With each day I fear them more and more. I cannot face the idea that each day brings the putrefaction of my flesh hours closer. I have definitely decided to die by my own hand, at a moment of my own choosing and soon. There is in me less fear of death than of old age. Having accepted this, I now speak to you of the Blood Oath League."

He looked up. "I want the league to kill ten men, the killings to be done before I die."

He waited for a reaction. There was none. He continued, "You are familiar with them. They are Japan's enemies, certain bankers, a particular journalist, certain businessmen and politicians of whom neither you nor I approve. Some are here in Japan, others are presently in the West, in America and Europe. I blame them for what Japan has become, a polluted and mercenary extension of the West."

After a while Nosaka said, "Please place the pearls in an empty tea bowl." He held out his hand for the monocle, took it from Kenpachi and examined it for cracks.

He looked at the film director. "If I refuse to help, will you still proceed...with all of it?"

"*Hai.*"

"I see. Well, we both know men who kill, do we not?"

Kenpachi bowed, aware that Nosaka's remark held a sinister implication: the old man was one of the few who knew that Kenpachi himself had killed twice, once in a secret ritual, once for the thrill of it.

Nosaka picked up the tea bowl of black pearls and began to stir them with a forefinger. "Men who hide behnd high walls and bodyguards with the smug assurance that theirs is the final truth and must be accepted by all. A past and present danger to Japan. Your words were my words at another time and I believed them as sincerely as you seem to now. Yes, I know the men you wish to kill and I despise them, perhaps more than you do."

He selected a pearl and rolled it between a thumb and forefinger. "We, the league, were fearless. We were made brave by knowing that there was nothing more glorious than to die for Japan. We believed in *geba*, the cult of divine violence, which promised a dying warrior immortality as a star in the constellation of Orion."

He stared into the small bowl of pearls as though seeing the past and the future. "We were heroes with but a single burning impulse, to lift Japan to a glory *higher* than the stars. Yes, *higher*. It was, I can tell you, a great experience and a great time in our history. Never have I felt as fulfilled, as alive as I did in those days with the Blood Oath League. I have thought of it often, especially now that I am old and have almost done with life. I, too, must prepare for death, for the day when the gods cut the cord binding me to this wheel of birth and death."

He looked at Kenpachi. "There are things I do not wish to leave undone."

There was a slight taunt in the film director's voice as he said, "There were three Americans who prosecuted you at your trial. Jude Golden was their leader. I have not forgotten their names."

Nosaka placed the tea bowl of black pearls to one side. "We forgive when it suits us and it has never suited me to forgive them. One can close one's eyes to everything except memories. On the day I was sentenced to hang I vowed to kill the three Americans. That vow kept me alive. *Hai.* No sooner had I thought those words than I knew that death would not come for me until I had disposed of Jude Golden, Salvatore Verna and Duncan Ivy."

He looked past Kenpachi to the wall beyond, at a *hora-gai*, a conch shell used hundreds of years ago as a horn to give notice of an attack. *Yesterday's enemy, tomorrow's friend.* By a twist of fate, Nosaka and the three Americans had been forced to become allies. That twist of fate was the cold war, as Japan joined forces with America against Japan's old enemies, Russia and China. Suddenly Nosaka's espionage skills were needed by an America bogged down in the Korean War and by a Japan anxious to keep communism at bay.

He had been allowed to live, given a pardon and gone on to prosper in business. The three Americans had even become his secret business associates. One was now an important labor leader in New York; the other two had become bankers. All three were corrupt and greedy and unaware that in his mind the unforgiving Nosaka had killed each one a thousand times. The impending death of Jude Golden was a sharp reminder that Nosaka still had an unfinished task. Or he himself could die and face the gods with nothing to offer but broken vows.

Nosaka's eyes returned to Kenpachi. The old man's catlike features grew more predatory. "You say Jude Golden is dying. How do you come to know this?"

"From his daughter who is called Jan. She is the producer of the American film which I have been offered, which would be done here, in the Philippines and in Hong Kong. She was to have come to Tokyo tomorrow to discuss the project with me, but she had to cancel our meeting. Her father was suddenly taken to the hospital with serious heart trouble."

Nosaka closed his eyes and sat rigid, hands palms down on his thighs. Kenpachi watched and remained silent. Finally the old man murmured, "Accept the American offer."

He has agreed to help me, thought an elated Kenpachi. He bowed. "*Hai, sensei.*" Master.

Nosaka opened his eyes. "I want the names of those you feel are fit

51

to do the task you now propose. Give me only warriors. When I have investigated them thoroughly, we shall then move on to the next step. Also, give me the names of the ten you wish to have killed. We must also begin to investigate them. When we strike there can be no room for error. As to your *seppuku*, when do you propose to do it?"

"I shall complete one last film, my masterpiece, and then I shall offer my life to Japan."

Nosaka bowed his head. "Let your *seppuku* follow the proper form. Traditional wine, witnesses, the sword handle wrapped in white and such. Above all, give much care to the choice of a *kaishaku*, he who will end your pain before it becomes unbearable. It is a special position, one to be filled only by a skilled swordsman and true *bushi*."

Dizzy with elation Kenpachi returned the old man's bow. For Kenpachi the weapons room became a meteor carrying him to an infinite and unimagined joy.

Bushido. The word coming from Nosaka had the force of a blow across the face and Kenpachi flinched as though he had just been struck. Suddenly he was afraid without knowing why.

"By joining you," said Nosaka, "I have not given you the right to amuse yourself at my expense. You will follow my instructions without deviation. Is that understood?"

"*Hai, sensei.*"

"True knowledge is being and becoming. No truth is yours until you have experienced it for yourself. In prison I was forced to unlock the powers trapped in my mind, or I would have died at the hands of the Americans. I released forces hidden in my soul, hidden in every man's soul if he would but seek them out. You must do the same. You must go beyond your limits and in doing so you will obtain absolute strength of body, mind and will."

"How?"

"Bushido. By the practice of kendo and karate, combined with *zazen*, meditation. Reach deeper within yourself than you ever thought possible. Look into your soul and explore death and become truly fearless. Above all, find a way to touch the universal mind, the one mind that we all belong to. For there you will be able to find him who would be your *kaishaku*."

Nosaka sighed. "Hundreds of years ago, one had to practice *zazen* for a minimum of ten years before beling allowed to begin the practice of the fighting form. Ah, the warriors of those days. They had such wills as to make mountains crumble before them and oceans dry up at a word. What is the first truth about Zen?"

52

"That there is no unity or One, that One is All and All is One. Yet the All remains All, the One remains the One."

"To know and to act are one. All of your past lives are in the One. Body and mind are to function as one..."

Kenpachi, now high strung with excitement, barely heard Nosaka's words. He vaguely saw the old man rise and walk to a pinewood chest, lift up the top and from inside remove several objects. Then Nosaka was kneeling in front of Kenpachi and handing the objects to him one by one.

"Benkai's Muramasa," said Nosaka, passing over the long sword.

Kenpachi's eyes were all whites.

"Saburo's knife," said Nosaka. "The one Benkai used to commit *seppuku* four hundred years ago. These are the jewels of my collection. All great weapons have souls of their own, powers of their own. These weapons have given me power which I have used to become successful. Now I give them to you. Use them with pride and never forget the glory and honor which they represent. When you do *zazen* keep both the sword and the knife at your side. Always."

Kenpachi, eyes bright with tears, could only nod.

"And now this." He handed Kenpachi a small black lacquered box edged in gold and silver. The top of the box had a grainy finish rough to the touch.

"Place your hand on it," Nosaka commanded. "Benkai's ashes are lacquered into the top."

Kenpachi, eyes closed, shivered.

"Do not open it," said Nosaka. "First purify yourself. Become fit for your *kaishaku*. Be worthy of him. You will know who he is when he tells you what is in this box. The man who is to be your second will be drawn to you by what is inside this. After you meet him you will then open the box, for you will immediately know the truth of what he is saying. Do not disobey me in this, for merely by looking at you I will, as always, know of your weakness. And this time I shall turn my face from yours forever."

"*Hai, sensei.*"

"If you must kill to keep this box do so without hesitation."

"*Hai.*"

"You have only a short time to acquire a new way of looking at reality. Practice Bushido and as I did in prison, send forth your spirit to meet that of the past samurai and beg their help. If your faith is strong you will receive what you wish for. Let the spirits of past warriors choose your *kaishaku*. Believe and they will come to you."

53

Nosaka smiled, remembering what he had accomplished in prison while living in the shadow of death. "I will show you how to use the way of the sword to make your spirit strong. I will show you how to find the hidden powers within yourself. That which you least know you will come to believe."

Kenpachi, holding the lacquered box in a tight grip, opened his eyes. He felt a new and vigorous force inside him and he now understood the need to consecrate himself. He would have to know his heart and mind as never before. He would have to deal in truths other than those he had always made for himself. Without knowing where the words came from he said, "Benkai will come to me. *He* will be my *kaishaku*. Honor and glory will be mine. Benkai will bring them to me."

*   *   *

THE Ikuba Castle *dojo*. Kenpachi had kept the old fencing hall as plain and as simple as it had been in Benkai's time. The one-room building had neither modern locks or electricity; the only source of light came from two windows and half a dozen paper lanterns hanging on bare walls. There were few decorations: there was a list of ancient swordsmiths on one wall and on another, two framed ink drawings of priests and birds done with exceptional skill by Benkai. Leather and wooden scabbards hung above the entrance, their lacquer dried and cracked with age.

It was a place that smelled of sweat and straw, a place where one felt the dead cold of the past.

Behind the *dojo*'s barred door and windows Kenpachi and Nosaka faced each other in the center of the floor. Both were in *seiza*, the formal kneeling position, buttocks on heels, back straight, hands palms down on thighs. Over kendo training clothes, a quilted cotton jacket and skirtlike trousers made of lightweight black cotton, each now wore the kendo armor—waist and hip protector of dark blue heavy cotton; a chest protector of heavy bamboo and leather which gleamed under a dozen coats of black lacquer; a hooded face mask with a leather flap to guard the throat and a steel grill to protect the face. Hands and forearms were protected by long leather gloves. The overall look was both medieval and futuristic.

With the left hand both men reached down to the mat and picked up the *shinai*, the lightweight, three-foot-long bamboo foil that was respected as a real sword.

They rose, still facing each other, and bowed from the waist, the *shinai* pressed against the left hip as though in a scabbard. For a few seconds they watched each other before sinking into a deep knee bend, to finish in a crouch, knees spread wide. Here Kenpachi and Nosaka slowly drew the *shinai* from its nonexistent scabbard and in a two-handed grip, right hand over left, pointed the weapon forward.

The bamboo foils touched and crossed at the tip.

Kenpachi's face was beaded with perspiration; a vein throbbed in the center of his forehead. *Zazen*, meditation, had not relaxed him. He was edgy, the result of a twenty-four-hour fast and a hard week's shooting on the American film called *Ukiyo*, the floating world, where pleasure was taken without a thought for the morrow. This was the first time in two weeks he had fenced with Nosaka, who had been out of Japan on business. Kenpachi would have to show a strong spirit.

The film director had also grown increasingly irritated over the matter of the black box. He wanted to open it now, today, but did not do so because he feared Nosaka's anger. Recent weeks of intense Bushido training, including long hours sitting in *zazen*, had left Kenpachi agitated and strained. Without telling Nosaka, Kenpachi continued the use of drugs, believing they heightened his awareness during meditation.

In sleep the director, exhausted by long hours on the set and by his increased martial-arts practice, saw into the dark caves of his own mind, saw evil at its most beautiful and ugliest and knew that all things were possible. Asleep, he enjoyed a profane and terrifying freedom.

Awake, he wondered if it was not madness to expect a stranger to describe the contents of a box he had never seen.

In the *dojo*, flickering light from the paper lanterns darkened the straw mats with long shadows which closed in on the two men. Saburo's knife and Benkai's long sword, still in scabbard, rested on a small wooden table near the door. Under dancing yellow flames from a lantern the scabbard's twin red dragons seemed to uncoil and slither about on the lacquered black wood.

The *shinai* of each crouching fighter was pointed at his opponent's throat. Each man's back was straight, his eyes unblinking, the head erect and both elbows held close to the chest. A slight grunt from Nosaka was the signal to begin.

They rose, each pushing the right foot forward, the *shinai* now aimed at the opponent's eyes, blocking his view as much as possible. Eyes first, said the ancient swordsman. Then footwork, followed by courage and strength. The eyes allowed you to detect your opponent's weakness, his fear, his technique, his spirit. Footwork enabled you to attack him with the speed and savagery of a hawk.

There were seven target areas in kendo: the left and right side of the head; the top of the face mask; both wrists and the left or right side of the chest protector.

Kenpachi attacked at once.

He leaped forward, *shinai* held high, then brought it down swiftly, aiming for the left side of Nosaka's head. The old man easily blocked the blow, knocking it away. Without stopping Kenpachi slashed first at Nosaka's right wrist, then at the left side of his chest. Each attack was blocked by Nosaka, who continually circled to his right, increasing the distance between him and his opponent.

With a shout Kenpachi pressed the attack, driving the old man back with a dozen quick, vicious strokes to the head, chest, wrists. Nosaka blocked, evaded and when he had knocked the last attack aside, stepped obliquely to his left and scored a clean slash against Kenpachi's right side.

His anger barely held in check, the film director aimed a thrust at Nosaka's throat; the old man sidestepped and at the same time tapped Kenpachi's right wrist. Kenpachi turned to face Nosaka only to have the old man make a small circular movement of his *shinai* that parried Kenpachi's weapon upward and to the right. A second later Nosaka again struck the director in the right side of the chest.

Kenpachi charged; this time his *shinai* was parried downward to the left. He never saw the next movement but felt the point of Nosaka's sword push hard against his throat flap.

"Patience," said Nosaka, stepping back out of range.

Patience. Kenpachi remembered the words which Nosaka had him memorize years ago, the words of the great Hideyoshi to his successors. *The strong, manly ones in life are those who understand the meaning of the word patience. Patience means restraining one's inclinations.* Reluctantly the director slowed the pace of the fight, attacking but not forcing an opening where there was none. Now he began to apply what he had learned in recent practice sessions with the Blood Oath League.

He began to score on Nosaka, each strike, clean, strong.

The two were in close quarters, weapons crossed waist level at the hilt when Nosaka shoved his hands forward to push Kenpachi back. At the same time Nosaka took one step back himself, weapon now raised high and Kenpachi, seeing the opening, quickly stuck him at the top of the face mask.

Ecstatic, the director pressed the attack, striking three more times at the head. A retreating Nosaka blocked each attack, his weapon held high. Increasing his speed Kenpachi leaped forward, faked a head strike, then struck at Nosaka's open right side. Score.

The old man countered immediately, going for Kenpachi's right wrist, forcing him to drop his hand low to avoid the strike. Nosaka, however, never followed up the wrist feint. Instead he scored twice—a thrust to the throat, followed by a head strike.

Neither man spoke. Talk was unnecessary. There was only the focus on combat, on the full use of body, mind and soul in a fighting form that traced its history back almost two thousand years. Kenpachi and Nosaka were aware only of the moment, that the difference between life and death lay in one quick movement of the wrist, that through kendo they were more alive than at any other time.

Sounds. The rhythmic clack-clack-clack of the bamboo weapons striking one another. The soft shuffle of bare feet across the straw mats. The *kiai*, the ferocious warrior cry designed to terrify the enemy and give courage to the attacker.

Nosaka, with his tigerish, implacable spirit, scored more frequently, mixing feints and evasions with a skillful combination of offense and defense. Kenpachi, more emotional and reckless, scored less. But it was obvious that in the past three months he had improved his technique and above all his *shin*, his spirit.

The match ended. An exhausted Kenpachi removed his face mask, breathed deeply and waited for Nosaka's criticism.

"Good," said the old man. Nothing more.

It was enough.

A jubilant Kenpachi bowed from the waist. "*Domo arigato gozai mashite, sensei,*" thank you very much, master.

"Your spirit has become stronger. Even now I feel it. The *seppuku* of such a man is a worthy gift to Japan."

"Your words mean much to me, Nosaka-san. But I am no closer to finding my *kaishaku*. It has been three months since you gave me the box, which as you know still remains closed. The film goes well. I shall finish it on schedule, perhaps a day or two sooner. It is my wish to die within twenty-four hours of its completion. The league will have done its work by then and my death would have much meaning. Some men in the league have said they would be honored to be my *kaishaku*. But when I mention the box, they have no answer."

Nosaka placed his *shinai* in a narrow leather carrying case and zipped it closed. "The league has killed five times for us. Two deaths here in Japan. One in Rome, one in São Paulo. And Duncan Ivy, first of the three Americans who put me on trial thirty-seven years ago, is now dead. Five deaths for the new Japan. What of the next killings?"

Kenpachi, who had knelt down and was folding his armor into a round leather carrying case, stopped and looked up at the *zaikai* leader. "Our

57

men are already in Paris. Within twenty-four hours the Frenchman Henri Labouchere will no longer be alive to finance and construct atomic reactors on Japanese soil. And the American Salvatore Verna will die before this week ends."

"Ah yes, Mr. Verna." Nosaka had a special hatred for Verna. The New York union official had not only tried to hang him but Verna's greed had recently forced Nosaka to abandon the building of a $600 million auto plant on Long Island.

The old man fixed his gaze on Kenpachi. "You will listen carefully to what I now tell you. Today is Sunday. Tomorrow you are scheduled to meet with the American producer Jan Golden, Jude Golden's daughter. There is to be some discussion as to whether or not you will do location filming in Hong Kong."

"*Hai*. She is against it. Each day's filming costs fifty thousand American dollars and we would be in Hong Kong for a week, perhaps ten days. She wants to save money. And time."

"You will insist on going to Hong Kong as scheduled. Do whatever you have to, but see that you go as originally planned."

"Miss Golden arrives in Tokyo from Los Angeles tomorrow afternoon. We are to discuss our differences over dinner."

"She is a woman and will be whatever you wish her to be."

Kenpachi smiled. "It disturbs her that she is attracted to me."

Nosaka carefully folded his *hachimaki* into a neat square. "Let your power over Miss Golden be equal to your longing for a glorious death."

His eyes went to Kenpachi. "Now I shall tell you why it is urgent that you go to Hong Kong as soon as possible. My business took me there, as it did to Manila, Singapore, Seoul and Jakarta. But it was in Hong Kong, during a meeting aboard my yacht, the *Kitaro*, that I first saw the boy."

"Boy?"

"Orito, my physician, was called to treat him. It seems the boy had some sort of trance or vision. One could even call it a rather lurid daydream. After Orito told me what the boy had said while supposedly in this trance, I came on deck to look at him. I didn't approach him. That I will leave to you."

The old man patted his neck with the folded *hachimaki*. "His name is Todd Hansard. Come, let us bathe while I tell you about him."

3

ON A hot July afternoon Frank DiPalma stepped into an air-conditioned 1927 Rolls Royce, the most magnificent car he had ever seen.

The elegant interior took his breath away. It was an eighteenth-century drawing room on wheels, with a painted ceiling of rococo cupids and upholstery of Aubusson tapestry, with scenes of chateaux, trees and gardens woven in silk and wool. Once the property of Victor Emmanuel III, the Italian king who had made Mussolini his prime minister, the Rolls belonged to Salvatore Verna, a New York union leader who entered the back seat after DiPalma and slammed the door behind them.

The front seat was empty. A chauffeur wasn't needed; the Rolls wasn't going anywhere. This afternoon the car was a meeting place.

It was parked in the garage of Verna's home, a Long Island oceanfront mansion lying between a hilly ridge and the sand dunes and shallow lagoons fringing the Atlantic shore. Not too long ago DiPalma and Verna would have punched each other out on sight. Then DiPalma had been a much decorated New York City narcotics detective, responsible for Verna's only prison term, a one-year sentence for refusing to cooperate with a grand jury. In retaliation the mob-connected Verna had put out a contract on him.

Now Frank DiPalma was a popular television crime reporter and Sally

Verna was still a corrupt labor leader. He was looking to DiPalma to keep him alive.

The garage door was raised, allowing DiPalma to take in the grounds of Verna's luxury home. Straight ahead was a collection of topiary sculpture—a large bear, lion and rhino expertly clipped out of dark green hedges. To the right three of Verna's grandchildren played in a swimming pool of Carrara marble edged in imitation Greek columns and black sphinxes. DiPalma had seen the mansion from the outside after being passed through the gates by a pair of armed guards. It was constructed of white marble, with a grand staircase visible through open french doors, and a patio ringed by stone cherubs riding stone dolphins.

A goddamn ice palace, DiPalma thought.

A private dock, a cabin cruiser and a pair of motorboats came with the estate, which had been built by a twenties bootlegger for his sixteen-year-old bride. Sally Verna had it all.

DiPalma stroked a silver-topped black oak cane, his trademark and favorite weapon; he was an expert kendoist and skilled in *escrima* and *arnis*, the Filipino stick-fighting arts. His mind wasn't on this meeting with Sally Verna; it was in Hong Kong with Katharine Hansard, the Chinese woman who had given him the cane, the woman he had once loved and had not seen in eleven years.

His mind was also on Todd, his son by Katharine. DiPalma had never seen the boy, only photographs of him. Yesterday DiPalma had received an urgent telephone call from her, begging him to come to Hong Kong immediately. Katharine feared for her life. And Todd's. The boy had had a vision indicating they were both in danger.

DiPalma was bone tired. There had been a piece of film which had to be edited and an assignment which had to be postponed and a station manager and producer who had to be convinced that if they didn't let him go he would go anyway, even if it meant getting fired. The script for an already filmed piece had to be rewritten and recorded in a hurry.

DiPalma had little time for Sally Verna. A half hour, no more. After that the limousine which had brought the former detective to Long Island was going to take him to Kennedy International Airport for the fourteen-hour flight to Hong Kong and Katharine. A sleeping memory awakened within him, thoughts of another woman who had once needed his help. Lynn, his dead wife. She had died in a hostage situation gone wrong, the result of a plot against DiPalma by a crazed and vengeful drug dealer.

Something else nagged at him. Katharine's father, a Triad leader, had vowed to kill DiPalma if he set foot in Hong Kong again. Her pregnancy by a white man had been shameful, a disgrace to a man in her father's

60

position. But he could not abandon Katharine. DiPalma had already failed one woman, burden enough on his conscience.

Frank DiPalma was in his mid-forties, six feet tall and bulky, a graying bear of a man with hooded eyes and a flat-faced look that women found handsome. He walked with a barely perceptible limp and had a sleepy-eyed, threatening sexuality. He had been a New York City cop for twenty years, most of it on the vice squad where he worked narcotics. Rising to the rank of detective lieutenant, he had served on DEA and FBI task forces and been an adviser on drug crimes to police departments throughout the United States and overseas.

Even after leaving the department DiPalma's reports on drug trafficking were required reading among drug enforcement officials worldwide.

Two years ago he had gone into television broadcasting. Capitalizing on twenty years of police experience, street smarts and an uncompromising honesty, he had become a media star at an unexpected age. With his polite menacing calm, the husky-voiced former detective reported on crime as TV audiences never knew it, speaking without exaggeration or sentimentality and always with a terrifying clarity. His sources of information, drawn from his past, were unmatched by rivals: from a mob hit man to a senator's mistress, from the chief of a Rome film studio to the head of the Justice Department in Washington.

The results were prize-winning investigative reports, high ratings, fan mail and enemies. The enemies were the Suits, the television and advertising executives whose advice he ignored while continuing to report what he considered was the truth.

"You let yourself be influenced by people you want to please," he had said to his attorney. Because of DiPalma's popularity and critical acclaim the attorney had twice been called in by the network to renegotiate a new contract. The most recent one was for six figures a year, with a three-year guarantee.

DiPalma said, "You *allow* yourself to be influenced. And it's usually because you're anxious to have somebody's goodwill. Well, I'll let you in on a little secret. I don't fucking care about the Suits' goodwill."

"Right now you don't," said his attorney. "When you're hot, you're hot. And when you're not, you're not. What happens when it stops, when the ratings go into the toilet and you stop winning prizes?"

DiPalma lifted his cane to his mouth, breathed on its silver top, then polished the metal with a black silk handkerchief. When he had achieved the desired luster he said, "Am I correct in assuming that I have lived over forty years without the Suits? And in that time did I not eat three meals a day, wear clean socks and cross the street without getting hit by an iceberg? I could walk away from broadcasting tomorrow if I had to and never look back."

For sure, thought the attorney. When the Suits had tried to get DiPalma to dye his hair, wear horn-rimmed glasses and a vest, he had walked. When they had told him he was overweight, needed to smile more and should take speech lessons, he had walked. Now they left him alone. Now they believed he did not need them. And so they wanted him all the more.

The attorney stroked his nose with a pinky finger. Independence wasn't for everybody. Frank DiPalma, on the other hand, wasn't everybody. Frankie boy knew the secret. Have the strength to stand alone in the midst of others and if you had to, against others. The attorney envied him for that. He disliked the big man for it, too. DiPalma reminded the attorney of what he himself might have been and wasn't.

*   *   *

IN the Rolls, DiPalma watched Sally Verna light a cigarette with a trembling hand. Verna was a balding, sawed-off bull of a man in his mid-sixties, with a small nervous mouth and a physique kept hard-muscled through weight lifting. For almost thirty years he had headed a New York automotive workers' union, one of the largest in the country. The union had become completely mob dominated; it had also formed alliances with other Eastern unions to give Verna and the mob extra-ordinary power.

In addition to controlling thousands of Eastern automotive workers, Verna and his underworld associates controlled freight handlers, security guards and clerks at half a dozen major Eastern airports. They also owned banks, real estate and mortgages in several cities, had investments in Atlantic City, Las Vegas and Caribbean casinos and administered a pension fund worth billions of dollars.

Verna himself held paying positions in at least six mob-dominated unions—local, regional and international—all of which allowed him to sell sweetheart contracts, with substandard wages and benefits.

Men in Sally Verna's position usually had others do their killings for them. But Verna was different. DiPalma knew that the cunning and unforgiving union leader had killed at least twice. Not because he had to, but because he wanted to. An associate had once betrayed him, then fled New York. Eighteen years later he returned, his appearance changed;

he believed he couldn't be recognized and the trouble between him and Sally was forgotten. As he sipped beer in a Queens bar, a man came up behind him and put three bullets in his head. Twenty patrons in the bar, however, never saw Sally Verna pull the trigger.

The informant who had helped DiPalma bring Verna before a grand jury fared worse. Verna learned his identity and had him taken to an Astoria warehouse and hung on meat hooks. The labor leader then personally tortured him with an electric cattle prod; to make the informant's death as painful as possible he was doused with water to give the prod a stronger charge. It took the man three days to die and Sally Verna was there each day, watching the informant scream and flop around on the meat hooks, which dug into his flesh whenever he twitched.

DiPalma wondered if Verna feared punishment for either crime.

Verna screwed his half-smoked cigarette into the ashtray of the Rolls and immediately lit another. "Wasn't sure you'd come." He picked up a hand radio lying on the seat between his legs. "I'll have somebody bring you a drink."

DiPalma shook his head. He hadn't had a drink in eleven years, not since that night in Hong Kong when a shotgun blast had shattered his left hip, almost torn his left arm from its socket and left him with a stomach that could not tolerate booze or spicy foods.

He said to Verna, "I'm here because I get paid for reporting. On the phone you said something about a very big story, something you could only talk to me about. And we both know you've got nothing to gain by lying to me."

"What's with lying? Hear me out, then decide for yourself. Think I'll skip that drink, too. Stomach's acting up. Before I go into this thing, we're meeting out here in the garage 'cause I don't want my wife seeing us together. She knows you and me bumped heads in the past. She's just getting over a heart bypass and I don't want her worrying. She's out sailing with my daughter and son-in-law. Gives me a chance to enjoy my grandchildren. *Enjoy*. Shit."

Verna blew smoke at the polished redwood steering wheel. "Understand you're going to Hong Kong."

DiPalma's eyes narrowed. "Since when did my travel plans interest you?"

"Hey, don't get me wrong. What you're doing over there is your business. I didn't ask and I don't want to know. I just heard you're going, is all."

"Nobody knows why I'm going and you're right, it is my business."

"DiPalma, it's not easy for me to come to you. I did it because the trouble I'm in might come down on my family and I'd like to stop that if I can. I got no right to ask you for a favor, but I'm asking. You're going to Hong Kong and you're the one guy I know can't be bought or scared off. Truth is, you go with this thing and you could run into problems."

"Such as?"

Verna studied him carefully. "Such as some very heavy people in Japan and their American friends coming down on you. People with money and power like you wouldn't fucking believe."

DiPalma looked at his wristwatch. "Sally, you have twenty-seven minutes. After that, I'm on my way to the airport."

Verna rubbed his balding head with a calloused hand. "Okay, okay. I want something from you, but I'm paying off with the biggest story you'll ever come up with. I want you to pick up a package for me in Hong Kong. It ain't what you're thinking, so don't jump salty. No dope, no jewelry, no cash. Nothing illegal. I'm not running a game on you. Sally Verna's brains ain't in his ass."

DiPalma turned in his seat until he faced the labor leader. The former detective's smile was chilly. "Sally, if I even *thought* you were setting me up or trying to get even for that fall you took, I would tear you on the dotted line right here and now."

"Hey, if it makes you feel any better, you can check out the package."

"As sure as the bear shits in the woods, I'd check it out. What's in it?"

"It's a file. Some records. Bank records, reports, correspondence. A lot of papers."

"So what's wrong with the mails? Or having one of your bent-nosed friends go and get it for you?"

Verna took his time answering. He didn't look at DiPalma. "There's an inside guy at a big bank over there who's been collecting stuff on the way the bank operates. It won't do him any good to be seen with me or any of my people. He wants like a third party, somebody neutral between him and me. He also ain't giving it away. We'll be paying plenty for that file."

"We?"

"I got a friend whose name I ain't gonna mention. Not yet, anyway. In any case, this stuff's too valuable to put in the mail or trust to just anybody to carry around. The guy who brings it back should be able to take care of himself. He's gonna need king-sized balls."

So you're warning me, thought DiPalma. He watched Verna drag deeply on his cigarette and saw the fear in his eyes. DiPalma had never really stopped thinking of himself as a cop, and much of a cop's knowledge was primarily guesswork. You combined that with speculation, supposition and you threw in a few "what ifs." This meant trusting your instinct. Instinct said that Sally Verna, a man who did not scare easily, was, at the moment, too terrified to lie.

DiPalma said, "About this story, how big is big?"

"Fair enough. I swear on the heads of my grandchildren it's the biggest story of your life."

"And to get it I have to bring you back a package from Hong Kong. What's wrong with just sending you back a postcard?"

"DiPalma, there ain't no free lunch in this world. You play, you pay."

DiPalma tapped Verna's knee gently with the cane. "You're forgetting something. You came to me, I didn't come to you. That means *you* pay. And I'm not a player. Not yet."

Verna snorted, sending twin spears of smoke from a heavily veined nose. "Have it your way. Ever hear of the Blood Oath League?"

DiPalma had to stop himself from laughing out loud. "Sounds like friends of yours. White on white shirts, bent noses and diamond pinky rings."

"Very fucking funny. A few weeks ago in San Francisco a banker named Duncan Ivy was killed."

DiPalma yawned and nodded. "Cops feel that one could be another Manson-type killing. Yeah, I remember. Ivy, his wife, and Ivy's lawyer and his teenage daughter, who apparently just happened to be visiting. Wrong place at the wrong time. Everybody sliced to pieces with knives, swords. Maybe machetes. No suspects, no motive."

Verna stuffed out an unfinished cigarette. "You don't know the half of it, buddy boy. The president of a Japanese aerospace company was down in Brazil for a business conference—"

"São Paulo. Same thing happened to him and two bodyguards. We've got a newsroom down at the station, Sally. Stuff coming in over every kind of machine you can think of. I've been known to read some of it now and then."

"So you know. You know about the Japanese reporter in Tokyo? Or the Japanese construction guy in Osaka? Or the Italian count in Rome who was trying to sell the Japanese government on building an airport that would have been the largest in the world?"

DiPalma rolled the cane between the palms of his hands and waited.

"The Blood Oath League," said Verna. "It killed them all."

"You make it sound like gospel. Maybe you'd better tell me where your information comes from."

"My information's righteous. Believe me, it's good. But like you said, you ain't a player yet, so let's just go easy on names. You don't go around giving away your informants, so don't expect me to be no different.

65

Not til you come on board. Let's just say I got a friend who's an expert on Japan. He's also tight with what you call 'the intelligence community.' He's fucking good at getting the facts, my friend. For now we call him Mr. O. 'cause he's always organizing."

"And Mr. O. has contacts with the French police?"

"Mr. O. is pretty fucking wired, let me tell you. You asked me about the Blood Oath League. For openers, it's Japanese."

Verna told DiPalma about the league, the old and new versions.

"Who's calling the shots on the new version?"

"Zenzo Nosaka. Same man who called the shots on the old one."

"Jesus." DiPalma's head flopped back against the seat. He focused on a pair of entwined cupids directly above him.

"You know Nosaka?" asked Verna.

Not just Nosaka, thought DiPalma, but Kon Kenpachi, his great and good friend. The two Japanese were inseparable and shared a deep interest in right-wing politics. DiPalma had never met Nosaka, but he had come face to face with Kenpachi more than once. The American and the Japanese hated each other. Both were linked by *ken*, the sword; it was the sword which had made them enemies.

Following the almost fatal attempt on his life in Hong Kong, DiPalma had regained his strength and the use of his left arm through kendo. His health had improved and kendo had become a fixation with him. He had a natural talent for sword and stick fighting. This, along with a cop's persistence, had led him to become an expert on samurai swords, their history, the men who forged them, the emperors and warriors who owned them.

With a growing reputation as a kendoist and sword historian, DiPalma was asked to speak before Japanese history groups in American colleges and universities, before groups of American businessmen and others interested In Japanese culture. He began collecting swords and writing his own history of their pedigrees, traveling to Japan to research the weapons and their makers. Then he wrote a book on Japanese swords and swordsmanship, which made his reputation. Western collectors, antique dealers, even Japanese, sought his opinion on a sword's authenticity.

Skilled at detecting forgeries DiPalma, while in Japan, pronounced a famed sword as merely an excellent copy. The sword belonged to Kenpachi, who denounced DiPalma as an ignorant and publicity-seeking *gaijin*. DiPalma was proven right and Kenpachi never forgave him. No white man could be superior to a Japanese kendoist in knowledge or fighting skill.

Kenpachi's hatred of DiPalma took a peculiar form. In the former detective's kendo club in New York, a mysterious fighter challenged him to a match. DiPalma accepted. The match was hard fought and dangerous but DiPalma defeated the man, who left without unmasking himself.

Later he learned that his opponent had been Kenpachi, who had flown to New York to challenge DiPalma. It was the flamboyant Kenpachi's style to make such a trip, to protect his pride by fighting masked. The defeat, however, was never forgotten. DiPalma became his sworn enemy.

DiPalma asked, "Did Kon Kenpachi's name come up in connection with the Blood Oath League?"

"No. Who's he?"

"Friend of Nosaka's. You asked me if I knew Nosaka. I don't, but I know of him. Son of a bitch is over eighty, wears cloaks and derbies and is one hell of a kendo man. Kendo's—"

"I know what it is. I spent time in Japan after the second World War. That's where I met Nosaka."

DiPalma, alert, sat up straight. It wasn't knowing a lot that made you smart; it was knowing what was necessary. The killings in Rome and San Francisco were facts and the other murders could be checked out easily enough. And Zenzo Nosaka was alive and well and fencing his ass off. On the surface, Sally Verna's story seemed to be coming together. His fear had to be caused by something or someone very special. Such as Zenzo Nosaka.

Why did Nosaka want Sally Verna dead? And how could bank records and correspondence in Hong Kong keep Sally alive?

DiPalma wondered about the two players Sally was protecting. There was Mr. O., who collected information, and there was the mystery man in Hong Kong, who was sitting on a special package Sally wanted brought to him.

Verna said, "I give you Nosaka and the Blood Oath League. You bring me back those records from Hong Kong. Like I said, check 'em out. Make sure you're not smuggling dope into the country or something."

"I have a question about your little package. Say I check out the papers and find you and your Mr. O. implicated in something naughty."

"For Christ's sake, DiPalma, ain't it enough you already put me in the slammer one time? Okay, okay, maybe, just maybe, my name and my friend's might turn up in those records. A few bucks may have changed hands, but that's it with us. For what I'm giving you on Nosaka, you can afford to forget about me and Mr. O. Fact is, I want your word that we ain't mentioned in any story."

I bet you do, thought DiPalma. Which was worse—breaking his word to Sally or keeping it? "Tell you what," he said, "let's put any promise like that on hold."

"What fucking choice do I have? Look, Nosaka's the big guy. Bring him down and you'll be doing the whole fucking country a favor, considering the way he does business over here."

"What about the way he does business?"

"Buddy boy, it's an offense against Jesus, I'm telling you. Payoffs here and in a dozen countries. Bribes to different governments, to guys down in Washington, to customs in any country you can name. Industrial espionage, blackmail. How the fuck you think Japan got to be so rich?"

DiPalma grinned. "I hate to tell you this, Sally, but he sounds a little like you and the boys."

"Listen, I didn't bring you out here to get zapped. I'm telling you about Nosaka, about him killing people, about him paying off half the fucking world. Japs call it *shieh lei*, bribes. Except nobody does it like Nosaka. And to do that he's got to move a lot of money around, I mean a lot."

"Through his bank?"

"You got it, buddy boy. And through a few other cute maneuvers, too. That's what I meant when I said you got to be careful on this thing. He's got heavy friends, people he's been payin' big bucks to for years. Bring him down and you can write your own ticket for the rest of your life, I'm telling you."

Easier said than done, thought DiPalma. Nosaka was one of the richest men in Japan, hell, in the world. He controlled companies that manufactured cars, trucks and electronic products. He owned international real estate and controlled a bank with branches in over fifty countries. He did indeed have friends in high places, including Washington. The price you paid for taking on somebody like that was to see a close-up of his ugly side.

DiPalma, an expert at reading faces and masks, knew that up until now Sally Verna had been doling out the truth in small doses. The labor leader seemed undecided as to which bridges to burn and which to cross. DiPalma gave him a push.

"Sally, we're running out of time. You're in bed with Nosaka, I don't know how, I don't know why, but you are and that's why he wants to ice you. From the top, Sally, and straight. What's joining you and the old man at the hip and why does he want to put out your lights?"

Verna turned from DiPalma to stare at a coiled hose hanging on the garage wall. The cigarette between his fingers was forgotten. "It was 1946. I was still in the army and in Tokyo working with the International Military Tribunal for the Far East. We went after Japanese war criminals. I bounced back and forth between the Central War Crimes Agency and the War Crimes Prosecuting Office. Shit, we were all hot to trot, a bunch of young wiseasses who were going to make the world safe for democracy.

"Me, Mr. O. and the others. We went after the worst of the Japs. Tojo, Dohihara, Hirota, Itagaki, Kimura, Muto. And Nosaka. We found the evidence, witnesses, we did the prosecuting. Nosaka we went after especially because he was with the Kempei Tai, a bunch of pricks. They were the army police, the Japanese gestapo and nothing but animals when it came to torturing people, especially American flyers. During the war Nosaka got around. Tokyo, Hong Kong, Malaya, Singapore. He was everywhere, dealing out pain and torturing for information. Men, women, children. Didn't matter."

Grinning, Verna turned to DiPalma. "On the day he was sentenced to hang Nosaka says to us, 'Your favor shall be remembered and the recipient is grateful.' Cute, huh? The Japanese don't come right out and say what's on their mind. They have to be polite even when they're mashing your balls between two bricks. What he was saying was he was going to kill us for what we had just done to him."

"How come he survived?"

"Hey, goombah, you're a big boy. Yesterday's enemy, tomorrow's friend. Comes the cold war and Russia and Japan change places. Russia's now the bad guy and Japan's the good guy, 'cause the fucking Japs hate communism. Nosaka was worth his weight in gold. A real smart cookie. All the time he was waiting to be hung he was giving us information, I mean real good shit. First he gives up some of his own people, guys we never knew about and couldn't locate until he tells us."

Verna stuck a hand under his T-shirt and scratched his chest. "America was scared of communism and Nosaka knew the names of all kinds of Communist agents, people in China, throughout the Pacific, all over. And his information was righteous."

DiPalma said, "One thing led to another, I bet. First his execution gets postponed, then his sentence is commuted and next thing you know Nosaka's on the street with pockets full of American money."

"What the fuck can I tell you? Russia grabbed all of Eastern Europe. North Korea and China went Communist. Then Russia gets the A-bomb, and now Washington is peeing in its pants. Nosaka became the greatest thing since sliced bread."

According to Verna there were many reasons why the little man in the cloak and derby was suddenly indispensable. He knew the names of the Japanese spies in Afghanistan, who for years had crossed the border into Russia and brought back information. The Japanese who operated in Switzerland and spied on Russia during the entire war. The Russian military men who, fearing Stalin, had defected to Japan starting in the late 1930s. The Japanese who, before Pearl Harbor, had been go-betweens for German spies in England and who knew about Russian agents buried deep in the British Secret Service.

"Another thing," said Verna. "The Germans captured a lot of Russian files, photocopied the stuff and passed it on to the Japs. And don't forget, it's always been official Japanese government policy to plan thirty years ahead. They did it back then and they're doing it today. Whether they won the war or lost it, they were ready to deal with whatever they had to deal with. And for them that meant knowing every fucking thing they had to know about everybody. That's a tradition which goes way back in their history."

"A man called Hideyoshi started it," said DiPalma. He looked at his watch. "How did Nosaka come to own you?"

"What makes you say that?"

"Because that's why he let you live. Men like Nosaka don't make threats lightly. He means every word he says. If you're telling the truth about his threat, you're only alive because he needed you."

Verna chewed on a thumbnail. "When he went into business, he needed connections in America. Private bills passed in Congress allowing him to do what he wanted to do in Japan, which was still under our occupation. We introduced him to people. Congressmen, bankers, lobbyists, businessmen willing to invest in Japan. In Nosaka. Paid off for him."

"And for you, Sally. For you and your friends."

"Like I said, no such thing as something for nothing in this world. Look, some people in this country wanted to see Japan on her feet again, with guys like Nosaka in charge. Japan was one country that would never go Communist, not with guys like Nosaka around. We had no trouble getting him together with the right people."

DiPalma rubbed his chin with the knob of his cane. "This bank of his, how much of it do you own?"

Verna blinked. "Son of a bitch. How did you figure that out?"

"You want me to take your name out of those papers I'm supposed to bring back. So-called bank papers. You're not that hard to read, Sally."

"With you around, I feel like I'm fucking made of plate glass. We're on the board of directors, me and Mr. O. We bring in other Americans, mostly military people. Everybody gets paid, stock, bonuses, whatever. The military guys are tight with the Pentagon and the CIA, so the bank's used to pay out money for American spy operations nobody's supposed to know about."

"Such as arms deals," said DiPalma. "What about drugs? Guns and drugs go together."

70

"Hey DiPalma, what do I look like? You expect me to answer a question like that? Anybody who wants to put money in Nosaka's bank can put it in. The bank does a lot of other things, too. Like it's a collection agency for Nosaka. Industrial espionage. The bank has branches around the world and the people who work in it are fucking spies. They steal business secrets and pass 'em on to Nosaka."

DiPalma nodded. Now that would make a good story. Industrial espionage. The dark side of Japanese business success and Nosaka right in the middle of it. One more question for Sally Verna.

"I get the feeling you did something recently to remind Nosaka of that little promise he made to you almost forty years ago. What was it?"

Verna stared straight ahead. His grandchildren were tossing a Frisbee near the topiary menagerie. "You might say I pushed a little too hard."

"I'd say you got greedy. That's your main character failing. And this time you did it to the wrong guy."

A look at Verna's face confirmed DiPalma's educated guess. Sally's explanation made it official.

A Japanese car manufacturer, Soami, had wanted to build a plant on Long Island. Soami was Nosaka's biggest rival, so he ordered Sally Verna to stop the plant, and he stopped it cold. He threatened Soami with strikes, with political trouble in Albany and in Washington, with trouble from the local zoning commission and unions allied to Verna. He threatened Soami's management with immigration problems. Soami pulled out in record time.

"That cleared the way for Takeshi, Nosaka's company, to come in. But I had my own ideas about that. I wanted to be taken care of."

DiPalma grinned. "You tried blackmailing Nosaka. You told him pay off or you'd blow the whistle about Soami."

Verna lifted a corner of his small mouth in a smile, in which his eyes did not participate. "Whatever I tried to tell him, he didn't buy. He ain't happy. Leave it go at that."

"I get the feeling he's a lot more than unhappy."

"He's not the only one. The emperor of Japan's not happy either. Last week this wacko Blood League sends him a letter saying that these killings are being done in his honor. Ready for that? The names of all the guys who've been killed so far are in this letter."

"Including Duncan Ivy?"

"Including him. Why did you bring up his name?"

"Because when you spoke about his death it seemed to bother you more than the deaths of the others. A lot more."

Verna pounded his thigh with a clenched fist. "Ivy worked the war crimes tribunal with me. He was also my daughter's godfather. When they got him and when his name turned up on the Blood League's list, I knew for sure the cocksuckers were after me. Letter to the emperor says it's all being done to bring back the old Japan. What the hell does killing half a dozen people have to do with the old Japan, I'd like to know."

DiPalma stretched. Time to go and leave Sally Verna alone with the dried flowers of his bad memories and even worse judgments. "Maybe you should ask Mr. O. about the old Japan. He seems to have pretty good connections with the Tokyo police. Here's the deal, Sally. Take it or leave it. No decision now. I want to think about our little talk. When I get to Hong Kong I'll call you and let you know if I'm in or out. If I'm in, you have your boy bring the file to me at my hotel. I'll be staying at the Mandarin but I don't want to get involved in paying this sucker, whoever it is. That's your problem. I don't want to be within ten feet of your money for whatever the reason."

Verna shrugged. "You're calling the play. If you agree to bring it back, I'll wire him the money."

"I'm in only if there's enough to stick it to Nosaka. Otherwise I'm not about to get involved. The network doesn't like libel suits, which is the least we can expect from Nosaka."

"What about keeping me out of it?"

"What about it?"

"You said—"

"No I didn't. And you know it. But if I can, I will."

Verna came as close to pleading as he ever had in his life. "DiPalma, if you don't keep me out of it, I'm a dead man."

The former detective thought of Katharine. And Lynn. And Sally Verna's wife, who had just had a heart bypass. He said, "You're out of it. Just one more thing: you've got good security here. Gates, walls, probably a first-class alarm system and enough headbreakers walking around on the grounds to start a small war. I've noticed a few guard dogs as well. That should be enough to stop anybody."

Sally Verna's voice was a pained whisper. "Those people are *ninja* And they don't give a shit about getting killed. What do you think the name Blood Oath League means? These guys are stone crazy and they deal in blood. My grandchildren are in and out of here all the time. I don't want anything to happen to them, but what can you do against *ninja?* Tell me, what the fuck can I do?"

72

IN the back seat of his limousine, heading for Kennedy, a tired Frank DiPalma stared through tinted glass at narrow sailboats slicing through a choppy Atlantic Ocean and wondered which boat contained Sally Verna's wife and daughter. Sally, of course, would not be grateful for DiPalma's promise to keep his name out of it. It was the union leader's style to hate those he owed. He couldn't stand to owe. But he owed his wife and grandchildren. This was the debt which DiPalma had agreed to help repay.

Frank DiPalma closed his eyes and settled back against the limousine's plush interior. Sally was a drowning man and his reaching out for DiPalma could pull them both down. The former detective turned his mind to Katharine and Todd. In Hong Kong he would go to them first, then deal with Verna's banker friend. If Verna was righteous, the man in the bank faced as much danger from Nosaka as DiPalma faced from Katharine's father.

Minutes later DiPalma slipped into an uneasy sleep and dreamed of a beautiful Katharine, who remained just out of his reach, a silent Todd in her arms.

And in the background Kenpachi and Verna's banker friend, his face masked, linked arms and laughed insanely and together beckoned DiPalma closer.

4

IN PARIS, a contented Henri Labouchere sipped Kir Royale, a mixture of champagne and crème de cassis, then closed his eyes and slid down into his scented bathwater, his broad back against the side of the huge, half-sunken rose marble tub. Tonight he shared the tub with his three-year-old son Nicholas, who with intense concentration was floating a black-and-white soccer ball between himself and his father. The ball was a birthday gift from Paul Gaspare, Labouchere's Corsican bodyguard.

Sliding doors on two sides separated the bathroom from the terrace where Gaspare now stood looking down on Avenue Foch. The bodyguard, who had been with Labouchere for years, enjoyed watching the whores on the elegant street work pedestrians and motorists for quick trips to the nearby Bois de Boulogne.

Of the twenty rooms in his Avenue Foch duplex, Labouchere's favorite was this bathroom. Ten years ago he had given this room to his first wife Delphine as an anniversary present, a bedroom converted at a cost of almost a million francs. There were gold faucets shaped like mermaids, authentic Louis XIII baroque mirrors, tables and chairs covered with a thin layer of gold. Delphine had chosen everything.

Over her objections Labouchere had selected the bronze and ebony empire style for the rest of the duplex, which comprised the top two floors of a ten-story building facing the Bois de Boulogne and the Metro station designed by art nouveau architect Hector Guimard. Riding the subway, however, was not for Labouchere or his Avenue Foch neighbors, who included Prince Ranier, several Rothschilds, deposed Iranian royalty, Christina Onassis and at least a dozen billionaire industrialists from as many countries.

Avenue Foch, a four-fifths-of-a-mile stretch running between the Étoile and Bois de Boulogne, contained the greatest concentration of wealth and power in the world. It was Paris's Golden Ghetto.

In the tub Labouchere opened his eyes. His empty glass was being pried from his fingers by his adored Nicholas. The Frenchman smiled and allowed his thick hand to be separated from the thin stem of the glass by tiny fingers. No one else was allowed to take anything from Labouchere with such ease. He smiled as Nicholas filled the glass with bathwater and poured it on the golden mermaid faucets, performing the task with a seriousness that amused his father.

Labouchere tilted his head back and inhaled deeply, trying to catch a whiff of Paul Gaspare's cigarette smoke from the terrace. The doctor had forbidden Labouchere to smoke and had cautioned him against rich foods, to help lower his blood pressure. He was allowed two glasses of wine at dinner and had to walk three miles every other day.

Labouchere had stopped smoking, but he kept an unlit Cuban cigar in his mouth for hours at a time. He avoided rich foods five days a week. Then, on weekends, he ate and drank as he pleased. Had he not done as he pleased throughout his life he never would have become a wealthy man. Nor would he have won the most lucrative contract of his life, a deal to build two atomic reactors in Kyoto at a cost of twenty-one billion francs.

Tomorrow morning a helicopter would fly him and Nicholas four hundred miles west to the port of Le Havre. Here father and son would join French and Japanese government officials and salute the three ships heading for Japan with construction supervisors, equipment and material and a dozen atomic technicians. On board would also be several hundred bottles of red wine from Labouchere's private vineyard near Bordeaux, his gift to the French workers who would be away from home for almost a year.

Tonight Labouchere had celebrated at Le Moi, his favorite Vietnamese restaurant, dining on pork with caramel, chicken with Chinese cabbage and crisp noodles. He felt entitled to enjoy himself; in securing the Kyoto contract he had attempted a difficult objective and achieved it. The doctor's orders cautioning restraint could wait until another day. In any case, a man who did nothing and caused no offense died as surely as the man who did as he wished and broke every rule.

Henri Marie Labouchere was in his late fifties, a beefy, horse-faced Frenchman with thinning brown hair parted in the middle and the hard, dark eyes of a man who preferred to distrust everyone rather than be deceived by them. His company, Canet-Banyuls, was France's number-one producer of nuclear power plants and its third leading manufacturer of turbine generators for conventional power plants. Canet-Banyuls's one hundred thousand employees also built transformers, electric motors as well as radar for combat aircraft and launching systems for French nuclear missiles.

Besides electricity and defense, Labouchere had guided his company into land-development projects in ten countries, the development of a French cable-television system and had recently concluded a licensing agreement with a major American soft drink company to bottle and sell its product throughout half of Africa.

Henri Labouchere's strength lay in his boldness, in his knowing what weapons to use and against whom to use them. Having decided to prey rather than be preyed upon, he found himself at home in an unjust world. He felt no guilt at his cutthroat business tactics, seeing a mirror of them in nature, where only the strong survived and the weak went to the wall. He had learned from the mistakes of his father, a man who had been betrayed by relying on the courage of others rather than trusting his own courage.

In love Labouchere had shown the same courage, choosing as a first wife a plain, unattractive woman who had been an assistant to his plant manager in Marseilles. The marriage, a shock to those who had expected him to marry for beauty or social position, had been a success until Delphine's tragic death from an aneurysm. She had been affectionate and loyal, with the courage to stand up to him and the sense to do it in private. She supported his every plan, became his most trusted confidante and disappointed him only in her inability to bear children. When she died it shocked Labouchere to realize how much he had depended on her.

At fifty-two, Labouchere married a second time. Sylvie, twenty, was a glacial, green-eyed beauty, who wanted to be important and admired as much as her husband. She was offered film and modeling contracts, all of which she turned down. Labouchere later learned that she had turned them down out of laziness, not out of a desire to be constantly at his side.

When Labouchere was fifty-three, Sylvie presented him with his first child, Nicholas. The industrialist found great joy in the boy, but also regrets over the childless years with Delphine. And guilt over the regrets.

Tonight in the tub Labouchere smiled and thought about his bold reaction when he had learned of Sylvie's infidelity two days ago. He had spoken of her betrayal to his bodyguard Paul, his only confidant since Delphine's death.

"Tomorrow I am sending her to New York to play among the wealthy Europeans and South Americans who infest Manhattan. I used a ruse. She is to select furniture for our Fifth Avenue apartment and, of course, do a little shopping. She suspects nothing. While she is gone, I shall make arrangements for the divorce and to secure permanent custody of Nicholas."

"How long will madame be in America?"

"At least two weeks. Should she find something or someone to amuse her, she will undoubtedly stay longer. In her absence I want you to gather all of the information I need regarding her lovers. There are two."

Labouchere's eyes held Paul's. "Get written confessions from each man. I do not care how, but I want from each one a written admission of his adultery with my wife."

"It is done, monsieur."

"*Bon*. When she returns, she returns to nothing. She will never set foot in this house again, nor will she anymore set eyes on Nicholas. Her settlement from me will be minimal. I will leave my mark on this whore. Can I rely on you, old friend?"

"Have I ever failed you, monsieur?"

*   *   *

WHETHER it was his failed second marriage or the Kyoto contract, Labouchere acted according to his belief that a successful man was always proud, aggressive and cunning. Above all, he was never to lack boldness at any decisive moment of his life.

To be the one French power company allowed to deal with the Japanese meant securing the permission and cooperation of the French president, prime minister and foreign affairs minister. It meant bribing French officials to withhold the necessary export licenses from Labouchere's competitors, leaving the way clear for him to obtain such licenses. And it meant being smart and tough enough to deal with the Japanese.

"You cannot bring the Americans into this Kyoto project," a Japanese businessman had told Labouchere. "You must understand this about Japan: there is a high sensitivity in my country to nuclear weapons, especially to nuclear weapons belonging to the Americans. Three atomic bombings of my country by America—"

"Three? *Mais non*, there have only been two. Hiroshima and Nagasaki."

"You are forgetting Bikini, my friend. In 1954 the American fallout from an atomic test at that Pacific island came down on a Japanese fishing boat, the *Fukuryu-maru*. One crewman died. With the memories of the war still fresh, it was as if a hundred thousand had died. As far as we were concerned, the Bikini test was the third atomic bomb to fall on us. Every August sixth the Hiroshima bombing is commemorated by demonstrations, protests, antinuclear speeches. You would do well to forget borrowing an American nuclear-powered ship to demonstrate the peacful use of nuclear energy on the high seas."

Labouchere shrugged. "It is forgotten. Let me say that I had no intention of bringing nuclear weapons into the picture. The Americans, however, have made great progress in peaceful uses of atomic energy. I merely wished to show—"

"Henri, listen to me. The contract was awarded to *you*, not to the Americans. We do not wish to involve ourselves at this time with the United States regarding atomic matters. Japan suffers from what you might call a 'nuclear allergy.'"

"Caused by the Americans."

"Dear friend, even French reactors for peaceful purposes will cause trouble in my country. There will be protests, angry newspaper editorials, even threats to your life."

"I am willing to accept this."

The Japanese said, "Certain people in my country feel that nuclear power in Kyoto will be of benefit to both business and to the consumer. That is why we are going ahead with this project."

Labouchere knew who those certain people were. In Japan, business dictated to the government, guiding it through the Sanken or council composed of two dozen of Japan's most powerful industrialists and bankers. The legislature, prime minister and all government agencies took orders from the Sanken, who represented the *zaikai*, the big business circles. This made Japan the ultimate corporate state, with big business deciding government policy at home and abroad. Any politician or government worker who disagreed with big business was booted out of office immediately.

The backing of the Sanken did not eliminate Labouchere's having to pay *shieh lei*, a way of life in Japanese business. Thirty million American dollars had been delivered in cash or placed in secret bank accounts by the Frenchman, who looked upon bribery as a legitimate corporate expense. In any case, the cost of the Kyoto project would probably double before its completion, yielding Labouchere windfall profits. Thirty million in *shieh lei* was peanuts compared to what the Frenchman would eventually take out of Japan.

As for Japanese opposition to the Kyoto project, Labouchere's friend had been correct. Antagonistic editorials, demonstrations at Labouchere's Kyoto and Tokyo offices and even threats to his life all materialized. None had the slighest effect on him; he had survived similar opposition in France and saw no reason why he shouldn't survive this.

These days the world was filled with crackpots, most of whom ended up with a policeman's club across the face. Labouchere was too rich and too powerful to concern himself with bearded crazies in jeans who preferred slogans to thought and rhetoric to an honest day's work. There was no way a handful of Japanese would stop the Kyoto reactors from being built.

But a few days ago a worried Paul had said, "Something's happening, monsieur, and I do not like it. It is a pattern and it concerns the Japanese."

The bodyguard told Labouchere of the killings. "Five, monsieur. Three Japanese, one American, one European. All businessman, all killed recently and not by guns or explosives. They were killed with swords, knives or bare hands. *Ninja* style."

Paul Gaspare neither worried needlessly nor scared easily. He was almost sixty, a small, dark man with a bulbous forehead and eyes which, in an enemy's words, were as hard as an erection. He wore in his jacket lapel the red ribbon signifying his military decorations for bravery at Dien Bien Phu and in Algeria. On his watch chain was the heavy gold medallion embossed with the Napoleonic eagle and Corsican crest. This indicated membership in the *milieu*, or Union Corse, the powerful Corsican underworld organization that made the Sicilian Mafia seem childish by comparison.

Gaspare, who had been with Labouchere for over twelve years, had also served with the Service d'Action Civique (SAC), which did the dirty jobs for De Gaulle that neither the national police or SDECE, the French CIA, would touch. Lebouchere had chosen his bodyguard not only for his bravery, but for his connections in intelligence, law enforcement and the underworld.

Labouchere paid attention when Paul said, "Your security is my concern. I have to look into every threat, no matter how trivial it may appear to be. A day or so ago I had a friend in the SDECE contact Tokyo about the threats you have received. He says we shouldn't worry about them, but there is something else he feels we should be careful of. It appears that Tokyo police feel a group called the Blood Oath League is operating again. It was pretty big around the second World War. Strong-arm stuff for businessmen, killings, spying, even a little blackmail. The Tokyo police don't have much, but they hear that the league might have been resurrected."

"Why? And by whom?"

"They don't know who's behind it. But they feel the reasons are the same as they were in the thirties and forties. Back then the targets were businessmen, reporters, politicians. The new league is just supposed to be after businessmen, Japanese and westerners. But at the moment Tokyo authorities can't get close to the group. They can't line up informants nor even infiltrate the league."

"The usual thing, I suppose," said Labouchere. "Kidnappings and ransom in addition to bloodletting."

"They kill. That's all they do."

Labouchere reached for a cigar and a lighter.

Paul said, "With your permission, monsieur, I'd like to put on a few more men, especially when you're traveling outside of France."

"But of course."

"I would also like a twenty-four hour guard on the flat. Say a couple of men with automatic weapons. They would be in a parked car downstairs. No one would notice. I can fix that up with the police so there would be no trouble. Building security is light, unfortunately. Some friends will make available hand radios and I think you should, perhaps, vary your routine. Leave for work at a different time each day and take different routes."

"I leave that to you, Paul. I shall do whatever you say."

The bodyguard looked up at the ceiling. "I'm wondering about the roof."

"Seems safe enough to me."

"It should be. It's more than twenty feet down to the top window. A sheer drop, too. Nothing to hang on to. No fire escapes, no ledges. But if we're talking about *ninjas*, these Blood Oath guys, I mean, we're talking about first-class athletes. Each of the men they're supposed to have killed all had tight security."

"But they didn't have you, my friend."

In the tub Labouchere struggled to his feet, waded over to the faucets and lifted up a giggling Nicholas. Holding the boy under one arm, the

Frenchman leaned over and pressed the lever releasing the bathwater, then straightened up and kissed his son on both cheeks. Nicholas had noticed the extra bodyguards around the flat, but had said nothing. He was observant, like his father, and showed every sign of taking the changes in stride. Labouchere liked that.

Labouchere was also pleased that for now Nicholas was too young to go to school. This reduced the chances of the boy's being kidnapped. At the moment let him stay home under guard. When a nurse took Nicholas for a walk, at least one armed man accompanied them.

Labouchere looked around the bathroom. *Merde*. No towels. The lack of efficiency in small things annoyed him. He expected perfect service in his home and no excuses. He was going to give the maid hell about it tonight. He turned toward the terrace to summon Paul to search the flat for bath towels.

Labouchere's mouth was open to call Paul when the industrialist saw three black-clad figures drop silently onto the terrace behind the bodyguard's back. Two rushed Paul; the other spun around and sped into the bathroom toward Labouchere, who was too surprised to move.

On the terrace one attacker kicked Paul in the back of the knee, then threw a wire over the Corsican's head and yanked it tight against his throat. At the same time the attacker jammed a knee hard against Paul's spine, pulling back on the wire with all his strength. The bodyguard, his air gone, the wire slicing into his throat, threw himself backward, sending himself and the attacker struggling toward the sliding glass door.

Both men collided with the glass at the same time, shattering it and sending shards flying into the bathroom and onto the terrace. They crashed to the bathroom floor simultaneously, both bleeding heavily. Paul, the wire embedded in his neck, attempted to push himself off the floor; his back was to his attacker, who lay writhing from side to side. When the bodyguard reached a sitting position he pulled at the wire with one hand and with the other clawed for the .38 Smith & Wesson in his belt holster.

The second attacker on the terrace moved faster. He wore a samurai sword slung across his back and in one motion unsheathed it, lifted the weapon high, then brought it down. The blade hit deep into the bodyguard's skull, sending pieces of bone and brain into the glass sprinkled on the yellow tiled floor. Paul, his head and face a mass of blood, slumped across the legs of the first attacker. The bodyguard's right arm twitched as he fought for life.

In the bathroom, the attacker who had rushed Labouchere came to a sudden halt, surprised by the sight of the naked Frenchman holding his son. The hesitation was brief. He also carried a sword across his back;

in a second the naked blade was in his hands and he swung.

Labouchere turned his back, using his body to shield his son. The blade dug into the beefy Frenchman's bare shoulder and he shrieked, then stumbled and fell forward into what was left of the bathwater. The attacker stepped into the tub, kicked his way through the now bloody water and lifted the sword high. He brought it down once, twice. Nicholas screamed. A bleeding Labouchere, still attempting to save his son, crawled toward him. The sword was raised again. And still once more. And then silence.

The attacker sheathed his sword, stepped from the water and looked down at his masked comrade lying under a dying Paul Casparc. He was dragged aside and the two *ninja* examined the bleeding man in black; his throat, side, neck and wrists had been badly cut by glass.

There was a brief conversation in Japanese before they carried the third man out to the terrace. Here he was tied to one of two ropes they had used to lower themselves down from the roof, with a makeshift harness around the bleeding man's chest and under both arms. Then they climbed the ropes and together pulled him up.

One slung the wounded man over his shoulder and, followed by his comrade, silently crossed the roofs of Avenue Foch, two shadows that soon blended into the June night.

   ⚜   ✳   ✿

IN the Bois de Boulogne the two Japanese, still masked, stood behind the dying third man. He was unmasked and bare chested and sat in a formal kneeling position, buttocks on heels, hands palms down on his thighs. He trembled with pain and his body was dark with his own blood, but he did not cry out. His eyes were closed and after a while he began to chant a prayer. His voice was strained, harsh, barely audible.

When his head slumped forward with pain, one of the two behind him stepped forward, sword high. A single, quick stroke and the wounded man's head flew off, disappearing into the darkness.

The butchering of the corpse continued. The executioner chopped off the dead man's hands, then wrapped them and the head in the corpse's black sweater. Next, the two attackers dropped to their knees and used their hands to scoop out a shallow grave in the soft earth beneath a nearby bush. The mutilated corpse was then placed in the grave and covered with earth, twigs, leaves.

83

Minutes later the two Japanese, one carrying a grisly bundle of the dead man's head and hands over his shoulder, jogged across a moonlit clearing and vanished into a grove of pine and birch trees.

5

WHEN TODD woke it was almost dark. Instantly his eyes went to the *bokken*, a wooden sword with the curved, tapered blade and carved hilt of an actual samurai sword, that lay bathed in moonlight on a chair beside his bed. Todd used the *bokken* in Koryu, an ancient fighting form practiced without armor in order to develop an exact and beautiful fencing technique.

While the lack of armor made the movements freer, Koryu placed greater pressure on the fencer to avoid being scored on. A higher form of fencing than *shinai* kendo, Koryu was performed with intense concentration. Each movement was executed with fierce pride.

A perspiring Todd sensed the threat of rain in the humid night. Nude, he pushed aside his sheet and mosquito netting, swung his feet to the floor and stood up. Both hands went to this throat. The throbbing pain that had sharply awakened him from a troubled sleep was still there. His skin tingled with an unnatural heat. His face smarted as though it had just been singed by fire.

When he had first opened his eyes there had been a horrifying second when he felt himself immersed in flames. Night and solitude now held only demons.

Something drew him to the *bokken*. He lifted it from the chair, hands on hilt and blade, and walked to the window. From behind bamboo blinds he watched guests step from expensive cars and enter the Hansards' Edwardian mansion or stroll its well-tended grounds, which were lit by paper lanterns strung between tall hedges, bamboo poles and red pines. Near the pergola, a covered walk formed by climbing plants, Todd's mother, lovely in a white Grecian tunic belted at the waist by an ultrathin Ciani gold lariat, was chatting with Hong Kong's governor, his wife and two of the American actors.

Todd's stepfather, several feet away, was talking to the film's attractive producer, Jan Golden, and a pretty Japanese actress in an Elizabethan knot garden of clipped shrubs and herbs. The boy noticed that his stepfather deliberately kept his back to the circular driveway as guests applauded a Chinese couple who arrived in a one-hundred-year-old horse-drawn hansom cab, complete with top-hatted driver. Todd watched them step down from the carriage and pose for photographers before disappearing inside the mansion.

The boy had seen the couple at his stepfather's bank. The man was a popular movie actor who produced and starred in one kung fu film a month and gambled away his profits. His wife was the beautiful star of a top-rated television soap opera shown in Chinese communities throughout the world. Todd knew she slept with his stepfather in exchange for the low-interest loans which financed her husband's movies. Ian Hansard had a craving for Oriental women.

Todd gripped the *bokken* with all his strength. There was a frightening bond between the boy and someone here at the party. *Who was it? And why?*

And there was the *ninja*. He had not told his mother what he had seen in his dream on the boat; it was a dream after all, a fleeting shadow on which no one could lay a hand. He feared for his mother, but he knew that he and all others were powerless in the face of karma. Destiny was destiny. Even the gods were forced to submit to fate.

Suddenly the pain in his throat grew keener. At the same time a deep impulse consumed him and he turned his back on the window. *Hai, someone connected to his nightmares, someone responsible for the uneasiness that he now lived with, was here in the house. Not on the grounds but here in the house.*

Todd faced the door and began to move instinctively. He crouched on his heels, knees spread wide, *bokken* gripped tightly at the hilt and aimed at the eyes of an imaginary opponent. Then he rose slowly, his gaze fixed straight ahead, his bare back streaked with silver moonlight.

With a cold ferocity he began the practice of Koryu.

                        *   *   *

KON KENPACHI stood beneath a cut-glass Georgian chandelier in the
crowded Hansard living room and forced a smile for the photographers
who had motioned him closer to Tom Gennaro and Kelly Keighley, the
two American male leads in *Ukiyo*. Unlike Kenpachi, who disliked being
ordered about by anyone, the actors seemed reconciled to the ordeal of
popping flashbulbs and shouted questions from reporters representing
Hong Kong's myriad daily newspapers. The Japanese director also found
his surroundings disturbing. His aesthetic sense was offended by the
clutter of the Hansard mansion, with its quilted white silk ceiling, red
damask chairs, Meissen porcelain and bay windows of Tiffany glass.

Any visit to China, and he had made several, always unnerved Kenpachi and left him uneasy. In his heart he knew the truth, that Japan
had built her civilization through the theft of China's secrets. Japan's
food and art, its music and science, its religion and even its martial arts,
all originated in China. For a time the Japanese people, having no written
language of their own, had spoken Chinese exclusively, as Western medieval scholars had used Latin. Today's Japanese language used several
thousand Chinese characters. Even the word *seppuku* represented the
Chinese characters for suicide.

The result of these centuries of pilfering was psychological dependence
and a cultural inferiority complex, which all of Japan's military aggres-
siveness and claims to superiority had failed to eliminate. Only one of
Japan's three invasions of China, in World War II, had come close to
succeeding. But when America had come to China's aid that invasion
too had failed, leaving the Chinese as conquerors of the people they
called "the monkey thieves," a slur on the Japanese who, a myth said,
were born of a Chinese princess kidnapped by a monkey.

Kenpachi knew that a case could be made for the Japanese as thieves
of other nations' technology and cultural ideas. The Japanese were im-
itators, not innovators; their strength lay in duplication or improving on
the achievement of others. China's existence reminded Kenpachi that
truth was too often a whore, someone you knew but did not want to
encounter in public.

An impatient Kenpachi had now been in Hong Kong for twelve hours
without seeing the boy Todd. Had the director purified himself these past
weeks only to be forced to bring the box to a half-white, half-Chinese

                              87

child? Yes, Nosaka was to be obeyed. The superior man was easy to serve, said Confucius, and difficult to please.

Kenpachi's curiosity about the small black box, carried to the party in a shoulder bag, was at fever pitch. Would he learn its contents tonight? Was his search for a *kaishaku* at an end?

To Kenpachi's right a second group of photographers had posed Jan Golden arm in arm with Ian Hansard and Hong Kong's governor in front of a cast-iron fireplace. Hansard was a member of the legislative council, which made Hong Kong's laws, set its economic policy and granted film-making permits. Kenpachi, who had been willing to do anything to avoid poverty, recognized that same wretched compulsion in Ian Hansard and therefore knew the banker was never to be trusted. As for the governor, Kenpachi had already posed with the pink-faced Englishman, whose bad teeth and malice were barely concealed by good manners.

Across the room Kenpachi and Jan Golden's eyes met briefly before she looked away to smile at the governor. She was in her mid-thirties, a tall, long-nosed woman with green-gray eyes and the habit of throwing her head back, causing her mane of auburn hair to swirl glamorously about, a gesture Kenpachi knew compensated for her short sight. She was ambitious, a hard worker and more knowledgeable about the Far East than any western woman he had ever met.

Kenpachi admired her willingness to allow a sort of nasty intent to surface, as he admired her talent for restraint or exaggeration when either suited her purpose. What interested him most about Jan Golden was her sexuality, which appeared offhand but which the observant Kenpachi knew masked a fear that her true and hidden sensuality was too strong for compromise. She was, he sensed, both repelled and attracted by him.

Kenpachi shaded his eyes against the popping flashbulbs and searched among the crush of reporters, photographers, dinner-jacketed men and elegantly gowned women for Wakaba, his Japanese bodyguard and chauffeur. The young, burly Wakaba, with kendo and karate skills matched only by a high-strung belligerence, was one of the first to meet Nosaka's strict requirements for membership in the new Blood Oath League. He worshipped Kenpachi and was insanely jealous when anyone came close to the director.

Wakaba had already offered to serve as Kenpachi's *kaishaku*, then join him in *seppuku*. But the bodyguard had failed the test of the box.

Kenpachi, increasingly edgy, glanced at the ceiling. One way or another, with or without Wakaba's help, he was going to find the boy and find him tonight. The box was a hot coal on Kenpachi's hip.

He felt a hand on his right shoulder and turned to see Tom Gennaro aim a finger at the reporters and photographers crouched in front of them. "Tell you people what I think of this man. I made the deal for this movie without seeing the script. And that's something I never do. I mean never."

A smiling Kenpachi bowed his handsome head, his mind still on Wakaba and the boy. Such praise was his due; all the Americans should be honored to work with him, especially on his final film. Still, there was respect for the talent of the Oscar-winning Gennaro, a dark, sad-eyed little man skilled at playing lethal outsiders. There was also admiration for Keighley, white haired and knife thin, who had a sinister sexuality popular with Japanese audiences.

Gennaro had undergone an immediate infatuation with Japanese culture and spent his off-camera hours touring temples, walking with geishas and practicing kendo with Kenpachi and Wakaba. Keighley's time was spent with his "secretary," a statuesque Venezuelan who was only seventeen and had been the actor's mistress for four years.

And there was Jan Golden, a woman of force who saw only a world of possibilities. Kenpachi and Nosaka were using her, but the situation was not without its small ironies. The American woman had shamelessly used Kenpachi's artistic reputation to get the high-priced Gennaro and Keighley to work for what she called "short money." With these three names on contracts it had been childishly simple to get whom she wanted for *Ukiyo*.

The original script, written by a former Vietnam war correspondent, had impressed Kenpachi, but it needed rewriting. The director was not satisfied with the story of two GIs, on leave in Tokyo from Vietnam, who become involved with a Japanese prostitute and steal money from the *yakuza*. Kenpachi's version, a brilliant rewrite instantly accepted by Jan Golden and the American stars, saw a young GI (Gennaro), team with the prostitute to steal money hidden by her lover, a Japanese gangster serving a prison term.

Both the American and the woman were now pursued across Japan by the *yakuza*, a mysterious and corrupt American (Keighley) and a female American journalist anxious to report the story. In the end it was Keighley and the journalist who betrayed Gennaro and the prostitute he had come to love.

"I'm wiped out," a tearful Jan Golden said after reading Kenpachi's version. "It's romantic, violent, sad, funny, it's everything. And I really care about the lovers. You've made it high tragedy and it works. At least I think it works. I mean it's, well, a bit downbeat. Couldn't we have one bit of hope at the end? A lighted match at the end of the tunnel, so to speak?"

Kenpachi shook his head. "As you have said, it is a tragedy and the essence of tragedy is sadness. We are dealing with the inevitability of events, destiny set in motion by the actions of those in the script. If you look closely, you will see a small triumph, the triumph of a man over those forces that seek to destroy him. Death cannot take away that tiny victory. The lovers, the American and the Japanese girl, now have convictions, beliefs. Convictions must bring suffering."

Jan Golden was silent. She had complete belief in his talent and besides, she couldn't deny a gnawing desire for him.

✳   ✳   ✳

KORYU.

Todd Hansard, chest rising and falling, held the hilt of the *bokken* close to his abdomen, the tip pointed at the throat of an imaginary enemy. In the moonlit room the naked boy paused before attacking again. The burning in his throat was ignored; he was in a dream state, free from mind and body, all other existences forgotten except that of *do*, the way.

He filled his lungs with air, then exhaled slowly. Then he attacked with a strong spirit; his life depended on a fraction of an inch of movement, on a single stroke of his blade. All that he was flowed from a secret place within him into the *bokken*.

He took three steps toward the door and stopped. He waited. Then, in Todd's mind, his opponent lifted his own *bokken* overhead and slashed downward. Quickly the boy stepped back on his left foot and struck the opponent in the head before the enemy's sword could complete its move. As the opponent took one step back, Todd, maintaining concentration, brought his *bokken* overhead. He held it there and waited. Then he and the opponent lowered their swords to point at each other's faces, held that position for seconds before pointing the weapons at the floor.

Each now took five small steps to the rear, brought up his *bokken* to point at the other's face and waited.

Todd attacked again. Three long steps forward. Stop. Watch the other man's eyes. Suddenly the opponent's *bokken* sped downward toward Todd's right wrist. Without thinking the boy stepped back diagonally on his left foot, evading the enemy's weapon. Then a step forward and Todd's *bokken* had cut the enemy's right wrist.

Five small steps to the rear and again the boy had his back against the window, *bokken* aimed at his opponent's throat.

Forward once more. Three long steps and stop. Eyes to eyes. This

90

time the opponent delivered a two-handed thrust at Todd's solar plexus. The boy parried the attack to the left and countered with his own thrust to the throat.

Spellbound, Todd had gone beyond time and space, beyond is and is not. He had transcended all existences to reach the plane of consciousness where thought neither mattered nor was necessary. He believed the enemy in front of him existed and sought to take his life. And because his own life could now end within the space of a heartbeat, the boy fought with a tension unknown to modern swordsmen.

Suddenly the room in front of him was filled with light. A second later it was dark except for a path of moonlight between the window and the door. But Todd retained his concentration. For him there was nothing between earth and sky but the sword. And the man he must kill.

*   *   *

Kenpachi quickly entered Todd's bedroom, then closed the door behind him. Wakaba remained on guard in the hall while the director pursued a paradox. Kenpachi was excited because he was about to see the boy recommended by Nosaka, the most clever of men. Yet common sense told Kenpachi that an eleven-year-old boy had no place in his plans. It was time to put an end to this business. Simply show the box to Todd Hansard and . . .

A shocked Kenpachi almost cried out, terrified by the power emanating from the naked boy across the room. Because he was half-hidden by darkness, the boy's spirit seemed all the more intimidating. Never had Kenpachi experienced such unity of body, mind and technique; not in Nosaka, not in the best of the fighters in the Blood Oath League. A boy. Was Kenpachi dreaming?

So completely had Todd given himself to his sword play that Kenpachi sensed danger; if he approached the boy now, the director would be killed. Frightened, yet willing to embrace danger, the Japanese did not run. Instead he stepped back deeper into the darkness, his hands fumbling with the shoulder bag.

91

*   *   *

TODD took three steps forward and stopped.

This time the enemy struck with all his strength, making contact with the tip of Todd's *bokken,* then sliding his blade along it in a thrust to the chest. Stepping back on his left foot, Todd parried his opponent's weapon. Immediately both fighters brought their weapons back to point at each other's throats.

Todd struck first. He sidestepped to the right and without hesitating leaped forward on his left foot and sliced the opponent's right side. Kenpachi inhaled sharply, marveling at a move of such outstanding skill and beauty.

The director could wait no longer. He stepped forward into the moonlight, the black box extended in both hands. He pushed the box toward Todd.

The effect on the boy was immediate; his cold savagery vanished and he dropped the *bokken.* Eyes bulging, he clutched his throat and backed away from a stunned Kenpachi. That was when the Japanese knew what the box contained.

Todd's face twisted in pain and he shook his head violently from side to side.

Kenpachi, overjoyed, bowed and said in Japanese, "It is yours."

Todd answered in Japanese in a drugged voice. "I do not want the bone."

According to ancient Buddhist rites, after the cremation of a body its ashes were searched for the *Hotoke-San* or Lord Buddha, a tiny bone found in the throat. The shape of such a bone foretold the soul's future. If the next birth was to be a happy one, the bone would resemble a tiny image of Buddha. But if the next birth was to be unhappy, the bone would be either shapeless or ugly.

Kenpachi's hands shook as he lifted the lid of the box.

The bone was half the size of a pinky finger and rested on red silk the color of fire.

It was yellowed. Hideous. Shapeless.

Kenpachi could only breathe the name. *"Benkai."*

Todd shivered. His eyes were closed and his arms extended, as though keeping Kenpachi at bay. "Keep the *Iki-ryō* away. Don't let it return to me. Please don't let it return."

With these words Kenpachi knew the pleasure of power. His practice of *bushido* and his meditation on death had brought forth the *Iki-ryō*, which now disturbed the boy. In life one dominated or one served. Therefore it was right and necessary that Todd obey the one who had assumed control of his existence. He had to obey Kenpachi.

He said, "You will answer. The point on Benkai's, on your Muramasa. Is its edge straight or curved?"

Todd's voice was a croak. *"Fukura-tsuku."* Curved.

"What is written on the tang?" The tang was the part of a blade which fitted into the hilt.

"D-date. The name of Muramasa. Province of Muramasa. My name. My-my..."

Todd, head back on his shoulders, dropped to his knees. His eyes remained closed.

"The five relationships," said Kenpachi. "Name them."

"Fi-five. Father and son. Husband and wife. Brothers, older to younger. Friend to friend. And..."

"Say it. I order you."

"Master and servant."

Kenpachi's eyes brightened. "Karma has said that the relationship between master and servant is to be found in the three worlds. What are they?"

"Three. Past life, this life, future life."

"You have lived many lives. On the normal plane of consciousness you remember nothing. But tonight is different and so I ask you: give me the name of two of Hideyoshi's chief spies."

Todd's breathing grew louder and he pressed clenched fists to his temple. Blood trickled from his left eye. "Spiiies." He drew out the word. "Spiiiies."

"Two."

"Hirano Nagayusu. Kasuya Takemori. They worked with the Buddhist priest Kennyo."

Nagayusu was the name Kenpachi wanted to hear and had doubted the boy could know. Nagayusu was Nosaka's ancestor. Kenpachi had found his *kaishaku*, his second. But while destiny had given him the half-Chinese boy, Kenpachi had yet to know what he had received.

What he did receive next was a warning. "The woman is a danger," said Todd. "Guard yourself well, mas—" He hesitated. The word came hard, but he said it. "Master."

Master. In life one could rarely ask for more than the happiness of a passing moment, and for this one moment Kenpachi was the happiest of men. Master.

"What of the woman. Who is she?"

"She was yours when I served you. Since then she has taken many births and is once more beside you. The woman is from the West."

There was only one Western woman in Kenpachi's life at the moment—Jan Golden. But how could she be a danger to him unless, yes, unless she was Saga, Saburo's treacherous concubine. And had been reborn to again betray the lord of Ikuba Castle. I am lord of Ikuba now, thought Kenpachi, and she shall not betray me.

If Nosaka didn't kill Jan Golden, then Kenpachi would. It was the only way to avoid becoming Saga's victim as Saburo had been four hundred years ago.

Wakaba opened the door. "She comes, Kenpachi-san. The mother."

Kenpachi snapped the black box shut and turned in time to see Todd, still on his knees, lose consciousness and fall forward to the floor. Frustrated, the director took a step toward the boy, then stopped. He didn't want to leave, but there was no choice. No matter. The boy was his.

Thousands of lives had prepared Todd for this moment. You are mine, the director thought. And I will have you. Nothing or no one shall prevent this. But first you must be purified, made ready for your role in my destiny, my *seppuku*.

Kenpachi stepped into the hall where Wakaba was staring at Katharine Hansard, now almost on them. Her eyes were narrowed with unspoken questions. Kenpachi had an answer. He slapped Wakaba's face.

"Fool," hissed Kenpachi. He spoke coldly in English. "You have wasted my time. You lead me from room to room and it is obvious that you have no idea where this telephone is. Meanwhile an important caller waits and I stand to lose a great deal of money because of your stupidity. Did you look in this room before summoning me?"

Wakaba, a hand to his cheek, shook his head.

"Of course not," said Kenpachi. "Had you done so you would have found nothing more than a sleeping boy. And please, do not blame the servant for your stupidity. You should have brought him with you instead of subjecting us both to your inability to remember correctly. For now I advise you to keep as far away from me as you can, at least until I find this caller."

Continuing his pretense of rage, Kenpachi walked away from Wakaba, leaving him in front of Todd's room. He strode past Katharine Hansard as though she did not exist.

Wakaba finally moved, following Kenpachi. He, too, ignored the woman, who watched the two men until they disappeared down the staircase leading to the ground floor and the party.

TWO

CHIKAI

In kendo, face to face
with an opponent.

6

IN HONG KONG Ian Hansard arrived at the snake restaurant shortly after 5:00 P.M. The restaurant, which served only snake meat, snake wine and snake bile, was in the western district, the area his wife was fond of calling "the real Hong Kong." Katharine loved the old three-story buildings with their carved balustrades and ornate balconies. And she enjoyed exploring the narrow side streets and alleys jammed with hawkers' stalls and shops of jade carvers, herbalists, calligraphers and coffin makers. Hansard found the district an eyesore filled with crumbling housing, toothless old whores, squatter shacks and foul-smelling slaughter houses.

More to his pleasure was the beautiful Oriental woman he was to meet in the snake restaurant. Dear God, what an absolutely smashing creature she was. Japanese, lovely and blessed with an eye-catching figure. Her name was Yoshiko Mara. Two days after the Kenpachi party, she had presented herself at Hansard's bank and requested his help.

"I am a designer," she said, "and I plan to relocate here from Tokyo. Labor costs in Hong Kong are cheaper and there is not the competition I face in my country from more established designers."

"Well, Miss Mara, what can I do to make your stay here in Hong Kong profitable as well as pleasurable?"

She crossed her legs before answering and Hansard's mouth went dry.

Her hair was blue black and her almond-shaped eyes were made more alluring by silver eye shadow. She wore a tailored gray suit with a slit skirt which showed a fair amount of thigh when she sat down. There was white lace at her throat and, God in heaven, she had on those ankle strap shoes that Joan Crawford always wore, the sort that put Ian Hansard instantly in heat. Yoshiko Mara was an extremely nice bit of crumpet.

"I have some money," she said, "but I shall need a small loan and perhaps advice on setting up one or two corporations. At least four businessmen in Tokyo spoke highly of you and recommended that I seek you out."

She gave Hansard their names. Ian Hansard smiled; damned if he didn't have her now. She knew he could help her and if she wanted that help she would have to be very nice to him. "I may well have a solution to your problems," he said. "Where will your showroom be?"

"Oh, I intend to have more than just a showroom, Mr. Hansard. I want to do both couture and ready-to-wear line. At the moment I can't discuss it, but there is some property in the western district which I may be able to get at a reasonable price. The property includes an abandoned factory which I intend to renovate and use for my ready-to-wear line."

"I say, that sounds exciting. By the way, do call me Ian. And since you're new to Hong Kong, perhaps I can show you around. It so happens I'm free for dinner tonight and we could discuss your plans over some rather excellent Cantonese chicken at a restaurant owned by a friend of mine."

Yoshiko Mara touched her small pink mouth with green-tipped nails and smiled shyly. She seemed most anxious to please. Ian Hansard had every intention of giving her that opportunity.

*　　*　　*

EXCEPT for Hansard and a trio of Chinese waiters engaged in a vigorous game of Mah-Jongg near the kitchen, the snake restaurant was empty. He had been to such restaurants before, but never one quite as unappetizing as this little room, with its dim lighting, low ceiling and stained, creaking floorboards. There were only a half a dozen wooden tables, which Hansard suspected had been looted from a trash barge. One wall was lined with built-in cupboards, whose drawers contained live snakes. Hansard could hear them hissing and thrashing about, which did little to soothe his nerves.

On either side of the cramped kitchen, walls of shelves were lined with large glass jars of snake wine, which was nothing more than clear alcohol containing decomposing snakes. While uneasy around reptiles of any sort, Hansard had come to share the Chinese belief in snakes as medicinal and rejuvenating aids. In the cold months he too ate snake to ward off influenza and had yet to become seriously ill during a Hong Kong winter. The meat tasted somewhat like chicken, only more succulent.

As for the aphrodisiac qualities of snake bile, Hansard had to admit there was something to what he had always treated as an old wives' tale. A drink of snake bile in Cognac did make him feel more amorous and ready for the old in-and-out. Perhaps one day he would be like those Chinese in their eighties and nineties, who claimed that snake bile enabled them to make love regularly and even father children.

Since Yoshiko had selected the snake restaurant for a drink Hansard guessed that the property she had in mind for her factory and showroom was nearby. Hong Kong's real estate speculators and their wrecking balls had already begun to reshape parts of the western district. As Hansard saw it, he and Yoshiko would have their drink; then she would undoubtedly take him over to the site she proposed to purchase and ask his opinion. Over the telephone she had hinted as much.

Professional matters out of the way, the two would then take the ferry across the harbor to Kowloon for dinner. Hansard had seen Yoshiko two days running and while he had not yet taken her to bed, he was certain that little pleasure would be his tonight. He screwed a Senior Service cigarette into a black ivory holder, then lit it with a thin gold lighter. A waiter looked at him, but Hansard shook his head. When Yoshiko arrived he would order. As the waiter turned back to his Mah-Jongg game, Yoshiko stood in the doorway. The Englishman's face brightened and he rose from his chair.

"You look absolutely lovely," he said.

Yoshiko wore a high-necked, long-sleeved dress of lavender silk, with a matching lavender headband to hold her lustrous hair in place. Her legs were bare and she wore gold sandals with wraparound gold laces that reached the knee. Fingernails and toenails were painted silver and she smelled of jasmine. Hansard stared at her with open longing and when she touched his arm, he coughed to clear his throat. He felt like a randy schoolboy, tongue-tied and nervous.

"I could use a drink," she said in a throaty voice that made Hansard tremble. "I have been rushing madly about all day, seeing people and trying to make decisions that could affect the rest of my life. Tonight, I just want to relax."

"Well, I must say the rushing about certainly seems to agree with you.

Not a hair out of place and your beauty appears to be completely intact."

"You are very kind. You have made my stay here in Hong Kong most enjoyable."

"The pleasure has been mine, I assure you. Well, let's summon a waiter and get ourselves squared away, shall we?"

Her hand reached across the table for his. "I've heard so much about snake bile. I wonder if it's all they say it is."

Hansard removed the cigarette holder from his mouth. "And what do they say it is?"

"Oh, they say it relaxes you, removes your inhibitions." She laughed. "They even say it makes you live longer."

That wasn't what she meant and they both knew it. Hansard squeezed her hand. He could afford to be bold from here on. He lifted a hand, and a waiter with hair like polished wood left the Mah-Jongg game to come over to their table. Hansard, his stomach knotted with excitement, ordered snake bile. Yoshiko's hand rested in his; the odor of her perfume, and thoughts of the night ahead, pushed aside his apprehension of snakes.

The waiter returned from the kitchen with a tray containing four small teacups and a bottle of Remy Martin. Then, as Hansard and Yoshiko watched, he went to the wall cupboards, where he slowly opened one of the sealed drawers and carefully removed a live, six-foot cobra. The waiter held the hissing, twisting snake at arm's length, his left hand tightly squeezing it just beneath the expanded hood.

Returning to Hansard's table, the waiter jammed his foot down on the snake's tail, stretching it taut. As the snake hissed louder and bared curved fangs, the waiter reached into a shirt pocket and removed a thin metal piece with a small hook at one end. Placing the metal piece between his teeth, the waiter ran his free hand down the length of the cobra's stomach, his fingers feeling for the bile sac.

When he found it he used the metal piece to make a one-inch slit over the sac, causing the cobra to tremble with pain and rage. Now the snake was at its most dangerous. Dropping the bloodied metal piece on Hansard's table, the waiter used two fingers to probe the opening in the snake. In seconds he plucked out the wet, thumb-shaped yellow sac that was the cobra's gall bladder, and dropped it into one of the teacups. Still squeezing the cobra below its flattened hood, the waiter now stepped back as a second waiter moved to Hansard's table. This one broke the sac, poured the clear bile into another teacup, then filled the cup with Cognac. Finished, he bowed, then stepped back to join the waiter holding the twisting cobra.

Yoshiko dipped a forefinger into the cognac and bile, then slowly

100

licked it, her eyes on Hansard. Again she dipped a finger into the teacup and this time touched Hansard's lips. He took her hand in both of his, licked the finger as she had done and devoured her with his eyes. She withdrew her hand and brought the cup to her mouth. She sipped, then held the cup out to him. She kept her hands on the cup as he took her hands in his and drank. There was a gentle pressure on Hansard's lips; Yoshiko held the cup against his mouth, urging him to drink more. Hansard, wanting her as he had wanted no other woman for a long time, drank all of the warm and bitter liquid, feeling its fire race through him, feeling his penis harden.

His eyes were closed and he never saw Yoshiko nod to the third waiter, who quietly locked the front door and stood with his back to it. A second nod to the two waiters near the table, one of whom still gripped the cobra, was returned.

Hansard swallowed the last of the Cognac and bile, opened his eyes and smiled at Yoshiko.

"Dear Ian," she whispered, placing the cup to one side and taking both of his hands in hers.

He leaned forward to kiss her. Suddenly with surprising strength, she yanked him forward toward her, leaving Hansard stomach down on the table, too startled to cry out. Leaping from her chair, Yoshiko then drove her elbow into his right temple, almost knocking him unconscious. As she stepped back, he rolled off the table and fell to the floor on his back, squeezing his throbbing head.

The waiter holding the cobra stepped forward and dropped it on Hansard.

The reptile struck without hesitation. Its head, the hood spread wide in frenzy, sped forward, fangs biting deep into Hansard's cheek. He screamed and pulled at the snake, but it clung to the Englishman's flesh, shooting its deadly venom into his face. Hansard twisted and writhed on the floor and desperately tried to push the snake away. His legs lashed out, overturning the table, sending teacups and the bottle of Cognac crashing to the floor. The venom worked quickly; Hansard's thrashing was followed by a seizure and then there was a muffled cry deep in his throat. He stiffened and spittle dribbled from his mouth. Then his eyes went up into his head and he relaxed and lay still.

The snake coiled and uncoiled over Hansard's chest and face, leaving traces of blood on the dead banker's clothing.

The waiter who had held the cobra went into the kitchen and returned with a garden rake and a meat cleaver. He handed the rake to another waiter and the two cautiously circled the cobra and the dead man. The hissing snake crawled away from Hansard's body, its gray hood red with the banker's blood, then stopped and rose in the air, swaying left and right, preparing to strike again. The waiter holding the rake struck first; he brought the iron end down quickly, pinning the cobra's head to the floor. Instantly the second waiter leaped forward and beheaded the cobra with a single stroke of the cleaver, driving the cutting edge deep into the floor.

Both waiters then rushed to Hansard's corpse and began to rifle his pockets.

Yoshiko picked up her purse from the floor and walked toward the door. The looters were forgotten; her mind was on the second person she had to kill tonight. At the door she stopped and turned. Her nostrils flared in disgust as she watched a waiter pick up the dead cobra's head and drop it into a jar of clear alcohol. The other waiter chopped up the cobra's body into sections for edible snake meat.

In Hong Kong nothing was allowed to go to waste.

Outside, Yoshiko walked to the edge of the western district before finding a cab. The driver understood English and she smiled and gave him Katharine Hansard's address on Victoria Peak, then opened the rear door and stepped inside.

*　　*　　*

In a kendo *dojo* above a tea merchant's shop on Queen's Road, Todd Hansard kneeled and concentrated on the practice matches. He wore kendo armor, but his mask and *shinai* lay on the mat. Suddenly his eyes widened and he flinched with pain; something was happening to his mother miles away on Victoria Peak. His head jerked under the impact of a blow to the temple, then snapped backward from a strike to the throat by a bare hand.

Todd clutched his throat and fought to breathe. And then the pain was gone. Now he felt the heat from the fire.

He leaped to his feet, raced across the *dojo* floor and disappeared down the stairs. The *sensei* and a few kendoists walked to the window and looked down the street, but Todd Hansard had already disappeared into the rush hour crowd.

Still in his kendo armor, Todd stood alone under the pergola on the grounds of the Hansard home. The climbing plants of the covered walk and the deep twilight hid the boy and his tears. Across the grounds flames had engulfed the bungalow behind the Hansard mansion, the bungalow his mother used as a sculpture studio. Hoses from the fire trucks were trained on the small burning building, their streams of water white arcs against the darkening sky.

Todd's mother was in that building, and he knew she had been murdered. The police, the servants and neighbors who whispered about a tragic accident were wrong.

Todd looked at the great white house, untouched by the fire, its windows now glowing a bright red. Her house. "Mother," he whispered.

Grief made the boy shrink from human company and cling to night and shadows. With an understanding that was becoming a curse, he knew that he could never share the sorrow of Katharine Hansard's death with anyone. It was a weight he must carry by himself, a sad endurance that would stay with him.

Yet within him was an awareness that pain and death could never be separated from life. To reject them was to reject life itself.

* * *

A deeper wisdom pushed its way into Todd's consciousness. It spoke to him of mujo, the impermanence to be found in all things. Whatever lived and was to be found between heaven and earth was subject to disease, decay and death, to inevitable and inexorable change. A samurai must remember mujo and be strong. All of life was a preparation for death. A warrior must contemplate mujo every day of his life.

103

＊　　＊　　＊

BUT Todd Hansard was still a boy, living partly within a normal adolescence, partly within an ancient destiny that sought to control him. His mother's love had offered the hope that he might one day escape his fate. But now she was dead and Todd was alone. And so it was the boy, not the warrior, who dropped sobbing to his knees, overwhelmed by a pain which clung cruelly to him.

7

A WEARY and unshaven DiPalma carefully picked his way out of the blackened ruins that had once been Katharine Hansard's studio. On the grass he looked back over his shoulder at the scorched chimney, at the iron sculptures twisted and melted by intense heat, at a charred, water-soaked couch. After a few seconds he turned forward and looked down, his attention caught by something on the ground. A pair of eyeglasses in a puddle, lenses smashed, a stem torn off. Katharine's.

He picked up the broken frame, placed his cane under one arm and wrapped the frame in his handkerchief. After pocketing the handkerchief he walked the several yards to where Todd stood beneath a cypress tree. DiPalma, eyes hidden behind mirrored sunglasses, had never taken a longer walk in his life. What the hell do you do when you don't know what to do?

At the tree, father and son stood side by side. Todd ignored DiPalma and continued to stare at the burned-out bungalow. He was taller than Frank had imagined, with something of Katharine's beauty in his face and with the strangest eyes. One blue, one violet, each vivid and deep colored and his gaze as pointed as an ice pick. Katharine had written of his intelligence, his interest in kendo and Japanese culture, even his having a touch of psychic powers. In recent letters she had called Todd *different*.

When they met for the first time earlier that day DiPalma had seen just how different his son was. Failure to save Katharine, which triggered new guilt over the death of his wife, Lynn, had left DiPalma depressed and suffering from his own ghosts. And so he had expected to meet an equally despondent Todd, a boy also saddened by two deaths. Instead Frank had met a composed, self-possessed and dry-eyed youngster, who had coolly shaken his hand and called him sir. Was the boy in shock or somehow managing to imitate the samurai he admired? Whatever the reason, Todd's composure was disturbing. And *different*.

DiPalma had been met at Kai Tak Airport by Roger Tan, a Chinese-American DEA agent he had known and worked with in New York and who was now stationed in Hong Kong. Roger had whisked him through customs and immigration without a baggage check, then taken him off to the side and told him about Katharine and Ian Hansard. Without saying a word DiPalma walked away. Roger Tan knew enough to leave the big man alone.

Tan walked to the newsstand, purchased a copy of the *International Herald Tribune* and turned to the sports pages. Fifteen minutes later the drug-enforcement agent, his head still buried in the paper, heard DiPalma say, "Let's go." Tan, who knew about Katharine Hansard and Frank, saw that DiPalma had been weeping. He also saw guilt and anger on that flat face and knew that the big man was at war with himself. Katharine's death would plunge him into war with others. Tan was glad he wasn't among them.

In the car Roger Tan had done most of the talking. He was in his early thirties, a short, broad-shouldered man with a round, boyish face and perfect teeth which he cleaned with mint-flavored dental floss several times daily. A federal drug agent for ten years, Tan was convinced that the agency was holding him back because he was Chinese and married to a white woman. He enjoyed passing on damaging or unflattering gossip about his superiors. He was also the only born-again Chinese-American DiPalma had ever met and held the highly original theory that Jesus had married, raised a family and spent time in China.

Roger Tan was correct about being the victim of bigotry. The bigotry, however, came not from DEA, but from the British on the Hong Kong police force, who had a racist dislike of working with the Chinese. For that reason Washington was reluctant to send Chinese-American drug agents to the colony. Unfortunately for Roger, DEA now needed intelligence on Asian drug dealers badly enough to assign him to the Far East.

Roger Tan was a good agent; he was also a vain man, one in constant need of praise from superiors and co-workers and a nuisance to them when he didn't get it. Frank DiPalma had failed to convince him that, race aside, insolence and abrasiveness did not help anyone's law-enforcement career. In the end DiPalma decided that Roger Tan would rather complain than not talk about himself at all.

As the car pulled away from the airport DiPalma said, "Forget the hotel. Take me to the Hansard place." After a long silence he added, "She telephoned me two days ago. Said she was afraid. Asked me to come as soon as I could."

"Figured it was something like that. Yes, sir, that's exactly how I figured it. You know Ling Shen hasn't forgotten his promise. The minute your plane touched down he knew about it. Bet a month's pay that somebody at customs or immigration's on the horn to him now, telling them you're back in Hong Kong."

DiPalma ignored the reminder that a death sentence hung over him in a land where such promises were always carried out. "Why does everyone think her death was an accident?"

"The evidence says so. She did metal sculpture and she used an acetylene torch. So you're talking about mixing gas and fire. Figure it out for yourself. The odds are strong that something can go wrong, especially, say, if she was a smoker."

"She wasn't."

"How can you be so sure? You haven't seen her in eleven years."

"Katharine was a nurse. She'd watched people die from lung cancer and she never forgot it. She hated the smell of tobacco and she wasn't the kind of woman to change her mind easily. What about Hansard?"

Roger Tan leered. Talking about Hansard was a chance to gossip, a chance to show off. "Found that sucker over in Kowloon, face down in Yuamatei Harbour. That's boat-people territory and most of them are illegal immigrants. They live like pigs, let me tell you. It's worse than any slum we've got in the States and twice as dangerous. They have these floating whorehouses if you're looking for cheap nookie, but I don't recommend it. Most of them are one-woman sampans and man, that boat does not stop rocking while you're pumping away. Ain't a day goes by some turkey doesn't get taken off over there or killed. Hey, they didn't just take Hansard's wallet and jewelry. They took his pants and shoes. I mean, shit."

"Cobra venom," said DiPalma. "Isn't that way out even for Hong Kong?"

Roger Tan chuckled. "Man, nothing is way out for Hong Kong. This town is in-fucking-credible. I'm not surprised at anything that happens here. Look, the boat people never leave the water. So they keep pets. So maybe somebody kept a cobra. Cops tell me the venom puffed up Hansard like he was a float in some parade. Face was bloated, purple, skin torn off. The man goes over there to play hide the wienie and ends up playing feed the cobra. Fucking funny when you think about it."

DiPalma looked out the car window at the ferris wheels of the Kai Tak amusement park. "You would think a guy as smart as Hansard would know better than to go strolling through Yuamatei any time, let alone late at night."

"I know a lot about this country," bragged Tan, "and I'm telling you the old guys knew how to run things. I'm talking about Genghis Khan. A mean fucker, but he made the country so safe they say a virgin with a sack of gold could walk from one end of China to the other."

He grinned. "'Course, there's no record of any virgin having started and finished the walk, but what the hell. Frank, Ian Hansard was a chaser. I know what I'm talking about. Strictly Orientals. No whites, no blacks, no plaids. Orientals only. So maybe he had something special going for him in Yuamatei."

DiPalma slowly turned his head and gave Roger Tan a hooded look. Tan, his eyes on the road, felt the weight of the former detective's gaze. After a minute Tan stopped chewing his lip and sighed. "All right, all right. So he was killed somewhere else, then taken across the harbor and dumped. So a dude in his position doesn't put his ass on the line chasing bimbos in a neighborhood that's worse than Newark and Detroit combined."

Tan made a left turn onto Lion Rock Road, slowing down for the flood of chinese who came there daily for the Kowloon city market, a huge concentration of indoor and outdoor stalls. He was still right about most of what he had said about Hansard's death, and set out to prove it.

"I know what I'm talking about when it comes to the boat people in this town. If they saw anything happen to Hansard, we won't hear about it. Like I said, they're illegal aliens from the mainland, with no papers, no ID, no visas, no nothing. The last thing they want to do is talk to the police. You said something about Katharine Hansard being afraid, that she had asked you to come to Hong Kong."

DiPalma used the fingertips of both hands to rub the sleep from his eyes. "Why were you investigating Ian Hansard?"

"You don't miss anything, do you?"

"You know a lot about his death. Cobra venom, the way his face looked, what was taken from his corpse. You said yourself Hansard had no wallet, no ID and not that much of a face. I think you were interested in him for some reason and ended up helping to identify him. Hong Kong is a hustler's town, the name of the game is get rich anyway you can. This place is money mad and Ian Hansard was in the money business. Since he and Katharine died at the same time—one hell of a coincidence by the way—I'd like you to tell me about Ian Hansard and the money business."

"That's your trouble, Frank. You don't come out and say what's on your mind. Okay. Hansard was chairman of the board and chief executive officer of Eastern Pacific Amalgamated Limited Bank. There are almost five hundred banks in Hong Kong, and Eastern's one of the biggest. It's got branches in over sixty countries. Hansard made a damn good living from Eastern and he was not very particular how he did it."

"So he was washing money. Who for?"

"The world. For openers, the Chinese underworld here and on the mainland. The Chiu Chau used him, which made Hansard a heavy hitter when it came to drug deals."

Hong Kong's Chiu Chau syndicates, named for a dialect spoken in southern China, had controlled most of Asia's narcotics traffic for over a hundred years. It was the Chiu Chau, protected by South Vietnamese politicians and military officers, who refined and distributed the powerful number-four heroin which created over twenty thousand addicts among American troops in Southeast Asia. The purity of heroin sold on American streets rarely exceeded 2 percent; number four's purity ranged from 80 to 99 percent.

Protected by Hong Kong's top government officials, the Chiu Chau also controlled much of the colony's organized crime. There were other secret societies in Hong Kong, along with criminal clans and gangs, but none matched the Chiu Chau for wealth, power and brutal efficiency. So tightly structured were the Chiu Chau that even the names of its half dozen leaders were unknown.

DiPalma said, "What about the Big Circle and the Red Guards?"

The Big Circle was a Chinese crime syndicate based in Shanghai; it had pulled off major bank robberies and hijackings in the colony, then invested the money in Hong Kong real estate, trading companies, dance halls, brothels and narcotics. The Big Circle was even rumored to own a few of the colony's banks.

As for the Red Guards, who had fallen out of favor on the mainland after Mao's death, some had drifted to Hong Kong and used their military training to pull off spectacular bank robberies and lucrative kidnappings.

109

Hong Kong police had captured many of them, but not all.

Roger Tan said, "There was only one thing Hansard was concerned about and that was whether or not you could meet his price. He charged one percent of anything he handled. Usual shit. Shift the money from one account to another, from one phony company to another, then maybe from one bank to another, from one country to another. And back again. Jesus, I'm telling you after that nobody could find the money. And that was only part of what the dude was into. The man was very heavy, and I mean heavy, into industrial espionage."

DiPalma took his hands away from his eyes. "Who's behind Eastern?"

Tan laughed. "Used to break me up. I mean Hansard pretending that Eastern was an English bank. Queen's picture on his office wall, British flag in the lobby, bagpipes playing in front of the bank. And every afternoon tea and cakes served to the bank officers in the conference room. Fucking joke. Eastern is owned by a man called Zenzo Nosaka."

DiPalma's eyes narrowed until they were almost closed.

"You've heard of Nosaka, I'm sure," said Tan. "Man's got more money than God and is older than water. We've got photographs of him and Hansard together. Couple of weeks ago Hansard drove down to Aberdeen for a business meeting on Nosaka's yacht, the *Kitaro*. That was around the time of the dragon-boat races. We had a couple of people in the crowd with telephoto lenses, but just to make sure we had a police helicopter fly one of our guys over the yacht and he gets a few shots of them together. Hansard's tied into traffickers, so we thought we might get lucky."

"Did you?"

"Bet your ass, got pictures of Hansard with known Chinese and European traffickers."

"And with Nosaka."

"And with Mr. Zenzo Nosaka."

"You mentioned something about industrial espionage."

"Yeah. See, Hansard could run his little laundry on the side just as long as he took care of business for Nosaka. That meant Hansard had to steal business secrets. And he had to wash and distribute money Nosaka used for bribes and payoffs. And he had to wash money for Nosaka's right-wing Japanese friends. I mean, I didn't go looking for any of this industrial espionage shit. I just tripped over it and included it in my report."

DiPalma said, "So you got lucky. You traced dope money to Hansard and that led to Nosaka. Don't knock it. You just might get lucky and get promoted."

"Sure. And hell could freeze over tomorrow morning."

"What I'd like to know is how a bank can be used to cop business secrets."

Tan pulled the car in a line behind other cars waiting to board the ferry that would take them across the harbor to Hong Kong island. "Shit, that's easy. A bank's always getting requests for loans. First thing they do is run a credit check. In no time at all they know all they need to know about you. Now if you just happen to work at a certain company and can get your hands on certain information, then maybe a deal is worked out. You come up with the information, you get the loan."

"And maybe you don't have to pay it back."

Tan shrugged. "A secretary needs money for her mother's operation. So she turns over her notes from a very important meeting. A guy in the research department wants a new sports car. So he turns over a file on a new product that's supposed to be top secret. A junior vice president wants to take his girlfriend to Bangkok, so he makes a tape recording of a certain sales conference and passes it on. Look, it can go down in a lot of ways, especially if a bank knows you're hurting for money and who isn't? You know how hard it is to get credit these days? You take a look at interest rates lately? Shit, Nosaka came up with a good idea."

"And Hansard was responsible for collecting that information for him?"

The car inched forward, then stopped. "From all over the world. Sixty-odd branches. Super-industrial-spy network. Real dynamite shit and I wasn't even looking for it."

"Who's on the board of directors?"

"Heavy hitters. Heavy, heavy hitters. Strong on American ex-military. Former generals, admirals, Pentagon, Defense Department and Intelligence people. A few European military brass in there, too. They bring in millions to Eastern."

"Where's the money coming from?"

"Money to be used in arms deals, private wars, expensive dirty tricks, drug sales. Money that must not be traced to anybody. And let us not forget tax dodging and a few other scams and schemes these heavy hitters are into and don't want U.S. banks to know about."

Roger Tan drove the car onto the ferry and turned off the ignition. "For the sake of argument let's say Hansard and Nosaka find themselves sitting on fifty million dollars of somebody else's dirty money. What do they do? They invest it in some stock or bond issue, but only overnight. In the morning they pull out with the interest on fifty mil, which is a nice profit. Meanwhile the money goes back into the regular account and everybody's happy."

"Which is what they did."

"You got it, crime fighter. They did it a few times a year, no more. Wait until there was a shitload of money in Eastern, then make that one overnight investment and get rich. Gave them plenty of money to pass out to the board and keep those fuckers happy."

"And Eastern's board gives Nosaka some very special Washington contacts. Neat. Real neat."

"Congress, Pentagon, CIA. What more do you need? Throw in London, Paris, Bonn. Those Europeans, remember? And you have got a man with a lot of connections." Roger Tan snapped his fingers. "Didn't tell you. A guy you popped a few years back, Sally Verna, he's on the board."

DiPalma acknowledged that revelation with a grunt. No surprises. Roger Tan's rundown on Eastern and DiPalma had put it all together. Sally Verna was on the board and Ian Hansard had been his inside man. Hansard knew of his wife's relationship with DiPalma. Through her he had learned that DiPalma was on his way to Hong Kong. So he had called Sally Verna, who then decided he had his messenger boy.

"What do you know about the Blood Oath League?" DiPalma asked.

"Fucking crazies. Strictly off the wall. The new kids in town and making trouble. Tokyo police telexed us. Wanted to know if we had anything on the league dealing dope to make money for guns. PLO, Red Brigades, they all do it. Couldn't help them. Don't know where the league's getting their bread, but it sure ain't through narcotics. I guess it's coming out of Japan, probably from guys like Nosaka and other right-wing creeps. Besides, from what I hear the league doesn't use guns."

It all came down to Nosaka, thought DiPalma. Katharine's death. The death of her husband. The Blood Oath League, the Eastern Pacific Amalgamated Limited Bank, Sally Verna and a file of incriminating information on one of the world's richest and most powerful men.

Roger Tan said, "What are you going to do about Ling Shen?"

"Fuck him. I want you to get me the names of Eastern's board and its chief stockholders. Also a list of the countries where it has branches."

"You think Nosaka had something to do with Hansard's murder?"

"Yeah." DiPalma squeezed his cane. "He's involved in Katharine's death, too. Somehow, some way, he is. Both were taken out in a hurry and probably for the same reason. Nosaka. He's the man. He's the one I'm going for."

The ferry eased into the dock at the Star Ferry Terminal. Roger Tan started the motor. "All of this is hard on the kid, him losing two parents at once. Well, at least Todd's got you and that should be some help to him. Poor kid. He's in a few of the pictures we took on the *Kitaro* that day. He fainted or something. Probably due to the heat. They had to get Nosaka's doctor to bring him around. Heat's a bitch in this town. A stone bitch."

* * *

ON the grounds of the Hansard home, Frank DiPalma, growing increasingly clammy in the noon heat, unbuttoned his jacket and loosened his tie. He wanted to step into the shade of the cypress tree behind him, but that would have meant walking away from Todd. Blue magpies and kites chirped and flitted among the leaves. The heat didn't seem to bother them.

He heard but could not see the Peak tramway, the funicular railway which lay beyond a nearby forest of bamboo and pine trees. DiPalma touched the jacket pocket containing the eyeglass frames that had once belonged to Katharine. He desperately wanted a drink.

A glance over his shoulder at the house showed that Roger Tan was still inside telephoning his office. Move your ass, Roger. Don't leave me out here alone. Todd had neither been hostile nor friendly. But DiPalma was certain that Todd would neither forgive him nor permit DiPalma to forgive himself. Was it time to accept responsibility for the boy? How do you go about that?

DiPalma had stopped being a father when his three-year-old daughter had been killed by a drug dealer. But the past had reached out for him and he was a father again, forced to do his best. With Katharine dead and Todd alone, he had no choice.

The heat reminded DiPalma of how Katharine had died. He closed his eyes. There was no more painful way of dying then to be burned alive.

Todd said, "My mother was dead before the fire started."

DiPalma opened his eyes. "What did you say?"

"She did not suffer, sir." The boy's voice had a trace of an English accent. He was formal, with good manners. For a few seconds DiPalma had the weird feeling that Todd has read his mind.

"She never stopped loving you," said the boy. "She knew you would come. It gave her hope."

DiPalma forced a smile. "Like they say, I needed that. By the way,

113

do me a favor and call me Frank. Nothing else makes sense. I haven't been a father to you and Mr. DiPalma is too formal."

Todd bowed his head. "As you wish."

"Your mother said you were different. She mentioned something about psychic powers."

Todd frowned. "Sometimes I see things. Different things. And then at other times I suppose I'm quite normal. Like the other lads."

"It's not easy for you to relate to other boys or even to most adults, is it?"

Todd smiled. "No sir, it isn't. You can't always tell people what you think. Especially if you yourself are unsure about what you're seeing. Am I being clear?"

"Perfectly. I want you to say exactly what you want to around me. Don't feel hemmed in or uptight. Be honest. And I'll try to be the same with you."

"I know you will, sir. I mean Frank."

DiPalma took a step toward his son. "Todd, you said that your mother was dead before the fire. How can you be sure?"

The boy hesitated and looked at the cypress tree. Then he looked at DiPalma. "You said be honest, did you not?"

"Always."

"I saw it, sir. I saw it in my mind. I felt it as well. The blow to the head and in the throat."

DiPalma studied his son. Todd had taken a chance and told the truth. He had risked being laughed at or dismissed. What DiPalma said next could keep communication open between them or cut them off from each other forever. "Todd, did you see who did it?"

"I did not see, but I know. I felt a presence."

DiPalma waited as Todd frowned. Then he said, "*Kunoichi.*"

"Women *ninja.*"

"Yes, sir. I felt it was a woman, one woman."

"Todd, your mother didn't smoke, did she?"

"No, sir. She hated cigarettes. She often tried to get my stepfather to stop, but he wouldn't."

"Thanks, Todd. And the name's Frank, remember?"

The boy smiled for the first time. "I'm awfully sorry. I shall try to remember."

DiPalma placed a hand on Todd's shoulder. He felt awkward, yet it seemed the natural thing to do. "Don't worry about the name. I've been called a lot worse things than sir. If you forget, it's not the end of the world. How do you feel about sleeping in that house alone?"

114

Todd's chin dropped to his chest.

"I thought so," said Frank. "I'd feel the same way. Why don't we go to my hotel? I can clean up and we can do some more talking, if you like. If you don't want to talk, fine. You don't have to. Truth is, I might not feel like talking myself."

The boy smiled at him again. Score one in the battle for hearts and minds, thought DiPalma. But from new truths new doubts grow. There was still tomorrow, next week, an hour from now. Each day meant dealing with an eleven-year-old son he had never seen until an hour ago. That was going to take some getting used to.

They walked toward the house and reached the mansion just as a limousine turned off the road and drove up the circular driveway. Roger Tan stepped from the veranda and joined DiPalma and Todd on the lawn. The car rolled to a stop and a burly Japanese chauffeur with a close-cropped head and dark glasses opened the back door. Two men and a woman got out and walked toward them. Frank DiPalma's jaw tightened and his hooded eyes grew hard. It was a look Roger Tan didn't like.

The first man out of the limousine was Kon Kenpachi. The second was Geoffrey Laycock, a British journalist. Behind them the woman hung back, reluctant to move away from the car. She fingered the oversized sunglasses hiding much of her face and stared at DiPalma. Finally Jan Golden came forward, eyes down on the ground and stopped behind Kenpachi.

Smiling, Kenpachi said, "Todd." The boy stood rigid, as though awaiting a command. DiPalma didn't like that. When the film director looked at the former detective the smile vanished. Then he turned to Todd and the smile was once more in place. They shook hands and DiPalma, suddenly jealous, knew they had met before. He also knew he didn't want Kenpachi anywhere near his son.

Kenpachi spoke to DiPalma but kept his eyes on Todd. "I understand you are the boy's natural father."

"That's right," said DiPalma.

"He and I get along quite well, don't we, Todd?"

As though hypnotized the boy replied, "Yes."

"We met the other night at his father's party and we've seen each other every day since then. I was the first to comfort him after the unfortunate death of his parents. You're still coming to stay with me at Ikuba Castle as we agreed, aren't you, Todd?"

DiPalma took one step forward. "I'll decide whether or not Todd goes anywhere."

Kenpachi studied the big man. "Ah, yes, the natural father at last makes his appearance. And as always when others are asleep."

Before DiPalma could reply Geoffrey Laycock stepped forward, his hand extended. "Dear boy, it's terribly nice to see you again. How long has it been? Ten years? Donkey's years, actually, since we've last seen one another and you haven't changed. You wouldn't happen to have a portrait of Dorian Gray hanging over your mantelpiece, by any chance?"

Geoffrey Laycock, a stringer for several London newspapers, was in his late fifties and had been a resident of Hong Kong since the end of the war. He was a potbellied little man, effeminate and quick-witted, with a pink angular face and thinning white hair combed sideways across the top of his head. A self-proclaimed devout coward, it pleased him to make outrageous statements and get away with them. DiPalma found Laycock's nervous vitality exhausting.

Laycock wore a polka-dot bow tie, a doughnut-sized gold medallion suspended from a gold chain around his neck, pleated pants and wing tip shoes. He carried a hand-painted bamboo fan against the heat. He tapped DiPalma on the chest with it, and with one eyebrow raised appraised the big man.

"I must say, Francis, you have become increasingly masculine with the years. Quite becoming. Quite. I can see the women pouncing on you with the intensity of a lapsed vegetarian attacking a T-bone steak. And speaking of beautiful people, I was interviewing these two on either side of me, when suddenly they decided to terminate the interview and dash up here to gaze upon your child Toddie. He does have smashing eyes, our Toddie. Absolutely smashing."

Laycock, folded fan against his lips, leaned forward to stare at the boy. "Jewels for eyes," he said. "Two exquisite and flawless gems." The journalist straightened up, flicked open his fan and began fanning himself once more. "Rude of me not to have introduced you two. Frank DiPalma, may I present Miss Jan Golden, film producer extraordinaire. Miss Golden—"

"We know each other," said Jan. "How are you, Frank?"

"Jan. What are you doing in Hong Kong?"

She smiled nervously. "I can see you don't read the trade papers. I'm producing a film here. Kon's directing. Actually, most of it's being made in Japan. We're only doing a week or so in Hong Kong."

"How's Hollywood?"

"Like somebody once said, you can take all the sincerity out there and stick it in a flea's navel. There are days when I'd like to chop it into little bits and shove it all through a six-inch hole."

"Sounds rough."

"Tide's always high and rising out there. For fear and loathing, you can't beat it. If nothing else, I've learned it's one place where sincerity definitely has its limits. But—" She smiled and shrugged. "It was my choice, wasn't it?"

There was something unspoken between her and DiPalma which caused Kenpachi and Laycock to watch them both. DiPalma broke the tension. "I'd like you to meet my son, Todd. Todd, this is Jan Golden."

As they shook hands she said, "Pleased to meet you, Todd. Geoffrey mentioned something about Frank being your father."

Todd gave DiPalma the warmest smile since their meeting. "Yes, he is my father."

With his back to Kenpachi, the boy looked up at Frank. "My mother wanted to be buried according to Fung Shui. Would you help me to do as she wished?"

It was a trust that DiPalma knew he must honor. "I will. We'll do exactly what she would have wanted."

Fung Shui, wind and water, were the unwritten Chinese spiritual laws which guided yin and yang, the female-passive and male-active elements in nature. It was an ancient Chinese custom applied to the construction of home, office buildings, highways or tombs. The most auspicious location had to be chosen and bad spirits appeased.

Kenpachi said, "Todd, is there anything I can do?"

"No," said DiPalma.

Before the film director could reply a police car entered the driveway and pulled up behind the limousine. Two British police officers got out, leaving a Chinese driver in the car. When the policemen reached the group on the lawn, the officer in charge looked boldly at Jan before stating his business.

"Inspector Jenkins. And this is Officer Cole. We've come for the boy."

Jenkins was the Welshman who had come to the Hansard mansion to speak to Katharine Hansard about her son fighting in the streets. Then Jenkins had been forced to bend the knee and bow his head and eventually crawl out of the Hansard mansion with his tail between his legs. Now he wanted his own back. Both Hansards were a lump of lead, leaving him only the boy on whom to take his revenge.

"I'm Todd's father," said DiPalma. "I'd like to know where you're taking him and why."

Jenkins combed his red mustache with manicured fingers and looked at his partner, a hawk-nosed Scot with tufts of hair sprouting from his ears and nostrils. Then he looked back at DiPalma with open contempt. Without a word Jenkins grabbed Todd by the elbow and almost jerked him off his feet.

DiPalma's speed and grace did not go with his size; the big man moved with a terrible swiftness. A blurred lifting of his right arm and the tip of his black oak cane dug into Jenkins's larynx. Eyes bulging, Jenkins gagged, took his hands off Todd and shoved the cane aside. A second later the inspector's right hand was inside his jacket and reaching for his shoulder holster.

DiPalma attacked again. A flick of his wrist and the cane cracked Jenkins on the right elbow. The Welshman yelped, jerking the hand back as though his gun were hot metal.

His partner drew his revolver, but Roger Tan stepped in front of him. "Stay cool, man," said the DEA agent. "This thing doesn't call for guns. Just stay cool."

The Scot spoke through clenched teeth. "Out of my way, bastard, or I'll put a hole in you."

Geoffrey Laycock, manicured white hands fluttering in front of his face, intervened. "Gentlemen, please. Must we have so much belligerence in this oppressive heat? Please, let us all take three very deep breaths and hold the last one for a count of ten before saying another word. Please."

For a few seconds there was only the sound of Jenkins's loud breathing. Red-faced with anger, he held his pained elbow and stared at Frank DiPalma with hatred. Finally he spoke with forced calm, the corners of his wide mouth flecked with spit.

"You, sir, are under arrest. The charge is interfering with a territorial officer in the performance of his duty. I understand that in the States you are Jack the Lad on telly. However, in Hong Kong you rank as high as whatever happens to be stuck to the sole of my shoe. Nor does your Chinese compatriot, who interfered with my partner, rank much higher. You fucking Americans think your money buys you the right to put your foot on our throats. Well, Jocko, I intend to put the lie to that. The ball's in my court now and when I get you down to headquarters I will personally make you pay for being so confident and stupid."

"Inspector?"

Jan Golden's smile was sinister, her eyes bright. "I witnessed what just happened. I saw you abuse Mr. DiPalma's son and I'll not only bring it to the attention of the American consulate, but I'll see that the governor is informed as well."

Jenkins shook his head in mock sorrow. "Oh dear, oh dear. Whatever

118

in the world do we have here? Why it's the liberated American woman bringing her righteous anger to the Far East. Bloody decent of you to give us yabbos an intoxicating breath of freedom. Now let me inform you of something. As far as I'm concerned you can get stuffed. Stay the hell out of my way or I will make you wish you had."

Geoffrey Laycock opened his mouth, but Jan Golden, the smile still in place, silenced him with a lifted hand. Stepping closer to Jenkins until they were almost nose to nose, she folded her arms across her chest, then spoke softly.

"Mister, if you arrest Mr. DiPalma, I will telephone the governor and tell him I am pulling my production out of Hong Kong as of today. Then I shall call the American consulate and tell them what I am doing and why. Finally, I shall call a press conference. I think the press will want to know that one million dollars and five hundred badly needed jobs are going to go flying out of your little town. All that hard work by your local film commission down the tubes. And when I finish spreading the word no one will want to come here and make a picture."

Jenkins concentrated on Jan's nose. He had been intimidated as soon as she had walked up to him. There was no getting around it; women with power, like her and Katharine Hansard, easily intimidated him. And Jan, with an instinct for brutal infighting, knew she had beaten him. Still smiling, she gently patted him on the cheek, then walked away.

Geoffrey Laycock stepped forward. "Dear God, it's all so heart stopping. Inspector, allow me to point out that if Miss Golden leaves Hong Kong under these circumstances, it will be terribly bad public relations for the territory."

"So it's taking her side, is it?" An angry Jenkins aimed a clenched fist at Laycock. "And I suppose your version of this little affair is destined to appear in those slimy rags you write for."

Laycock raised both eyebrows. "This is one of the governor's favorite projects, not to mention being a favorite of the legislative council. You'll not be first in their hearts for having botched it up. Furthermore, your opinion to the contrary, Mr. DiPalma is an important journalist and any difficulty encountered by him would undoubtedly be looked into by his American television network. Dear boy, we both know that the Hong Kong police department cannot stand close scrutiny at this time. Or at any other time. But, of course, you are free to do as you please."

Jenkins said to no one in particular, "There is a Chinese couple waiting at the police station who claim to be an aunt and uncle of the late Katharine Hansard. They have identification supporting this claim, which under Hong Kong law makes them the boy's sole kin."

DiPalma said, "I'm the boy's father. Besides, when Todd was born Katharine's entire family disowned her."

"We've only your word that you're the boy's father."

"Check hospital records. Check—"

Jenkins shook his head. "Mister, I don't have to check a bloody thing. My orders are to bring the boy down to police headquarters and that's what I intend to do. Any opposition from you is in clear violation of the law."

"I'm afraid he's right," Laycock said. "You'll simply have to let the boy go."

DiPalma shook his head. "Katharine's relatives cut off any contact with her years ago. There's no secret about that."

"Ah, but the law, dear boy, is, if not blind, then afflicted with a severe case of cataracts."

Roger Tan said, "To get custody of Todd, you'll have to let him go. You stand in their way and they'll have the right to come back here with a small army and do whatever's necessary. If that happens, Todd could get hurt. And you can't sneak him out of Hong Kong because that makes both of you fugitives. Your best chance is to find proof that you're the natural father."

DiPalma said, "Eleven years ago they ran me out of this town. Ran me out. The game was played by their rules and I lost. Wasn't allowed to see Katharine before being put on the plane. Never saw Todd. And now I get here too late to help Katharine. Too goddam late. Even if I come up with papers saying I'm the natural father, I'm going to end up playing by somebody else's rules. Well, I think I'll change the rules. Todd, go with them. I'll see you soon."

DiPalma, followed by Roger Tan, left the group and walked toward the house. At the veranda a knot of servants scattered and made a path for them. When the two men had disappeared inside the house Jenkins said to Todd, "If it isn't asking too much, your worship, would you mind getting into the fucking car?"

Todd slowly walked ahead of Jenkins and his partner to the car. Kenpachi had drifted over to the limousine, where he and Wakaba, the chauffeur, now talked quietly in Japanese. Jan Golden and Geoffrey Laycock were left alone with each other. And while Jan stared at the house, Laycock stared at her.

"My dear," he said sympathetically, "the only way to be happy by means of the heart is to have none. You loved him once, didn't you? I saw it in your eyes. They say there are two great moments in a woman's life. The first is when she falls hopelessly in love with a man. And the second, of course, is when she leaves him. You, my precious, have obviously had your great moments with Mr. DiPalma."

"He asked me to marry him. I said yes. And then I walked away."

She looked at Laycock. "I'm sure you'd like to know why."

Laycock, eyes bright with anticipation, leaned forward.

Jan Golden smiled through her tears. "I just bet you would." And she walked away from him.

8

THE LIMOUSINE carrying Jan Golden, Kon Kenpachi and Geoffrey Laycock entered Statue Square, the location of Hong Kong's most powerful banks. A tap on the window from Laycock's fan directed Jan's attention to the chunky gray silhouette of the Bank of China, whose doorways were guarded by forbidding stone lions. She drew deeply on her cigarette and allowed the British journalist to tell her what she already knew, what she had learned from her father: that China owned a dozen banks and controlled over 20 percent of Hong Kong's deposits; that China had billions of dollars invested in Hong Kong businesses; that China and not the British Parliament controlled Hong Kong's very existence.

"China can take back Hong Kong without firing a single shot," Laycock said. "A telephone to the Queen and it's done. Whole damn colony is nervous about the treaty coming to an end, you know. Fifteen years from now, in 1997, Britain's ninety-nine year lease expires and China gets the bloody territory back. All four hundred square miles and some two hundred thirty-five useless islands. The mere thought of a Communist takeover strikes the fear of death in us all, especially among the posh set. Having grave effects already, I must say. Stock prices dropping, Hong Kong dollar sinking, fewer investments being made and that rather telltale sign— money moving abroad in suspiciously large amounts."

Suddenly the limousine braked, almost throwing Jan out of her seat. A cream-colored minibus had cut in front of them without warning. Fucking Hong Kong traffic. Worse than anything Jan had seen in Paris, Rome or New York. The minibuses were small, privately owned vehicles which were allowed to compete with regular buses and trams. They could stop anywhere. A prospective passenger had only to hold out his hand or stand in the road and flag them down. To get off, one simply yelled at the driver.

To calm her nerves Jan lit another cigarette, then opened the window to allow the smoke to escape. Twenty minutes ago the limousine had left the Hansard mansion to return to location filming in Wanchai, once a popular red light district for American servicemen on leave from Vietnam. Laycock had begun babbling about Hong Kong, past and present, while Kenpachi buried himself in a leather-bound copy of his script. He used a felt-tip pen to make notes in the margins. The notes were in Japanese, beautifully formed characters running down the left side of each page.

If the notes were to himself, fine. But if they were dialogue changes or called for new camera setups, Jan wanted to be consulted. Meanwhile, Kenpachi had shut her and Laycock out. A director had the right to concentrate on his work without being interrupted; Kenpachi would be in deep shit if he didn't take his craft seriously. Jan suspected, however, that at the moment Kenpachi simply wanted to avoid talking to her about Frank DiPalma. Christ, what a shock that had been. She hadn't known the two men knew each other, let alone hated each other's guts.

As for Geoffrey Laycock, the man would not shut up. Jan bore the brunt of his running commentary on Hong Kong; her mind, however, was on Frank DiPalma. Kenpachi and Frank. The story of Jan's life. The man she wanted versus the man she needed. And as always Jan would make her choice according to her passion.

She knew that the immediate pleasure was always her undoing, that it drew her into what was often nothing more than the encounter of two weaknesses. But like everyone else, she did what she wanted to do. For her, pleasure lay in the knowledge that love was only temporary, that it would not last. With Frank DiPalma, love had threatened to last and so a frightened Jan had left him. She had not wanted to change. And yet she could not forget him.

In the stalled traffic she stared through tinted glass at the domed and colonnaded Supreme Court Building on the east side of Statue Square. It was a lovely example of Edwardian architecture by Aston Webb, the man who had designed London's Victoria and Albert Museum and the facade of Buckingham Palace. The building reminded her of Frank DiPalma. Surrounded by banks, glass and steel high-rises and even a Hilton hotel, it went its own way with dignity and grace. And with strength.

Geoffrey Laycock covered a yawn with his fan, reminding Jan of something Kon Kenpachi had said about Frank. Something to do with sleep. She looked at Kenpachi, still wrapped up in his script. She wanted answers now, not when Kon was ready to give them to her.

She said to Geoffrey Laycock, sitting across from her, "Kon's in another world at the moment, so perhaps you can help me. Something was said back there about Frank only showing up when people were asleep. I understand that Japanese and even Chinese often disguise the truth in their remarks, especially if the truth happens to be unpleasant. Do you have any idea what that sleep business was all about?"

Laycock's eyes widened. The fan waved briskly. "Death, my dear. In this case, sleep is a euphemism for death. Surely you know Mr. DiPalma's reputation. People dying around him and all that."

Jan could have kicked Kon for making that crack about Frank. But right now she didn't want to risk an argument. Making a picture was tough enough without antagonizing your director.

Laycock frowned. "I believe, yes, it was three. Frank suffered the loss of three partners while serving as a policeman. And he himself also sent a few men to their eternal rest. Strictly in the line of duty, of course. Some people looked upon him as a walking albatross, rather a black cloud of sorts."

"He killed to save his life or somebody else's," she said. "There wasn't a cop in the department who wouldn't have been glad to have Frank DiPalma as a partner."

"I cast no aspersions, I fling no brickbats. I merely report what has transpired. You are aware, of course, of the deaths of his wife and daughter?"

"They were taken hostage by a drug dealer, then murdered. Are you blaming Frank for that?"

"Absolutely not. I'm merely answering your question. People around Mr. DiPalma do tend to fall into 'the big sleep', as they say in detective thrillers. New York Hispanics nicknamed him 'Muerte', death. Another colorful street name for him, I'm told was 'Mr. Departure.' May I ask how you and Frank became acquainted?"

"We met at the network. I was in charge of all series and made-for-television movies produced in New York. Frank was hired as an investigative crime reporter."

"Quite accomplished at it, I hear."

"The best. Surprised the hell out of everybody. No one has better contacts, not even reporters with ten times his experience. The camera doesn't scare him and his crew love him. They know he's good and that they'll get to work on some exciting stuff, so they walk through walls for him. You can't compare him to most of the people in television. What they lack in brains they make up in stupidity."

The limousine started up again, leaving behind white-clad Englishmen playing cricket in Statue Square Park. Kenpachi was still buried in his script.

"A few of Frank's stories have gone on to make the newspapers," said Laycock. "Our English-language papers here have carried one or two. There was that rather odd one where he solved the murder of a young black child. She had been struck in the head by a bullet while lying in her pram. Somehow Frank learned the killing had been done by a local drug dealer. Apparently the dealer had money stacked floor to ceiling in a closet, and the rats had gotten at it. Eaten almost a hundred thousand dollars, if I recall. Bloody dealer became enraged, drew his pistol and began firing at the rats. A stray bullet killed the child. Amazing how Frank was able to go into the ghetto and in hours discover who had done it."

"Frank knows everybody. I've never seen a reporter with a better information network."

"I concur. And he does take advantage of every opportunity to enlarge that network, doesn't he?"

"What's that supposed to mean?"

"Please don't take offense. I was merely referring to the way in which he handled the story on the killing of the three judges in Palmero, Sicily."

Jan said, "Frank risked his life to get the story. He could have been killed."

"Indeed. I mean, after all, it did involve the American and Sicilian Mafia. Three judges murdered while trying Sicilian heroin traffickers and our Frank finding out that the hit man was an American living in Manhattan."

"Frank used to be a narc, remember? Somebody he knew owed him a favor and gave him a tip. He followed it up at the risk of his life."

"And he was clever enough to bring in an important American senator to share the acclaim. If I remember, the publicity from this case aided the senator in getting reelected. Very, very clever of Francis. And you say he's had no journalistic training?"

"None. His parents were Sicilian immigrants who ran a small produce market in Queens. He drove a truck for his father, fought the head breakers who tried to muscle in on the family business and managed to get in a couple of years of college before losing interest. He left school, got drafted by the army and was sent to Europe to work in the army's criminal-investigation division. Got out, bummed around Europe for a few months, then came home and became a cop."

Laycock sniffed behind his fan. "Not much formal education, apparently."

"Mister, the army can be one hell of an education. I should know. My father was an army officer and I learned plenty being around him."

"Forgive me. I meant no offense. I merely—"

"Mr. Laycock, I was born in Japan. My father did three tours of duty there and I was with him on two of them. By the time I was fourteen I had lived in six countries and in seven American states. When I grew older, I attended three different colleges and never learned as much as I did when I was an army brat."

"How did you become a film producer, if you don't mind my asking?"

"No, I don't mind. I had a failed marriage on my hands because my husband preferred gambling to me. I also was rather sick to my stomach at the constant rejection that went with trying to become an actress. I wanted glamor, money, power, fame, freedom. They all seemed to go with being a producer, so I became one."

"And the husband?"

"A trip to the Dominican Republic and ten minutes in front of a sleazeball of a judge, who tried to get me alone in his chambers, took care of that little matter. I think I married Roy because he had a year-round tan and good teeth and made me laugh. The trouble was, that outside of knowing every headwaiter in Manhattan and being able to shuffle a deck of cards with one hand, the bastard couldn't pour piss out of a boot with the instructions printed on the heel."

Laycock giggled. "Oh, I say, that's marvelous. Absolutely marvelous. Frank must have been quite a change from your husband."

"Roy was a lightweight. Frank's heavy duty."

Kenpachi closed his script and placed it on the seat between him and Jan. "Why don't you tell her why Mr. DiPalma will never leave Hong Kong alive."

Jan's head snapped toward Kenpachi, then at Laycock. The cigarette slipped from her fingers and she quickly brushed it off her skirt. Laycock picked it up and stubbed it out in the ashtray.

"I'm afraid there's more than a bit of truth in that. I'm surprised Francis never told you any of this himself."

127

"He used to say never put your business in the street," said Jan. "It just wasn't his style to open up that much. There were some clips at the network, something about him being in a shoot-out here in Hong Kong. Does it have anything to do with that?"

"Sad to say, yes. I supposed you could call it an example of Laycock's law, which is to say that just when it's darkest, things go black. It all started some eleven years ago when Frank was investigating a Chinese drug dealer in Manhattan, a lad who was a right nasty piece of work himself. Definitely mental, he was. Had the tendency to burn people alive if they displeased him. Francis was in hot pursuit and Nickie Mang knew it. Our Nickie moved back and forth between Hong Kong and America and so far had managed to avoid arrest.

"Then one day Francis learned that Nickie was returning to America by way of Canada and was bringing with him a rather large consignment of heroin. In addition, Nickie was also bringing with him a lovely new Chinese bride. Well, the worst occurred. There was a shoot-out in the Canadian woods and several of Nickie's associates lost their lives, as did his new bride."

Laycock sighed. "Not to put too fine a point on it, our Nick was now in a foul mood. He escaped the ambush and made his way to New York, where he did the last thing anyone expected him to do. He showed up at Frank's home in Queens and took his wife and daughter hostage. Frank, unfortunately, was seen as the man responsible for all of Nickie's woes, not the least of which was the demise of the late Mrs. Mang. Laycock's law turned out to be very much in evidence from here on in. Frank was still in Canada tying up loose ends in this case. By the time he managed to get to New York, it was all over. Nickie had killed Mrs. DiPalma and the little girl. He then surrendered.

"Poor Francis. He suffered the tortures of the damned and didn't know there was more to come. Now you would think that our Nickie, having proven himself sufficiently antisocial, would have been retained in custody without bail of any sort."

Jan said, "Are you telling me they let him out on bail?"

"Laycock's law, remember? I believe the proverb goes 'Laws, like the spider's web, catch the fly and let the hawk go free.' Mr. Mang's bail was set at one million dollars, an astronomical sum at the time. No one thought he could meet it. They were wrong. Once unchained, our Nick fled what had now become America's inhospitable shores and went to ground in Hong Kong. Seething with righteous anger, Frank took off with the idea of returning him to American justice."

Laycock snapped his fan shut. "Somehow Francis catches up with our

Nick and starts back to the airport with him. Between Hong Kong island and Kai Tak Airport some of Nickie's associates attacked them and fired off a shotgun at Frank. Wounded him grievously. Damned near killed the man. Believing Frank to be dead, Nickie and friends started to drive off. Ah, but Francis was not dead. He clung rather perilously to life. By a miracle he found the strength and will to draw his revolver. Emptied the gun at the villains. Didn't hit a soul. However, he did manage to hit the gas tank of the car containing Nickie and his frineds. There was an explosion and Nickie and cohorts were scattered about the countryside."

"What about the Hong Kong police? Where were they while all this was going on?"

"'The gods are moved by gifts and gold does more with men than words.' Euripedes. There is a great deal of money to be made in Hong Kong and sometimes the making of it is helped by having the police on your side. This is an advantage which does not come cheap. Our local constabulary, sad to say, too often becomes corrupted. Alas, Francis was left on his own. Rumor had it that the police kept Nickie Mang's friends aware of Francis's whereabouts at all times. Another rumor says the police were paid handsomely to sit on their hands. Now we come to the romantic portion of our tale, equally as sad and as unfulfilling. While recovering in a Kowloon hospital, Francis met a lovely young Chinese nurse."

"Katharine Hansard."

"At the time, Katharine Shen. Her father Ling Shen headed the important Triad here. A Triad is—"

"I know. My father had contact with them during the war. They began as patriotic societies meeting in temples. That was a long time ago. Today Triads are little more than thugs and head breakers. They live off extortion and payoffs and whatever else brings in money without working too hard."

Laycock studied Jan before answering. Then, "A taste for truth and she spares nothing. Be that as it may, Katharine Shen and Frank DiPalma were drawn toward one another, with the result that she soon found herself *enceinte*. Preggers. You know, of course, that the Chinese regard themselves as the world's superior race."

Jan looked at Kenpachi out of the corner of her eyes. "As do the Japanese."

"Quite. Well, then, you have some idea of just how embarrassing Katharine's pregnancy was to her father and family. He, in particular, regarded it as an acute slur on the house of Shen. Fact is, Ling Shen was ready to kill our Francis. For that matter, the American government was not too fond of Francis either."

"Why? Since when is falling in love a crime against the United States?"

"You see, dear girl, we were at that point in time, 1970-71, when your President Nixon and his secretary of state Mr. Henry Kissinger were opening China up to what they rather pompously called 'the free world'. Secret meetings, coded cables, scrambled telephone calls. Very high-powered goings on. Diplomatic relations between America and China, which had ceased when the Communists came to power, were now about to resume."

"Christ," said Jan. "I can smell it coming. Go on."

"Think of it. China in the American camp and keeping an eye on the Russian bear. Do you know how many divisions this is worth to your country? In the light of that fact, Francis and Katharine, of course, became expendable. Shen set the ball in motion. He had enough influence in mainland China and Hong Kong to have them pressure your country. Simply put, the powers that be combined to have Francis booted out of Hong Kong. Furthermore, back in the States he was denied the necessary visas to reenter Hong Kong. The White House, Peking and Hong Kong. A most unholy trinity and a most powerful one. Our Francis never had a chance. He was not allowed to make waves. Time passed and both he and Katharine settled into new lives. They kept in contact with one another over the years, but the damage had been done. The world had used them ill."

"And Frank never saw his son until today."

"Yes."

"I don't care what you say, there was more than just 'contact' between them over the years. Frank came back to Hong Kong knowing what might happen to him. There has to be a reason for that."

"I'm afraid I can't shed much light on the reason for his return. Katharine did save his life, more or less. The death of his wife and child had to be a shattering experience. And there was the severity of his wounds. The doctors despaired of his life. He was broken in body and spirit. Then along came Katharine and he had a reason to live."

Jan closed her eyes. "And he never told me any of this."

"It was Katharine, by the way, who encouraged our Francis to take up Japanese fencing. Quite good at it, he is. You saw the business back there with the cane. He knows a bit about Japanese swords as well."

"*Gaijin*," said Kenpachi. "Nothing more, nothing less."

"*Gaijin* means—" began Laycock.

"I know what it means," said Jan. "Outsider. Alien. It's the name Japanese give to foreigners. That's your mistake, Kon. If you knew Frank DiPalma, you'd know it doesn't bother him to be an outsider, that he doesn't care what people think of him."

130

"Shen thinks of him. At this very moment, I would imagine that Shen is thinking of your Mr. DiPalma."

"You sound like you want him dead. I don't like that, Kon. I don't like it one goddamn little bit."

Laycock said, "Mr. Kenpachi does not exaggerate. To save face, Shen must kill Francis. Things have not gone well with Shen of late. Triad chiefs hold power on the basis of performance, nothing else. A mistake here and there and a chief can still retain his position. Too many mistakes, however, and he would find himself removed. Often this means a permanent removal from the world as we know it. The word is that if Shen makes just one more mistake, he will be sent to join his celestial ancestors."

"And failing to kill Frank DiPalma constitutes a mistake?"

"Dear girl, in Hong Kong, life is real and indeed quite earnest. Recently someone sent Shen a message by way of reminding him how much his authority has eroded of late. They kidnapped one of his lieutenants, then returned the fellow to Shen the next day. He was still alive. However, both hands and feet had been cut off."

"Christ."

"I read it as a power struggle of some sort. Definitely a difference of opinion between incompatibles. Fascinating business, these local crime wars. A provincial form of amusement."

"Am I alone on this one?" Jan said angrily. "Frank's walking around Hong Kong in danger of being done in by some damn weirdo and all you two can do is sit there."

"What do you expect us to do?" said Laycock. "I, for one, am no threat and Mr. Kenpachi, for another, was hired by you to direct a film, not flex his muscles on anyone's behalf. If Frank wants help, I'm sure he'll ask for it. He didn't have to come to Hong Kong and he most certainly doesn't have to stay."

Jan sighed. "I know him. He's here for a reason and he's not leaving until he's ready. He's filled with guilt over Katharine and the only way to get rid of that is by taking care of Todd. You can put money on it. You won't get him out of Hong Kong so easily this time. Shen or no Shen, Frank will do what he came here to do. And he'll leave when he's finished. With Todd."

She took her sunglasses from her purse, put them on and looked through the window. She didn't see Kenpachi's face as he stared at her with cold disdain. Nor did she see the eye contact between the director and Geoffrey Laycock and the tiny smile on the journalist's face before his fan came up to hide it.

131

She now hated Hong Kong because of the danger it represented to Frank. A part of her knew that she had made a mistake in leaving him. But it was her style to persist in certain mistakes, especially mistakes concerning men.

Laycock was right; there was nothing she could do for Frank DiPalma. Except remember how much she owed him and hope with all her heart that he would leave Hong Kong as soon as possible.

The limousine slowed down. They were in Wanchai, on Lockhart Road, the main thoroughfare, with its tattooists, its pungent cooking odors, topless bars, massage parlors, gaudy hostess clubs and Chinese ballrooms. "The Wanch," as it was known to the locals, was shopworn and tacky, Times Square with egg rolls, downtown Los Angeles with sweet and sour sauce.

Jan could not wait to say good-bye to the neon lights, the schlocky souvenir shops and particularly to the pushy bar girls with their bared nipples. Kenpachi had insisted on shooting here because The Wanch had played a part in the lives of lonely GIs during the Vietnam war. He was right, but she still detested the place.

Ahead Jan saw the cameras and lights, the crew and actors in front of a cheap hotel which was to be the scene of a sad farewell between Tom Gennaro, a GI on leave, and the Hong Kong bar girl with whom he's spent the night. Jan was glad to be back on the set, in her own world and away from other people's problems. Especially Frank DiPalma's.

The limousine stopped. Jan took her compact from her purse, checked her hair in the mirror and touched up her lipstick. When Kenpachi's chauffeur opened the door, she left without saying a word to the director or to Geoffrey Laycock. She headed straight for Stephen, her production manager.

Smart man, Stephen. Always had a lid or two of grass stashed somewhere. Jan wanted something to make her worry less about Frank Di-Palma, to give her some hint as to why she still wanted to go to bed with Kon Kenpachi. Bring on the Acapulco gold, she thought. There were times when reality needed fine tuning.

9

FRANK DIPALMA stood at a bay window in the living room of the Hansard mansion and watched the limousine carrying Jan Golden disappear down the tree-lined road from Victoria Peak. A telephone receiver was squeezed between his jaw and shoulder, and his little black book of addresses and telephone numbers was opened face down on a nearby jade cabinet. A seven-foot Martineau clock, its long trunk encasing a brass pendulum, struck one in the afternoon. Time. It had softened his anger toward Jan for walking out on him. It had even lessened the pain. What it hadn't done was free him from her.

From the start there had been this difference between them; DiPalma measured love by it fidelity and seriousness, Jan measured it in terms of sensuality and an almost theatrical compulsion. She was elaborate and inexplicable, and he loved her. She was ambitious, conniving, impatient and unreliable. She was also honest, caring, generous and loyal. The mystery which was Jan Golden was one that Frank despaired of solving.

And because in their courtship she had fled from him, he had instinctively pursued her.

In bed, on their last night together, Jan had warned him, "Frank, there's not enough time to do all the things I want to in this world. What I'm saying is, I can't give too much time to anything. Or anybody."

"So you expect a lot out of life. What you end up with is something else again. Meanwhile we've got something here and now. And you know it."

"Frank, with me you'll always be chasing two rabbits. And the guy who does that never catches either one."

"What do you want me to tell you, that I won't play the game unless there's an easy way out? Look, we come into the world crying, we bitch like hell while we're here and most of us go out terribly disappointed. There are no easy answers for anybody. My father told me that life's a choice between boredom and exhaustion. He ended up working himself to death, which is a hell of a way to prove a point."

"I'll exhaust you, Frank. God knows I don't mean to, but I will. The only thing I know for sure is that I'm always at war with myself. Always have been and can't tell why. But I've never met a man like you, a man stronger than I am. I don't know if that's good or bad."

"Do you love me?"

"Today I do."

"Today's the day I'm asking you to marry me."

"Jesus, what am I doing?"

"Yes or no."

"Yes." And then she was in his arms, her mouth on his, her tongue spearing his. By saying yes to DiPalma, to the moment, she now had a moment without fear, without uncertainty, without doubt.

In the morning when he awoke she was gone. Later that day he learned that she was en route to Los Angeles, to begin work on a three-picture deal she had quietly signed with a Hollywood studio. It would have done no good to call, so he hadn't. He recognized that Jan had done what she wanted to do, as always. All DiPalma could do was forget.

In the Hansard home Roger Tan was talking in singsong Cantonese to a pair of Chinese servants. Roger had learned something interesting about Ian Hansard's love life; days before his death the banker had been seen with a beautiful Japanese fashion designer, who had come to him for money and financial advice. Her name was Yoshiko Mara. A *woman* ninja *killed my mother said Todd.* No matter how trivial or personal, nothing happened in Hong Kong without the Chinese knowing it. And the Chinese loved to gossip, especially about *gweilos.*

A telephone call to the DEA office had produced a list of Eastern Amalgamated's board of directors. There had been no time to read it. At the moment, DiPalma had something more important to do. To get what you wanted you made the other guy see the light or feel the heat. DiPalma wanted his son and he knew how to go about getting him.

He shifted the receiver to his other ear. Instantly he heard, "Hello, Frank? You there?"

"Yes, senator. Sorry to wake you, but I need your help."

"You must need it real bad. It's one in the morning. Unfortunately, I'm still up. Getting some things ready for a breakfast meeting with the vice-president. I owe you one, that's for sure. Wasn't for you I'd be drinking myself to death in some second-rate Washington law firm."

"You and my father were friends, senator. He would have wanted me to help you."

"Your old man and me were more than just friends, Frank. Couple of ginzos who started out dirt poor and ended up doing okay." He laughed, a deep, warm sound. "Hey, paisan, we did it, didn't we. Fucking bastards in the party thought I was too old to run. Told me I couldn't win. But you put me back on the Hill with that Palermo thing. Feel younger than I have in years. Hell, if it wasn't for you, I'd probably be a dead man by now. Being out of work can kill a man my age. Was my wife serious? Are you really in Hong Kong?"

"Yes, senator, I am."

"What's cooking over there?"

DiPalma chose his words carefully. "Biggest thing I've gone after since I became a reporter. Might be something I can bring you in on."

Silence. And static. Then, "Something in it for me, you say. Anything you care to talk about?"

"Not right now. But if it's what I think it is, it's going to be incredible. Right now I need you to do one thing for me. One phone call."

"It's done. Just tell me who."

DiPalma rubbed the corners of his eyes with his fingertips. "First, let me tell you it concerns my son. Somebody's trying to take him from me."

"Jesus, I didn't know you were married."

"I'm not. The boy's mother is dead. Happened here yesterday. Senator, you've been to China."

"Three trips. Last one with the vice-president early this year."

"The papers say China wants U.S. arms."

Again the deep, warm laugh. "Like people in hell want ice water. What's that got to do with you?"

"Senator, I want my son. I'd like you to make that call for me now. Tonight."

"Where to?"

Frank touched the lump in his jacket pocket that was Katharine's glasses. "I'd like you to call Peking," he said.

135

10

IN HER hotel room Yoshiko Mara showered, sprinkled perfume on her wet body, then toweled herself dry. After shaving her legs and armpits, she styled her wig with a blow dryer and painted her fingernails a pale blue. Forty minutes were spent on makeup, most of it on the eyes, Yoshiko's best feature. She used three different colors of eye shadow, starting with white in the corners, then mauve on the center of the eyelid and finishing with a dark purple as she moved deeper into the socket. Coloring completed, she added false eyelashes and carefully painted them a dark brown. The result was provocative and beguiling.

The makeup done, Yoshiko stood nude in front of the bathroom mirror. Her body was slender and hard, with broad shoulders and lean but muscled arms. Her legs were those of an athlete, with solid thigh muscles and developed calves. Smiling, she stroked her flat stomach, allowing her fingers to brush the top of her pubic hair. It was a body that had given pleasure to both men and women. It was a body that promised fulfillment, no matter how forbidden the desire.

She raised her arms shoulder high, the backs of her hands toward the mirror. Her smile faded. Both forearms were scarred. This was why she wore long-sleeved dresses and blouses, to hide her body's only imperfection. She was twenty-eight and the ugly scars, which ran from wrist to

137

elbow, had been with her for half of her life. She had gotten them when she had not been called Yoshiko, when she had lived in Hakone, the mountain resort southwest of Tokyo.

Hakone, with the districts of Fuji and Izu, formed one of Japan's most popular recreation areas. Together the three districts were a huge national park, offering swimming, hiking, skiing, boating and saltwater springs. Hundreds of thousands of Japanese and foreigners came here, most of them drawn by Mount Fuji, the majestic, long-extinct volcano whose snowcapped beauty could be seen from every resort, hotel and lodge in the surrounding countryside. Hakone, famed for its therapeutic hot springs, lay at the base of Mount Fuji; the peninsula of Izu, with its beaches and rocky seaside cliffs, lay to the south.

Yoshiko was the only child of parents who owned and operated a small Hakone resort and souvenir shop near a centuries-old hot spring. Like others in the region, both parents were passionately Japanese, with a strong, almost mystical attachment to nature. Both were religious zealots and politically conservative. Years of living such a narrow life had made them prisoners of their own experience, no longer able to recognize their intolerance.

Despite her strict parents, Yoshiko grew up undisciplined and resentful of the restrictions placed upon her. From the age of eight she was forced to work in the resort, where she cleaned toilets, made beds, scrubbed floors and waited tables. When her work displeased her parents she was beaten or forced to go without food. Occasionally she was made to stand silently in her father's office, facing the wall, while he went about his business. During one beating Yoshiko fought back, breaking her father's thumb. In retaliation he blindfolded the child, tied her hands and feet and left her in a locked closet for three days without food or water.

At school Yoshiko was an indifferent student, with a reputation for defying authority. She arrived late, missed classes and hid movie magazines and photographs of professional athletes in her desk. She fought other students, sometimes played brutal pranks on them and wrote bold love notes to older boys. The more punishment was inflicted on her, the more defiant she became. Her only interests were drama and sports, especially karate and kendo.

At thirteen she became the resort guide for guests who wanted to explore the region. Yoshiko took them to Matsugaoka Koen, the pinewood park, to the Dogashima Walk, the trail leading down the side of a ravine to beautiful cascades; to the azaleas and cherry blossoms of Kowakidani, and to Owakidani, the Valley of the Great Boiling, where the air reeked of sulfur and clouds of hissing steam spurted from crevices in the rocks and a stick pushed into the earth caused steam to shoot up into the air.

Yoshiko enjoyed being a guide. It took her away from her parents, whom she hated, and from the resort, where she was treated like a slave. She took pride in her knowledge of the trails, parks and temples and in her ability to walk tens of miles without tiring. Above all there was the excitement of meeting people from Tokyo and foreign countries and learning that there was a world beyond Hakone.

At fourteen Yoshiko was seduced by a guest at the resort. He was Zenzo Nosaka, the wealthy businessman who came to Hakone for the hot salt springs that would calm his nerves, smooth his skin and prevent stomach trouble. Drawn by Yoshiko's girlish beauty and unbridled energy, Nosaka found her to be as invigorating as his twice-daily saltwater baths.

For Yoshiko the seduction was an electrifying experience, an arousal beyond fleshly joys. It was the first indication that she might have power over others, a power stronger than her parents had over her. Nosaka was influential and rich, yet she quickly sensed that his desire for her was so strong that he would leave nothing undone to satisfy it. Despite his age he was an expert and vigorous lover whose sensuality exploded upon Yoshiko. From this point on, sex would not only become a source of power for her. It was to be her greatest slavery.

Nosaka made several trips to the resort, delighting Yoshiko's parents. Each time she secretly went to his bed, leaving it at sunrise to return to her own room. By now sex had become indispensable to her, a necessary function performed without guilt. There was no question of having betrayed her parents. No bond existed between them and Yoshiko, who had long wished to see them dead.

Between Nosaka's visits she took lovers from among other resort guests, giving herself to men and women for the only reason which mattered, her own pleasure. Yielding to her strong sensuality gave Yoshiko confidence as well as the endurance to survive a miserable life. To make love was to live. To make love was to enjoy being cruel to those who loved her too much. Now there was no longer any boredom. Yoshiko had found her own wisdom and her vision of the world would never be the same.

She was upset when Nosaka's visits stopped. But in his place came Kon Kenpachi, to whom Nosaka had spoken of Yoshiko. The handsome Kenpachi, a glamorous and famous film director, easily overwhelmed her with his sensuality. For the first time she felt herself a victim in bed, vulnerable to one who would always be her master. She became obsessed by him; his lovemaking increased her sexual hunger until her longing for him pushed aside any feelings she had had for anyone else.

139

During his visits to Hakone and Yoshiko's secret trips to meet him in Tokyo, Kenpachi not only taught her about sex but introduced her to drugs, art, music and the world of filmmaking. He gifted Yoshiko with new kendo armor and improved her fencing technique in private workouts at his castle. While it was one of many such affairs for him, it was the first true love affair for Yoshiko and became her whole life.

Toward the end of the resort season, when her parents left on a two-day business trip to Tokyo, Yoshiko and Kenpachi together climbed Mount Fuji. It was a demanding climb, 12,350 feet to the peak of what had once been one of the world's mightiest volcanos. During the climb they passed the ten rest stations and followed the custom of having their walking sticks burned with the sign of each station as proof of having reached all ten. At the eighth station they spent the night alone in a stone hut, where they ate a cold supper packed by Yoshiko, made love and fell asleep in each other's arms.

They arose before dawn and climbed to the top of the snow-covered peak. Here, with a handful of other climbers, they watched the incredible *goraiko*, the world's most beautiful and moving sunrise. They could see the blue Pacific Ocean, other mountains and strings of villages which lined the coast. But it was the *goraiko* which left them speechless. Yoshiko had never been happier.

That night, back at the almost empty resort, they lay naked and exhausted in Kenpachi's bed. Yoshiko did not want the morrow to come. Tomorrow her parents would return and Kenpachi would be off to Tokyo. She wanted to go with him, to leave the despised resort behind. She had tasted freedom with Kenpachi, and now she did not want to be separated from him.

At the sound of a key in the bedroom door Yoshiko and the film director froze. When the door opened, her father stood in the entrance, a carving knife in his hand. Paper lanterns on the walls gave his horrified face the look of a demon.

He walked toward them, speaking with terrifying calm. "You have shamed my house. I cannot allow either of you to go unpunished."

Reaching the bed he slashed Yoshiko, the nearest target. She covered her face with her arms, shrieking as the blade sliced into both forearms. From the other side of the bed Kenpachi rolled onto the floor, snatched a walking stick from a chair and raced around the bed to confront Yoshiko's father.

Holding the stick overhead the director yelled, *"Kiaiii!"* The father swerved toward Kenpachi, away from the hysterical, bleeding Yoshiko. When he swung the blood-stained knife and pointed it at Kenpachi's stomach, the director brought the stick down on the father's wrist, breaking it. No longer rational, Kenpachi used the stick as a samurai would have used a sword.

Kenpachi smashed the father in the temple, across the nose, in both sides of the rib cage. Bleeding from the nose and ears, the father dropped to his knees. Now completely out of control, Kenpachi stepped forward and dealt the father a final blow, in the back of the head.

Backing away from the dead man, Kenpachi reached the bedroom door and pushed it closed. When he tore his eyes away from the corpse to stare at the blood-covered Yoshiko, he blinked. She was composed, with a hint of a smile on her beautiful face as she stared down at her dead father.

Kenpachi saw only the ruination of his career and prison. He began to shiver and the walking stick slipped from his hand.

And then he remembered Nosaka, who had always been his savior.

On a deserted road several hundred yards from her parents' resort, Yoshiko, her forearms wrapped in strips of torn sheets, stood with Kenpachi in the chilled darkness and watched the two cars speed toward them. It had taken the cars only forty-five minutes to reach Hakone from Tokyo, normally an hour's drive or more. When the glare of the headlights blinded Kenpachi, he waved his arms wildly. Quickly the lights were switched off and both cars slowed down. One rolled to a complete stop and cut its engine. The other made a U-turn and stopped, its engine still running.

Kenpachi led the sprint to the car with the running engine. When they were in the back seat, the driver jammed his foot down on the gas pedal. The car leaped forward, racing back to Tokyo. Through the rear window Kenpachi watched four men leave the first car and start toward the resort.

He relaxed. He was going to get away with it. His fears slithered away from him like a whipped dog. Nosaka would erase the business at the resort as though it had never happened. The entire matter was made of sand; the tide of Nosaka's influence would wash it away. For Kenpachi, it was all in the past and the past was gone.

He looked at Yoshiko, dazed by a painkilling injection from Doctor Orito. Orito worked swiftly, silently. He had already cut the bloodied bandages from one arm and had almost finished cleaning it. As for Yoshiko, never had she appeared so alluring. Her beauty and youth were breathtaking. The thought of making love to her now, this instant, so aroused Kenpachi that his penis grew rigid. He looked out at the pine trees racing past the car window to calm his lust.

But the glass held Yoshiko's reflection and because she was denied to him, he had never wanted her more. Orito was working between them,

141

his back to Kenpachi, who dropped both hands to his lap and squeezed his hard penis, feeling a joyful pain, squeezing, squeezing, squeezing until there was a blissful release.

Kenpachi closed his eyes. His head flopped back against the seat. He was still weary from the climb of Mount Fuji and so he drifted easily to sleep. *Yoshiko.*

* * *

IN Tokyo she lived with Kenpachi at Ikuba Castle for almost two years. She grew taller and more beautiful, a beauty improved by Kenpachi's advice on makeup and fashion. He decided that long sleeves would best hide her scarred forearms and that she should wear only the best wigs made of human hair. Yoshiko, however, remained undisciplined, with little patience for serious work and study.

Formal schooling bored her, with its Japanese approach to learning through endless repetition and imitation. Kenpachi tried and failed, to teach her calligraphy, the ancient form of penmanship, and *ikebana*, the traditional art of flower arranging. She made several attempts to learn *sadō*, the tea ceremony, before giving up entirely.

Both Yoshiko and Kenpachi were reckless, sensual and short-tempered. But she lacked his intelligence and sophistication, his artistic gifts and capacity for hard work. Kendo and karate slightly interested her and she decided that when older she would work in films. She did not need schooling for that. In any case, she no longer had to account to anyone for her actions; she was free to do as she pleased. Both parents were dead, the victims of a fire which had all but destroyed the resort.

As her stay at the castle lengthened, she spent less and less time with Kenpachi. He had his filmmaking, composing, acting and circle of friends with whom Yoshiko had little in common. And there were his other lovers, none of whom lasted long for Kenpachi's promises were written on the wind. Left alone, Yoshiko explored the gigantic and supercharged city that was Tokyo. The crowded pavements and heavy traffic shocked her; the constant movement left her dizzy.

But at night the city was at its best. Then it became a gigantic pleasure palace wrapped in miles of neon lights. A dazzling richness of theaters, pachinko parlors, night clubs, turkish baths, movie houses, restaurants, homosexual bars and bowling alleys. Tokyo after dark was a fleshpot, an unending orgy of sensual gratification.

142

On her own Yoshiko wandered the Ginza, the broad, long avenue of department stores, hostess clubs, bars and dance halls. In the Akasaka district she was befriended by geishas and dancers who frequented the coffee shops when they were not working in nearby nightclubs. In Akasaka she met strippers and homosexual prostitutes, who took her to the Sensoji temple to hear the one hundred and eight tolls of the great bronze bell. Here Yoshiko stood with hundreds of others crowded around a monstrously large incense burner and hoped that its heat would cure their pains and illnesses. She held her forearms in front of the burner, but her scars did not go away.

In Shinjuku, site of Ikuba Castle, she met students, homosexuals and young people drawn by trendy shops, foreign films, coffee bars and promises of sexual freedom. Here also she met Juro, the student who became her lover. Slim and handsome in his black school uniform, the twenty-year-old Juro brought her dolls and American-style hot dogs and made her laugh. He worked hard at his studies and played the guitar for her in his room and told her of his plans to enter government service. In bed Yoshiko educated him.

With Juro, her self confidence was restored, her sensuality reawakened. Kenpachi had become bored with her; she could not see beyond a small circle, a weakness he could no longer tolerate. He made fun of her lack of education, calling her *yabo*, uncouth and peasantlike. The lovers he really preferred were *iki*, sophisticated and refined, men and women with elegance and experience.

Yoshiko retaliated by seeing Juro and others behind Kenpachi's back. But Kenpachi learned of her infidelity and took a horrifying revenge.

One evening, after a candlelit supper with Yoshiko in the main hall, something they had not done in weeks, he invited her to the master bedroom. Here he showed her the entrance to what had once been Lord Saburo's secret tunnel, which had been sealed off for years. Recently Kenpachi had commissioned the reopening of the entrance; it was once more possible to use the tunnel, to follow it from the castle to a nearby Shinjuku park.

Hand in hand the two stepped through a wall closet and entered the tunnel. Kenpachi held a flashlight as they went down a small ladder leading to what was once an earthen room. The room was at the mouth of the tunnel and, except for one unfinished portion behind the ladder, was now lined with cement and bricks. Yoshiko giggled. This was the sort of fun she and Kenpachi had enjoyed at the beginning of their relationship.

There was a little light in the room, but the section behind the ladder was dark. Kenpachi and Yoshiko faced it together, his arm around her shoulder. When he shone the flashlight on it, Yoshiko screamed. *Juro.* Wild-eyed with fear, the bound and gagged student whimpered at the sight of her. He was almost entirely walled up behind fresh bricks and mortar; only his shoulders and head were still visible. Two men stood beside the wall. Yoshiko recognized them from the car which had taken her and Kenpachi from her parents' resort.

She wanted to run, but was held by Kenpachi's iron grip. "I think this is one history lesson which will leave an impression on you," he said. "In the days when Tokyo was Edo, human sacrifice was common. It was also considered necessary. *Hai,* very necessary. Human pillars. People buried alive in the foundations of important new buildings. Castles, villas, temples, even courthouses. It kept evil spirits away. It ensured that the gods granted the building eternal life."

He brought the flashlight up to Juro's terrified face. "Officially, of course, such sacrifices were forbidden. Nevertheless, they were carried out, usually in secret. Flesh and blood added to a new building to give it life. Sometimes a servant would beg his master for the honor of pleasing him by being buried alive. Think of it. Tons of earth and stone slowly pressing every ounce of life out of you and you unable to move."

He shone the flashlight on Yoshiko. "I gave you life. I took you away from the pigsty into which you had been born. And you repay me by reverting to the slut you were when we first met. I own you. You are mine, to do with as I wish for as long as I wish. You need to be taught a lesson. I assure you it will not be boring. Please stand in front of your lover."

Too paralyzed to speak, Yoshiko shook her head.

Kenpachi shoved her away. She stumbled, tripped and fell to the ground.

"You will not die," he said. "But you will place the finishing touches on this human pillar. It won't be the first time, will it, my darling?"

Yoshiko blinked tears from her eyes. *The first time.* After Kenpachi had killed her father, Yoshiko, inflamed by bloodlust, had picked up her father's carving knife and run bleeding down the hall to her mother's room. And cut her mother's throat.

"Finish entombing your lovely little student," said Kenpachi, "or join him."

Juro whimpered, moaned and pleaded with his eyes, while a weeping Yoshiko lay on the floor.

"If you're still on the floor twenty seconds from now," said Kenpachi, "the two of you will die together."

Slowly she pushed herself to a sitting position, then stood.

144

And began to complete the entombment.

As Kenpachi and the two men watched, she carried bricks to the unfinished wall, covered them with mortar and was almost finished when Kenpachi said, "Stop."

Kenpachi walked over to Juro, grinned, then placed gold coins on the student's head and shoulders. Money to spend in the next world. *But in this world there would be no reprieve.*

Kenpachi backed away from the wall and said without looking at Yoshiko, "Your task is not yet completed."

She screamed, then fainted.

She awoke in bed, with Kenpachi brutally making love to her. Too drained to resist, Yoshiko attempted to close her mind to any emotion. She willed herself to think of Juro, of what Kenpachi had forced her to do to him. She tried to make her will deny herself any feelings of pleasure. And failed.

To her shame, her sexual response to Kenpachi began to grow. Her body remembered the gratification he provided and sought it once more. Against her will she abandoned herself to him, calling his name, begging him to do whatever he wanted.

In the morning, she lay in bed and told herself that last night had been a bad dream. But she saw her broken nails and the dirt on her body from the tunnel and knew that Juro had been walled up alive in the bowels of the castle. Kenpachi reminded her of the role she had played in the human-pillar ritual and in the death of her parents. Her choices now were silence, prison or death at Kenpachi's hands.

And then he told Yoshiko that she would have to leave Ikuba Castle.

Shocked, she could barely get out the word. "Why?"

"Because I am getting married."

She clutched his arm. "What will become of me? Where will I go?"

"I shall give you money. From time to time I shall, perhaps, find you a small film role. But do not return here unless I summon you. Is that understood?"

"I am frightened. Please do not send me away. How shall I survive?"

"If the need is strong enough, you will find a way."

*   *   *

SHE survived through her beauty and cunning. There were jobs in a fried-fish and rice shop, in a souvenir shop, and for a time she teamed with a lover to work as a *chindonya*, a street musician hired to lure customers to the opening of new bars and restaurants. When Yoshiko left him she stole money and jewelry left to him by a dead wife. Friends found her work as a club hostess, a masseuse in a turkish bath and in nude shows, all prostitution fronts.

She appeared in *sutorippu*, strip shows, pornographic films and posed for erotic magazines. There were affairs with women, including an Australian stewardess who committed suicide when the relationship ended. Another relationship finished when a dance-hall bouncer, with whom she was living, was beheaded during a gang war between rival *yakuza* mobs. Sex was her only concept of power but it was a concept which had to be paid for.

She lacked acting talent, but because of her beauty Kenpachi was able to find bit roles for her in legitimate films, with Bunraku, the puppet theater, and with a small Kabuki company. He also placed her with dance companies, first Kagura, which performed festival dances at Shinto shrines, then with a Bugaku group. Here, masked and costumed in red, with a silver rod in her hand, she learned the bold and stately dances which sometimes lasted for hours. While Yoshiko performed adequately, she was late for performances, was caught stealing and had to be let go.

Kenpachi never left her life. An American, whose sports car she had stolen, was persuaded by Kenpachi not to have her arrested. And when Yoshiko stole the wallet of a nightclub owner with underworld ties, it was Kenpachi who talked the *yakuza* out of killing her. She attended parties at Ikuba Castle, in Kenpachi's Tokyo duplex and in Kamakura, the seaside town where he owned a beach house within sight of the Great Buddha. He invited her on film locations, slept with her and gave her money. Yoshiko never stopped loving him. But she knew that everything he gave her only prevented her from ever being free of him.

She was twenty-one when he told her that until further notice she was to work for Zenzo Nosaka.

"What does such an important man want with me?" Yoshiko asked.

"In the West it is called industrial espionage," said Kenpachi. "However, Japanese laws do not recognize such a thing. We think of it as gathering intelligence, nothing more. Nosaka-san has constructed his own intelligence network, one which functions through a bank owned by him. You will do exactly what Nosaka-san tells you, is that clear?"

"*Hai.*"

"You will be well paid. Nosaka-san is to be your *daimyo*, your lord. Obey him without question. If you don't he will kill you. Do you understand this?"

"*Hai,* Kenpachi-san."

It was a satisfying job, one which allowed her to achieve much while earning excellent money. With information provided by Nosaka's bank, Eastern Pacific Chartered Limited, she sought out Japanese businessmen who either willingly sold company secrets or who were targets for potential blackmail. She traveled to London, Paris, Geneva and Rome, sometimes as a courier transporting cash or information, sometimes as a "model" or "fashion designer" who quickly made friends with executives and engineers able to provide company information. And with Eastern Pacific furnishing background data on each assignment, the advantage was Yoshiko's.

In San Francisco, she convinced an executive with a microchip company to sell a piece of property to Eastern Pacific, which paid him four times its worth in exchange for valuable information. She traveled with Japanese research teams, who aggressively gathered information, then reported back to the government and to big business. She attended conferences and conventions in Japan and abroad, where she met managers, engineers, sales chiefs and executives and told Nosaka what she had learned.

Through him she received invitations to parties and press conferences, meeting politicians and journalists whose conversations and casual remarks became part of Nosaka's intelligence files. When ordered to, she spied on his employees. Once she learned of an executive's plan to release damaging information to the press on the company's industrial waste disposal program. Shortly after she informed Nosaka, the executive died of what was diagnosed as heart failure.

When a Russian pilot defected and landed at an American air base in Japan with a highly advanced fighter plane, only American military personnel were allowed to examine it. Yoshiko, however, obtained a copy of the file, which contained a detailed analysis of the aircraft, which Nosaka then passed on to Japanese intelligence in exchange for future favors.

If Nosaka was intimidating, he could also be generous. For the first time Yoshiko had everything she wanted. Prostitution and petty thievery were no longer necessary. She could afford clothes by the finest Japanese and foreign designers, as well as an American car. She purchased an expensive flat on Omote-Sando Boulevard not far from the holy Meiji Shrine, where the entrance to the gates were made of seventeen-hundred-year-old Japanese cypress. Omote-Sando, with shops that sold foreign fashions and ultramodern clothing, was a favorite with Japan's smart set and Yoshiko could now take her place with the best of them. Above all she could indulge her passion for antique jewelry. As for lovers, Yoshiko no longer went with them for money, but for pleasure.

There was a price for this luxury and comfort. She came to fear Nosaka as she had never feared Kenpachi. She knew of the Blood Oath League; on Nosaka's orders she had joined the league's secret training sessions in the martial arts. Yoshiko was a modern *ninja*; she had to be prepared to fight and, if necessary, die. Like it or not, she had chosen the way of the warrior, which was death.

Some part of her wondered if Kenpachi could bring himself to actually kill her. After all, there was a bond between them, a past with which neither wanted to lose contact. Yoshiko had no such doubts about Nosaka. If need be, he could have her killed without a moment's regret.

Which was why she had not hesitated when he had ordered her to murder the Hansards and bring their son back to Tokyo. The boy, Todd Hansard, was important to Kenpachi. Why, Yoshiko did not know, nor was it necessary that she know. Her duty, *giri*, was unquestioning obedience to Nosaka. Her fear of the old man made her feel ugly and lose her power of reasoning. That fear had also made her cruel and murderously effective in her work.

＊　　＊　　＊

IN her Hong Kong hotel room, Yoshiko put on a Norma Kamali dress of white cotton, with wide, thickly padded shoulders and full, flared calf-length skirt. Her small waist was accented by a four-inch-wide belt of black patent leather with tiny leather buttons. She wore sheer white stockings and black-and-white slingback sandals with high heels and the toes cut out. In addition to hoop earrings of white gold, she had chosen two favorite pieces of antique jewelry—a Victorian bracelet of gold leaves in enamel, set with blue sapphires, and a gold-and-enamel pendant by Giuliano, the great Italian jeweler who had worked in nineteenth-century London. Her watch from Harry Winston in New York cost more than she had earned in her entire life until going to work for Nosaka.

Yoshiko packed her luggage but decided not to summon a porter until after she heard from the Chinese couple hired to pose as Todd Hansard's relatives. They were due to telephone from the lobby any minute, letting Yoshiko know that the boy was downstairs in a waiting car. Then it would be time to have the luggage taken downstairs, pay the couple and take the car to Kai Tak Airport. Here a private plane would fly her and Todd back to Tokyo, where he would be taken off her hands.

Kenpachi had insisted that Yoshiko telephone before leaving Hong Kong. He had to know that the boy was in her possession. The highly strung Wakaba was waiting by the mobile telephone on location in Wanchai.

Did Kenpachi intend to use the boy as a human pillar or in some equally frightening ritual? Such a man was capable of anything. There was a concealed side to him, something that Yoshiko found beyond her comprehension. It had to do with violence, but not the cold-blooded, calculated kind she could expect from Nosaka. Kenpachi's veneer of talent and good looks hid something animalistic and demonic.

Some in the Blood Oath League knew why Kenpachi wanted the boy, but no one would tell Yoshiko. She might have pressed Kenpachi for an answer, but Nosaka was also involved and it was wiser not to ask questions at this time. If they wanted Yoshiko to know, they would tell her. If not, then the matter was best forgotten.

Nosaka. He had warned her to be careful, to leave nothing incriminating behind in a hotel. Yoshiko had almost finished inspecting the bathroom when she heard a soft knock at the door. She closed the medicine chest and listened. She was not expecting anyone and she had no friends in Hong Kong.

Caution. She walked into the bedroom, reached in her shoulder bag and removed the fan Nosaka had given her from his collection of ancient weapons. It was efficient and deadly and she had spent hours learning to use it. A second knock brought her to the door. She said in English, "Who is it?"

"Soon." The Chinese man and his wife, who were to bring the boy to Yoshiko.

Yoshiko touched the knob but did not open the door. "You were to telephone me from downstairs."

"I tried to call you, but your telephone is out of order."

"Just a minute." She crossed the room, picked up the telephone receiver and held it to her ear. The line was dead. She relaxed. The fan was in her hand when she opened the door.

"Miss Mara? Yoshiko Mara? I'm Captain Fuller, Royal Hong Kong Police. This is Inspector Jenkins. Sorry to bother you like this, but may we come in." He turned to a Chinese policeman in the hall. "That will be all, Deng. Please escort Mr. and Mrs. Soon downstairs, if you will."

Shocked, Yoshiko placed both hands behind her and backed into the room. She had been tricked. How much did they know?

The English officers, both in plain clothes, stepped forward, followed by a single uniformed Chinese policeman and someone else, a large gray-

149

haired American who watched Yoshiko with eyes that reminded her of the cobra that had sunk its fangs into Ian Hansard. He closed the door with his walking stick, but not before she saw the Soons being escorted toward the elevator by a Chinese officer. *Something was wrong. Had Yoshiko made a mistake or had she just been betrayed?*

Captain Fuller, the officer in charge, was fortyish, tall and stoop-shouldered, with a triangle of a mustache under a flat nose, and a determination to be discreet and helpful. He could have been a school principal offering Yoshiko amnesty if she would admit her part in a girlish prank. The second Englishman, Jenkins, combed his thick red mustache with his fingers and eyed her with undisguised lust. The Chinese officer maintained the attitude of a servant who knew his place, remaining a respectful step behind the Englishman.

The American with the walking stick had positioned himself against the door, his half-closed eyes following her every move. The sense of danger coming from him was strong enough to make Yoshiko blink.

Fuller said, "We were wondering if you could aid us in our inquiries. It concerns the deaths of Mr. and Mrs. Ian Hansard and a claim by the Soons to be Mrs. Hansard's only relatives and therefore entitled to the custody of the Hansards' only son."

To save themselves, they have led the police to me.

She smiled at the policemen, who had formed a semicircle around her, and brought the fan from behind her back. A flick of her wrist and the fan, made of ivory, silver, gold and iron, snapped open. She fanned herself with it slowly. "I am sorry, but I cannot help you. I have never seen Mr. and Mrs. Soon in my life."

"That wasn't the impression I got out in the hall," said the American.

Fuller sighed and his nostrils flared in disgust. The introduction was made reluctantly. "Forgive me. This is Mr. Frank DiPalma from America. We are told that he is Todd Hansard's natural father."

Yoshiko brought the fan up, hiding most of her face. *Hai,* she knew this one. He and Kenpachi-san were enemies, rivals in the way of the sword and now rivals for the boy. Yoshiko's eyes brightened above the fan. Did Kenpachi-san want the boy in order to revenge himself upon the hated American?

"Originally," said Fuller, "the Soons presented themselves as Katharine Hansard's relatives. But at Mr. DiPalma's request, we questioned them and now it seems they no longer make such a claim. At the same time, they did mention something about turning the boy over to you."

He smiled to show her that he, too, found such an idea to be contrary to reason and absurd.

Jenkins, still resentful of DiPalma, said, "Maybe we should mention that Mr. DiPalma has friends in high places. We've received telephone calls on his behalf from Peking, London and even our very own governor. Everyone asks that we cooperate with him to the fullest extent, which we'll bloody well do if we know what's good for us. Mr. DiPalma is here to show us that power can be a serious fact. Has some fanciful theories, he does. Thinks a beautiful woman like yourself murdered the Hansards."

DiPalma's husky voice made Yoshiko uneasy. "Ask her how she came to know the Soons," he said.

"She's answered that," said Jenkins. "She said she'd never seen them in her life. You weren't listening."

DiPalma rubbed his unshaven jaw with the silver head of his cane. "Oh, I was listening, all right. Heard every word. You'll probably tell me that at the door she thought she was talking to the bellboy."

Yoshiko bowed her head. "As you say, the bellboy."

DiPalma's smile was edged and abrupt. "Nice move. I feed you the straight line and you follow through with the punch line. Maybe we ought to work up a little act. Well, let's see how you handle this. Somebody saw you beat Katharine Hansard to death, then set fire to her bungalow."

"DiPalma, really." Jenkins looked at DiPalma and raised his eyebrows. "Keeping secrets, are we? And why haven't you shared this little bit of news with us before now?"

"Kunoichi." DiPalma drew the word out, turning it into a hoarse and jarring accusation. Yoshiko, caught unprepared, was left shaken and uncontrolled. How could the American know about her unless there was the spirit of evil in him. She had to escape from this room, from this demon.

The fan in her hand was a tessen, a war fan with a razor-sharp iron tip hidden beneath gold paint. It was not merely a woman's weapon; centuries old, it had been carried into battle by two feudal generals.

Yoshiko turned first to Captain Fuller. Her nervous smile appealed for sympathy and concern, a silent plea which found him off guard. His hands were at his side and he was defenseless when she backhanded the fan's cutting edge across his throat, tearing loose the cartilege. He spun around, spraying Yoshiko and the Chinese policeman with blood.

As Fuller crashed into a writing table, Yoshiko kicked the Chinese officer in the groin, then quickly drove her heel down hard on Jenkins's right ankle. Both Jenkins and the Chinese officer doubled over, and as Jenkins bent down, Yoshiko slashed at his eye with the fan. His hands came up too late to protect his face. Leaving the Welshman screaming

151

behind her, she leaped over the prone Chinese at her feet and sprang at Frank DiPalma.

When she was almost on him, Yoshiko spun around and with her back to him lashed out with her right leg, kicking at his groin. DiPalma stepped to his left and deflected the kick with a quick, whiplike blow of his cane to Yoshiko's calf. She went down with her leg beneath her. Then, on the floor, she reached out and backhanded the fan at Frank's right knee.

Take the fang from the snake and the snake is harmless, said the stick fighters. The war fan was Yoshiko's fang. DiPalma went after it. Her backhand attack was met with one of his own; he swung the cane down in a short, powerful arc, putting his bulk into the blow, smashing into her wrist and breaking it. Yoshiko fell backward, clutching her useless wrist. Awkwardly she tried to scramble to her feet.

Gripping the cane with the silver knob exposed, DiPalma stepped forward and in the same motion brought up his right fist in an uppercut, driving the knob under Yoshiko's jaw. She landed on her back, then rolled over. She tried to rise to her knees, then fell back as the first bullet tore into her side.

DiPalma screamed "No!" but Jenkins, a two-handed grip on his revolver, continued firing until the weapon was empty. Two more shots entered Yoshiko's chest, sending red stains across the white dress. Another shot missed and hit the television set, causing it to explode. A fifth shot hit Yoshiko high in the shoulder and the final shot entered a sofa.

Jenkins, face covered in blood, moaned, "Bitch! Fucking bitch! Fucking, fucking bitch!"

DiPalma ran to him. "You didn't have to do that. The fight was over."

Jenkins kept his face turned toward Yoshiko. "My eye. You bloody bitch."

It was his right eye. There was too much blood for DiPalma to see the damage, but the eye didn't look good.

"Oh God, the pain," said Jenkins. "Can't see. Can't..."

Jenkins fell back against DiPalma, who helped him onto the bed.

The police were banging on the door with their gun butts.

He let them in, two Chinese officers with drawn guns who shoved him inside and ran toward the bodies.

"Call an ambulance," said DiPalma. "I think Fuller's dead and so's the woman. Jenkins and the man on the floor can use some help. What about the phone?"

"It is working again, sir," one of the Chinese officers said. "We have reconnected the line. The break we caused was merely temporary, as you suggested."

DiPalma stared down at Yoshiko's body. "Yeah. As I suggested." He had wanted her alive. She was only a mule, a courier who was carrying Todd somewhere else, to someone else. She was a link in a chain which DiPalma had wanted to follow to its source. Jenkins's anger was understandable, but by blowing her away he had slammed the door in Frank DiPalma's face.

In death Yoshiko's wig had fallen off. DiPalma crouched over the corpse. He stared at the face, then at the Adam's apple. Jesus, was it possible?

As the Chinese policeman tended to Jenkins and the other officer, DiPalma looked under Yoshiko's dress.

He stood up. A Chinese came over to stand beside him. "Captain Fuller is dead and Inspector Jenkins may have lost the sight of his right eye. Chang will be all right."

"The guy who got kicked in the balls?"

"Yes. Inspector Jenkins said the woman did this. Do you know who she was?"

DiPalma shook his head. "No idea. Tell you this much. Captain Fuller's not the only dead man in this room. Yoshiko Mara's not a female. She is a man. One very dead man."

11

IN WANCHAI, a restless Kon Kenpachi walked across the aged stone floor of the temple, leaving his crew to light the next scene. At the entrance he leaned against the pillar and stared at the crowd which had lined the street to watch the filming. He was inside Chai Kung Woot Fat, the Temple of the Living Buddha, where the interior was covered with thousands of mirrors. According to local custom, the Chinese recovering from an illness left a mirror here bearing a lucky inscription. Kenpachi wanted to be sure the camera lights did not reflect in the mirrors nor cause distracting brightness. Satisfying that demand took time, and Kenpachi was not a man who liked waiting. Especially now, when his mind was on Yoshiko and the boy.

Another local custom had delayed the afternoon's filming even longer, costing Kenpachi time needed to shoot on the temple steps in available sunlight. A Chinese funeral procession had marched in front of the temple, with musicians playing oboes and cymbals, mourners in white hoods and relatives of the deceased bearing roast pigs as gifts for the gods. A furious Kenpachi had pushed his way through spectators, then locked himself in his limousine until the procession passed.

To Jan Golden, the funeral cortege meant overtime costs. "This is going to run into money, said the monkey as he peed into the cash register."

At the temple entrance Kenpachi fingered the viewfinder hanging from his neck and watched the Chinese onlookers applaud Tom Gennaro, who had just left the limousine which doubled as his dressing room. Gennaro, with a Chinese girl friend, had a scene in which he left a mirror inside the temple, in gratitude for having survived a grenade attack in Vietnam.

Kenpachi looked past the crowd to his own limousine parked in front of a furniture-making shop. No signal from Wakaba. Which meant no telephone call from Yoshiko. Damn her. It was late afternoon and still no news of the boy. Kenpachi found Sakon, Yoshiko's male name, to be thoughtless, forgetful and unsure of himself. Worse, the male side, despite Sakon's physical beauty, was dull and as common as dirt. Only as Yoshiko, complete with women's clothes and makeup, did Sakon become spontaneous, defiant, sensual. His female side was his greatest talent.

If the relationship between Nosaka and Yoshiko would never be other than master and servant, the relationship between her and Kenpachi was less easy to classify. Sakon had always loved Kenpachi. It was Sakon's only humanity. But Kenpachi had freed himself of love by concentrating on his own problems. Still, Sakon was more than a source of pleasure. He was a passion which Kenpachi had never been cured of, a beautiful object and pleasing delusion to which Kenpachi had permanent title. But deep in his heart Kenpachi knew the real reason why he needed him. It was only with Sakon that he truly felt himself to be loved.

At the temple entrance Kenpachi heard Jan Golden call his name. But before he could turn to answer her, blaring automobile horns cleared the street and two police cars pulled up in front of the temple steps. Three policemen walked up the steps and stopped in front of Kenpachi.

"Mr. Kon Kenpachi?" The officer was British and middle-aged, a small, hairy man with a tanned, wizened face and an air of troubled nobility.

"I am, yes."

"We would like you to accompany us to police headquarters. We think you might be able to help us with our inquiries."

"I do not understand."

"It will be explained to you when you get there. One of our officers was murdered. Two others were hurt, one rather badly."

"What's this got to do with Mr. Kenpachi?" Jan Golden stood beside the Japanese film director. She was vigilant, protective.

"Our business is with Mr. Kenpachi, if you don't mind."

Kenpachi willed himself to stay calm. "I must tell my crew—"

"Sorry, but there's no time for that. The killing of a police captain is

156

a serious matter. We would very much like to get to the bottom of it. The *individual* who did it is dead. Bit of confusion there, especially about gender. Seems you and this individual were acquainted and that's what we'd like to talk to you about."

It was several seconds before Kenpachi realized that the "individual" was Sakon. Numbed, the Japanese let the policeman guide him by the elbow down the temple steps and into his car. In the back seat, between two Chinese officers, Kenpachi showed no sign that the news of Sakon's death had been a staggering blow. He closed his eyes, placed his hands palms up on his thighs and went into *zazen*, meditation. With the strength from Bushido, he resisted his attachment to the memory of Sakon and struggled to free his mind-spirit from sorrow and fear.

With the cast and crew Jan watched the car with Kenpachi pull away. Directly behind it was a second car, which slowly made its way past the Chinese lining both sides of the narrow street. And then the crowds filled the street behind the second car, blocking Jan's view. But not before she had seen Frank DiPalma sitting alone in the back seat.

12

DIPALMA HANDED his black oak cane to Todd, who sat across from him in a restaurant located in the Landmark, a trendy new building whose five floors were filled with banks, boutiques, jewelers, restaurants and airline offices. They had just finished dinner on a suspended balcony overlooking a giant indoor plaza, where a circular pool-fountain contained water which shot up when the noise level around it increased. The restaurant, Todd said, had been a favorite of Katharine's. It was decorated to resemble a seventeenth-century pub, with flintlock pistols and pictures of highwaymen on the walls and Chinese waitresses in knee britches and three-cornered hats.

DiPalma and Katharine had come here together eleven years ago. Then the Landmark had been the site of a hotel, with a quiet bar and a Filipino pianist who sang only Broadway show tunes written before 1945. In those eleven years Hong Kong had lost so much of its past to the real estate developer and the wrecking ball.

As DiPalma watched, Todd gripped the cane as though it were a *shinai*. Silver knob resting in the palm of his left hand, the last three fingers squeezing while forefinger and thumb gripped the stick loosely. Right hand exactly one fist away, last three fingers holding the *shinai* tightly, forefinger and thumb relaxed. Both thumbs pointing downward.

Nice grip, DiPalma thought. Strong enough to withstand the weapon being knocked out of his hand, yet flexible enough to give slightly when struck. Katharine had said Todd was an extraordinary kendoist for his age. DiPalma wanted to see just how good the kid was.

A waitress cleared the table, leaving behind a fresh pot of tea. When she had left, DiPalma poured tea into small pewter cups, cooling his by filling half of the cup with milk. His stomach couldn't stand anything too hot or too cold. Todd raised the cane overhead, then slowly brought it down until it almost touched the table. He did this several times, smiled at DiPalma, then placed the cane on an empty chair.

DiPalma returned the smile. "Very good. *Jodan*, wasn't it?" *Jodan* was the upper-level stance, fists in front of the forehead before attacking or defending. It was one of the five basic postures in kendo, though not the most commonly used.

"It's not for everyone," said Todd. "But it suits me quite well. Sometimes in a match, I feel as though my *shinai* is a real sword. So I draw it from an imaginary scabbard in the Katori style and the *jodan* stance seems to blend in of its own accord."

DiPalma was familiar with the Katori method of drawing a real sword. Thumb and forefinger pulling against the outside edges of the handguard in a screwing forward action, making the sword leap from its scabbard and stop in an overhead position. The draw, a quick one, was hard to block and achieved a longer reach than other styles. Holding the sword overhead also meant less distance between the blade and target, making the Katori overhead cutting stroke one of the swiftest in kendo. It was a style of swordsmanship which had flourished during the sixteenth and seventeenth centuries and was scarcely practiced today.

"Why does *nito*, the use of two swords at once, appeal to you?" Todd asked.

DiPalma stirred his tea. "Most people won't fight with two *shinais* at once. Too hard to control. Me, I enjoy it. The short one lets me control the opponent's weapon and when I've blocked it or knocked it aside, he's got nothing to use against my long weapon. If you know how to use it, a short *shinai* is a good defense. Still, you score with the longer weapon. It's got the reach."

"But there is a time for the use of the short sword. When your opponent is close and there is no room to use the long sword. Or when you are fighting in a confined space. Also it is good to have both a short and long sword when fighting several opponents at once. Kenpachi-san says I must start to practice with two *shinais*."

Kenpachi-san says. DiPalma caught it at once: defiance under Todd's politeness. A potential for insolence which didn't go with the boy's well-bred exterior. Todd's attitude toward Kenpachi was just as inconsistent. The boy appeared to fear him, while at the same time deferring to him as though he were his commander in chief. Or *daimyo*. DiPalma didn't want Kenpachi in Todd's life for any reason. Kenpachi had all the courage necessary to become corrupt and corruption was contagious.

DiPalma had told Todd about the confrontation at Yoshiko Mara's hotel but not about Yoshiko's connection to Kenpachi. He didn't want to make Kenpachi look bad in the boy's eyes. Putting his foot down too soon on Todd would only make DiPalma look the fool. Was this really the first day he and Todd had spent together?

There was no one with whom DiPalma could fully discuss Katharine's murder and that included the Hong Kong police. DiPalma's sole eye-witness to her death was Todd, who had seen the killing through his extrasensory perception. Frank believed him. But the police wouldn't and in their place neither would he. In a cop's world only facts mattered.

When the police had questioned him about what had happened at Yoshiko Mara's hotel, DiPalma had kept his explanation to a minimum. "I ran a bluff and it worked. Nothing more, nothing less."

"Forgive me if I fail to view the matter quite so simplistically," said the questioning officer, a round-faced superintendent with pebble glasses, wavy hair and a tendency to speak to his folded hands, which rested on his desk. "One of our officers has been butchered by a female impersonator. Another has been blinded in one eye and currently lies in hospital in a state of shock. 'Nothing more, nothing less,' you say. I say there's more. For example, what made you 'run a bluff', as you put it, on someone you had never met and ostensibly knew nothing about?"

"To begin with, Yoshiko Mara or Sakon Chiba, as we now know him to be, lied about knowing the Soons. I was in the hall and heard him speak to Mr. Soon. Chiba knew him, all right. And was expecting him. Your men believed her lie. They wanted to believe."

The superintendent raised his eyes from his hands to DiPalma. "And why would they want to do that?"

"Because they didn't like being forced to cooperate with me. Because they wanted to show me who's boss. It was an ego thing. Made them feel better. Fuller was polite, but he was only going through the motions. Anything to keep me quiet. In his own little way, he made sure I knew it. Jenkins? As far as he was concerned, Chiba or Yoshiko had just won the 'Miss World' contest. Jenkins's tongue was hanging out. He had found his dream girl. All he saw was a beautiful woman, not somebody who could kill two people."

161

"If you don't mind, I would rather be spared any criticism of my men at this time, thank you. I suppose we'll just have to work on being more distrustful in future."

In his polite way the man's throwing stones, thought DiPalma. "I think a smart cop distrusts everybody he doesn't know."

"All well and good, but we had no hard evidence linking Chiba to the deaths of the Hansards."

"Katharine Hansard told me she feared for her life and Todd's."

The superintendent nodded. "That telephone call is on record, yes."

"Around that same time, Chiba shows up in Hong Kong dressed as a woman and using the name Yoshiko Mara.

"We found the different passports in his hotel room. Go on."

"Katharine's frightened. Chiba's in Hong Kong. Katharine and her husband die. And Chiba hires the Soons to bring Todd to him. You have the Soons' confession. I think that links Chiba to the death of the Hansards."

Without lifting his eyes from the desk, the superintendent steepled his fingers under his chin. "Suppose, just suppose, someone else and not Chiba disposed of the Hansards. Theoretically speaking, of course."

"Chiba had the stomach to do his own killing. He proved that in his hotel room. I saw him do it and so did two of your men."

"Hmmm, quite. Anything else?"

"Ian Hansard and Chiba were seen together. At Hansard's bank, at a restaurant, by Hansard's chauffeur. And Hansard's servants knew what was going on."

"He did have a reputation for womanizing," said the superintendent.

"Not just women," said DiPalma. "Oriental women. Made Chiba's job a lot easier."

The superintendent looked up. "I assume it's Mrs. Hansard you are most concerned about?"

"And Todd."

"That would explain your 'running a bluff' regarding *her* death, as opposed to that of her husband."

The superintendent wore his mask well, DiPalma thought. A clever man who didn't appear clever. Choosing his words carefully DiPalma said, "I came to Hong Kon at Mrs. Hansard's request, so I guess you're right. Her death is the one which concerns me."

"Yes, I suppose it would be. After all, you did father a child by her. Seems odd that Chiba would kill to secure the boy. Why not kidnap him instead?"

"Katharine loved Todd. If someone had snatched him, she would have stopped at nothing to get him back. Dead parents can't come looking for a missing child."

"Good a theory as any. Odd sort of chap, our Mr. Chiba. Telex from the Tokyo police said he had been an *onnagata*, a male actor who played women's roles in Kabuki theater. Also performed female roles in Noh plays and in Japanese dance companies. Lives as a woman most of the time."

"A woman with the fighting skills of a well-trained man," said DiPalma.

"A *ninja*, I believe you said. *Kunoichi*."

DiPalma leaned back in his chair. There was no hesitation; he made up his mind immediately. No mention of Todd's mystic visions or nightmares. To do so would make him and Todd appear to be fools twice over; once for believing in those visions and twice for having said they did.

DiPalma said, "For the sake of argument, let's say Chiba or Yoshiko Mara eliminated the Hansards. It means he had to know a few things about them. About Ian Hansard's interest in Oriental women, about the best way to use that information. He had to know when and where to strike at Katharine Hansard. And he had to have people here who could help him with Ian Hansard's murder."

"And how do you know Chiba had help in killing Ian Hansard?"

"Because Hansard was killed by a cobra and I don't think Chiba came through customs with a cobra in his purse."

The superintendent permitted himself a smile. "Fair enough assumption. So Chiba had friends in Hong Kong."

DiPalma leaned forward. "He had more than that. It appears that he arrived here and was handed all the information he needed, all the intelligence, all the background, all the contacts. Chiba not only fought like a *ninja*, he also dealt with the Hansards as a *ninja* would. Get the information first, then make your move. He wasn't here long enough to get that smart on his own."

"Chiba did seem to move about Hong Kong in an efficient manner. If what you say is true, he managed to amass quite an amount of data on extremely short notice."

DiPalma shook his head. "No way. The telex you received from the Tokyo police department and the one Roger Tan got from DEA's Tokyo office both say the same thing. On his own, Sakon Chiba did not have the brains to walk into a strange city and take out two people he never saw before."

"Unless someone else was doing his thinking for him, as you seem to imply."

"The telexes say that Chiba had a police record. Petty crime. Porn actor, male hustler, petty thievery, ripping off tourists. Minor drug dealing. Car theft's the heaviest thing on his sheet. The man didn't touch anything that involved a lot of thought and planning. He was a loser until four years ago."

"And what do you suppose turned him around?"

DiPalma looked at the ceiling. "I wish I knew. All of a sudden, no more stealing wallets from johns, no more hot-wiring cars, no more shoplifting. Enter prosperity. Chiba suddenly buys a flat in a very expensive Tokyo neighborhood. He acquires a half interest in a Tokyo boutique. And he wears designer dresses with expensive-looking jewelry. No more arrests, no more trouble with the police."

The superintendent's fingers drummed on the desk. The conversation was becoming interesting. "Born again, as you Americans might say. And with a frightfully large amount of American dollars in his or her possession. Ten thousand was the amount, I believe."

"And four passports," said DiPalma. "Each with a different name, each a first-class piece of work. And none of them stolen, I bet. That would be sloppy and nothing about the born-again Sakon Chiba is sloppy. Loser into prosperous citizen. Somebody took over his life and turned it around. Nothing in Chiba's past indicates he would do this well on his own. Something else: I saw him fight. He took on three men. Killed one, crippled two. Whoever trained him trained him well."

"That alone would seem to confirm your suspicions of his being a *ninja*. Or does it?"

"Superintendent, I've made several trips to Japan and I've seen most of the martial arts in action. I've been taken around by some important people, but not once did I see a *dojo* where they taught the use of a war fan. If it's taught these days, it's taught in secret. I never saw fan fighting, I never even heard rumors about it. It was part of past history."

"Until now."

The superintendent removed a large brown envelope from a desk drawer. After looking inside, he held it out to DiPalma, who took it and turned it upside down. The folded war fan slid into his hand.

"Anything you can tell me about it would be of interest."

DiPalma turned the fan around in his fingers, slowly opened it and when it had reached its full length he examined it again, fingers brushing the handle and both sides. The fan was made of a thin but strong metal and was silver coated, with a cutting edge hidden beneath gold paint. A gold ring hung from an ivory handle inlaid with gold and silver. One side was painted with lilies, orchids and azaleas; the other was decorated with a snow-covered landscape and a hillside temple red with the setting sun.

"It's called a *tessen*," said DiPalma. "Japanese for war fan. Or iron fan. Samurai used it as protection when entering the home of someone they didn't trust. Catching a man's neck between sliding doors was an old trick. To avoid that, you held the open fan in front of your head. Kept the doors from closing on you. Good weapon in its own right. Could be used against knives, swords, sticks."

He placed the fan landscape-side up on the superintendent's desk and with his forefinger tapped the hillside temple. "Those markings on the front. Hard to make them out. Here, just under the roof."

"What are they?"

"Markings from Kuan Yue, the Chinese god of the martial arts. The god of war."

The superintendent allowed himself a tiny congratulatory smile. "I bloody well know who he is myself. Favorite god of the Chinese underworld. And you'll find a statue of him in every police station in the colony, including this one. Always struck me as peculiar, policemen and criminals praying to the same god to protect them from each other. Why should Kuan Yue be appearing on a Japanese war fan?"

DiPalma picked up his cane and sat down. "Because Japan built its civilization on what it took from China."

"The Chinese never let us or the Japs forget it," said the superintendent. "It's one reason, among many, which makes the Chinese rather arrogant, not to mention insufferable. If rumors are to be believed Japan's still going in for 'borrowing' these days. Only it's called industrial espionage. No law against that in this part of the world, unfortunately. Done in Hong Kong all the time as well. You were saying?"

"Those markings probably mean a military man commissioned this fan. Kuan Yue's name was added for good luck. All Japanese military strategy for hundreds of years was based on the Chinese *Book of Changes*, on Chinese theories of yin and yang, on the ideas of Chinese generals and philosophers. The spear, the bow, the sword, they all came to Japan from China."

"I see. Where would one go about securing a fan like this today?"

"You couldn't. It's a museum piece, a collector's item. Almost four hundred years old. Probably late sixteenth century. The sort of piece even a top antique dealer would have a hard time coming up with."

The superintendent wriggled his small mouth before answering. "Could Chiba have stolen it, perhaps?"

You're coming around, DiPalma thought. Slowly but surely you're

165

coming around. "You're saying somebody with Chiba's record wouldn't ordinarily own something like this."

"I suppose that is what I'm saying, yes."

DiPalma stood up. "Might be a good idea to telex Tokyo again. See if a fan matching this description has been stolen from a museum or a private collection."

The superintendent rose. "You've been most helpful. I regret the relationship between you and my department got off on the wrong foot. Difficult situation, being forced to obey an outsider. But you're really not that much of an outsider, are you?"

"I've walked your road, if that's what you mean. I didn't throw my weight around because I enjoy seeing people jump. My son was involved. You probably know about Katharine and me, about what happened eleven years ago."

"I do, yes."

"I owe her."

"The debt you owe to the past can be discharged by assuming custody of the boy, I grant you. But then there is Ling Shen. Your only chance against him is to take the boy and leave Hong Kong now, this minute."

"Katharine's funeral is three days from now. Peking's making the arrangements. I promised Todd I'd be there with him. I don't have to tell you that the most important thing in life to the Chinese is to be buried in the right way."

The policeman nodded. "I quite understand. Unfortunately, the Triads hold power in Hong Kong second only to that of Peking and the bankers. I will assist you in any way I can, but Shen is an implacable foe and I'm afraid that once his heart is set on revenge he cannot be dissuaded."

He patted his wavy hair and, being a pragmatic man, mentally began to steel himself for the furor certain to erupt from America and points elsewhere when Mr. DiPalma was dispatched by Shen, as would inevitably happen. DiPalma's concern for his child and his sense of obligation to the late Mrs. Hansard were both admirable. Very human. But being human was no solution.

DiPalma said, "I can give you a few places in Japan to start asking about the fan."

The superintendent folded the fan and returned it to the envelope. "In exchange for what?"

"For tying Kon Kenpachi to Katharine Hansard's murder."

"Mr. Kenpachi is not a murder suspect at this time. Which is why we released him after getting his statement."

"The telexes—"

"Said that Mr. Kenpachi had aided Chiba regarding past arrests, nothing more. Kenpachi's presence in Hong Kong during Chiba's stay appears to have been a coincidence, not a conspiracy. As far as we can determine the two did not meet during their respective stays here. You seem inclined to believe the worst of Kenpachi, which is your prerogative. But there is no evidence to indicate that he had any reason to want the Hansards dead. For that matter we're having trouble establishing a motive for Chiba. The only thing anyone appears to have wanted out of this is your son and with all due respect, I, for one, cannot see why."

"Chiba had the number of Kenpachi's mobile phone—"

"Which was the main reason we brought Mr. Kenpachi here for questioning. He had an explanation for that. There was to be some discussion of Chiba playing a role in Kenpachi's new film. They'd already spoken once on the phone and were to speak once more. No face to face meeting, said Kenpachi. Strictly business, strictly over the telephone."

"In Japan, Kenpachi bailed Chiba out of trouble more than once. Tokyo police also said that the two lived together and had been seen in each other's company off and on for a long time. There's a good chance they could have been more than just strange bedfellows."

The superintendent dropped the fan into his desk drawer and pushed it shut. "We have gossip columns in this part of the world and we are well aware of Mr. Kenpachi's sexual proclivities. Here in the East such practices are not looked upon as they are in the West. Sensuality, in all its aspects, is simply considered a matter of the flesh. To quibble about the form it may take, say the Orientals, is to condemn a man for eating with his left hand instead of his right. In any case, given the state of the world these days, it would seem that chastity's the only perversion."

DiPalma brought the silver head of his cane up to eye level and studied it. "Ask yourself why Chiba went crazy when we came for him in his hotel room. Ask yourself why the word *ninja* set him off and made him want to kill every one of us."

The superintendent was a long time answering. "Judging by his reaction, it would appear he was afraid. Afraid for himself, perhaps. Afraid of someone other than the police. It could well be that you were correct, that he had been trained and financed by someone whose identity he couldn't possibly reveal. His actions did appear to be those of a wild man."

"Chiba was scared shitless. I've seen that look before."

"Could he have been frightened of you?"

"Like I said, his money, his life-style and martial-arts training came from somewhere."

"Your bluff successfully spooked Chiba, but it also closed the door to further questioning. Or I should say Jenkins did, speaking of the actions of a wild man. So now Chiba's dead and Kenpachi's free to return to the glamorous world of films."

He extended his hand to DiPalma, who took it. "I won't insult your intelligence by suggesting you change your mind regarding the funeral. But do take care. Shen is ruthless. Things haven't gone well with him of late and more than ever he is determined to save face. He will not appear at his daughter's funeral. In eleven years he has had no contact with her whatsoever. That should give you an idea of his determination. She must have loved you quite dearly to do what she did, knowing what her father's reaction would be."

They parted in silence as the superintendent recalled the death of his own wife and remembered that to love well meant forgetting slowly.

*   *   *

IN the Landmark's balcony restaurant Frank DiPalma sipped lukewarm tea and said to Todd, "You're right. Benkai was very good with two swords. Where did you learn about him?"

"I have read about the great swordsmen. Hayashizaki, Ittosai, Shimpachi Nikai, Bokuden, Musashi and Benkai. Kenpachi-san has given me a book on the life of Benkai. Benkai once lived in Kenpachi-san's castle as bodyguard to Lord Saburo who built the castle."

"Is the book in English or in Japanese?"

"Japanese."

"When did you learn to speak Japanese?"

Todd looked embarrassed. "It would seem I have a knack for it. I began picking up words and phrases from my kendo instructor and when he noticed my interest, he insisted on our conversing in it. I suppose it's come easy for me. I don't know quite why."

Japanese hadn't come easy to DiPalma, who had spent years learning a language once described as making Chinese appear to be a puzzle for retarded children. Japanese was one of the world's most difficult languages; it was imprecise, with a massive vocabulary and a system of writing DiPalma still hadn't mastered. Yet his eleven-year-old son could speak Japanese and God knew how many Chinese dialects.

DiPalma thought of Sakon Chiba and his ties to Kon Kenpachi. "Kenpachi mentioned something about your visiting Ikuba Castle."

"We talked about kendo. At Ikuba Castle there is still the original *dojo* where Benkai trained and taught swordsmanship. It is something Kenpachi-san feels I must see. And there is the room where Lord Saburo and Benkai committed *seppuku*. I must go there. I must..."

His eyes widened and he held his breath. And just as suddenly, he relaxed and turned to DiPalma. "Benkai was *kaishaku* to Lord Saburo."

"Do you know what *kaishaku* means?"

Todd nodded gravely. "A *kaishaku* acts as second to one committing *seppuku*. It is his duty to end the pain of the one taking his own life. A *kaishaku* must be of strong character and a very good swordsman."

DiPalma was impressed. "Katharine said you knew a lot about the martial arts. And about Japan. *Seppuku* goes back a long way. No one knows for sure how long."

Todd stared down into his untouched cup of tea. "At least fifteen hundred years. It began with warriors who would strangle themselves because they could not live with the shame of defeat. Other warriors burned themselves to death by setting fire to their own homes."

"Does this mean they will live forever?"

"The soul cannot die. We are born again and again until we free ourselves from the wheel of birth and death to become one with the Ultimate Reality."

DiPalma smiled. "Your mother and I talked about this a few times. Like you, she believed in reincarnation. In karma. I don't mean to challenge you or anything, but I find it hard to accept that. Seems to me that when you're dead, you're dead. A door shuts behind you. The book's closed."

"You can never die," said Todd with cool certainty. "You cannot even imagine your own death. You can imagine anything else, but not your own death."

"Oh, I can do a pretty good job of imagining my death. I see myself lying in an expensive coffin, silk lined, hands folded across my chest and me in a neat black suit. I see flowers, maybe a few beautiful women sniffling in the front row and a fat, bald-headed man playing the organ."

Todd, half-smiling, leaned back in his chair. "But there it is. The truth. You see yourself lying in the coffin. You are the witness, the onlooker. You cannot be dead and be the witness as well."

"Hey," said a grinning Frank DiPalma, "you are sharp. Let me play with that one for a while."

"I'd like to talk to you."

DiPalma turned to see Jan Golden standing by the table, taking long, angry drags on a cigarette.

"Jan. You know Todd." The boy stood up. "Miss Golden," he said politely.

Jan ignored him. "We have to talk, Frank. Now."

"This is my first day with Todd. Maybe you and I can get together tomorrow. A lot of things happened today and—"

She removed DiPalma's cane from a chair, and sat down. "That's what I'd like to talk to you about. What the hell are you trying to do to me?"

"I don't understand."

"I'm talking about your having Kon arrested for no reason. I'm talking about you delaying my movie and costing me a damned fortune."

"And how did I manage to do that?"

"Kon's disappeared."

DiPalma looked at Todd, who sat quietly watching them. The boy's composure was impressive.

"I spoke to him at the police station," Jan said. "Right after that he left. I thought he was returning to the shoot, but he never showed up and nobody knows where the hell he is. A day's shooting, fifty thousand dollars, down the tubes." She slumped in her chair, a hand covering her eyes. "A drink, please."

DiPalma summoned a waitress and ordered a Rob Roy. Jan dropped her hand from her face. "He said it goes back to this rivalry you two have in kendo. Says you don't miss a chance to drag his name through the mud."

"He's a liar," DiPalma said. He felt Todd's eyes on him, but did not turn to look at his son.

Jan fumbled in her purse for her cigarettes. "Frank, I know you. You're Sicilian. You don't forget. You told me that, remember? Something else you told me, too. You said more than once that you wished you could go back in your life and change a few things. Make them right, you said."

"I wasn't thinking of Kenpachi when I said that. I was thinking of my wife and daughter. I was thinking of the partners I lost." He looked down at the table. "I was thinking of Katharine."

He lit her cigarette and watched her drag deeply on it. "Frank, all I know is I saw you with the police when they came for Kon. And down at the police station they think you're hot shit. Strictly heavy duty. Somebody to be scared of. You made a telephone call, to Senator Joseph Quarequio and everybody in Hong Kong sat up straight in their chairs. Or they're lying on their backs with their paws in the air and it's all because of you. That's a lot of power, my friend. It's the kind of power that usually ends up hurting other people."

"Jan, Kenpachi wasn't arrested on my say-so. He wasn't arrested at all. He was brought in for questioning, that's all. And only because a friend of his killed one police officer and blinded another in one eye. The man who did it—"

"A transvestite. I know."

"He had the number of Kenpachi's mobile phone."

She stubbed out her cigarette and reached for another. "And that's enough to involve Kon?"

"Kenpachi and the killer were tight for almost fifteen years. Yeah, I'd say that's enough to pull Kenpachi in for questioning ten times over. Especially when the two are in the same city at the same time."

She used her thumb and pinky to remove a tobacco strand from her tongue. "He knows we were supposed to get married and that it didn't work out. He thinks you're jealous of me and him working together, that you might make trouble for us."

"Do you really believe that?"

She looked away. "I told him about us. I felt he should know. Especially with this business of"—she stared across the table at Todd—"this business of what happened to your son's mother. Kon swears he had nothing to do with it."

The drink arrived. Jan snatched it from the tray and drained half of it at a gulp. Her lush, autumn red hair hung free and Frank was drawn to it. She said, "This has not been the best day of my life. This is serious. Delay, delay, delay. Then Kon goes up in a puff of smoke and a half hour ago I get a cable from Tokyo saying our permission to film in the Bank of Tokyo and the Mitsukoshi department store has been withdrawn. The bank doesn't think the film would be good for its image and the store, which gets three hundred thousand customers a day, says we would interfere with business. We need substitute locations in a hurry, not to mention rewrites. And the hurricane season's on the way. Might strike Japan this month, maybe sometime next month. It's going to hurt any exteriors we've got planned, especially some shooting Kon wants to do on the coast."

She held up a finger. "Now get this. I had the perfect *mix* on this film. The right American and Japanese actors, a great script, the director I wanted. Sometime this afternoon my production manager gets a cable from New York. An actor who's due to show up in Tokyo next week for filming has changed his mind. Seems he's been offered the lead in a new Arthur Miller play and is determined to do it even if it means breaking his contract with me. John Ford was right. Actors are crap."

She emptied her glass, set it down and stared at it.

It was Todd who broke the silence. "I am sorry about your father, Miss Golden."

Her head jerked up. She stared at him, then at DiPalma. "How did

171

he know about my father? Did you tell him? Frank, are you spying on me?"

DiPalma forced himself not to look at Todd. He had never discussed Jan's father with the boy.

Tears formed in her eyes. "God, I really need this on top of everything else. He's back in the hospital again. Something wrong with his pacemaker. Frank, I'm sorry I ran out on you. It was wrong, I know it and I'm sorry. Nothing I can do about it now. For the time being this movie is my life. What I'm saying is this is my chance to be somebody, do something besides grow old. You and Kon, well, what I'm saying is, please don't spoil it for me. If there's something between you and him, I'd appreciate it if you'd let it go until the movie's done. That's all I'm saying."

Her hand reached across the table for his. He took it because he was dog tired, ready to drop and because he didn't have the energy to explain that despite what he still felt for her he didn't trust her. Frank DiPalma had loved Jan and so it had been easy for her to deceive him. It wasn't anything he cared to go through again.

In believing Kenpachi she was deceiving herself. Taking out her frustrations on DiPalma was part of that deception. If she failed to deliver a good film on time and within budget, her career as a producer would suffer, perhaps permanently. In Hollywood, where failure was a crime, few people got a second chance. She needed Kenpachi. She was also attracted to him, or she would not have tracked DiPalma down. Anytime Jan fell in love, it was a love that knew no limits and could not be controlled. The hurt and disillusion would follow, but for now she would fight for Kon Kenpachi even if it meant fighting against Frank DiPalma.

He remembered what his father had said, that in love you never got to choose.

"I didn't know you and Kenpachi were here in Hong Kong," DiPalma said. "I came here because Katharine asked me to. After her funeral I'll be leaving for New York. Believe what you want to believe, but I think you know me well enough to know I wouldn't lie to you."

She stubbed out another cigarette. "I'm sorry. I'm upset and I just felt like bitching, that's all. As if we don't have enough problems, we sent prints of some of Kon's past films to New York for his retrospective at Lincoln Center next month and they haven't arrived. Kon's earned that showing and I'd hate to see anything go wrong with it."

She stood up as did Frank. "Hell of a way for us to meet after all this time," she said. "I didn't tell you how well you look."

"You too."

172

"I hear a lot of good things about what you're doing. They say you'll win another Emmy this year for sure. What will that be, your fourth?"

"Third, if it happens. Good luck with the movie."

Jan smiled at Todd, who rose and shook her hand. Then she kissed DiPalma on the cheek and left the restaurant. Frank's eyes followed her down the balcony stairs and across the plaza. *In love you never get to choose.* When she had left the building he turned around to ask Todd how he knew about Jan's father's illness.

But the boy had disappeared.

13

IT WAS dark when Kon Kenpachi knelt in front of a low table in the small room, struck a match and lit the four white candles. The flames sent long shadows across the low ceiling of the snake restaurant, the site of Ian Hansard's murder. Except for Kenpachi and his bodyguard, Wakaba, the restaurant was now empty. Wakaba locked the front door, then closed the thick wooden shutters over the two windows which faced the street. After peeking through a crack in the shutter, the bodyguard returned to the door and stood with his back against it.

At the table Kenpachi regarded the candles, which were surrounded by incense sticks and flowers—lilies, blue orchids and chrysanthemums—Buddhist ceremonial offerings to the dead. The ceremony was for Sakon, who was represented by an empty coffin, the head of which pointed north and touched the table. Sakon's body was still in police custody; there would be an autopsy the following morning. Kenpachi could not claim it without calling more attention to himself. He would have to perform the ceremony without Sakon's corpse.

Kenpachi's favorite photograph of Sakon stood in the coffin, resting on a white silk handkerchief. It had been taken at the top of Mount Fuji over ten years ago, when Sakon had been a teenager with an unspoiled and vulnerable beauty.

175

Assisted by Japanese from Nosaka's Eastern Bank, Kenpachi had hastily arranged the death rites to honor Sakon and to let his spirit know that it would be revenged. For the policeman who had done the killing there would be no pardon, no forgiveness. The murder of Sakon would be repaid with samurai justice; Sakon had died a warrior's death in service to Nosaka and Kenpachi. His death now made him a *kami*, a god, whom Kenpachi would soon meet in the next world. The filmmaker did not want to encounter Sakon without first observing the code of Bushido.

The death rites.

Because he now purified himself for his forthcoming *seppuku*, Kenpachi, using Buddhist rituals, acted as his own priest. Before entering the restaurant he had pasted a piece of paper with the words *mo-shu*, in mourning, on the front door. Now, at the table, he picked up a pen and pulled a blank sheet of white paper toward him. He dipped the pen into a bottle of black ink, then drew a circle in one continuous stroke, filling the entire page with its outline. Within the circle he drew three large comma-like shapes, each chasing the tail of the next.

As Wakaba watched, Kenpachi patiently filled in one comma, then drew a stork and a turtle inside the others. The stork and the turtle were both symbols of eternal life. Finished, he rose and carried the design, a *mitsutomoe*, over to the coffin and laid it near a photograph of Sakon. A *mitsutomoe*, with its three commas, represented the three treasures of Buddha—Buddha himself, his teachings and those who followed them.

Another table near the coffin held fruits, sweets, vegetables and tea, as well as a pair of sandals, a pearl necklace, a jeweled brooch and a kimono. As prescribed by ritual, Kenpachi, as Sakon's only survivor, had paid for these himself.

Publicly he had shown no grief. Now sorrow fell on him and for the first time since learning of Sakon's death there were tears in Kenpachi's eyes.

He knelt at the second table and began to wrap the gifts in white paper, strong, beautiful and handmade. Following tradition, he used one sheet of paper, working precisely and seeing that the last fold came out on top of the package and extended all the way around. He wrapped the sandals, the kimono, tea and *manju*, bean-jam buns. Then he rose and presented the wrapped packages to Wakaba, who accepted them and bowed from the waist.

Kenpachi now stood at the coffin and chanted Buddhist incantations he had learned from his mother. Then he closed his eyes and performed *kuji-kiri*, the magical signs made by *ninjas* to gain self-confidence and to strengthen the spirit in times of danger. Frank DiPalma was the danger facing Kenpachi; he had led the police to Sakon. Ling Shen would dispose of DiPalma within hours. But if Shen should fail...."

Kenpachi linked his fingers together in one of the eighty-one ways known only to a *ninja* and recited a Buddhist sutra used by *ninja* for over a thousand years. As he recited he alternately made five horizontal then vertical lines in the air with his knitted fingers. *Kuji-kiri* increased a *ninja's* perception; it allowed him to read the thoughts of others, to see into the future and to predict death. Through *kuji-kiri* a warrior achieved "the eyes of God," becoming all-knowing, all-seeing, all-wise.

Eyes closed, Kenpachi spoke the mystic words. Arms extended, fingers linked, he envisioned *jigoku*, the Buddhist's hell, for the policeman who had shot Sakon... and he saw something else.

Opening his eyes, he reached into the coffin and took out the two weapons, Bankai's long sword and Saburo's *seppuku* knife. He whirled around, weapons held high overhead, and whispered to Wakaba, "Open the window on your left, then stand aside."

Wakaba pulled the shutters open, then stepped out of Kenpachi's line of vision.

On the darkened street, Todd stood and stared into the restaurant. He saw the sword and the *seppuku* knife held by Kenpachi. In the candlelight the two blades shimmered and glowed. Todd began to shake, his eyes riveted on the blades. Kenpachi made no move toward him, but held the weapons aloft and stared at Todd until the boy jerked his head away and was gone.

Jubilantly Kenpachi turned to face the coffin. In death Sakon had still managed to bring the boy to him.

*   *   *

FRANK DiPalma lay still in bed and listened. He had been awakened by a knock on the door of his hotel suite. In the darkness he reached for his cane, then sat up and turned on the night light. His watch read 11:10 P.M. The knocking continued, soft, but insistent.

He got out of bed, put on his robe, then walked into the sitting room and paused at the door before opening it. "Hello, Todd."

"Forgive me for disturbing you, sir. May I come in?"

"Sure."

DiPalma stepped aside, flicked the light switch and closed the door behind his son. The boy looked as if he had been rolling around in a coal bin. His hands and clothing were smudged and there were scratches on both arms. A package which he clutched to his chest was streaked with black marks. It was the size of an attaché case and was wrapped in yellow oilcloth.

DiPalma sat down in an imitation Hepplewhite chair, shoved both hands in the pockets of his robe and waited. Todd was an unusual boy, with a touch of the unreal about him. He had been surprised when his son had walked away from the restaurant without warning, but for some reason he hadn't worried. Todd could take care of himself.

What bothered Frank DiPalma was Todd's self-control. His parents were killed violently and an attempt had been made to kidnap him. Yet the boy maintained the calm of a neurosurgeon. Or a samurai warrior. Either the kid had ice water in his veins or he had managed to bury the hurt deep inside.

Todd held out the package. "Please. It is what you want."

"It is?"

"The papers from my stepfather's bank. The files you were supposed to bring back to New York."

Frank DiPalma sat in his chair and didn't move a muscle. He had been caught unawares before in his life, but never like this. It was time to start asking questions. "Where did you find them?"

"They were hidden beneath an iron door in the floor of my mother's studio."

"Explains why you're dirty."

"Yes, sir. The man who originally built the main house used the bungalow as an ice house and to store his opium. He was an opium trader, you see. The iron door in the floor protected the files from burning. Everything is here in the attaché case. I'm afraid it's locked. Only my stepfather had the key."

Frank DiPalma took the package from Todd. "In a world of paper clips and letter openers," he said, "there is no such thing as a locked attaché case."

He peeled off the soiled oilcloth, dropped it into a waste basket and reached for a brass letter opener. "How did you know I wanted these files? I never mentioned it to Katharine."

There was a moment of silence. He turned to look at his son, whose head hung as though he had done something shameful.

"Bothers you, having this thing," DiPalma said. "This telepathy business. This extrasensory perception."

"My mother called it second sight or thought transference. She said it is both a gift and a curse. It comes to me without warning. Sometimes

I see frightening things. At the restaurant I saw something bad about Miss Golden's father. He will soon die."

"His heart is bad."

"He will not die that way."

"How will he die?"

"*Ninja.*"

Frank's eyes narrowed. "Is his name in these files? Is that why you ran away from the restaurant?"

"His name is here, yes. And it is on the list given to you by your friend, Roger Tan."

The list. He could have kicked himself. He had forgotten all about it. Back at the Hansard home, Roger had given him the names of Eastern Pacific's directors and Frank, busy with the call to Senator Joseph Quarequio, had never even glanced at it. He placed the unopened attaché case on the desk and walked to the bedroom closet. The list was where he'd left it, inside his jacket. Two pages of notebook paper in Roger's handwriting.

Jude Leonard Golden, Jan's father, was the fifth name from the top. Salvatore Verna and Duncan Ivy were there too, along with retired military officers from America, England, Europe and Japan. If Sally Verna was telling the truth, the men on this list were a part of Nosaka's industrial-espionage network and were also involved in his murky financial transactions.

Frank, with Todd looking on, studied the list further. Jude Golden had to be Mr. O., the organizer who Sally Verna claimed had worldwide contacts in the intelligence and law-enforcement communities. And he was Sally's partner in a bid to buy the late Ian Hansard's hidden banking files. This was not an educated guess. Jan had given him the proof, her birth in Japan a few years after her father's tour of duty as a war-crimes prosecutor. She had also told him of her father's lifelong love of the Far East, of his business dealings throughout the Pacific, of the lavish Japanese-style home and gardens Jude Golden owned in Connecticut, complete with Japanese serving girls. And like Duncan Ivy, Jude Golden was a banker.

After the three of us convicted Nosaka, he vowed to kill us, said Sally Verna. Me, Ivy, Mr. O.

No doubt about it, thought Frank. The third man, Mr. O., is Jude Golden. Money had brought the Americans and Nosaka together; money had also made the Americans forget that Nosaka was the fox and they were the chickens. Nosaka, however, had a long memory; he would keep the vow he made forty years ago, because it was the only way he could die with honor. At his age, an honorable death had to be something he thought about often.

Nosaka's calling the shots on the new Blood Oath League same as he did on the old, said Sally Verna. He wants to build a new Japan by killing people.

Jan could be one of those people. All she had to do is be in the wrong place at the wrong time, like Duncan Ivy's lawyer, and she's cut to pieces by a samurai sword. Just let her be caught with her father when the Blood Oath League comes for him and she's dead. Frank crushed Roger's list in his fist. Damn Kenpachi for bringing Jan this close to Nosaka.

Kenpachi, the superpatriot, the would-be samurai. The Blood Oath League would certainly get his vote. He believed in violence, flag-waving. He had been one of the first to come out in favor of the controversial new history textbooks, which gave a watered-down account of Japan's aggression during World War II. He had demanded a resurgent Japanese militarism, calling the war his country's days of glory. Kenpachi had ended one speech by cutting his arm and using his blood to draw a Japanese flag on a white handkerchief; when he held it up to a group of Japanese war veterans they cheered him to the skies.

He favored those films which showed the Japanese military as peace loving, the Allied forces as brutal and treacherous. And in typical Kenpachi fashion, the filmmaker had produced, directed and written a documentary showing wartime prime minister General Hideki Tojo not as sadistic and power hungry, but as a gentle and scholarly father figure. It was like claiming Charles Manson was a lovable camp counselor whose charges sometimes got out of hand.

If Nosaka was behind the Blood Oath League, Kenpachi knew about it, and approved. Jan was definitely in over her head. She was holding a wolf by the ears.

But Todd...Todd was a different story. He believed Todd's powers and yet he didn't believe. He believed because Katharine had believed, because his instinct said the boy was not a liar.

"You didn't eat at the restaurant," he said. "Are you hungry?"

The boy grinned. He was going to break a few hearts when he grew older. "I could eat, sir. If you please."

"Well, we've got twenty-four-hour room service, they tell me. What'll it be? Hamburger, ice cream, french fries, milk, soft drink. You name it."

"All of that sounds good, sir."

"All of it. Hey, why not. Your engine can't run on empty. I'll order, then we'll see what's in this attaché case."

He telephoned the order then turned to the locks. No problem there. Both locks quickly yielded to a letter opener.

The leather case, new and unmarked, was packed with folders. There were folders for memos, correspondence and bank records. There were folders for records of conversations, for dummy corporations, for customs personnel on the take. It was the history of Zenzo Nosaka's industrial-espionage network, enough to place him under investigation in the Far East, Europe and the United States. The lawyers at DiPalma's network would stay up nights checking every line. He would put his own investigative team on the file to verify as much as possible. He had more than enough to go on. When his team finished, they would have a story hot enough to guarantee Frank more than two minutes and twenty seconds on the eleven o'clock news.

Shieh Lei, Sally Verna had called it. Bribes. Ian Hansard had made an impressive case for Zenzo Nosaka as an industrial spymaster without equal. Nor were Hansard's hands clean. He was the one who had set up charities, ecology groups and wildlife organizations in America, England and Europe, fronts for dispersing payoffs to industrial spies on Nosaka's payroll. Hansard had been a bagman for Nosaka, carrying large sums of money from Hong Kong to foreign countries when the information and the person selling it were important enough.

There was more, showing Hansard's direct involvement in Nosaka's spy network. Bank information on loan applications, credit checks, business mergers, business expansions, money for research and development. All the transactions involved people in a position to pass on information about their companies, people who could be bought or blackmailed. Hansard had had a sense of humor. Beside one name the banker had written, "seeks the cure for poverty at our expense."

The former military men on Eastern's board had close contacts in defense and nondefense industries and Hansard had used them to gather information for Nosaka. They also had their fingers in secret arms deals, which involved laundering millions through Eastern Pacific Amalgamated. Naturally the bank took its commission on these details.

One page of names caused Frank's eyebrows to rise. We meet again, he thought. In his hand were the names and account numbers of several class-A narcotics traffickers, men whose annual volume of business topped that of most companies listed on the stock exchange. Frank recognized each name and knew its history. There was the Bolivian cocaine dealer he had failed to make a case against some years ago, a man who paid his country's generals fifty million dollars in protection every six months. And it didn't surprise Frank that a Mexican heroin dealer, whose beautiful twenty-five-year-old daughter was his mistress and second in command, had washed over six hundred million dollars in Nosaka's bank in nine months. The bank's fee, three percent, came to $18 million.

Not only was the bank delivering intelligence, it was also making windfall profit.

The file was worth millions. Hansard dealt in big bucks and wouldn't have sold information like this for peanuts. As to why Hansard suddenly decided to go into business for himself, the answer was in the attaché case. Bank books and false passports. The bank books showed hefty deposits in numbered accounts or under dummy corporate names in banks around the world. They belonged to Ian Hansard; Frank knew a hustle when he saw one.

The passports made it official. There were six, three for Hansard, three for Katharine. Three false names each, all passports officially stamped and with recent dates. There were no passports for Todd.

Was it the Blood Oath League that had made Hansard decide to take the money and run?

Frank flipped through some of the other pages. Nothing on the league. Which didn't mean it wasn't there. In any case, Sally Verna would help him with that, in exchange for the file and for keeping him and Jude Golden out of any story. Frank would look at the file again tomorrow and this time he wouldn't miss a page. Hansard the great record keeper was sure to have something on Nosaka and the Blood Oath League.

He would have to move fast. The sooner the word got out on Nosaka, his industrial-espionage network and the Blood Oath League, the better it would be for the former prosecutors, Sally Verna and Jude Golden. The glare of publicity might save their lives. On the other hand, it might not. Nosaka could decide to carry out his vow in any case.

Whatever happened, Frank stood to gain. This story would blow away every reporter in the business, not to mention the network libel lawyers, who would go over it with a fine-tooth comb. From any angle, the story was dynamite. A major war criminal who should have been hanged forty years ago would be hanged now. Not with a rope, but by the media. Nosaka was nothing more than a hood involved in the legalized thievery that was business. He deserved to go down, to be shamed before the world, to be dragged through the courts in countries where he had stolen business secrets. The disgrace would weigh heavily on the proud Nosaka. I love it, Frank thought. I fucking love it.

Then he remembered Katharine. Finding her killer mattered more than dumping on Nosaka. Sakon Chiba had been the instrument; somebody else had pulled the strings. Frank was going to let his investigative team run with Hansard's files while he looked into Katharine's death. It would gnaw at him until he found the answer.

There was a knock at the door. He put the files back into the case and closed it. "Feeding time," he said to Todd. "Let them in and have them put it down on the coffee table. You should be comfortable on the couch. Tomorrow I'll give these files one hell of a toss. Go through them from beginning to end."

"Yes, sir."

"Hey, Todd, no more of that sir stuff, remember? I know they brought you up to say it and it's great, but there's no reason for you to call me that. I hear sir and I look aound to see who you're talking about."

"I understand . . . Frank."

My son. The words were strange, a foreign language. They would take some getting used to.

Todd opened the door, then leaned back to protect himself. Frank was out of his chair and rushing toward him, but it was too late. Three armed men pushed into the room and slammed the door behind them. One grabbed Todd from behind, an arm around his neck, and pressed a Colt .45 to the boy's temple. Frank froze in the center of the room. Ling Shen, he thought. I'm going to die a long way from home.

The other two men moved quickly. They separated, keeping distance between them, then stopped and crouched, guns in a combat grip and trained on Frank. One had a Walther PPK; the other held a .357 Magnum revolver fitted with a laser-targeting device which threw a brilliant beam of red light on the spot the bullet would hit. The beam was aimed at Frank's throat.

Frank's stomach reacted first, rumbling as though he hadn't eaten in a long time. Then knotted. Under his robe the perspiration dripped from his back. His eyes were on the man with the magnum, but he also picked up the light coming from the top of the weapon. He had stared into the barrel of a gun before, but none held the terror of this one. Prison guards armed with laser-targeting rifles had put down riots without firing a shot. The sight of that red beam on his body unnerved the toughest convict.

The man holding the magnum was tanned and slight, with small plump hands, silver hair and cool gray eyes. He wore a three-piece pin-striped suit and wine-colored tie, and spoke with an Australian accent. *Australian.*

"Hands behind the neck, Mr. DiPalma. Good. Now kneel facing me. Splendid."

These were not Shen's men. They were Caucasians. But they were still dangerous, especially the Australian, who seemed to find a primitive pleasure in his work.

"We've come to relieve you of Mr. Hansard's case," said the Australian in a nasal twang. "Him havin' gone to Jesus and all, I doubt if he has much use for it. And you, boyo, are not the rightful owner, so you'll forgive us if we don't ask your permission to go dashin' off with it. By the way, the food in this establishment is as bad as I've ever tasted. We called downstairs and canceled your order, for which you should be thankin'- us. Now we'll be gettin' to the heart of the matter and havin' the case." He jerked his head toward the desk and the man with the Walther placed the case under his arm.

"I take it every scrap of paper is in place," the Australian said. "You haven't had it long enough to hide anything, have you?"

"It's all there."

"I'll take your word for it, guv. You appear to be an honorable man, a rarity in this devious world of ours. Now listen and listen well, for I'll not be repeatin' what I'm about to say to you. We're leavin' here with the lad. And the case, of course. The lad's going on a trip, but a brief one. He'll ride downstairs with us in the lift, then in the lobby he'll be released to return to you. You don't have a say in the matter, so I hope you'll find these arrangements satisfactory."

"Whatever you say."

"Splendid. You are to wait here in this room until your son returns. Any deviation from this plan could bring something terminal down upon you and the boy. Do we understand one another?"

"We do."

"It pleases me that we do. Two lives depend upon you controlling your heroic impulses. Now one last item of business and this meeting will be adjourned."

He nodded. A signal.

The man holding the attaché case crossed the room to the couch and picked up the phone from the coffee table. A sudden move and the cord was jerked clean from the wall. Then he went to the bedroom and yanked out the second telephone.

Then the three men and Todd were gone, leaving Frank DiPalma alone.

It was fifteen minutes before Todd returned to Frank's room to find him packing his one suitcase.

"I thought you were going to stay for my mother's funeral," Todd said.

Frank stopped. "I am."

"But you're packing."

"We're going downstairs to reception. I want another room." He pointed to an ashtray setting on the edge of his bed. "Bugs," he said.

Todd picked up one of the small metal disks in the ashtray.

184

"There was one in each of the phones," said Frank. "One behind the bed, one under the couch, one in a lamp near the desk. No way of knowing if I got them all."

"How did you know they were here?"

"Our Australian friend in the tailored suit told me. That crack of his about the food, about his canceling our room service. And his mentioning that we hadn't had the files long. Hell, there were ears all over this place. I'd feel better if I had a new room."

Todd's eyes widened. "That was clever of you, sir. I mean, Frank."

"Todd, anybody with the brains of a radish could figure that one out. What I can't figure out is who hired those shooters. They're high-priced talent. They're slick, they've got access to good equipment and damn good weapons. Hell, they're pros. It was almost a pleasure to watch them work. Almost."

*   *   *

IN the hotel bar, DiPalma began dialing long distance. "Got to call Sally Verna first. Our new room can wait. He was hoping that file would keep him alive. All I can do is warn him that somebody else has it now. I owe him that much. Why don't you find a waitress and order a sandwich or something."

"I'll wait here for you, if you don't mind."

Frank tried three times to reach Verna and failed to get through each time. After the third attempt he dialed a telephone-company supervisor, who put him in touch with two other phone-company employees. It took fifteen minutes of being shuffled around before he finally learned that the New York area had been hit by a severe summer storm and telephone lines were down.

DiPalma hung up. "That's that. OK, how about that sandwich."

Todd was staring straight ahead. Frank followed his gaze, but saw nothing special. Just a handful of Chinese and one or two Europeans at the tables and at the bar. Then he realized that Todd was not staring at anyone in the bar. He was staring at something only he could see.

"*Yamabushi*," he whispered.

Mountain warriors. Another name for *ninja*, who had always trained in secret mountain strongholds.

"The *yamabushi* have come for him," said Todd.

Frank looked at his son and grew alarmed. The boy was sinking deeper into a trancelike state.

185

He grabbed Todd by the shoulders. "They've come for who, Todd. Who have the *ninja* come for?"

But Todd did not answer. He kept staring into space and Frank DiPalma was suddenly afraid.

14

LONG ISLAND, NEW YORK

THE JULY storm which struck the New York area brought with it warm, heavy rains, moisture-laden air and flash floods so severe that Manhattan police in rowboats had to rescue motorists trapped on deluged transverses in Central Park. The storm had formed over the Caribbean, started west, then changed direction and moved northeast. It traveled along the Atlantic Ocean, more than four hundred miles wide, and brought sixty-five-mile-an-hour winds.

Flash-flood warnings were posted for portions of New England, northern New Jersey suburbs and parts of Long Island, which was especially hard hit. Here the heavy downpour caused rivers to overflow and raised sea levels, threatening homes and halting train service to New York City. Schools and airports were closed and fishing fleets stayed tied up in port. Telephone lines were down and entire communities were without electricity.

It was not the driving rain or strong winds which left Sally Verna's oceanfront home isolated, without telephone or electricity. All power lines and burglar-alarm systems connected to the white marble mansion had been deliberately cut from outside by six black-clad figures, who made their way in the downpour and darkness down the hilly ridge, rain slicked and treacherous, then over sand dunes and sodden beaches until

187

they reached the wall protecting the west side of the mansion. Tonight no one stood guard on the ridge or on the swaying dock or on the beaches and lagoons. And no one stood guard outside the walls.

Using ropes and grappling hooks, the *ninja* scaled the walls and dropped down on the estate grounds. The house was well lit by an emergency generator in the garage. Three *ninja* trotted to the topiary animals cut from the hedges and followed them to the garage and the generator, their target. The other three went for the second target, the guards patrolling the grounds.

Dogs. Outside the garage. And barking. One of the *ninja* crept forward until he could see the snarling dogs. German shepherds, ears close to their skulls, fur darkened by the rain, teeth bared. No handlers, just the dogs. Their barking could not carry in the storm and wind. And they were indecisive about attacking. Taking advantage of their hesitation, the black-clad raider removed poisoned meat from his pocket and tossed it to the animals.

The dogs sniffed the fresh beef, then wolfed it down.

The *ninja* watched, and waited.

When the dogs slumped to the ground, foaming at the mouth, he ran forward, picked up one of the dying animals and ran back to his companions. He tossed the dog to the leader, then returned for the second animal, now dead. Seconds later the two men stood on the edge of the swimming pool and heaved the animals into the wind-driven water. A guard coming upon a drowned dog would not be as suspicious as finding a dog with its throat cut.

At the garage a *ninja* with only his slanted eyes visible under a hooded mask, peered through a window at two men straddling opposite ends of a workbench and playing cards. He turned to his companions and signaled with his index fingers. Two guards inside with the generator. Each *ninja* carried a sword across his back, but they would not be used until they reached the main house. A blade left blood and blood would alert a guard.

There were two entrances to the garage, a wide one for cars and a door facing away from the mansion. Two *ninja* positioned themselves on either side and the third pounded the door with a clenched fist.

From inside came an irate voice. "Yeah. All right, all right. Fuckin' crazy to come out in this shit's all I gotta say."

The door opened and a chunky man shaded his eyes against the rain. "You mind gettin' inside before we all drown—"

One man grabbed his shirtfront, yanked him out of the doorway, then rushed past him into the garage. Then another grabbed him from behind, yanking a forearm hard into his throat, and slipping his other arm under the man's left armpit and behind his neck until the palm of the left hand was pressed against the man's right ear, pushing his head into the forearm. Now he couldn't breathe.

Inside the garage the second guard was killed almost instantly. A *ninja* sneaked up behind him as the guard examined the ten cards in his hand and gave serious thought as to whether he should knock with eight points or try for gin and get off the schneid. He never saw the attacker reach out; he felt only his hands and by then it was too late. The *ninja's* left hand cupped the guard's chin and the palm of his right hand was hard against the back of the guard's skull. The left hand pulled the chin, the right hand pushed the head. Quick. Strong. And the guard's neck snapped.

The dead guards were hidden inside the Rolls-Royce. While one *ninja* crouched inside the doorway, the others disconnected the generator. The garage went dark. A grunt from the man in the doorway signaled that the mansion had also gone dark.

Static crackled on a hand radio lying on the work bench. A voice called the name of the dead men in the Rolls.

At the doorway the three Japanese waited, listening to the heavy down-pour on the garage roof and the roar of the ocean and the shrieking winds. Then the leader heard the sound he was waiting for: a rock tossed against the side of the garage. A pause, then two more rocks hit the garage and the second team of *ninja* joined the others, reporting to the leader.

Four outside guards were now eliminated. Two dogs poisoned. The bodies of men and animals hidden to prevent discovery and alarm. On the bench the radio squawked and a man's voice came cursing through the static. Ignoring the radio the *ninja* leader stepped out into the storm, ran to a hedge and crouching low at its base followed its outline toward the house. The rest followed him in single file, protected by rain and darkness.

*   *   *

SALLY Verna, a camping lantern in one hand, walked to the top of the grand staircase and looked down at Petey George, who was walking up the stairs toward him. A large handsome man in his forties, who kept in excellent shape by boxing regularly, Petey George was in charge of man-sion security. He was carrying a valuable painting upstairs, away from the flooding first floor that was pissing Sally off no end. The painting, a

189

thirtieth-anniversary gift from Verna to his wife, was a Caravaggio which the union leader had purchased in Florence and spent a fortune having restored in Milan.

Petey George walked past Verna's light and moved down the hall into darkness. Fucking Petey, thought Verna in admiration. Moves like a cat and makes his way around in the dark like an owl. Petey George didn't have an ounce of fat on him, and he had the hands of a classy welter-weight, something you didn't find on big men. Petey could have gone far in the ring if the commission hadn't pulled his license for throwing two fights.

Verna hadn't seen a storm like this hit the island since Hurricane Agnes in 1972, which killed a few people, and caused three billion dollars worth of damage. Tonight's storm was a ball buster, too. Sally watched two men nail planks across the terrace doors to keep them from flying open. A third man, sawed-off shotgun in one hand, held up a camping lantern, giving them light to work by.

There was broken glass on the carpet. Minutes ago the terrace doors had burst open and the wind had knocked down a mounted, glass-en-closed papal guard uniform, blessed and personally given to Sally Verna by Pope John XXIII. The treasured blue-and-yellow uniform, designed by Michelangelo, was now upstairs in the bedroom with the Caravaggio painting and other expensive art treasures.

Fucking storm. It had hit Sally like a kick in the balls. His basement was flooded and in the patio one of the stone cherubs had been blown off his dolphin, losing its head. The roof was leaking in two places and he had enough broken windows to keep a glazier in champagne for a year. His boats were probably getting the shit knocked out of them, if they weren't already at the bottom of the ocean. And no electricity, no telephone.

His wife Chiara was in bed and not well, but she was cheerful and trying not to complain. *Arte di arrangiarsi,* she said. We make do. We survive with style. It was the saying Italians fell back on when things went wrong. Chiara, a round, energetic woman with eyes as blue as the waters of Capri, believed in surviving, in resisting, in never giving up. Which is why she was alive with a heart that was growing weaker after years of giving to Sally, to the three kids and to anyone else who appealed to her generous heart.

Sally could not imagine life without the Admiral, as he called her. She was a descendant of Admiral Andrea Doria, Genoa's most famous seafaring man after Christopher Columbus. Chiara's most prized pos-session was a gilded silver plate said to have belonged to Doria and used by him at a banquet honoring Emperor Charles V. To impress the holy Roman emperor, Doria had tossed the gilded silver tableware overboard as it became dirty. He had done this every day during a twelve-day feast.

Petey George joined Verna at the railing overlooking the staircase. Together they watched the men nail planks over the terrace doors. "Talk to me, Chootch," Verna said in Italian, using Petey George's nickname. "What's with them bastards in the garage? It's like the Cotton Club in here. Dark as a nigger wedding."

"Sent Enzo and Rummo out there to see what the fuck's going on."

Verna's hand was in the pocket of his robe, resting on a .38 Smith & Wesson. "And if they don't come back?"

"If they don't come back, I go out there myself."

"No, no, no. You send somebody else out there. I want you right here keeping an eye on things. What's happening with the rest of the people we got outside, for which I'm payin' through the ass."

"Wish I knew. Radios can't do shit in this weather. They get wet, that's it. *Finito.* You got the storm, the wind, this, that. If you ask me, I don't think they're walking around. The dogs might be out in this shit, but hell, a dog ain't all that smart or he wouldn't be a dog. No, I think we got people hiding out in the garage, maybe the pool house, maybe in a car. And they don't wanna answer. Long as they don't answer, they can say they tried but the storm, blah, blah, blah. I think they're nice and dry somewhere."

"So you think I'm worryin' 'bout nothing."

"Hey, who in his right fuckin' mind's coming out in this weather. Roads are a disaster and you can forget about getting a boat through those waves. You got power lines down and you're taking your life in your hands goin' near them."

Petey George patted his thick, gray hair. "Not to worry, goombah. We got a dozen guys all over the house. No pussies. We got shooters. We got guys in both rooms on either side of you and your wife. Just you two, them and the grandchildren up here, nobody else. First pair slanted eyes we see—" He cocked his index finger. "Boom. That's all she wrote."

Sally Verna clapped him on the shoulder. "Think I'll look in on the grandchildren, then maybe lie down awhile. Thank God Chiara's resting. Says the rain relaxes her. My daughter got through before the phone lines went down. Claims she and Jim got the last available room in Manhattan. Hotels are jammed. Says they'll try to get out here tomorrow, but I told her not to worry. The kids are safe with us. Told her to stay in the city and spend money. She says her motto is Buy 'Til You Die and Shop 'Til You Drop."

191

Petey George smiled. "Maybe I should get married. Kid I'm going around with now comes into one trust fund when she's eighteen, another when she's twenty-five. A cool million and a quarter. Smart girl. Says going around with me is 'perverse and corrosive,' whatever the fuck that's supposed to mean. Some kind of vocabulary this kid's got. Some kind of ass, too. Gave me this badge that says 'Mozart. 400 Years Old and Looking Good.' One time she—"

The shot came from downstairs, from the back of the mansion. One shot. A gun was in Petey George's hand and he was past Sally Verna and running down the stairs three at a time. "In your room, Sal, and stay there. Lock the door and don't open it for anybody but me. Go!"

*   *   *

IN the kitchen a guard named Gino Riviere had gone in search of a cold beer. He placed his .38 on top of the refrigerator, opened the door and using the beam of his flashlight finally located a six-pack of what was still fairly chilled beer. Gino needed the brew. He was sweating buckets— no air conditioning, locked windows and doors, the heavy humidity. Right now he'd give his left ball for the beer and maybe a dip in the ocean. The ocean would have to wait. Tonight it was the end of the world out there. Gino would settle for the beer, then it was back to watching the back door like he was being paid to do.

He slipped the flashlight under his sweating armpit, popped the top of a Bud and tilted his head back to drink. He never saw a shadow slide from under the large kitchen counter. Getting a firm grip on Gino's ankles, the shadow yanked hard. For one second Gino was suspended in the air. He dropped the beer and reached out for the top of the fridge.

A hand came down on the .38, but the gun was knocked to the floor and went off, sending a bullet into a spice rack. A second later Gino was slammed into the red-tiled floor, his skull cracking. The shadow scrambled forward, lifted a fist shoulder high and drove the knuckles of a bone-hard fist into Gino's temple three times, killing him.

Shouting men were drawing closer. Footsteps rushing toward the kitchen. The shadow stepped over Gino's body, hurried across the kitchen and opened the door leading to the flooded basement. Stepping down the stairs in the pitch dark the shadow, with his excellent night vision, pulled a foot-long bamboo tube from his belt and eased into the waters of the flooded basement. He swam around and behind the staircase,

192

keeping close to the basement wall where the protruding tube could not be seen. His job was to create a diversion. The shot would do.

In the kitchen Petey George and half a dozen men looked everywhere. Closets, freezers, cupboards. Under tables and counters. And found nothing.

"Got to be here," said Petey George. "Son of a bitch has got to be in here. Didn't come past us and the fucking door's locked from the inside. Take a look in the basement."

Someone did, shining a flashlight down on the smooth black surface of the water. "Zilch, Petey. Fucking basement's flooded all the way up to the stairs."

Petey George pushed through and stared down into the basement. "Tear this whole fucking house apart. But find the bastard. We got a visitor. Maybe Gino got drunk, maybe he slipped, but I don't believe it. I think somebody's in here who shouldn't be in here."

"But how the fuck he get past us?"

"Just find him. He's here somewhere and his ass belongs to me. Find him."

*   *   *

IN the downpour two guards in hooded ponchos huddled under an overhang above the front door. A shit job being out here, but you didn't argue with Petey George. Even with nothing moving in this storm he still wanted men outside. Two men at all times on the door, to be relieved every couple of hours. The two on guard now had stopped parading back and forth. Fuck it. The wind was strong enough to pick you up and carry you to New Jersey and the rain was so heavy that the feel of it on your body was like being struck with a stick. Up yours, Chootch. You come out here and drown for a change.

One of the guards pointed. Two more men in ponchos coming toward them. Enzo and Rummo, the lucky bastards, back from the garage. Maybe there would be some light now. The guard called out, "What's happening with the lights? You guys shoulda stayed in the garage. What are you, schmucks?"

The men in hooded ponchos kept walking until they were almost on them and then they attacked.

193

THE living room was on fire. The second *ninja* diversion. Orange flames danced brightly against the blackness. Smoke floated up to the high ceilings, remaining trapped there. Petey George shouted, "Come on, come on, move your ass. We got fire extinguishers around here somewhere. Let's get on this thing, okay? Where the fuck is everybody? Where's Enzo and Rummo?"

"They're back."

"No shit. And how come I don't know they're back. How come they don't tell me what's happening with the generator?"

"Jesus, Petey, why you asking me? They come in 'round the same time this fire starts. I seen them go upstairs same time I'm calling you about the fire. Hey, I thought maybe they went to speak to Sal or change clothes or something."

Petey George looked toward the front door. "Who's out there? Who saw Enzo and Rummo come in?"

"Ivan. Richie."

"Get 'em. Bring them here."

"Now?"

"Hey assface, anytime I tell you something it's now. Don't worry about the fire. We got insurance."

"It's just that we ain't got that many guys on the fire and if it gets out of hand—"

"If it gets out of hand, we'll all line up and piss on it. Now you gonna move your ass or what. And check the kitchen. I left Paulie and Dee out there. Just see if everything's all right."

The guard left and Petey George watched the fire. He was getting some very bad vibes, the kind you got in the ring when you hit a guy with your best shot and he wouldn't go down; he smiled at you and told you to do it again and kept smiling, kept coming forward and taking your best, then he slipped a punch and hooked to your kidney and you knew it was going to be a long night.

Generator gone. No word from the garage. No radio contact with the outside guards. Gino dead. No marks on him, but stone dead. And now this fire.

The messenger returned. "Can't find them."

"The fuck you can't find them."

"I mean there's nobody out front, nobody in the kitchen."

Petey George looked up at the second floor, where Sally Verna was. Where Enzo and Rummo had gone.

He drew his .38. "Forget the fire. You, Tony and Abe, come with me. Upstairs."

* * *

IN the master bedroom Sally Verna sat up in bed. *Smoke*. At his side his wife slept peacefully. Verna slipped out of bed and into his robe. A smoke alarm went off. He didn't like it. There was Chiara to worry about and the grandchildren. Taking them outside in this storm wasn't anything he wanted to do. Maybe it was a false alarm. Probably somebody playing around with the electricity.

"Grandpa."

Verna's youngest grandchild, his favorite. Five-year-old Vanessa.

"*Grandpa, please.*" Something was wrong. The kid sounded in pain. Maybe the fire was scaring her.

And then she screamed.

Petey George's warning was forgotten. Lantern in hand, Sally hurried to the bedroom door and yanked it open. The three grandchildren stood in their pajamas, weeping. There was a red welt on Vanessa's face. She had been struck. Hard.

Verna stepped into the hall and went down on one knee, arms extended, inviting Vanessa to run to him. But she didn't. Instead her eyes went to something behind him. Sally turned to follow her gaze and saw two men in ponchos who had been hiding on either side of the door, their faces hidden by hoods.

Each held a samurai sword high overhead. The one on the right struck first, bringing the blade down on Sally's neck. The second hacked at the union leader's shoulder, slicing through thick muscle and into bone, spraying the squealing children with blood. In the lantern's light both blades rose and fell several times.

When it was over the *ninja* fled down the hall, disappearing into the smoke pouring from rooms on either side.

Petey George and his men rounded the corner to see the screaming, blood-stained children and to see Chiara stagger to the door and look down at the bloodied remains of her husband. The gray-haired woman's eyes turned up in her sockets and then, moaning, she slid to the floor.

195

Petey George crouched over her, feeling for the neck pulse. The other men ran along the hall banging on doors, kicking at them, opening them. "Holy shit," said one. "They're all dead in here. Cut up. Jesus, they're dead."

"They hit us," one of the weeping children said. "They hit us to make grandpa come out."

But a numbed Petey George didn't hear a word. He held Chiara Verna in his arms and gently closed her eyes with his fingertips. His tears fell on her still warm flesh and he held her closer, tighter, and slowly rocked back and forth. Even with the fire so near Petey George had never felt so cold and alone in his life.

15

DIPALMA, WITH Jan Golden at his side, climbed the faded stone steps and entered Chai Kung Woot Fat Temple. It was midday, lunch break for the production company, and except for a handful of American and British crew members guarding the equipment, the temple was empty. The crew on guard sat cross-legged on the floor near the entrance, eating Chinese food from paper cartons and washing it down with Coca-Cola. They were complaining about the temple rule prohibiting beer and wine. DiPalma watched an Englishman make the sign of the cross over a can of Coke. "Christ turned water into wine, didn't he," said the Brit. "So why can't he do the same with this, seeing as how we're on holy ground, or so I'm told."

Inside DiPalma welcomed the peace of the cool, mirrored temple. It was an escape from Hong Kong's heat, crowds and noise. Noise. Jackhammers and construction cranes, the high-pitched falsetto of Cantonese opera singers in a nearby rehearsal hall, the disco thud-thud-thud from round-the-clock topless bars. Street vendors, attracted by crowds watching the filming, loudly hawking bowls of noodles, oysters grilled in their shells and chicken blood cooked and eaten as soup. You don't live in a town like this, thought DiPalma. You only survive.

Jan led him past dolly, crane and tripod cameras; past lights, cables, props and cans of raw stock, unexposed film. It was DiPalma's first time in the Temple of the Living Buddha and he was impressed. Thousands upon thousands of mirrors from grateful worshippers who had recovered from illnesses. Mirrors that by candlelight became lustrous stars and glorious jewels. DiPalma had stopped going to church long ago, but it bothered him to see the temple invaded by a film company. It was a thought he chose not to share with Jan.

Jan herself seemed to belong to the temple. Her reddish hair caught patches of candlelight and shimmered with a fiery radiance. By candlelight her face assumed a mysterious elegance and DiPalma could easily imagine her as a temple goddess, arms spread wide, blessing the harvest. Her clothes were Japanese designed; she had been wearing them long before they were seen on the mannequins in Henri Bendel's window or in West Broadway shops. Their original and oversized silhouettes managed to compliment her figure, while looking both seductive and sophisticated.

She wore an Issy Miyake white linen jacket and skirt, with a Rei Kawakubo T-shirt of black cotton and carried a shoulder bag of deep red eelskin. The effect was one of confidence and relaxed assurance. Today she was all of these things. DiPalma had watched her finesse, then, stroke, finally crack the whip with cast and crew, selecting the right approach at the right time and improvising with the skill of a great jazz musician.

In a flurry of long-distance telephone calls Jan had refused to cave in to a bullying studio executive who demanded that the due date on *Ukiyo*'s answer print be moved up; insisted the studio marketing head clear any program for promoting the movie with her before implementing it; optioned a new book and two original screenplays; and confirmed the arrival of several Kon Kenpachi films in New York for his Lincoln Center retrospective. She also confirmed the rental of sound stages in London to be used for interiors, and wrote a check for the Knightsbridge penthouse she had rented.

On the set she confronted a Chinese actress who had wept uncontrollably when criticized by Kenpachi for fluffing her lines. She agreed to speak at the Hong Kong press club and suggested a cutaway to Kenpachi, a shot of a hairy-faced, toothless old Chinese woman in the crowd outside, to be inserted between segments of the temple scene. Kenpachi agreed. She impressed the Chinese extras by speaking a few lines of their language to them and applauded when they finished shooting, causing them to break into rare smiles.

They loved her. Cast, crew, extras. DiPalma could dig it.

At the back of the temple, away from the crew members, Jan removed a small mirror from her purse and placed it on a table among dozens of other mirrors. "For my father. You're only supposed to leave a mirror here when someone's gotten over an illness. I guess I'm jumping the gun. But he's gotten worse and I figure I have nothing to lose."

And it's me who has to tell her, thought DiPalma. About her father. About Todd.

Jan stared down at her mirror. "I thanked the gods in advance for keeping him alive for one more year. I thought, why be greedy. Just ask for a year, no more. Don't ask me what gods, because I don't know. Right now, I'm desperate enough to try anything. One of our interpreters did the Chinese inscription for me."

DiPalma said, "Jan, something happened in New York yesterday, something you should know about. That's why I phoned you this morning."

"And you couldn't talk about it over the phone, you said."

"No, not over the phone. Has to do with a man named Sally Verna. Salvatore Verna."

She looked at him out of the corner of her eye. "He's a friend of my father's."

"I know. Or rather I didn't know for sure until last night. He's dead, Verna. Slaughtered in front of his grandchildren. His wife died of a heart attack when she saw his body."

"You're joking." Her fists tightened on the strap of her shoulder bag. "Jesus, you're not joking. Not you. Oh, God. Poor Sal. And Chiara. Who would do a crazy thing like that. Do they know?"

"No," said DiPalma. "But I do."

She flinched. Her lips parted.

DiPalma said, "Before I left New York Sally told me that a group called the Blood Oath League was out to kill him."

"The what?"

"Blood Oath League. A World War II secret society. Japanese. They were into assassinations, head breaking, espionage. They were connected to some very rich, very right-wing Japanese. And to the Kempei Tai, the Japanese gestapo."

"My father told me about the Kempei Tai. First-class bastards."

"According to Sally, the Blood Oath League's back in business and the man who ran it then is running it now. A man who was also in the Kempei Tai. A man who should have been hung as a war criminal, but who got lucky with a little help from his friends. Zenzo Nosaka."

She nodded, sure of what he was going to say next. "You're going to tell me that Kon's mixed up in this somehow. That because Kon and Nosaka are close friends—"

"Jan, hear me out. I didn't come here to talk about Kon."

"God, I wish I could believe that. No offense, Frank, but you do have a reputation of getting those who got you. I just somehow see you getting back at Kon for something that happened while the two of you were beating up on each other with bamboo sticks."

"You're reaching, Jan, and you know it. Yeah, I got even with some people. Dealers trying to blow me away. Informants who jerked me around. The sleazeball who killed my partner and left me to break the news to his wife and four kids. And the guy who killed my wife and daughter."

She took his arm. He tried not to smell her perfume. "Shitty thing for me to say," Jan said. "I'm sorry."

DiPalma thought: Kenpachi. She's sleeping with him. DiPalma's stomach started to burn.

He said, "I came here to warn you about your father. I got it from Sally, and it's beginning to look like he was being straight with me. Just after the war Kenpachi's friend Nosaka vowed to kill three men, three Americans who got him convicted of war crimes, who worked like hell to get him hung. That would be Sally himself, Duncan Ivy—"

"And my father," said Jan.

"Sally's dead and so's Duncan Ivy."

"I don't know about Sal, but Duncan and his wife were killed by some kind of California cult."

DiPalma shook his head. "No way. Cops, the press, they were all guessing out there."

She released his arm. "For your information, my father, Sal, Duncan, Nosaka, they've all been doing business together for years. I don't know the details and I'm not really interested. Some of it has to do with banking and running interference for Nosaka in the States. What I do know is that my father and Nosaka are definitely not enemies and haven't been for a long time."

DiPalma remembered the secret bank records he had read last night, the records Sally Verna and Jude Golden had been prepared to use against Nosaka. "The honeymoon between your father and Nosaka is over." He told her about his talk with Sally Verna, about the secret bank records and about having them taken from him at gunpoint by a well-dressed, silver-haired Australian.

"Australian?"

"You know him?"

"I think so. Rolf Nullabor. He works for my father."

"Left-handed, gray eyes, the kind of guy who'd freeze a kitten in a block of ice and drop it in a punch bowl."

200

Jan sighed. "That's Rolfie. A regular mean machine."

"What's he do for your father?"

"In charge of security. Bodyguard. Courier. Nobody you'd want to meet in a dark alley, that's for sure. Sadistic son of a bitch. He caught some kid driving a snowmobile on our property once. Fifteen-year-old kid. Had a dog with him. Rolf the weird poured gasoline on the dog, then burned it alive. Then he broke the kid's back. Literally broke his back. A warning to trespassers. A rotten little shit, that Rolfie. A few years ago he came on to me. Made my skin crawl. I said, 'You like sex and travel?' He drooled, oh, how he drooled. 'Indeed I do,' he said. 'Then go fuck off,' I said. Frank, the man turned eight different colors and I knew right then and there I'd made a mistake. Not in turning him down. Oh, no. My mistake was in being a wiseass, but you know me. Anyway, he got back at me in his own little way. He started leaving notes in my apartment. They'd be in the fridge, in the drawer with my underwear, in the pockets of my clothes, in my purse and even on the pillow during the night while I slept."

She shivered, remembering. "He was coming into my apartment as if there were no front door, let alone three locks. Now here's the part that really freaked me out. He left a couple of nude photographs of me behind and man, that's when I really climbed the walls."

DiPalma said, "How'd he get pictures like that?"

"How the hell would I know? I certainly didn't pose for them, if that's what you're thinking. Rolfie's an absolute nut on any new gadget or piece of machinery that comes on the market. I guess he had some kind of long-range camera."

"Maybe a hidden camera with a timer, some place where you'd never think to look. A miniature camera. Maybe he followed you and took the pictures when you were in a health club, or with some boyfriend."

"All I know is I practically went broke changing the locks on my apartment. Fat lot of good that did. Rolfie managed to find a way in any time he felt like it. I never caught him at it and yes, I did go to the police."

"What happened?"

She looked at him as though he were naive. "You're a cop and you ask me what happened? Nothing happened, that's what. No fingerprints on the notes or on the photographs or in my apartment. Except mine and those belonging to the man of the hour. No witnesses, no proof. The only thing that came out of it was I guess the cops got off looking at the pictures. Eventually Rolfie got tired of playing games and the whole thing died down. Except ever since then he's been calling me 'Butch

Cassidy, the daughter Hopalong never mentions.'"

DiPalma tapped the worn stone floor with his cane. Why steal the files when they were being brought to you? "Weird Rolf. I wonder if even he's enough to stop the Blood Oath League. That's what I wanted to see you about. Pass the warning on to your father. The Blood Oath League plans to kill him."

"Frank, listen. You say Sal's dead. Okay. But it's very hard for me to believe that my father's going to be killed by someone who's been his friend for almost forty years. I mean, I make my living in the world of make-believe, but I don't know if I can get behind what you just told me."

"I might not have believed it either except for one thing. Todd."

She looked around. "Where is he?"

"Across the street with Roger Tan. Gave him money and told him to pick out any stereo cassette he wanted. My treat."

Jan grinned. "I don't believe it. You mean he actually wants one of those box radios, those ghetto blasters?"

"Last thing in the world I would have thought he'd go for. Guess there's a part of him that's like any other kid."

"That's a strange thing to say. What do you mean a part of him? Why not all of him?"

DiPalma waited a moment before speaking. It was nitty-gritty time. "Todd's got colors of his own. I guess the word is unique. I'm still trying to get used to him, frankly. He told me who killed his mother. The police didn't know and there were no witnesses. And Todd was miles away when it happened. But he knew. Turned out he was right. *Ninja*, he said. He also said *ninja* would kill Sally Verna. Happened just that way."

Jan gave him a doubtful look. "Todd told you about Sal *before* the murder?"

"Before. I finally got through to New York this morning. Had trouble with the storm last night. Jesus, I could not believe it. The kid flat out hit it. Sally's grandchildren were witnesses. They couldn't make out the faces of the guys who did it, but they did say swords. They saw Sally killed with swords. That's the way the Blood Oath League took care of business in the old days. That's what Todd says is going to happen to your father."

"I don't believe it."

"Jan, Todd told me that I was in Hong Kong to get his stepfather's secret bank records. I mean he told *me*. I never mentioned that to anybody, not even to Katharine when I spoke to her from the airport. And

202

if you remember, last night he said he was sorry about your father's illness. Jan, I didn't tell him that. I didn't know about it."

"Kon did say that Todd's unusual. Said he's a true samurai. Said they have a special relationship. Came about awfully fast. They've only known each other a matter of days." She looked at DiPalma. "You're asking me to believe Todd's psychic, that he can read the future."

"Like I said, he's been right so far."

"Or very, very lucky. Look, how can I telephone my father, who's sick enough as it is, and tell him to be alert for something called the Blood Bath League—"

"Blood Oath League."

"Whatever. I mean what do I tell him, that some kid had a vision about an old friend doing him in?"

I tried, thought DiPalma. I opened the door; she has to walk through it. "All I can do is tell you. I can't make you believe. Truth is, it's not the kind of thing I believe in myself. But I can't ignore the kid's record. He's batting a thousand. On target every time. What's more he doesn't go around bragging about it. You want anything out of him, you drag it out."

Jan said, "Speaking of keeping things quiet, there's been nothing in the papers about what happened in the hotel yesterday. I mean you would think that a cop and a drag queen found dead in the same room might merit some attention from the press. And don't tell me nobody knows about it. There are no secrets in Hong Kong, which happens to have one hundred and twenty-five newspapers. Even my interpreters were able to describe to me the fan used for homicidal purposes by one Mr. or Ms. Chiba. Kon's not talking, but that's to be expected, of course."

"Of course," said DiPalma. "Why the sudden silence? The police are partially responsible. They don't want to call any more attention to me than necessary. It's one way of avoiding telephone calls from Peking, London, the States. Anything about what happened in the hotel would be linked to Katharine's death. And the death of Ian Hansard as well. Hong Kong banks don't like nasty stories about bank presidents. Tends to make customers nervous."

"And we can't have that, can we," said Jan. "Now why do I get the feeling you're not telling all?"

"I don't know. Why?"

"Come off it. Let's have the rest of it."

"The rest of it. Let's see. The rest of it is that the press is waiting for the rest of the story, or so a police superintendent told me this morning."

"I don't understand."

"Me and Ling Shen. That's what everybody's waiting for."

Jan chewed her bottom lip and shifted her weight from one foot to another. "You could leave Hong Kong. Now."

"I've been told that."

"I see. So I'm supposed to get spastic worrying about whether or not you're going to be killed anytime soon. Here we go again. Golden's Rule. Never face the facts."

"Katharine's funeral is day after tomorrow," said DiPalma. "Then I'm off to Tokyo, to find out who sent a Japanese drag queen to kill Katharine. And why."

He was going to mention Kenpachi's name when Jan stepped closer to him and the film director was forgotten. Keep walking and keep smiling, Tiny Tim always said. But DiPalma didn't move. He was thinking what it would be like to warm his hands in the fire that was Jan's hair. And he didn't move because he felt the heat of his own hidden fire, his craving for her. Desire and want. The father of all misery.

She touched his face. A tear crept from beneath her dark glasses. "Don't die. If that happens—"

She threw herself into his arms and clung to him, her nails digging into his back. DiPalma's heart leaped. Slowly his hands came up to touch her. But then she broke away and walked toward the temple entrance. She never looked back. But then she never did.

*   *   *

DIPALMA stood at the top of the temple stairs and watched Todd hand his new box radio to Kenpachi for his approval. They stood at the base of the stairs, together with Jan, Roger Tan and Wakaba, the chauffeur. Wakaba had his back to the group as though irritated by what was going on. Once he looked over his shoulder at Todd as though he could wring his neck, then turned back to stare at the crowd. To DiPalma the bearish and surly Wakaba appeared to be playing the role of a woman scorned. With a switch-hitter like Kenpachi in the picture anything was possible.

Kenpachi pressed a button on the big radio. Marvin Gaye sang about "Sexual Healing." Don't I wish, thought DiPalma, remembering the feel of Jan near him. He watched Kenpachi hand the radio back to a pleased Todd. He said something to the boy, who nodded in agreement. Now it was DiPalma's turn to be jealous. Suspicious. Guarded. Watchful.

Twenty years as a cop told DiPalma that Kenpachi knew more about

Katharine's murder than what he told the Hong Kong police. Kenpachi and Sakon Chiba in Hong Kong at the same time. Chiba knowing Kenpachi's telephone number. Too many coincidences. And what did Kon Kenpachi want with DiPalma's son? Was he interested only in Todd's knowledge of kendo and ancient swordsmen? Was he thinking of using Todd in a movie? Was he planning to get back at DiPalma through Todd?

The least you could say about Kenpachi was that he was unpredictable. DiPalma knew all about his mystical side. His desire to be a samurai, his love of mysticism, blood rituals in particular, and his infatuation with his own beauty. Kenpachi also revered the memory of Yukio Mishima, Japan's internationally known author and, like Kenpachi, a superpatriot with a longing for what Mishima called "restoring Nippon to its true state."

In November 1970 Mishima had committed *seppuku* on a Tokyo army base, an act which in Kenpachi's opinion made the author nothing less than a god. Kenpachi's first book had been a flattering biography of Mishima, after whom he had named his first son. The director had called Mishima *kensei*, sword saint, a tribute usually reserved for only one other, Miyamoto Musashi, the legendary seventeenth-century samurai known for *Go Rin No Sho*, A Book of Five Rings. Dealing with the practice and strategy of swordsmanship, the book was one which DiPalma had read and reread and never stopped learning from.

Calling Mishima "sword saint," DiPalma knew, was merely more evidence of Kenpachi's love of excess. Musashi was the greatest swordsman in a nation of outstanding swordsmen. After the forty-seven Ronin he was Japan's most popular hero. Mishima had never risen above mediocre in the martial arts.

Something else DiPalma did not like about Kenpachi. Word was he had killed people. No one knew for sure how many, but DiPalma had heard that rumor more than once. Kenpachi was beyond being flaky. DiPalma had to keep Todd away from him.

Roger Tan, perspiring in the heat, waved to DiPalma, then held up a hand to keep him in place. Something the DEA agent wanted to say in private. Something he didn't want anyone to hear.

"Freaking heat. What's good for crotch itch? Checked in with my office while you were inside. There's a message from Geoffrey Laycock. Says he has to see you toot sweet."

"Did you tell him we're checking on Katharine's funeral arrangements?"

"Yeah, I told him. He says not to worry, Peking does good work. If they say do something, it's done. He wants to see you anyway. It's about the fan, the one that faggot used to cut up on the cops."

"What about it?"

"Gone, Jack. Disappeared. Walked right out of the police station."

DiPalma angrily whacked the step with his cane. Todd and Jan looked up at him, as did Kenpachi.

Roger Tan said, "Laycock says he'll bet you a new tiara the fan's on its way back to Japan."

"Let's go talk to him."

Together they walked down the stairs. Todd turned off his radio, then lifted a hand in farewell to Kenpachi and joined his father. Kenpachi smiled pleasantly at the boy and ignored DiPalma. Jan lifted her dark glasses to peek at DiPalma. "Take care, Frank."

He nodded and let it go at that. For some reason he didn't like talking to her around Kenpachi. And since DiPalma was walking away, he gave Jan a smile. Look at me, Tiny. Walking and smiling.

Then DiPalma stopped. He did not like the way Wakaba was looking at Todd. There was nothing inscrutable about Wakaba's face. He loathed the boy. Why? DiPalma took a few steps toward Wakaba, coming between him and Todd, then stopped. Now he and the chauffeur were eyeball to eyeball. And it was DiPalma who was getting the dirty look.

Kenpachi barked a command in Japanese. Wakaba said, "*Hai*," and stepped back as though obeying a military command. Then he spun on his heel and walked away to stand behind Kenpachi, arms folded, eyes all but closed.

DiPalma knew the type. Short fuse, malignant, capable of murderous hatred. Kenpachi was smirking and saying it all without saying a word. *He can kill you. It is something I would very much like to watch.*

DiPalma played the game. He said nothing; they understood each other. He didn't like Kenpachi, Kenpachi loathed him. And that would never change. As for the chauffeur, guys like him either tried to punch your ticket or they ignored you. When they brought it to you, they brought it good. Cold-blooded, unfeeling, remorseless. Words didn't impress them.

He walked back to Todd, who looked up at him with pride. And gratitude.

"Thank you, Frank," he said.

There was more to it, much more. Only Todd and maybe Wakaba understood. Hearing his son thank him for what he had just done made DiPalma feel better than he had in a long time.

16

MYSTIC, CONNECTICUT

JUDE GOLDEN knew he would not win tonight.

Nijo, the youngest and prettiest of his three Japanese serving girls, had become a tough opponent. After weeks of coaching she had become more daring in her strategy, unpredictable in her moves, increasingly difficult to trap. Go, with its four-thousand-year history, its squared board and black-and-white stones, was one of the most demanding and engrossing games ever invented. Westerners played it poorly. Orientals alone could truly understand go, whose rules were simple but whose variations exceeded the number of atoms in the universe.

Nijo, despite her lack of experience, had a feel for the game; she was a deliciously treacherous adversary.

Jude Golden's heart condition had forced him to live in the most comfortable of his homes, in a red brick Victorian mansion on the outskirts of Mystic Seaport, a restored nineteenth-century Connecticut whaling village of cobblestone streets and white clapboard houses. Each of the mansion's three stories reflected his wealth and love of ease and comfort, his love of New England and Japan.

The first floor was New England, with maple, walnut and mahogany furniture dating from the 1830s, blown glass, long-cased clocks with metal disks and seventeenth-century Dutch silver tankards, two-handled cups and beakers. The second and third floors, both closed to visitors, were Japanese, Golden's private sanctuary. One floor contained straw-matted rooms divided by sliding doors, folding screens and shoji, wooden frames covered with rice paper. Golden slept and ate here, attended only by Japanese serving girls.

The top floor was an Ali Baba's cave of straw-matted rooms filled with tea ceremony utensils, jewel boxes, samurai swords with elaborate scabbards, lacquered screens, porcelain, pottery and costumes and masks from Kabuki and Noh plays. If New England was Jude Golden's wife, Japan was his mistress.

He had been born and raised sixty miles west in New Haven, but a love of clipper ships, kept on display in the harbor for tourists, had always drawn him to Mystic. In New Haven, where he was chairman and the largest stockholder in one of New England's most successful banks, he owned an Italianate mansion with a landscaped garden on Hillhouse Avenue, the street Charles Dickens had called the most beautiful in America. And he owned a condominium within walking distance of the ivy-covered buildings and green courtyards of Yale.

But his heart was in Mystic, where from his Victorian mansion he could smell the salt air from Long Island Sound and be alone with his Japanese artifacts. He loved to roam the cobbled streets lined with quaint nineteenth-century seaport homes, rigging shops, sailmaking studios, and talk with coopers, who made barrels and tubs by hand as their ancestors had done a hundred years ago for whaling expeditions. There was always something new to discover at the Mystic Marine Life Aquarium with its two thousand varieties of fish. But best of all were the tall ships in Mystic harbor.

Jude Golden owned the most beautiful of the old clipper ships. It had cost him three-quarters of a million dollars to restore the *Jan Amy*, a former China clipper named for his daughter and only child. The ship had once carried on a flourishing China trade in tea and opium, and before that had run slaves and sailed from the Atlantic coast around Cape Horn to the California gold fields. Now she rode proudly at anchor, first among equals, long, narrow and built for speed, and with a cloud of sails—skysails and moonrakers, topgallant and royal sails. She was his proudest possession.

In a straw-matted room on the mansion's second floor Jude Golden watched Nijo move to capture another of his stones. If she succeeded she would have three. Tonight's game was her best. But Golden was determined to end up the winner, to put up a real fight. For the first time he noticed that Nijo, who was seventeen, wore different color nail polish on each finger. A far cry from her namesake, a thirteenth-century

Kyoto noblewoman who copied pages of Buddhist scriptures as an offering to Shinto shrines.

Nail polish and Buddhist scriptures. To Jude Golden Japan was incongruous, cultured yet crude, a mixture of mysticism and technology. In Japan illusion and reality were indistinguishable; everything meant more than it appeared to mean. The Japanese way of life was at once sophisticated and simple, immensely appealing, and Jude Golden was caught in its maze of hidden meanings.

He could not live in Japan; he was tied to America by family and career. But he could not erase from his mind the best of Japan, its mysterious past and elegant eroticism. He would have them both, the money to be made in America, the satisfaction of immersing himself in things Japanese.

Jude Golden had gone after money by fair means or foul, with an insatiable hunger. Now, on the edge of death, he saw that he had really been driven by fear. Fear of failure, fear of anti-Semitism, fear of his father. Too late he realized what he had had to do to acquire his great wealth. There was no crueler joke in life than getting what you wanted. And the cruel joke in his case was Zenzo Nosaka. Because of Nosaka, Jude Golden's past had become his present, bringing with it shadows and pain.

Jude Howard Golden was in his early sixties, a tall, square-faced descendant of Russian Jews, with graying, thinning hair and a whining cordiality which often hid the fraudulent man behind it. He headed the third largest bank in the East, founded by his father. Until his recent heart attacks, Golden had traveled thousands of miles on bank business each year, adding new names to his file of over ten thousand foreign politicians and businessmen whom he knew personally.

Under his leadership the bank's overseas branches increased, its stock doubled in value from 1970 to 1980 and its credit-card and traveler's-check operations had become one of the most successful in America. His father and other Jewish immigrants had started the bank in 1920, the year Jude Golden was born. It was their answer to the snobbish anti-Semitism of the New England corporations and commercial banks of that time.

"A long time ago," his father once said to him, "I believed that money was the only thing in life that mattered. Then I was right. And now I am just as correct. With it we Jews create our own golden age. With money we bring order to our lives. I tell you something: when it comes to money we share the same religion with the goyim, except they are too stupid to realize it."

His father, a hard-driving man who had arrived in America penniless, never forgave an insult. Jude Golden grew up watching him make the WASP banking world pay for its snobbery and discrimination. Under the elder Golden, the fledgling New Haven bank aggressively sought out mergers during the Depression, bought shares in foreign banks, built the tallest building in New Haven and was one of the first banks to make loans to multinational corporations.

Jude Golden's father lived long enough to become one of the most influential bankers in the East and to savor the WASPs' sending their Ivy League-educated sons to him to learn banking. But Jude was not as strong or as uncompromising as his father. He was a man of fragile health, insubstantial character, sly and secretive.

He was also calculating and shrewd, with an excellent memory and a talent for gathering useful information. With a law degree from Yale and his father's influence he went into World War II with a lieutenant's commission and was assigned to the Judge Advocate General's Office. He was stationed first in Hawaii; then when the war ended he was sent to Japan to try war criminals.

Jude Golden would always look upon that time as the happiest of his life. To convict the Japanese warlords, generals and admirals who had once terrorized the world, was so exhilarating that he ignored his health and worked harder than he ever had in his life. Zenzo Nosaka was one of the biggest convictions Golden worked on, a man almost in a class with Himmler and Martin Bormann. On the day Nosaka received his death sentence Golden and the other members of his team celebrated with sake until they passed out in a geisha house.

But Nosaka didn't hang. The United States needed him to fight a new war, the cold war.

"How the world turns," said Salvatore Verna. "We team up with Uncle Joe to kill the Japs and now we're teaming up with the Japs to go bang-bang at Uncle Joe. Somebody tell me if I'm crazy or what."

"Life is licking sugar off broken glass," said Duncan Ivy.

"Hey Dunk, I think maybe you been in this here fuckin' country too long. Either that or somebody told you you were profound when you were a kid and you ain't been able to let go the idea."

"Salvatore, my friend, I was merely pointing out that in life things go right and they go wrong. Up and down, the waxing and the waning. Sun and shadow. Constant change, with uncertainty as the only certainty."

"Your ass. How's that. In any case Nosaka goes back to his cell to beat his meat for the next twenty years when all he should be doing is hangin' by his nuts for what he's done to people."

Jude Golden said, "Nosaka will go free."

"You're crazy," said Verna. "They ain't hangin' the bastard, that's all. He's still gonna be inside looking out for a long time."

"The word is *free*," said Jude Golden. "Mark my words. It's the old story of the camel. You let him put his nose in your tent so he can keep it warm. Then his head's in. Next comes his front paws. Then one hump, followed by the other hump. Before you know it, the camel's inside and you're out in the cold. Nosaka has his nose in the tent. Watch what happens next."

Jude Golden's father had told him how the medieval Jews had come to control banking. All other occupations had been closed to them and there were laws preventing Christians from earning interest. The Jews had no armies, but they had their brains and knew that to protect their banking business they would have to know all about the goyim. So with banking came one of the first and most efficient spy systems. Even the goyim came to learn that ignorant bankers did not survive and that a banker without means of espionage was a banker doomed to failure. Knowing a single important fact and knowing it in time offered a banker more protection than he could receive from a battalion.

Realizing the importance of Nosaka's information, Jude Golden knew that the Japanese would not hang. American intelligence agencies had to keep him alive because they were hungry for anything they could get on Russia, the new enemy. Golden also knew that Nosaka could eventually talk himself out of prison. Once free, in the pragmatic tradition of Japan, he would turn for help to those who had tried to kill him.

Little favors at first. Then larger favors and each time there was a payment in exchange for services rendered. The camel now came bearing gifts. But as Jude Golden came to see, Nosaka was still a camel intent on having his own way. Golden, Verna and Ivy's association with him was so prosperous that the Americans were blinded to the knowledge that one day there would be a big bill due.

It was Jude Golden's father who told him that he was committing his worst sin for a man he should have despised.

"He was with them, the Nazis," said the elder Golden. "That makes him *dreck*. There are some things a man should not do even for money."

"Nosaka's breaking no law in his own country."

"You think that means you're breaking the law?" The old man touched his chest. "You are breaking the law in here. Here. From the army you know people in the spy business all over the world and you use them to help this Jap bastard and make yourself rich."

"I do it for the bank. Your bank."

"You don't fool me, sonny boy. You do it for yourself. Commitment you don't got. Except maybe to yourself, to your Japanese girl friends. You think because you are involved with the bank, you care. Well, I tell you what is commitment. You take a plate of ham and eggs, excuse the expression. The chicken lays the eggs and that makes him involved. The pig he furnishes the ham. That makes him committed. When you get like that pig, then you are committed to something. Now you ain't."

"If I'm not committed to the bank, why is it making more money than ever?"

"I tell you why. Because you like to plan, to scheme, to set a thing in motion, then sit back and watch what happens. Mr. Organizer. You are on the sidelines watching us poor bastards fight in the pit, which is a bad something to say about your own son, but I'm too old to lie. Lie down with dogs, you get up with fleas. That Jap is worse than a dog and he does not change. I tell you, he is the same man he always was. And don't tell me about legal in Japan. Some things just are not right. Not right."

Jude Golden could have told his father that times had changed, that things were different now and the idea of right had changed. But he said nothing. Even his father knew Jude Golden had been born weak and that weakness intensified during the years with Nosaka. After the death of Jan's mother, it was Nosaka who had sent the first of the young Japanese "comfort girls." She was replaced by others, girls recommended by Japanese business associates, girls selected by Golden himself during his trips to Japan. During their stay with the American banker they were treated well, given cash and gifts, and served him with the submissiveness due a Japanese man. The girls were the same, none older than twenty-four, attractive, able to sing, dance and play Japanese musical instruments.

It was a comfortable, well-ordered world. Golden had money, a touch of Japan in his Connecticut mansion and his beloved clipper ship within walking distance of his home. Nosaka's vow to kill him was meaningless. Until a bad heart, the worst of Golden's many illnesses, all but gave out. The sharp pain in the left arm, a terrifying tightness in his chest, the difficulty in breathing. He knew without question what it was and that it was serious.

Two heart attacks within months. The best heart specialists held out no hope; it was only a question of when. His eyes were going to close in death and all of his treasures would be lost to him forever. Approaching death forced him to see his life for what it was, a house built on quicksand, a series of shortcuts. He had allowed Nosaka's manipulations to become his curse.

Commitment. Too late for that now. He was committed to Jan, but

212

she no longer needed him. She was on her own, a successful television producer who was determined to make it in movies. He had written the obligatory checks to Israel, hired minorities to work in his bank and allowed his employees to buy stock. What else could he do? He thought of his father, of what he might say, and that was when Jude Golden decided that before he died he would destroy Nosaka.

Once committed to the idea, help came. Private reports from Japan included information on the murders of two Japanese businessmen. The murderers could have been terrorists, but the use of swords or knives reminded Golden of the Blood Oath League. When other businessmen were hacked to death in Rome, São Paolo and Buenos Aires, Golden checked with Japanese sources and learned that the Blood Oath League was indeed operating again. At least two people told him that Zenzo Nosaka, if not the leader of the new league, was a financial backer. But Nosaka was too important to challenge without overwhelming proof, and so far Jude Golden didn't have it.

Golden the organizer fitted the pieces together. Nosaka was old and, like Golden, facing death. It was time for both men to put their houses in order, to prepare for that journey to an unknown place. The Japanese industrialist was a descendant of samurai, an ultranationalist, and the spilling of blood for Japan's greater glory was nothing new to him. Then and now the purpose of the Blood Oath League was the same. In Japan the past and the present, as always, was one.

Which also meant that if Golden and his fellow war-crimes prosecutors had forgotten the promise made to kill them, Nosaka had not. The industrialist had now decided to act on that promise.

Golden had to act, too, but how? How could he effectively destroy the man who was Japan's most effective spymaster since the legendary Hideyoshi? This became the commitment Golden's father had always wanted him to make.

Ian Hansard, the English banker in charge of the Hong Kong branch of Nosaka's bank, came up with the answer. Golden had helped form the bank, had sat on the board with Verna and Ivy and had drawn in other prominent Americans, men with information and connections for sale.

At Golden's last meeting with Hansard, the Englishman had complained bitterly about Nosaka, giving Golden the weapon he needed to fulfill his commitment.

"I didn't think he'd actually go through with it," said Hansard. "Letting me go and all. But he's certainly planning to do it. Already the bastard's ordered a few of my duties transferred to some Japanese in the bank and he's given me vice-presidents, two to be exact, that I neither requested or need."

"That's the Japanese way," Golden said. "You're a *gaijin*, a westerner, an outsider. The Japanese pick your brains, then do it their way. As soon as they learn all you have to offer, the game's over. You're gone."

"I'm beginning to get the picture. Don't like it one little bit. It's me who's made this bank successful, not bloody high-and-mighty Nosaka. My brains, my sweat, my hard work. And what thanks do I get? Out on my arse with nothing to show for it."

Jude Golden said, "Oh, please, let's not be dramatic. You'll have plenty to show for it. Like those numbered accounts in Panama, Zurich and Amsterdam."

Hansard puckered his small mouth. "I don't know what you're talking about."

"The hell you don't. We're all victims in this life, but you really don't have to overdo it. I've always lived with the thought that to believe is to believe the worst, so I've made a point of knowing everything there is to know about people I do business with. And wouldn't you know it? Most of what I learn comes under the heading of the worst. Take you, for example. Those numbered accounts I mentioned. Even Nosaka doesn't know about them. If he did, you might have a problem."

Hansard chewed on a thumbnail. "Fascinating. Absolutely fascinating."

"You've been playing fast and loose with Nosaka's money. I could say stealing, but that's a strong word. Working your magic, shall we say, in such out of the way places as South America, Africa and the Arab world. Oh you're smart. You don't do a thing here in Hong Kong or anywhere in the Pacific where Nosaka spends most of his time. You're wheeling and dealing where he can't see you, where the lines of communication are stretched pretty thin."

Hansard said, "You do have a long nose. But that's an affliction with your people, isn't it? Hell hath no fury like a Jew who's been outfoxed by a wog." He lifted his drink. "I give you Zenzo Nosaka, who's bloody well put the sharp end to us all, you included. So what do we do now? May I inquire how you got on to me?"

"You mean how did I come upon your creative accounting? First let me say you're very good with computers and yes, I know you erased all the tapes. And the phony companies you formed to do business with your own bank are dissolved immediately after serving your purpose. And that business of going after unclaimed bank funds in those out of the way branches. Clever. You always manage to hire the most believable false claimants. Though in the matter of certain loans to companies which have no intention of repaying, companies in which you have a hidden interest, well, I'd go a little slow in that department in the future if I were you. But that's just my opinion."

"You've made your point. Now what do you intend doing about it?"

"Surprise. Nothing."

Hansard waited.

Golden said, "*You're* going to do something about it. Oh, in answer to your question about how I came to know. Bekaa Valley. Lebanon."

Hansard looked shaken. "How in God's name did you learn about *that?*"

"As you might put it, us Yids stick together."

Hansard frowned and then the answer came to him. "Mossad. You've got the bloody Israeli secret service working for you. Christ, I should have known."

"The PLO makes millions off the marijuana it grows there," said Golden. "You launder their money. Quietly. For twice the going rate. And not through Eastern Pacific, which costs Nosaka a pretty penny. You're supposed to do everything through him while in his employ. I believe that's one of his rules. You know how the Japanese believe in teamwork and toiling for the greater good."

"What is it I'm going to do regarding your newfound knowledge of my activities?"

"Get me everything you know about Eastern Pacific, about Nosaka's industrial spying, bribery, payoffs, blackmail. Anything that's damaging."

"That's all? Why don't I stick my head in a cannon or try wing walking on a cross-Atlantic flight. Are you mad? On second thought, I can't bloody well say no, can I?"

Golden said, "Our arrangement won't work if I attempt to blackmail you. I don't want that. I've learned one thing from Nosaka: make the game worth the candle. I want the best job you can do, nothing less. My health's bad and that's a major problem, one I don't care to go into right now. Before I go, I want to get Nosaka. I have reason to believe he's out to kill me."

Hansard smiled. "Is he, now. Pity."

"You don't seem surprised."

"You haven't exactly endeared yourself to me these past few minutes."

"That could change," Golden said.

"Oh?"

"When you have all of the information you think could ruin Nosaka, information that could bring him to trial in a dozen countries, then

215

contact me. Don't write or telephone me about this until you have it all. There's a chance Nosaka might be bugging my phones or watching me. When you have what you think I want, let me know and we'll do a deal."

"Will we now. What to your mind constitutes a deal under these circumstances?"

"Three million dollars for you. Cash on delivery."

Hansard blinked.

"Take it or leave it," said Golden. "One way or another you're finished with Nosaka."

Hansard leaned back in his chair. He cleared his throat and swallowed hard. Three million dollars. Just like that. And Golden could easily afford it. Ian Hansard, he said to himself, you may just be in luck, in real luck.

＊   ＊   ＊

IN the straw-matted room Jude Golden removed the oxygen mask from his face and turned off the tank. He breathed easier; the slight constriction in his chest was gone and his face felt less heated. He glanced at his watch, then back at the go board, where he had surrounded one of the few white stones left to Nijo. 11:15. Almost time for the nurse to buzz him on the intercom with her annoying reminder that bedtime was twelve midnight sharp.

The midnight bedtime was the only compromise he and the implacable nurse had been able to work out. Golden, a lifelong insomniac, rarely went to bed before four or five in the morning, preferring to nap during the day. The nurse, black Irish and hard as nails, had insisted he turn in no later than nine. To make sure, she had injected him at 8:55 with what she called a "sleepy-weepy." With that safely in his bloodstream, she then smugly dismissed him for the night.

Golden defeated her easily. Even with the injection he slept no more than three hours, then immediately buzzed the nurse and woke her up. A few nights of this warfare and a midnight bedtime was agreed upon, provided he had napped previously. Thereafter he rarely disturbed the nurse before her normal wakeup time of 6:30 A.M.

On a corner of the go board nearest her, Nijo fought capture and defeat. Rigid with concentration, she sat with both hands in her lap, focused on the cluster of small black and white stones. Two more moves and Golden would close the trap. In true Japanese fashion she would not give up without an intense struggle. Surrender was out of the question;

Golden would have to defeat her decisively. To do otherwise was to risk losing her respect and what Nijo did not respect she ignored.

There was a dignity and grandeur about her that could have kept Golden watching the beautiful girl for hours. He was drawn by her perseverance, by her belief in herself. She had the courage for action and to be near her made Golden regret that he had not taken a more active part in life. There was something healthy and invigorating about Nijo. Even the other girls were drawn to her; despite being the newest and youngest, Nijo had quickly become their leader, the one who insisted they try new foods, visit new shopping malls, imitate the new dance steps seen on television and risk the new fashions, American or Japanese. In a dark and dead world Nijo was vital and garden fresh and Golden, who usually tired of girls after a few months, was infatuated with her.

The telephone rang. It was a private phone, kept locked in a honey-colored box and carried with Golden wherever he went in the mansion. The unlisted number was changed frequently, and the lock combination only Golden knew. As Nijo watched, Golden drew the box to him and began spinning the lock. Seconds later he lifted the top of the box and reached inside for the telephone receiver.

"Dad? It's Jan. Hello?"

"Gyp, how are you? What are you doing calling me on this line?" Gyp was short for Gypsy, a nickname given to Jan because of a teenage addiction to wildly colored skirts, head scarves and hoop earrings.

She sounded worried. "Are you all right?"

"As all right as can be expected. We've had a big storm here. Did some damage to the ship, but nothing that can't be repaired. Why? Do you know something I don't know?" He smiled at Nijo and mouthed *my daughter*. Nijo bowed and returned his smile.

Jan said, "Yesterday when we talked there was some trouble with your pacemaker. I tried the hospital, but they said you had checked yourself out."

"False alarm, Gyp. Not to worry. Sounds worse than it was. Had a few anxious moments, but it seems my pacemaker's functioning as it ought to. Right now I'm relaxing with one of the girls and enjoying a fast game of Go. You know me. The original night owl. What time is it there?"

"A little after one in the afternoon. Dad, let me ask you something. Where is Rolf Nullabor right now, this moment?"

Golden toyed with his obi, the sash he wore around his summer kimono. "I had the impression you weren't too fond of Rolf. Why the sudden interest?"

217

"I don't give a damn if he lives or dies, if you want to know the truth. Just tell me if he's in Hong Kong or not."

Golden looked at Nijo. Should he send her from the room? And then she slowly pulled her kimono down from her shoulders, baring her breasts. Lovely. Small, firm breasts. Grecian in proportion. Totally unlike the udders which passed for breasts in America.

Golden watched as Nijo took a vial of oil from the pocket of her kimono. She poured some into the palm of one hand and slowly oiled her breasts. Golden's throat went dry.

"Dad? Are you there?"

Golden watched Nijo squeeze her right breast, now shiny with oil, and stroke the nipple with a lavender-tipped thumb. "Here, Gyp. Right here. You mentioned Rolf. Yes, he's in Hong Kong."

"Oh, God. He was right."

Something in her voice jerked his thoughts away from Nijo. "Who was right? Have you talked with Rolf?"

"You've got to be kidding. I wouldn't go near that ding-a-ling with a whip and a chair. Someone I know claims Rolf robbed him last night at gunpoint. It has something to do with a group called the Blood Oath League and with your friend Nosaka."

Golden picked up a black stone from the go board and began kneading it between thumb and forefinger. "Who are we talking about?"

"Frank DiPalma. He's in Hong Kong. He says you and Sal know why he's here. I heard about Sal and Chiara, by the way. Frank says the Blood Oath League killed them, that Nosaka was behind it and that you're next."

"DiPalma, DiPalma. That would be the television news guy. Crime reporter. Big fellow, gray hair, raspy voice."

"Daddy, no games, please. You know damn well who Frank DiPalma is. I've told you about him, you've seen him on the tube, so let's stop the bullshit."

"Never did get to meet him."

"Let's not go into that," said Jan. "I didn't want to discuss my family with Frank. He's a reporter and will bird-dog a story until he gets what he wants. I ended up playing dumb, rather than hurt you."

"Hurt me? How?"

Jan said, "Dad, before grandpa died I remember you and him arguing about Nosaka. I wasn't that interested, but I do recall one thing. Grandpa thought Nosaka was a shit. But you said business was business and that Nosaka was no worse than anybody else. Maybe so, maybe not. I really don't have all the facts, but Frank did tell me that Nosaka planned to kill you, Duncan and Sal. You've probably forgotten that you told me the same thing a long time ago. I didn't tell Frank because I don't want him coming after you. Also, I have a movie to make. It's my first and if I don't do it right there won't be a second. I don't want Frank complicating my life at the moment."

"But you called me," said Golden.

"You're my father. You're damn right I called you. Daddy, Sal and Duncan are dead. You're the only one left and I'm worried. And for God's sake don't talk to me about coincidence. I'm getting bad vibes from all of this."

Nijo pushed her breasts together, bowed her head and touched the nipples with the tip of her tongue. Golden closed his eyes in order to concentrate. He wanted desperately to keep Jan away from anything to do with Nosaka. When she had hired Kenpachi to direct her first film there had been no thought of Golden going after Nosaka, his longtime business partner. That came later, after the murders of Duncan Ivy and the others, after learning that the Blood Oath League had been resurrected with Nosaka behind it. Kenpachi, unfortunately, was too close to Nosaka; the two shared right-wing political views, for all Golden knew, Kenpachi, too, could be involved with the Blood Oath League. The film director intended to go overboard for his beliefs.

But for Golden to talk his daughter out of working with Kenpachi meant telling her things Golden didn't want her to know. Things about himself and the way he ran his business life. Things about himself and Nosaka.

Time enough to tell her when he had the files, when he knew exactly what he had to use against Nosaka. It was unlikely that anyone as stubborn as Jan could be convinced to fire Kenpachi, unless she herself caught him with the smoking gun. Jan was stubborn, ambitious, determined to succeed and unwilling to be controlled by her father or any other man.

Her life was movement and freedom; she scorned indecision, inactivity. It was more prudent to let her finish the film and get rid of Kenpachi, leaving Golden free to go after Nosaka. Jan would have the career she wanted. And Golden could fulfill a commitment his father would have been proud of.

Golden said to his daughter, "Rolf was in Hong Kong to get certain bank records for me."

"With a gun. Why send Rolf for those records when according to Frank he was bringing them back for you and Sal?"

Golden closed his fist around the black stone. "Sal only wanted to use the records to blackmail Nosaka, to make him back off and leave us

219

alone. I want to finish Nosaka permanently. There's a difference. In any case, I saw no reason to argue the point with Sal. I mean why cause *tsuris* if you don't have to."

"Let me get this straight. You let Sal think the two of you were partners, in agreement on whatever it is you're planning, when all along you had your own ideas of how to go about it."

"Jan, please."

"Always turning it to your advantage, aren't you. Everybody's some kind of commodity to you, nothing more. Sal was your friend and you strung him along. Daddy, that sucks."

Japanese history and Hideyoshi taught me well, he thought. Send two teams of spies after information, with one team assigned to watch the other. Yes, Golden and Sal had agreed on the value of Hansard's records. The difference lay in how each proposed to use them. Golden wanted to draw blood. Sal would never have agreed. But, then, his opinion no longer mattered.

Golden said, "Jan, if Nosaka's after me—I say if—then nothing's going to stop him. I know the man. Sal's way would not have worked, believe me. With Nosaka it's hardball, or you don't play."

"So Frank's right about Rolf. And you're saying he's right about Nosaka. What about Kon Kenpachi. Is he involved in any of this?"

"Far as I know, Kenpachi's not involved. And yes, Rolf is bringing the bank records to me. I don't want you to worry about Nosaka and me. One way or another, it'll work itself out."

As he spoke Nijo moved the Go board aside, then leaned over and oiled the soles of his feet. The effect was soothing; the tension of thinking about Nosaka slackened. Then Nijo lay down at his feet and took his big toe in her mouth. The effect was galvanizing; a pleasurable jolt sped up his leg to his brain, invigorating him in seconds.

Nijo removed the toe from her mouth, blew on it, filling Golden's body with an exquisite chill. He trembled as she rubbed the oiled sole of his foot against her oiled breast in slow circles. It was a delectable sensation.

With an effort he forced himself to speak to his daughter. "Jan, the man who gathered those bank records for me was Ian Hansard. But he died just before DiPalma arrived. How did DiPalma come up with those records?"

"Through his son, who by the way, predicted Sal's murder and also predicted you'd be in trouble with the league. Seems the boy has ESP or something like it."

Nijo, now lying on her back, closed her eyes and pushed off her kimono. Naked, she used one hand to rub Golden's left foot against her breasts. With the other hand she began to masturbate.

Golden opened his kimono and cupped his hardening penis.

"Psychic powers," he said. "I didn't know DiPalma was married."

"He's not. He fathered the boy, Todd, by a Chinese girl."

"Ah yes. Katharine Hansard. Who also died recently."

Jan said, "She was killed by some Japanese transvestite, who was shot to death by a policeman. Apparently Todd helped Frank find this transvestite. Frank says there might be something to the boy's predictions. Dad, I want you to take care of yourself. Just be on guard, okay?"

"That department's well taken care of. I have alarms, closed-circuit television, armed guards, you name it."

Nijo fingered herself faster. Golden's penis was hard and warm in his hand. He couldn't stop looking at her.

"Gyp, I've got to run. Some hag of a nurse is hovering over me with my medicine and I can't get out of it. I'll be fine, believe me. Rolf will see to that. You just hurry up and finish that film of yours so I can see it before I die."

"Dad, you know I will."

"One other thing I want you to do, Gyp. If this boy of DiPalma's comes up with any predictions you think I ought to know about, get on the horn, will you?"

When he had hung up, the nurse Southy buzzed him on the intercom. "Twenty minutes, Mrs. Lyons. Then come upstairs."

And then Nijo, her face contorted, climaxed, pulling his foot into her breasts, pushing her pelvis off the floor, the thumb and forefinger of her right hand pinching her clitoris. Then she fell back against the floor and rolled over to embrace Golden's feet and ankles. Submissive. *Hai. And he was her lord.*

Golden took her in his arms, pulled her on top of him and fell back to the mat, mouth on hers, loving her, loving her.

No bad memories, no thought of death, no reality. Only Nijo, who was in his life so that he did not have to deal with himself, and who was in his arms and was all he wanted to know.

)

＊　＊　＊

NIJO lay awake, her back to Jude Golden, who was snoring slightly. Both lay on the floor, on the comfortable Japanese futon. She stretched out patiently. The injections given by the nurse had now taken effect, and he slept deeply.

Shortly before 1:00 A.M. she sat up, looked down at Jude Golden with loathing and wiped her mouth with the back of her hand, wiping away the taste of him. Nude, she rolled away from the bedding and sat up, her arms wrapped tightly around her knees.

Nijo stared at Golden's form in the darkness. She hated the touch of him, hated the medicine smells and the old-man odor which clung to him, his sickly white flesh, his pretense of knowing Japan and the Japanese. He was a *gaijin*, an outsider, a Westerner, a barbarian. He would never know Japan nor understand its people, not if he lived to be a hundred.

She wept and thought of the day when she would return to Japan. She no longer lived in the present; her life was a future shaped by dreams of what Nosaka-san would do for her after the hated *gaijin* was destroyed. Squeezing herself more tightly, she rocked back and forth, back and forth, and did her best to stop thinking about home.

17

FRANK DIPALMA, amused, watched the two Chinese policemen, seated on the far side of the crowded tearoom, busy themselves with a fan-tan game and pretend not to be interested in him. Both wore light green summer uniforms with red tabs on the shoulders, indicating they spoke English. Neither was a good actor. DiPalma knew their game the second he walked through the door. He had seen customers near the entrance glance at the cops, then at him and back at the cops. No secrets in Hong Kong, paisan.

In fan-tan an unknown number of buttons are placed under an inverted cup, then counted out in groups of four. The players then bet on how many buttons are left in the last group to be removed, a number always between one and four. A lack of interest in their game indicated the cops were in the tearoom to sit on DiPalma. The younger of the cops would lift up the cup, slide out his buttons, then look at DiPalma out of one eye as if to say *hey was that a smart move or what?*

It was the older one who finally stopped pretending. He shifted in his seat until his back was against a marble-backed bench and drank his tea looking directly at DiPalma. DiPalma grinned and showed a palm in greeting; the cop looked through him as though he were invisible. DiPalma liked that. A real professional.

223

The same, however, could not be said for Geoffrey Laycock. From the moment DiPalma, Todd and Roger Tan had entered the small tearoom on Pottinger Street, a ladder street because of its vertical steps, the British journalist had been restless. He had been sitting alone, shifting around teacups, saucers and teapots, nervously drumming his fingers on the table. Even after they sat down with him he continued to toy with cups and saucers, eventually snapping at a waiter in perfect Cantonese to bring new cups and saucers, and be quick about it.

Surrounded by whirling ceiling fans, potted palms, blackwood tables and brass spittoons, Laycock in his white linen suit reminded DiPalma of an island colonial official gone native. The jittery Brit seemed to belong in the tearoom, with its Chinese menu in characters and traditional Chinese teacups with small lids instead of handles. Laycock was a reminder that at the beginning of this century his country had ruled a fourth of the world's area and population.

The waiter returned with the fresh cups and saucers. Laycock said, "I'll be mother, shall I?" and began to pour.

In deference to DiPalma's stomach, Laycock had ordered green or fermented tea, slightly scented and taken hot and straight—no lemon, sugar or milk. The lid on the cup was adjusted so that only the liquid passed into one's mouth.

Laycock sipped his tea and sighed. "Orgasmic. Positively orgasmic." He glanced around the packed tearoom before concentrating on DiPalma and Todd. The boy, wearing a connected headset, had given his full attention to the new radio on his lap.

Laycock whispered, "A contact in the police station told me about the fan this morning. Apparently it disappeared during the night. Of course no one has the slightest idea how this came about."

"Of course," said DiPalma. He wasn't surprised. Hong Kong was Hong Kong. Almost everything here was for sale, including the police. A war fan like the one used by Sakon Chiba could easily have been traced to its owner. DiPalma scratched an eyebrow. Hell, it still could be traced. He knew what it looked like. All he had to do was get out of Hong Kong alive, go to Tokyo and start asking questions. But he wasn't going until after Katharine's funeral two days from now. Fuck Ling Shen. DiPalma owed Katharine. And he owed Todd. He would have to take his chances for the next two days and hope that bird dogs like the two cops sitting by the front door would discourage Shen or at least slow him down. Even as the words flashed into his mind DiPalma knew that it wasn't true. Shen was going to have to make a move or lose face. And maybe lose his life for no longer acting like a true leader.

Laycock jerked his head toward the entrance. "You have company, old sock. Albert and Victoria are pretending to be caught up in the mysteries of fan-tan while contorting themselves into permanent paralysis by sneaking a peek at you. Rather transparent, wouldn't you say?"

"It would warm everybody's heart if I got dusted somewhere besides Hong Kong. Frick and Frack are sitting on me in the hope of discouraging Shen."

"Vain hope, wouldn't you say?"

"Fucking optimist we got here," said Roger Tan. "Is that why you're acting strung out? Nervous Nelly afraid she'll get caught in the cross fire?"

The Englishman fingered his bow tie and slowly turned toward Tan. "Oh dear. Vexed and cheesed off, are we? I'll wager it has something to do with requesting a transfer out of Hong Kong and having it denied."

"That's how you get shit on your mustache," said Tan. "You're looking for love in all the wrong places. But you're still smiling. Nobody happier than a golden-shower queen who's made it to the store in time for the one-cent beer sale."

Whoa, thought DiPalma. He watched Laycock's face redden, then saw something else, a look Laycock had never shown before. Eyes narrowed into a steely gaze. Face an unyielding mask. DiPalma had seen that look before, on men who were stone killers. Like the Cuban in Washington Heights who had killed his mother, then cooked pieces of her flesh and fed them to his dogs.

The look passed from Laycock's face. He relaxed, laying a small, damp hand on Roger Tan's forearm. "I do apologize, dear boy, for telling tales out of school. My problem, you see, is that I'm never at my best from sunrise to sunset."

He turned to DiPalma. "I'm also in a flap over you, dear heart. I do so want to be the first to get your complete story, which includes Shen. We're all waiting for the other shoe to fall. Have a vested interest in it, you might say."

"What's a vested interest?" asked DiPalma.

"Various and sundry wagers. Bets have been placed as to how long you'll manage to stay alive in Hong Kong. There were some who bet you'll live no longer than one hour. Forgive the pun, but they were dead wrong. Those who wagered you'd go to Jesus yesterday are also out of the running."

"How did you bet?"

"*Moi?*" Laycock's hand was over his heart.

"How much?"

The journalist looked at the ceiling. "How much." He gave DiPalma a thoughtful look. "A strong show of faith on my part, actually. Two thousand Hong Kong dollars at ten to one that you would live until Saturday."

"The day after Katharine's funeral. Yeah, that's a show of faith, all right." He sipped his tea. "So tell me about the fan."

"Nothing to tell, old boy. Gone, vanished, missing. No one seems to know a thing about it. Chiba's remains are still in custody, however. No one's come forward to claim them."

"Not even Kenpachi?"

"Not even Kenpachi. Oh, I did hear something about Chiba. Seems he did quite a bit of traveling. Europe, California, the Middle East and even throughout Japan. No one seems to know why."

"With the Japanese nothing is what it seems to be. For all we know, Chiba could have been an Avon lady or a Bible salesman. Something else for me to check out when I get to Tokyo."

"I'll give you something to check out in Tokyo," Roger Tan said. "Check out Japanese influence with Chinese Triads."

"What for?"

"Because nothing happens in Hong Kong without the Triads being in on it. Because a Japanese fan walked out of police headquarters with the help of one of the Triads in this town."

DiPalma leaned forward.

Tan said. "Triads own this town, Jack. And they own the cops or enough of them. You got cops who are in the Triads. I hear tell that one or two high-ranking cops are *Cho-kuns*, Triad subchiefs. You want to reach the cops for something that isn't kosher, you have to deal with the Triads or you don't deal at all."

Roger Tan stood up and stretched. "Better get my ass down to the office and show my face. If I stay out too long my supervisor gets antsy and starts checking my expenses too closely. Man's got it in for me. Sooner I get out of this shit hole, the better. Frank, check with you later." He tapped Todd on the shoulder. The boy looked up from his radio and smiled.

When Roger Tan had gone Laycock said, "Getting to be rather testy, our Roger. Still, he could well have a point. About the Triads and that fan."

DiPalma finished his tea and put the cup down. A hand went up in refusal, halting Laycock's attempt to refill the empty cup. "Roger's sharp. Good head for collecting intelligence, but not the most diplomatic guy around. Frustrated over not being promoted. But he does know his stuff.

Time for Todd and me to get rolling, too. Got to finish checking on Katharine's funeral arrangements. Chinese funerals are hell to arrange. Christ, I hate to think what it would be like having to do all this without Peking's help."

Laycock said, "Delightful thing, power. Both a means and an end. Sometimes I think it exists only in its perception or in the opinion of others. Sometimes I wonder if it really does corrupt. Well, dear boy, do keep in touch. And do your best to stay alive at least until Saturday."

He poured more tea for himself. "They say gambling causes you to lose your money or your character. At this stage of my life I so much want to hold on to what little I possess of both."

✳   ✳   ✳

DIPALMA leaned forward in the taxi and threw up. Then, breathless and shivering, he fell back against the seat and forced his eyes open as wide as possible. His eyelids weighed a ton; he stared through slits, barely able to see as far as his knees. His ears rang and with the ringing came a whistling sound which reminded him of a boiling teakettle. He felt chilled, as though he were sitting naked in snow. Seconds ago he had been perspiring, his shirt drenched and leaving a wet imprint on the leather seat. He willed himself to move his hand, lifting it from his thigh and placing it on his stomach. No feeling in the hand. Not a goddamn bit of feeling in either hand.

He hadn't felt this sick in a long time. Not since the shooting eleven years ago in Hong Kong.

From miles away he heard the Chinese driver curse him in very obscene Cantonese. And he heard a worried Todd, seated beside him, call his name and lay a hand on his cheek. Todd then said something in Cantonese to the driver, who angrily waved him away. It was late afternoon and the driver, who had yet to be paid after driving DiPalma and Todd around for hours, was losing patience in the heat and traffic.

Having driven several places to confirm Katharine's funeral arrangements, DiPalma and Todd were now returning to the hotel. From the tea shop they had gone to see the Fung Shui man, the diviner selected by Peking, who after consulting the spirits of nature and animals, had selected the auspicious date and time for the funeral rites. Then there had been a forty-five-minute drive south to Stanley Village, the coastal fishing community which was one of Hong Kong's oldest settlements.

Here, where Japanese had interned their British prisoners during World War II, DiPalma and Todd had visited the monks in the two-hundred-year-old Tin Hau Temple, dedicated to the colony's popular goddess of the sea.

The unpretentious temple, whose main hall contained three walls with black-and-gold statues of gods, had been Katharine's favorite. She had come here to pray for DiPalma's recovery eleven years ago and had returned every year since then. This was Hong Kong's miracle temple; during World War II bombs had landed directly on top of the temple but did not explode.

And here, under a canopied shrine, was a statue of the god Wong Tai Sin, who generously granted his followers' wishes and was one of Hong Kong's most popular deities. Wong Tai Sin cured illnesses and also gave his devotees advice on horse races.

This is where Katharine wanted her services held, Todd said. And she wanted to be buried in China, just across the border in Shenzhen, in a special cemetery for Hong Kong residents who preferred to be buried on the mainland.

"To be buried in her ancestral homeland means favorable Fung Shui for my mother," said Todd. "This must be done according to the spiritual laws she lived by. Elements of heaven, ocean, fire, wind and earth have been consulted by the Fung Shui man. He has used *ch'i*, the breath of yin and yang, to decide upon the day and upon the place she will occupy in the cemetery."

"It'll be done her way," said DiPalma, understanding none of it.

The temple reminded him of that day in the Kowloon hospital when he had tried to get out of bed for the first time since he had almost been shot to death. Katharine had watched him as he hopelessly tried to stand up on crutches. Not once did she make a move to help him.

Then DiPalma had attempted to walk. A child could have done better. Three very awkward steps, agonizing steps, followed by disaster. One crutch slipped from under his arm and when he tried to cling to the other with both hands he lost his balance and dropped to one knee. It hurt like a son of a bitch. That was it. No more. He was giving up. He turned toward the bed.

Katharine blocked his way. "Crawl toward the window. Don't go near the bed."

DiPalma needed someone to be angry with and she was it. "Get the hell out of my way."

"Knock me out of the way. Because I'm not moving. Crawl, fly or roll on the floor. But get to that window any way you can, because you're not coming back to this bed."

He could have hit her with a crutch. Gone for her head and enjoyed doing it. "You get off watching people crawl? Well, I ain't a comedian. No laughs from this boy. Not today. For the last time, get out of my way. I'm not ready to walk to that window or any other fucking window and maybe I'll never be ready. Come back tomorrow. I always limp on Thursdays."

"I'd rather see you limp today." She folded her arms across her chest. "Because if you limp, Mr. Comedian, you're walking."

He clung to the one crutch and stared at her for long seconds. Then he pulled the other crutch toward him and gave her a hateful look, hating her yet knowing she had done more for him than anyone else in his life. He turned his back on her and began to limp toward the window. Ten feet between his bed and the window. The longest ten feet of DiPalma's life.

There was pain every inch of the way and more than once he wanted to quit, fall down and rest, but she was watching and he kept going until he made it. He saw the sun, the gray water of the harbor and a black, ugly freighter about to overtake a sailboat. He was exhausted, drained. And ready to cry, because there were no words for what he had just done, for what she had made him do. He looked over his shoulder at her. Another time he might have been ashamed for a woman to see him weep. Not now. She was weeping, too.

In DiPalma's mind there was no doubt that if he had stayed on the floor that day or gone back to bed he would never have walked again. Nor would he ever have loved again.

*   *   *

IN the taxi DiPalma sucked in air through his open mouth. His head had split into fragments and his legs and arms had lost all feeling. The terrible thirst which had plagued him since early afternoon had returned. He had blamed that on the heat. It couldn't be his diet. Since the shooting his diet had been fairly bland; heavy on dairy products, boiled vegetables. A wild time at the dinner table was two pieces of fruit with his meal.

Something else had caused this terrible thirst. Since leaving the tearoom DiPalma had gone through half a dozen glasses of milk, a couple of bottles of Perrier, club soda. No ice. And still the thirst would not go away.

When the cap stopped for a red light DiPalma stiffened with cramps and doubled over. *Jesus.* He heard Todd yell and DiPalma forced his eyes open. Had he passed out or just come close? Todd wasn't calling him; he was arguing with the driver, who kept shaking his head. Now Todd held up his radio so that the driver could see it in the rearview mirror. Silence. A few words in Cantonese and the driver nodded. A bargain had been struck. The cab speeded up, then the driver made a U-turn away from the hotel, back the way they had come.

DiPalma, fighting for breath, looked at his son. "Hos-hospital."

"You are dying," said Todd. "Ling Shen has poisoned you."

"Hos, hos..." DiPalma couldn't form the word.

"No," said Todd. The boy's eyes bore into DiPalma, who wanted to scream. But his eyes closed and he climbed toward a starless and grotesque night.

18

GEOFFREY LAYCOCK had spent a pleasant evening in his kitchen preparing himself a first-class Chinese meal.

Because Chinese cuisine was the greatest the world had ever known, he had trained to become a superb chef, specializing in Cantonese cooking which called for food to be cooked quickly and lightly, preserving the flavor and original taste. By 10:00 P.M., after four hours of cooking, Laycock was ready to dine on food that would have pleased the notoriously finicky empress dowager of the Ching dynasty, who before she was deposed in 1912 enjoyed a daily meal of one hundred dishes, all of which her eunuchs first tested for poison.

Laycock had brought a plastic bag of live frogs from a Hong Kong market, sliced off their legs and deep fried them in a crunchy batter mixed with crushed almonds. After dipping them in sweet-and-sour sauce he munched on the legs while preparing the rest of the meal in his large, well-equipped kitchen. Working to cassette tapes of Placido Domingo, Mozart and Willie Nelson, Laycock boned and sliced small eels, then braised them in wine and garlic. This was a Shanghainese dish, the only diversion from his Cantonese menu. Next he prepared shark's fin soup, to be eaten with onion cakes.

For the main course he prepared Hakka-style stuffed duck. He deboned the duck through a hole in the neck, then stuffed it with lotus seeds, chopped meat, rice and pigs' brains stewed in wine. Dessert was to be a sea-swallow's nest, whose dried saliva lining was said to have rejuvenating powers. The nest, while tasteless, would be flavored with coconut milk, honey and almonds.

Cooking finished, Laycock showered, shaved his legs, then slipped into a red-and-gold gown and gold slippers, gifts from Hong Kong's most popular opera singer, a charming woman with whom he often smoked opium.

In the living room he set a service for one on a small table by the window. From here he would dine and look down on Murray Barracks, which the occupying Japanese used as their headquarters during World War II. For a few seconds Laycock stared at the timber-and-stone building with its deep verandas and allowed the memories to wash over him.

The smell of the meal he had cooked intruded on the hazy dream that was his past. He clapped his hands together. Time to enjoy a well-earned repast, his reward for a job well done. Was he not a good cook, and was not cookery an art, a noble science, and were not cooks gentlemen? Laycock lit incense sticks, which jutted from a tiny sandbox on the window sill, then lit two lavender candles on the table. From a teakwood cabinet he selected tapes by Mozart, Aznavour and the Clash. Music. The pleasing melancholy. The speech of angels.

When the doorbell rang, it made a most unmusical sound. An exasperated Laycock slammed the tapes down on the top of the cabinet. Who had the nerve to call at this hour, unannounced and uninvited. He had well and truly earned this meal, especially after all he had gone through in the past twenty-four hours. Whoever it was put a finger on the doorbell and kept it there. Bloody cheek.

Laycock crossed the living room and squinted through the peephole. He caught himself frowning, which he knew wasn't good for the face. He stopped and smoothed the skin between his eyebrows with the heel of his hand. He opened the door.

Roger Tan took his thumb off the bell.

"Your timing is foul," said Laycock. "Be brief, then be gone."

The drug agent's eyes took in the red-and-gold robe and the gold slippers. "Shit, I wouldn't have missed seeing this for anything. You wear that when you go to get your Pap test?"

"That's the trouble with masculinity. You must prove it over and over again. We are all as God made us, only worse. Speak your piece, Roger, though I fail to see why this couldn't wait until tomorrow. You could even have tried telephoning. But then stupidity is such an elemental force, isn't it?"

"Well, it is a bitch being butch sometimes. I just dropped by to tell you that you fucked up. Blew it."

Laycock folded his arms across his chest. "Your vanity is insufferable at times. Such as now. Just what is it you know and I don't?"

"Frank DiPalma's still alive. You didn't kill him. Came close. Real fucking close. But Frank...well, he is a cat with nine lives."

Laycock pressed his lips together and hugged himself. He took deep breaths, then clenched his teeth and fought to keep himself from trembling. Without being aware of it he backed into the living room. All thought of food was forgotten.

Tan entered the apartment and kicked the front door closed behind him. He stopped and sniffed the air. "Smells good. Private party?"

Laycock cleared his throat. "I happen to be alone."

"Well, if you're celebrating, you jumped the gun. Frank's still with us. Barely alive. There's a chance he might not make it, but if he does, well, you know where that leaves you and Ling Shen. Up shit's creek, the both of you."

"I'd like to sit down."

"Hey, why not. We'll both sit down." Laycock sat down on a black metal chair near the kitchen. Roger Tan sat down on a brown leather couch, then removed a Beretta from his jacket pocket and casually placed it on the coffee table in front of him.

There was amused contempt in the drug-agent's voice when he said, "You're not going to give me any trouble, Miss Priss, are you?"

Laycock, head down, mumbled, "No."

Tan leaned back, hands behind his neck. "Worst you can do is hit me with your purse or give me a hickey."

He stared at the ceiling and did not see the Englishman look up. Laycock's face held the same hard look he had worn when insulted by Roger Tan in the tearoom. Then he smiled. "So you think I tried to kill Frank DiPalma."

"Know you did, Miss Priss."

"And what put you on to me?"

Tan kept his eyes on the ceiling. "Teacups, saucers and teapots." He looked at Laycock. "You were playing around with them when we walked in the tearoom this afternoon. You were signaling somebody. You were telling whoever was watching you from Ling Shen's Triad that you felt it was all right to proceed with killing Frank."

Laycock folded his hands under his chin. "*Moi*, the golden-shower queen, a taker of life? Surely you jest."

"Hey queenie, you're a member of Shen's Triad and we both know it."

"Now how can that be, dear boy, when Triads are Chinese only. No *gweilos* need apply."

"Wrong. That's what Triads like the world to think. Oh, I admit not many Europeans get past the membership committee. Damn few, in fact. But you did."

Laycock said, "For your information, Triads were founded in seventeenth-century China by Buddhist monks to fight Manchu invaders. Early freedom fighters, you might say. Patriots risking their lives for the greater good. Since then—"

"Since then they've become hoods. Dope, whores, extortion, counterfeiting, pornography. And political corruption. There was a time they practically ran China. If you weren't in a Triad or a secret society you damn sure had no chance of ever being a successful politician. You like my gun? You keep staring at it."

"Makes me nervous. What is it with you Americans and your guns? A penis substitute?"

"Yeah, well don't worry about my dick, Miss Priss. Worry about yours, because it is definitely caught in the wringer. You were supposed to burn Frank and you didn't. You know what that means. Means your ass is grass and Ling Shen's the lawnmower. Means you're dead. Am I getting through to you?"

Laycock said, "I sit here enthralled by your rhetoric. Could it be that I underestimated you after all?"

"My specialty is intelligence and if I say so myself, I am fucking good at it. There's a book, not many people know about it, called *Zhong-guo Bi-mi*. Written in the last century by a Japanese secret agent named Hiraya Amane. Amane was the first Jap to really get on to the Triads. See, Japan's been spying on China for years. Knowing Japan, they're probably still doing it. China's a lot bigger than Japan. Potentially a hell of a lot more dangerous, too."

"You know, of course," said Laycock, "that China has dominated this part of the world for hundreds of years and that Japan's military and economic success of the twentieth century are looked upon as nothing more than a blink of the eye insofar as time is concerned. That Japan's moment in the sun will pass and China will again rule the East as she always has."

Tan continued as if Laycock had said nothing. "China's always been fucked up. Warlord against warlord. Emperor against prime minister. Dynasty against dynasty. Intrigue up the ass. No end to it. Japan wanted a united China under its control. How do you bring that about? You spy. You work your way into the secret societies, into the Triads."

"Fascinating. Do go on."

"You take Chinese immigrants who come to Japan and you turn those suckers. Make them your agents and send them back to China to collect information and pass it on."

Laycock said slyly, "Don't forget the Chinese politicians, rebels and generals who wanted power. They came to Japan for tea and sympathy, not to mention money and bullets. And received a helping hand, did they not, albeit for future considerations."

Roger Tan missed the dig. He was too interested in the sound of his own voice. "All this shit went down before World War II started. By the time the war was on, Japan had so many agents in the Triads, in Hong Kong and all over China, that it was a fucking joke."

"May I correct you on one point," said Laycock. "The full name of the Amane book is *Zhong-guo-Bi-mi She-hui Shi*. Still being used as a source for intelligence in China, by the way. And yes, he was the first to discover the secret language and rituals used in restaurants and other public places by Triads all over the world. If you don't mind, dear boy, I would like to enjoy my food before it gets cold. And you can tell me more about secret societies and Americans being poisoned in Hong Kong in July."

Tan stood up. "I'll bring the food. You keep your tail glued to that chair." He pocketed the Beretta. "One dish at a time. What do you want to start with?"

"Let's have the soup for starters. First pot on your right facing the stove. Should be a low flame under it, which you can turn out. Place it in one of the puce-colored bowls you'll find on the cooking table."

"Puce?"

"The moronic know it as light purple. I'll need a spoon and napkin, please. And kindly refrain from picking your nose while your are serving me. I suppose it's too much to ask you to wash your hands. And you say Frank DiPalma is still alive."

Tan walked into the kitchen. "Barely. His kid saved him. Kid knew they'd never make the hospital in time, so he had the driver turn back to Causeway where they'd just come from. Stopped at an herbalist, who made a special tea. Todd forced that into Frank, made him vomit some more to get rid of most of the poison."

Laycock, who had not moved from the chair, nodded. "Clever. A bright lad, our Toddie. Should go far."

Roger Tan returned from the kitchen with a bowl of soup in one hand. "Keep the bowl in your hand and walk over to the table. Bring back one spoon. Make sure I can see both hands at all times."

He walked to the couch and sat down, his eyes on Laycock. When the Englishman returned to his chair with the spoon, Tan took his hand out of his pocket. "Twenty-four flavored tea. That's what they called it. Fungi, roots, stems, seeds, different kinds of grass. Todd mixed it by himself. Didn't need the herbalist. Poured it into Frank. Then called a police car. Wasn't for the kid Frank would never have lived to see the hospital. As it is now, Frank's in deep shit."

Laycock blew into a spoon of shark's fin soup to cool it. "If you don't mind my asking, how did I poison DiPalma? Certainly the tea wasn't poisoned. We all drank it and by his own admission DiPalma had to make several stops after leaving the tearoom. He could have been poisoned anywhere. Perhaps it happened when he took a cold drink from a food stall."

"We didn't use the same teacup," said Tan. "You used one set of cups to signal whoever was watching. Told them it was a green light. You got Frank to come to the tearoom, which is probably a Triad front, and you made sure he got a certain cup to drink from. A cup from a new set, a cup which was coated with poison before you filled it with tea. Whatever they gave Frank had no odor, no taste and worked like a time-release cold capsule."

Laycock patted his lips with a napkin. "There are many such poisons in China. They say there's one which creates a monstrous thirst in the victim. Seems the more liquid he drinks the more effective the poison becomes. I'd like my eels, please. They're in a covered dish in the oven. Just bring the dish. I'll eat from that. Have you figured out why I would want to kill DiPalma? He and I are supposed to be friends, after all."

"Bullshit. You're in a Triad and they've got first call on whatever loyalty you may have. Truth is, you're not even that loyal to them. You're doing what one man tells you to do and you've been doing that for a long time."

"The eels. Who might this supreme authority be whom I serve with such slavish devotion?"

Roger Tan stood up. "You said it, I didn't. You've got your nose so far up this guy's ass, if he farts he'll blow your brains out. Nosaka. Zenzo Nosaka. Still want those eels?"

Laycock said, "Yes, please." He watched Roger Tan back into the kitchen, keeping his eye on Laycock all the time. Mr. Tan was quite full of himself at the moment.

Laycock ate the eels with his fingers, an ignominious approach to a superb dish. The more he thought about having the meal interrupted, the more he began to dislike Mr. Tan.

Tan said, "The teacups got me started. Not every day you see a white man go through that ritual the way you did. Not one mistake. When I got back to the office, I went to work with computers, printouts, telephone hookups. Know what I found out? You were a British prisoner of war here during the Japanese occupation. You went over to the other side. Betrayed your people. Naughty, naughty, Miss Priss."

Laycock licked his fingers. "I wanted to survive. It was that simple, yet not so simple. I was quite impressed with Colonel Nosaka. He can be most persuasive. The Far East has always appealed to me. Always felt comfortable here."

"Exotic Orient and all that shit. So you stayed alive during your internment by sucking Nosaka's cock."

Laycock raised his eyebrows. "You do have a way with a phrase. We were lovers, yes. I did truly love him. Actually when I was young I did have a certain pristine beauty. You could say that I was crystal."

Roger Tan chuckled. "Fucking unreal. Crystal. Anyway you couldn't go home after what you did, so you stayed right here in Hong Kong and became Nosaka's man inside Ling Shen's Triad."

Laycock drank wine sauce from the eel pan. "Seemed like a good idea at the time. Would have been the height of folly to present myself in Britain, considering my past behavior. Parents had disowned me. And my native land had always been rather hard on us fairies. Blackmail, imprisonment, social disgrace. That sort of rot. All in all, it seemed wiser to stay here."

He placed the eel pan on the rug beside his chair. "There were three kinds of Triads during the war years. One was more or less loyal to Chiang Kai-shek. A right old sod he was. Devious, obstinate, corrupt. Startlingly uneducated. Egotistical and vindictive. But an expert at manipulating the secret societies for his own purposes. The secret societies, with their mystic mumbo-jumbo and ties to Confucius, just about controlled China. They were rather dangerous to play around with but Chiang played and won."

Laycock crossed his legs. "There is a heavenly duck in the kitchen. I would like that served now. The wine with it, of course. You'll find a bottle uncorked on top of the fridge. A delicate little Beaujolais, since Chinese wines leave something to be desired. In the light of recent events, I shall refrain from offering you a glass."

When the duck arrived the Englishman sat cross-legged on the floor and ate it from the pan. Roger Tan allowed him a fork, but no knife. "Now the second type of Triad," said Laycock, "did not allow the war to interfere with business-as-usual. They remained committed to their usual illicit enterprises and prospered. To do so meant coming to an arrangement with the Japanese. You know, espionage, handing over wanted men and women to the Japanese military police, eliminating anyone who was a bother to the Japanese, that sort of thing."

He pointed his fork at Roger Tan. "Which brings us to the third type of Triad. One hundred percent loyal to the Japanese, they were. They, too, made a profit here and there. But in effect, they were an arm of the Japanese military police. There is one thing that bothers me. How did you learn about my association with Nosaka?"

Roger Tan said, "Made a phone call."

"To whom?"

"Jude Golden."

"Ah."

"Computer coughed up a lot of shit on Nosaka, including his war-crimes trial and the names of the guys who prosecuted him. Two of those guys are dead, by the way. Frank thinks Nosaka's behind it. But that's another story. Golden's the last one. He told me about that trial, about a certain British POW who had turned traitor and should have been hung. But he lucked out, this English guy. Nosaka made him part of his deal. If the Americans wanted his cooperation, they had to make sure this English guy got off. British high command was pissed, but what could they do? In those days America had the Marshall Plan and if you wanted money it was the only game in town."

Laycock pulled a crisp bit of skin from the duck. "Quite. I remember America's generosity to what was called 'war-torn lands.' But in the process your country did throw its weight around. Fortunately, it was to my benefit."

"It was that, all right, Mr. Phillip Tibber."

Laycock froze, his greasy fingers over the duck. Then, "I see. You have been busy, haven't you?"

"Golden's a smart dude. Knows a lot of stuff. His daughter's here in Hong Kong doing a movie. Frank used to bang her. Anyway, her old man says you ain't who you claim to be. Says you took the name Geoffrey Laycock from a dead two-year old child who's buried in a little English town called Chalfont St. Giles."

Laycock held his wine glass up to the light. "I do wish you'd learn how to handle one of these. You hold them by the stem when presenting it to whoever is to drink out of it. Spares them the hideous sight of your fingerprints. Chalfont St. Giles, is it. Must remember to send flowers. I wasn't aware Mr. Golden was in possession of so much information about me."

"Standard procedure for spies. Use the name of a dead kid, somebody who can't be traced. Have phony papers made up with that name and you're home free. Golden says you've had plastic surgery."

"Is nothing sacred? Very well, yes. A nip and a tuck in Morocco. More than a nip and a tuck, actually."

"Golden told me something else. Said Nosaka's got this fantastic collection of old Japanese weapons. Stuff even a museum doesn't have. See, I'd mentioned that you'd got us over to this tearoom to talk about a certain missing war fan. Well, one thing led to another and he tells me about Nosaka's collection."

Laycock giggled. "Very well, you have me. The fan does belong to Nosaka. And I helped him to retrieve it from police headquarters. There, are you satisfied?"

"You and a certain cop, whoever he might be. You didn't walk into police headquarters to get it. Somebody brought it out to you."

Laycock staggered to his feet, glass in one hand, wine bottle in the other. He giggled again. "Best police money can buy. Right here in old Hong Kong. Nosaka tells me, I tell Ling Shen, Ling Shen tells the constable who shall remain nameless and *voila!* the war fan tiptoes out the door."

Tan shook his head sadly. The faggot was getting looped and talking good noise. "Why did that drag queen kill Katharine Hansard?"

Laycock gulped wine and rocked back on his heels. "But you see, dear boy, he killed them both."

The drug agent blinked. "Both?"

"Little Toddie had to become an orphan and that's all there was to it."

"Why?"

Laycock waved him away. "It's all so beyond you, dear boy, but briefly, Kenpachi wants the boy for some little ceremony he's planning. *Seppuku*, it's called. The lad is to be a participant."

Tan scratched his chin. He didn't like what he was hearing. This was weird shit.

"A minor correction," said Laycock. "Ian Hansard went to his reward for another reason as well. He was planning a bit of blackmail aimed at Nosaka and involving certain bank records. Even if Kenpachi had no use for the boy, Ian Hansard would have ended up a lump of lead. Mustn't cross Nosaka, you see."

He sipped more wine. "My turn. Obviously, with DiPalma lying at death's door, you've had no opportunity to discuss any of this with him. And you've come here alone. Why is that, pray tell?" He rocked back and forth on his heels, but did not go down.

"Simple," said Tan. "I want out of Hong Kong and you, my man, are my ticket to ride. I've got a statement typed up right here in my pocket. Don't have everything in it. You've just added a few things, but we'll get around to including them. Ain't sharing the glory with nobody. Not the cops, not the agency. This dumb chink is bringing you in alone. Only I ain't so dumb."

"You are sadly Americanized, old boy. You lack the subtlety and restraint traditional with your people. Pity."

"I got your pity, sweet meat. I plan to tie you into the murders of the Hansards, tie you into Ling Shen's drug trafficking, tie you into Nosaka's stealing business secrets. You are also gonna tell me what you know about whatever the fuck it is Kenpachi's planning to do with Frank's kid. If Frank ever gets onto that, oh boy."

Laycock looked down at his robe. "Blast. Grease spot on my sleeve. I do wish someone would tell DiPalma that the past is irrevocable. He seems to be consumed by thoughts of two dead women, the late Mrs. Hansard and his own departed wife. It does make him something of a bother."

"He feels he owes them. That's Frank's style."

"I'm sure he's sincere, but sincerity has its limits. Bury the past. Look to the future, I always say."

"Couldn't agree with you more. Your future lies in cutting a deal with me. You show your face on the street right now and Shen's liable to blow it off. You ain't got but one choice and that's to 'turn'. Sooner we get out of here and down to DEA headquarters, the better your chances of living to get that robe cleaned."

"Having no wish to become a dead queen, I submit myself to your tender mercies."

"You can start by turning around so I can cuff your hands. Behave yourself. I don't want to work up a sweat kicking your ass."

Laycock set the wine bottle and glass down on the metal chair, sighed and turned his back to Tan. "Godawful, it is. Here am I, Mrs. Tibber's little boy, about to be paraded through the streets looking as colorful as a tropical parrot. Most regrettable. Oh well, just another shitty day in paradise."

He glanced over his shoulder. Roger Tan was almost on him, the cuffs in his right hand, his left hand empty. Laycock looked ahead and smiled.

And lashed back with his right leg, driving his heel into Tan's right shin. The drug agent dropped the cuffs and clawed at his jacket for the Beretta.

Laycock spun around with astonishing speed and in the same motion jabbed the stiffened fingers of one hand into Tan's right eye. When the

240

drug agent brought both hands up to the pained eye, the Englishman kicked him in the testicles, folding him in half. A straight punch from Laycock crushed Tan's nose. A right uppercut to the cheekbone, followed by a vicious left hook to the right temple, and the drug agent spun round and dropped like a stone.

Laycock removed the Beretta from Tan's pocket, released the clip and the single bullet in the chamber and put them into the deep pockets of his robe. He picked up the platter containing the remains of the duck and carried it into the kitchen. Returning to the living room he poured himself a glass of wine, then sat down in the metal chair and watched Tan roll over onto his back and moan.

Laycock said, "And what do you think of the old queen now. Interesting style of combat, wing chun. Never ceases to amaze me even after all these years. Doesn't have the force-against-force style of the Japanese forms. Lacks the pyrotechnical displays of the Korean fighters, with their spinning and leaping kicks. Wing chun is simpler, quicker. No brute strength. Low kicks, straight punches and always immediate counter-attacks. Never block. Just counterattack."

A glassy-eyed and slack-jawed Tan attempted to sit up.

Laycock sipped more wine. "Did you know that wing chun is said to have been invented by a Buddhist nun? Imagine that. A second woman came along and refined it. Marvelous origins, wouldn't you say? One of the deadliest fighting forms ever to come out of China and it was born of two women. Bruce Lee trained in wing chun, you know. That should tell you something. But I suppose it doesn't, you being so virile and masculine."

Tan fought for breath. "Ling Shen. Gonna kill...kill you."

Laycock stood up. "Which reminds me. Must make a telephone call. You stay there on the floor and try not to throw up on the rug. Leaves a smell no matter how many times its cleaned. Shame your computers didn't warn you about us old queens. You'd be surprised, dear boy, how violent some of us Nellies can be. I do my wing chun in places not open to the general public, not even to most Chinese. Believe me when I tell you I've run across gays who could tear masculine fellows like yourself apart with ease."

Laycock sat on the couch behind Tan and made his call. He spoke in Cantonese and the call was a brief one. When Laycock hung up, he looked down at Roger Tan. "Well, I suppose you understood what was being discussed."

"Shen told you to finish it, to go to the hospital tonight and—"

"Finish DiPalma. Quite. Seems if DiPalma is around to see the sunrise, Ling Shen's life is forfeit. And so is mine. DiPalma must not be allowed to leave the hospital alive. Simple enough, isn't it? I see by your eyes that you would like to prevent this from happening. Don't see how, dear boy."

"Guards, guards on DiPalma's door."

"Been taken care of. Starting"—Laycock looked at his wristwatch—"five minutes from now, DiPalma's hospital room will be unguarded. I'm afraid you won't win your laurels tonight after all."

Laycock leaned over the coffee table and pulled a dark wooden box toward him. He lifted the top and took out Nosaka's war fan. A snap of his wrist and the fan was open. Its metal cutting edge glittered.

Laycock, the fan held coquettishly in front of his face, stood up and walked over to Roger Tan. "The paths of glory lead but to the grave, dear boy."

19

NUDE, KENPACHI crossed the room and switched off the light shortly before midnight. Except for two candles burning in the living room the director's suite was totally dark. In the living room Kenpachi had placed a thick red rug four feet square and enclosed it on three sides with a white screen. The candles in front of the screen were each four feet high, wrapped in white silk and resting on bamboo stands.

Benkai's long sword, the Muramasa, still in its scabbard, rested on a low wooden stand, the jeweled hilt wrapped in a white silk cloth. To the right of the sword was a small table holding a bowl of rice wine, Saburo's unsheathed *seppuku* knife and the black lacquer box finished in Benkai's ashes and containing the *Hotoke-San*, the bone taken from Bankai's throat after his cremation.

It was time for *zazen*, the daily meditation that was to prepare Kenpachi for his own *seppuku*.

He stepped on the rug, knelt facing Benkai's sword and bowed, his forehead touching the floor. Then he sat back on his heels, eyes closed, back straight and palms on his thighs. He was alone. Wabaka was on guard in the hall and the hotel switchboard had been ordered to hold all calls until further notice.

Zazen.

Surrounded by objects which had been used in Saburo's *seppuku*, Kenpachi sought to unfasten the ties that bound him to life and to increase his growing contempt for death. Nosaka's instructions came to mind. *Look into your soul. Explore death. Become truly fearless. Above all, find a way to touch the universal mind, the one mind to which we all belong. From there you will be able to find him who would be your* kaishaku. *You must go beyond your limits.*

Kenpachi thought of the boy who was to be his *kaishaku*. Todd was not only the epitome of youthful beauty but a reminder of the ugliness of the old. The young were free, strong, warm. The old were decrepit, remote, subdued. Had not Bushido, the warrior's code, taken much from Buddha, and had not Buddha's three warnings spoken of death and old age?

*　　*　　*

Did you ever see in the world a man or woman eighty or ninety years old, frail, crooked as a gable roof, bent down, resting on crutches, with tottering steps, youth long since fled, with broken teeth, gray and scanty hair or bald-headed, wrinkled, with blotched limbs?

And did the thought never come to you that you are also subject to decay, that you also cannot escape it?

Did you never see in the world a man or a woman who, being sick, afflicted and grievously ill, and wallowing in his or her own filth, was lifted up by some people, and put to bed by others?

And did the thought never come to you, that you also are subject to disease, that you also cannot escape it?

Did you see in the world the corpse of a man or a woman, one or two days after death, swollen, blue black in color and full of corruption?

And did the thought never come to you that you also are subject to death, that you cannot escape it?

* * *

UNLIKE his beloved mother, who had wasted away of cancer, Kenpachi would escape disease and decay. As for death, most people died too soon or too late. He would die at a time of his own choosing, raising himself to glory and immortality, and his voice would be heard in Japan forever.

Kenpachi shared Nosaka's belief in the *Hotoke-San*. The sight of the ugly and shapeless bone had caused the boy Todd to become temporarily possessed by a samurai warrior who had been dead four hundred years. It had forced the boy to acknowledge Kenpachi as his master, and it had brought out in Todd the fear of being enslaved by the demon *Iki-ryō*.

Tonight Kenpachi sensed the presence of the *Iki-ryō* in the bone, though not as strongly as had the boy. Born of evil thoughts, the *Iki-ryō* was a ghost which now sought a home in something as deadly as itself. Kenpachi's practice of *zazen* had enabled him to sense the demon's desire to leave the bone and come to life fully, to rejoin the soul and mind of Benkai.

The boy, more sensitive than Kenpachi, had known this instantly. Which was why he recoiled when Kenpachi had held out the box to him. Todd had resisted the *Iki-ryō*'s claim on him. But the boy was *bushi*, a warrior; he must be made one with his ghost, and then he would become the implacable Benkai, pledged to obey his master.

For a few seconds there was resistance in Kenpachi's mind. He feared the *Iki-ryō*. Could he control the boy after he had become possessed?

Only five or six weeks of scheduled work remained on the film. Kenpachi had not changed his mind about committing *seppuku* when the film was done. For maximum impact, his work and his life must end at the same time; that was how his mother had died. He would issue a *zankanjo*, a death statement explaining his disgust with modern Japan and his sincere hopes for the return of Imperial Nippon. The *zankanjo* would be delivered to the emperor, with copies to the press. Such a courageous death would mark Kenpachi's last film as art of the highest order. And the film itself would forever remind Japan that it was Kenpachi who had forced it to seek out its past greatness.

The right *kaishaku* was essential. Kenpachi needed someone other than the brutish Wakaba or the maniacs of the Blood Oath League. They idolized Kenpachi enough to behead him. But they were also proof that in life too much was often not enough. Wakaba, jealous of all who came

245

near Kenpachi, desperately wanted the honor of being his second. He had even begged to be allowed to commit *seppuku* with the film director.

Wakaba, high strung and loyal, would give his life for Kenpachi tomorrow. His love for the film director bordered on idolatry. Wakaba could easily kill the boy, believing that in doing so he was saving the director from being defiled by a *gaijin*.

But it was Benkai, who lived in Todd, whom Kenpachi wanted for his *kaishaku*. And so there could be no fear of the *Iki-ryō*, Wakaba or anyone else. Including DiPalma, who was either dead or dying. A samurai must not be a coward; he must bear all calamities and never flee.

Zazen.

Kenpachi concentrated his mind on the *Hotoke-San*, closing out all thoughts of family, career, life and death. For him there was only the small, hideous bone. And the demon within it.

In front of the tall white candles a perspiring Kenpachi lost all sense of his body and began slipping in and out of consciousness. Then he began to grow alarmed; he sensed he was no longer alone in his suite. He heard a noise, a screeching that was neither animal nor human. It began softly, slowly, then gained power until it filled the room with such a grating noise that Kenpachi began to shudder. The suite's windows and doors were locked, but an icy gust blew out both candles, leaving Kenpachi in frozen darkness.

Eeeeeeiiiiii. The screeching stabbed his ears. There was the smell of burning flesh and Kenpachi grew sick.

Then, suddenly, the screeching sound stopped. But the room remained cold and there was that nauseating odor. The silence in the room was one of imminent horror.

Exhausted, Kenpachi slumped on the floor and passed out, but not before he realized that he had succeeded in driving the *Iki-ryō* from the bone and had sent the demon in search of Benkai.

*   *   *

WHEN Geoffrey Laycock stepped from the elevator into a sixth-floor corridor of the Connaught Road hospital it was five minutes past midnight. He was dressed rather smartly, he thought, in the khaki uniform of a police lieutenant, complete with swagger stick and holstered pistol on a lanyard. Completing the disguise were a false mustache, dark glasses and a cap pulled so low it pushed his glasses painfully into the bridge of his nose. Despite a slight case of nerves he found the playacting exciting. He saw himself with the military bearing of the young officer he had been during the war. He was Jack Hawkins in *The Cruel Sea*. British pluck personified.

On the other hand it was doubtful if Hawkins had ever sneaked into a hospital with the intention of sending someone on to a better world, which is what Laycock intended doing to Frank DiPalma. It was DiPalma's life or Laycock's. Ling Shen had little tolerance for failure.

In the corridor Laycock encountered two Chinese nurses. As he passed them he brought a folded newspaper to his face, but they ignored him, chattering away. Halfway down the corridor the Englishman stopped in front of the EXIT door leading to a staircase. After making certain he was unobserved he pushed through the door and closed it behind him. Then, fanning himself with the folded newspaper he began walking up the stairs. On the eighth-floor landing he stopped in front of the door leading to the corridor and cracked it.

The corridor was empty. There was the smell of medicine and sickness, which Laycock despised, and there were empty wheelchairs and a walker here and there. The receptionist was around the corner and out of sight. Even if he was spotted, who would give a second thought to a policeman on the floor, given the precarious state of DiPalma's health. Most important of all, DiPalma's room, three doors away, was unguarded. As Ling Shen had ordered it to be.

Laycock closed the door and leaned back against it. He unfolded the newspaper and regarded the small black box containing the hypodermic needle. The needle was filled with the same poison that had been smeared on DiPalma's cup at the tearoom. Except this time there was more, much more. Not to worry. Laycock would do his deed and be gone. Needle at the base of the skull. Thumb on the plunger and Mr. DiPalma was off to join the angels.

Laycock removed his cap and massaged his forehead with his fingertips. Patience. The art of hoping. Of course everything would proceed as planned. No reason for it not to. Hadn't he shown patience back at the flat, when he had forced himself to eat in order to catch Roger Tan off guard? And being alone in the flat with Tan's corpse until Ling Shen's men arrived had required patience as well. And a strong stomach. Laycock was not keen on keeping company with the dead.

A bit of White Dragon Pearl to soothe the nerves would be most welcome. The chalky white heroin, mixed with a barbiturate called barbitone, was ground into powder, then mixed with regular tobacco. It was by far the colony's most popular brand of heroin, more popular than opium and produced a better high. Laycock was not addicted to heroin, as were many in the colony. Ninety percent of Hong Kong's prison population were heroin addicts.

The Englishman was twirling his cap on his forefinger when he froze. He cocked his head and sniffed the air. And smiled.

He put the cap back on his head, turned and cracked the door. There were rushing footsteps at the far end of the hall. Someone yelled *fire*. Laycock stepped into the hall, pulling the door closed behind him. The smell of smoke was stronger out here, as it was supposed to be.

Laycock walked to DiPalma's room and with his hand on the knob looked left, then right. No one was nearby, no one was watching him. And no one saw him enter the room, close the door behind him and walk toward an unconscious Frank DiPalma.

*　　*　　*

JAN GOLDEN switched on the small lamp beside her bed, sat up and screwed her cigarette into an ashtray. Then she shook another loose from the pack, lit it and inhaled. She put on her glasses and picked up her wristwatch. A little after midnight. She dropped the watch back on the table, stood up and drew her robe tighter around her. It was going to be a long night. Especially if Frank DiPalma died.

She had the room next to his, with a creaky air conditioner that furnished little in the way of cool air. The sealed windows hadn't been washed in months. There was a private bath, but the toilet was sluggish and the wash basin had permanent stains. The bathroom mirror was cracked and a tiny wastebasket under the basin was overflowing with mildewed rags. It was the tackiest place Jan had slept in since her affair with the Yugoslavian conceptual artist who lived in an unfurnished railroad flat on Manhattan's Ninth Avenue and kept a gerbil named Dali. Love, or something like it, had allowed her to tolerate several weekends in that roach farm. Love now had her pacing the floor of a Hong Kong hospital room; in her own way she loved Frank DiPalma. And the thought of a world without him was terrifying.

Todd was in the room next to hers. Where else could either of them spend the night except here? Waiting. Jan remembered Frank's face when he had been wheeled back to his room after the doctors were through with him. Unconscious, with a dark purple discoloration of the skin due to poor circulation. Cyanosis, a doctor had said. Also caused by a shortage of oxygen in the bloodstream. Narcosis had been another effect of the poison, a stupor so deep that no one knew for sure when Frank would regain consciousness. If it hadn't been for Todd...

Goddamn Ling Shen.

She walked to the window and looked down at the parking lot. In the scanty light she watched two white-clad interns leave the building then climb on bicycles and pedal off the parking lot. She had sent her own driver home, with instructions to call for her at 7:00 A.M. and take her to the set. But if Frank died or didn't come around...Jan closed her eyes. Right now the film was the last thing on her mind. Frank dead. She leaned forward, her forehead pressed against the cool glass.

Which was worse—not loving, or loving and not telling. He mustn't die before she spoke to him again. She thought of what he had done for her. Dealing with Ray when he had attempted to blackmail her. Dealing with the network executive who had tried to rape her. The award-winning documentary she had done on prostitution, with his help. And the chance to go into films. Frank had been supportive and protective, never asking questions, never accusing. In return she had hurt him.

She was sleeping with Kon now. It had happened the night she had angrily sought out Frank in the restaurant, the night Kon had appeared at her hotel room after having disappeared from the police station. Jan had gotten what she wanted, a great fuck, but something had been missing. It was as if Kon had been standing outside of himself watching himself perform. And as physically satisfying as it had been, Jan, when it was over, felt even farther away from ever possessing him.

That's me, she thought. Run away from the ones who want you and run after those who don't and hate yourself for it. Love only had one great enemy and that was life itself. Jan's sensible and farsighted side told her that Frank DiPalma was best for her, that she could be with him without being known only through him. That wasn't possible with Kon. Everything about Kon was erotic. His talent, his unpredictability, his unwillingness to be cured of his passions. Sooner or later, Jan said for herself, this bastard is going to destroy me. Just like the other bastards did. But the wildness in him drew her like a moth to flame.

Both men, she suspected, knew her secret, that when Jan fell in love she would submit to anything, endure anything. Frank would never use that knowledge against her. Kon would. Would he ever. And if she were in trouble, who could she depend on? The Sicilian, who else. Kenpachi's concern was only for himself. A classic case of a man whose love for himself came first.

But why fool herself? That was Kon's appeal. He was as dangerous as

249

a Grand Prix racecourse; he was an irresistible challenge to women drawn to the exotic, the outrageous, the unexpected, and there were enough of them to keep men like Kon busy for months. Why hadn't she married Frank? Because it would have meant demanding more from herself than she had up until now.

She walked into the bathroom and looked into the mirror. Christ, did that face belong to her? She needed sleep, lots and lots of sleep. And when had she last eaten? A fish dinner in the room had gone untouched. Just coffee and cigarettes. No wonder she looked like a frog in a blender, red and green and going through life at a hundred miles an hour.

She touched her nose. Jewish girls were supposed to do something about long noses. Jan hadn't. She and Streisand. This is it, folks. Take it or leave it. You look like Wayne Gretsky the hockey player, Frank had said. Meryl Streep, Jan had said. She looks like Gretsky too, said Frank.

I need Frank, I want Kon. Didn't some actor once tell her that being drunk or on location never counts. Maybe when the movie was finished she and Kon would be finished. Maybe it would be a good idea to finish with Kon sooner than that. He was into some off-the-wall shit, talking about black magic, ghosts, reincarnation and the beauty of death. Jan saw nothing beautiful about Frank dying.

She ran cold water in the basin, cupped her hands and splashed water on her face. She dried her face and had reached for a jar of cold cream when she heard the sound of breaking glass coming from Todd's room. Then a thud. Had he fallen out of bed and hurt himself?

"No! No!" shouted a frightened Todd.

Jan heard him whimper. She ran from the bathroom, stopped a moment to belt her robe, then stepped into the hall. She never noticed that there were no guards at Frank's door.

At Todd's door she hesitated, fist poised to knock, then turned the knob and pushed. The door was stuck. She gripped the knob with both hands, threw her body against the door, then stumbled into the room as the door flew open. She turned on the light and rushed to the boy.

Todd lay on the floor, backed into a corner and trembling. The night table was turned over. Lamp, dishes and drinking glasses were scattered on the floor. Avoiding broken glass, Jan crouched barefoot beside the boy and reached to take him in her arms. He was terrified, completely unnerved.

Nightmare. Of course. First his mother dies, then his stepfather and now his natural father is critically ill from being poisoned. Jan's heart went out to him.

A cringing Todd, knees drawn up protectively, edged as far away from her as possible. *"Iki-ryō."* he said.

"What?"

There was no warning. He shoved her aside violently, sending Jan flying back against the bed. She struck her elbow painfully. Todd scrambled past her and raced to the door. Angry, yet concerned for him, Jan pushed herself off the floor. Todd was pulling at the doorknob. Stuck.

She stepped on a piece of glass, cut her bare foot and cried out. But she reached Todd, pulled at him and was thrown off. Jesus, the little bastard was strong. Now he had the door open, pulling it so hard that it banged into the wall. Jan ran after him.

In the hall she watched him push Frank's door open, then lean back, hands covering his face. There was something in the room Todd didn't want to see.

Jan, limping, came up behind the boy. She placed her hands on his shoulders, preparing to turn him around and read the riot act. He wasn't helping Frank by bursting into his room like a wild man. That was when Jan felt the icy air. The cold was a shock. It jolted her and she staggered a few steps back into the hall.

It reminded her of the worst of the New England winters she had endured, when twenty-six inches of snow and winds strong enough to overturn cars piled up drifts twenty feet high and the mercury dropped below zero. Frank's air conditioner must have gone insane.

And there was something else. A smell that the incredible cold could not hide. A burning smell, so nauseating and repellent that it made Jan sick to her stomach. Eyes closed, she backed away from the room, hands cupped over her nose and mouth. Then she stopped, opened her eyes and looked into the room.

And screamed.

* * *

Was he awake or sleeping? Todd no longer knew. But his skin was dark and hairy, his forearms rock hard with muscle and the Muramasa, gripped in both hands, was held high overhead. He was in a man's body. A Japanese man. He was squat, bearded, powerfully built and poised to strike, to bring the sword down on the bared neck of a man bending over Frank DiPalma, who lay unconscious in a hospital bed. Todd's father was in danger. Seconds away from death. Todd had to save him.

But the sword would not come down. Todd's arms remained

251

*inflexible, unyielding. None of his great strength could bring
the awesome weapon into play.*

*He grew fearful. It was not right that he should feel fear.
He must conquer it.*

*And then he felt the presence of the Iki-ryō, felt it probe him,
felt its baseness and unspeakable hatred. Frightened, he resisted. Fought with his mind. Tried to will it back into the
past. Were he to accept the Iki-ryō he would become the instrument of its depravity. But he would also possess a power
that would allow him to grasp the world.*

*The Iki-ryō spoke. "Accept me. I am the ghost of the living
and I alone can save your father. I will keep him away from
shi, from death. But first you must accept me."*

*At the side of his father's bed Todd saw the stranger take a
small black box from inside a folded newspaper, open it and
remove a hypodermic needle. He held the needle to the light
and pushed the plunger, sending a thin stream of clear liquid
across the room. He turned back to Todd's father.*

*"Yes," said Todd. "Save him. I accept you, but save my
father."*

*A searing heat enveloped the boy's body and he screamed.
For an instant he saw himself as iron hardened in fire, a blade
thrust into flame to create a classic weapon worthy of a samurai.
Then the heat vanished, leaving behind a great cold. He saw
his past lives, and all time came to stand as one within him.
The unknown that was the past and the unknown that was
the future became known to him. His name was not Todd. He
was Benkai. He was samurai.*

*　　*　　*

Thumb on the plunger and DiPalma would be with the angels. Laycock,
hypodermic held high in his right hand, reached down with his left to
turn DiPalma over on his side. Had to get to the base of the skull. Hide
the needle hole in the hairline. But turning this walrus over was no easy
task. Laycock would have to use two hands.

The cold. The overpowering stench. Where on earth did they come from? Laycock felt himself being squeezed in an iron grip and opened his mouth to cry out, but no sound came from his lips. Terrified, he looked over his shoulder and saw no one. But if there was no one behind him, then who was squeezing the very breath of life from him?

He was being pulled across the room, toward the window. An irresistible pull, growing stronger, faster, and suddenly he was jerked across the room as though on wires, leaving his feet like an adagio dancer. He was spun around in midair. He witnessed himself flying, *flying* toward the window, and he screamed. A woman screamed, too. And then Laycock was driven through the glass, feeling excruciating pain as shards of thick, broken glass tore at his flesh. For a second he hung suspended eight stories above the ground, then fell still screaming toward the parking lot, feeling and hearing the rushing wind, feeing himself being suffocated by the wind pouring in his face, and then came a great pain that filled his mind and body as he felt nothing more.

He hit the top of the metal flagpole, which passed through his back then emerged from his stomach. The Englishman slid down the pole, coming to rest in the center. His bleeding body hung on the bent flagpole, arms and feet dangling, and his lifeless eyes opened and focused on a hazy moon.

20

TOKYO

IT WAS dawn when Frank DiPalma and Obata Shuko, a Tokyo police captain, walked side by side along a quiet alley in Rokubancho, one of dozens of small, quiet communities hidden away behind Tokyo's noisy main thoroughfares. Like other villages in the heart of the city, Rokubancho maintained its separate identity with lanes too narrow for cars and an almost total absence of street names. While this was discouraging for visitors, it gave those who lived there a sense of secure isolation.

At this hour DiPalma and Shuko were alone on a winding street of temples, low houses, shops and villas whose walled gardens were topped by trees thick with leaves. The flapping of birds' wings caused DiPalma to look up at the gray sky. Wood pigeons. Nearby the Imperial Enclosure, a parklike island of three hundred acres, surrounded the Imperial Palace.

He had seen photographs of this secret valley of willow groves, pine trees, brooks, ponds, wild birds and rustic paths, all of it solely for the pleasure of the imperial family. But neither he nor anyone else, Japanese or Westerners, were allowed inside. For that matter, few Japanese or westerners were allowed where Suko was now taking DiPalma. DiPalma was on his way to a swordsmith, to participate in the forging of a blade, an honor he had dreamed of for years but had never imagined would be granted him.

There were elements of a religious ceremony in the swordsmith's task: he purified himself, wore special robes, prayed to the gods before he began, then cut himself off from the outside world until he had finished.

From the beginning of sword making in Japan, each school attempted to keep its manufacturing techniques secret. Few written records existed; instructions were passed from father to son, from master to disciple, and men had been killed for attempting to steal information. Poets, emperors, shoguns and warriors all praised the sword maker.

While DiPalma was well aware of the sword's mystique among Japanese, he insisted on remaining a realist. There was no magic in the sword. And what magic there was in the swordsman was nothing more or less than a skill honed by thousands of hours of practice. The sword was a well-crafted weapon; it came alive only in the hands of a trained warrior. Nothing supernatural about that. The cryptic approach to *ken*, the sword, struck him as pretentious, verging on superstition. He could tolerate that attitude in the Japanese. In westerners it was presumptuous.

The attempt in Hong Kong five days ago to kill him had done more than leave him physically weak. It had done something to his head, to his mind, and DiPalma didn't like it. At night he shivered and dreaded falling asleep, fearing he would die when he closed his eyes. He had lost weight and had trouble digesting his food. Was it his imagination or had there really been changes in Todd? He seemed to have grown more surly since they had left Hong Kong.

DiPalma owed his life to his son. Todd had given his new radio to the Hong Kong cab driver in exchange for driving to the herbalist. The boy had forced the tea down DiPalma's throat, making him puke his guts out, saving his skin. Maybe the kid was just having a delayed reaction to his dead parents.

Dai-sho, Shuko called the two of them. Big sword and little sword. Shuko was looking forward to seeing Todd fence. So was DiPalma.

The poison which almost took him out had not yet been identified by the hospital; it probably never would be. There were poisons used in China that went back a thousand years and the people who knew the ingredients weren't telling. Bruce Lee was rumored to have died from such a poison administered by Hong Kong gangsters when he had refused to make films for them. There were as many rumors about Lee's death as there were Chinese in Hong Kong. One thing was sure: no poison was found in Lee's system.

The poison had affected DiPalma mentally more than physically. It had left him feeling depressed, without mental energy or spiritual fire, the things that had made him a good cop. Instead of going after Nosaka, he had to force himself to start contacting people and asking questions. He had ignored the Hong Kong reporters who had called to tell him that Ling Shen was dead. The Triad leader had been found floating in Victoria Harbor with over fifty stab wounds in his body.

DiPalma had only spoken to his network once, taking the first call when he arrived in Tokyo, then ignoring the rest. He had taken only one call from his TV investigative team; they had been worried sick, especially after hearing about the poisoning. They were digging into Nosaka, as DiPalma had requested, and getting some good dirt. He was only half-glad to hear from them, politely listened, then said he'd call back and hung up. Only Roger Tan hadn't called.

Shuko had given DiPalma a juicy piece of news. Sakon Chiba, the transvestite, had not only been a close friend of Kenpachi's. He had also been an industrial spy for Zenzo Nosaka. Chiba, Kenpachi, Nosaka and the Blood Oath League were now linked together. DiPalma should have been jumping for joy. He should have been out pounding the bricks and going for Nosaka's jugular. Instead he was going through the motions and trying not to be scared shitless when the sun went down and he had to go to sleep.

Jan was due to arrive in Tokyo the following day. Filming was shifting to Tokyo for the next four or five weeks. She had stood beside him during the funeral ceremonies, had held his hand in the car when he couldn't stop shaking. He needed her now, but she belonged to Kenpachi. He desperately wanted a drink.

Three days in Japan and he had yet to practice kendo, yet to see any of his Japanese friends except Shuko. DiPalma had met him years ago at a law enforcement conference in Hawaii and the two had hit it off immediately. Both were kendoists and shared a passion for Duke Ellington. Among Shuko's huge Ellington collection was the piano used by the Duke when he began his career as a jazz musician in 1916.

The two men kept up their friendship through letters, telephone calls and visits. For Shuko the relationship proved invaluable when his sister Nori was kidnapped. Nori was the wife of a Japanese importing executive assigned by his company to New York. They lived in New Jersey with other Japanese who had moved to the suburbs to escape New York's crime. Crime, however, found Nori in a shopping mall not far from her home. She was kidnapped and held for ransom. Shuko, devoted to his sister, asked for DiPalma's help.

DiPalma met him at Kennedy Airport, drove him to New Jersey and acted as interpreter for Shuko with the FBI and local police. At the request of Shuko and his brother-in-law's company, DiPalma was allowed to act as go-between, contacting the kidnappers and arranging for the delivery of the ransom. Nori was returned safely and the kidnappers captured twenty-four hours later. It was a favor neither Shuko nor his brother-in-law would ever forget. DiPalma also received a letter of gratitude from the Japanese ambassador in Washington. He had made some very useful friends.

This morning Shuko was about to repay the favor.

The two made a comical-looking duo walking along Rokubancho's walled streets—DiPalma, large, gray-haired, strained but still forceful looking with his hooded eyes and flat, ugly-handsome face, moving in long strides; the small, bandy-legged Shuko, with jet black hair and unlined face, almost trotting to keep up with his companion.

DiPalma stopped. He was having second thoughts. "I appreciate what you're trying to do, Shuko-san, but I'm not sure it's going to work. What can I get out of watching the making of a new blade?"

"Not watch. You do. You clean your soul. You wash the poison from your mind. You become *bushi* again."

He walked away from DiPalma and never looked back to see if he was following. DiPalma caught up to him. "Such things exist for others. They do not exist for me."

Shuko said, "Duke Ellington said that a problem was a chance for you to do your best."

"Duke Ellington never drank tea in Hong Kong. At least not where I did."

"There are things about the sword you do not understand. You have much information, but you have little knowledge."

"Shuko-san, there are things about my own son I don't understand. He saved my life because he knows more about herbs than an herbalist. Where did he learn that? He and San told police they saw Laycock throw himself out of the window. If they hadn't, I'd be in jail accused of murder. As it was, the police had a hard time believing that anyone had the strength, not to mention the insanity, to throw himself through glass half an inch thick."

Shuko looked at him. "Ah, but he did. Or so it would appear."

"It's as if Laycock was possessed. The man just went crazy. And speaking of possessed, my son's nightmares are getting worse. Same dreams. Either he thinks he's Benkai or Benkai's after him. We can't seem to get that straight."

"You know, of course, that Benkai was said to have been possessed by what we call a ghost of the living."

"*Iki-ryō*. Yes, I know it. Someone's secret thoughts, evil thoughts, leave him and go out and make trouble."

"You do not believe?"

"No." And that's all there is to it. Nothing logical about a thing like that. Just part of the local mythology. But DiPalma wasn't buying it.

DiPalma said, "Something else I do not believe and that's reincarnation. Would you tell me how someone can be alive forever and not know it?"

They passed burlap-wrapped bales of rice stacked in front of a restaurant. "Reincarnation is accepted by many," said Shuko. "India, China, Japan. Africans. Sufi mystics. It appears in Persian philosophy, in Greek philosophy. Once it was a part of early Christianity, but the Christian fathers eliminated it from the teachings."

"Why?"

"Too rational, my friend. Reincarnation meant that you alone were responsible for your fate. This gave the church less authority. To keep its power, the church dispensed with karma and reincarnation."

Shuko gave him a shrewd look. "As for why we do not remember our past lives, may I say that your existence does not depend on your memory. You cannot remember your childhood. Does this mean you did not exist as a child? Do you remember the details of your life as a very young man? Can you remember all that you did last year?"

DiPalma smiled. "You have a point, Shuko-san."

"It is a blessing that you do not remember, my friend. It would disturb us, make pretenders of us, be the cause of great foolishness and much harm."

DiPalma thought of Todd, who could remember his past lives and suffered for it.

He said, "How much farther?" His limp was beginning to bother him.

"Soon. The walk is part of the preparation. It allows you to compose your mind, to subdue impulses. Too often the mind is resistant to all supervision. We say it is as wild as a monkey who has been stung by a scorpion."

"At the moment I don't feel in charge of my own monkey. Shuko-san, may I ask a favor of you? While I am with the swordsmith will you please take Todd to your *dojo* and ask permission of the *sensei* for him to fence? It might help the boy while I am away."

"It will be done, my friend."

"Thank you. How long will I be with the swordsmith?"

"We have arrived, DiPalma-san."

The American stopped and looked around. They were in a narrow street of walled houses, a street without a name. A street of hidden houses without numbers. Without Shuko, DiPalma was lost. One door was ajar. There was no need to ring the old-fashioned brass bell hanging beside it. He was expected. Through the open door DiPalma saw bonsai, dwarf trees, and twisted pines and a small pond. From the other side of the wall came the faint sound of someone chanting. DiPalma had to walk through that door. And didn't want to.

He waited for Shuko to urge him forward, to tell him that there was magic in the sword, that he could find his soul in the blade. DiPalma turned around. Shuko was gone.

DiPalma looked at the door. It slowly opened wider until he could see the entire garden. He limped toward the empty doorway, the tapping of his cane the only sound in the narrow street.

*　　*　　*

THERE were three processes in producing a blade: forging the steel, then tempering and sharpening it. DiPalma was to assist only in the forging, the first and most difficult step. The rest would be done over a period of weeks by the smith, his assistants, and by professional sword polishers. After that came the mounting of the blade, which meant adding the guard, hilt, collar, ornaments and decorated scabbard. The finished weapon would be a highly prized *daito*, a long sword with a two-foot blade.

Inside the forge, a small two-room house in the middle of the garden, DiPalma stared at a single blade hanging on the wall beside the deity shelf. It told him which school of sword making was practiced here and also gave the blade's history, all in characters eight hundred years old and written in gold inlay on the tang.

December 2, 1192. Sukesada, sixty-three years old, smith of the Sagami Province. Made for Minamoto Yoritome. The tester was Tenno Nitta. Three bodies with one stroke.

DiPalma took a deep breath. To call this blade rare was an understatement. It was matchless, unparalleled in its workmanship and place in Japanese history. From such blades Japan drew its feeling of moral strength and oneness with the past. DiPalma stepped closer. Courage, integrity of heart and spirit, self-control and honor. All in this one blade. The virtues which made up the moral code of Bushido. And it was important to remember that the strength of those who carried this sword lay in their contempt for death.

Minamoto, for whom the sword was made, was Japan's first shogun, the military strong men who ruled the empire and the emperor for over seven hundred years. Tenno belonged to a professional group who tested a sword's sharpness by slicing metal, wood, clumps of straw and human flesh. Records were kept of each test, noting witnesses, date, tester's name and how many bodies were cut with a single stroke. The blade on the wall had been tested by cutting through three corpses or three condemned criminals.

A dejected DiPalma had not asked the name of the smith he was to meet. Why bother when nothing was going to come of it. He had agreed to the visit only to avoid offending Shuko. The honor which had been granted the American was lost on him until now, until he came face to face with the swordsmith in the forge. That was when DiPalma's cane slipped from his hand and his jaw dropped. He was visibly shaken. He was in the presence of a living immortal.

In Japan the swordsmith enjoyed a status above all craftsmen. The country possessed only a handful of men with this skill that was so much a part of its history. Standing above them all was the legendary Tendrai, whose blades were said to rival those of his twelfth-century ancestor, the great Sukesada. Tendrai was never seen, refusing all requests to be interviewed, photographed or observed at his ancient task. Ten years ago, when the emperor had declared him a living treasure, an honor given to few, Tendrai had consented to come to the Imperial Palace. But the palace photographer took his orders that day from the smith, not the emperor. One photograph, no more. DiPalma recognized Tendrai from Shuko's copy of that rare photograph.

In recent years Tendrai's health and sanity were the subject of wild rumors. He was said to be blind, dying of cancer, the victim of a severe burning accident which had webbed the fingers of one hand together, preventing him from ever forging another blade. Old age and the loss of his skill were said to have caused him to commit suicide. Both hands were supposed to have been cut off by a wealthy man who became enraged when Tendrai refused to make a sword for him.

DiPalma now stood before this man who was a link between the Nippon of the past and the Japan of today, tomorrow, the future. Tendrai was the heart of Japan, a reminder of *giri*, eternal duty, of self-discipline, of all that was worth preserving from the old Japan. DiPalma felt light-headed, aware that he stood in the presence of someone very special.

Tendrai was imposing, a big man in his late seventies, white haired and heavily jowled, with large gnarled hands and the air of a man whose authority was seldom resisted. He took a long hard look at DiPalma, examining him with eyes that bored holes in him. The ex-cop was used to people trying to stare him down on the streets and he usually won the game. Not this time.

It was DiPalma's place to bow first and he did so, bending from the waist. *"Sensei."* He did not trust himself to say more.

Tendrai's face remained impenetrable, as though nothing had been said. Then he looked at his *sakite*, his two assistants, and left the forge. He and DiPalma were to speak to each other only once. Instructions came from the *sakite* and were to be obeyed instantly and without question. The atmosphere in the forge was one of strict religious ritual and DiPalma soon understood that talk was neither welcomed nor necessary. He was in a place where all that mattered was thought and action.

They began immediately.

DiPalma followed the *sakite* to the main house, a two-story wooden building near the forge. Here, in a large room covered with mats, all four men stripped nude, then purified themselves by pouring cold water over their bodies. Next they put on orange robes, black conical hats tied under the chin and *tabi*, white split-toed socks and clogs. Everything was done in silence, including the walk from the house back to the forge.

Inside the forge Tendrai led the way to the room with the deity shelf, a collection of small statues, vases, teakwood box, scroll, fresh flowers and amulets, all dedicated to the god of Tendrai's forge. In front of the shelf the three Japanese bowed from the waist and remained in that position. DiPalma thought, why not? and bowed, feeling hypocritical, yet not knowing what else to do. This was not the time to say that he believed in only one world and one life with nothing beyond.

Tendrai stood up, inhaled and exhaled. It was time to go to work.

The object was to weave numerous fine threads of steel into one perfect unit. DiPalma watched as a melon-sized chunk of steel was heated in an open furnace, then removed to be flattened. Tendrai wielded a large hammer with a thick, wooden head, pounding the reddened metal in huge, powerful strokes. Minutes later he was relieved by one of his assistants. DiPalma swung the hammer last. It was heavier than it looked. After only three strokes his shoulders ached and he knew there were going to be blisters on his hands.

He was relieved when one of the assistants tapped him on the shoulder. The steel was flat enough. Using tongs, Tendrai picked up the steel and thrust it into a bucket of cold water. DiPalma was kneading a sore bicep when he felt a sharp pain in his ribs. One of the *sakite* had jabbed him with an elbow and was glaring at him. DiPalma recognized that look from his early days of kendo practice. His instructors would glare at him when he made too much of an injury. Reacting to pain in front of an opponent would only make him attack you more. DiPalma let his hands fall to his sides.

The assistant then looked at Tendrai, who nodded. The assistant then pointed to the hammer. Instead of resting DiPalma would now go first. Silently he picked up the hammer.

He pounded the quenched steel, bringing the hammer down with all is strength, ignoring the three Japanese watching him. DiPalma, the steel, the hammer. That was his world. It took his mind off the edginess he felt in Tendrai's presence. Besides, he began to enjoy the glow and the warmth coming from the furnace.

Stop.

It was a command from one of the assistants. DiPalma was so consumed by his hammering that he failed to notice he had broken the steel into pieces. Now the exhaustion hit him and his lungs burned and he couldn't stop his stomach from rising and falling. Someone pried the hammer from his hands, which were bleeding. He had broken the steel, had done it by himself. He looked over at Tendrai. Still the stone face, but the eyes didn't seem as hard now. Or was it his imagination?

DiPalma watched one of the *sakite* place the pieces on a steel spatula, which Tendrai picked up and carried to the fire. The smith's face was red from the flames, but his eyes never blinked and he looked into the fire as though seeing something. In a while an assistant went to the smith, who handed the spatula to him without a word. DiPalma noticed all communication was in silence and that the Japanese did everything without any wasted effort. The second assistant took his turn holding the spatula in the flames, and after a time he simply looked at DiPalma, who had had the sense to do what the rest were doing, which was to watch what was going on. He stepped forward, crouched and was handed the spatula.

At first the fire was painful. It was blisteringly hot on his face and the warm spatula handle was hell on his bleeding hands. But he wasn't going to walk away. It became important to do all that was expected of him, to see it through to the end. In his whole life it had always been balls forward. Even if the poison had done a number on his head, he wasn't going to shame himself in front of Tendrai.

That was when the fire became hypnotic. DiPalma stopped thinking about the heat and his hands. The problem now was to avoid falling asleep. To keep awake he recalled the names of the great swordsmiths of the past. Enshin, Chikamura, Arikuni, Iesuke, Jumyô, Hideyoshi, Gisuke, Kanehira, Kanetomo. Muramasa, the Emperor Go-toba. Daruma, Naotane.

Someone tapped him on the shoulder. He looked up to see an assistant point to the spatula, then to the hammer. Time to pound the pieces again.

DiPalma brought the spatula over to an anvil resting on the earthen floor. Neither of the assistants moved, so he guessed he was still on. Tendrai stood to one side of the anvil and motioned for DiPalma to squat across from him and hold the spatula on the anvil. Both men were now fitted with thick eyeglasses, a protection against flying sparks; the steel was white hot and at its most dangerous. DiPalma's glasses were all but opaque; it was the world as viewed through egg white.

Tendrai's pounding of the steel shook DiPalma's arms, forcing him to tense his muscles and grip the spatula harder. Sparks flew and struck his face, his hands and arms. Through his thick glasses he watched them flit and take off like miniature comets. It was a beautiful chaos and he wondered if the creation of the universe had been anything like this.

An assistant took the spatula from him, while another hammered the steel. Then it was DiPalma's turn to swing the hammer and by noon the steel, reheated and pounded over and over, had become a solid piece, six inches long, two inches wide and a little over half an inch thick. At this point work stopped and and the two men ate a lunch of cold vegetables, noodles and hot tea brought to them by servants. DiPalma and the Japanese ate in the forge, in silence. When Tendrai finished, he stood up. The *sakite* set their food aside, as did DiPalma, who had had an appetite for the first time since the poisoning. It was back to work.

The flat rectangle of steel was heated, cut in the middle, then once more folded and pounded into a rectangle. At the same time a second chunk of steel was being prepared in the same fashion. Heated, broken into pieces, then pounded into a small, flat rectangle. Toward late afternoon both rectangles were heated and joined together, then cut, folded and pounded. DiPalma had sweated buckets; his robe and the light garment under it were drenched. There was blood on the robe from his hands.

When had he made such good use of his time? When had he been so fulfilled and satisfied? The effort was everything; the struggle had never been so pleasing. It was as if Hong Kong had never happened. He could do anything.

When he saw the metal take the shape of a stick, DiPalma was as keyed up as when he had joined the police academy. Tendrai had shaped it, using a metal hammer and lighter strokes. After a while he stopped and held out the hammer to DiPalma. When the smith stood up and stepped aside, DiPalma hunkered down over the blade and hesitated. He felt a heat that had nothing to do with the burning furnace. He felt exhilarated, yet calm. Confident, yet humble. He wondered if it were true that in Japan man had no need to pray, for the soil itself was divine.

In a trancelike state he pounded the stick-shaped metal. The blade had become DiPalma's life and the hammer in his bleeding hand was an extension of his body. He was experiencing truths that could not be expressed in words, could not be felt anywhere except in this forge. See with your heart. Feel fully. Believe in what you feel.

DiPalma brought the hammer down on the blade until someone shook him and he opened his eyes. It was night and the door to the forge was open. He was lying on the floor in the room with the deity shelf. One of the *sakite* had come to wake him. A shocked DiPalma sat up quickly. What in hell had happened? He scrambled to his feet and rushed to the room where the furnace still burned, where Tendrai sat at the anvil shaping the metal into a rough blade. The smith used a *sen*, an ancient form of shaver, which he gripped by two handles. Occasionally he paused to use a file, then returned to using the shaver.

DiPalma rubbed his eyes. How could he have been so stupid as to have fallen asleep? Was he still that weak from the poisoning? More important, what did Tendrai think of him? DiPalma wanted to run and hide. Physically he felt like his old self. And the embarrassment was going away. He was starting to feel confident. Strong. Strong in body and mind. Maybe he could explain to Tendrai about Hong Kong.

DiPalma entered the room as Tendrai dipped a hand into a pot, then brought it out and smeared clay on the blade. The smith looked up and stopped. Here it comes, thought DiPalma. Tendrai beckoned him closer, pointed to the balde and stood up. What the hell? He wasn't going to kick DiPalma's ass after all. And it hit the ex-cop. They knew he was sick. Sleep had been as much a part of the cure as helping to forge the blade.

Sleep. *He had not worried about dying.* He had closed his eyes, had not thought of poison, of Ling Shen, of the hospital. It was an effort for DiPalma now to remain composed. He squatted down behind the crude-looking blade, dipped his hand in the dark, thin mud, a special mixture of Tendrai's, and smoothed it along the blade. The clay would be allowed to dry, then scraped off by Tendrai so as to give the blade the desired tempered pattern. After that, the blade would be heated once more, the curvature corrected. The polishing was the last step.

An assistant stood in front of DiPalma and bowed. There was something final in the gesture. DiPalma got to his feet. Fatigue was forgotten. His fear of dying was gone. He wanted to stay in the forge until the blade was finished and mounted, until the task was complete. He did not want to leave. But his part in the making of the *daito* was over.

Saddened, he bowed to the assistants. He walked past them, through

265

the forge and out into the night where Tendrai waited for him. The smith said, "That which touched you when you lay dying has been driven away."

DiPalma thought of what Jan had told him at Katharine's funeral. *Icy cold. And a stench that went beyond putrid. And if I didn't know better, I'd swear something invisible yanked Laycock through that window. Through plate glass that's supposed to be unbreakable.*

DiPalma bowed. How could someone have gone through a window like that on his own? He said, *"Domo arigato gozaimashita, Sensei."*

Tendrai said, "It now lives within him in whom it once lived." He gave a slight nod, then turned and stepped into the forge. A servant led DiPalma to the bath. When DiPalma had bathed, he returned to the room and found his clothes. Cold water was waiting for him in the same wooden buckets which he had used to purify himself hours ago. He poured water over his aching body, dried himself and dressed. And thought about Tendrai's words.

A servant led him from the house and through the garden. DiPalma stopped to stare at the forge and to listen to the sound of the hammer on the crude blade. Then he followed the servant to the garden door leading to the street.

Outside, Shuko stepped from the shadows and bowed. DiPalma returned the bow and then they smiled at each other. The American looked over his shoulder at the smoke rising above the wall behind him. Then in silence the two men began walking along the narrow street.

21

JAN GOLDEN stood on the ramparts of Ikuba Castle and looked down on the cars pulling into the cobbled courtyard for the party. A Cadillac Eldorado caught her eye. As it rolled to a stop the driver put his hand on the horn and kept it there, playing the first few bars of "The Yellow Rose of Texas." Jan swallowed the last of her Campari and soda. There were times when the Japanese *gaijin compurekksu*, western complex— the feeling that anything Western was better—was a real pain.

She watched two Japanese couples leave the Eldorado. Exactly what Kon would have on his guest list. The men were *yakuza*, straight from Warner Brothers casting in their pin-striped suits, spats, dark shirts, white ties and slouched fedoras. This was everyday wear for them, as well as an expression of their admiration for American movie gangsters. Their women, slim and pretty and neo-punk: spiky hairdos streaked with pink and green, leather jackets, stiletto high heels and designer jeans. Straight from downtown L.A., thought Jan. Or the Mudd Club in Manhattan.

She was alone on the ramparts, relieved to be outside and away from the castle which was mobbed with Kenpachi's friends, acquaintances and admirers. Originally the party had been planned only for the film's cast and crew. A casual buffet dinner, followed by a tour of the castle for those who had never been inside. It had been a typical Kenpachi impulse;

267

as a rule Japanese rarely invited foreigners into their homes. There was always the fear that the home might prove too humble or Japanese customs appear bizarre.

Then Kon had changed his mind and the casual dinner became a party celebrating his Lincoln Center tribute in three weeks. Typical Kenpachi. Impulsive, self-centered, unpredictable. In minutes the guest list expanded to include Japanese and foreign press, members of the Japanese film community, Japanese and foreign models, sumo wrestlers, baseball players, gays, *yakuza*, Kabuki performers and several tough-looking young men with hard eyes and short haircuts. Members of Kenpachi's kendo club, Jan was told.

This last group kept to themselves, giving the impression of being an elite, men of high mark. They didn't smile and scarcely spoke to anyone. Jan put them down as goons when one shoved a waiter to the floor for no apparent reason, then kicked him in the side before being pulled away. Kon's reaction had been to curse the waiter. That was when an angry Jan had walked outside. She had had enough of Kon's gross behavior for one night.

On the ramparts she drew her shawl around her shoulders, placed her empty glass on top of the wall and began to walk. She felt like a fly on the wall; she could see the grounds, the arriving guests and the white wooden castle, but no one looked up at her. A handful of people strolled on the grounds, but most were inside, in the matted rooms with the original gilded ceilings and their sunken panels of waterfalls and seashores.

Jan had been impressed with the care that Kon had lavished on the castle. Its vast corridors were highly polished and the rooms, separated by sliding doors, had been redone to gleam with the gloss of lacquer and gold as it might have been in Lord Saburo's time. Golden brassware, Edo period sculptures and colored paintings completed the *daimyo* effect that Kenpachi sought. Was Kon's career really on the downswing, as Jan had heard? If so, it was going down in style.

But there were times when his style was hard to swallow. Tonight, for example, Kon had decided to show off his skill as an *onnagata* and attend the party dressed as a woman. Jan had thought he was kidding until she watched him put on the makeup and assume the role. She watched fascinated as he sat in front of the mirror and began coating his eyebrows with softened wax, then covered his face and neck with white pigment.

Then he brushed on blue eye shadow, powdered his face and drew in thick, dark eyebrows. After he had brushed on eye liner he drew a small red mouth and leaned back to admire his beauty. And he was beautiful. Jan found herself wondering what it would be like to make love to him *now*, then closed her eyes. It was wrong, or was it? Japan could really turn your head around.

She opened her eyes to see Kon being helped into a dazzling kimono by a servant. The kimono was made of red, black, blue and white silk, with designs of birds, flowers and deer sewn into the fabric. Jan couldn't take her eyes off the garment, which was belted at the waist by a wide gold sash with a tiny, round-faced doll attached just over the heart. For Jan to speak would have broken the spell. She still had not accepted the idea that Kenpachi would go through with it, that he would appear in front of his guests in full drag.

But was it full drag? Wasn't she viewing his world through her own mind? When men did that to her she became angry. Did she have the right to judge Kenpachi by her standards?

The wig was the last piece of apparel. It was heavy and elaborate, covering his forehead and reaching down to his shoulders. It was topped by a diadem of blue sapphires and blue silk flowers. When it was in place Kenpachi covered his forearms and hands with white pigment, then took a fan from a drawer and snapped it open. He stood up, fanned himself and looked down at a stunned Jan.

Then he began to walk. Not like a man, but as a woman. Knees close together, feet slightly pigeon-toed. Body swaying, head moving gently from side to side and elbows at the hips. The effect was staggering. Kon Kenpachi had disappeared, to be replaced by a woman so feminine that Jan, who knew the truth, now began to doubt her eyes. It left her ill at ease. The degree of Kon's sexuality never failed to surprise her. If it is physically possible, he had said to her, it is not unnatural.

But in the end it was more than Jan could handle. That and Kon's flirting with several of the men at the party and his cruel attitude toward the servant who had been kicked by his friends. So she had taken her drink and gone outside to stare at the stars and think of Frank DiPalma. She had to laugh at the thought of Frank in a dress. And as tough as he was, Frank would never push an old man to the floor and use him for a football.

Most of the men closest to Kon impressed Jan as on the edge, barely keeping their violence in check. Head cases like Wakaba. Wakaba hadn't been on the plane when it left Hong Kong. He's delivering a message for me, Kon had said in a way that closed the subject. Jan hadn't been interested enough to pursue it. If she didn't see Wakaba again in this life it was fine with her.

She remembered the scene at the temple between Wakaba and Frank, who had delivered a message of his own. Don't bother my son. Why did

Wakaba hate the boy? Jan shuddered to think of what might happen to Todd if Wakaba ever caught him alone.

Jan owed Todd a great deal. He had saved Frank's life, first by forcing him to drink the herbal tea, then by entering his hospital room in time to stop Laycock from poisoning him a second time. Again and again Jan had asked herself what had happened in that room, and had failed to come up with a reasonable answer. She remembered the incredible cold, the horrendous smell. And she could never forget Laycock's throwing himself through the window. But the glass had been so thick that the police had failed to break it with a hammer.

Had Todd really saved his father a second time or had something occurred which couldn't be put into words? It really doesn't matter, Jan thought. Frank is alive. I'll take that and be happy.

From the ramparts she looked down at Kenpachi's gardens, swimming pool, guest cottages and private theater. Kenpachi's wife and children rarely came here and then never without an invitation. He talked about them quite freely, boasting of the children's scholastic achievements, praising his wife for being a good mother.

"But you see," he said to Jan, "my choice was to be faithful to others or to myself."

Jan was about to ask if it mattered whom he hurt by such a choice when she remembered that she had done the same thing all her life. It was a shock to find out how much she and Kenpachi had in common.

Near a stairway leading from the ramparts down to the courtyard she stopped to light a cigarette and then looked back at the castle. Kon had stepped into the courtyard. Still looking like a beautiful woman, moving as though he had been a woman all his life. She watched him greet newly arrived friends, saw them accept him as though a feminine Kenpachi was nothing extraordinary; then he walked across the courtyard toward Jan. She dropped her cigarette on the wooden walk, stepped on it and moved back deeper into the darkness. She didn't want Kon to see her.

She watched him pause before the fencing hall, just below her, then look around before entering. Jan relaxed. He hadn't seen her. Lights went on inside the *dojo*, paper lanterns which cast a soft orange glow on the window facing Jan. She could see that someone else was in there.

Todd.

Jan stepped forward. What was the boy doing here? And why was he hiding where he couldn't be seen? Kenpachi and Todd stood facing each other, and Kon was doing all the talking. She couldn't hear a word, but she saw Todd nod in agreement.

270

A taxi crossed the drawbridge, then glided into the courtyard, catching the party guests in the glare of its headlights. Jan ignored it; her mind was on Kon and Todd. Why was the boy at Ikuba Castle without Frank? Had Kon brought the boy here on his own? For what reason? An angry Frank could easily send Kon Kenpachi to the hospital and Jan's film right into the toilet. Why couldn't Kon stay away from the boy?

The taxi made a U-turn and stopped, motor running, headlights still on. A man left the back seat and slammed the door hard enough for the sound to carry up to the ramparts and draw Jan's attention. She looked at him and flinched. *Wakaba.*

He set a suitcase down on the cobblestones, paid the driver and turned around to look up to where Jan was hidden in the darkness. She cringed against the stone wall and pulled her shawl tighter. *Don't let him see me.*

Wakaba's left hand was bandaged and there was a white patch on his forehead. Did the bandages have anything to do with the message he had delivered in Hong Kong? And Todd. What if Wakaba saw him? Jan remembered how Wakaba had glared at the boy in Hong Kong. What if Kon's chauffeur came across the boy alone tonight on the castle grounds? Todd would be safer away from Ikuba Castle.

She saw Kenpachi's hardnoses, led by the man who had kicked the waiter, step into the courtyard and noisily greet Wakaba. There were smiles all around as Wakaba and the hardnoses shook hands and slapped each other on the shoulder. She felt her skin crawl; they were scary.

The light in the *dojo* suddenly went out. Todd was a child; he had no business being with a grown man who hosted parties dressed like a woman. Maybe it was time she barged into the *dojo* and broke up whatever was going on. Kon wouldn't like it, but to hell with him. Jan owed it to Todd. And to Frank.

She had her foot on the top of the stairs leading down to the courtyard when the door to the *dojo* opened. Jan froze. Kon stepped out alone. Wakaba greeted him, shoved a bandaged fist in the air and smiled. Kon, still a woman, minced over to his bodyguard, who bowed from the waist as the hardnoses watched in respectful silence. Jan felt as if she were witnessing some secret ritual.

Kon and Wakaba began talking quietly in Japanese. Wakaba did most of the talking, the messenger boy making his report. Kon reached out and touched Wakaba's bandaged forehead, then asked a question. Wakaba clenched his bandaged fist and seemed to talk tough. The hardnoses listened and nodded as Wakaba delivered his report. Jan wondered if Wakaba had delivered Kon's message wrapped around a brick.

Two photographers stepped from the castle doorway, followed by a

271

mannish-looking Japanese woman wearing a fedora and tuxedo. The woman called to Kenpachi, who raised his fan in acknowledgement. He looked back at Wakaba, tapped him on the shoulder with the fan, then began his swaying, knees-together, toes-in walk to the castle. One of the photographers looked around, said something in Japanese and the other photographer nodded in agreement. Jan guessed that it was too dark outside even for a flash camera. Or maybe they wanted pictures posed against an indoor backdrop. Whatever the reason, Kon, the mannish-looking woman and the cameraman disappeared inside the castle.

Most of the hardnoses strolled after Kenpachi, but two remained behind to talk with Wakaba. Jan began to tiptoe down the stairs. Wakaba hadn't yet spotted her. He was staring at the *dojo*, at Todd. The boy stood in the doorway, thin, vulnerable and Jan, now at the bottom of the stairs, looked at him, then at Wakaba, and opened her mouth to cry out. At that moment two leather-jacketed bikers roared into the courtyard on powerful Hondas, and there was no way Jan could be heard over the rumble of those ear-shattering machines.

She ran toward the *dojo* as Wakaba started toward Todd.

*   *   *

DIPALMA walked quickly along the narrow Rokubancho lane, staying behind Shuko, who suddenly stopped and flattened himself against a low stone wall. DiPalma, cane held high, did the same. Seconds later came a white-shirted delivery boy on a bicycle, a tray of covered metal dishes balanced on the palm of his right hand. Without looking back, Shuko stepped into the lane and DiPalma followed. At the corner they again backed into a wall, this time making way for an old man pushing a cart of steaming roasted sweet potatoes, a favorite Japanese delicacy.

Now the two men walked slower, peering into the windows of a pachinko parlor, a coffee bar, a Korean restaurant. They were searching for Todd, who had disappeared from Shuko's home.

As they searched, Shuko continued to tell DiPalma the story of his ties to Tendrai and the swordsmith's ties to Nosaka and the Muramasa long sword which had once belonged to Benkai.

Earlier Shuko had taken Todd to his kendo club, then after practice brought the boy home. Leaving Todd with his wife and two sons, Shuko then made the long walk through the winding streets of the village to Tendrai's forge, where he picked up DiPalma. At 10:00 P.M., when the two men returned to Shuko's home, Todd was gone. No one had seen him leave. The boy could easily get lost in an area without street signs, house numbers and with few streetlights. An embarrassed Shuko had accepted full responsibility for Todd's disappearance. For the first time DiPalma felt a wave of panic.

DiPalma had telephoned their hotel, the New Otani, the largest in Asia, with a ten-acre Japanese garden dating back to the seventeenth century. There was no answer in the room.

Shuko had sent out his teenage sons to look for Todd, before teaming with DiPalma to search in a different direction. DiPalma had needed something to take his mind off Todd; in the dark and deserted streets he had asked Shuko about Tendrai. How did the police captain know a man who had gone to great lengths to hide himself and his work? Shuko had never spoken of this relationship and might not want to speak of it now. A conversation with a Japanese often found him parrying, modest, evasive, silent and, when need be, a liar. Lying was not only accepted but was considered a social grace! It was often used to save face and spare others' feelings.

"Tendrai-sensei is my uncle," said Shuko without breaking stride.

A surprised DiPalma stopped dead in his tracks, then rushed to catch up to the little man. "Then your sister is his niece."

"*Hai.*"

Jesus, thought DiPalma. All these years and not one word about being related to the greatest living swordsmith in Japan. Typically Japanese to be so damned closemouthed. Yet neither Shuko nor Tendrai had forgotten what DiPalma had done for the niece. Today that favor had been repaid. Forging the blade had brought out DiPalma's true strength, his inner fire, and given him back his confidence. Now he couldn't wait to go after Nosaka, and Katharine's killer.

Shuko said, "Tendrai-sensei knows of your interest in the sword. He knows of your writings and your research. And he is also aware of your conflict with Kenpachi. I am to ask you to do a service for sensei."

"Tell Tendrai-sensei it will be my honor."

Shuko stopped. There was a force behind his words which had not been present until now. "He asks that you destroy the Muramasa blade belonging to Benkai."

DiPalma shook his head. "That sword doesn't exist anymore. It was destroyed in the great earthquake of 1923."

Superstition said that a giant catfish lived beneath Japan and when he lost patience with the sins and stupidity of human beings, he would rear up in righteous anger, causing earthquakes and tremors. The quake which

273

struck Tokyo on September 1, 1923, was a calamity. More than half of the city was destroyed and over one hundred thousand people died. It was the son of Emperor Taisho, Hirohito, who supervised Tokyo's reconstruction.

Shuko said, "Benkai's Muramasa was never destroyed. It is now in the hands of Kenpachi."

"Are you sure?"

"Tendrai-sensei told me and I do not question how he came to know. The way of the sword is his life. It has made him exceptionally perceptive."

"I won't question that. Tell sensei he has my word. I will destroy the Muramasa. How did Kenpachi come to own it?"

For a long time Shuko didn't answer. They passed a movie theater, a library, their eyes searching in every dim alley for Todd. Then Shuko spoke with surprising emotion.

"At midnight on August fourteenth, 1945, the Emperor Hirohito recorded a message announcing Japan's surrender to the Allies. The message, which was to be broadcast the following day, would end World War II for Japan. Atom bombs had been dropped on Hiroshima and Nagasaki, killing over one hundred thousand people. This was the weapon which your President Truman called 'the source from which the sun draws its power.' It could, of course, destroy my country, the land born of the rising sun.

"Shortly after the emperor finished the recording, a group of fanatical officers decided to kidnap him, destroy the record and break off all negotiations with the Allies. They wanted the war to continue until the last Japanese was dead. For them destruction was better than surrender. Nosaka was one of those officers, these military gangsters, who lacked all common sense.

"Of course, those plotters needed the support of others and desperately tried to convince their fellow officers to join them. But one young officer, let us call him Gappo, resisted Nosaka and told others to do so. Obey the emperor, said Gappo, and consider the living. This angered Nosaka, who decided Gappo must be taught a lesson.

"In feudal wars, a samurai knowing he faced a difficult battle would sometimes kill his wife and children. This prevented him from thinking of the three things no warrior should remember in battle: those whom he loved, his home and his body. With all that he cherished gone, the warrior was prepared for *shini-mono-gurui*, the hour of the death fury. From this point on he would neither ask nor give any quarter.

"Nosaka waited until Gappo had left his family unguarded. He then entered their home and, using Benkai's Muramasa, slaughtered Gappo's wife, mother and eldest son. Two children escaped because Gappo's wife gave her life to gain time. Nosaka then told Gappo he had killed his entire family, that Gappo now had nothing to lose and was free to join the plot against the emperor. Gappo, however, could think of nothing but revenge. He drew his sword, but Nosaka struck first and beheaded him with the Muramasa."

Shuko stopped walking and continued to stare straight ahead. "Gappo was my father and the brother of Tendrai-sensei. Sensei, like his brother, also wanted revenge. The emperor, however, made him vow never to harm Nosaka. All members of our family were bound by that vow, for Nosaka became important to Japan's survival. The plot to kidnap the emperor and stop the surrender failed, but the situation was still quite dangerous and the emperor knew it. Should Nosaka be murdered he could easily become a martyr to the rebels, who might redouble their efforts to keep Japan fighting. The emperor did not want this to happen.

"When the war ended Nosaka immediately began helping the Americans. In return the Americans aided Japan and protected her from Russia. In the last few days of the war, Russia was ready to invade our country and eliminate the monarchy. Without the monarchy our country cannot survive. America, backed by the atom bomb, ordered Russia to keep away from us and it did. Any occupation of Japan by Russia would have been permanent and unbearable. America, once our enemy, suddenly became our most needed ally. And the emperor, who had rebuilt Japan after the earthquake, knew that to rebuild Japan after the war meant securing the aid of men like Nosaka, men on whom the Americans depended.

"I cannot tell you how difficult it was for Tendrai to turn his back on vengeance. It took all of his strength to do this. He was asked to place Japan and the emperor first and he did so. But it meant that he must retire from public view, to stay within his forge and draw his strength from it. I suspect that he must also have remained there in order to hide his shame. And in the forge he knew he would never run into Nosaka and be tempted to kill him."

The two men resumed walking. Shuko said softly, "My sister and I owe our lives to our mother's sacrifice. Tendrai-sensei, perhaps, made an even greater sacrifice."

DiPalma said, "He gained more. Blows bring out the fire in a piece of flint. And I have seen how blows shape steel into a sword. The deaths of those he loved and his vow to the emperor were blows which shaped Tendrai-sensei and brought out his greatness. By keeping his vow he has become Japan's finest swordsmith. Which is the most glorious achievement, to have killed Nosaka or to have become Tendrai-sensei?"

275

Shuko smiled. "You have learned much in the forge."

"I *feel* more, but I cannot put it into words. Perhaps feeling is enough. I'm calmer, more relaxed. Shuko-san, something has just occurred to me. When the Muramasa is destroyed, does this mean Nosaka will be destroyed as well?"

Shuko avoided a direct answer. Instead he said, "The evil you suffered from has gone. Sensei knew of it merely by conversing with me. He has told me that you will be confronted by the Muramasa and if you do not destroy it, it will destroy you. Such an evil sword always finds its way back to its original master, for like is drawn to like and—"

In the darkness ahead a woman screamed in English, "Run! Get out of here!"

DiPalma stepped forward past Shuko and listened. He knew that voice. "Run, Todd, run!"

The woman was Jan and she was terrified.

DiPalma, the black oak cane in his right hand, ran toward her.

22

FROM THE top of a broad flight of stone steps Wakaba looked down into the blind alley where Todd and the woman now stood trapped.

In his hand was a *balisong*, the Filipino "butterfly knife" that was his favorite weapon. His little finger undid the hinged lock at the hilt; freed, the blade's cutting edge was face down. With his knife arm dangling at his side, Wakaba slowly descended the stairs into the alley, a deserted cul-de-sac of shuttered shops, turkish baths and snack bars. His shadow, cast by a single streetlight, reached out for the woman, whose frightened face was colored silver by moonlight.

Wakaba grinned as she put an arm around the boy and drew him close, then edged toward the darkened window of a silk shop. It was pointless for them to run; both were trapped in a dead end and the only escape was past Wakaba. He felt no pity for either one. They threatened his dreams and his life with Kenpachi in this world and the next.

The woman began to beg. "Don't do this. Please don't do this." She brushed tears from her eyes and looked wildly around.

Baka, thought Wakaba. Fool. Rokubancho's shops had been closed for hours and would attract no pedestrians. There were no private homes here, no nightclubs; the street was not a thoroughfare. The only passersby were drunkards, who tumbled down the stone stairs to lie unconscious on the pavement until kicked awake in the morning by an angry shop-keeper. A human scavenger might join filthy long-tailed cats in prowling through plastic trash cans lined up at the bottom of the stairs. None of these intruders would be of much help to the boy and the woman.

The sight of Todd and Kenpachi together in the doorway of the castle *dojo* had made Wakaba almost physically ill. He had vowed never to allow a *gaijin* to take part in the suicide of any Japanese as great as his master. Why couldn't Kenpachi-san understand that using a foreigner, a mere boy, as his second would only corrupt the most honorable act of his life?

Fiercely jealous of all who came near Kenpachi, Wakaba saw himself as the only one who deserved to behead him. He loved Kenpachi violently; he was even willing to commit *seppuku* with him, to open his own *hara* so that the world could see the strength of his soul center. Only Wakaba had served the film director with honor and unswerving devotion, even when it was dangerous to do so. Love, a selfless and pure love, made the bodyguard determined to spare his master the disgrace of being be-headed by *gaijin*.

Before Kenpachi had befriended him, Wakaba's life had been dark and empty. The bodyguard's mother had been a prostitute, his father one of her customers. At thirteen Wakaba was on his own, a boy whose great strength and psychotic behavior made him uncontrollable. He suf-fered headaches, epileptic seizures and had a reputation for random sadism which made him feared even among Tokyo's most violent men.

From their first meeting in a Ginza nightclub, Wakaba had never stopped worshipping Kenpachi. By putting Kenpachi on a pedestal, Wak-aba had lifted himself up higher than he had ever been. The film director was beautiful, world famous, brilliant and a samurai, all that the burly bodyguard admired. What drew the two men together was cruelty; neither restrained that impulse, drawing from it a savage, and necessary satisfac-tion.

Once connected to Kenpachi's power, Wakaba vowed to live through him until one or both of them died. For the bodyguard there was no greater joy than to be consumed in Kenpachi's fire. The director's hyp-notic voice, the drugs he fed him, the touch of his hands eased Wakaba's terrible headaches. The epileptic fits became fewer and less severe. Under Kenpachi's direction Wakaba improved his reading and writing and de-veloped his martial-arts skills with Tokyo's finest instructors.

Nor did the film director ridicule him when the hulking Wakaba confessed that he had always wanted to do something gentle and beautiful with his hands, that he had always yearned to carve delicate combs out of aged, fragrant wood. Kenpachi had sent him to the workshop of a man who was the eighteenth generation of his family to fashion such combs. Under his instruction Wakaba produced beautifully crafted combs from sweet-smelling wood, often spending hours on a single piece carved in an extraordinary shape of his own design. Kenpachi set up a workshop for him in the castle dungeon and arranged for Wakaba to sell dozens of pieces of his striking work to Japan's most famous people.

This grateful bodyguard gave the filmmaker unqualified obedience even when it meant risking his life, as in Hong Kong, where Wakaba had brutally dealt with the British policeman who had killed Yoshiko. Only Wakaba's martial arts skills and the *balisong* prevented him from becoming the policemen's second victim. Instead, Kenpachi's curse of *jigoku*, the Buddhist hell, had been realized. Yoshiko had been avenged.

Tonight Wakaba had decided to kill the boy without further delay.

The bodyguard had borrowed a car from the Blood Oath League members who had greeted him in the courtyard, then followed the woman's limousine to Rokubancho. Here the gods smiled on Wakaba; the narrow streets forced the woman and the boy to leave their vehicle and walk. Here there were no hotels or elaborate Western-style guest lodges, with their well-lit lobbies, security guards and crowds of tourists. At night, in Rokubancho's cramped and dark streets, the woman and the boy would be easy to kill. *Hai*, the gods intended for Wakaba to get rid of the two *gaijin* and spare Kenpachi-san a dishonorable death.

The driver of the limousine remained behind the wheel, unwilling to get lost in Rokubancho's meandering and signless streets. Besides, the boy had claimed to know the way to the house belonging to his father's friend. Let the foreign child and the redheaded woman wander around in darkness, in an area of Tokyo known only to those who were born there. The driver pulled his cap over his eyes and slumped down in his seat. He never saw Wakaba leave his car and jog noiselessly into Rokubancho.

In the Rokubancho alley Wakaba, the long-bladed knife hidden behind his thigh, stalked Jan and Todd. The sight of the boy not only angered Wakaba but made him feel alone and want to destroy everything around him.

As for the woman, Kenpachi had planned to kill her; Wakaba would now do it for him. She, too, was an enemy, the reincarnation of Saga, who four hundred years ago had betrayed the lord of Ikuba Castle.

Wakaba heard running footsteps and spun around in a crouch. He held the knife in front, thumb on the blade, and waited. Seconds later DiPalma and Shuko turned the corner, saw Wakaba, Jan and Todd, and slowed down. DiPalma motioned Shuko to hang back.

"He has a knife," the American whispered.

Wakaba looked over his shoulder at the woman. The American had heard her screams but he could not save her or the boy; Wakaba would kill them both, even at the cost of his life. Their deaths would be his final gift to Kenpachi.

But Wakaba did not expect to die. There was nothing to fear from either the woman or the boy. He had only contempt for the big American, the *gaijin* who played at being a swordsman and who had once defeated Kenpachi in a kendo match. Kenpachi fenced with enthusiasm and practiced karate diligently, but his skills did not approach those of Wakaba. The bodyguard was a born fighter who had never learned to fear.

He found Western men inferior; they were unwilling to fight to the death and believed that a foe should be shown mercy. A *gaijin* was a coward and a weakling. Wakaba spat in the direction of the big American and waited.

DiPalma, cane at his side, slowly descended the stairs. He had been physically drained, played out from the long hours in the forge and from walking Rokubancho's serpentine streets. The feeling was gone now; he felt relaxed, calm. The gut feeling that Todd was in trouble had been proven true, but the tension was gone. Something like the heat felt in Tendrai's forge passed over him, then disappeared.

As DiPalma walked down the staircase he kept his eyes on Wakaba's face. He saw neither fear nor indecision in the bodyguard, only a determination to kill, a conviction that nothing could stop him.

At the bottom of the staircase DiPalma, holding the cane away from his body, circled to his right. Wakaba, scornful, scarcely moved. He looked with contempt at the American's cane; the *balisong* had opposed tougher weapons. The *gaijin* had only seconds to live.

Wakaba tossed the knife from hand to hand, changing grips, blade up, blade down. Then he sandwiched the knife between his palms and went down in a crouch.

The attack was swift, unexpected. Jan cried, "Oh God!"

Wakaba leaped forward and swung the knife low, slashing at DiPalma's left knee. The American moved without thinking; he stepped to his right and quickly backhanded Wakaba across the face with the cane, crushing his nose. Bleeding heavily, the enraged Japanese hesitated briefly, then charged, thrusting his knife at DiPalma's heart.

DiPalma stepped aside and cracked Wakaba on the right knee. The Japanese grunted, stumbled forward and spun around to face the American, who had backed out of range.

DiPalma remembered his training. See through the opponent. Look strongly into his mind. See his fears, his doubts, his weaknesses. Pay only passing attention to the opponent's size and physical skills; to observe them too clearly was to be beaten before the fight began.

He looked into Wakaba's mind, saw the anger which prevented him from concentrating properly, saw the overconfidence which told him his opponent was of little consequence. He saw Wakaba's chief weakness, his inability to think. The bodyguard relied on his immense strength, his technique, the pleasure he received from hating.

Wakaba tossed the knife from hand to hand as he inched toward DiPalma. His right leg dragged slightly. He had been hurt and wanted revenge. His plan was to take the *gaijin*'s cane, then slice his throat and genitals. Wakaba bent his knees, ready to spring forward.

In kendo the three best opportunities to attack came when the opponent was about to make a move, after he had made the move and when the opponent was waiting.

The three methods of attack were to go for the opponent's weapon, his technique or his spirit.

DiPalma decided to do what Wakaba least expected—attack first and break the bodyguard's seemingly unbreakable spirit. He saw Wakaba's knees bend, his nostrils flare and his knife hand start to come up. Preparation.

Screaming at the top of his voice DiPalma charged and brought the cane down on the bodyguard's bandaged hand, once, twice, shattering the hand. Before Wakaba could withdraw DiPalma struck him on the elbow, faked another attack on the ruined hand, then unleashed a vicious head strike. The head strike never landed; the bodyguard, to protect his tortured left hand, leaned back and out of range.

Wakaba continued backing up toward the trash cans near the stairs. With his sleeve he wiped blood from his fractured nose and face. His left arm was useless. His right knee throbbed and had begun to swell; his damaged nose now forced him to breathe through his mouth. Inside he could feel the power gained through his anger begin to ebb. The *gaijin* had left him confused and frustrated. Wakaba no longer faced a weak enemy, but one who attacked with murderous precision, with a spirit strong enough to force a retreat. But the bodyguard would die before he surrendered.

The tiger of wrath raged within Wakaba; to feed his anger he had only to look at the American's son. Suddenly, he conceived an idea which so possessed him that it blotted out the pain. There was one sure way of defeating the American, one which would break his spirit and leave him too shaken to continue fighting.

Wakaba would kill the American's son before his eyes.

The *gaijin*'s will was not free; it was strongly attached to his son, something Wakaba had seen in Hong Kong and again here in the alley. The pain of witnessing his son's death would be a suffering the American could not overcome. But to get to the foreign boy, who stood at the opposite end of the alley, Wakaba would first have to deal with the American.

His leg brushed one of the plastic trash cans. *Hai*. There was a way to take care of the American.

DiPalma advanced slowly toward the bodyguard, the black oak cane held shoulder high in a two-handed grip. He had learned to end a fight quickly, to put an end to it before the uncertain occurred. Wakaba was hurting, dragging his right leg, making no attempt to use his left arm. He's still dangerous, thought DiPalma. He's too stubborn and stupid not to be.

DiPalma was inching closer when Wakaba suddenly dropped his knife and in a single motion grabbed a trash can by the handle and flung it across the alley at him. Trailing garbage, the container hit DiPalma in the hip, knocking him off balance. A second trash can crashed into his chest and arm. The cane was sent flying across the alley and landed in a shop doorway. DiPalma, fighting panic, turned to run after it as a third can hit him between the shoulder blades, sending him stumbling to finally fall on his hands and knees.

The American looked over his shoulder as still another trash can was flung at him. He rolled over, the concrete painfully scraping his face and hip; the container sprayed him with broken glass and empty beer bottles. On his back DiPalma watched as Shuko reached the bottom of the stairs, leaped forward and attempted a roundhouse kick to Wakaba's rib cage.

Obsessed with destroying the boy, the bodyguard threw himself to the pavement, landing on his right side. At the same time he kicked up with his left leg, driving deep into Shuko's stomach. The policeman was lifted off his feet, then dropped to the ground, the wind knocked out of him.

Wakaba scrambled toward his knife, scooped it up, then pushed himself off the pavement. Looking neither at Shuko or DiPalma, he half-limped, half-ran toward the closed end of the alley, toward Todd.

DiPalma was on his feet, frightened and frustrated almost to tears. He glanced away from Wakaba, to the oak cane lying only a few steps away. Todd was doomed. He and DiPalma were at opposite ends of the alley. With or without the cane DiPalma would never reach his son before the bodyguard. Todd was going to die and there was no way to stop it. Unless—

DiPalma ran to the shop doorway. "Todd!" he yelled.

With all his strength DiPalma hurled the silver-knobbed cane toward the boy, arching it high enough to fly over Wakaba's head.

As soon as the cane was in the air DiPalma's heart sank. It was a poor throw, off line, too far away from Todd. It floated softly, turned twice in midair, then began its descent. As the boy ran to catch it, Wakaba angled toward him, ignoring Jan, who backed along the windows of the darkened shops. Once behind Wakaba, she bolted toward DiPalma.

The cane hit the ground, bounced twice, then rolled away from Todd.

Wakaba shouted, "I will not let you be *kaishaku* to Kenpachi-san! You will never violate his *seppuku!*"

He was almost close enough to touch when the boy dived for the cane. He landed on his stomach and stretched his arm until his fingers closed around the silver knob.

Wakaba, leaning forward, slashed down at Todd's back.

But the boy, cane clutched to his chest, quickly rolled a few feet away and sprang to his feet. He was now between Wakaba and DiPalma and could have run. Instead he stood his ground and with both hands held the cane near the knob, the tip aimed at Wakaba's stomach. "Goddamn it, run!" yelled DiPalma. "Get out of here!"

But a fearful DiPalma could only clutch Jan and watch as the bodyguard, slowed by his injured knee, turned to face Todd. Wakaba limped closer, and, incredibly, the boy inched forward to meet him.

DiPalma shoved Jan aside. "Back off, Todd! Stay away from him!"

The boy did not answer nor did he turn around. Instead he continued to stare at Wakaba. And continued to move forward.

Wakaba had the distance he wanted. He slashed at Todd's neck with all his strength. As Jan screamed, Todd stepped left and crouched. The knife passed over his head. At the same moment he backhanded the cane against Wakaba's damaged knee, causing it to buckle.

With one knee on the ground, Wakaba, off balance, braced himself against the alley floor with his knife hand. He and Todd now faced each other, their heads at the same height.

As though he had done it hundreds of time before, Todd jammed his foot down on Wakaba's knife hand, pinning it to the ground. Then, with his hands wide apart on the cane—right hand on the knob, left hand near the tip—the boy gave a savage yell that paralyzed DiPalma and drove the cane lengthwise into Wakaba's throat.

The bodyguard dropped like a stone. He twisted and turned, his eyes bulging.

"Oh, my God," whispered Jan, hands clutching her own throat.

Stunned, DiPalma ran to his son, who gazed down at Wakaba with cold satisfaction. The boy's eyes were half-shut and the ghost of a smile played on his mouth. He stood supremely confident, a war lord who had pronounced judgment and meted out punishment.

DiPalma reached for the cane, but Todd clung to it with surprising strength and glared at his father. Then the boy relaxed and removed his hands from the cane. A second later his eyes turned up in his head and he collapsed in DiPalma's arms.

DiPalma knelt, eased his son to the ground, then felt the boy's neck for a pulse. It was erratic but strong. He wiped sweat from his temple, then smoothed the boy's damp hair. Katharine had understood their son in a way he never would.

He looked up to find Jan and an unsteady Shuko standing behind him. But before he could speak Wakaba rolled over on his side to face Todd. Only minutes ago he had shouted at Todd: *I will not let you be* kaishaku *to Kenpachi-san. You will never violate his* seppuku.

DiPalma looked at the bodyguard and in that instand he understood and knew. The horror of it chilled his blood. Kenpachi was planning to commit suicide and wanted Todd to behead him. DiPalma's son was to be the film director's *kaishaku*. Wakaba had to answer some questions and answer them now.

But the bodyguard was dying. His eyes had an unnatural brightness and his face was dark from lack of oxygen. Todd had crushed Wakaba's larynx and now he was drowning in his own blood.

The bodyguard reached for Todd with a trembling hand and willed himself to form a single word.

"Benkai," he rasped. Then his hand flopped to the ground and he was silent.

23

ZURICH

KEN SHIRATORI stepped from his chauffeured Mercedes and stopped to listen to the bells of the Grossmünster, the eight-hundred-year-old cathedral whose Gothic twin towers were the symbol of the Swiss city. He was late for an 8:00 A.M. breakfast meeting. The bells, however, reminded him that there was no escape from memory. For a moment the Japanese businessman stared into the past, then shook his head and dismissed the memory. He had no time for dead and dying things. He belonged to the future.

When the bells finished striking, Shiratori, flanked by two Swiss bodyguards, walked into the office building he owned on Bahnhofstrasse, Zurich's elegant avenue of banks, deluxe stores, high-rises and cafés. Until recently he had traveled with at least one security man. But the recent murders of Japanese and western industrialists had convinced Shiratori to keep a minimum of two guards with him at all times. He wasn't sure if he believed in the existence of the Blood Oath League, the group which rumor had credited with the killings. But he knew that to ignore danger was to increase it.

This morning a cold wind blew off the elongated lake from which the city took its name. Shiratori wore neither a topcoat nor a sweater. And he had refused to use the car heater during the drive from the Dolder

285

Grand, the fairytale castle of a hotel located on a wooded hill which looked down on the city. He had also denied a request of his bodyguards to close the car windows. The muscular Swiss could only turn up their coat collars, blow into their cupped hands and softly curse in Romansh, a language spoken by only one percent of the Swiss. The bodyguards had a name for Shiratori. "Old Split Foot." The devil. What else could you call such a warm-blooded prick.

Before any major business deal, Shiratori always suffered a chemical imbalance; his skin reddened, his body temperature shot up, and he perspired so heavily that he was often forced to leave the conference table and change into a dry shirt and clean underwear. His increased body warmth neither made him physically ill nor affected his judgment. He had been master of himself since boyhood; he had learned long ago that what lay in his power to do also lay in his power not to do.

This morning he was to meet with a consortium of Italians and French who had agreed to invest two hundred million dollars in Shiratori's most ambitious project, a $500-million Tokyo theme park that would include Japan's most modern golf course. He had all the money he needed, money, in fact, that had been easy to come by. Shiratori's toughest problem had been finding available land in Tokyo, where real estate prices topped those of Paris, Zurich and Manhattan. The Grossmünster bells reminded him that in acquiring the needed land he had also destroyed Japanese traditions and made enemies.

Ken Shiratori was in his early forties, a lean man with delicate features spoiled by a harelip which he attempted to hide with a mustache. He was the son of a Japanese airline pilot and a French actress; his response to his mixed parentage had been to develop a brutal instinct for making money and exercising it without passion or feeling. He owned Japan's largest chain of hotels, held large blocks of stock in a well-known beer company and was a partner in a baseball team. He also controlled a real-estate corporation which bought vast parcels of land throughout Japan, then built *danchi*, cheap apartment houses.

To do this, Shiratori uprooted thousands of poor and lower-class families, leveled hills and destroyed sacred trees and small parks. He had little reverence for tradition, seeing the old Japan as obsolete and outdated.

"Japan's obsession with its past is weakening," he had said in a speech to a group of admiring young Japanese businessmen. "Habit and custom should not be beyond criticism, nor should the dead rule the living."

Shiratori made no secret of his *gaijin kompurekksu*, his belief that western culture was superior to that of Japan. He spoke fluent English, wore his hair in a permanent, ordered his clothes from Rodeo Drive in

Beverly Hills and Saville Row and had an American wife. He was a champion speedboat racer and had spent a small fortune outbidding other Japanese promoters for the right to import top American show-business talent.

To Shiratori, being first meant being faithful to his instincts; his life was dedicated to rising above the snobs who still looked down on him for not being "a true Japanese." He boasted that neither fire nor war could avenge him as well as he could avenge himself.

Apart from his lavish Tokyo homes, he kept a suite at New York's Hotel Carlyle and condominiums in Los Angeles, Acapulco and Honolulu. His favorite western city, however, was Zurich. He felt at home among its fabled "gnomes," the bankers who had made the city a world financial center and to whom money was the elixir of life. The Swiss were indifferent to Shiratori's mixed parentage, his ruthless business tactics, his determination to invest his own traditions.

Life in the bankers' town pleased Shiratori enough to spend four months of the year here. His French wife loved Zurich's medieval quarter, with its maze of narrow, sloping streets and old houses with wrought-iron signs. He preferred the new Zurich, especially the Bahnhofstrasse, the beautiful broad street which ran three quarters of a mile from the main railroad station to ice blue Lake Zurich, and which was one of the world's most expensive shopping avenues. Through the gnomes' influence, Shiratori had purchased an office building on Bahnhofstrasse, where vaults of gold were buried under the pavement and the summer air was sweet with the smell of linden trees.

Without consulting Shiratori, the gnomes inserted a clause in the purchase agreement, giving them the right to buy a twenty percent interest in the building, at a price to be set by them. He was forced to go along; nothing could be done in Zurich without the bankers' approval.

The gnomes earned their forced partnership by helping Shiratori to finance his ambitious amusement park. They found the last two hundred million dollars he needed and arranged dummy corporations so that European investors could remain anonymous. Accounts were then set up in Swiss banks and abroad and the money flowed back and forth until no French or Italian tax man could trace it.

The gnomes also found Shiratori a first-class law firm and acted as his financial advisers on the amusement park. Some Japanese saw the gnomes as cold-blooded and pitiless, obsessed with greed and gain. Shiratori saw them as brilliant and energetic, bold princes in rimless glasses and close haircuts. Willingly he paid their multimillion-dollar fee and gave them two percent of the amusement park's gross.

The park, called Cosmos, had a science-fiction theme. It was the world of the future, time unborn, the existence yet to come. It was Shiratori's world and he had planned it carefully, first consulting scientists in six countries, then turning to American and British film technicians who had worked on the most successful science-fiction films of the past ten years. Cosmos was going to be the finest park of its kind in the world. It was also going to be the biggest problem of Shiratori's life.

In gaining title to the land he had been as ruthless as the gnomes, using money, influence and perseverence, his own brand of courage. But land was scarce in Tokyo, where too many people were packed into too little space. The press, citizens' groups and politicians attacked Shiratori for "stealing" precious real estate and evicting families in the name of profit. Shiratori shrugged off the critics. He was building a new Japan, and only the ignorant would oppose that.

To drive home his point he selected a particular parcel of land to be leveled first. Besides cheap wooden houses, a beautiful pagoda and a small park, it also contained an ancient Buddhist temple, whose bell was said to have been blessed by Lord Buddha himself. Emperors and shoguns had worshipped here and some claimed to have witnessed miracles within its walls. Shiratori ignored all the pleas to save the temple. Neither censure, threatening letters nor media criticism could change his mind.

Thousands of Japanese who lived near the temple signed a scroll asking that the temple be spared. A delegation of temple monks, accompanied by reporters, attempted to present the scroll to Shiratori at his office; he refused to see them. The land had been legally purchased and the proper authorities had given their approval to Cosmos, which could be expected to draw tourists from all over the world. As the for the golf course, Shiratori was already in touch with golf associations in America and Europe about staging a tournament. The prize money would be double that of any current Western tournament. Like it or not, the land and anything on it belonged to him to do as he pleased.

Then Shiratori heard about the three monks. His Tokyo lawyer showed him the letter.

"I received it in the mail this morning," said the lawyer. "No return address. Postmarked yesterday. Not much to it. Three monks are going to set themselves on fire the day you begin demolition of the temple."

"I guess I should be grateful," said Shiratori. "This proves there are at least three men in the world dumber than me. A perfect example of conscientious stupidity. Don't bother me with this nonsense. Just wipe your ass with it and flush it down the toilet. Nothing's going to happen. I'm not about to help them get the publicity they're looking for. No comment. And that's official."

"What if they're serious? What if they carry out their threat to kill themselves?"

"God will forgive me. That's his business, isn't it?"

But on the morning of the demolition Shiratori arrived at the temple site feeling uneasy. His anxiety grew when he saw the thousands who had gathered along with extra police and the press. Outwardly he appeared detached, even amused. Nothing in the world was permanent. Nothing lasted forever. He had never shared the "true Japanese" idolatry of the past and never would. No one was going to stop that temple from coming down.

But he felt a foreboding which grew when the temple bells started to ring. The crowd, which had been restless, suddenly became silent and Shiratori, his engineer and construction foreman all turned to stare at the temple entrance. Half a dozen monks in saffron robes, their shaved heads bowed, stood chanting on the temple stairs. Several others now left the temple, playing flutes, drums and cymbals. The last to leave were three monks, holding prayer books and beads.

While the three monks knelt outside the entrance, the bells continued to ring and ring until Shiratori wanted to put his hands over his ears. Suddenly he hated that sound. To hell with the monks. He opened his mouth to give the order, to tell his engineer and foreman to proceed. That was when the crowd groaned. Several men and women cried out. Shiratori looked at the temple. And felt sick.

It happened too quickly for anyone to interfere. The three kneeling monks struck matches and touched them to their robes, which were already soaked in gasoline. All three were immediately engulfed in flames. A shocked Shiratori watched as many in the crowd prevented the police from going to the monks. People screamed, fistfights broke out and the three monks fell to the ground, wrapped in pale blue fire.

The bells continued to ring as the observing monks chanted louder, their droning voices ominous to a now frightened Shiratori. A rock grazed his cheek and a bottle sailed in front of him, cracking a tinted window of his limousine. Now rocks and bottles rained down on his crew, who backed away from their equipment and looked toward him with pleading eyes. The crowd surged toward Shiratori and the handful of employees around him. Without waiting to be told by the police, he fled the temple site in his limousine.

The burning monks stayed in his mind for days. As did the temple bells.

A week later, after an official investigation and dozens of negative press reports, the temple was destroyed. Shiratori, meanwhile, looked at what he had and wondered why he was not happy.

IN the lobby of his Zurich office building Shiratori and his two bodyguards walked toward the private elevator that was held open by a uniformed Turk who spoke six languages and had been a university professor in his native Istanbul before fleeing a repressive Turkish government. The elevator was used only by Shiratori and kept locked when he was not in Zurich. The Turk held the keys and was so grateful to Shiratori for the job that he had vowed to die rather than surrender the keys to "improper authorities."

Shiratori felt perspiration run down his forehead and chin. His hands were damp and his skin heated as though he were standing in front of a roaring fire. He was also becoming sexually aroused. He smiled. His body was signaling him that he was ready to confront the gnomes, the Italians, the French and the dozen lawyers waiting in the conference room.

He stepped to the back of the carpeted, polished oak elevator as a bodyguard pressed a button. The door closed on the smiling Turk, who held up the keys. Shiratori ignored him. There were other things to focus on. He had to change into a fresh shirt before entering the conference room. The one he now wore was wringing wet. A good sign.

The elevator ride would be a swift one. Silent, too. Thirty-three floors nonstop in seconds. Shiratori wished it was faster.

The elevator began its ascent, picked up speed, then slowed down and stopped.

Shiratori angrily pushed past a bodyguard and banged the starter button with his fist. Nothing. Again he pounded the button, then again. The elevator did not move.

"Shit," he said in English. "Get on the goddamn phone and call the Turk downstairs. He's supposed to make sure this fucking thing is working whenever I'm in Zurich. Tell that wog I want this elevator moving and I want it moving now."

Felix, the older bodyguard, slid back a stainless steel panel below the elevator buttons. For a few seconds he said nothing. Then, "Mr. Shiratori, we have a problem."

"I'm not interested in problems. I'm only interested in results."

"There's no telephone."

It had been removed, its wire neatly cut.

290

Felix and the other bodyguard, Stephan, exchanged looks. Felix tugged at his earlobe, a lifelong habit when bothered by anything suspicious.

Shiratori backed into a corner and rubbed his palms on his thighs. He was losing control. The perspiration had stopped. He looked at his watch. Eight-twenty. He had to get out of this damned elevator. He reached for his cigarettes.

Felix looked up at the ceiling. "I wouldn't do that, Mr. Shiratori. Smoking, I mean. Don't know how long we'll be trapped. Better to conserve what fresh air we have. There is a trapdoor on top. Maybe one of us can get out that way. Maybe see how close we are to one of the floors."

He turned to Stephan. "You're the gymnast around here. Or you used to be when you were a schoolboy."

Stephan smiled. "That was years ago. But I try."

Shiratori wrung his hands and nodded. His voice became soft. He knew he was on the edge of hysteria. "Do whatever you can to get us out. I do not like to be closed in. I must have air."

"We'll do our best," said Felix. "Stephan, time to make like a monkey or like you are escaping from a jealous husband."

Felix squatted and Stephan, in his stocking feet, sat on his shoulders. Felix then rose to his full height, pushing Stephan close to the ceiling. He reached overhead, unlatched the trapdoor and threw it back. The sound of the door hitting the top of the elevator echoed along the darkened shaft. Felix wobbled as Stephan, grunting, pulled himself through the opening and disappeared. Shiratori braced himself against a wall as the elevator rocked gently. Stephan was walking around on top.

Felix called out, "Hey Stephan, lose some weight while you're up there. You're heavy."

Stephan's voice had an echo. "Maybe I go jogging before I come back down. Very dark in this shaft. Let me get my cigarette lighter and I—"

Suddenly the car rocked so violently that Shiratori and Felix almost lost their balance. It jerked on its cable and scraped the sides of the concrete shaft.

Felix cleared his throat. He didn't want to criticize Stephan in front of this Jap bastard, but what he was now doing on top of the elevator was dangerous. "Stephan, I think—"

Shiratori was raging. He shrieked at the ceiling. "Are you mad? I order you down from there this minute, or you're out of a job. And I'll see to it that you never—"

Something hard, wet and red flew through the trapdoor and bounced off Shiratori's shoulders, landing on the thick carpet.

Stephan's head. Eyes wide with disbelief. Neck and chin slick with warm blood.

Whimpering, Shiratori backed into a corner, hands over his ears. The bells. The bells. And death.

Retching, Felix stared down at Stephan's head. And when he heard the noise above him, he tried to do everything at once. Tried to remember his training.

Turn to face the enemy. Draw the PPK Walther. Thumb off the safety. Empty the gun into the bastard.

The *ninja* was faster and more cold-blooded. He dropped through the ceiling, landing on Felix's back with both knees. In pain and out of breath, the bodyguard fell forward, striking his head against the wall. He was on his knees, dazed, the PPK Walther still in his hand, when the black-clad figure slit his throat from behind in one smooth gesture.

Then the *ninja* leaped on a screaming Shiratori.

Moments later the *ninja* returned the knife to the small of his back, bent his knees and gracefully leaped toward the ceiling, where dangling arms caught his wrists and pulled him up. Then he disappeared through the opening, and the door closed.

In the darkened shaft three black-clad figures began to climb the elevator cable with the ease of acrobats.

24

Tokyo

THE SMELL made Jan sick to her stomach. Turning her back on the fire now burning in the temple courtyard, she removed a tissue from her shoulder bag and held it over her nose. A few seconds later she thought, to hell with it. Where is it written that I have to stand on top of my crew while they work. Shading her eyes against the blistering sun, she crossed the courtyard and stood near a pond filled with water lilies and shaded by yellowing gingko trees.

From here she watched the second unit film two Buddhist priests as they burned a collection of dolls in the center of the temple courtyard. Women and girls surrounded the priests as they fed dozens of damaged and worn dolls onto a large metal tray of hot coals. It was an ancient and moving ceremony, but the odor of burning plastic forced Jan to watch from a distance.

To the Japanese, dolls were not mere toys. They demanded love and consideration at all times. Childless women and spinsters kept dolls to alleviate their loneliness, treating them as babies. In time such affection was said to create a soul within the doll. That was why when a doll began to fall apart, it could not be treated like trash.

Proper respect called for destruction by purification through fire or water. Some women and girls floated old dolls on a river or allowed the tide to take them out to sea. Others, like those Jan now stood watching, brought their dolls to be purified in a temple fire. For a small donation Jan's crew had been allowed to film a doll-burning ceremony in a run-down neighborhood of flimsy wooden houses with sliding paper doors.

Because locks were useless on such doors, one member of the household stayed home at all times to guard against burglars. Today dozens of them leaned out of windows and stood in doorways watching the actors and crew. To win the neighborhood's cooperation, one Japanese crew member had gone out into a street near the temple and, as the local people gathered around him, acted out the entire film, even to the point of falling down when "shot."

At the moment Jan could easily have shot Kon Kenpachi. He had had an 8:00 A.M. appointment with the Tokyo police, the fifth straight day the police had talked to him about the late Wakaba. It was now past noon and no word from Kon. Not even a quick telephone call letting Jan know when he might return to the set. With production costs now running close to sixty thousand dollars a day, Jan's first movie could fall apart for lack of a director.

What had saved her so far was Sam, her efficient production manager, who had quickly shifted to the backup shot, the doll-burning scene in the temple courtyard. It was something a second unit could handle without Kenpachi. Under a first assistant director, a second unit shot exterior footage—crowd scenes, car chases, floods, avalanches—scenes which didn't need major stars or a director. The doll burning was to be used as a cutaway while Tom Gennaro and Kelly Keighley discussed the *yakuza* money stolen by Gennaro's Japanese girl friend.

Gennaro and Keighley were due to go before the cameras this morning. Instead they sat around bored, until both decided to go off and amuse themselves until Kon returned. Both actors had a star's ego; when they were ready to work, everyone else should be ready. By talking to each man, Jan had managed to cool them down, but they couldn't be controlled for long if they had nothing to do. Gennaro was off on a side street throwing a football with some of the American and British crew. Keighley, with his teenage Venezuelan mistress, was strolling under the weeping willows which lined the bank of the Sumida River.

Jan believed in keeping to a tight production schedule, something she had learned in television, where there was no such thing as working too fast. A producer never allowed actors, especially expensive actors, to become bored. Bored actors gave boring performances. Without a strong director or producer, actors could easily lose interest in a film. Worse, they might attempt to take over a production.

But if God had wanted actors to direct themselves, he would have made them all fat and bald and named them Hitchcock.

In the week since Wakaba's death, Kon had spent so much time with the police that the crew had nicknamed him "Monopoly Man."

"'Cause he don't pass Go, he don't collect two hundred dollars, but he do go directly to jail."

Not funny. Without Kenpachi, Jan had no movie. She couldn't fail, not the first time out. In Hollywood, if you blew it there was no mercy. Failure was a contagious disease. Anyone who came down with it was ostracized.

"Don't you ever come up short out here, girl," a black casting director had told Jan on her first trip to Los Angeles. "That's the same as admitting your feet stink, your breath's bad and you don't love your Jesus."

Why were the police leaning on Kon? He hadn't killed Wakaba. Todd had. In self-defense and in front of witnesses. God knows he was a nice enough kid, but after what Jan had seen him do to Wakaba she suspected him of having more than a homicidal touch in his soul. In Hong Kong she had almost passed out at the sight of Geoffrey Laycock lying skewered in the middle of the hospital flagpole. But when Todd had looked out the window at the dead Englishman, Jan thought she had seen a smile on his face.

The Royal Hong Kong Police, who had seen everything in the way of violent crimes, had never seen a man die as Laycock had. And the hospital staff on duty that night had been horrified; some, like Jan, had to be sedated.

Todd had been unmoved. He had stood by Frank's bed and stared down at his unconscious father as though he, Todd, were the father, the protector, and Frank the child, the one in need of protection.

In Tokyo, this same boy kills a knife-wielding grown man who outweighs him by over one hundred pounds. Also spooky. Jan had tried to tell herself that the boy had acted out of nerves, that his adrenaline had been pumping in the alley and he had just gotten lucky. But the more she thought about it, and connected it to the incident at the Hong Kong hospital, the more she believed that Todd had known exactly what he was doing.

Todd Hansard was beginning to look less cuddly and more creepy-crawly. Frank must have noticed. He never missed much.

What was behind Wakaba's incredible hatred of Todd? The two had never laid eyes on each other until a couple of weeks ago, when *Ukiyo* moved to Hong Kong for location shooting. When Jan asked Frank why Wakaba had hated his son, the only answer was, "The man was a wacko. Let it go at that."

Which immediately told her he was holding something back. His hooded eyes seemed more veiled than normal and he stared at Jan as though challenging her to doubt his answer.

Over drinks at Ikuba Castle she had asked Kon Kenpachi the same question. His answer had been more detailed, yet simple.

"Jealousy. The greatest of all punishments. I'd offered Todd a small part in *Ukiyo* and refused to do the same for Wakaba."

Jan didn't know whether to laugh or cry. "Kon, I've heard of people dying to get into show business. But *killing?* No offense, but it makes Wakaba sound as if he had the brain of a crouton."

"There is a little more to it than that."

She sipped an almond-flavored French liqueur. "With you there always is."

"I would very much like to star Todd in a film of his own."

"Are you serious?"

"It's not something I'm prepared to discuss for publication, but I do have a project in mind for the boy. I admire the way Steven Spielberg works with children. He has a very good way of telling a story from their point of view, while managing to retain the interest of adults. That's the sort of thing I have in mind for Todd. The boy has a certain magnetism, a brooding quality, which I feel could transfer quite well to the screen."

Jan said, "But he's never acted before. How do you know he can do it?"

"It is my business to know such things. Besides, most of my films depend on casting performers who have not lost their beauty, their vigor." His eyes glazed over and his voice grew soft. "Beauty, youth and death. So irresistible."

"You mean like James Dean, Valentino, Jean Harlow."

He nodded vigorously. "Yes. That is exactly what I mean. And now they are beautiful for all time. As is our own Yukio Mishima, whom some now consider a god. Through death one can live forever."

Jan hated this kind of talk. But Kon was a performer and performers all had a touch of the fanatic in them. She said, "I take it you haven't discussed Todd's movie career with Frank."

Kenpachi swallowed his drink, then refilled their glasses. "Mr. Di-Palma's life and mine run counter to each other in every possible way. He does not like the idea of his son being in my company."

Jan reached over and touched Kenpachi's arm. "Babycakes, you have not exactly spent your life in mad pursuit of clean living."

"I can assure you I have no sexual interest in the boy, if that's what you are insinuating. Wakaba was jealous, yes. But no relationship I had with other men ever pleased him."

296

"Sexual or otherwise?"

"Sexual or otherwise."

"Were you and Wakaba ever lovers?"

A faint smile crossed Kenpachi's face, but it told her nothing. "Pleasure articulates itself," he said. "Pleasure finds its own voice. Then a day arrives when that voice becomes silent. Intoxication is temporary and inevitably fades. Wakaba found this part of our relationship difficult to accept."

"I see. Today a chicken, tomorrow a feather duster. Sooner or later everyone in Kenpachi's life has to get up and give his seat to someone else."

She swallowed more almond liqueur. She felt relaxed, daring, she wanted to challenge Kon. Why not? Why have an affair if you can't kick each other in the shins once in a while?

"From what I could see," Jan said, "Wakaba was very loyal to you. Yet you're treating his death as if it were nothing more serious than dropping a piece of toast on the floor. No tears, no long face. Is it because the show must go on or what?"

Kenpachi gave her an ugly look. For a second she feared he might strike her. Then he said smoothly, "Wakaba attempted to kill the boy. I shall never forgive him for that. Todd is of immense importance to me."

"Speaking of movies, ours is running behind schedule. You've been off to see the police every day since Wakaba's death. Meanwhile we're losing time and time is money."

"Perhaps this is something you should discuss with your friend, Mr. DiPalma."

"I don't get it. You're saying my movie's behind schedule because of Frank DiPalma?"

"Captain Shuko is his friend. And it is Shuko who insists on my appearing in his office whenever the mood strikes him."

"If I read you right you're saying Frank blames you for the attempt made by Wakaba to kill Todd. And that he's using Shuko to get back at you."

Kenpachi looked at Jan with contempt. "On the subject of DiPalma, your mind is not exactly possessed by wisdom. The day will soon arrive when you will be forced to concern yourself with those things you do not wish to know at present. Has it not occurred to you that DiPalma feels extremely guilty in the matter of Katharine Hansard's death?"

"He's told me so, yes."

"Then does it not make sense that this guilt may have settled his mind in the matter of the boy?"

"Anything's possible, I suppose."

"He would not be the first man who did not want to accept responsibility for his own actions. Why should you be surprised that he wishes to unload this guilt on others. You know why he's here in Tokyo."

Jan said, "He's investigating Katharine Hansard's death."

"For which he holds Nosaka-san responsible. And to get at Nosaka-san, DiPalma is having me harassed by Captain Shuko in the hope that I will soon tire of such treatment and help them to destroy a very great man. DiPalma is even going so far as to pry into Nosaka-san's business affairs."

"Frank says Nosaka's deep into industrial espionage—"

Kenpachi slammed his fist on the table, making Jan jump in her chair. "You are now in Japan. Here, industrial espionage does not exist. What information our government and businessmen gather is for the good of our country as a whole. Much of what we gather is public knowledge, available to anyone who will take the time to collect it. We do not spy. Do you hear me? *We do not spy.*"

Jan held up a hand in a stop signal. "If you don't mind, I'd appreciate not being yelled at. Call it what you want to over here. What Frank's concerned with is the effect of Nosaka's actions in America and maybe in a few other countries as well. He has a right to his opinion same as you. I'd rather not go into that at the moment. You said something about Shuko getting involved in all of this because Frank asked him to. Assuming Shuko's not a moron and he's not being paid off, why should a man in his position do something so dumb? You'd think he'd be the first to come out on Nosaka's side. Let's face it: Frank's a foreigner here, an outsider. Shuko and Nosaka are both Japanese, or they were the last time I looked."

Kenpachi rose and stood with his feet apart, hands folded across his chest. Just like Yul Brynner in *The King and I*, thought Jan. Except this time the king has only one subject to put in her place. Me.

"Shuko is scum," said Kenpachi. "He's looking out for himself, not for Japan. During World War II, his father was an army officer who brought disgrace upon himself at a time when his country needed him. Shuko's father betrayed Japan. For this he was executed by Nosaka-san. Shuko, who is not a man, has never stopped hating Nosaka-san for doing his duty. That is what Shuko and DiPalma have in common. Both are too weak to accept responsibility for their own karma. Both now seek to blame Nosaka-san for their own weaknesses."

"Frank never mentioned this to me."

"And if he had?"

She took her cigarettes from her purse, shook one loose and lit it. She blew smoke toward the lacquered ceiling. "I don't know. I really don't know."

"I understand that the women of your country think for themselves."

"I'm still working on the difference between reasons that sound good and good, sound reasoning. Get to the point."

"The point, my dear free-thinking American, is that you should reason for yourself and do so independently of Frank DiPalma. If you will investigate you will find that the emperor himself approved of Nosaka-san's killing of Shuko's father. The emperor placed Nosaka-san under his personal protection, where he still remains. Shuko and all members of his family are forbidden to harm Nosaka-san. This does not, however, prevent them for enlisting others to do their dirty work work for them."

"You mean Frank?"

"He carries two dead women with him at all times, does he not? He even seeks to involve your father in this charade."

Jan lifted her chin. "My father *is* involved. I didn't need Frank to tell me that."

Kenpachi stepped closer. "Because your father and Nosaka-san are business associates does not involve them in a criminal conspiracy. Is it not possible that the files now in your father's possession are nothing more than forgeries?"

"And who would go to the trouble of forging files on Nosaka's bank and other businesses?"

He dropped to his knees beside her and grinned like a schoolboy. "Mr. DiPalma would. His is a nature which craves revenge."

Jan touched her forehead to his. "Passionate Sicilian nature and all that. Don't forget people like him love to wear bright colors and pointed shoes." She leaned back. "Now that we've disposed of the obvious, let me tell you that my father thinks the files are genuine. And it wasn't Frank who put the files together. It was Todd's stepfather. Meanwhile, dad's gone to a lot of trouble to protect those files."

"And what exactly has he done to protect them?"

Jan sighed and reached for her drink. "Checked himself into the hospital again. He says, or rather the weird little man who heads his security says, the hospital's the safest place. Easy to guard, that kind of nonsense. The weird little man, someone called Nullabor, feels he can better protect my father in the hospital than in either of dad's homes. From what I can gather, the files are within reach at all times."

Kenpachi kissed the palm of her hand. "I assume when you say protect, you're referring to the Blood Oath League?"

Jan nodded. "I have to tell you, I really don't understand what's going on. Part of me says dad's getting paranoid in his old age. The other part says two of my father's friends are dead and they weren't tickled to death. Salvatore Verna and Duncan Ivy. Jesus, I'd known them all my life. So what do I do? Is my father right or not?"

"I can see the confusion in you. Your mind is a collection of shifting winds. Has DiPalma said anything more about your father?"

She finished her drink before speaking. "That's just it. Frank and I haven't seen each other or spoken since . . . since what happened to Wakaba. True, he's running all over Tokyo digging into Nosaka's life. But I feel a draft coming from Frank. A definite draft since that night. He doesn't seem to want to confide in me any more than he has to."

Kenpachi cupped her chin in his hand and gently turned her face toward him. "To confide in you is perhaps to confide in me. Or he could be jealous of our relationship. I think you still have an affection for DiPalma and find this difficult to accept. In any case, you cannot put him out of your mind."

Her smile was weak. "Moving right along, let's talk about the rains that are supposed to hit Tokyo next month. They could cause us more delay. You'll be taking time out to fly to New York for the Lincoln Center retrospective, which is going to be something. The Japanese ambassador's flying in from Washington and we've got requests from over three hundred press people who want to cover—"

Kenpachi, still on his knees, used his tongue to make circles in her palm. Jan shivered, remembering previously experienced pleasure with him. And humiliation. She cleared her throat. "We're putting together a collection of clips from your old films. I'd like to include a clip from *Ukiyo*. Did I tell you that the studio wants to rush *Ukiyo* into December release to qualify for the Academy Awards? They're talking about a formal dinner, a knockdown, drag-out bash at the Metropolitan Museum of Art in New York after the world premiere—"

He silenced Jan with a kiss. There was nothing more for her to say. What did they have in common? The movie, of course. And a love of Japan. And a willingness to accept in themselves what they would never tolerate in others. Both were too often dominated by desire and when that desire was satisfied, both believed they possessed everything.

Was there any answer to the question of desire? Or had Jan, in walking away from Frank DiPalma, turned her back on the answer? Since seeing him again she had recalled the time when she had possessed his heart and had given him hers.

She dreaded going to bed with Kenpachi. And longed for it. Was humiliation the pleasure she got from him, or the means by which the pleasure was attained? One thing was certain: Kenpachi's sexual mastery unnerved her, for with it came a sense of shame.

In a drugged haze Jan was brought to the brink of orgasm several times, only to have Kenpachi back off, deliberately to deny Jan her climax. After the third or fourth time Jan did as he ordered. She begged. And after she had done so, Kenpachi lovingly kissed her eyes, her mouth and neck, her breasts, her stomach. When his tongue found her clitoris, she closed her eyes and clawed the sheets. But again he stopped, deliberately preventing her orgasm.

This time, however, she did not have to beg. He inserted a *ri-no-tama*, two small metal balls, into her vagina. He had used them before. One ball contained a vibrating metal tongue, the other a small amount of mercury. The slightest movement sent sensual tremors through her and along her spine. Without waiting for Kenpachi's orders, she drew her legs toward herself slightly, then straightened them. She repeated this, slowly at first, then faster, thrashing about on the bed until she arched her back with an orgasmic cry which went on and on and on.

Then she collapsed back on the bed, drained and breathless. Only when she opened her eyes did she realize that Kenpachi had been watching her with casual disdain. But his attitude did not register as distasteful, for the drugs they had both taken in an ancient bowl of red wine had left her mind clouded and uncertain.

Kenpachi now removed the metal balls and entered her, making love with an insistence and skill that brought her quickly to within reach of another climax, until he pulled out and began to kiss her thighs. Once more his tongue found her clitoris. Eyes closed, Jan stroked his hair and called his name over and over. The waves built up again, unstoppable. Kon's denial only increased her longing for him, for orgasm, for release, for Kon.

She opened her eyes to drink in his beauty, to feast on the sight of what he was doing to her, and in that instant the orgasm seized her and she called his name and with all her strength pressed his head between her legs.

She exploded, eyes closed, touching that thin line between ecstasy and death, and not caring if she died.

Kon called Jan's name. Slowly she opened her eyes to see him standing naked beside the bed while hands and tongues caressed her body. The drugs . . .

With an effort Jan forced her eyes away from Kon and looked down at the naked Japanese man and woman who were making love to her. She wanted to stop them, to cry out, to push them away. But then she felt warm with pleasure again and Kenpachi was forcing her to drink more wine, and soon she was slipping into a shadow world and there was nothing to feel anymore.

When Jan awoke in the morning, Kon and the man and the woman were gone. The shame of the previous night was too strong to believe it had never happened. For a few minutes she curled up in bed and wept. She had no idea who the other man and woman were and she dreaded the thought of seeing them again. She had never done this before. Never. She had fantasized about it, but had never done it. It was as though Kon had read her mind, discovered her secret thoughts and brought them to life. She had never made love to a woman before, had never gone to bed with a man whom she did not know.

But she had done so last night and enjoyed it. With an effort she made her way to the bathroom, turned on the hot water and stood under it for a long time. She shivered with fright, not at what had happened, but at its effect on her in the future. The night could not be undone.

        *   *   *

IN the temple courtyard Jan was joined by several staff members. Together they watched a young Japanese mother in fashionably baggy jeans and T-shit lead her weeping daughter away from the crowd surrounding the bonfire. Jan signaled her second-unit crew to film them against a temple wall where the woman knelt and hugged the tearful child.

The Japanese girl was adorable in pink kimono, gold sash and clogs. She looked like a doll herself as the kneeling mother softly spoke to her and pointed to the black smoke spiraling above the courtyard. Was she telling her that the doll had gone to heaven? The mother kissed her daughter's tears, then took the child's left hand in hers and linked her left pinky finger with her daughter's.

Jan's turn to cry. Smoke gets in your eyes, she said to no one in particular, and reached into her bag for another tissue. *Yubi-kiri* it was called. Linking your pinky fingers and making a promise to be fulfilled in the future. A child's game. When Jan was a child and living in Japan on an army base with her father, they had played *yubi-kiri*. What had she wished for then? Long life? To be forever happy? A date with the Everly Brothers?

Time to take herself in hand. Link pinky fingers with Jan Golden. No one else was going to save this movie.

She looked around and began to issue orders. Neil Weiner, her personal assistant, was ordered to find Kenpachi. "Start with the police

302

station. If he isn't there, find him anyway. Don't speak to me until you locate him. Time he and I had a full and frank exchange."

Then she turned to Debbie Elise, her secretary. "Leave a message for Frank DiPalma at the New Otani Hotel."

Debbie looked up from her note pad, then dropped her eyes. Jesus, thought Jan, they're all so goddamn well informed around here about my personal life. Aloud she said, "He's probably out. I hope he's out because I don't want him to say no. Just leave a message. Say I want to have a drink with him. Today if possible. Have him leave a message at my hotel."

Jan was going to find out for herself if Frank was using the Tokyo police to dump on Kon. At sixty thou a day she was damned if that would go on.

Then it was her production manager's turn. "Is there any way we can set up another shot this afternoon, something which does not involve the active participation of Kon Kenpachi?"

"Tough one," said Sam Jonas. "Permits we need for the park scene tomorrow aren't due to come through until late this afternoon. Gennaro and Keighley are ready for the Ginza scene, but you can eighty-six that. They only agreed to do this picture for a chance to work with the Monopoly Man."

"Sam, do me a favor. As long as you're on this picture, kindly do not use that term around me, okay? I mean it's about as funny as AIDS."

"How's this for funny. Guy sees a sign on the Ginza says Karate-Judo. He says it's the name of that Mexican actress who used to be married to Ernest Borgnine."

"Sam, please?"

"Okay, okay. Look, I'll push for the permits today. No promises. I may have to grease a few palms."

"Grease, already. We can break for lunch, which gives you time to get lucky."

"Got lucky last night. Model from L.A. who's over here doing a cosmetic commercial for Japanese TV. She's getting five thousand dollars a day and I had to pay for dinner."

Neil Weiner trotted up to Jan. "Found him."

Jan turned her back on Sam Jonas. "Where?"

"I think I found him."

"Think?"

"Police station says he left there at ten-thirty."

Jan looked at Neil from the corner of her eye. "Ten-thirty, did you say?"

"Oh, shit. Messenger bearing bad news loses his head. You have to

303

understand, I'm getting all of this through one of our interpreters. I did make her repeat it to me and I did write it down. The local law says Mr. Kenpachi departed their circle of warmth around ten-thirty and, wait for it, was returning to Ikuba Castle."

Jan brushed past him. "You come with me. I think it's time we kick ass before I lose control of this movie altogether. If I didn't know better I'd swear Mr. Kenpachi's retired on the job, for which I am paying him very big bucks."

At the cramped noodle shop which the production company had rented as a temporary headquarters Neil Weiner dialed Ikuba Castle. Jan dragged heavily on a cigarette and paced back and forth. What the hell had gotten in Kon? He was on a picture and couldn't afford to be away from the set for an hour. His appearances at the police station had cost her more time and money than she cared to think of. Her grandfather was right. Your friends come and go, but your enemies just keep on growing in numbers.

And don't forget the August rains. Or typhoon. She had hoped to be finished before they arrived. She desperately wanted *Ukiyo* ready by December, time enough to qualify for the Academy Awards. She felt good about this film. And in that case, why not go for it. Gennaro was acting his ass off and Keighley had never been better. If Jan got the New York critics to rave over *Ukiyo*, she'd have the studio by the balls. Then they would have to give her the promotion she wanted. Marketing, they called it these days. Whatever it was, it was the only game in town. Studios were so hung up on marketing that if the marketing boys didn't like a script, it wasn't made. Dumb? But Hollywood wasn't called fruit-and-nut city for nothing. As Jan's agent told her a long time ago, nobody in Hollywood ever gets fired for saying no.

Jan wanted a strong trade campaign geared strictly to the Academy Award nominations. Then she wanted gossip columns, still an effective way of creating want-to-see. But before she could get any of that she needed a finished movie. Edited, scored, dubbed, looped and printed before the third week in December. The more she thought about what she stood to lose, the more pissed she became at Kenpachi.

"No answer," said Neil, the receiver pressed to his ear.

"What the hell do you mean, no answer. He's there. The police said he's there."

Neil looked through the noodle-shop window. "Notice anything?"

"Yeah. I notice we have no fucking director."

"Monopoly Man's friends are among the missing. Everyone of those clowns has hauled ass away from here. Now why's that, I wonder?"

Neil was right. Some of the tough-looking characters Jan had seen at

304

Kon's party the other night had been put on the film as extras, drivers, security. The Bananas, someone from L.A. had called them. Yellow and always hanging around in a bunch. Wakaba had been one of them. Gorillas with flattop haircuts. Even the other Japanese avoided them.

Kon practiced karate and kendo with them during film breaks. They were good. Almost too good. Watching them fight gave Jan the feeling that they really worked at it.

And now they were gone. Drifted away like the movie smoke now rising above the temple walls.

Jan said, "Kon's at the castle. And the Bananas have slithered off to join him. Get my driver."

"I'll go with you."

Her back was to Neil and he could not see her face. He could not see the fear. This morning the Bananas had leered at her when she arrived on the set. Burning with shame Jan had hurried by them and into the noodle shop. *One of them had been in bed with her last night.* That son of a bitch Kon. She decided right then to fire his friends, then thought better of it. If he wanted them on the picture, they were on and there was nothing she could do about it. Not at this stage of filming. She was stuck with them, she could only pretend that she didn't know what the hell they were carrying on about.

"Stay here," she said to Neil. "My driver knows the way. I'll be all right. Kon and I need to clear the air."

Neil looked down at the floor and scratched his head. So you know, she thought. So what. Fuck you very much for thinking of me.

She hurried to find her driver.

＊   ＊   ＊

AT Ikuba Castle the drawbridge was down. Strange, thought Jan. Kon said he preferred to keep it up all the time to insure privacy. Not only was it down, but there were several cars on it that probably belonged to the Bananas. The castle gate, two huge steel doors, was closed against the outside world. In the center of one large door was a smaller one, also closed. Jan hesitated before leaving her limousine. Her nerves screamed cigarette. She lit one and smoked half of it before leaving the car.

She wished she had brought Neil with her. Better yet, she wished Frank was with her. He was in her thoughts more and more.

305

She walked across the drawbridge, carefully picking her way along the cars, wishing she had worn flats instead of heels. At the iron door she stamped out the cigarette and closed her eyes. If God had wanted us to be brave, why did he give us feet? She opened her eyes and pounded on the small door.

The sound echoed across a quiet courtyard. Jan looked behind her. All those cars and not a peep from inside. Weird. She was about to knock again when the grating of the handle on the other side of the door made her jump. The door opened wide, and what Jan saw in the courtyard made her jaw drop.

One of the Bananas glared at her as she looked past him into the courtyard. A naked Kon, his body glistening with oil and perspiration, knelt alone on a red carpet. A samurai sword, its blade polished to a jewellike perfection, lay in front of him on a small, low table.

He knelt in the center of a square formed by four bonfires. The Bananas stood outside the fires watching. Instinctively Jan knew she had seen something she was not supposed to see.

The man who had opened the door stepped through and angrily shooed her away. A second man joined him. Both looked as though they wanted to kill her.

Turning, she ran along the drawbridge toward her car and never looked back.

25

FROM THE front seat of Shuko's parked Datsun, DiPalma and the Tokyo police captain looked across the traffic-clogged street at the Takeshi Building, Zenzo Nosaka's corporate headquarters. The dark, bulky structure, its eight stories looking more Victorian than Japanese, stood on the corner of Marunouchi Square, Japan's industrial and banking nerve center. There were other corporate high-rises near it and the adjacent banks held deposits totaling billions of dollars. But somehow the squat, funereal-looking Takeshi building intimidated every structure within blocks. If the taller, more graceful buildings were like flamingos, Nosaka's stronghold was an alligator.

From where DiPalma and Shuko were parked it was possible to look past the Takeshi building and down a wide mall leading to the Imperial Palace and lined with oddly shaped pine trees propped up to withstand the autumn typhoons. At one in the afternoon every foot of the mall was packed bumper to bumper with cars, yellow taxis, buses and trucks. The pollution was eye burning. According to Shuko, Tokyo pollution was strong enough to corrode metal.

Sitting here reminded DiPalma of his days as a cop, when he had pulled surveillance and lived on soda and pizza. He smiled, remembering the first rule of the game. Make sure you pee before it starts, because when surveillance starts you can't move. You keep an empty milk carton on the floor of the car. You'll learn to love it because it's your toilet.

In the back seat of the Datsun a Japanese cameraman aimed a hand-held camera at the Takeshi Building. This was as close as DiPalma could get. Nosaka's corporate headquarters was off limits to both Japanese and western press. Nosaka himself hadn't given an interview since the end of the war. The only photographs of him had been taken with his permission at kendo matches. The Alligator was well guarded. Uniformed, armed men checked everyone who entered the lobby. If the guards knew DiPalma was filming the building there would be heavy trouble.

The cameraman was a twenty-one-year-old Tokyo film student who called himself Ford Higashi after John Ford, his favorite director. Ford spoke English, used dated American slang and worked with earphones turned up loud enough for DiPalma to hear every note of the score from Errol Flynn's *The Sea Hawk*. Ford did a lot of work for the Tokyo correspondent of DiPalma's network, a bone-thin, preppy-looking Canadian named Donald Turney. Turney, twenty-nine and ambitious, was the son of a Canadian diplomat who had played a role in the release of the American hostages from Iran. Young Turney had never stopped looking for a story to top the one his father had lived, which was why he had tried to force DiPalma to include him. The ex-cop wondered if things in Tokyo were really that slow.

"Ford says the shoot he's doing for you has something to do with Nosaka," said Turney. He tried to sound commanding.

DiPalma had been about to leave his hotel room when the phone rang. He didn't like Turney's tone. "I'm on my way out."

"DiPalma, I want in. You're on my turf."

"You're on my time."

"Hey, guy, don't hardball it here. You're a long way from home. Over here you're not destiny's child. You're just a wayfaring stranger who can very easily get caught in the crunch. Do I make myself clear?"

"Ain't this a bitch. Good-bye, Mr. Turney."

"Suit yourself, friend. But as soon as I hang up, I'm calling New York. And then we shall see what we shall see."

DiPalma, receiver in two fingers, extended his arm and let the receiver fall.

A day later Turney called again. He didn't sound so tough this time. "New York says we ought to try and work something out. Should be enough glory to go round. Might be good for the both of us. You scratch my back and I'll scratch yours kind of thing."

"New York told you to fuck off. They said if you've got any sense you'll keep away from me. I've got a team on this thing in New York, I've got friends here who are helping me. You're deadweight. And I don't need you."

"Mister, I can hurt you in this town."

"If you do, don't ever let me find you. Call New York and ask them if I mean it." He dropped the receiver again. Let Turney get his information from Ford. Such as it was.

Before the film student had arrived, DiPalma had sat in the car and told Shuko some of the results of a week's investigation. "Nosaka's not too popular here, though no one's willing to speak out publicly against him. I've got two people on film who agreed to talk if their identities were kept secret. We shot them sitting in darkness."

"I do not need to know their names, DiPalma-san. But I would be interested in what they had to say."

"Fine. I found them through a friend, Rakan Omura."

"*Hai.* He is the antique dealer for whom you have done certain investigations."

DiPalma nodded. "And from whom I have purchased swords. I checked out a couple of Madison Avenue antique dealers for him in the past. One was a thief, the other was okay. I also put him in touch with someone at the Metropolitan Museum in New York and he's gotten rich off that. Sells them thousands of dollars worth of stuff every year. Seems he sells to Japanese businessmen as well, including two who used to work for Nosaka. One, whom we'll call Joe, feels Nosaka's definitely behind the Blood Oath League. He says two of the men who were killed were business rivals of Nosaka's. Ken Shiratori was one."

"The man who was murdered in Zurich last week."

"*Hai.* Apparently Nosaka wanted a fifty-percent share in Shiratori's amusement park. Shiratori turned him down and did it in a nasty way. Nosaka was very insulted because Shiratori did it in front of a roomful of people. What you have here is not just killing for a new Japan or an old Japan. What you have is killing for money, for good old-fashioned greed."

"Did the second man also speak of Nosaka's greed?" asked Shuko.

"*Hai.* But he had a personal story to tell me. The second man we will call John. John and I have practiced kendo together in Tokyo in the past, but we do not know one another outside of the *dojo.* He has read some of my writings on the sword. He agrees and disagrees, but this is his privilege. In the matter of *ken*, the sword, you Japanese are not easy to please. Anyway, John contacted Omura-san and asked to speak to me. However, I cannot reveal his name nor use his face in my film.

"John told me about Nosaka's bank, where he was once an executive.

309

He says the bank gathers business intelligence and washes money. John sees no harm in any of this. Like most Japanese, he considers knowledge important to Japan's survival."

Shuko said, "I do not understand. If John sees no harm in what Nosaka does, why then did he want to see you?"

"To tell me about his dead son. He blames Nosaka for the boy's death. The boy was an excellent fencer and a member of the Takeshi *dojo*. What attracted him to this club was the spirit of its fighters, their belief that Japan must again become a great military power."

"Did Nosaka tell him this?"

DiPalma nodded. "According to John, his son heard patriotic speeches from both Nosaka and Kenpachi. Everyone connected with the Takeshi kendo club is superpatriotic. Very far right. Which was fine with John's father. He felt the same way. Then sometime this year the boy told his father that he had joined a secret nationalistic group which would revive Japan and make it first among nations once more. Kenpachi was involved, the boy said. And Nosaka was putting up the money. Other than that, everything had to remain a secret. The boy had taken an oath in blood to reveal nothing."

"The Blood Oath League," said Shuko.

DiPalma loosened his tie and looked around for the tardy Ford Higashi. Shuko's Datsun had no air conditioning and the fumes from the traffic were stifling. He said, "At first, John was proud of his boy. This secret organization, whatever it was, seemed just the thing the country needed to get it back on course. Then came the killings. Suddenly John started to get nervous. Talking tough was one thing. Spilling other people's blood was another. But what could he do about it? He was scared of Nosaka and his own son was involved in whatever was going on. In the end John simply told himself to believe in Nosaka. Until his son died."

"When did this happen?" asked Shuko.

"Around the time Labouchere, the French businessman, was killed in Paris. The French police have an unclaimed body in their custody. A Japanese male. The head's missing and so are both hands. Neither the French nor Japanese police have been able to identify him. The boy, of course, is John's son. Since his death, the heart's gone out of John. He has retired, given up kendo and spends a lot of time saying prayers for the soul of his son."

"Did Nosaka contact his father?"

"*Hai*. The boy had told his father that the Takeshi fencing team was scheduled to give exhibitions in London and Brussels. From either city Paris is less than a hour's flight away. When the boy did not return from the tour, his father spoke to other members of the *dojo*. Their silence and press reports of the mutilated body confirmed his worst fears. Nosaka paid John a visit and forbade him to claim the body. Nosaka didn't say why. He didn't have to."

Shuko looked straight ahead. "And the father obeyed. Tell me, what is the religion of the dead boy's parents?"

"Shinto."

"They die each day that their son is denied the proper burial rites."

"*Hai.*" DiPalma stared at the Takeshi Building. That was the son's karma. Just as it was the karma of the dead Wakaba to lead DiPalma and Shuko to this building. On Wakaba's corpse they had found a passport stamped with his arrival from Hong Kong less that two hours before his death. And an airline ticket to Geneva the following day, where he was to join the Takeshi team for a fencing match. Information in the ticket envelope indicated that Geneva was the first stop on a six-city European exhibition tour by the Takeshi kendo club, Japan's best.

Like many Japanese corporations, Takeshi encouraged its employees to practice the martial arts in order to strengthen their spirit and make them better workers. Outsiders were not allowed to join the team or observe its practice sessions. This rule, however, did not apply to Kon Kenpachi.

DiPalma's talk with "John" had convinced him of two things: the Takeshi team, backed by Nosaka's money, was the Blood Oath League. And Kenpachi was a member. It hadn't taken Shuko three seconds to draw the same conclusion.

The bandages on Wakaba's forehead and hand, along with his passport and its Hong Kong exit stamp, had bothered DiPalma. The bodyguard should have been with Kenpachi. Instead he had left Hong Kong *after* his boss. Why? And those wounds. Deep gouges made by a sharp instrument. The more DiPalma thought about it, the more his curiosity grew. From Shuko's office DiPalma telephoned the Hong Kong police superintendent.

"Jenkins attempted to fight off his attacker," said the superintendent, "but obviously he wasn't quite good enough. He'd been gardening at the time. Tried to fight the bastard with a hand gardening tool. We still have it. Bits of blood and flesh on the steel end."

"What happened to Jenkins?"

"Tongue cut out. Blinded in his remaining eye. Spinal cord slashed several times, leaving him paralyzed waist-down for life. He's alive, but that's all to be said for him. He's living in hell."

When DiPalma hung up, he said to Shuko, "I told him you would send blood and tissue samples from Wakaba. My guess is Wakaba was acting for Kenpachi, who wanted revenge. Jenkins did kill Sakon Chiba."

"*Hai.* I will question Kenpachi about this and send a report on to Hong Kong. I must also question Kenpachi about Wakaba and what occurred with your son in the alley."

In Shuko's parked Datsun, DiPalma thought of Todd, now at the Tokyo police headquarters under the protection of Shuko's fellow officers. DiPalma had requested this favor; his excuse was that Wakaba's friends in the Takeshi kendo club might want revenge and try to harm the boy. That was a lie. An indispensable one but still a lie. Todd did not have to fear Wakaba's fencing companions. He had to fear Kenpachi.

To get his hands on Todd, Kenpachi had been willing to kill. That was why he had ordered Katharine's death.

I will not let you be *kaishaku* to Kenpachi. You will never violate his *seppuku.*

In the alley DiPalma had heard Wakaba make this threat. Jan had heard it but she didn't understand enough Japanese to get it. To her, his shouting had been the raving of a loonytune, nothing more. As for Shuko, he had been too far away to hear anything. He had been at the opposite end of the alley, recovering from the effects of a kick in the stomach.

DiPalma himself could hardly believe what he had heard, but he knew it was true. Every frightening word of it. It was true because Wakaba's last act on earth had been to point at Todd and call him Benkai. Benkai who had beheaded the first lord of Ikuba Castle four hundred years ago.

Shuko had remained silent. And when Jan asked DiPalma what it meant, he had ignored her and walked away with an unconscious Todd in his arms. Jan was now too close to Kenpachi for DiPalma to confide in.

How could he tell her or Shuko that his son was quite possibly a reincarnation of an ancient samurai warrior? Would they believe this warrior was alive in the body of an eleven-year-old boy? And about to take part in another *seppuku* within the walls of Ikuba Castle? Would anyone believe this story? Shuko might, but he would be obligated to report it to his superiors.

Kenpachi would deny it, then select another time to come after Todd. The film director already had too many advantages. Todd was drawn to him and he had Jan.

DiPalma had come to Tokyo to find evidence linking Nosaka to Katharine's murder. The evidence now pointed to Kenpachi, who would be more on guard than ever.

DiPalma saw no reason to tell Shuko of his conversation with Andy

Pazadian, a Tokyo DEA agent he had worked with on past drug cases. The conversation with Pazadian might prove offensive to the police captain.

In Pazadian's office the two Americans had begun by talking about Roger Tan.

"Looks like he's dead," said Pazadian, a dark and stocky Greek in his mid-forties with pointed ears. "No trace of him. Gun he signed out for was found in the apartment of a Geoffrey Laycock."

"I knew Laycock."

"So I hear. Gun was in the pocket of one of Laycock's dressing gowns. Looks like Laycock's apartment was Roger's last stop."

"Any rumors floating around Hong Kong on Roger?"

Pazadian straightened a paper clip and used it to dig wax out of an ear. "We hear things. None of it's good. Triad's supposed to have done him in. We think it was Ling Shen's Triad, the same clowns who were supposed to whack you. Roger's log says he made long distance calls here to Mystic, Connecticut, to a Jude Golden. His daughter's here in town doing a movie."

DiPalma nodded and waited for the rest. Pazadian wasn't as bad as Roger Tan, but he did like gossip.

"She a friend of yours?"

"Acquaintance would be more like it. What did Roger and Jude Golden talk about?"

"Roger's notes say they talked about Laycock's true ID. Turns out he was a prisoner of war in Hong Kong under another name. Speaking of names, guess who's name was also on Roger's desk?"

"I'll bite, who?"

"Mr. Zenzo Nosaka, who I hear you're in the process of checking out."

DiPalma said, "That's why I'm sitting here watching you scrape wax out of your ear." He told Pazadian about Nosaka's industrial-espionage network, its worldwide dirty tricks. He didn't mention Katharine, but he had a hunch Pazadian knew all about her.

Pazadian leaned back until the front legs of his chair were off the ground. "Industrial espionage is not, repeat, not a crime in this country. It's part of Japan's defense against Russia and China, its two biggest potential enemies. That's why it doesn't do you any good to knock this kind of spying to a Japanese. To them knowledge is power and all knowledge improves their country's chances of survival. Fucking Japanese are obsessed with knowledge. Any kind of knowledge. Military intelligence or stealing silicon chips, it's all the same to them. Japan can't survive without either one. You and I may think something's wrong, but we don't count."

DiPalma said. "Nosaka's no one-hundred-percent patriot. He's out for himself. Japan gets what's left over."

"All well and good, paisan. But you ain't gonna get a living soul in Japan to dump on the guy. Look, Japan lost the war, remember? They don't like losing. So to make sure it doesn't happen again, they're in the spy business up to their eyeballs. Especially when it concerns Russia, who ain't but a hop, skip and a jump away. Fact is, Japan's paranoid about Russia, which has a lot more nuclear bombs and a helluva lot bigger army than she does. There's a twenty-four-hour underwater watch off the Japanese coast for Russian subs and who's to say the Japs are wrong? They also keep an eye on China and the Chinese spies in this country. Lots of them around."

"So you're saying that espionage isn't a dirty word in Japan."

"Not today, not yesterday, not tomorrow. Russia and China are tough-ass neighbors. Wouldn't you keep an eye on those fuckers if they were on your doorstep? Look, by law Japan can't have a large army, nuclear weapons, a big navy, none of that shit. Losing the war was a nightmare to these people. They had never been conquered, never been occupied, never had to surrender as a nation."

"Surrender is not in the Japanese vocabulary," said DiPalma.

"Not until Hiroshima and Nagasaki put it there. Anyway, with no national defense to speak of, the best protection they can have is espionage. Espionage equals national security. You don't believe me? I'm telling you it does. That's why the Japanese government is behind it, behind all of it. They don't tell guys like Nosaka to go out and do piggy things, but you can bet your ass they don't take it quite as hard as we would if Nosaka gets caught with his hand in our cookie jar."

"So that's why Japan has so many research institutes, think tanks, data bureaus, trade councils, business groups. All of them into industrial espionage, and if they come across anything the Japanese military might be interested in, they just pass it along."

"Hooray for the Italians. Now you want to hear what we get out of it?"

"We?"

"My country 'tis of thee."

DiPalma said, "Let me guess. Free espionage."

Pazadian pointed the wax-coated end of the paper clip at him. "You probably know the difference between pussy and parsley, you're so smart."

"Nobody eats parsley."

Pazadian grinned. "My wife thinks that joke is sexist. I fucking love

314

it. Anyway, you're right the first time. We get a lot of information we might not come up with otherwise. Like information on drug smuggling in this part of the world. Like information on Arab terrorists and Latin American guerillas being trained in North Korea. Like stuff on various arms deals, gold smuggling. And we get a lot of shit on Russia and China. All from them spy-happy little Nips. It goes without saying you and me never had this little talk."

The little talk that DiPalma and Pazadian never had also revealed that ninety percent of all Japan's spying went to boost the economy. Gathering military intelligence was an afterthought. Information poured into the country from every corner of the globe on new technology, changing markets, trade unions, consumer demands, current and future research, ecology and politics.

How did the Japanese do it? DiPalma wondered.

"The most curious people on God's earth, bar none," said Pazadian. "They want to know everything and I do mean everything. And when they know it, first thing they do is sit down and improve on it. Show them a better way and they'll take it. None of this Let's do it this way, 'cause that's how it's been done all these years. Shit like that you get in the West, not here. And they work hard. I mean to the point of pissing blood. Always, always open to new ideas and they know how to read intelligence, how to use it. Patient like you wouldn't believe and they don't miss a fucking thing, no matter how small."

Pazadian laughed. "You know what's funny? They spend one-tenth of what we do on research and development. One-fucking tenth. And look how it pays off."

DiPalma said, "Military or industrial espionage. All the same, you say."

"Right you are. Japanese government treats it as one and the same. You got a lot of government agencies promoting this intelligence gathering. Ah, you're writing this down I see. Pearls of wisdom from my ruby lips."

"Not quite. Go on."

"Government agencies. Yeah, well there's M.I.T.I. Ministry of International Trade and Industry. Very heavy duty and they can play tough. They are not backed by the government. They *are* the government. Always sending research teams around the world, attending conferences, going over stuff that's public information, asking questions. They've got scientists and laboratories for them to work in and lotsa dudes who just sit around all day and analyze shit. That's M.I.T.I."

DiPalma looked up from his notes. "I hear there're schools here that train people to be corporate spies."

"You're telling me. How about more than four hundred detective agencies in Tokyo alone that stay in business by ripping off other people's business secrets. This does not include agencies in Osaka, Kyoto, Yokohama and God knows where else. Intelligence gathering of one kind or another is just about the most important thing you can do in Japan."

"And you say there's no law against it."

Pazadian waved him away. "None at all. They got a law that says if it involves copping other guys' patents, that's a no-no, though I wouldn't want to be hanging by my dork from a very tall building while they brought some guy up on this charge. If it's not copyrighted, Japanese law says it's up for grabs. Coke dealer once told me, 'If it's worth having, it's worth stealing.'"

"And it's official, I mean the government—"

"Will you come off this shit about the government? Hey, like they don't care. The end justifies the means. Get there any way you can and we'll worry about the details later. Only the Japanese government doesn't worry. The guys who set up this operation in the first place, this research bureau so called, were top World War II spies. Patriots. You get where I'm coming from? They were patriots."

DiPalma closed his notebook. "So Nosaka's a hero."

Pazadian turned his hands palms up. "Nobody says you got to sit on the curb and clap as he goes by. That's just how it is. Just as I think it's gonna be a cold day in hell before anybody accepts what you told me earlier. It ain't gonna be what the Japanese *believe* about Nosaka killing people. It's gonna be what they *do* about it."

He leaned forward in his chair. "Winners don't get asked if they're telling the truth. And little old Nosaka is a winner, a very big winner."

*   *   *

IN the front seat of Shuko's Datsun, DiPalma turned around to look at Ford Higashi. The young cameraman had been late; he had gone to see a screening of *The Searchers*. This was the fifty-fourth time Higashi had seen the John Ford western, a favorite of American directors like Francis Ford Coppola, George Lucas and Steven Spielberg, themselves current favorites among Japanese film students. *The Sea Hawk* theme was still blasting on Higashi's earphones.

Higashi shot the Takeshi Building from top to bottom, shot people entering and leaving, shot the guards making scrupulous ID checks, shot limousines and Rolls-Royces pulling up and company executives getting out. When DiPalma returned to New York he would write copy to go with this footage. That copy would be more potent if he could only get his hands on the Hansard files now in Jude Golden's possession.

"*Daimyos* of the twentieth century," said Higashi in English, the camera still pressed to his eye. "Modern warlords, man. Groovy guys."

"Who?" asked DiPalma. Shuko, whose English was barely passable, turned to look at Higashi.

"Talking about cats like Nosaka," said Higashi. "Dudes like him have money, power, cars, women. Anything they want. Guys who work for him are like his samurai, dig?"

DiPalma quickly translated for Shuko, who nodded and said in Japanese, "Such samurai now conquer the world with attaché cases and expense accounts instead of swords."

Higashi nodded and continued to film the Alligator. "That's why you got all them Datsuns, Sonys and Hondas in the States." He took his eye away from the camera to look at DiPalma. "Bet you didn't know that the first Tokyo businessman, I mean heavy businessman, was a samurai."

DiPalma smiled and translated for Shuko, who said, "*Hai*. The oldest department store in Tokyo, Mitsukoshi, was founded almost five hundred years ago by a samurai named Hachirobei. One day he found himself destitute, so he pawned his *dai-sho*, his two swords. He also sold candles, shoes, women's clothing, ribbons. Other samurai insulted him, spat on him, until they saw how much money he made. Hachirobei's family crest is today still used by the corporation which owns that store and other businesses."

DiPalma said, "'John' told me that Japanese business does not use terms like manager, assistant manager, managing director like we do in the West. What they use are the same ranks that samurai armies used a thousand years ago. It amounts to a military chain of command in modern business."

"Efficient," snapped Shuko. He said the word with pride. "Insures discipline. Sometimes a certain businessman can be a *Sa-konye* or *U-konye*. General of the left or the right. Also captain of the left or the right. And other military ranks, of course. A simple system, yes, but an efficient one."

"Right on, my man," said Ford Higashi. Then, "Hey, hey. Wow. Numero uno himself."

He looked at DiPalma. "The *daimyo*."

DiPalma swiveled in his seat to face the Takeshi building.

Nosaka. Stepping from a limousine. A little man in a derby, dark suit, bow tie and walking stick. He stopped to say something to the chauffeur who had opened the door, then walked toward the entrance. Two massive bodyguards dwarfed him.

The guards cleared the way, opening doors, shooing people to one side. Some stepped aside without being asked and stared at Nosaka as though he were royalty. As though he were a *daimyo*. And then he disappeared inside.

"Wow," said Ford Higashi, collapsing back against the seat. "Far-fucking-out."

DiPalma had to fight from being impressed. It was in Nosaka's bearing, the way he walked, the way the guards and pedestrians had reacted to him. He was Japan's exotic past come to life. The empire builder. Surrounded not by human beings but by instruments to be discarded when they had served their purpose.

DiPalma looked at Shuko. The police captain, eyes narrowed and hands gripping the steering wheel, stared straight ahead. And also into the past. Not at Japan's past brought to life in a modern warlord, but at the man who had murdered his mother, his father and other members of his family. And who could not be touched because of a vow made to the emperor forty years ago.

*   *   *

FROM a fourth floor window facing the street, Nosaka and a male secretary watched the Datsun pull away from the curb and enter the heavy flow of traffic. The secretary held a telephone receiver in his ear and said in English, "Yes, Mr. Turney, I have passed on your request for an interview to Mr. Nosaka and he will consider it. He is most grateful for your call regarding your colleague, Mr. DiPalma. No, we have no statement to make at this time. Such things are handled through our public-relations counselor. His name?"

He looked at Nosaka, who nodded once.

"His name is Mr. Yoshinaka. His address—no. We prefer that all requests for interviews be submitted in writing, along with a list of prospective questions. Mr. Yoshinaka does not accept telephone requests for interviews."

After the secretary had hung up, he and Nosaka stood side by side and watched the Datsun until it disappeared into the shimmering heat waves rising above the frantic traffic in the mall.

318

26

NOSAKA LOOKED up from his desk and out into the walled garden behind his villa. The sliding door to his weapons room was open, and an aroma came from a pine branch burning in a Korean stone lantern used as a censer. Near the lantern a servant tossed chunks of bread into a pool filled with carp. Nosaka believed that the huge fish, which the Japanese prized for their courage and determination, brought him luck. They made him feel bold and victorious.

He rose and stood in the open doorway, admiring the dwarf bamboo trees, peonies and camellias now blood red in the setting sun. When the world threatened to overpower him, the garden was his retreat. Surrounded by its beauty, and stillness, all passions were forgotten and he found peace within himself. It was the one place on earth where he felt content, where he did not wish for more than he already had.

A hanging weight-driven pillar clock read 6:30 P.M. Kenpachi was thirty minutes late, not unusual for him. When would he learn that men counted up the faults of those who kept them waiting. Since possessing the Muramasa blade the film director had grown more arrogant, even disrespectful. Nosaka found Kenpachi's vanity increasingly difficult to stomach. Kenpachi was convinced that his *seppuku* would bring Japan to a standstill, that it would trigger an outburst of patriotism not seen since World War II.

319

"The emperor will be moved by my death," said Kenpachi. "He will declare me a hero. I will be buried in Yasukuni Shrine with other warriors who have given their lives for Japan."

Such arrogance made him charismatic to the Blood Oath League. Convinced that he was sincere in wanting to die for the glory of the nation, the members became even more willing to risk their lives for him and Japan. Nosaka, however, found Kenpachi none the wiser.

Nosaka returned to his desk to resume examining a saddle which, if purchased, would cost him more than most of the weapons in his collection. There were other saddles among the swords, daggers, armor, spears and bows in his weapons room. But none equaled the one he now peered at through a magnifying glass.

It was carved from dark wood and covered with rich gold lacquer. The pommel was ivory with silver inlay and there was blue velvet padding which prevented a horse from being chafed. The stirrups, shaped like half shoes with turned-up toes, were made of silver with gold inlay. More than four hundred years old, the saddle represented matchless craftsmanship and incomparable beauty. It was one of only three made by the great Muramasa.

Like his swords, spears and knives, Muramasa's saddles were also said to be possessed by the evil which haunted the brilliant but unbalanced swordsmith. During the year an antique dealer had owned it, his wife had been injured in a severe fall, he had suffered a serious automobile accident and a beloved granddaughter had died in her sleep of unknown causes. In a quivering voice, the dealer had confessed that, to him, the Muramasa curse was all too real.

Nosaka did not fear the evil in a Muramasa weapon nor in the exquisite saddle. Nosaka was samurai and he feared nothing. Fear was a source of superstition, born of uncertainty and he had never been less than absolutely certain of his own worth. He was immune to any form of dread or panic. His arms collection, much of which he had donated to Tokyo museums, contained many Muramasa weapons. Over the years they had given him the forcefulness and vitality which had made him one of Japan's wealthiest men. On his death the remainder of his collection would be distributed among the country's museums.

Meanwhile he kept the choicest weapons in his hilltop villa. If he purchased the saddle he would keep it here too. He stroked its pommel, then leaned closer with the magnifying glass to focus on the left stirrup. *Hai.* He recognized the workmanship and became excited. Such intricate, serpentine use of silver, such complex, mystifying patterns no other sword maker had been able to duplicate. Muramasa. Nosaka's heart began to

320

beat faster. He must have this saddle. He stroked it with a shaking hand. Kenpachi was forgotten. With this saddle Nosaka would now own at least one sample of every creation by Muramasa. With this saddle the cycle of collection was complete.

Kenpachi arrived ten minutes later dressed in a white Yves St. Laurent suit and sunglasses with a tiny diamond in the corner of one lens. He made no apology for being late, nor did he indicate a wish to change into a kimono, as was his usual custom when visiting Nosaka. When he bowed to the older man, it was so casual as to be disrespectful. Nosaka's offer of tea was refused.

They sat on the matted floor on opposite sides of a low table. A restless Kenpachi fingered the viewfinder hanging from his neck and looked past Nosaka into the garden. It was clear that he felt himself now being summoned to Nosaka's home.

As Kenpachi chewed a thumbnail, Nosaka pointed to a small tape recorder on the table. "They met in the park near Toshogu Shrine," he said. "One of my operatives, a woman pretending to be a mother, brought her baby to the park for fresh air and sat three benches away. She taped their conversation with this machine. Its microphone is powerful enough to pick up any conversation two hundred yards away. With astounding clarity, as you will hear."

He pressed a button on the machine then slid the recorder toward Kenpachi.

*   *   *

Sounds. Schoolboys playing baseball. Airplane overhead. Barking dogs. Squealing girls awkwardly attempting to maintain their balance on roller skates. A cassette radio comes into range and Elton John singing "Rocket Man" drowns out all other sounds.

"—believe the walls have ears," said Frank DiPalma. "Especially in Tokyo."

"You said something about maybe being followed. Are you serious?" It was Jan Golden.

"I'm kicking over rocks and peeking into Nosaka's life. Damn right, I'm serious. He's the twentieth-century spymaster. Hid-

eyoshi come to life. He's a fool if he isn't spying on me. In his place I'd do the same. I don't mean to rush you, but I have to get to the police station and pick up Todd. We're having dinner with Shuko. It's our last night in Tokyo. Tomorrow we leave for New York."

Jan Golden said, "I didn't know. Well, I guess it's a good thing I called you. Especially since I'm not too sure you would have called me. I have to ask you something about Kon."

"You're asking me about Kon Kenpachi? Christ, the Japanese are right. They say the unexpected often happens."

"Frank, this picture's a bear. A ball breaker. We've got between three and four weeks' shooting left and I need my director. Trouble is he's spending so much time down at the police station, my crew calls him Monopoly Man. You know, do not pass go, do not collect two hundred dollars—"

DiPalma chuckled. "Go directly to jail. Funny."

"Kon says you're behind it. He says you're doing a number on him through Captain Shuko."

"What do you say?"

"Didn't make sense to me, a foreigner coming to Japan and ordering the police around."

"Shuko's a good cop. Nobody tells him what to do. He's on Kenpachi's case for a reason. Wakaba tried to kill my son. And he was also tied into something very nasty. That's why Shuko's talking to Kenpachi."

"Does this nasty thing involve Kon?"

"Let's hear why you want to see me."

"Around noon today, when Kon still hadn't showed up, I dropped in at Ikuba Castle. I couldn't get him on the phone and anyway I felt it was time he and I had things out in the open. In private. At the castle I saw something I don't think I was supposed to see. I saw Kon naked, kneeling in the courtyard on a red rug—"

"In the center of four fires. Noon, you say. Makes sense. The ritual—"

"What ritual?"

Silence.

DiPalma said, "You saw a Buddhist austerity ritual, something Kenpachi probably learned from his mother, who was a Buddhist priestess. And you're right, you weren't supposed to see it. Kenpachi was making a deal with the gods for his next life."

"His what?"

"First he punishes himself. Fires, hot sun. He has to suffer. It's a trade-off. He suffers in exchange for what he hopes the gods will give him in his next life. It's literally a matter of life and death."

Jan said, "You're telling me Kon plans to die soon? That's ridiculous. The man has everything to live for. He wouldn't kill himself. That much I know."

Silence.

Then she said, "I need him, Frank."

"Everybody invents their own dreams, what can I tell you."

"I'm in trouble, aren't I? With Kon, I mean. That's why you've avoided me the past few days. That's why you brushed me off in the alley the night Wakaba was killed. You know something about Kon and you don't want to tell me."

Silence.

"Look, I can keep a secret," she said. "If you want me to say nothing, I'll say nothing. Just tell me. Please."

DiPalma said, "If I ask you to walk away from Kenpachi, leave Tokyo and come back to New York with Todd and me, would you do it?"

"Walking away from the movie?"

"And you'd never do that, right? Nobody walks away from a movie. Jesus, why am I wasting my time? You've spent your life doing exactly what you wanted. Just push the right or wrong of it aside and keep on trucking."

Jan said, "I'm scared to death of one thing. And that's watching people only half as good as me come along and succeed in this business after I've failed. Look, if suffering were the answer, the world would have been a better place years ago. So don't ask me to suffer any more than I have to. A month. That's all I need. Maybe less, if Kon can get his act together. Just let me get the film in the can."

She wept. "Frank, I'm so close, so close. I can't walk away.

Not now. Ask me anything else."

"That's the only thing worth asking. You don't want me to understand, you want me to approve. Wakaba might have smoked you if he'd had the chance. And remember Kenpachi's fag friend, Sakon Chiba?"

"The drag queen who tried to kill you in Hong Kong."

"He managed to kill a cop before he got smoked by another cop named Jenkins. Jenkins isn't doing so well now after Wakaba paid him a visit. Did you notice Wakaba stayed behind in Hong Kong when the rest of your company left?"

Jan said, "Kenpachi told me Wakaba had to deliver a message for him."

"He definitely delivered. He cut out Jenkins's tongue."

"Are you serious?"

"He also gouged out Jenkins's one remaining eye, then cut his spinal cord. Jenkins is now paralyzed for life. And blind. And speechless."

"I think I'm going to be sick."

DiPalma said, "There's no doubt Wakaba did it. His blood and tissue samples match those found on a garden tool near Jenkins. Wakaba was also a member of the same Blood Oath League which killed Sally Verna, Duncan Ivy and plans to kill your father."

"How do you know this?"

"An airline ticket to Geneva was found on Wakaba's body, along with a schedule of kendo matches to be played in three European cities by the Takeshi kendo team. Nosaka's team. And the team Wakaba worked out with. At the same time the Takeshi team was putting on a show in Geneva, a Japanese businessman was killed in Zurich. The two cities aren't that far apart. There's a lot of violence around the late Mr. Wakaba and his friends. I think that's reason enough to request Kenpachi's presence down at police headquarters. Wakaba was his boy, remember?"

A nervous Jan said, "Slow down. You're saying that Kenpachi's involved in the Blood Oath League. What about Nosaka?"

"He's still on my list. Kenpachi and Wakaba both practiced

kendo on Nosaka's team, the Takeshi team which is connected to the Blood Oath League. I think Kenpachi owes a few people some explanations. Jan, your father's in danger. And if you keep hanging around—"

"You're pushing me, damn you! I don't want to hear any more. I can't listen to you or anybody else. I have to do what I think is right. That's it. That's it."

*   *   *

NOSAKA switched off the machine. Interesting, he thought. Kenpachi had lost his arrogance. He stared at the machine and looked worried.

Nosaka said, "This was recorded less than two hours ago. Miss Golden ran weeping away from Mr. DiPalma, who did not follow her. As you can see, Mr. DiPalma is aware of your plan to commit *seppuku*. His awareness of the austerity ritual, his leaving the boy at the police station as he goes prying into my life. He knows. And I am sure you noticed how the woman led DiPalma closer to the Blood Oath League. Closer to us."

Kenpachi, frowning, hugged himself. "She knows nothing. How—"

"Think upon what you have just heard. Analyze what was said and not said. Miss Golden caused Wakaba's death. She interfered with his plans to kill the boy, then led him to the alley where he died. Wakaba in death is proving to be something of a liability. Why did you not ask my permission before revenging yourself on the policeman Jenkins?"

Kenpachi dropped his eyes.

"Insolence ill becomes a stupid man," said Nosaka. "Wakaba's wounds at the hands of Jenkins triggered DiPalma's inquiry. Suspicion causes a man to store facts and bits of information in his brain. DiPalma, a former policeman, easily becomes more suspicious than most. Especially when the woman reports to him what she has witnessed in your courtyard. What was your explanation to her of what you were doing?"

"I told her it was a religious ceremony for the soul of Wakaba."

"Obviously she does not trust you or she would not seek out DiPalma. He is strongly attracted to her. Even now he attempts to warn her. But she rejects his warnings. She is ambitious." Nosaka smiled. "He does not want her to die as did the other two women he loved. He is willing to risk his life for her. That is why the two of them are dangerous. Do you

325

think you can make the film without her?"

Kenpachi shook his head. "No, *sensei*. All that is necessary for the film comes from her. Money, actors, the important American studio. I need her."

"And she needs you. Still, I feel DiPalma will find a way to use her against you. He can ruin your plans for a glorious death and do harm to me."

Nosaka rose gracefully from the floor and turned his back to Kenpachi to look out at the garden. The light of a setting sun bronzed the businessman's small, catlike face, making it appear more timeless than old, more infinite than human. "Two men, one woman," he said. "Both cannot have her."

He looked over his shoulder at Kenpachi. "I will tell you why I have not harmed DiPalma while he is here in Japan. He is going to bring me the Hansard files. Security is very strong around Jude Golden and too many people know about the Blood Oath League—DiPalma, Shuko, Jude Golden, his daughter. I would rather not use the league now. You will convince the daughter that the files in her father's possession will be more effective if given to DiPalma who, after all, is a journalist."

Nosaka turned back to face the sun. "After we have taken the files from DiPalma, then you may kill him. In America. It is best that it be done as far away from us as possible. Since you now possess the power, I suggest that you have the son kill the father. The *Iki-ryō* came to you in Hong Kong where it killed Laycock. Now have it kill DiPalma."

Nosaka walked to a nearby wall, removed a *tessen* and began to fan himself. It was the same war fan that Yoshiko had used to kill a Hong Kong policeman.

27

DAWN, GRAY and muggy over Ikuba Castle. On the horizon a rising sun spread its fiery reflection across the top of the blue hills and the muddy Sumida River, now rain swollen and overflowing its banks. On all sides of the castle rice fields, roads, marshes and plains were black with Hideyoshi's cavalry and foot soldiers, an army made confident by an unbroken string of victories.

Like the ninja who had preceded him, Hideyoshi, the Crowned Monkey, had used rain and darkness to "steal in." Ikuba Castle was surrounded, its garrison outnumbered and cut off from any escape.

In the daimyo's quarters Todd, who was Benkai, watched his lord prepare for seppuku. Stepping onto a thick red rug enclosed on three sides by a white screen, the lord dropped to his knees, pulled the kimono off his shoulders and bared his chest. Todd nodded at a steel-helmeted guard wearing leather armor, who stepped forward and removed the lord's sandals.

The averted eyes of the guards told Todd how harrowing was his own appearance. There was the arrow in his left eye; his

327

kimono was soaked with his own blood, and the woman's head hung from his sash by her long black hair. He was a terrifying sight, one to be feared more than the attacking ninja or Hideyoshi. Fear had robbed the castle guards of all judgment. Nothing mattered except to obey Todd, who was Benkai.

Smoke floated from beneath the barred oak door to the daimyo's quarters. And smoke drifted down from the gilded ceiling, from the burning rooms above the daimyo's quarters and through the open window above the courtyard; the ninja were attacking throughout the compound. The smoke did not hide the dead ninja destroyed by Todd when they had attempted to enter the daimyo's quarters through the secret tunnel.

Other ninja kept trying to reach the daimyo from in the tunnel and the hall, where the nightingale floors "squeaked" under their sandals.

Suddenly the hall became silent and then came the sound of racing men and the door shook under a roar from many throats and from the thrust of a battering ram.

The daimyo was doomed. He could retain his honor and avoid the shame of capture and disgrace only through seppuku.

Todd, who was Benkai, said, "A samurai must choose between disgrace and glory. Seppuku is the way to glory."

"Hai!" shouted the guards.

Todd looked at his lord, who smiled at him and offered him a katana, a long sword with a white cloth around its jeweled hilt. White, the color of death.

With both hands clasped tightly around the hilt, Todd lifted the sword and gazed into the dazzling light which enshrouded its razor-edged blade.

Bowing his head, the daimyo waited.

Todd looked at him, waited, then swiftly brought the blade down on Kenpachi's neck.

*   *   *

NEW YORK

Todd opened his eyes. He was terrified, breathless, unable to see. He fought for air, breathing deeply through his mouth. Then light attacked his eyes and he raised his arms against the harsh brightness. *Did the brightness mean that the sword was near him once more?* He feared the sword. He wanted to hide before it found him. Before he had to kill.

"Easy," said DiPalma, who had turned on the light in Todd's room. "Another bad dream. Just relax. You're awake now. Just take it easy."

He crossed the room and sat down on the bed. He had almost said *Nothing to worry about. Those things are far behind you.* But he knew better and so did Todd. This was not the first nightmare the boy had suffered during his ten days in New York.

They were in DiPalma's comfortable Brooklyn Heights flat, among beautiful old brownstones and tree-lined streets overlooking New York Harbor and the southern tip of Manhattan. DiPalma had been born and raised in Brooklyn, had married and been a cop here. He preferred Brooklyn to Manhattan; it was more peaceful, less pretentious.

Todd said, "Perhaps it is better to accept what will happen."

No games, thought DiPalma. Not with this kid. He said, "Kenpachi?"

"For the first time in my dreams I held the sword. And I killed him. I was the *kaishaku*. I was Benkai. It was so real. The smells, the screams of dying men, the wounded horses. And the dampness from the rain, the perfume from the giant camellias."

DiPalma nodded, silently urging him on. "I saw armor, pieces of leather and iron held together by colored silk cords. I saw riderless horses in the courtyard with blood on their wooden saddles. Not horses. Ponies. *Hai.* Small, ugly ponies. I saw a general lying in the courtyard beneath the *daimyo*'s window. He wore a *kabuto*, an iron helmet with horns on top. He had been carrying a *saihai*, a baton with blue paper streamers. The *ninja* had killed him in the first attack."

Sweat stood out on Todd's forehead. "I am being told to kill a second time."

DiPalma playfully rubbed his son's head. "Dreams are only true while they last. You're awake now. Sleep can't hold you forever. Sooner or later it has to let you go."

"It was so real tonight," said Todd. "For the first time I knew for certain that I was Benkai. I was myself, but I was him as well."

There must be something more I can do for him, thought DiPalma. *Something*.

He said, "How'd you like to go for a walk?"

Todd looked at the small clock on the night table. "Now?" It was 3:35 A.M.

DiPalma shrugged. "Why not? Might relax us both." He didn't add that it would also prevent Todd from doing what he had done in Hong Kong and Tokyo—leaving the apartment at night alone.

Todd grinned. He looked like a boy again. "I'd like that. I would enjoy that immensely. The night can be peaceful, you know. If it's not too much trouble, may we have some ice cream?"

"Now that's going to take some doing this hour of the morning, but we'll try. Give me a few minutes to throw on some clothes and we're on our way."

In his bedroom, where a balcony offered a stunning view of the Manhattan skyline, DiPalma stopped dressing to look at his cane, laid across the arms of a stuffed chair. An excellent weapon. But he thought about the .38 Smith & Wesson he was still licensed to carry. What was Kenpachi waiting for? Why hadn't he tried to take Todd away from DiPalma in New York? Why hadn't the Blood Oath League tried to kill him?

In his closet he rummaged around for a good pair of walking shoes. He didn't own jogging shoes or sneakers for the same reason he didn't own a single pair of jeans. He hated uniforms. Moccasins were just as comfortable and more stylish. Especially if they were handmade in Milan. He selected a brown pair and sat down to put them on.

Ten days ago, he had worn these shoes to his first network meeting since returning from Japan. At DiPalma's request a handful of network brass had sat in on the meeting, which had included his investigative team, producer, editor and the station manager. In a conference room overlooking Sixth Avenue, DiPalma had held his audience spellbound. He began with an explanation of why he had gone to Hong Kong and ended with a rundown on Nosaka's industrial-espionage network. He recounted the attempt on his life, the story of the Blood Oath League, of the file that could bring criminal charges against Nosaka.

He told them about Katharine and Todd.

But he said nothing about Todd's nightmares or that the boy might be the reincarnation of a four-hundred-year-old samurai. Or that he had killed a man. He mentioned Jude Golden, but said nothing about Jan. Or Kenpachi's planned *seppuku*.

When he finished, the room was silent.

Then Raffaela, his chief researcher said, "Do you think this Blood Oath League or Kon Kenpachi will still try and kill you?"

"Yes."

"Because of the file?"

DiPalma nodded. "I think everyone here knows about Sally Verna and Duncan Ivy. That should give you an idea of just how the Blood Oath League plays the game. Which is why I'm the only one who's to go after those files or who's to contact Jude Golden. I want that understood."

A vice-president said, "Didn't you forget to mention that Jude Golden is Jan Golden's father?" He threw out the question as if to say "Gotcha."

DiPalma looked at him until even the men around the vice-president began to shift uncomfortably. When the vice-president turned his face toward the ceiling, DiPalma rasped, "I didn't forget. I *don't* forget."

He looked around the table. "My team's been on this thing the past three weeks. I'd like the rest of you to hear what we've come up with. I'd appreciate it, however, if you'd hear us out before asking questions."

"Question before we start," said another vice-president, looking down at his manicured nails. "Will you be on the air while you're preparing this one? When you were away we didn't get our usual numbers in your time period. Compliment to you, of course. But we prefer to be on top looking down, instead of on the ground and staring up at someone else's ass."

DiPalma said, "I'll be on the air tonight. That's what you're paying me for."

The vice-president forced a smile. "No offense, Frank. We need you, that's all. Mind telling us what we can expect?"

"Something we were putting together before I left for Hong Kong. Piece on a teenage dope dealer."

The vice-president reached for a pencil and began to make small interlocking circles on a blank pad. He kept his eye on the pencil. "Teen age dope dealer. You've done one or two of these before, haven't you, Frank?" A quick smile at the pencil. "No offense."

"This dealer's seventeen and a Brazilian countess. She owns a penthouse in an East Side building full of rich Europeans and South Americans. Her drugs come into the country by diplomatic pouch and she only sells to the foreign jet-setters she meets at private clubs. She's been on the cover of Vogue and Harper's Bazaar, she's turned down two movie contracts and she clears over a million a year dealing. Her family's wealthy and she doesn't need the money. She does it for kicks, for the power. I'd say she's different from other teenage dealers I've done, wouldn't you?"

331

Those around the "suit" who had asked the question looked at him, then turned away. Someone said, "I think we got our numbers back. Welcome home, Frank."

Rafaella said, "We have her on film shooting a 'speedball'. That's coke and heroin combined. She's one of the most beautiful women I've ever seen in my life. And totally crazy. Completely out of her tree."

Someone else said, "She sounds fascinating. How did you happen to get her?"

DiPalma looked down at the table. That was the suits for you. Either at your throat or at your feet. "Let's get back to Nosaka and the Blood Oath League. We have a few things we'd like you to listen to. We'll try and make it as brief as we can because I have some film I'd like you to see."

Marshall Harris, DiPalma's producer, joined the team in presenting the facts collected on Nosaka's relations with congressmen, lobbyists, businessmen, journalists, and how he had used them to build an industrial empire. Newspaper clips told of past arrests of Nosaka's industrial spies in America and abroad. Each time the spies had pleaded guilty, avoiding a trial and further publicity. Fines had been imposed, but no one had gone to jail.

Then it was DiPalma's turn. He explained the role of the Japanese government in backing industrial espionage. He reported on Nosaka's role as a war criminal, how America had used him as a cold-war spy, how Nosaka had organized his bank as an espionage network. Then DiPalma showed film footage of Nosaka's corporate headquarters, factories, businesses and home. He showed them film clips of the Tokyo research bureaus, trade-commission headquarters, detective agencies and business institutes specializing in industrial espionage, many of them with government sanction and support.

There were interviews with "Joe" and "John." And footage of a Japanese management school for business trainees. "Nosaka has a secret interest in this school," said DiPalma. "As you can see, it's hidden in a wood north of Tokyo. Very private, very secluded. What the school does is turn Japanese businessmen and women into warriors. Twentieth-century samurai dedicated to keeping profits high and cutting costs to the bone. The training is brutal, a marine boot camp for executives who want to get ahead. They train in everything from English to the martial arts, to penmanship, speed-reading, positive thinking and how to get the most out of the people working under you.

"Japanese companies spend a lot of money to send their people here. Courses run ten days or two and a half weeks. The only thing you learn is how to make your company rich. You do that by letting the instructors humiliate you until you learn to obey without questioning. Either you pass the course or, in most cases, you lose your job. Give you an idea of how tough it is. Trainees sign insurance forms in case of accidents. And there are accidents.

"Everybody's tested twice a day. Builds character, they say. Food is putrid. Try doing a fifteen-mile forced march on a bitter rice soup and a potato. Anybody here want to put his or her career on the line with a seventeen-day stay in a joint like this?"

Jokes were made but they were all clearly impressed. Then the lawyers had their say. Like all cops DiPalma had no love for lawyers. He had spent enough time in courtrooms watching them distort and delay and fuck up the judicial system until it had become nothing more than their private money-making machine. How many times had DiPalma seen a case postponed because a lawyer was awaiting the arrival of "Mr. Green," a very important witness. Meaning the lawyer hadn't been paid and until he was there wasn't going to be any goddamn trial.

In the conference room, the lawyer who gave DiPalma the most trouble over the Nosaka story was a man named Kenner. He was the youngest network legal gun and therefore had the most to prove. Even though it was the last week in July, he wore a three-piece suit. Fingering a gold sovereign on his watch chain Kenner said, "Before we label this a go, I want to make sure we're not shooting ourselves in the foot. Especially with the big names involved. Nosaka, Kenpachi. Heavies. With all due respect, Frank, while you're saying this thing can fly, my job is to make sure it doesn't fly up and hit us in the face. Still, what I've seen and heard here is mucho effective. Mucho. Up to a point, that is."

He hooked his thumbs in his vest pockets. "Would you like to know what would soothe my troubled breast, Frank?"

He waited.

DiPalma didn't look up from the table.

Kenner cleared his throat and said, "I'd greenlight this sucker if we could do a criminal number on Nosaka which would stick. Get where I'm coming from? We need a jockstrap, Frank. Something to give it support."

DiPalma said, "The Hansard files support it. All the dirty tricks are spelled out there. Everything about the money, who got it and why."

"What about the Blood Oath League?"

"It's in there."

Kenner threw up his hands. "My point, you see. Corroboration. That's our jockstrap. Those files. If we're going to take on Congress and retired

333

generals and maybe the CIA, we need a nice big pile of rocks to throw at them. Libel suits are hard on the blood pressure, Frank. Lay those files on us. If they're top shelf, state of the art, then it's green light."

*　　*　　*

IN his bedroom DiPalma unscrewed the top of a vacuum cleaner, then reached inside and pulled out the .38 in its ankle holster. A pair of handcuffs dangled between the trigger and the guard, making it impossible to fire the weapon. DiPalma took out his key ring, found the tiny key he was looking for and unlocked the cuffs. If the Blood Oath League decided to make a move while he and Todd were taking their early morning stroll, the gun could make a difference.

Todd was quite the little fighter himself. At DiPalma's kendo club the boy had shown that his skill was out of the ordinary, that what he had done to Wakaba was no fluke. Watching his son fight had left DiPalma both proud and uneasy. No eleven-year-old should be that good. His skill was uncanny, superior to all but two or three fencers in the *dojo*.

When he appeared for practice everyone slowed down or stopped fencing to watch him. Todd practiced tirelessly and with such solemn demeanor that the *dojo* nicknamed him Little Buddha. The more DiPalma watched him, the more ambivalent he became. Todd was a remarkable fencer and he was DiPalma's son. But he was *too* good.

When DiPalma fenced with Todd he felt uncomfortable, nervous. But then the boy's aggressive style and strong spirit forced him to concentrate on the match. Where did Todd get his strength from? And where did he learn to handle a *shinai* with such incredible agility? DiPalma used his long reach to keep the boy at bay, but Todd managed to score on him twice, to the applause of the *dojo*. And DiPalma was considered one of the top three fighters in the club.

Only old Hidiya-*sensei* was totally able to control Todd. Hidiya, who had run the *dojo* for over twenty years, had trained in Japan's top fencing schools and university clubs; he had served as a police instructor and competed in tournaments held in the presence of the emperor. Hidiya had twice fought his way to the finals of the all-Japan championships. He had also trained championship fencers and instructed all over the world.

Watched by the entire *dojo*, Hidiya and Todd fought an electrifying match. The silent men and women watched intently, then broke into loud applause again and again as the man and the boy brought to life the finest movements of medieval Japanese swordplay. Hidiya alone scored, but several times he was forced back by Todd's aggressive tactics.

When the match was over the applause erupted and went on for a long time. Hidiya removed his helmet and did something he had not done in a long time. He smiled. He looked at Todd as though seeing him for the first time. The applause, the cheers and whistles drowned out his words to Todd and the boy's reply. DiPalma, however, knew Hidiya did not consider this a routine match.

Hidiya said to DiPalma, "Your son speaks excellent Japanese. Whoever taught him also taught him a bit of old Japanese, words that are not used in daily conversation. They date from many, many years ago, from a form of Japanese which is not spoken anymore. One can easily see that he has practiced the sword in past lives."

DiPalma nodded and said nothing. He did not trust himself to speak. Benkai, Wakaba had said. Did men tell the truth when they knew they were dying?

DiPalma sat in the stuffed chair and took off a moccasin. He had almost fastened the wide leather strap containing the holstered gun around his ankle when Todd said, "You will not need that."

DiPalma looked up to see the boy standing in the doorway.

Todd said, "You are in no danger until she has given you the files."

"She?"

"Miss Golden. She will see that the files come to you."

DiPalma leaned back in the chair and eyed his son. Like it or not, fate led or dragged you along a prescribed path, forcing you by its terrible power to play the game. He wondered if his son saw death for him. It was a question the former cop did not have the courage to ask.

Reaching down he removed the ankle strap, attached the handcuffs to the trigger guard and returned the gun to the vacuum cleaner.

Then father and son walked silently out into the warm night.

28

TOKYO

THE SOUND of the rain had brought Jan out of a sleep so deep that it took all her strength to open her eyes. Slowly the room began to assume form. There was the ceiling with its sunken panels of painted waterfalls and seashores. And there were cedarwood folding screens inlaid with mother-of-pearl, bamboo screens, mats on the floor and the smell of burning incense sticks.

Across the room Kenpachi, nude, stood at a window looking down into the courtyard of Ikuba Castle. Until today he had been a miracle worker. They were now into August with only ten more shooting days to go and only one day behind schedule. Kon had cut scenes from the script, rewritten others and inspired the cast and crew members to work like demons.

The rushes were great. Jan knew they were great because the studio execs, who had not seen them, telephoned her long distance every day to tell her how great they were. The jungle drums were beating. Word was out that Jan had come up with a winner. A few weeks ago, when Kenpachi was spending hours at police headquarters, those same drums were pounding out the message *Don't dress*. Don't expect the Kenpachi project to happen. Now *Ukiyo* was chiseled in granite: it was absolutely going to happen.

A few execs were going to meet her in New York next week at the Kenpachi retrospective, where she would show them the rushes and talk about a new contract. No options. A firm three-picture deal. Play or pay. If the studio decided not to go ahead with the new deal after she signed it, they would still have to pay her the full amount. Based on what Kenpachi had done these past few weeks, Jan was now a heavyweight. And her first picture wasn't even in the can.

Her agent in New York had telephoned her to say he was being shown some outstanding new properties. Books, plays, original scripts. "No fingerprints on them either," he said. "You've got first look."

Kon, Kon, Kon, she said to herself. Make the fucking rain stop, why don't you?

Days before the rain arrived Tokyo had been covered by the *shitsuzetsu,* the wet tongue, the warm moist air from the tropics which preceded the August rainfall. The wet tongue had been hell; Jan had not stopped perspiring the whole time it had hung over the city. With the rain, which started the night before, had come predictions that it would last anywhere from three days to three weeks. With four more days of exterior shooting to do, the last thing Jan needed was a deluge.

She sat up in bed and lit a cigarette. Shouldn't smoke on an empty stomach, but what the hell. Her hand shook. She was doing too many drugs. With Frank she had rarely done more than an occasional joint. Why couldn't she just say no to Kon? Simple question, simple answer. She didn't want to.

Kon was the right temptation at the right time. He was all that was alluring and forbidden about Japan. To experience him was to experience this country in ways few people ever did. And yet...

When they had started filming she had been hungry for him. Now she was sick with the thought of what he made her do in bed. The excuse was, of course, the movie. She needed him. The truth was she wanted to stop sleeping with him, but she didn't know how. Pleasure was a sin and sin a pleasure and none of it came without remorse.

Her affair with Kenpachi was taking its toll. She felt ashamed, emotionally drained, helpless, dependent. And none of it could be undone. She worshipped Kon's talent and she found his beauty unspeakably desirable. There were times when she wished she didn't.

As the rain became torrential, she punched out her cigarette in an ashtray and put her hands over her eyes. Why did the rain have to happen now? Why did it have to prevent her from finishing the movie and getting out of Japan? Away from Kon.

"It will stop soon," he said.

She dropped her hands. He was smiling down at her. His hair was wet.

"Have you been out in that rain?" she asked.

"Yes. I went to the *dojo* to meditate."

"I wish you'd meditate this rain away."

"Get dressed," he said. "It will stop within the hour."

She shook her head. "No way. This is just the first day. According to the weather report, we're in for a few more days like this."

"It will stop. We can go to work on schedule today."

"Kon, I know you're into the occult and I know you meditate, but what makes you think the rain's going to stop?"

"I know. That is enough. Just as I know you are going to meet some important men next week in New York at my retrospective."

"Come on. You could have heard that from anyone on the picture."

He sat down on the edge of the bed and stared into her eyes. "Did you tell anyone?"

"No, I didn't. There're so many egos on a movie. The last thing you want is resentment or jealousy."

Damn him. Lately he knew too much. About the weather, the film. And her. But give him credit, he had come through for her when she needed him. A week from today she and Kon would break off filming to fly to New York for the retrospective; Jan would also make a quick side trip to see her father. Then back to Tokyo for three days' work, followed by a wrap party at Ikuba Castle, a party which Kon had promised cast and crew would remember as long as they lived.

Kon looked into her eyes, stroked her forehead with a soft hand, and Jan relaxed. Her fear of him was gone. "There is something I want to discuss with you," he said. "When I arrive in New York, DiPalma will be there and I think he will do his best to harm me."

Jan felt herself grow tense. It always came back to Frank.

"I have nothing to hide," said Kenpachi. "Nor does Nosaka-san. I think this can easily be proven with your help."

"My help?"

"Your father has certain files, you told me. Suppose DiPalma were to be given those files or allowed to examine them. Suppose he were to see for himself that Nosaka-san and I are innocent of all wrongdoing?"

The drugs. Lack of rest. In her weakened state Jan tried to look away from Kon's eyes. She couldn't help herself, however. He had mastered her.

Kenpachi leaned closer. "The files...your father...DiPalma..."

29

DIPALMA STEPPED from the gangplank onto the deck of Jude Golden's clipper ship, the *Jan Amy*, where three men wearing baseball caps and cradling shotguns blocked his path. They were polite and impressed with his celebrity; DiPalma, after all, was a cop, a part of their world, and he was on the tube, which gave him status. But the guards had a job to do and Rolf Nullabor, who stood near one of the masts, was watching.

DiPalma had to undergo his second security check before being allowed to see Jude Golden. The first had occurred at the base of the gangplank. Here guards had relieved DiPalma of his .38 pistol and ankle holster and had gone over him with a metal detector. Such was television fame that other guards, who had been sitting in parked cars, had opened the doors to get a glimpse of DiPalma.

On board the *Jan Amy* he submitted to a second search with a metal detector, while his face was checked against two separate photographs. More stares, this time from guards scattered around the deck of the tall ship from bow to stern. Even a man at the top of the masthead trained his binoculars on DiPalma. Only Rolf Nullabor seemed unimpressed.

When a guard started to lead DiPalma to Jude Golden, Nullabor's Australian twang stopped him in his tracks. "Forgetting something, aren't you?"

341

The guard frowned.

"His cane, you stupid cunt!" shouted Nullabor.

"It stays with me," said DiPalma.

Nullabor shook his head. "Not on board my ship, mate. Oh, and one more thing. I'd like you to drop your pants and unbutton your shirt. I need to be satisfied that you're not wired for sound, as it were."

DiPalma gave him a long, hard look. Then he said, "Golden knows where to reach me."

He turned and walked toward the gangplank.

Nullabor pushed himself away from the mast. "And just where do you think you're going?"

DiPalma continued walking.

*   *   *

JUDE GOLDEN leaned forward in his chair, one arm extended. "May I?"

DiPalma handed him the cane.

The tall banker turned it around in his hands. "Well made. Strong. Silver knob, not silver plated. Nice. Katharine Hansard had excellent taste."

He returned the cane to DiPalma.

They were below deck in the captain's quarters, a dark wooden room with a low ceiling, two bunk beds and a rolltop desk bolted to the floor. DiPalma found the room depressing, reminiscent of a police holding cell. The stuffy air circulated by a small electric fan trained on Jude Golden. Golden had dismissed two pretty Japanese girls, sending them on deck, but DiPalma could still smell their perfume. And the marijuana. For a heart patient who needed a full-time nurse, Jude Golden still believed in unrestrained satisfaction.

"Sorry about Rolf," said Golden. "He's only doing his job."

"So was Martin Borman." DiPalma didn't care if Nullabor heard him. The Australian stood guard outside in the passageway, looking like a neatly pressed autumn leaf in maroon jacket, wine-colored shirt and slacks and tan suede shoes.

"And you would have walked away without seeing me rather than give up your cane," said Golden.

"In Hong Kong Nullabor got a kick using that laser gun of his. I walked away today rather than hurt him."

Golden studied DiPalma. "I believe you. Rolf just might push the wrong person one of these days." The banker popped several pills in his mouth, swallowed Perrier from a battered pewter mug and closed his eyes. He pinched the bridge of his nose. "My daughter's called me four times the past week. Wants me to turn the files over to you. Failing that, I'm to allow you to study them at your leisure. Says it's important to her, but won't say why."

He opened his eyes. "She sounds... I guess the word is *disconnected*. Not herself. Not the real Jan. Rather like someone standing on top of a tall building without quite knowing how she got there. I've turned down your requests to see me because I thought we had nothing to talk about. I know you want the files, but why should I waste your time and mine when I have no intention of giving them to you."

A helicopter swooped low over the tall ship, then banked right. Golden looked up at the ceiling.

"Mine. Rolf's idea. Eye in the sky, he calls it. Moving me hither, thither and yon, that's Rolf. The hospital, New Haven, here. Disconcerts the enemy, he says. Keeps the bastards off balance." Golden smiled, showing even, white dentures. "He's a shit, our Rolf, but he's my little shit. Let's talk about my daughter."

"Let's not," DiPalma said.

Golden frowned. "Didn't you have an interest in her once upon a time?"

"Once upon a time I had an interest in Gene Autry and Hoot Gibson. Times change. I want those files, Mr. Golden. It's the only reason I drove up here in this heat."

Golden leaned back in his chair, linked his fingers together and began to twirl his thumbs. "Frankie, I've played every game of intrigue that comes to mind and a few that haven't yet been labeled. In the process I've learned how to keep what was mine and acquire whatever else I needed that didn't belong to me. You haven't a prayer of separating me from anything I choose to hold on to. My daughter was intent on my seeing you. Why? That's the question I'd like answered, if you'd be so kind."

"She's there, I'm here. How would I know what's on her mind?"

"Ah, we've decided to stonewall the old gray fox. Mr. DiPalma, I detect a sense of the dramatic in you. Tell me, do you figure to strike some sort of defiant pose and so impress me with your fighting spirit that I will simply wilt and press those files upon you? Those files, Mr. DiPalma, give me strength. With them, I feel powerful. I can break Nosaka like that." He snapped his fingers.

"Why haven't you?"

"Reasons."

"If you're waiting until Jan's out of Japan and no longer involved with Kenpachi, it may be too late."

Golden aimed his chin at DiPalma. "Explain."

"She's attracted to Kenpachi. It's not that easy for her to break away."

"I'm aware of her personal life, thank you. It's something she and I do not discuss. She'll be here tomorrow, by the way. Something to do with a trip to New York for a tribute to Kenpachi. Maybe I can talk her out of returning to Tokyo. Maybe I can talk her into putting this Kenpachi business behind her."

DiPalma shook his head. "Jan can't be talked out of a damn thing and you know it. That's one reason why you haven't moved against Nosaka. She's in trouble until she gets out of Japan, away from Nosaka's friends. Also you don't want to look bad, so you've been trying to clean up those files so you don't look like a prick."

Golden sighed and adjusted a yachting cap on his large head. "I had no idea how many people were involved until I read those files. Not just me and Sal and Duncan. Nosaka's using quite a few people in this country, men of substance and stature. They not only take his money, but in some cases they've come to depend on his reports."

"People like the CIA?"

"Among others. Jan's bound to catch some of the fallout. I'd at least like her to have that one movie under her belt before I play God. There's another reason I haven't turned the files over to you and probably won't. Some of these organizations and individuals are presently investigating you, Mr. DiPalma. Did you know that?"

"No, I didn't."

"Rather important people, some of them. They're trying to find something on you, something to discredit you just in case you do get your hands on those files. I don't know if you're the man to stand up to that kind of pressure. Some of them have already been in touch with your network. I see by your face you weren't aware of this. We live in a world, Mr. DiPalma, where there are fewer and fewer secrets. I promised Jan I'd see you. I didn't promise I would turn over the files to you. And now that I think about it, I don't exactly like your attitude regarding my daughter. It strikes me that you don't care as much about her as I thought. At least not as much as you care about the Hansard files."

"Doesn't it bother you that Jan sounded scared?"

"Scared? What the hell do you mean by that?"

"I don't work for you, Mr. Golden. I don't have to be nice to you. You know what I mean by scared."

Golden's nostrils flared. His face to turned red. "I was right. You do know something you're not telling me. I could have Rolf beat it out of you."

DiPalma tilted his head back and looked at Golden from under his hooded eyes. He smiled.

The banker said, "She's all I care about. If it wasn't for her—"

"You wouldn't have seen me. I know." DiPalma leaned forward. "When did you say Jan was returning to Tokyo?"

"Day after the Kenpachi thing. You're right. She won't leave that film until it's finished. Christ, she's an obstinate bitch sometimes."

"Kenpachi's close to Nosaka. Would you say he knows about the Blood Oath League?"

Golden sat up in his chair.

"Kenpachi's planning to commit *seppuku*," said DiPalma. "Probably when he finishes the movie."

Golden moved his jaw. He rubbed the area over his heart and did not speak for a long time. Then, "How do you know?"

"His bodyguard told me before he died."

"The one your son killed. Where is your son?"

"At my *dojo* with friends."

"I hear tell he's a rather unusual boy."

"Kenpachi wants to use him as *kaishaku*. I'm sure you know about his interest in Todd. You know so many things, Mr. Golden. Do you know that if Jan's anywhere near Kenpachi when he commits *seppuku* she could be killed? Do you know that Nosaka has never stopped hating you for forty years and that maybe he just might hate Jan, too?"

"You've told her this?"

DiPalma sighed. "Does it matter? Look, you say she sounded uncomfortable. She senses something's wrong about her relationship with Kenpachi and that's all she knows. In Japan, your mind plays tricks on you sometimes. Things are never what they seem there."

"Makes sense now," Golden said. "Kenpachi sending the *onnagata* to kill the Hansards." He studied the ex-cop. "They say your boy's special."

"So's Jan."

Golden kept quiet for a long time. "You still love her, don't you."

DiPalma did not leave the clipper ship for another hour. When he did, he carried the Hansard files with him.

30

NEW YORK

IN A CAFÉ at the corner of Broadway and Sixty-fourth Street Jan walked to a row of telephone booths and entered the one nearest the kitchen. On the metal shelf beneath the phone was a glass of champagne, a bottle of Dom Perignon, and a single rose in a thin, crystal vase. She took a card from under the vase and sat down in the booth to read it. *Thanks. Frank.* Removing a handkerchief from her bag, Jan blotted the tears and waited for his call.

She remembered the champagne and sat up. As she sipped it she looked across the street at the crowd milling around Lincoln Center, the performing-arts complex on Manhattan's Upper West Side. Tonight the mob ignored the richly wrought chandeliers and Marc Chagall murals, which could be seen through the glass front of the Metropolitan Opera House. Dozens of uniformed police prevented the hordes from pushing each other into the dancing waters of the Lincoln Center fountain, glowing with blue and green lights.

For the hundreds gathered in front of Avery Fisher Hall, tonight had nothing to do with culture. Their numbers swollen by audiences leaving ballet, theater and concert performances, the crowd was waiting for a glimpse of the celebrities attending the Kon Kenpachi retrospective. Jan wanted to tell them they were in for a long wait. None of the stars, the beautiful people, Japanese dignitaries, politicians and film critics would

347

be leaving before midnight. The projector had broken down, speeches were running long and after the tribute a champagne buffet and press conference was scheduled to begin at 11:00 P.M.

The telephone rang as Jan was pouring herself a second glass of champagne. To calm down she drained half of it in a gulp, took a deep breath and felt her pounding heart before reaching for the phone.

"Jan?"

"Frank? Frank, is that you?" She was getting teary again without quite knowing why.

"I see you made it," he said. "How's the champagne?"

"State of the art. I love it."

"Wanted to thank you for the files."

She thought of Kenpachi. "If it helps you, why not? Dad says you promised to keep him out of it if you could."

"I'll do my best."

She fingered the rose. "Your best isn't too shabby. It's really good to be back in New York. Nice to see Blacks and Puerto Ricans on the street, to read a menu in English, even though I miss the Tokyo cabdrivers. They all wear white gloves, jackets and ties and are very, very polite."

"Wasn't sure you'd be here. Your father said this was a big night for you."

She shook her head. "Not for me, kiddo. Big night for Kon. We put together forty-five minutes of clips from his films, plus a rough cut of a scene from *Ukiyo*. Went over big. Meanwhile a bunch of actors, directors and film critics are onstage telling him how great he is."

"How'd you manage to get out?"

She laughed. "'And with one leap she was free.' That's a line from a script. Seems a writer had his hero in trouble and couldn't get him out, so he simply typed 'and with one leap he was free' and turned the script in. No, what I did was wait until the lights went down, mumbled something about the little girl's room and off I went."

DiPalma said, "Sort of a coincidence my getting the files just about the time Kon bops into town."

She tugged on the telephone cord. "You got me there, paisan. Christ, I wish I could sit down and just talk over this thing between Kon and myself. I admire his talent, which I suppose makes me a star fucker of sorts. And I do need him for this movie, which mercifully is coming to an end in three days."

Jan looked toward Lincoln Center. "It's just that lately...oh, God, I sound like something out of 'Twilight Zone.' He seems to have a force in him, something that draws you to his way of thinking, whether you feel like it or not. Sounds unreal, I know, but there it is."

"I understand," said DiPalma. "Maybe I understand better than you know."

"Know something? In New York he doesn't seem all that special to me. But in Japan, Jesus. Over there on his turf the man is definitely *extraordinaire*. Could be it's just Japan, I don't know."

She looked at the rose. "Three days. Then it's a wrap, thank God. I'll spend time in London for the editing, music, looping. Then it's home, home, home. Speaking of home, where are you by the way? I mean, calling people in public telephone booths sounds like the sort of work you did before you sank to the level of television journalism."

"I'm in a hotel. Why do you ask?"

"Because, Mr. DiPalma, you sound a bit edgy. Look, if you say so, I won't mention any of this to Kon. I'll just tell him you have the files—"

"Oh, he'll know soon enough, believe me. I just don't want anyone to know I have them until I have another chance to go over them. I've spent almost twenty-four hours going over every line. Don't think I've slept more than three hours during that time. Man, I could crash right now. Put my head down on the desk and not move for days."

Jan frowned. "Why the big push? Don't you have an office and an apartment, a very nice apartment if I remember correctly?"

"According to your father, certain people are trying to cut a deal with my network about these files. At the moment I can't trust anybody. So before I turn them over to the lawyers, who are having shit fits about libel, I want to see just what I've got here. Todd doesn't mind the hotel. Hell, he's crazy about room service. Especially ice cream."

"How is Todd? Is he still having those nightmares?"

"He'll be okay."

She twisted the telephone cord around the fingers of her free hand. "Frank, I'd like to see you."

He didn't answer immediately. "When?"

"Tonight. It's the only time I've got, I'm afraid. I have a breakfast meeting with some studio people, then right after that Kon and I fly back to Tokyo."

"Movie's got to have an ending."

"I have done some crazy things in my time, as we all know. I'm thinking. Wouldn't it be nice if I didn't have to go back."

Silence. Then DiPalma said, "You don't have to go back. Why don't we both be crazy. You bring the champagne over to the hotel and we'll sit around and see if we can't come up with a reason for your not returning to Tokyo."

"Are you serious?"

349

"Italians are always serious about champagne."

"Do you know what you're saying?"

"Hotel Buckland. East Sixtieth off Park. Room 309. Ask for Harry Rigby. If anybody at the desk says anything, tell them you're in charge of pest control."

A tearful Jan hung up and clung to the receiver with both hands. She hadn't been this happy in a long, long time. She was free of Kenpachi. She had a first-class production manager in Sam Jonas; let him take charge of the last three days of filming. So what if she missed the wrap party at Ikuba Castle. She would lie. God knows lying was the indispensable part of making life endurable. Kenpachi's contract called for final cut, so let him edit the film without her.

Tonight, boys and girls, Jan Amy Golden was going over the wall. As of now she was free of Kon. And whatever kind of number he was doing on her head.

Frank.

Jan picked up the champagne, turned and dropped the bottle. Shocked, she collapsed back into the telephone booth. Kenpachi, backed by two squat, muscular Japanese, reached into the booth and took the yellow rose from the vase. After he inhaled its fragrance, he smiled at Jan. And crushed the rose.

*　　*　　*

TODD placed the file folders in the attaché case that had once belonged to his stepfather, closed it and looked at Frank DiPalma. The ex-cop had fallen asleep face down on his desk. The boy's unnaturally bright eyes burned into his father's back. There was a .38 on the desk near the ex-cop's right hand and his black oak cane rested on top of a nearby wastebasket.

Todd cocked his head and listened to the voices which urged him to kill his father, to let the *Iky-ryō* come forth as it had in Hong Kong. The boy suddenly stood rigid, eyes closed, and began to perspire heavily.

The room grew frigid and icy winds pulled at the drapes and fluttered the pages of a newspaper on the desk near DiPalma's head.

Minutes later Todd left the hotel carrying the attaché case. He walked to the corner of Sixtieth Street and Park Avenue, where he stood waiting in the August night. A bus stopped in front of him and a passenger got off. When the bus pulled away, a limousine glided to a halt at the bus stop and the rear door opened. Todd stepped into the car, which headed downtown, then turned right on Fifth-seventh Street and sped downtown on Seventh Avenue.

At Forty-second Street, the limousine turned right and slowly cruised toward Eighth Avenue. Todd shuddered at the sights—porn movie houses and bookstores, street peddlers selling stolen jewelry, blood banks, video-game arcades, junkies and prostitutes. At the corner of Forty-second Street and Eighth Avenue the limousine stopped and a squat, muscular Japanese in a tuxedo and wearing dark glasses got out and began to walk back toward Seventh Avenue.

In the middle of the block he stopped in front of a young Puerto Rican boy lounging in front of a record shop whose windows were covered with steel shutters. The boy was slim and dark-eyed and wore a tank top with the word Menudo spelled out in rhinestones. Beneath that were photographs of the five Puerto Ricans who made up the wildly popular rock group. After a few words the boy followed the Japanese back to the limousine.

With the Puerto Rican boy now inside, the limousine pulled away from the corner, turned right and headed north on Eighth Avenue.

＊　　＊　　＊

THE telephone jarred DiPalma awake. He sat up quickly and looked around for Todd. The boy was probably asleep in the next room. It was probably Jan calling to tell him she'd changed her mind and wasn't coming over. Jan Amy Golden. Last of the free spirits. When it comes to her, he thought, I got it bad and that ain't good. The first one to get over a love affair is the luckiest.

Still groggy, he crossed the room and snatched at the receiver.

"Frank?" A male voice, familiar.

"Charlie Griffith. They asked me to call you."

An alarm went off in DiPalma's head. Griffith was a fireman he'd known for years, an old friend who had finally gotten the captain's rank he deserved.

"There's been a fire over at your kendo club," Griffith said. "We found a body. Just a kid. Burned pretty badly. Looks like it was your boy. I'm sorry. I'm really sorry."

DiPalma looked toward the bedroom. "Griff, hang on a minute, will you?"

He stood up and walked to the bedroom. At the door the hairs on the back of his neck stood up. He opened the door and looked inside the room. Twin beds. Both unslept in.

DiPalma tore himself away from the room and picked up the phone. "Yeah Griff, I'm listening."

"Kid had ID on him. And a Buckland hotel key in his pants pocket. Note had your name and this room number. I was hoping he had no connection with you. Some of the kendo people came down here the minute they heard about the fire. They said only one kid had a key to the *dojo*. Only one kid had the instructor's permission to come in here and practice anytime he wanted to."

DiPalma's voice was husky. "Be right down. Thanks for calling."

He hung up and stared at the bedroom, then covered his eyes with one hand and wept.

31

TOKYO

AT MIDNIGHT, in the *dojo* of Ikuba Castle, Nosaka stepped away from a bare wall and walked to the center of the matted floor where Todd stood alone, naked except for a *fundoshi*, a white loincloth. The boy wore his hair in ancient samurai fashion, the back braided, then oiled and pulled forward across the top of his shaven skull. There was a wolflike brightness to his eyes and a sense of power emanated from him that filled the room.

Outside, a strong southern wind drove the heavy rain against the castle buildings. Water poured from the castle roofs down onto sand and rock gardens, turning them into black whirlpools. Pine trees ringing an ornamental pool bent beneath howling gusts that drove sheets of water across the cobblestones and onto the parked cars. The drawbridge was up and the huge iron gates were locked, isolating the walled castle from Tokyo. Within the compound every building was dark, except the *dojo*, where two men stood guard at the entrance.

Inside Kenpachi and half a dozen members of the Blood Oath League stood in the shadows cast by paper lanterns and watched Nosaka complete the ritual which would signify Todd's emergence as a samurai. Nosaka had been selected as the boy's sponsor, an honor comparable to that of godfather or guardian.

Dressed in the traditional gray kimono of his clan and wearing a *hachimaki* tied around his forehead, the industrialist handed Todd a *hakama*, the loose black trousers worn by feudal samurai. After Todd had put them on, Nosaka handed him a green ceremonial gown embroidered with storks and tortoises, symbols of longevity. The stork was said to live a thousand years, the tortoise ten thousand. Nosaka then lifted a hand and an earthenware cup of rice wine was brought to him on a tray.

Nosaka took three sips, then handed it to Todd, who did the same. Nosaka then took another three sips and returned the cup to the tray. Lightning flashed brightly, and the courtyard lit up as though it were day. Then came thunder, an ear-shattering crack.

Nosaka clenched his fists and attempted to stay calm. The thunder and lightning triggered a storm of wind and waves in his mind, leaving him again restive and unsteady. He had begun to feel this way with the purchase of the Muramasa saddle. But just as quickly he had rejected the idea that the saddle had anything to do with his distress.

In buying the saddle he knew that some would say he had completed a cycle of evil, that he was now surrounded by base objects which could produce only suffering. But he remembered the power he had drawn from Muramasa's weapons over the years. Especially from Benkai's sword. For the past three days Nosaka had lived in Ikuba Castle, watching Kenpachi draw that same power from the sword and from the bone which had once been in Benkai's throat. This was the power Kenpachi had used to control and manipulate the boy's mind until the fearsome Benkai, long buried in his soul, had emerged.

There had been no resisting Kenpachi. He had convinced the American woman to return to Japan against her will. Nosaka had only contempt for her weakness. She was easily manipulated, she with the untrained western mind found in fools who lived to serve their own feelings. She was not like Nosaka, who had always been master of himself.

Yet tonight he was in danger of yielding to a fear of evil. For the first time in many months he felt his age; exhaustion weighed so heavily upon him that it seemed to be pushing him into the grave. He shivered in the warm *dojo*. Everyone else, even the boy, was perspiring; the tropical August storm had brought with it steamy, dank air, more uncomfortable than the hottest summer heat.

Nosaka felt a coldness that brought to his mind the *Iki-ryō* and the reason it had not killed DiPalma despite Kenpachi's control of the boy.

Nosaka had said, "The *Iki-ryō* saved DiPalma's life in Hong Kong because the boy felt a loyalty to his father. Having given life the *Iki-ryō* cannot take it back. It can never be used to kill whom it has saved."

Kenpachi angrily turned his back on Nosaka. "Then DiPalma is invincible."

"No. He can be killed. Remember, the boy was not then Benkai. His sense of loyalty to his lord was not as intense as it is now. True, if the *Iki-ryō* refuses to kill, it will not recant. It is also possible that DiPalma has been purified in Tendrai's forge. The power of the sword can manifest itself in many ways. The American, however, is mortal. Never forget that he can be killed."

In the *dojo* a clap of thunder startled Nosaka and he shivered again. Others in the ancient fencing hall threw each other quick, nervous glances. Only the boy stood calmly, impassively waiting for the ritual to conclude. When it was over he would be Benkai.

Even now his swordsmanship surpassed that of anyone else in the Blood Oath League. Only Nosaka and Kenpachi had not been shocked. By drawing blood from three opponents, Todd had also won the respect of league members. The purification rituals of the past three days had included fencing with actual swords. Now no one wished to spar with Todd; even to fight him with wooden swords could mean death. He had knocked two men unconscious and had to be forcibly prevented from clubbing a third to death.

The following afternoon Kenpachi would complete the film for the American woman, who now slept drugged in his bed. Hours later he would host a party in the castle for the actors and crew. There would be other guests, including Nosaka. All would be held hostage until Kenpachi had completed his *seppuku* and a film of it shown on Japanese and American television.

All in the Blood Oath League had taken a vow neither to surrender nor bargain for amnesty. Fear of disgrace, Nosaka knew, would make them keep that vow at the cost of their lives. This was the league's strength and its greatness. This is why it would live long after Kenpachi's *seppuku*. Just as Benkai had lived for hundreds of years.

The lightning flashed, followed by thunder. And by something else. Alarmed, Nosaka looked around the *dojo*. No one else seemed to have heard it.

It was a harsh whisper, a ghostly utterance which made Nosaka's flesh crawl.

"*Shini-mono-gurui.*" The hour of the death fury. Giving and taking no quarter. The deepest commitment a samurai could make before going into battle. Killing those closest to him to free himself for a fight to the death.

The words made Nosaka sick to his stomach. With an effort he faced Kenpachi, who held out the Muramasa blade in its scabbard to him. The final part of the ritual. As sponsor Nosaka was to hand it to the boy, thus officially designating him samurai.

Suddenly Nosaka backed away. Everything in him said reject the sword, flee. Kenpachi was speechless. Everyone watched Nosaka back to the door and open it, letting in the wind and rain. Paper lanterns fluttered and one tore loose to bounce across the matted floor. Todd's robe billowed and his face became wet and slick with rain. While others around him cringed before the terrible storm that had invaded the *dojo*, he stood firmly in place, arms folded, his eyes riveted on the Muramasa held by Kenpachi.

Nosaka staggered out into the warm, heavy rain. He smelled the stench of the *Iki-ryō* and felt its icy chill and heard Kenpachi call his name. Nosaka was supposed to witness his *zankanjo*, a written vindication of Kenpachi's suicide and the murders by the Blood Oath League. He was also to serve as witness when Kenpachi signed his will.

But white faced with cold, Nosaka now stumbled through the downpour to his limousine, where a bodyguard quickly opened a back door.

The car horn blared and the huge iron gates slowly swung open. The heavy drawbridge dropped. Lightning illuminated the courtyard as the car swung around in a half circle, sped past the *dojo* and rumbled across the bridge before disappearing in the darkness and rain.

32

NEW YORK

WHEN DIPALMA opened his eyes it was almost dawn. He lay motionless, still hearing Todd's voice. For the third consecutive night he had dreamed about his son. Tonight's dream, however, had been the most vivid of all. Todd had pleaded with his father to come to Japan and save him.

DiPalma sat up, turned on the bedside lamp and looked at the digital clock-radio. Almost 4:30 A.M. He slipped into a robe, then walked out to the balcony to stare at New York harbor. From the darkened waters came the sound of a tugboat's horn as it guided a freighter out to sea. A chain of barges, looking like a string of giant black pearls, floated across the horizon. A single gull spread its wings against a pale sky before squealing and dropping to skim the water for food.

DiPalma looked east toward a rising sun. Toward Japan. Toward Todd.

*　　*　　*

The greased braid of hair had been pulled across the top of the boy's shaven skull. His outstretched hands held a sword whose

357

jeweled hilt was wrapped in white silk.

Todd wept and begged his father to come to Ikuba Castle before it was too late.

Then Kenpachi entered the dream. The film director knelt before the boy and smiled. As though on command, Todd gripped the sword, lifted it high in the air and brought it down on Kenpachi's bared neck.

Blood spurted and covered the boy's face. As the blood cleared it washed away his skin, leaving the skull bare. DiPalma heard Katharine's voice behind him, but when he turned, he saw only fire. He looked back at Todd, who was now a skeleton.

The skeleton spoke. "There is a way, my father. Steal in as did the yamabushi. *Steal in." And then the dream was over.*

*   *   *

ON the balcony DiPalma closed his eyes and tried to concentrate. In each dream the boy had been in Ikuba Castle. But there was something about the last dream which bothered DiPalma.

Then he remembered. *Todd had once told him about this dream.* There were slight differences between his version and DiPalma's, but basically both were the same. Until now he had believed his son was dead. But with the final dream he knew Todd was alive, reaching out for him with a will almost as powerful as that of the great swordmaker Tendrai.

DiPalma opened his eyes and began to pace. The dead boy found in the burned out *dojo* was not his son. Now it made sense. Todd's missing dental records in Hong Kong. The delay in forwarding his medical history. Someone didn't want DiPalma to have those records. Todd was alive and DiPalma knew where to find him.

He raced from the balcony into the bedroom. Fumbling through a drawer in the night table he found his address book, then sat on the bed. When he had the name he wanted, he pulled the telephone toward him and dialed Tokyo.

*   *   *

Rolf Nullabor looked at his wristwatch, then at Jude Golden's nurse. They stood outside the sliding door to Golden's room on the second floor of his Victorian mansion. Golden had overslept, which annoyed the nurse, a stickler for punctuality. He was due to get his first shot of the day and she was not about to let him avoid it. Nullabor had been summoned to help her.

Nullabor loathed her as he loathed most black Irish. She was too authoritarian for his taste, and, besides, much taller than he. Hell-bent on giving Golden his injection, she might enter when he and Nijo were doing the old in-and-out. Better to warn Golden first, just in case the little Jap beauty was sitting on his face while saying her morning prayers.

Nullabor removed his shoes. The nurse did the same, though it was a custom she found pagan, as she did Jude Golden's penchant for collecting Oriental concubines.

Nullabor knocked on the wooden frame. "Mr. Golden? Nursie's here. Wakey, wakey."

He grinned at her. "Could be he and his friend are locked in a convoluted discussion concerning the adverse effects of thermonuclear warfare on plant life."

She folded her arms across her ample bosom and eyed him with loathing.

Nullabor knocked on the frame again.

"Well?" the nurse said, thrusting her head back and forth.

"Well, me bleedin' arse," said Nullabor as he slid back the door. Across the room Jude Golden lay on his side, his back to the door.

"Mr. Golden, Princess Di is here with her magic wand. Time—"

The looseness of the banker's body, the stillness surrounding him. Nullabor had seen it before. It meant only one thing.

He crouched down and turned Golden over on his back. The banker's lips were blue, his face discolored. Poison. He had not died an easy death.

A search of the house failed to turn up Nijo.

Nullabor did find the other two Japanese girls, but they could tell him nothing. They too had been poisoned. Nijo had covered her tracks well.

33

TOKYO, EVENING

DIPALMA was silent as Shuko drove fast over the rain-slicked roads leading from New Tokyo International Airport into the city. Even without the rain and heavy traffic the trip would take over an hour. The U-shaped, ultramodern airport was forty miles outside of Tokyo in Narita, a town built around a tenth-century temple dedicated to Fudo, god of fire. Airport traffic on this road was bad enough. The eight million pilgrims who came yearly to worship Fudo made it worse.

Rain slapped the hood and windshield like waves from an angry sea, and gusts rattled the car. It skidded several times, causing DiPalma to push his feet against the floorboard and stiffen his arms against the dash. Off to one side he saw an overturned truck, its cartons spread out along the highway as though being offered for sale. In a lane leading back to the airport a car had been blown into the path of an oncoming bus, halting traffic. DiPalma could not recall a worse storm in his life.

On the phone from New York he had told Shuko everything. Todd's reincarnation. Kenpachi's planned *seppuku*. And DiPalma's dreams.

"The circle is complete," Shuko had said.

"I don't understand."

"Tomorrow Kenpachi finishes the movie. And tomorrow is the day when Lord Saburo committed *seppuku* over four hundred years ago with

Benkai as his *kaishaku*. Karma, DiPalma-san. What is, was. What was will always be. Past, present and future. The same."

DiPalma rubbed the back of his neck. The fourteen-hour nonstop flight had been rough. But there had been no more dreams. This meant Todd was dead or no longer wanted to contact him. One thing was certain; belief in the unknown, which DiPalma had begun to accept in Tendrai's forge, was now stronger than ever. There was a Japan which could not be seen, which could only be felt, which could only be experienced.

When Shuko braked behind a truck load of pigs, DiPalma said, "What would happen if Kenpachi's death were not honorable, if he were to die at the hands of someone not worthy to be his second?"

"It would be bad karma. It would be the judgment of the gods condemning him to an unhappy life in the next world. His death would be useless and of no value. Even Mishima is not a hero to everyone."

The truck pulled away and the pigs began thrashing about. Shuko said, "And you know a way into the castle?"

DiPalma hesitated. "I think so. There is only the dream to go on. And what Todd told me weeks ago about the tunnel."

"The tunnel is supposed to have been destroyed in the great earthquake. If it has been rebuilt, it has been done so in secret. And most illegally."

"Kenpachi would do it and not think twice."

Steal in. Was the dream real or just wishful thinking? DiPalma leaned forward and wiped steam from the windshield. The heavy rain prevented him from opening the windows, turning the car into a sauna on wheels. He leaned back in his seat. *Was the dream real?*

Shuko said, "After your telephone call I spoke to Tendrai-*sensei*. I told him of our conversation. About the dream."

DiPalma waited.

"Tendrai-*sensei* told me to do as you ask. Without question."

"Did he say anything else?"

"He did not have to."

DiPalma rolled down his window and let the rain hit him in the face. He had his answer. "How long has the party been on?"

"It was scheduled to begin thirty minutes ago. Most of the people attending worked with Kenpachi on the film. Others are friends."

"They won't stay when he starts to kill himself."

"He will keep them hostage. Kenpachi needs an audience."

DiPalma nodded. "When we go in we'll have to be careful."

"I will have six men. They will be armed with automatic weapons and sidearms. Unfortunately, I am not allowed to give you a gun, DiPalma-san. You know our laws."

362

"Strict as hell. Wish we had laws like that. I'll take my chances with this." He held up the cane. "Did you tell them what we were going to do?"

Shuko smiled. "No. It was not necessary. They will obey me without question. I also did not tell them that a *gaijin* will be our leader."

DiPalma grinned. "Can't wait to see how they'll take that."

"They have a duty to me. Just as you have a duty to your son."

And to Jan, thought DiPalma. She had not come to the hotel after the Kenpachi tribute, nor had she called. Was it Jan acting up again or had Kenpachi taken her over as he had Todd? Kenpachi had to be responsible for her recent behavior. DiPalma tried not to think that Kenpachi intended to kill Jan.

The car came to a halt in a sea of traffic. DiPalma grew alarmed. "We're not going to arrive in time."

"Karma will bring us to the castle or keep us away," said Shuko.

He closed his eyes.

After a few seconds DiPalma did the same.

*　　*　　*

HAND in hand with Kenpachi, Jan walked down the long polished corridor toward light softened by a sliding rice-paper door. The corridor was lit by pine torches hanging from walls decorated in ancient hand-scrolls, colored silk drawings of horses, landscapes and flying geese. They walked in silence, as did the men who followed them. Instead of shoes all, including Jan, wore *tabi*, the split-toed white ankle socks. Jan also wore a golden kimono with a brilliant red sash and her hair had been done in the ancient fashion, an elaborate styling of cascades and cocoons containing fragile oyster shells. Her face was coated in white makeup, leaving a small red mouth.

She had been dressed by Kenpachi, who had also done her makeup.

"Tonight you must look the role of the *daimyo*'s mistress," he had said.

She was in a daze, hypnotized by the pounding rain, by the drugged wine she had drunk from an earthen cup, by Kenpachi's words. She had reached the point where she believed he could speak to her without words as he had done in New York. Then he had simply stared at her as she cringed in the telephone booth, dreading his touch and wanting to cry out for Frank.

But no sound had come from her. Kenpachi's piercing eyes were all she remembered until Japan, where she woke up one morning in his bed and suddenly realized that New York, Lincoln Center and Frank had happened three days ago. Depressed and frightened, she had searched the castle for a telephone. She had to speak to Frank. But when she found an empty room and a phone, she was unable to make the call. She was too guilty, too ashamed, too weak.

Something in her cried out for Frank, but she had betrayed him once more and had to be punished. So she punished herself by walking away from the phone and by doing as Kon ordered.

Now, in the corridor, she forced herself to gather up the pieces of her life. The film was over, in the can. But where was the satisfaction she should have felt? There was a party in the castle. Yes. That's where Kon was taking her now. To the party.

She slowed down. Her steps faltered, but Kon's strong grip pulled her along the corridor. She had slowed down out of panic; she wondered if she could ever leave Kon. Would he let her go? *Frank.* A tear slid from a corner of Jan's eye to become a pearl on her white-coated face. The worse thing, she knew, was being unable to forgive herself.

When they reached the sliding door at the end of the corridor, someone behind them stepped forward and opened it. Jan tensed. There were dozens of men and women attending the wrap party. Several decorated, sliding doors leading to other rooms had been pulled back to create one large room whose low ceiling was sectioned off by dark wooden beams; the only light came from paper lanterns and tall candles in bamboo stands.

As the conversation suddenly stopped, Jan tried to concentrate her mind, to think clearly. The silence was all wrong. And why were people staring at her and Kenpachi? What was wrong with her? She looked at Kenpachi. He was dressed oddly. White kimono and matching headband. And behind them were a dozen men dressed in white kimonos and armed with samurai swords. Some had a short sword tucked in their sashes. She remembered that Kon's parties were bizarre affairs, but tonight's was even more weird. *Why?*

Kenpachi and his men pushed guests back from the entrance. Those who did not move fast enough were slapped, kicked, threatened with the swords. Jan saw it all through a haze. A woman shoved; the man beside her stepped forward and was kicked in the stomach. A guest who was trying to reason with Kon's friends was punched in the mouth. Two women were struck with the flat of a sword.

The guests, holding drinks and plates of food, now ceased to eat and drink.

Kon released Jan's hand and stepped inside the room. Someone else

364

took one step forward to stand at his side. *Todd*. What was he doing here? Why was he dressed in a black kimono with the top of his head shaved? And carrying a sword. He looked bizarre, a miniature version of an ancient samurai on one of the hanging scrolls in the corridor. He gave off an air of being too formidable to oppose. Even the hard-looking men around Kenpachi, men older and bigger and armed with swords, seemed to be afraid of Todd. Why were they afraid of a boy?

Kenpachi folded his arms across his chest and coolly surveyed the room. "Listen carefully and do not speak. From this moment on, all of you are my hostages."

There was mumbling from the guests. Kenpachi waited. The mumbling faded.

"You are my hostages and will remain so until my purpose has been realized. I will retire to my bedroom to await the arrival of a television crew who will film the reading of my *zankanjo*." He hesitated. "And my *seppuku*."

"My *seppuku*," he repeated. "I—"

An American stunt man, high on pills and Cognac and bored with Japan after weeks of filming, staggered toward Kenpachi. Several Blood Oath League members rushed toward him, but Kenpachi's command stopped them.

The stunt man stood in place and weaved. Pointing at Todd he said, "Fuck you suppose to be, something from *Fantasy Island?*" He giggled. "The plane has landed, boss."

He threw his arms wide. "Fuckin' wild party, right? Shit, I'm ready for that." He charged Kenpachi, who took one step back. Todd stepped forward. He wielded the sword in its scabbard, like a club, bringing it up hard between the stunt man's legs.

The big, blond American doubled over, and Todd delivered a series of blows so quickly that the horror of it shocked Jan into consciousness. The boy struck the blond man across the face, then in the right temple, spinning him around and dropping him unconscious to the mat.

The silence in the room deepened to grim helplessness.

Kenpachi smiled. "You have seen what my *kaishaku* can do. Had he taken the blade from the scabbard, the fool on the floor would have died, for a bared blade has the right to blood. Actually I am happy that his blade was not soiled by this man's blood. Benkai, my *kaishaku*, has been purified for me and by me. But I see an object lesson is in order."

He nodded at a guard, who stepped forward and cleanly hacked off the stunt man's head. Women screamed and Jan almost fainted. She was now propped up by two of Kenpachi's men.

Kenpachi clapped his hands once. Todd stepped forward, picked up the head by its long, blond hair and held it high in one hand. His sword was held high in the other. Slowly the boy walked back and forth in front of the guests.

Kenpachi said, "Look at it! Look at it or I will have another killed until the rest do as I say. Take your hands away from your eyes and never turn your backs to me when I am addressing you."

He waited as the guests kept their eyes on Todd.

Kenpachi said, "I shall now retire to my quarters to await the television cameras. One of you will be executed every hour until my *seppuku* is shown on Japanese and American television. I suggest you pray the storm does not delay the arrival of the press. As for any rescue, this castle is a fortress. It is impregnable. There is no way in or out except through the front gate, which is now locked. The drawbridge is up. You cannot escape and I strongly suggest you do not try."

He clapped his hands again. Several of his men stepped forward and pulled a handful of guests from the stunned group. One of those shoved toward Kenpachi was Nosaka.

Kenpachi looked them over. "You will be taken to my quarters where you will have the honor of witnessing my *seppuku* and the reading of my *zankanjo*. Everyone else will remain here under guard. My men have orders to kill anyone who resists or causes the slightest difficulty. I go now to join Japan's immortals, those whose blood has watered the tree of Nippon's greatness. In the future you will worship me as a god and you will be proud to tell others that you were present here in this castle on this most auspicious occasion. Long live the emperor!"

Outside in the hall he said to a terrified Jan, "Tonight, Saga, I shall kill you before you have the chance to betray me."

He led the way back down the vast corridor. Jan was roughly dragged behind him by an incredibly strong Todd.

34

TOKYO, NIGHT

DIPALMA stood in the dark, fetid-smelling shack and watched as two uniformed Japanese policemen tore at the floor with crowbars. He and Shuko trained flashlights on the planking. As chunks of it came loose, they were tossed outside where Shuko's men waited in the downpour. There was no room inside for a pile of wood or an extra man.

The shack was an abandoned caretaker's hut in a grove of trees on the edge of a Shinjuku park. It had neither electricity nor heat and anything valuable had long since been stolen or removed. A locked door had protected a bare room covered with dust, cobwebs and rat droppings.

After the break-in DiPalma had taken a crowbar, pried loose the window boards and stared out into the rainy darkness. Shuko stood beside him silently. At first the policeman saw nothing. Then lightning lit up the center of the city and he saw it clearly.

Ikuba Castle. Barely a quarter of a mile away.

As DiPalma continued to stare through the window, Shuko ordered his men to tear up the floorboards in search of the trapdoor to a secret tunnel, a tunnel that DiPalma said led to the castle.

Rain leaked through the roof and plastered DiPalma's gray hair to his skull. Wind whistled through cracks in the shack. Once or twice the men glanced at DiPalma, then dropped their eyes back to the ground. He knew what they were thinking. But no one would say it in front of Shuko.

They were digging because the *gaijin* wanted them to, because he believed there was trouble in the castle. What kind of trouble? They were all fools and the biggest fool was Shuko, who was letting his friendship for the *gaijin* ruin his career. His career would be finished when it was learned that he had attempted to sneak into the home of a man as important as Kenpachi-san, a man with very important friends. The smartest man in the park tonight was the one Shuko had assigned to sit in a police car and monitor the radio. Poor Shuko. *Hai*, the life of a fool was worse than death.

They don't have to like me, thought DiPalma. All they have to do is keep digging.

When the trapdoor, moss covered and made of iron, was discovered under the floor, the atmosphere suddenly changed. As the men pulled at the door, the policeman assigned to the radio rushed into the shack and spoke excitedly to Shuko. When he had finished, the men in the hut looked at DiPalma, who said, "Kenpachi has made his move."

Shuko nodded. "As you said he would. Copies of his *zankanjo* have been delivered to the press, to the emperor. A police car drove up to the castle where someone threw a head down from the wall. It was the head of a man, a westerner. Shall we enter the tunnel now?"

DiPalma nodded. "Tell your people at headquarters we're going through. We can't take too many with us. Too noisy, might alert Kenpachi. You, me and four of your men. Leave two here to wait for reinforcement. Tell them to be on guard in case Kenpachi attacks us from this end. We're to have at least fifteen minutes before anyone follows us."

He spoke softly, in perfect Japanese, never raising his voice.

This time no one waited for Shuko's instructions.

DiPalma removed his jacket, tie, shirt, then his shoes and socks. He took coins and keys from his pants pocket and placed them in his jacket. As he looked down at the opening in the floor, Shuko and four policemen also stripped to the waist.

DiPalma, flashlight and cane in hand, was the first to descend the wooden ladder leading down into the pitch black tunnel.

*   *   *

KENPACHI stood at his bedroom window, peering into the darkness at the stone walls ringing Ikuba Castle, and cursed under his breath. *Hai*, the castle was impregnable, but he did not like the rain. Four hundred years ago the rain had helped to defeat Saburo. It had hid the *ninja* attack and enabled Hideyoshi's armies to steal in undetected. Damn the rain.

And damn the press, which had not contacted him. The telephones were working. Kenpachi had spoken to the police, who were now outside the walls in their little cars, and he had spoken to someone at army headquarters, telling him what he planned to do at Ikuba Castle. He had attempted to reach the emperor and failed. No matter. The emperor had a copy of Kenpachi's *zankanjo*. The emperor would understand and approve. Kenpachi had prepared himself. He was pure enough to be a worthy sacrifice to Nippon. And he had Benkai. He must calm himself, remain in control and act the *daimyo*. Then, when the television cameras arrived, he would show the world how a warrior died.

He turned from the window to see Todd walk away from the hostages in the bedroom and stand in front of the closet leading to the secret tunnel. Kenpachi had not mentioned the tunnel to the boy, but he had no doubt that the boy knew of its existence. Even most members of the Blood Oath League did not know of the tunnel.

Todd grunted. His voice was deep, a man's voice.

"What is it?" said Kenpachi. He felt an ominous forewarning.

"*Ninja*." Todd's eyes were glued to the door. "They are coming through the tunnel."

Kenpachi pressed his fists to his temples. It must not happen again. How did they find out about the tunnel? He looked pleadingly at Nosaka, whose face held a strange smile. Kenpachi had to forcibly restrain himself from asking the industrialist what to do next.

But was not Kenpachi *daimyo* of Ikuba Castle?

He pointed to the closet. "Kill them, Benkai! Do not let them capture me alive!"

✳   ✳   ✳

IN the tunnel DiPalma led the way through ankle-deep water. The beam of his flashlight sent rats scurrying. The air was sickening and for the first time in weeks his stomach began to trouble him. He was weak from lack of food. His feet, cut by rocks hidden by the water, were in agony but he dared not stop.

He had slipped once and fallen, tasting rancid water and mud and he had almost vomited. He had willed himself not to throw up, to keep running. Concentrate. *Hai.* Concentrate on Katharine, on Tendrai's forge. He thought of all his years of kendo practice, remembering how he had wielded the sword until his arms ached, until he could not lift them, but somehow had continued to fight.

The darkness threatened him, brought him close to panic. Where was the darkness leading him? Was he leading five men to their death because of a dream?

The tunnel seemed to grow longer, to go deeper into the earth. His mind played tricks. He was lost inside a dragon and would never see the sun again. The tunnel was a fake, designed to lure the castle enemies to their deaths by leading them in circles. DiPalma would starve to death under the earth. *There is nothing around you but dirt, foul water and rats. The rats will feed on you after you die.*

He ran, breathing through burning lungs, and heard only the splashing water. He ran because if he stopped, he would lie down in the water and warm darkness and never rise again.

He thought of Hong Kong, of the day in the Kowloon hospital when Katherine had forced him to walk. Crawl, she had said. Limp. But don't lie where you have fallen.

DiPalma ran. *Splash-splash-splash.* He led and the others followed, taking their strength from him; they too were tired. They were ordinary men, not *ninja*. But with the right leader, they could equal the *ninja* in spirit.

When DiPalma thought his heart would shatter, when it seemed all the breath had left his body and his legs could not longer function, he felt the cool air.

In the beam of his flashlight he saw the small red brick room at the end of the tunnel. Drawing the cool air into his burning lungs, he staggered forward and out of the water, up an incline, then stumbled into the room and collapsed. Seconds later a mud splattered Shuko and his men followed. The sweating, dirty men looked half-dead.

Shuko, too tired to speak, touched DiPalma. The gesture said, You have led us well.

DiPalma turned away, listening. His hand went up, commanding silence. All the flashlights were turned off. A second command and the men dragged themselves to the wooden ladder leading upstairs, flattening themselves against the wall, waiting.

In the darkness DiPalma leaned against the ladder and felt the vibrations as someone stepped on it and began to climb down. When the man touched bottom, DiPalma reached out, grabbed his shirt and yanked him close. He covered the man's mouth with one hand and kneed him twice in the groin. Then he smashed him in the head with the knob of his cane.

370

A scuffle told DiPalma that a second man was being dealt with by Shuko's men. There was a clang as a sword fell to the floor.

Then there was a scream, an animallike screech, and in the darkness DiPalma heard someone leap from the ladder and land near the tunnel. Quickly DiPalma yanked his flashlight from his belt and switched it on.

Todd.

Standing at the mouth of the tunnel, teeth bared, the Murasama held overhead.

A wolf at bay, exuding more evil than any man in the small room had ever seen.

More flashlights were switched on and DiPalma heard the click of a safety catch. He shouted, "He's my son! Don't fire!"

He ran his flashlight over the floor and found a dropped sword. With the sword in his right hand, the cane in his left, he inched forward. "Keep your lights on him! On him, not me! Try to blind him if you can! And don't go near him. He's dangerous. He doesn't know what's he's doing!"

Two of Shuko's men climbed the ladder to get out of the way. The others, pistols and rifles aimed at Todd, edged along the walls, keeping far away from the boy and his sword.

With a ratlike quickness, the boy scurried to his left, out of the light and into a patch of darkness. Before the flashlights could find him again, Todd leaped out of the darkness and at his father.

The boy attacked, slashing at his father's left knee. *Clang.* Their blades clashed as DiPalma blocked the swing and felt the vibrations from Todd's powerful stroke race up his arm. Todd faked a stomach thrust, then slashed at DiPalma, who sidestepped, but was still cut on the wrist. A second's delay and he would have lost a hand.

He had no choice but to accept a frightening truth. Todd was now the more skilled fencer. And he almost matched DiPalma in physical strength.

More terrifying, Todd was no longer his son or Katharine's. He was now a deadly swordsman, a merciless fighter, a cold-blooded warrior committed to serving his *daimyo*, Kenpachi, to the death.

Dai-sho. Two swords.

Karma. Fate.

Father and son inched toward each other, each holding three feet of curved, razor-sharp steel.

Because Todd was concentrating on the kill, Shuko's men could do as DiPalma ordered. Quickly running behind DiPalma all aimed their flashlights at Todd's face.

The boy turned white in the garish light. He cursed, his face tight with hatred. An arm came up to shield his eyes. For that one instant he was helpless.

DiPalma switched weapons from one hand to the other. The cane in his right hand, the sword in his left. He charged, pushed aside Todd's sword with his own; then, with a mighty shout, he brought the cane down on the Muramasa, breaking it in half.

As though pierced by a blade, Todd screamed in pain. He staggered back toward the tunnel, followed by the light. DiPalma smacked his wrist. Todd dropped the broken sword, then DiPalma dropped his cane and sword and rushed him. He wrapped his arms around the boy's shoulders and lifted him off his feet. Todd kicked, twisted and fought with such unexpected strength that both father and son crashed into a wall, then fell to the cement floor with Todd on top. Cursing, the boy jerked an arm free, punched his father in the temple and almost knocked him unconscious. Before DiPalma could move, Todd punched him again, breaking his nose. The boy's strength was astonishing. Todd could beat him to death with his fists and DiPalma knew it.

With blood streaming from his nose DiPalma shouted, "Shuko! Shuko!"

The police captain, followed by his men, rushed forward and pulled at Todd.

Maddened, the boy fought back. He shoved one man back into the tunnel, dropped another to the cement floor with a kick to the groin and smashed his elbow into the face of a third. DiPalma pushed himself to his knees. Unbelievable. Todd was holding his own against six grown men.

Sucking air in through his mouth, DiPalma hesitated a second, then leaped on Todd, tackling him from the rear. As the boy went down, Shuko grabbed an arm and hung on. Three men fell on Todd's legs, pinning him down. DiPalma grabbed the other arm. Todd continued to fight. Face down, he thrashed as a policeman cuffed his hands behind him.

A jerk of Todd's wrists and the cuffs were broken.

"Cuff him again!" DiPalma shouted, then told them to put on a third pair.

DiPalma turned the writhing boy over on his back and tied his ankles with his sash. A strip of cloth was torn from Todd's kimono and shoved into his mouth.

DiPalma looked down at his wild-eyed son, who flung himself about on the damp concrete, rolling left, then right to escape his bonds. There was something bestial about the boy which made DiPalma shudder. His face was hideous, almost unrecognizable.

"He is Benkai," whispered Shuko. "And he has been strengthened by the *Iki-ryō*, by thoughts of evil and darkness."

"Kenpachi."

"And Nosaka, who gave Kenpachi the Muramasa."

DiPalma picked up a flashlight and flashed it around the brick room until he found what was left of the Muramasa. Then, as the policemen watched, he took the sword and smashed it against the wall until the blade was broken from the hilt.

Todd had grown calmer, but he followed every move made by his father.

DiPalma stepped in front of the tunnel and, after once more looking at Todd, hurled the jeweled hilt far back into the darkness. When he heard it splash in the flooded passage, DiPalma turned and picked up his cane.

Without a word he began to climb the ladder.

*　　*　　*

IN Kenpachi's bedroom the only light came from the four large white candles near the white screen and rug on which the film director was to die. Nosaka concentrated on a single candle and prepared himself for the warrior's task. Gone was the fear of twenty-four hours ago when he had jumped at the sound of thunder, when he had been terrified by the sight of the Muramasa blade. Gone was his sense of shame at having fled the *dojo*.

During the purification in the dojo, *I came to know the boy as Benkai. Thus he and I were enemies for he served the lord of Ikuba Castle as my ancestors had served Hideyoshi. I fled Benkai the swordsman whom none could face. I beg your forgiveness.*

Muramasa's words. Spoken by Nosaka and accepted by Kenpachi. Admitting that the boy was Benkai had flattered Kenpachi; it was an admission that Kenpachi's power had brought Benkai to life.

And so Nosaka was a hostage, an observer at Kenpachi's planned *seppuku*. In truth, Nosaka was here to carry out Muramasa's commands. He was here because the hour of the death fury had come, a time calling for courage and greatness. Nosaka, descendant of samurai, of feudal warriors, of Nippon's first spies, was ready. Muramasa had commanded him.

Muramasa had also told him that Kenpachi was not samurai and unfit for a warrior's death.

And Muramasa had revealed to him the glory of the evil deed he was

373

about to commit, evil bred of all the evil Nosaka had ever done. Urged on by his karma, he could only obey. His karma, born of the sinister and demonic, had been nurtured by the Muramasa weapons he had collected. Muramasa had said that Nosaka's karma now called for him to dye his hands in blood. Now.

In the bedroom Nosaka stepped up to a guard and pried a sword from his fingers. The guard nodded respectfully, assuming that the charade of Nosaka as hostage was over.

The gray-haired man held the sword up to his catlike face. As rain continued to pound the castle, he stared at the candlelit blade. *To know was to act*. He smiled at the hostages and guards, then began killing them.

He plunged the sword into the stomach of a shocked politician, withdrew it and slashed a guard across his right side, sending him bleeding and spinning toward the door. As screaming hostages scattered throughout the bedroom, another guard charged Nosaka. He sidestepped his rush and cut off the guard's sword hand.

A Japanese reporter tried to run but tripped over a teakwood chest. As he frantically tried to crawl away he knocked over a tall white candle, extinguishing its flame. Nosaka raced to him, lifted the sword high and brought it down, splitting the reporter's skull. Nosaka then chased an American actress, who fled toward the door. Two steps and he was on her. He hacked her across the back of the neck, dropping her to her knees.

Muramasa was pleased, but demanded more victims.

"*Nosaka-san!*" Kenpachi's voice broke as he cried out. Too stunned to move, he stood near the screen and the candles, his eyes shimmering behind his tears. Why had this man whom he revered, to whom he owed everything, suddenly turned insane. It was beyond understanding. It was a mystery so impenetrable that it left a shocked Kenpachi on the verge of a breakdown.

Nosaka had brought the boy to him. Nosaka had given him the bone from Benkai's throat. And Nosaka had given him the Muramasa blade. Kenpachi must reason with him before it was too late. Nosaka would not harm him. The old man loved him; it was time to show that love, to cease this slaughter which had already defiled the room and made it unfit for an honorable death. Those killed by Nosaka had not died in battle. They had died at the hands of one who was crazed and therefore impure. No one should have to die in such a manner.

Such a swordsman was the instrument of gods who wanted to punish.

Kenpachi held out his hand. "*Sensei*, I ask that you give me the sword.

You have my respect, my love, and so I beg you not to defile this room any further. Please hand me the sword."

Nosaka let his sword hand drop. Only two people in the room were still alive. Kenpachi and Golden's daughter, who cringed near the tunnel entrance. Those who had not fallen victim to Nosaka's sword had fled the room.

Kenpachi, the pretender who would be a samurai. And his whore, who had betrayed the castle. Muramasa wanted them dead. Nosaka walked slowly toward Kenpachi.

Kenpachi ignored a growing fear and took one step toward Nosaka. Only one step. Smiling, Nosaka stopped and stared into the film director's eyes. Returning the smile, Kenpachi bowed. There was nothing to fear from his protector, from his mentor, who had been his whole world. He tried not to think about the horrible karma of one killed by the man Nosaka had now become. Such a death meant thousands of years of torment to come.

Nosaka's sword arm came up slowly. Then, as Kenpachi reached for the weapon, Nosaka speeded up his motion. The old man's face was a mask of revulsion. He could no longer stomach the unworthy Kenpachi. He struck. His sword stroke was strong and aimed at Kenpachi's neck.

The razor-sharp blade, a prize from Nosaka's collection, bit into Kenpachi's flesh and sliced his head from his neck. Blood spurted high into the air, then fell to the floor. The head flew into the screen, knocking it back into a candle. The candle fell to the mat, where its flame was doused by Kenpachi's blood.

In the dark room Kenpachi's headless corpse stood erect, blood spewing from the neck. Then it fell forward. The legs twitched and a straw sandal fell from one foot. In the light of one of the two candles still erect, the eyes in Kenpachi's severed head shone with an unnatural brightness. There was disbelief on his handsome face and his lips continued to move, as though still pleading with Nosaka.

Jan screamed, drawing Nosaka's attention. Smiling and happier than he had ever been, he shuffled toward her, the sword held high over his right shoulder. She backed away from the tunnel entrance and edged toward the window overlooking the courtyard. Nosaka slowly stalked her.

Jan knocked down a bamboo screen, then looked back at Nosaka. She wept and shook her head, but Nosaka kept coming. He stopped directly in front of her, alert, ready to move left or right. The window, the rain, the thunder and lightning were at her back. *To know was to act.* Nosaka lifted the sword high.

The closet door leading to the tunnel shattered, then gave way as

DiPalma pushed his way through and into the bedroom.

"Frank! Oh, God, Frank!"

Nosaka's eyes narrowed and he turned to look at his new enemy. *Kill him, said Muramasa. You are my beast of prey. You are my wolf who slinks from shadow to shadow in search of a quarry. You are my sword arm.*

DiPalma gripped his cane and stepped toward the old man. He thought of Katharine and Todd, of what Nosaka had done to Shuko and Tendrai. And to others.

A life for a life. A wound for a wound. It was time for judgment, for punishment.

Nosaka's confidence grew. The stick could not stand against the sword. He sneered, aimed the point of his sword at DiPalma's throat and inched forward.

DiPalma, barely able to breathe through his broken nose, stepped forward slowly. Judgment and punishment.

Suddenly DiPalma lashed out with his cane. Not at the old man, but at the two remaining candles, and knocked them to the floor. One flame went out immediately. DiPalma stepped on the other with his bare foot. Now the bedroom was totally black.

Nosaka froze, confused. Then he began to swing the sword wildly in all directions, calling out Muramasa's name, hearing the voice of the great swordsmith. Lightning flashed and in the brilliant light Nosaka, who was facing the window, never saw DiPalma behind him. DiPalma lifted his cane. Thunder crashed as he brought the cane down and in that instant the room became dark again.

Nosaka grunted. The sword slipped from his fingers and fell to the floor.

In the darkness the cane was raised twice more and brought down in powerful strokes. Each time it found its target.

Shuko and his men entered the bedroom from the tunnel and in the beam of their flashlights found DiPalma near the window, his arms around a weeping Jan. A few quick commands from Shuko, and his men, guns drawn, fanned out across the room. From here they moved into the hall, where they encountered guards with swords who had come to deal with Nosaka. Shots were fired. A guard fell, then the swords were dropped to the floor in surrender.

In Kenpachi's bedroom Shuko shone his flashlight beam from corpse to corpse, from the dead to the dying. He lingered briefly on Kenpachi's severed head, then moved on. He was looking for Nosaka. The American, pressing Jan tightly against him, jerked his head toward the window.

Shuko looked out into the rainy night. He heard the sounds of his men taking control of the castle and moving out into the courtyard. There were more shots. A guard on the wall screamed that he had been wounded. In the darkness flashlights were trained on two of Shuko's men as they struggled to lift the huge crossbar which locked the iron gates.

Then, in the courtyard below the window, a flashlight found Nosaka's rain-soaked body. Something dark and wet seeped from beneath the old man's skull, then was washed away by the rain.

As Shuko stared down at the dead industrialist, DiPalma held Jan and stroked her hair.

"It's over," he said. "It's all over, Jan."

And immediately sensed that it wasn't.

EPILOGUE

DECEMBER

IN Manhattan's Metropolitan Museum of Art, DiPalma held Jan's hand as they and Todd followed a small group of formally dressed men and women through a gallery lined with ancient Greek gravestones. The museum was officially closed. But tonight it was the scene of a private champagne supper following the world premiere of *Ukiyo*. As with most premieres, things had gone wrong.

Some people had attempted to get in by using counterfeit tickets. A mounted policeman's horse had accidentally stepped on a photographer, and the film had been delayed because a studio VIP had been delayed. The elaborate supper would also be late. With little else to do DiPalma and the other guests wandered through the galleries.

DiPalma had shocked Jan by his agreeing to wear a tuxedo, to join the rest of the penguins, as he put it. Jan looked beautiful in a black dress which left her shoulders bare. Her only jewelry was a string of pale blue pearls and her wedding ring. DiPalma had thought they needed the rest a honeymoon would give them, but he wasn't pushing it. The film was important to Jan and she had to go on tour with it. After the first of the year, they planned a vacation in Aruba, if she could get away.

DiPalma had worried about her sitting through the film too many times. It could trigger bad memories. Tonight she had remained silent

379

through the two-hour showing, but she had never let go of his hand.

Marriage had calmed her down. She didn't like parties any more and had lost all interest in Japan. She had sold her father's homes and was resisting pressure to move to Los Angeles. She clung to DiPalma, whether out of love or need he did not know, nor did it matter.

In the museum she looked at a collection of Greek coins. "I may not go on the tour," she said. She was upset at the thought of being apart from him.

"Your decision," he said. "I'll go along with whatever you want."

She touched the glass case covering the coins. "Was Nosaka insane?"

"Yes. He killed Kenpachi's wife and children before coming to the castle. Shuko said it was part of a samurai ritual. Said Kenpachi had an impure death. No sense going over all that. He killed six people, all told. What made you think of him?"

"I was thinking of my father. I wanted him here tonight. And I thought of what you did for him."

"All I really wanted from the files was enough to make a case against Nosaka and his spying. Nothing more. Shuko said the files were mine. Nosaka sure wouldn't be using them. No sense hurting anybody."

He grinned. "Besides, I think Shuko wanted to increase Nosaka's bad karma. But don't quote me."

Jan looked around. "Where's Todd?"

DiPalma looked left, then right. "Around somewhere. Hasn't smiled since we got back from Japan." He stopped a white-jacketed waiter, took a glass of champagne from a tray and handed it to Jan. "Good at his school work, though. Put him in private school. Thought it might be less of a culture shock. He's still strong on kendo. Does his homework. Good kid. Except he just won't smile. Doesn't make friends either. I don't push it. Wouldn't help him if I did."

Jan took his arm. "Don't worry. He'll smile. He's going to be gorgeous, I'll tell you that. A regular little heartbreaker. Let's find him."

They found him in the next gallery. He was staring at a wall hung with medieval Japanese weapons. DiPalma felt Jan's fingers dig into his arm, but she said nothing.

Jan began to shiver, then rub her bare shoulders. DiPalma felt cold, too. It was freezing in here. Near the entrance a frowning guard squinted at a thermostat. "Jesus, that's weird."

DiPalma was afraid. "What's weird?"

Jan huddled near him.

The guard shivered and continued to look at the thermostat. "Impossible. One minute it's warm, the next minute the goddamn thing goes crazy. How can it be forty in here—"

He looked at DiPalma. "Sorry. What did you say?"

DiPalma stared at Todd, who now stood in front of a glass case that contained an ornate, Japanese feudal saddle.

"That saddle," said DiPalma. "The one the boy's looking at."

"What about it?"

"Tell me about it."

"Everybody's fascinated by that thing. Just got it in this week from Japan with a lot of other stuff. It's on loan from a museum over there. Some guy died and left a bunch of things to the government. Happens all the time."

DiPalma knew.

From across the room Todd smiled at him and Jan. The room grew colder.

The guard hugged himself and hopped from foot to foot. "One of the rarest saddles in Japan, that thing. Done by a real expert. Man called Muramasa."

PULSE
POINTS

PULSE
POINTS

SUZANNE TOPPER

St. Martin's Press
New York

In loving dedication to
Sid,
who would have been proud

This is a work of fiction. All of the events, characters, names, and places depicted in this novel are entirely fictitious or are used fictitiously. No representation that any statement made in this novel is true or that any incident depicted in this novel actually occurred is intended or should be inferred by the reader.

Design by Martha Schwartz

Library of Congress Cataloging-in-Publication Data

Topper, Suzanne.
    Pulse points / by Suzanne Topper.
        p.   cm.
    ISBN 0-312-01501-1 : $19.95 (est.)
    I. Title.
PS3570.O66P8   1988
813'.54—dc19   87-29355
                                                               CIP

First Edition

10 9 8 7 6 5 4 3 2 1

There are one hundred points of measurement in the weight of a gem carat. Flashing rays bursting from skillfully cut facets imply an unquenchable internal fire. Such a high-quality stone pulsates with life.

And life imitates the gem.

PROLOGUE

Rome, Wednesday, October 10, 1979, 2:20 A.M.

IT WAS AN HISTORIC BED BUILT BY A MASTER CRAFTSMAN IN THE mid-sixteenth century. Its four corner posts were embellished with museum-worthy carvings of male and female figures entwined in sexual abandon. The fine walnut headboard was largely concealed by plump, down-filled pillows. Silken draperies were tied back at the rear sides.

The massive bed had provided sheltering rest for genera tions of the Corchese family, the site of ecstatic passion, the wonders of births, survivor of those who had lain upon it. Its legs remained sturdy, but of late the frame, headboard, posts, and canopy had commenced creaking, subtly swaying as though sympathetic to the weakening life-force of its present owner.

The old man's perspired and pallid face was revealed in the glow of the bedside lamp he switched on. *"Ho la nausea,"* he complained, his normally powerful voice subdued by the clutch of pain in his chest.

"Hush, Ugo. Have no fear. It is a spasm of gas. Merely that." His considerably younger, stout blond mistress sought to soothe him as she sat up, one full breast exposed by her twisted nightgown.

Every breath had become an effort.

"Do you suppose I have food poisoning?"

"Most likely the fish," she said, the while stroking his perspiring brow. She didn't attribute his illness to this, but there was no point in being cruel.

"I am allergic," he whispered. Nevertheless, there was naked fear in his dark eyes.

His impending death shook loose powerful memories. *Why, I am young again*, he thought with astonishment as scenes of the past flitted by his mind's eye. He gasped and his mistress wrongly attributed this to his illness.

The old man shivered mightily. His mistress' concerned face hovered above his, momentarily blocking the unwanted visions from sight. The interruption of her presence was welcome. He had heard tell that the spun thread of one's life invaded the mind shortly before death. He did not want to die.

"Is it a bit easier, *caro?*"

How desperately he wanted it to be so, but he tasted the acridness of bile rising into his mouth, and was struggling to rid himself of it when a new wave of pain crunched within his body, as if his ribs were being compressed inward. His disheveled leonine head of iron-gray hair hid his pained face as it sank onto her bare breast.

"*Un medico,*" he urgently whispered. "Send for—"

His body convulsed against her. Then as the pain subsided he quietly rested, conserving his strength, which in the past he had trusted to never fail him. An irreligious man, he fervently prayed in silent desperation. Only his eyes communicated vitality in the slackened contours of his face, until finally his lids eased shut and he moaned as the woman raised his head and supported him in her arms.

His breathing came in labored rasps, his faint pulse throbbed irregularly. Tears overflowed his eyes as he turned his fever-bright unseeing gaze directly upon his young mistress. "Daughter?" he pleaded. "Is it you? Angela Maria . . . ?" His weight upon her breast grew heavier, and with the emission of a hissing sound came the final escape of his warm breath. He was dead.

She disentangled herself from the burden of the old man's weight. Shivering from a sense of moment, she leaned over his body to reach the table holding the telephone. She squinted to dial the prearranged number.

"Come quickly . . . *subito, subito!*" she spoke into the mouthpiece.

"Who is this?" the man who sleepily answered asked.

"Serafina Musso. You told me to call you the moment . . ."

Instantly awake, excitement raised his voice to a shout. "Il principe? Is he?"

"*Sì.*"

"*Morto?*"

"I . . . I think so." She shuddered and crossed herself, looking back at the hulk of a man lying face down across his massive bed. "He doesn't move."

"Wait half an hour to be safe. Then summon his physician and a priest."

She was sobbing. "I did as you instructed . . . seduced him. Now what of me?" The woman was frightened. "You told me his heart was weak, but I am not a murderer."

"No, you are not," he said. "You will be paid our agreed-upon fee. Don't call me again. Your money will arrive in the mail."

For the past several years he had cultivated his plan, finally implementing it when his associates grew impatient waiting for the old man to die.

Ugo Ferrante, il Principe di Corchese, was dead. The plan was about to unfold.

His wife stirred on her side of the bed. "Who were you talking to?" she asked.

He despised her for being a gossip, and didn't answer.

"Men!" Her scornful voice was muffled by the pillow.

Astonishingly, he felt himself growing hard. As he visualized Ferrante in his death throes, his semen spurted onto his pajamas. Momentarily, he thought of his own mistress as he hastened to the bathroom to cleanse himself. Glancing into his own eyes in the medicine cabinet mirror, he winked as one conspirator to another. If one regarded the event with practicality, he had acted in old Ugo's best interests.

What better way for any man to die?

B·O·O·K

I

· 1 ·

Fifth Avenue, New York, 10:00 A.M.

FERRANTE WOULD OPEN FOR BUSINESS—BUT NOT AS USUAL. THE sole owner of the international retail jewelers lay dead in Rome.

Throughout the store there was a prevailing numbness among the staff, a foreboding of invasive change. A shift of management, which was likely, portended displacements, possible loss of positions long held. Anyone who hadn't already learned of the old man's death during early-morning radio and television newscasts was soberly informed of it upon entering the sparsely furnished locker room where cardboard-bearing slotted racks hung alongside the centrally positioned and much-despised time clock.

Here employees huddled together in mutual nervousness. Their subdued voices were rife with conjecture.

"I can't believe it happened," a man said.

"It hurts so much. Not because the old man died, mind you. He never came to New York, so what's to mourn?"

Someone said flatly, "We'd better mourn for ourselves."

"That's right."

There was a hum of agreement.

"Listen, we've said it all, and we'll drive ourselves crazy guessing what's going to be."

There was an angry protest. "We have to be prepared."

"Much good that's going to do you, me, or any of us."

"Perhaps we'll hear something later in the day."

"Your guess is as good as anyone's."

"Shit!"

People started to move away. The store would shortly be open for business, and they were adhering to their daily routine. Some of the sales personnel went to the main selling floor where they were accustomed to earning six percent and higher commissions, according to their years of employment. Since the merchandise sold at prices which were thousands of dollars at a minimum, should any of them lose their jobs, the loss of income would be a severe jolt. Hoping against the worst they could imagine happening, they began lighting the counters and cases, oblivious of the opulent displays of jewelry these contained. Normally, every morning was a show as exciting as the rise of a theater curtain because the lights were so cleverly positioned that quality stones sparkled and revealed depths of color that could never be seen in even so concentrated a brightness as natural sunlight. *Today was different.*

The huge bronze-framed shatterproof glass doors hadn't yet been opened. Standing nearby, guards attired in discreet business suits grouped together discussing their own speculations. They wore their working clothes since uniforms would be more attention-getting and render their function less protective of the stock. This morning they wondered how well they themselves were protected. And so it followed all through the building, which was entirely occupied by the fine jewelry department store known as Ferrante-New York. Worried persons discussed the death in staff lavatories, in the silverware department, in the china and figurine section, in the divisions of watches and clocks, glassware, crystal, engraved stationery, gold-fitted leathergoods, jewel-clasped precious metal handbags called *minaudières*. And in the special shop, small and self-contained, abutting the main floor and called the Àtrio.

It was a generally observed rule that the apricot velvet-paneled customer elevator was off-limits to employees with the particular exception of Mr. Vincent Bregna Salinari, president and chairman of the board. Today the custom was ignored as several of the designers, craftsmen, and office workers rode it upward for its greater privacy, making uneasy guesses about what would imminently happen.

Ferrante-New York was generally perceived as being a branch of the far older Roman shop. This wasn't so. It existed as a separate corporate entity with its own officers and directors. Although the deceased Ugo Ferrante had been sole owner of both enterprises, there was but a shared sisterly umbrella connection with the Italian business. The reason for the separation was obscure so many years after its inception in the 1930s.

The building itself was a contradiction. Situated between Fifty-fifth and Fifty-sixth Streets on the east side of Fifth Avenue, the store was wedged between two tall office structures, of which the southern one had been erected on land occupied by several townhouses when Ferrante-New York began doing business. A strip of land behind the commercial tower was subsequently purchased by the store, and a wing now extended behind it, accommodating a side-street employees' entrance.

On the Fifth Avenue side, the Renaissance facade was elegant Italianate with rose-hued marble slabs and, at street level, opalescent white marble framed two glittering show windows and the doorway. It was upon entering that there was a calculated shock to a visitor's eye. Ornate iron gates were folded open during store hours on either side of heavy plate-glass doors with electronic sensing devices concealed in their bronze framing. Within, the spacious two-story main selling area was in the modernistic decor of its construction era. Chrome patterns pointed two stories upward like giant silver candlesticks upon mauve silken walls.

A balcony extended across the rear, sheltering an enclave of private viewing rooms for the store's more affluent customers. Directly above, there was a small office where estate jewelry might be discreetly sold to Ferrante. Also on the mezzanine, the security division was located close by a marble staircase leading down to the street-level sales floor. Here, on the south side of the building, was the little shop of special designs called the Àtrio.

Over all, hung from a stark white ceiling, angular lighting fixtures focused upon display counters where workers continued fussing nervously with jewels gleaming against black velvet. All of the salespeople had found themselves *busy work*. They experienced a need to keep occupied. The atmosphere of impending change was making them apprehensive.

The outstandingly beautiful young woman alighted from a cab on traffic-jammed Madison Avenue, and a middle-aged business man hastily stepped out of her path when she dashed by him in great haste. He appreciatively stared after her slim figure as she long-legged it west on Fifty-fifth Street.

Gaia Gerald, the youngest of the Ferrante-New York jewelry designers, was making her hurried way toward the store's employee entrance. She was late this morning for the first time ever during her four-year employment that had suddenly thrust her from the ranks of amateur student into the realm of professionalism. Despite later success at designing a unique jewelry collection, she was continually haunted by a sense of loss—inadequacy. This was a state of mind which was long ago imbued in her.

This ingrained feeling was very much akin to the emotions she experienced earlier in the morning when she heard the report of Ugo Ferrante, il Principe di Corchese's death on the portable radio she'd been listening to in her bathroom. Her hand involuntarily shook and she had to stop brushing her teeth. Unexpectedly, she emitted a wrenching sob, startling to herself. After all, she had never even met the old man. Yet, her reaction was predictable—a grieving that frequently overcame her: pretending that she was part of other people's families. This habit of childhood had carried into her twenty-sixth (nearly twenty-seventh) year. She had transferred surrogate grandfatherly attributes to Ugo Ferrante simply because he was head of the firm she worked for—her sole sense of family.

Her startling green-flecked irises returned her mirrored gaze. It was a questing for comprehension. More composed, she wiped away a tear with the back of her hand before stroking a coat of mascara on dark lashes that needed no artificial lengthening. A nagging discontent was her strong nose, but she had never considered plastic surgery. Her artistic soul recognized that it was effective counterpoint in an otherwise pert face: round cheeks ending in a slightly pointed chin, and a lush-lipped triangular-shaped mouth. The prominence of her nose saved her features from mere prettiness. She was a striking beauty. A whisk of a comb through dark brown curls that defied control. Strands of hair bounced onto her forehead, escaping the confines of her high-swept, well-shaped coiffure, which tapered at mid-neck.

Her more immediate mental attention was focused upon memories. Of her childhood. A time of unending sadness. Deprivation. As a lonely youngster, she had created an inner world of fantasy that intruded to the present time.

She had never known any family, let alone her grandfathers. It was why, subconsciously, although she was extraordinarily fulfilled in her designing labors, she had projected Ugo Ferrante to represent a pseudo-grandfatherly figure. She'd wept as if he were her blood relation because it was her emotional necessity to do so.

On any other morning, she would have been thinking of Dominic Perrini. He occupied most of her thoughts when she wasn't contemplating the creation of a new jewelry design. Dom, whose habit was to remind her that he was older than she. He who had fascinated her from the instant of their first meeting.

His attitude was such that she always felt there was an air of mystery behind his chiseled, attractive features. His skin was swarthy (darker than hers), as though given hue from a Mediterranean sun. Was the mysteriousness she imbued him with a figment of her imagination? Merely because he refrained from offering her the attention she desired? All she could say was that she extravagantly admired him, perceiving power in his rugged handsomeness. It impressed her that he

stood half-a-head taller than she. This was an implied protec-
tiveness, as though to say that despite how she wanted to
consider herself mature, a part of her would always remain
a little girl.

Except for traces of gray, his full head of hair was as dark
as hers. His physique was without paunch, he wore his
clothes well. More than his figure, it was his face—mostly his
dark occasionally brooding eyes—that so captivated her.
What secrets were unrevealed? she wondered.

And when Dom occasionally smiled, the relaxation of his
sometimes stern countenance was precious to her. She *knew*
she'd glimpsed a sentimentality he preferred to keep hidden.
How great her pleasure to unobtrusively gaze at him, becoming enormously embarrassed should he notice. Assuredly, he
was not only a private man, but a complicated one. Wasn't
that part of his fascination for her?

She enjoyed that his humor (the little she knew of it) was
never crude. Yet, Gaia struggled within herself to never let
him realize how the other side of his wit—a sharpness, often
to the point of being caustic—could devastate her feelings.

Gaia was positive that he wasn't ever intentionally mean to
her. Mean? No, that wasn't so, she told herself. Dom excluded
her from the personal side of his life because he sheltered her.
But from what? a small unbidden voice would protest within
her. He never mentioned a wife or a family. He'd told her he
never wanted that from life. Was this his method of distanc-
ing himself from her?

She was in love with him.

On any other morning, walking more than a mile from her
Murray Hill neighborhood of sedate apartment buildings and
well-tended brownstones, Gaia would have been receptive to
the swift changes from one area of the city to another. She
would have breakfasted at home, the aroma of yesterday's
pizza wafting from open-front Lexington Avenue stores nauseating her. Rapidly passing seedy corner juice stands, she
would have hastened farther north than Grand Central Station and the Pan Am building on Park Avenue. Choosing a
steeply inclined side street, with her limbs flying, she would

have cut through to the avenue's wide sidewalks, absorbed in the joyful momentum of her pace; her eyes would have glowed as if reflecting the sun's morning radiance on glass-walled office towers. They reminded Gaia of aloof diamonds haughtily flashing spectrums of colors against a bright morning sky.

With a trained artist's perception, she appreciated the spare linear detailing of the contemporary buildings, but upon crossing Park Avenue, she would invariably gaze back at the rococo twin spires of the Waldorf-Astoria, thinking they were as delicately designed as old fine jewelry set off against the cool, clean lines of modern buildings like a cameo against shiny black glassy facades.

West then to Madison Avenue, and her excitement would mount, her creative juices already flowing, loosening that indefinably mysterious preserve within the truly talented who are on the verge of conceiving something highly original.

Reaching Fifty-fifth Street, she would have bounded toward Fifth Avenue along the north sidewalk to reach the store's employees' entrance. She was humble about her talent because it was such a privilege to be a Ferrante-New York jewelry designer.

But on the morning when Ugo Ferrante died, Gaia walked slowly, almost hesitant to enter the store. When she would normally have cheerily greeted the guard on duty, today she silently passed him by, her eyes averted. She couldn't shake off a pervasive foreboding. This day—was it because she was saddened by Ferrante's death?—remembrance of the forlornness of her youth, more than its poverty, was very much with her.

It was already late, and the locker room was deserted. Selecting her time card, she regretted that the clock would punch in the late time of her arrival. Preparing to insert the card into the stamping mechanism, she reconsidered. It was not her nature to be devious, except that she was aware that the wonderful job she'd assumed to be permanent might very well not be. She was, after all, the junior designer in terms of years of employment. If economies were about to be made by new ownership, it followed that she would be the first to be discharged in the design department.

Try as she might, she was unable to convince herself that her job wasn't in jeopardy. Washroom attendants and cleaners would be newly on a par with higher-echelon commissioned sales clerks, jewelry appraisers, model-makers, lapidists, stone cutters and setters, cashiers, bookkeepers, secretaries, minor executives, guards—all those whom she thought of as her work family. The most elite of all were the name designers. She was the youngest. The most expendable.

She returned her unstamped card to its place in the rack. Better to let it be assumed that she had neglected to check in because of confusion over the news.

If this had been an ordinary day, she would have gone to her cubicle-size studio, actually a white-painted plywood sectioned-off portion of the larger design area, otherwise divided into walled rooms for the senior designers. Seldom interrupted here, she was always so eager to sketch her ideas that she barely noticed her isolation in the windowless space. Illumination was from a fluorescent ceiling bulb and a draftsman's-type lamp clamped on to her standing easel. Too uneasy to bear being alone this morning, she directly headed for the main sales floor.

Fairly recently there had been those who decried the decor as being out-of-date, and considerable discussion ensued about refurbishing at substantial cost. Until Miles Tuchelin, the store's talented youthful director of promotion and advertising, became the man of the moment, convincing the board of directors that he would glorify its period style. He inveigled the major fashion and decorating magazine editors to spark a revival of Art Deco.

This accomplished, Ferrante-New York was the earliest beneficiary. Tuchelin generated an enormous swell of publicity for the store. The candlestick motif on the side wall remained prominent. Silver and mauve continued to be used as signature colors, including on distinctively striped gift-wrapped packages tied with metal-shot silver ribbons and hand-delivered to each of the editors.

* * *

When Gaia opened a service door to walk out on the main floor, she immediately saw that people were crowding through the Fifth Avenue entrance. She could tell further that few of these were regular customers. It was too early in the day for serious shoppers. These people were curiosity seekers, because they had heard news stories of the owner's death. Probably, it was already spelled out in newspaper headlines in morning editions.

It was her intention to proceed to the southernmost corner of the floor on the avenue side, where there was a small enclave with a low ceiling. It resembled a fancied-up closet and had previously been used as a wrapping section until Miles Tuchelin implemented a better idea. He publicized it as the Àtrio, meaning "antechamber" in literal English translation, but since it led to no room beyond, the word was incorrectly used. It was where the jewelry of Gaia's design was sold.

"*Àtrio* has a good sound. There's a definite ring to it, don't you agree?" he'd enthusiastically asked her.

There were those who were openly amused by Miles—at his expense and behind his back. Gaia wasn't one of them. It distressed her that much of the humor was a cruel jibe—in her opinion—at his physical appearance. He was short, and his wiry figure seemed to be in perpetual motion. Miles was liable to unexpectedly show up anywhere in the store. A shock of orangy-red hair was laughingly referred to as the flame at the head of a match. Gaia declared that this was the expression of others' envy. Perhaps some persons would rather forget just how much he'd done for the store. She indignantly took his side, often chiding staff members for their disrespect.

Oddly, by the way they reacted, she became aware that some among them were envious of *her*. As for herself, she acknowledged that it was Miles who first saw commercial merit in her jewelry when she was too timid to take her ideas to Michael Vanderman, the head of the design department.

Gaia remembered pleading with Miles: "Please promise me

you won't say anything to Mr. Vanderman. I didn't do these pieces on assignment, so he knows nothing of them. I don't want him to know I've been designing for myself during store hours."

"If you don't see the potential of what you've got here, I sure do." Miles smiled as he picked a glistening, golden star.

"Stop teasing me, Miles. You asked to see what I've been working on, so I showed you. Now let me put everything away. It could be just my luck that, of all times, he'll decide to walk in here while everything is spread on my work table. I should never have shown you what I've been playing around with. Mr. Vanderman would be furious. He's been reluctant to let me design anything totally on my own, and he'll know I went behind his back."

"Did you do it to deceive him? Were you evil?"

"No, of course not. I had ideas that I sketched."

"What's so bad about that?"

"I did it without permission. Oh, don't you understand that nothing good can come of this? Besides, I'd get the goldsmith in trouble who made these designs up for me. I'm going to bring them back to him to melt down."

Miles gripped her arm as she would have reached toward the table. "Any jewelry designer, including Vanderman, would be proud of these."

"Why? Mr. Vanderman is a world-famous master of design. He uses priceless, fabulous stones. All of *my* work is unimportant."

"Gay, Gay, Gay!" he remonstrated, mispronouncing her name, though she was too upset to notice. "What you have here *is* important! Take this star in particular. It's dimensional, sculpted . . . its points jut out like brilliant rays. The moonstone you've positioned at its highest peak works wonderfully, although I would much prefer to see a fifteen-point diamond set there. Depending on the size of the star, of course. The largest would require a carat or more."

"You're not joking, are you?"

His reply was brisk. "Do I ever?" His eyes narrowed

speculatively. "Of all the pieces, the star is the strongest. We'll use it as the leader."

"Whatever you're planning, Miles, this time it's hopeless. It will never be put on sale at Ferrante. It's not . . . grand enough."

"Hush up and let me consider. What I want you to do is design several interesting-looking chains . . . three of them, each heavier weight than the next. The stars will also be in three sizes. Have the chains end low on the chest." He pointed to the middle of his tie. "I'm going to convince the powers that be to feature your jewelry. The star will be a great pendant. Fantastic! All the beautiful people will be wearing them. And I'll promote it everywhere until they do."

"You know very well that Mr. Vanderman won't allow—"

"And what makes you suppose I'm about to ask his permission?"

"Okay then, if you plan on speaking to Mr. Salinari, he's a hidebound traditionalist. He'd never agree."

"Exactly! Which is why I'm going above our stodgy president, directly to the board of directors. Say, isn't your friend one of the board members?"

Gaia hoped that she wasn't blushing. "I am acquainted with one of the directors," she admitted, feeling heated and uncomfortable although Miles had already turned away, forever on the move. She would have wanted to read his expression, to see how much he knew. "I hardly ever see Dominic Perrini." She thought to add, "He's often out of the country."

This last was certainly true. Didn't she receive his gifts purchased during his frequent travels? Pearls from the Orient, cashmere from Scotland, something funky from London, perfume from Paris. And when he *was* in New York, she never had the romantic dinner date hoped for. Always, after a functional meal, he dropped her off at her apartment building, to return alone to his Mercedes, perhaps finding his night's companion elsewhere. She thought of Dom Perrini every night when she got into bed—alone, except for sensual reveries. Her body ached with desire until her own fingers and seductive imagery eased her passion.

* * *

She preferred not to question Miles about how he'd accomplished it. His drive was compulsive. Within a week carpenters were brought in to hammer behind a screen during store hours, a necessity because of security requirements. Within a month, the Àtrio was a reality. Advertisements and publicity articles began appearing in *Vogue*, *W*, *Harper's Bazaar*, and *New York* magazine. For Gaia, the ultimate thrill was when, on page three of the *New York Times*, she saw a line-boxed ad containing a photograph of the pendant and the copy: "The Gaia Star. Available in the Àtrio at Ferrante-New York."

Sales of the Gaia Collection in the beautiful new Àtrio were higher in percentage than any other jewelry line sold in the store.

"You have to admit that I did well by you," Miles boasted.

"Except for one thing."

He seemed surprised. "Yeah? What's that?"

"My name."

"What about it?"

"You always mispronounce it. It's *Guy-ah*. When I was a small child, an Italian-born nun told me how to say it."

"Oh, come on." Miles didn't like being corrected. "I called you Gay as a sort of pet name," he assured her, although it wasn't true. "Anyway, I'll bet your folks didn't always say 'Gaia.'"

She didn't answer.

Gaia snapped out of her reverie. She glanced at her wristwatch. It wasn't yet 10:30, and people were continuing to stream through the Fifth Avenue entrance. Walking as quickly as she could manage in the crush, Gaia noticed that the unexpected horde was being watched over with special alertness by the plain-clothes guards, each of whom she recognized. Busy sales personnel at those counters featuring expensive jewelry had little to do other than occasionally answer ridiculous inquiries.

"How much is that necklace?"

This, about a piece of some twenty-four precisely matched

four-carat diamonds of superb coloration in combination with smaller diamonds of no less quality, all flanking a magnificent centered emerald.

"One million dollars."

A silly grin. "I didn't know it was real."

The saleswoman put her fingers to her temples and, looking across at Gaia, shook her head.

As she progressed toward the Àtrio, Gaia listened to anxiety-spawned rumors spreading like a contagious disease from tongue to tongue. A replacement staff would shortly be imported from Italy.

Wrong! The stores in Rome and New York were going to be permanently shuttered.

Absolutely incorrect! Ferrante would merge—with Tiffany, Bulgari, Cartier, Harry Winston, Van Cleef & Arpels, H. Stern. Take your pick, depending upon who told you.

Nonsense! Didn't everyone know the business was going to be sold to a European conglomerate whose other properties included coal mines in Kentucky, an Australian publisher, a French couture house, a fat farm in Capri, and Las Vegas gambling operations?

Impossible! The privately held majority stock was going to be floated on the over-the-counter market.

Not so! A New York real estate magnate had already tendered a $10 million binder for the land and air rights. A sixty-story condominium and office tower was going to be erected on the site, and Ferrante-New York would ultimately occupy considerably smaller space upon the building's completion. Ergo, a loss of jobs.

This was why Vincent Bregna Salinari had arrived early and gone to his office.

A fierce loyalty to the store built within Gaia. Forgotten for the moment was her own earlier fear of being discharged, a fate she'd felt was inevitable. Despite her association with Dom Perrini she knew she would never ask him for favors, not when he was generally unavailable to her. It was a matter of pride.

As she neared the Àtrio, a telephone rang inside the small shop. When she entered, she saw that Clarise, the head salesperson for the Gaia Collection, was speaking with quiet seriousness into its mouthpiece. She spotted Gaia and motioned with the receiver aloft in her hand. "It's for you."

"Who's calling?"

"Etta Spring."

The president's private secretary . . . With a heavy heart, Gaia reached across the counter for the receiver, stretching its curled cord as she brought it over, preparing herself for the woman's cigarette-harsh, grating voice.

"Mr. Salinari wants to see you in his office at once."

There was no chance to reply as the connection broke off. Gaia saw Clarise regard her questioningly, and she turned away so as not to meet her eyes. She wished to absorb this hurtful moment in relative privacy.

She had been summoned because he was going to fire her. What other reason could there be?

· 2 ·

WHY ME? GAIA'S HEART HAMMERED HER NERVOUSNESS. SO, SHE was going to be dismissed, just as she'd feared. The other jewelry designers were safe because of their seniority. She was the youngest; it was unfair.

Mona Hof, flamboyantly clothed, middle-aged, and stocky, used odd color combinations in her overpowering eye makeup. Her cheeks were dusted with a plum shade, and her mouth was over-painted in orangy-red. She sprawled like an overgrown plant in her batik-decorated studio. Her jewelry designs were as preposterous as the woman herself, but she had a following. Her designs sold well.

There was prim-looking Greer Hadley. Ever a purist, her clientele was attracted to her traditional designs, which relied upon high-quality gems and superior workmanship. It was her specialty to create necklaces that might be ingeniously separated into a pair of bracelets, or earrings a woman could attach to a platinum frame and wear as a pin.

Then there was taciturn Henry Phelps, Ohio-born and Paris-trained, whose work showed intricacy and cleverness. He was famous for concealing watches in imaginative bracelets heaped with gems. His rings garnered him renown for the use of gemstones in unexpected combinations: large-carat diamonds set into imperial jade bands, the finest black opals with rare Burmese rubies, aquamarines with diamonds and sapphires, magnificent gray-hued pearls with emeralds. His work was unusual and instantly recognizable, highly prized in private jewelry collections.

And lastly, Michael Vanderman himself, head of the department, an Englishman, long residing in New York, wielding absolute control over the design associates. In his youth he'd been employed by De Beers in London, and was subsequently apprenticed to the master jewelers on Bond Street, where sales were likely to be made to Eastern potentates with fortunes to spend. Brooches for emirs' turbans, jeweled medallions for their tunics, matched sets of necklaces, dangling earrings, lavish brooches, and important rings for their women, often in multiples for entire harems. Then, too, of course, by appointment to the British royal family, tiaras were reset with family-owned jewels. Gems presented by foreign rulers were to be set into brooches designed for Their Majesties, requiring personal consultation at Buckingham Palace. When Michael Vanderman decided to cross the Atlantic, he became a valuable asset to Ferrante-New York.

Well what chance, Gaia asked herself, do I have against them? There was no question that if cuts in staff were to be made, she was the one to be first discharged. She walked, head up despite her nervousness, toward Salinari's domain.

The chief executive's penthouse office was the most imposing of any of the rooms on Ferrante's uppermost story. Within his suite, a ceiling had been removed to accommodate the arched supports transported, under Vincent Bregna Salinari's personal orders, from a medieval Italian palazzo, necessitating the bribing of workmen and truckers, as well as a questionably honest Roman customs inspector paid to look anywhere but in the outsize crates awaiting loading in an airport cargo warehouse.

The lower level of Ferrante-New York was given over to general administration offices. A special stairway was sealed from general access by a barred gate. When a coded card was inserted in a magnetically activated security lock, one gained access to the stairs that led to the firm's jewelry-manufacturing factory, further protected by a steel-grilled electronically fortified door that was equipped with a buzzer. Anyone who had successfully reached this point was scrutinized through a television screen.

Beyond this was a series of rooms in the wing on a side street. One with northern exposure was given to stone sorting, and was equipped with special blue-tinted high-intensity fluorescent overhead lighting. There was a medium-size safe built into a wall. Behind a closed door was the grimy cutter's area with rough-surfaced wheels and polishing equipment. Another room was given to model making and jewel setting. Here were stone-surfaced bench tables, burners, pots for softening wax that would be compressed into molds according to designers' sketches. While some casting work in metal was farmed out to specialists in the West Forty-seventh Street jewelry district, there were in-house artisans to work on the finest pieces in eighteen-karat gold, platinum, and palladium.

By contrast, Vincent Bregna Salinari's office suite was furnished with a noteworthy collection of Italian Renaissance antiques requiring precise temperature and humidity control. Visitors were apt to be uncomfortable in the climate that was more beneficial to architectural and decorative treasures and richly framed old masters than human beings. Salinari considered himself an authoritative custodian, but there were those who claimed his unhealthy pale appearance was due to excessive inhalation of the chilled dry air, better suited to inanimate objects.

But for all of Salinari's vaunted knowledge of art, he was considered lacking in understanding of the intricacies of the fine jewelry business. For example, there was the time when he vetoed purchasing loose diamonds from the De Beers combine in London because it offended him that a package of stones is sold as is, with no substitutions allowable for the quality carat stones preselected by the seller. Such manner of trade has been traditional throughout decades, and De Beers protects its monopoly by buying the output of competitive sources, including the choicest stones produced by Russian mines, in order to keep them from flooding the market. Vincent Bregna Salinari, out of ignorant conceit, proclaimed he had been personally insulted. Didn't they appreciate his stature and know with whom they were dealing?

An accommodation was hastily made. Salinari was induced to sail from Southampton on the *QE2* (he refused to fly), and a Belgian agent was commissioned by Ferrante-New York to make the purchase instead.

At first, Salinari chose to pretend he had never heard of the store's De Beers acquisition. When he could no longer do so, he argued violently with the head designer, seeking to save face.

"All work must cease immediately," he loudly decreed. "I refuse to sanction your going behind my back."

"The project is too far along to stop," Vanderman replied, standing his ground.

Of course, Salinari had to back down. It was common knowledge that he was only a figurehead. Furious, he assuaged his lost dignity in a renewed rudeness to Etta Spring, his mature, hard-smoking secretary, who couldn't talk back. Theirs was a longtime relationship, and strictly business. What she thought of him, no one knew, but she was not generally liked. One of her functions was to act as a buffer between him and the employees.

On his way out of Salinari's office during the De Beers confrontations, Michael Vanderman had muttered to Etta that the London incident had been a near debacle. The store had come close to being cut off forever from the internationally recognized diamond broker's carefully controlled output.

"The old fool has sawdust where his brain ought to be," he complained. "I'll never understand how he holds on here. President and chairman of the board, indeed!"

From behind a cloud of cigarette smoke, she made no reply.

Etta Spring, for her part, knew exactly how he did it.

He was a corporate figurehead—selected by the board of directors because of his dry, uncommunicative personality, which was well-suited to their intent—and he acceptably circulated—at arm's length from his wife—in the upper echelons of the socially elite.

Salinari was his mother's family name.

In boyhood, Vincent considered that he was vastly different from his father, whom he despised not for being a minor hood, but because he was limited by innate stupidity. Vincent's father hung his head, shoulders hunched. His lips were slack, his limited vocabulary was thick with slurring and, at times, difficult to comprehend. Vincent was enormously embarrassed to be the son of such a father—embarrassed and, silently, deeply furious.

However, Vincent's withdrawn character chiefly derived from his mother's compensating domination over both him and his sisters. He was almost slavishly obedient to her; he feared her wrath. His resentfulness built within him like a poison, as potent as the poverty and teeming humanity-packed environs of Mulberry Street.

A school expedition in the fourth grade provided his first trip away from Brooklyn. It was to the Metropolitan Museum of Art. The upper Fifth Avenue location impressed him and he returned alone, time and again, to the museum. Guards throughout the galleries began recognizing the tall, delicately slim, and shabby boy, but he ignored their greetings. He did not like these men in their gilt-touched dark uniforms. Too many times Vincent had seen neighbors being arrested by young arrogant policemen, and he harbored a deep fear of any authority.

One day when he stood before a full-length classical painting of a semi-draped young woman, her lovely face inherently luminous, a guard approached Vincent from behind, touched the now fifteen-year-old boy on the shoulder, and said, "Your mother must be just as beautiful."

He shuddered as if the man's fingers were electrically charged. Tears surfaced in the boy's eyes, and the guard assumed his mother was dead; but before he could ease the tense moment, Vincent dashed out of the gallery.

He sullenly returned to his family's cold-water apartment,

relieved to find it unexpectedly empty, for he was burdened by the shame of his mother's grotesque deformity. Her twisted mouth, congenitally drawn downward, slanted toward the left side of her long narrow face, rendering her expression perpetually dissatisfied. Her dull black hair was brushed close to her skull, fastened at her scrawny neck in a bun from which strands were forever escaping. With no one to hear, he shouted foul street words and curses at the dirty walls, venting his fury at their poverty. He couldn't know that something traumatic had happened before he'd returned home.

His father had been murdered.

Gregorio Bregna, Vincent's father, ran errands for one of the leading crime families, of which Antonucci Perrini was don. Perrini considered loan sharking and protection scams his largesse to the immigrant community. Both were *services* required to safeguard individuals and shopkeepers—who quickly became the helpless victims of that "protection."

Bregna had never even footed the bottom rung of mob hierarchy; months before, Perrini had decided he was the logical choice to be sacrificed—an expendable patsy in a caper.

"Woman, I am big shot," Bregna had stupidly bragged to his wife. "Signor Antonucci Perrini respects me so much that he is giving me my own candy store."

A candy store proprietor too inefficient to reorder stock, whose egg creams were deplorable, whose bubble gum machines were always empty. Perrini's men were here because the true purpose of the business existed in the store's back room, where a bookie operation thrived on a rival gang's turf.

"That half-ass motherfucker," the bookies complained. "Ya can't even depend on him to have a pack of smokes in the brand ya want. He's always just out of whatever y'ask him for."

So his nickname became Just Out. When Perrini was told, he laughed so hard that he gagged, and had to be slapped on the back. It was the only time anyone had dared to touch him.

There was a preplanned escape route in case of trouble: through the store's back door and along an alley to an emer-

gency dash up a fire escape, then across two adjoining rooftops to the inside stairs of a tenement a block north, there to
emerge on a safe street. It was a plan that had been worked
out in committee when the shop was leased. The men in the
store used it at the crucial moment—except Just Out. He was
riddled with bullets while mixing one of his atrocious egg
creams on an otherwise sunny afternoon.

The hood who'd shot him stood with the gun still smoul-
dering in his hand, a smile fixed upon his pock-marked face.
"The flavor ain't piss chocolate no more," he'd said.

It was not a rub-out to be avenged.

Vincent Bregna Salinari buzzed his secretary, Etta Spring,
on the intercom. "Locate that young designer girl. Send her
directly to me. Tell her I require her presence without delay."

"Do you mean Gaia Gerald, sir?"

"At once!" he shouted.

Gaia rapped upon the carved wooden door.

"Enter!"

She hesitated, her heart beating rapidly although her long
fingers already gripped the curved door handle. She was motivated by a familiar reaction to authority that she hadn't permitted herself to dwell upon these past several years.
Powerful bittersweet memories can never be contained. In a
flash of revelation, she realized she had only fooled herself
when she believed that because her life was creatively fulfilled
by her designing work, she was immune to past achings of
inferiority.

It was as though she had known all along that someday she
would again stand unprotected and afraid. With her hand still
on the handle, she wrestled with her fears, seeking the courage not to turn heel and flee.

She had never revealed the terribleness of her unhappy
childhood. To speak of it would have overwhelmed her with
painful memories, rushing out of control, as if each were a
frame in a motion picture film gone wild, running backwards
at increasingly faster speed. How much wiser she'd been,
schooling herself to be cautiously reserved, a close acquain-

tance rather than an intimate friend—no matter how often she yearned for it to be otherwise.

Except with Dom. Simply because she was in love with him. She had loved him totally, recklessly, from that unexpected moment during her adolescence when he entered her life. She owed him all that she was, but her feelings toward him extended far beyond gratitude. Her adolescent ardor had grown into the strong passions of a grown woman. She had earlier unquestioningly accepted his advice when there was a career choice to be made. Why then hadn't she thought to phone Dom before coming up here? She remained standing outside of Vincent Bregna Salinari's office, victimized by her apprehension. Gaia squared her shoulders.

In adult years she had determined to develop a strong personality. No one had suspected the tremendous effort involved before she could psych herself to appear as a guest on the TV talk shows on which Miles booked her to publicize the Gaia Star. In the Àtrio, Clarise never imagined Gaia's inner struggle to overcome timidity when she engaged in conversation with an admiring customer, but how charmingly she'd win that customer over!

The voice from the inner side of the door was recognizably impatient. "Why don't you come in, Miss Gerald?"

She turned the handle, swallowing hard. As the door shut behind her, she faced the thin aging man who remained seated behind his broad ornate desk at the far end of the Oriental-carpeted room. The carpet's busy patterns did not harmonize with the other furnishings. The room, however large, gave the impression of pushing in upon its overabundant decor.

Renaissance oil paintings by great masters competed for wall space with finely stitched scenic allegorical tapestries of an earlier era. Statuary flanked well-preserved cabinetry and stacks of ornate gold church vestments. Remaining partially crated was a section of a stained glass window of remarkable artistry depicting gossamer angels floating above the Christ figure. Its rich coloring was dissipated in the artificial lighting.

Any knowledgeable curator immediately would have marveled at the collection, while frowning at the disarray in which the parts were thrown together. The ineffectual display so denigrated the importance of each individual piece.

Although Gaia had never been in the room before, she instinctively knew that Vincent Bregna Salinari was incapable of seeing this disorder. During her employment, she'd heard rumors that Salinari's collection was actually acquired with Ferrante money that had been covered by the clever bookkeeping assistance of his secretary, Etta Spring.

Whatever the rumors, the sheer arrogance of the man facing her was unmistakable. He stared at her coldly from behind his desk. Worried as she was about her future, she experienced embarrassment recalling the way the staff mocked him for his false pretensions.

She had heard that he and his wife kept separate bedrooms. There were those who said that he didn't dare exercise his real sexual preference, and that the collection was the only emotional outlet for a man who'd been relentless in the pursuit of financial and social success.

But then Gaia thought, What does any of this matter to me?

"Be seated." A bony hand gestured toward an upholstered straight-back, armless "audience" chair.

Gaia precariously balanced herself upon its front frame, wary of its sagging seat. Although she was slim, the chair creaked, warning of its unsteadiness.

For a considerable time there was an anticipatory silence, Salinari's technique in managing an interview, a practice she'd also heard rumors of.

Gaia fidgeted, her hands in her lap, fingers gripping fingers. More than at any moment since becoming a name designer, she wanted to remain at Ferrante's. Her newest piece—a sun and moon pendant—was about to be introduced in the Àtrio. Her Àtrio! Unless she managed to save her job this would be taken from her.

"Shall we settle down?"

"Yes, sir."

He cleared his throat, and peered at her through laced fingers held before his pale face. "Why are you staring so hard at me, young woman?"

She drew a deep breath. "I'm sorry, sir. I wasn't aware of it." He seemed as nervous as she. Perhaps there was some slight hope.

"Do you enjoy designing jewelry?"

"Very much." She leaned imperceptibly forward. "I'm happy my designs are an asset to the store."

He sounded impatient. "I didn't ask you that."

Her spirits sank.

"How have you reacted to il Principe's death, may I inquire?"

She answered him quietly, "I have been mournful."

There was no change in his facial expression. "Then you do understand?"

She was puzzled. "I'm sorry, I don't."

"You know absolutely nothing?" It irritated him that he was being used as an errand boy. This was what his father had been. He must be especially careful, however, not to allow his animosity to spill over on this young woman. He needed to cultivate her. "My dear, I have great news for you."

Salinari reached for a cigarette and lit it with a silver desk lighter. He belatedly remembered to offer her one.

"No thank you. I don't smoke."

He continued observing her from behind each puff of smoke. Strangely, she was becoming aware that of the two of them, he was acting the most nervous.

"The hell with it!" His voice seemed strangled as he ground the cigarette into an ashtray. "An attorney should be telling you this, but since I am head of the firm"—his voice strengthened as he recited his corporate position—"the duty falls to me. My dear, simply said, you are an heiress."

"An . . ." Blood suddenly pounded through her veins. She experienced a pulsation in her throat. Her face whitened.

He hurriedly came around the desk to grasp her, and continued speaking. "Under Italian law, you have inherited the New York store. It is separate, you know, from the one in

Rome. You own all of the stock in the American corporation."

She swallowed, unable to speak, shaking her head from side to side in protest. "It can't be," she said. The room seemed to sway.

"Why do you protest your good fortune?" He poured a glass of water for her from his carafe, and her hand visibly shook when she accepted it. "I can understand that you are in shock, my dear." He drew up an armchair for her. "But believe me, once you become accustomed to this, you'll find it's not difficult to be rich. You are many times a millionaire."

Gaia sipped the water, then set down the glass. "I can't believe . . . no, there's a gigantic mistake, Mr. Salinari. . . . Surely a relative—"

"That you are. Ugo Ferrante, il Principe di Corchese, was your maternal grandfather."

"That's impossible! I mean, it's . . . I . . . I am not his heir . . . because I am an orphan. I have no family." It was her most guarded secret, and she felt herself tremble as she whispered the words aloud.

He turned paler than his normal complexion. "Even orphans have antecedents."

"Mine are deceased. I contacted an organization that tries to reunite people like me with their natural parents. They made a search. The report they gave me was negative."

Salinari panicked. At this point he *had* to gain her trust— for his own sake.

"I sympathize, dear girl. This is overwhelming news indeed. It is logical for you to be upset."

"If it is true that I am Mr. Ferrante's granddaughter, wouldn't he have acknowledged me when he was alive? Why was it kept hidden?"

"I don't know." Salinari was edgy. "Come now, you should be elated. You are a wealthy young woman."

Gaia shook her head. "May I use your phone?" she asked.

"Miss Spring will answer when you pick up the receiver. She'll connect you with your party."

Gaia turned her back to him and spoke softly into the

mouthpiece. "I want to talk to Mr. Dominic Perrini." She gave Etta Spring the number.

"I couldn't help but overhear. You're calling Dom?"

"Yes." She looked at him in momentary surprise. But of course he would recognize the name. Dom was a director of Ferrante-New York.

"It was he who informed me of your inheritance."

"*He*—Dom—he . . ." Then into the phone she said, "Etta, please cancel the call." She placed the hand piece back into its cradle.

If her inheritance was valid, although she couldn't imagine that . . . if Dom had known, or believed that she was Ugo Ferrante's heir . . . why hadn't he told her? Pieces fell into place . . . or almost did. She tried to think clearly. It was difficult to believe that she really was his kin. Although . . . there was the coincidence of how Dom had urged her to study jewelry design—how he arranged that she come to work at Ferrante-New York. She couldn't help but speculate: Was it for his profit or hers?

The aspect of suspecting Dom was new, shocking, and repulsive to her. Gaia couldn't possibly feel bitterness toward him. Hadn't Dom always been caring, looking out for her best interests?

"My dear girl," Vincent Bregna Salinari was saying, "remember you can count on me to be your friend. Should you ever need my help—"

"It's too late," she replied tonelessly, "if my grandfather is already dead."

· 3 ·

Sister Mary Agnes, one of the younger nuns, rapped for attention on the head table in the dining hall of the Children's Home of Little Flowers.

"Today is our dear Gaia's birthday," she announced to the less-than-interested children, until their whoops of pleasure had to be quieted when they learned each would receive an unaccustomed portion of chocolate ice cream and a cookie. "Gaia is seven years old today!"

The nun was a good-hearted, simple young woman with an uncomplicated trust in her faith. She was, therefore, deeply puzzled when she was reprimanded by the mother superior.

"How did you know that today is the child's natal day?"

"I saw it in her records, Mother."

"Which means you invaded a file folder that you were not authorized to see."

"No one told me that I shouldn't have."

"What else did you read about the girl? Speak up."

Mary Agnes nervously fingered her rosary beads.

"Do you solemnly swear, under penalty of expulsion from the order, that you will never reveal what you saw?"

"Yes, Mother, I do."

"One thing more. Should the Gerald girl ever question you,

the ban on divulging information—particularly to her—is not to be forgotten by you."

"It won't be."

"You are dismissed."

The nun crossed herself. "Thank you, Mother."

"Don't be so foolish as to ever bring this up again. Now leave me and remember to keep silent."

For many weeks thereafter, the sensitive Sister Mary Agnes worried through long nights of sleeplessness. She felt that the admonition had been unjustified. As she recalled, none of the entries in the file folder had seemed unique. It contained what every orphan's dossier detailed so far as possible: what was known concerning parentage; date and place of birth; medical records; handwritten and typed reports; a birth certificate if available. Now curiosity consumed her like a passion, and she recognized this was a mortal sin.

She attempted to rationalize it because of her concern over the unhappy little girl whose emotions were so blocked that she couldn't even manifest delight at her own birthday party. In the quiet of her bed, the young nun reaffirmed her intention to help Gaia, whose name had strangely never been placed—not once—on an adoption list. Why was this? She was, on all scoring, highly desirable. Gaia was beautiful, healthy, intelligent; she had no obvious defects, medical or otherwise. The nun was sorely tempted to sneak back into the small close office where the dusty seldom-used file cabinets were stored and study the file more closely—but knew that she wouldn't. She was tremendously afraid of the consequences she might suffer, and prayed to Jesus to shelter her in anonymity in the sight of the mother superior.

Until Gaia was about three years old, she didn't realize she was bereft of both her parents. There was enough constant activity in the Home of Little Flowers to occupy her days, however predictable with their never-varying routine. There were early-morning and evening prayers and catechisms, which were intended to solidify into a granite-like spiritual foundation. Young roots, however, can force themselves through the hardest of substances to outer channels of nourishment. For Gaia, Sunday Mass provided lovely unregulated hours in which she could freely indulge in forbidden thoughts and flights of fancy.

She would look hungrily around the church, staring at the people streaming in through the huge front doors. She was especially in awe of women in fussy hats and bright-colored clothing. She could not at first comprehend why the orphanage children were separated in a block of side pews from the other congregants. She observed other youngsters seated in center pews among grown-ups, men as well as women. Upon returning to the Home, Gaia's ensuing questions confounded the nuns, who supplied only sketchy answers.

"Because they have parents. That's why."

"Why do they?"

"It is how God decreed."

"Why don't I have parents?"

"Because! Gaia, it is time for your nap."

The child hadn't been difficult until now.

By the nature of their calling, the nuns were accustomed to accepting rigid discipline, but it was frequently painful for them—as it was for the children—when they had to resist the urge to offer a motherly embrace, to kiss an upturned face, to lavishly compliment a small virtue. Despite widely circulated belief spread by half-told whispers, this stern dictum was not handed down by diocesan authority. It was a ruling enacted within the Home as a necessary means of obtaining order and avoiding favorites. The Home sheltered 340 children when there was full occupancy, and a spare cot was rarely available.

This was intended to be a temporary holding residence, and its children were not considered to be hapless victims of fate and society but blessed by its patron saint, Theresa of the Little Flower. The very name of the orphanage was meant to be a hopeful infusion of religiosity for each of the otherwise abandoned children. Hadn't they, thanks to Christ and the Catholic Church, a roof over their heads, food on the table, clothes to wear? Of course, because the garments and shoes were charitably donated, they rarely fit.

Gaia Gerald was the only child held over year after year. The mother superior had privately spoken to Father Burney about this.

"The child is well formed, intelligent, and would be of a pleasing disposition was she not so unnaturally confined. Why may she not be adopted?"

"I understand the reason better than you."

"By whose directive is she kept here?"

"Not by anyone in the Church."

The mother superior was appalled to realize that a lay power could be stronger than the ecclesiastical. "Who can be so cruel?" she protested. "An orphan's prime time of adoptability is in infancy. It happens that Gaia came to us when she was past two years old, but there is still opportunity! She is an exceptionally pretty girl. In fact, several times I initiated adoption inquiries on her behalf. One time I was positive I'd accomplished a match between a fine young couple and Gaia. Poor lamb, she was tearful when she was interviewed by them. It was heartbreaking the way she sobbed for her blood parents, whom her file shows as deceased. I remember thinking then that Gaia had touched upon something by intuition. Yet this couple was delighted with her. Suddenly, without explanation, they refused to take her. I questioned them and they appeared frightened . . . no, *terrified!* I had the distinct impression that their fear had nothing to do with the child's tears. They withdrew their application to adopt her, reacting as if they'd been threatened."

The mother superior wasn't worldly, but neither was she stupid. Father Burney recognized this and wanted to change the subject. "The second-grade textbooks that were delayed will be delivered next week," he said. "I personally checked into that for you."

Her thoughts lingered with Gaia. "I suppose there may be some person, organization, entity . . . whatever . . . powerful enough to keep this child from entering a normal household."

"It is wiser, Mother Superior, not to contemplate."

"Do you know what or who?"

"I don't."

* * *

Until her twelfth year, the orphanage was Gaia's entire world.

It had formerly been a privately owned estate, abandoned when the city of Chicago sprang up around its wrought-iron fence. As the neighborhood changed, the fence became more of a protection than a decorative border of a wealthy family's preserve. The property was donated to the Catholic diocese, and ultimately the ornate rooms within the red-brick Georgian structure were stripped; chandeliers, paintings, and other moveable features of architectural grandeur were removed to the residences of the hierarchy.

Separate dormitories for males and females were created when the already sizable third-floor bed chambers were enlarged, and lines of cots were installed with footlockers wedged beneath each. The upper floor beneath the attic contained a warren of maids' rooms that served for the sisters, who doubled and tripled in their occupancy of these. Because it had originally been a home of wealth, Little Flowers fortunately contained enough bathrooms to service the building's increased population. The former ballroom, an especially high-ceilinged extension in the rear above the kitchen, with two dumbwaiters serving between the levels, was converted into a dining hall. The beautiful, tiny elevator of the mansion was at all times off limits to the children and to all but elderly infirm nuns. On the second story above the sweep of curved staircase, the layout was given to classrooms and offices, with sufficient space remaining to be converted into a chapel for daily prayers. But on the Sabbath, whether in good weather, rain, near tornado, or snow, the children were marched to a nearby parish church in long silent lines, admonished to be quiet by accompanying nuns.

Although the poverty of the neighborhood left little of beauty for most beholders, in the eyes of a secluded orphan it was a place of extraordinary excitement. Gaia began to register certain observations: Parents were divided into mommies and daddies, and together with their children comprised little families. Sundays, therefore, became cherished days for her, not for religious reasons—the nuns' rigorous overemphasis on prayer had destroyed whatever sustenance she might find in church, and she rebelled against the fact that children were never allowed to decide whether or not to go, but had to silently obey. For Gaia it enabled her to see *The World*.

But she was convinced that she was an outcast—that she would never enter The World. Other girls and boys received special visitors; couples appeared to take them away from the Home. As she grew older, Gaia increasingly longed for this to happen to her. Whatever reasoning had previously possessed her to reject any substitutes for her real parents was no longer dominant in her mind. She was terribly lonely and yearned to belong. Year after year, she was disappointed.

There were no mirrors allowed in the dormitories. One night when she was denied dinner for an insignificant behavioral rebellion, she climbed the stairs and went directly into a deserted bathroom nearest to her dorm. She locked the door and took off her clothes. There was a full-length mirror set in the wall and she posed, studying her body from various angles. Her fair skin had the sheen of fine soft velvet, particularly against the contrast of her curling dark shoulder-length hair. There was a disappointing excess of bulging tummy, and specks of brown nipples were mere hints of breasts. Gaia was fascinated by the bosoms of *outside* women; the nuns' bodies were undefinable beneath their loosely fitting habits.

Turning before the reflection of her naked body, Gaia's eyes were bright with the pleasure of doing something she knew would have shocked the nuns. She craned her neck to better inspect her buttocks. Her hips and waist were still childishly fused together, without definite indentation at the waist. She regarded the soft folds of her crotch where pubic hair would soon grow, although she had no knowledge of that. She only knew that she felt remarkably happy in a strange, warmly invigorating way as she stared at her body. Because the other children were still at dinner she knew her privacy was insured for about ten minutes more.

She recalled how a boy and two girls had been caught together in this same bathroom after the sternest demands that it be instantly unlocked. They had hastily and confusedly piled out, partially unclothed. One girl carried her underpants in her hand. Gaia had witnessed their exit from the bathroom, following them with her eyes as they were yanked along the corridor. They claimed to have been playing "doctor." Gaia was intrigued as to what that game had been and why it was punishable.

She'd turned and shyly asked another girl what was wrong. "Here!" she hissed, sliding her hand between Gaia's legs. "This," she whispered, and laughed. Gaia could never thereafter forget the quick thrill of sensation the unexpected thrust of that hand had produced.

Her heart beat hard and she was suffused by the deliciousness of experimentation as her fingers tentatively touched the smoothness of her vulva. Giving herself over to pleasure, she explored herself. Her hand darted away when her fingertips became moistened; she didn't know what the wetness meant, she only knew she desired to prolong it. She brought her fingers up higher and they brushed against her clitoris. Sudden rapture engulfed her, and she closed her eyes, massaging herself in heightening excitement. Then she felt a strange shuddering release. Her cry was muffled by the arm she flung against her mouth.

She didn't know how many minutes had elapsed, and she became horribly frightened. She frantically drew on her underpants and managed to get into the remainder of her clothes and be out of the bathroom before anyone came upstairs.

By this age she had decided her true parents were as unreal as fairy-tale characters. Nevertheless an image of a beautiful woman's face persisted, whether imagined or remembered She drew sketches of this lovely face in the margins of her notebooks, each rendition slightly different, but somehow the same. She studied the drawings as if she hadn't made them herself, wondering who the woman could be. The portrait resembled her, but she didn't recognize this.

Through those lonely years, Gaia never allowed herself to feel *this is all there is for me and it can never be better.* She tolerated the dreary life-style she'd grown used to, knowing she was still legally a dependent child. But she still hoped, still dreamed.

She was an anomaly among the nuns, whom Gaia felt were starched, sexless shadows of women. Whenever she reached out to them in need, she met a benign solicitude without substance. She felt, sensed, was *positive* that her own mother had resembled the stylish *outside* ladies, but differently, with a kindness and caring that she craved. Taped onto the wall behind her cot was one of her sketched portraits. She had taken to calling this woman "Mother," and held imaginary conversations, pouring out her hurts, seeking counsel for her problems, gazing into the kind, liquid eyes she herself had drawn. But because there could be no answers, she grew increasingly withdrawn.

Was it a dream, an enveloping aura of contentment that was totally false, or were her earliest memories of being in a pastel crib valid? Were there plush stuffed toys that squeaked when pressed and wonderful framed pictures of fairy-tale scenes upon the walls to which strong arms carried her in a sleepy bedtime tour? At times that period of her life (if it had ever been) seemed so close at hand that she would stretch her far memory attempting to recall all of it, especially the blurred images of the parents she'd lost. In vain, the threads of her recollections unwound like an elusive scent upon the wind.

Had there truly been a perfume that she remembered, a unique scent she associated with hummed lullabies and a soft loving touch? The earthy floral essence was unforgettable. Before dawn she would waken from a dream with her nostrils filled with it. Then morning brought reality and she knew where she was.

Years later when she worked in Ferrante-New York, she would spend her lunchtimes in nearby department stores and exclusive boutiques sniffing testers of expensive perfumes without ever recognizing the familiar remembered fragrance. But in the Home, when Gaia thought about her future, she had no idea that she would become a jewelry designer. Her focus was then more on the immediate. She desperately wanted to escape, to belong within a family where she would be loved. Where her love would be returned.

At a special meeting in a State Street law office attended by a representative of the orphanage, and state of Illinois and city of Chicago social workers, a determination was reached.

It was Miss McEvoy, a portly social worker from Springfield, who began the meeting with a query. "Why has this lovely child been consistently overlooked for adoption?"

Sister Mary Agnes was designated by the mother superior to represent the Home in concert with its attorneys. She had been cautioned against speaking too freely. "Do not volunteer information," they had told her.

Mrs. Porter, a Chicagoan, put aside a prepared mimeographed file, a copy of which was available for each participant. "The child's scholastic record appears to show that she is slightly below average."

Despite the outraged glances of the lawyer present, Sister Mary Agnes couldn't hold herself back. "That is because the girl doesn't apply herself."

"Is Gay"—Mrs. Porter mispronounced her name—"lazy? Is she subnormal intellectually? Does she require remedial counseling?"

"Certainly not!" Sister Mary Agnes flushed with indignation. Ignoring any eye contact with the lawyer and, thereby, his urgent signals to desist, she blurted out a defense of the Children's Home of Little Flowers. "Our way is to reason with them and to pray for them."

"Quite evidently you missed the boat with this child," Mrs. Porter said, and Miss McEvoy assented by nodding her head.

James Farraday rolled his plated imitation gold pen between his fingers. He was painfully aware that he was a junior employee of the firm, assigned to conduct what was supposed to be a perfunctory meeting.

The state social worker consulted her notes. "If she were an unintelligent or unattractive youngster, the lack of friends and poor schoolwork might be understandable. However, when I spoke to this child I was impressed that she is a clever little one, although pitiably shy. Somewhere in these papers I came across a notation of her I.Q. Here it is . . . I must say it seems odd to me that it is decidedly above normal while her schoolwork is poor. In my experience such a vast discrepancy between the two is explainable. Possibly, just possibly, the girl is desperately unhappy, and who wouldn't be, living almost an entire lifetime in an orphanage?"

The nun's mouth was already half opened when Farraday positively cleared his throat. She took the warning.

"Are both of her parents deceased?" Mrs. Porter questioned. "I see no report one way or the other."

Farraday hastily replied. "As you can see, there was an automobile accident involving them both. The baby was thrown clear onto a grassy shoulder and, remarkably, was uninjured."

"You are reading what I have before me, but I ask of you, what did happen to the man and woman? No medical disposition of either of them is indicated."

"Ah . . . they apparently died."

"There's no statement about that," Mrs. Porter observed.

"Are you inferring they may be alive?" Miss McEvoy asked.

He looked up from doodling on his pad. "How can one tell after so many years have passed?"

"Yes," Miss McEvoy countered, "but what I'm thinking is that if they, one or the other, had survived, wouldn't they have claimed their child?"

"Who can tell?" Mrs. Porter shrugged. She was a good twenty-five years older than the Illinois social worker. "In my years of service I've come across so many strange, almost unbelievable situations that each new time something odd turns up I tell myself I am no longer amazed." She momentarily glanced at the nun. "Why aren't notations of the parents' death certificates included in the file, if not photostats of the certificates themselves? Did they both, in fact, die? If not, what happened to them? I want to see the original file, not mimeoed editings."

Farraday spoke up. "I already requested it."

"So where is it?"

"Somehow the file has been misplaced at the Home."

"Funny, isn't it, that it was around when the mimeoed info was turned out."

Sister Mary Agnes' voice turned husky. "It has been lost since then."

"A 'convenient incredibility.' " Mrs. Porter smiled.

"I assure you there isn't the remotest chance of that," Farraday protested.

"How do you know? Did you personally search the Home for it?"

He swallowed. "I want that file located as much as you do."

"We've already looked high and low," said the nun. "It appears to be irrevocably lost."

"With no photostat copies of it?"

"None."

"Know what my guess is? I'll bet it's right here in this law office." Mrs. Porter made a move as if she was ready to take off for the file room.

"I assure you, such a thing would never happen here," Farraday said. "Besides, we never possessed the original folder."

"Then it is apparently still somewhere in the Home."

"It couldn't be," he said. "I was over there when the sisters hunted through their file cabinets for it."

"Did you open the furnace door when a fire was lit?"

"Really, Mrs. Porter." Sister Mary Agnes appeared shocked. "I must protest."

"Okay, have it your way. 'Misplaced' is a more convenient description of its whereabouts because 'lost' or 'destroyed' are so final, isn't that so?"

"There's no sense blaming the sister," Farraday insisted.

"No, she isn't personally the one who likely tore it up or stuffed it into the furnace, or did whatever happened to it."

The young lawyer spread his fingers wide, palms down on the table. "I'm sorry," he said.

"How very polite you are." Mrs. Porter scraped back her

chair to stand up. "As you may realize, with the file disappeared all possible explanations of why Gaia Gerald was never adopted, presuming that her parents are deceased. Also we'll never know, will we, whether proof existed that they were . . . oh, let's say, for example, undesirables . . . and don't suppose I'm suggesting they were." She was angry. "But I'll tell you one thing, the reasons for the girl's withdrawn behavior aren't particularly mysterious. Not to me."

The nun's face turned beet red. "I've already told you, she is purely recalcitrant. It is her nature to be so."

"Why?"

"Because we overly spoiled her. I certainly did when I first entered the order."

"I'll bet."

Miss McEvoy addressed her peer. "What do you suggest we recommend?"

" 'Implement' is more like it. The girl must be placed in a foster home immediately. By the time a child is her age, adoption is more difficult. And in this case, with no substantive information about her background . . ." She shrugged. "At any rate, I want her placed in a nonreligious environment. Maybe she'll perk up. For the present I suggest holding off on any psychiatric aid. I have a hunch this one is spunky and will work things out for herself if given half a chance."

Jim Farraday worked as second assistant to Sean O'Brien, one of the partner attorneys.

"Stop by my office later this afternoon," O'Brien said when he came upon the younger lawyer in the elevator lobby where he was courteously escorting Sister Mary Agnes after the meeting broke up. Once the social caseworkers had gathered up their papers and departed, the nun continued to sit in the rigid posture she'd assumed as the proceedings evolved.

"Sister?" He leaned over her. "Are you ill?"

Her face was lowered, concealed by the black cloth folds of her wimple. When she looked at him he saw her cheeks were moist from tears.

"It's so unfair," she said. "The Children's Home of Little

Flowers is one of the finest institutions, and the reports those ladies are bound to make will give us a poor reputation. How am I going to face Mother Superior and tell her?"

Farraday was curious on his own account. "Sister," he asked, "what *did* happen to Gaia Gerald's documents?"

Her facial muscles contracted as she made an effort to forestall further tears. "That's what is so terrible," she said. "They simply disappeared, although we knew the file was kept in the cabinet."

"Who typed the material excerpted from it and did the mimeographing? Was it the same person?"

"Yes. One of our volunteers who does office work."

"I'd appreciate speaking to her."

"That is impossible, Mr. Farraday."

"You must certainly understand, Sister, that if this individual isn't produced for examination, the Home will irrevocably suffer, because in order to raise funds it must never lose public trust."

She was remorseful. "This lady cannot be interviewed."

"Why not? It must be explained to her that she is not under accusation, but we ought to find out whether or not she can shed light on this mess by at least describing the missing contents from memory if the file itself cannot be found."

"I'm afraid I am very upset and not making myself clear. Such an interview is impossible because the lady in question is dead."

"Shit!" Farraday was too stunned to realize what he had said. He stared questioningly at the nun.

She crossed herself. "May God accept her soul into heaven. The poor dear must have been the victim of robbers. She was discovered shot to death in her apartment. She must have returned home unexpectedly and surprised a thief."

"Where did she live?"

She looked perplexed but reluctantly replied, "Lake Shore Drive. Why would that—"

"Hmm," the lawyer mused. "She was evidently a person of wealth. Why would she volunteer for typing and filing?"

She was embarrassed. "In all likelihood she wished to atone

for her unsavory life-style. It was said that she was a kept woman, the consort of gangsters who stayed with her whenever they passed through Chicago."

"Her connections make our missing documents more and more interesting."

"I can't imagine any connection."

"Nor can I, but it's an intriguing conjecture, don't you agree?"

Later that day Farraday detailed this conversation to Sean O'Brien. "Should we pursue this, sir?" he asked.

The older man chomped on his cigar. "Don't see how or why," he said.

"Well, I wanted you to know."

"Fine, but I can't see any reason to investigate. The nun has to be correct in her theory. Chippy sins and does charity work to compensate. For any one of a dozen nonassociated reasons, one of her hood boyfriends bumps her off." He relit his cigar as its ashy glow extinguished. "No, there's no reason to be suspicious. Merely coincidental, that's all."

The Lake Shore Drive apartment building, like many city multiresidences, had its share of less than desirable tenants. According to the lease signatory for apartment 11F, it had been rented to a New York man by the name of Vincent Roselli.

No sooner than the ink was dry on the lease, he'd installed his "sister," Franci La Pierre, in the apartment. Frequently, his male business associates, in the course of their travels, would stop off as overnight guests.

Late one night she received a particular telephone call from Vincent Roselli.

"Darling, here's what I want you to do," he told her. "Get your fanny out of the sack, and stay out of Marshall Fields for a change. You're gonna volunteer to do a real good deed.

"Can you type? Great! The Children's Home of Little Flowers is an orphanage that needs a clerical volunteer. It's a charity that friends of mine have a real interest in.

"It happens there's one little girl there we want to take

specially good care of. Her name is Gaia Gerald. We don't want her to be taken out of the orphanage by mistake until the situation is right.

"So you're gonna lift her records . . . the whole file. Give me a ring when you've gotten hold of it. I'll send over a Chicago guy I know to pick it up."

Franci did as she was told. Several weeks later she placed her call to a Brooklyn phone number. "Tell Vince," she said, "I've got what he wants. His guy can pick it up at the apartment."

Several days later she was found dead. Her killing was played up in newspaper headlines as the break-in and murder of a mysterious high-class woman.

It remained in police records as an unsolved crime.

· 4 ·

GAIA HAD SPENT THE PAST TEN MINUTES CONSIDERABLY ILL-AT-
ease in Vincent Bregna Salinari's grandiose office. If she was
an immensely wealthy heiress, why wasn't she feeling elation? Was her disquietude because she was unsure whether or
not Dom had manipulated her to accept employment as a
junior designer at Ferrante-New York, when, all along, he
might have known that upon il Principe di Corchese's death,
she would inherit? If so, how could he have kept the information that she'd had a grandfather from her?

Or, it also occurred to her, just possibly all she had recently
heard from Salinari about being old Ugo's granddaughter
might not, in fact, be true. Her head had begun aching as her
thoughts became mired in confusion.

When the desk phone rang, Salinari answered the call. "It's
for you," he said, holding out the receiver to her.

"Hello?" she answered doubtfully.

"Merrill Ross here. I'm head of the estate department of
Bari & Battaglia."

Gaia wasn't aware until after she'd spoken that she'd
blurted out, "Then you'd know for sure, wouldn't you?"

"I beg your pardon?"

"I mean, do you have . . . what proof is there that I am
. . . that is, that I've genuinely inherited from Mr. Ferrante?"

"Precisely. I see." He cleared his throat. "I am going to read
the pertinent clause of bequest to you. It is numbered 'Third'
in the will." He paused and cleared his throat. "I further give,
devise, and bequeath, absolutely and forever, to the living
offspring, *per stirpes*, of my deceased younger daughter, Angela Maria Ferrante Gerald, one half of my entire estate, to
wit: the retail jewelry firm and all of its assets, said firm being
known as Ferrante-New York, a corporation existent under
the laws of the state of New York, United States of America,
said incorporated business being entirely separate from the
Roman retail jewelry enterprise operating under the name of
Ferrante-Roma. To reiterate what has previously been stated
in the preceding clause, namely 'Second,' the Roman store
and all of its assets are totally unconnected to the American
business, and are exclusively bestowed upon my living elder
daughter, Silvia Ferrante di Malvestiti Wood, or in the event
that she shall have predeceased me, to her sole offspring, her
daughter Mara di Malvestiti."

"But . . . I am not mentioned in the will."

"Yes, you are."

"I didn't hear you read my name aloud."

"Angela Maria Ferrante Gerald was your mother."

"My . . . she is . . . deceased, you said."

"Correct."

"What proof is there that I'm her daughter?" Gaia was all
too familiar with a contradictory document, a paper that had
shaped her thinking for too many years—a paper she had
studied so often that she knew its sparse contents by heart,
paragraph following paragraph, word for word.

"Why do you question it?"

Impatience flared, her emotions thawing from the deep
freeze of shock. "Are you telling me, Mr. Ross, that you don't
have proof?"

"Ms. Gerald, I do understand your doubts. You seek confirmation that your mother was, in fact, Angela Maria Ferrante Gerald."

A chill coursed through her as she listened to him speak the name. Was this the woman whose perfume was a distinct memory, although her face, figure, and voice were maddeningly distant? It was a beautiful lilting name. *Angela Maria.* Her mother? As much as she hoped it was so, she had to know for a fact, one way or the other. "I'm afraid I didn't hear my own name mentioned in the will."

"Yes, you did. At least, it is there for all legal purposes."

"I don't understand."

" 'The living offspring, *per stirpes,* of my deceased younger daughter, Angela Maria Ferrante Gerald.' The expression *per stirpes* alludes to living filial siblings. Had you brothers or sisters, the inheritance would be shared equally among you. Since you are the sole child born to your mother, that is not applicable. In this instance, you inherit the whole. Without question, you are the legal heir of the New York business, inheriting through your maternal parent."

"How do you know that?"

"Because Giuliano Rinzini has researched it to his satisfaction."

"The Italian lawyer?"

"Yes."

"From so far away?"

"Believe me."

"How could he have found out what I was unable to?"

A degree of annoyance surfaced in his voice. "I have before me an international telecommunication. I won't bother reading it to you, but it says that an investigative search has discovered that Angela Maria Ferrante Gerald and her husband, Hugh Gerald, were killed in an automotive accident in Illinois on June 2nd, 1955. They had one child, a daughter by the name of Gaia. It is you who have survived them."

She gasped. If this were so . . . she at last knew about her parents. And—she struggled to clear her thoughts—it meant she had an aunt, Silvia, and a closely related cousin, Mara. Except it wasn't true. It couldn't be.

Hadn't she memorized the document that was the only fruit of her own search into her past?

ADOPTION REGISTRY ACCESS

OBJECTIVE: To reunite adopted children and their natural
parents.

SUBJECT: Gaia Gerald.
It must immediately be noted that subject was never an
adoptee, having resided in an orphanage until the age of 12
years, and thereafter in foster homes.

DATE AND PLACE
OF BIRTH: Both date and place of subject's birth are
unverified due to missing birth certificate, although year of
birth is presumed to be 1953.
A search was made of birth records in Chicago and
environs for year 1953. Following are births of infants with
surname of Gerald:
John Quentin Gerald, b. January 15
Sean Joseph Gerald, b. May 29
Geraldine Gerald, b. July 10
Roger and Cathleen Gerald, twins, b. September 17
Eileen Gerald, b. December 21
Of the three females, Geraldine, Cathleen, and Eileen,
Geraldine seemed the most hopeful to pursue because of
similarity of initials to subject Gaia Gerald, but Geraldine
Gerald FitzHugh, presently married, was located and
positively identified through her parents.

SUBJECT'S
PARENTS: Names unknown, due to missing birth certificate.

RELIGION: It is presumed that subject's antecedents were
Catholic, because subject was placed on August 4, 1955, in
care of the sisters in the Children's Home of Little Flowers,
a Catholic charity-supported institution in Chicago, Illinois.
A difficulty in resolving this search successfully is that the
Home's file on subject has either been hopelessly misplaced
or must be presumed to be permanently lost/destroyed.

INTERVIEW: The mother superior, administrator of the
Home, has recently died. Request was made of the Catholic
diocese, but they can only supply names and addresses of
subject's foster parents in pay-for-care situations subsequent

to what is presumed to have been subject's twelfth year, and prior to her running away from last-placed foster home at the age of fifteen years.

RESOLUTION: Subject has refused, upon questioning, to offer explanation of where or with whom she lived at time of unheedful departure from a foster home. ARA therefore refuses to make further inquiries in an attempt to discover subject's origins. Subject's refusal to provide requested information upon her claim that it is not pertinent to her search for her natural parents is deemed to be indicative of a questionable life-style.

ARA considers this case irrevocably CLOSED.

Gaia felt that the stand taken by the board of governors of ARA was unwarrantedly unfair. She wasn't about to explain to them that she was withholding information concerning her life following her departure from her last-assigned boarding home because, above all other concerns, she was intent upon protecting Dominic Perrini.

· 5 ·

GAIA STOOD AT THE HERMETICALLY SEALED WINDOWS IN VINCENT Bregna Salinari's office, hardly more certain about her status following her conversation with Merrill Ross. To be declared the sole owner of Ferrante-New York was so overwhelming that she subconsciously resorted to the trick of mind that had comforted her from childhood on. She empathetically gazed down on crowded Fifth Avenue, trying to associate herself with individuals she spotted on the opposite sidewalk, and imaginatively placing herself within another's persona, an existence that presumably offered fewer problems than her own. She saw several young women pausing to gape at the Ferrante building. Would they envy her? What would they say if they knew her immediate reaction was a powerful head-ache?

She remembered how much simpler it had been to have small-girl dreams of what her life would be when she was an adult. She had hungrily looked at life as a forbiddingly expen-sive bakery, devouring trayfuls of pastries with her eyes. Now it seemed she had been given the entire establishment. Reality was beyond her wildest flight of fancy. It produced a far greater emotional upheaval than winning a lottery's grand prize because, in her case, she hadn't even bought a ticket. She was unprepared.

The rustle of his presence distracted her attention from the window view. Dom Perrini briskly entered the office ahead of the secretary's phoned announcement of his arrival, its harsh ringing seeming to echo around him as he strode across the long room. Tall, spare of body, his powerfully moving musculature visibly interacted with the play of his well-cut navy blue suit. Dark hair, slightly graying at his temples, face strongly structured, jawline firm, almost stern. The penetrating brightness of his deep-set eyes softened as they focused upon her.

He came toward her, arms outstretched. She felt renewed in his embrace. "I got here as fast as I could, *cara.*"

Was he looking at her strangely? She mustn't speculate on that at this moment. "Thank you, Dom." Her voice was small. She was suddenly so nervous that her body stiffened against her will. Sensitive to her reaction, he released his hold.

"I am delighted for you, Gaia."

She attempted a smile that came off weakly. "I guess I'm overcome by all that's happened."

"That's understandable . . . such a surprise."

This awkwardness between them was itself unreal. She had to ask him, and right away, but each word was weighted with lead as she spoke it. "Did you know about my inheritance before today?"

Was it her imagination that Dom and Salinari briefly glanced at one another?

"Wouldn't I have immediately told you?"

Gaia observed Dom's previously caring facial expression assume remoteness. She felt as though a cold hollow substance had settled in the pit of her stomach. With her hands pressed against her body, she sought to reject her reaction. He *couldn't* be involved in ways that she was unable to perceive and might only guess at. Not Dom! She thought of how it had been in the beginning.

By the age of fifteen, Gaia remained stubbornly positive that *somewhere* in the large city of Chicago, there had to be a better quality of life for her. Admittedly, she had seen very little of the metropolis. Thrust from one foster home to the next—no more palatable than the one she'd recently been extracted from—she knew only neighborhoods where an air of despair hung over the low-rise apartment buildings, where the residents were either on relief or had such poor-paying jobs that they barely subsisted. There were some people who found a way to supplement their incomes. They boarded foster children.

Gaia was one of these unfortunates, taken in only because she was a commodity, denied the love her heart cried out for, tolerated because of the social-service checks which were supposed to pay for her upkeep. The money was considered income and was never used for her needs.

She still retained her sketch of a woman's face, and it became increasingly important to her. She communed with it silently as a means of keeping her spirits up. She was unhappy, but never knowing happiness, she had no basis for comparison.

There had been the horror of finding herself one of seven foster children used as unpaid factory help, blatantly circumventing child-labor laws. Frequently forced to fake illness in front of her teachers in order to remain out of school, Gaia was set to operating a handpress that turned out plastic novelties. But Gaia resolved to break free; she loved school—it was her sole escape. On days when she was allowed to attend, she was too shy to ask for help from the teacher, but on the day the class essay was entitled "How I Spend My Day," Gaia wrote descriptively. She was shortly thereafter taken to a new set of foster parents.

Once she looked up her surname, Gerald, in the Chicago telephone directory. She did this at the corner cigar store because none of her homes could afford private phones. There were many listings. She had no money to spend for phone calls, but one address was close to where she then lived. Steeling her courage on her way home from school, she detoured to an apartment house as shabby as the one in which she lived. With her heart thumping, she rang the doorbell of the apartment to which a tenant directed her.

"Mrs. Gerald?" She looked into unfriendly eyes.

The woman was slovenly. Gaia slipped her hand into her pocket and held tight to her folded portrait.

"Who wants ta know?"

Without another word, Gaia turned away. In the street she brushed tears from her eyes, using the back of one hand. Not even to herself did she want to acknowledge that she was crying.

Each time she was removed to another home, her circumstances worsened.

A father began to take an unfatherly interest. "You're a good-looking girlie," he said, holding her around the waist.

His wife had seen them. She notified the agency immediately.

In her following situation, Gaia was less fortunate.

It was winter when she was taken to an apartment in the depressed vicinity of the orphanage. The building's furnace was more often broken than not. Throughout the winter, she was forced to care for the adults, running their errands, carrying home groceries, purchasing cold remedies at a local pharmacy.

"You're spending too much. D'ya think money grows on trees?" the woman complained.

"It's not my fault. The medicine is expensive."

"Idiot!" She was upbraided. "Who said to pay? Lift the stuff."

"What do you mean?"

"Take it off the shelf."

Gaia was appalled. "Without paying?"

"That's right!" She was given a shove toward the door as the woman padded off to the bathroom.

While the woman was at work in a commercial laundry, every afternoon upon school letting out Gaia hastened back to minister to her foster father. If he is so sick, she thought bitterly, how does he find the strength to go out and buy liquor?

Her newest father did, in fact, drink since morning, always

with his eye on Gaia as she worked around him. Today he'd strike. When she returned upstairs after carrying his empty bottles to the street garbage can, he was ready. Rising naked from the bed, he attempted to drag her to it, yanking at her clothing despite her kicks and screams. He was lying atop her, one big hand pinning her arms against the pillow, while she struggled in vain to keep her legs locked together. Neither heard his wife enter; Gaia's screams muffled all sound.

There was no defense for Gaia against the woman's wrath as her fists, her nails, teeth, and ready objects battered her. Nor would she cry afterward. She wouldn't let herself. She wouldn't show her feelings to anyone anymore. The social worker's professional attention was as clinical as the hospital where she was taken for treatment.

Her next foster home was that of Mike and Selma Wikowsky. Theirs was a three-room apartment, and she would bed down on the living room couch once the Wikowskys vacated the room at night. Plainly furnished, the most expensive item was the television set. The couch sagged, but that hardly mattered to her tired body when, past eleven, Mike Wikowsky tore himself from the screen and stumbled into the bedroom where Selma already slept. Picking up the beer cans he left scattered on the bare floor, Gaia lay a sheet across the rough upholstery fabric, covered herself, and fell asleep.

It was her responsibility to rise before they did, and hastily wash in the bathroom where the basin continually leaked, creating brown rust spots on hexagon-shaped tiles that were otherwise grayish no matter how vigorously Gaia scrubbed them. The kitchen ceiling and some of the upper wall showed remnants of past leakage that had never been painted over. There was a gas stove that emitted fumes, a cracked porcelain basin, and a small work area that Selma always crowded with food containers no matter how many times Gaia put them away in the old-fashioned glass-paned cabinets. The floor was covered with linoleum of an undetermined color, and standing in one corner with two uncomfortable chairs fronting it was a rickety table where they ate their meals. Of course, Gaia had to eat after they had finished, there being no room for her. It was hardly a punishment. Mike Wikowsky was a noisily unpleasant eater.

At fifteen, she was of an age to legally obtain working papers for employment after school and on weekends at a neighborhood supermarket. Her hours were from half past three until the early evening. The Wikowskys preferred when she was required to remain overtime until the midnight closing. It meant she would bring in more money for them— they never let her keep her wages.

Gaia accepted her work schedule without complaint. Her long hours gave her less time to spend in the drab apartment where she was never met with any love or affection.

The manager took advantage of her youthfulness and, mostly, her inexperience. Whenever the store was short a packing boy, she would be chosen to handle her station unassisted while the boys worked at the other counters. Accustomed to unquestioningly implementing the commands of those who assumed the role of her superior, she hauled heavy-weight cartons from her packing ledge after expertly inserting the bulky items on the bottom, and stuffing fragile eggs in crannies that offered them some insulation.

Customers found her pleasant, willing, and quick at the cash register. There were those who chose to wait in the line leading to her counter. She greeted them cheerfully, the natural lilting cadence of her young voice belying her solemn deep unhappiness. It no longer disturbed her when her name was mispronounced. She was too hardworking to care, too exhausted afterward.

But when customers initiated conversation with Gaia, her responses were muffled. It was the residue of a lingering shyness, a need to protectively hold whatever little was hers in privacy. Mostly there were questions. What year of high school was she in? What did she want to be when she graduated? Gaia didn't know the answer to that. Aside from her unsubstantiated daydreams, she was aware that she had developed no important skills. And there was clearly no money for college.

Her high school guidance counselor, knowing from her record that she was a boarded-out orphan, felt it was kinder not to instill great ambition in a child so limited in opportunity. Yet Gaia was special! Primarily, she had an artistic talent that, sadly, would never be developed. Beaten down by circumstances, the pretty dark-haired girl was never likely to glimpse the luxurious world of fashion, wherein the counselor speculated she would excel. A pity, because she had a decided flair for the proportions of design, a sense that is necessarily inborn. Moreover she showed a natural artist's feeling for the uses of color.

Alas, the counselor had already considered and abandoned any options for Gaia within the creative commercial realm. Without funds to maintain herself, it would be nearly impossible for her, even if she were to be so fortunate as to secure an art school scholarship, for these were usually only partially subsidized. Even if she could obtain an extremely rare full scholarship, Gaia would have to live without financial support, because in less than three years she would no longer be a ward of the state. There would be no further boarding situations available to her.

The counselor, like a physician who must become inured to the condition of dying patients lest she become emotionally involved in hopeless cases, couldn't even hope for the best to happen. What did Gaia have to look forward to—a predictably dreary marriage, which would likely never enable her to escape this depressed neighborhood? There were few alternatives. The counselor had seen one option the prettier girls of the neighborhood exercised: selling themselves on the streets. Gaia was suitably endowed to compete there. She prayed that the girl wouldn't be tempted to test herself in that market.

As for Gaia, she sometimes let herself visualize a future of great promise, although her vision was vague and unstructured. She had no idea where she was headed. Her emotional mainstay, the sketch of a lovely face that she used to pretend was her mother's, no longer seemed important to her. She would close her eyes and see herself happy and smiling. But the truth was that the future frightened Gaia. She had already experienced the worst of human nature in a succession of foster homes. Where in the world might she expect kindness? Thinking this, she was wary. She'd close her eyes again, fantasizing. It was her escape.

Girls her age were using cosmetics, but Gaia didn't. It wasn't a matter of saving money, although that was important. At the Wikowskys', makeup or even nail polish was considered indicative of moral looseness. And appearing as plain as possible would keep her foster father from showing interest in her.

Her past experience had left her extremely suspicious and fearful of men. There were those younger ones who wanted to date her, except she foresaw what going out with them would predict. She wasn't willing to present herself as a body and not a person to anyone. And yet her need for human warmth and understanding was so poignant that if any one of them had showed even the smallest touch of genuine caring, she might not have consistently refused them.

Once a week she carried home shopping bags laden with foodstuffs purchased with her employee discount. Each time Gaia inwardly cringed, anticipating the predictable routine. Miscalculation and shouting invariably ensued in the small kitchen of the third-story walk-up.

"You didn't give me enough change," Gaia was accused.

"Yes, I did, Mrs. Wikowsky. Let me add it for you."

"So's you can finagle the figures? I know your sort, trying to get away with stealing."

"I am honest!"

"So you say."

"Please . . . let me show you."

"Shut up!"

"If you'll let me, I can—"

"Leave it!"

Gaia worried that Mike Wikowsky would hear his wife's raised voice above his blaring television and plod into the kitchen to witlessly side against her.

"Okay," Selma eventually admitted grudgingly. "I guess it figures out to be correct. Mind you, be careful the next time.

If I ever catch you . . . say, why are you home early tonight?"
It was seven-thirty.

"The manager said business was slow."

"Well, you better eat your supper, but take it easy, huh? Without your overtime pay we've gotta stretch what's in the fridge for the whole week."

"Thank you, Mrs. Wikowsky." Damn, there she'd said it again. Appreciation for scant favors! How come, Gaia frequently asked herself, both of the Wikowskys were grossly overweight if they couldn't afford to pay for food? They weren't exactly underweight when Gaia first entered their household, and now they had grown fatter since she'd been working at the supermarket.

She opened the refrigerator, looking for the leftover ham from the Wikowskys' dinner. But when Mike walked into the kitchen to deposit a plate in the sink, reaching over her shoulder for a can of beer, she realized he had just devoured the remaining ham in an afterdinner sandwich. He barely glanced at her, and padded back to the television. She fried a couple of eggs and toasted bread. How wonderful it would be, Gaia mused, to sit at a brightly decorated table in the company of interesting people who would converse with her. She was so lonely eating by herself, although even in the Wikowskys' company she felt alone.

There were school lessons to prepare, homework for tomorrow's classes, Gaia remembered as she poured herself a glass of milk. Slowly sipping it, she looked around the disorderly room. Something had been spilled on the floor earlier and not wiped up. There was a peculiar smell. No wonder there were always roaches in evidence. She took out a mop and pail and swabbed away. Rinsing the mop, she contemplated the two hours' minimum time required by her studies. After wiping and drying the table, Gaia spread out her work. She sighed. Would it make any difference in her life if she failed in school? She lowered her head to her crossed arms. It was probably why Selma never complimented her on good grades when she signed her report cards. Gaia closed her eyes.

After a short while she raised her head. Something within her refused to tolerate defeatism.

I won't be fifteen forever. Things have got to change. One day something wonderful will happen.

The buzzer sounded a jarring vibration in the kitchen where Gaia had begun studying, and she heard Selma unlatch the door. That anyone had rung the bell was a surprise. This was a neighborhood where visitors would bang knuckles on doors when they made their infrequent appearances at friends' apartments.

A man's unfamiliar resonant voice issued from the corridor. Was she imagining that he asked for her? She told herself that was ridiculous and vigorously shook her head as if this would clear it. Apparently she was having another fantasy. But once again she seemed to hear him say, "Gaia Gerald." *She really had!*

Selma Wikowsky began excitedly shouting to her husband, who came to the door mouthing curses because he was being pulled away from the television.

The door creaked on its hinges. Selma's high-pitched voice queried, "Are you the numbers man? Did Mike win?"

"I had better come inside your apartment while we talk," the man said.

"Oh yeah?" This from Wikowsky. "So's you can rob us?"

"Hardly. I have one thousand dollars for you with your name on it. Interested?"

"What for?" Mike Wikowsky was suspicious. "Nobody gives nothing for nothing."

"It has something to do with *her*," Selma said. "He asked if Gay was here."

"One thousand dollars, for me to take her with me."

Trembling, and with her heart pounding, Gaia kept her ear pressed to the kitchen door. The man's strong voice was unfamiliar. She was certain that she had never heard it in the supermarket.

Husband and wife spoke in lower tones between themselves. Then Wikowsky boldly asked for a larger sum. The man resisted raising it, and Selma began to bend. When it became apparent to them both that it was the thousand or nothing, Mike Wikowsky was ready to settle for the cash. Even so, he made another try for more.

"It's all you'll get from me. I could take her without paying you a dime." The man's deep voice was sufficiently firm to be a barrier, a spiked fence that couldn't be climbed over.

Selma sounded worried. "What'll we tell the authorities when the social worker comes 'round and she ain't here no more?"

"We'll say she ran off . . . we don't know where." Wikowsky outstretched his palm to receive ten crisp hundred-dollar bills.

Selma shouted. "Gay! Gay, come here."

Gaia tentatively pushed open the kitchen door. Directly in her line of vision, she saw a tall well-dressed man, but it was neither his towering over the Wikowskys nor his chiseled face that brought a movie actor's handsomeness to mind, causing her to catch her breath. Gaia gaped at him. She had never seen anyone like him. He was hatless beneath a bare electric bulb, and his thick dark-brown hair was the same color as his deep-set eyes that momentarily flashed light as he looked at her. Had he recognized her? Ought she to know him?

Flustered and overcome by shyness, she nervously watched him, memorizing his face as if he might disappear: the tautness of his well-formed jaw; the forward thrust of his nose, prominent but balanced by his high cheekbones; the clean-shaven skin that hinted at blue shadows of beard. His full upper lip was sensuously mobile, now extended taut in annoyance; and although it was stretched into an expression of harsh impatience toward her foster parents, Gaia's impression was that the same lips could bespeak tenderness. A young girl's romanticizing? Not entirely. She had never seen anyone exuding sheer physical confidence like his. She was mesmerized and felt exuberant, weightless.

"Are you Gaia Gerald?" he asked her, using an entirely different, more gentle tone.

She nodded. She couldn't have spoken if her life depended upon it.

"I have traveled a very long way to find you."

"Are you my father?" she blurted out, and was immediately embarrassed that she had let him see that she regarded him as an older man.

A semblance of a smile flitted across his face. "No, *cara*. Shall we say that I am a friend. I want you to always think of me as that, as well as your guardian, which I shall be when I take you to live with my mother."

Her reaction was the easy compliance of floating in a dream. "Where does she live?"

"In Brooklyn. It's a part of New York City."

She fell silent. There was a magnetism drawing her, undeniably binding her to this stranger. She wanted to go with him just for himself, not only because he was taking her away from the Wikowskys and from her dreary surroundings. "I'll pack my things." She turned away.

"Bring nothing with you."

She paused, glancing uncertainly back at him.

"I'm taking you to an entirely new life, Gaia, where you will learn to be a proper young lady. You will wear beautiful new clothes, like other girls your age." As he spoke she noticed that a movement of his right hand brought prismatic fire to a large diamond set in a gold ring. "Are you willing to go with me?" His eyes took on additional brightness when he searchingly looked at her.

She was choked up and nodded. Only later would she wonder at her total abandonment, her absolute faith in the honesty of his face. That night she questioned nothing.

"Just take a jacket for the night air," he suggested.

She instantly returned with a faded sweater, and followed him out of the apartment without saying good-bye, without a backward glance. A cab, its meter running, was waiting in the street. Such an unusual sight in this neighborhood brought a crowd of spectators. Gaia felt as though she were the princess in one of her remembered cherished fairy tales as she swept into the taxi while he held the door open for her to precede him. She had never been in a taxi before.

They were nearly at the airport when she abruptly drew in her breath. "Oh!" she exclaimed, stricken.

"What is it? Did you leave something behind that you already miss? Don't worry about it. We'll replace it in New York."

She shook her head sideways to indicate that this wasn't what was troubling her. They were then traveling along a dark stretch of road. Without being able to see her, Dom Perrini sensed her agitation and movement.

"Be calm," he said quietly. "You have absolutely nothing to fear."

Her voice was small. "I don't even know your name."

"Dominic Perrini. I apologize for not informing you before."

"Mr. Perrini, I was nervous . . ."

"That's understandable. You are making a journey in the night with a man who's a stranger to you." His hand touched one of hers. "Will you call me Dom?"

"Dom is a fine name," she replied seriously. "I'll be proud to call you that."

"Thank you."

They had turned onto a multilane highway. Oncoming headlights fleetingly sliced into the cab in shifting blocks of light. Gaia looked in his direction. His face was then in darkness, and she wondered what his expression was. She fervently hoped he wasn't smiling at her immaturity. She wished that she were already a woman—to appeal to this handsome man as a woman.

"Gaia! Haven't you heard a word I've said?"

"I—I'm sorry."

"*Cara*, I really think you ought to pay attention." His voice held a mild rebuke. "After all, you are the beneficiary."

"Why wasn't it *you* who told me?"

"For your own good. I understand you, Gaia . . . better than you do yourself. If I had been the one to break the news of your inheritance, can't you see that you would have suffered an even greater emotional reaction? Having Vincent inform you, it became a matter-of-fact statement."

"Why didn't you tell me I had a grandfather while he was alive so I could get to know him?"

"For one reason, because he was an extraordinarily disagreeable man."

"Don't you think I could form my own opinion? He left me part of his estate. Didn't he want to meet me?"

"Leave it alone, Gaia. I don't propose to discuss it any further."

"Why not?"

"It isn't like you to question me."

"Tell me this: When did you first find out that he'd died?"

"Very early this morning when I received a phone call from Rome."

"From whom?"

"The estate lawyer who is also the executor."

"Was I mentioned?"

"You assuredly were."

"It puzzles me that I am not referred to by name in the will. The lawyer here in New York read the bequest clause to me."

"That you aren't named is immaterial."

"So Merrill Ross said."

"What's important for you to realize is that your position in the store has substantially and unalterably changed. You have a responsibility to oversee operation of the business in a smooth manner so that the transition of ownership won't be evident in the day-to-day running of Ferrante-New York."

"Yes, but Mr. Salinari is president of the firm. I want only to continue designing jewelry. It is what I enjoy doing."

"You still don't comprehend, do you?"

Just then Vincent Bregna Salinari began a nervous coughing in a tense hacking explosion.

"Will you explain it to me?"

"It's simply this. You will be taking an active role in the

store's management. And I emphasize, it is absolutely essential that you do so."

"Oh no, Dom. I'd rather not."

"*Cara*, have I ever given you bad advice?"

"No you haven't, but you must realize that all I know how to do is to design jewelry. It's what I was trained for."

"I promise you, I will be beside you all the way to guide you."

She hung her head, momentarily defeated.

"Gaia, look at me. *Cara*, we both know that your life hasn't been easy. Now you will be given the marvelous opportunity to make up for all those bad years."

"It's been a wonderful life since you entered it," she admitted.

"Then trust me."

Their eyes made contact. "I always have."

"Why not now?"

She swallowed, aware that Salinari was raptly attentive to what she was about to say. "Because, frankly, I'm scared. I've been so happy being a designer. I found myself through my work. I don't want to give that up. Dom, I have no experience in running a business."

Salinari broke in. "She's absolutely right. Matters ought to remain as they are for the good of Ferrante-New York."

Dom gave him a short look and turned back to Gaia. "It is the board of directors who will make that decision," he affirmed.

She experienced discomfort about what he would say next. Salinari appeared to be on the verge of agitated collapse.

Dom softly asked her, "Don't you guess who is going to be the new president and chairman of the board?"

She tried to speak but her throat was too tight.

"You are."

"Whether or not I want to be?"

"Yes."

· 6 ·

THE NUMBER WAS PRESELECTED. IT HAD BEEN PROGRAMMED INTO the miniature cellular-type telephone, slim enough to fit undetected into a man's pocket or a woman's handbag. Its power to transmit was fed from strategically placed hidden transmitters throughout the metropolitan area.

"The plan is underway," the caller said.

"Excellent! Any hitches you're aware of?"

"None apparent. She left the executive office and immediately went to her design studio, where she remains alone."

"What about the staff?"

"Word has been spread among them of her inheritance. There are signs of jealousy."

"Which was to be expected. Be advised, the directors are already on their way to the store. Nothing must be allowed to interfere with the real business at hand."

"Understood."

"Besides the girl, where are the other protagonists right now?"

"Salinari is in his office. Perrini wanders about the building."

"Unless Gaia Gerald cooperates, she will have to be removed. Is that clear?"

"She's an innocent pawn."

"That makes her no less of a danger."

"The greatest danger is to herself."

· 7 ·

GAIA'S WORKROOM WAS HER SANCTUARY, MORE SO THAN THE
Àtrio, where her clean linear jewelry designs were exclusively featured. Despite a sense of pride in her accomplishment, she was naturally modest and invariably received the
compliments of customers with a trace of embarrassment. So
it was within her own smallest portion of the store where
Gaia was most content . . . or had been until today.

It had always excited her to be here where her creative ideas
flowed and could be expressed. She hardly noticed that her
studio wasn't windowed or as spacious as Michael Vanderman's. Mona Hof had furnished hers in expression of her
flamboyance, swathing the walls with outrageous batik in
pulsating jungle-print motif and color. That wasn't for Gaia,
nor did she have a collection of Art Deco objets d'art that had
become Greer Hadley's signature of style. She hadn't assumed the cool contemporary modernity that inspired Henry
Phelps to work at his drawing board. Gaia was happy just to
work in proximity to the great designers, all of them considerably older than she, and world-renowned for their talents.

But no means would Gaia become a mere imitator, as impressed as she was by their individual style, their artistic
creations. She funneled her imagination into her designs.
While she worked her concentration grew so intense that she

was actually unaware of her surroundings. An idea would pop into her mind, and with her shoulders hunched she'd commence a series of developmental sketches, each taking the pattern a step further in laborious sequence. This was how she had designed the Gaia Star. Her head was afloat in an ethereal, glittering cloud of imagination, an aspect of style she captured, defined, and detailed on paper.

The white floor-to-ceiling-partitioned enclosure was compact, its minimum of space efficiently utilized beneath overhead fluorescent lighting. There was a high draftsman's combination easel/desk with shallow drawers for artist's supplies. A tall stool positioned before it was on casters so it might be propelled from the easel to the waist-high slate-surfaced jeweler's work table upon which were strewn miscellaneous tools familiar to the jewelry trade. Here she manipulated wax molds, using her long slender jeweler's tweezer to lovingly and reverently remove gems from their folded paper packets, selecting those she wanted to work with and positioning each in the pliable wax castings to roughly approximate the design she had in mind. On the table were pieces of precious metal, jewelry findings, and her own loupe that she would frequently clamp to her right eye, squinting the other as she viewed stones with magnification to reveal their internal structure. Like so many imitation cabochon jewels, sugar-glossed candies from an opened bag of M & Ms were frequently spilled across the table. She nibbled these for energy whenever she became so engrossed in a project that she postponed eating lunch.

And there were the other times when Gaia felt creatively fallow. Then her focus would shift from the immediate to wander in a far-distant direction. Anyone looking in would have assumed she was doodling across the blank page of her sketch pad because she was between ideas. They could not have understood the emotional pull that gripped her, often before she herself was aware of it, as without conscious intent she drew the head and shoulders of a lovely woman. It was an identical likeness to the one she had long ago pasted on the wall above her cot at the orphanage.

Every other Friday she had a set routine. After cashing her paycheck and depositing a variable portion of it, depending on what bills she had to pay, she hastened up or down Fifth Avenue, crossing from one side of the avenue to the other, occasionally dangerously heedless of oncoming traffic in her compulsion to scrutinize the window displays of competing fine jewelers: Cartier, Bulgari, H. Stern, Tiffany, Harry Winston, Van Cleef & Arpels. Observing their design trends would preserve her uniqueness, of which she was fiercely protective.

She denied herself the time for a sandwich, and munched a frankfurter on a roll, swilling it down with a Pepsi purchased from a brightly colored, umbrella-topped curbside vendor's cart. Afterward she hastened to the nearby department stores' perfume counters, never relinquishing the hope of someday rediscovering the elusive scent that haunted her memory. One afternoon at a crowded counter in Bendel's, her eye caught sight of a picture frame. It was cloisonné, with a white ground and delicate pastel flowers. After purchasing it, Gaia hastened back to her studio, where she immediately inserted the pencil sketch that she thought of as her mother's likeness. Whenever she was upset, she extracted comfort from its presence.

Gaia looked at it now, her eyes misting over.

People had been dropping by to offer their congratulations. How word of her inheritance had spread so rapidly, she couldn't imagine.

Miles Tuchelin, the short, wiry director of advertising and promotion, was the first to enter. He always seemed to draw peripatetic energy from his flaming red hair, and his presence lifted her spirits.

Gaia thought Miles was the most talented person at Ferrante. He was marvelous at devising window displays, clever print advertising layouts that were noted industrywide for their sales pull, and promotions involving prominent personalities, as when expensive jewelry was frequently loaned (transported by Brink's) to a fashion magazine's photographic

sittings to be draped upon the sensational body of some actress or other who was more well-built than talented.

And of course without him, there would have never been
the Àtrio, the display area for jewelry of her design. Without
his sure hand, she would have had far less success.

If Miles had a flaw that Gaia could discern, it was that he
lacked constancy. Always off on a new idea, he constantly
prowled the store's departments, apt to know that a twenty-
dollar silver toothpick was outselling the gold version at seven
times the price. By his impact advertising, he could swing a
trend to high-priced Montana-cornflower-blue sapphires,
moving a glut of them, faceted and unmounted in the second-
basement vault. Then, just as quickly, his attention turned to
promoting another project. Be that as it may, Gaia was grateful to him for championing her first design to achieve renown: the now familiar Gaia Star.

Miles had come in, embraced her, and had uttered congratulations she was too numb to hear, let alone remember.
Following his departure, every member of the design staff as
well as most of the factory technicians had come by to speak
with her.

The stocky, graying, tired-looking Etta Spring had stopped
by last. It was hard for her to get away from Salinari's tight
control of her hours, but she wanted to offer her personal
congratulations, she said. But her words were somehow without enthusiasm. "I wish you the best of good fortune." She
gave a faint smile. "I didn't mean it as a pun, you know. You
already have the fortune."

Once more alone, Gaia considered it odd that of all the
well-wishers, none offered condolences. Ugo Ferrante, il
Principe di Corchese, had died and no one thought to mention
it.

She was alone at last, nervously pacing back and forth in
the scant floor space, her movement suggestive of the ham-
pered energy of an animal trapped in a cage. Her fingers were
tightly curled under, forming knotted fists of tension, her
nails stabbing into her palms.

Undoubtedly there were major decisions that she'd shortly be expected to make when she assumed the helm of Ferrante-New York, decisions she felt inadequate to formulate and invoke. She grew a bit calmer, remembering that Dom had promised he stood ready to guide her whenever necessary. For this she was extremely grateful. Hadn't he, after all, been her dependable advisor since their first meeting? She felt guilty for having doubted Dom's purposes for even a moment. Without him as her buffer, she would be far more bewildered than she already was.

She briefly wondered about Salinari. As she was going to assume his corporate titles and office, his resentment of her must be enormous. She thought again of Etta Spring's wry, tired face. But she could not manage to concentrate long upon this or any other matter. Her mind whirled as she considered the enormously difficult job being thrust upon her. She'd considered herself lucky to be a designer. In the arts there are few demarcations between male and female opportunities, beyond the talent to make the most of them. From this day forth, there would be irrevocable change so far as that was concerned.

She would not only be compelled to deal with men in an area in which she felt unfamiliar, but being a woman suddenly finding herself in a high position within a man's world was bound to subject her to sexual bias, if not outright resentment, from which she had heretofore been free. When it came to her setting internal company policy, would her former coworkers be any more tolerant because she had risen from their ranks? She thought not. There had been recent times when she discerned some pettiness directed toward her from the sales personnel simply because she was a relatively elite designer. She'd been smart enough never to show offense. When she tried to convey that, like them, she was working at a job, they were intentionally dense in their understanding. This confounded her. She had never been envious of their high-percentage commissions that earned them sums often many times more than her fixed wage. Now that was totally reversed.

But then, a relatively small income had never been a problem. Not when Dom had given her an exquisitely furnished co-op apartment in a choice building, nor when he regularly ordered lavish gifts to be delivered to her. The most extravagant was a recently bestowed white fitch coat, its rare pelts breathtakingly marked with the drama of pure white and shaded black striping. She protested, but he would hear none of what she had to say, shouting at her over the phone that he expected her to wear it as she would any other coat. Fearful of seeming unappreciative, she expressed her gratitude, but he abruptly cut her off.

"It is your right to possess the best of everything," he told her.

"I don't deserve—"

"Never make yourself subservient to any son of a bitch, including me."

By the time she opened her mouth to reply, he had already hung up.

The coat was draped across a chrome valet in a corner of her studio. What greater luxuries might her newfound money buy? Yet there was one thing more Gaia yearned for that remained unattainable. Something no amount of wealth might acquire for her.

Dom Perrini.

There was never any mistaking the knowing expression, almost a slyness in the eyes of those who took it for granted that her relationship with Dom meant they were having an affair. Whether it was Vincent Bregna Salinari or Miles Tuchelin, or anyone else, she recognized the unspoken assumption: a romance between the young designer and a fascinating man of the world. It was an irresistible combination.

"You'll like New York," she recalled him telling her in the airplane as she stared wonderstruck at a late-night view of the electrified grid of streets and illuminated tall buildings from the tip of Manhattan to midtown, where cleaners still toiled in lighted offices.

They landed smoothly and left the near-empty plane. Dom

firmly gripped her arm as she hastened along with many rapid steps to accommodate his lengthy stride through the terminal. They walked beyond the taxi lineup to where a liveried limousine waited. An attentive chauffeur snapped to attention, greeting them both by name. Dom supplied the driver with an address. Turning to Gaia, he smiled, seeing how impressed she was by the car.

"It's not mine," he said. "An associate loaned it to me because it isn't safe to leave a car parked at an airport. Otherwise I'm not the type to use a chauffeur."

"Is that because it's the way an old man travels?"

He laughed. "Something like that. Now remember, I'm taking you to my mother's house in Brooklyn."

"Do you live there, too?" She was hoping against hope he would say that he did.

"No."

"Where *do* you live?"

"For a little girl you ask a lot of questions."

"I'm sorry."

"You don't ever have to say those words to me. I imagine in your short lifetime you've voiced far too many apologies."

She marveled that he could tell. He had touched the core of her long-held resentment, but unsure of how to reply, she remained silent.

"You'll be enrolling in school. There will be no need for you to take any after-class jobs. Just concentrate on your studies."

She nodded, overwhelmed. The car hummed over a beautiful mysterious bridge. Gaia looked behind her, marveling at the view, but was silent. Was this really happening to her? Who was this man, and why—

Dom broke through her reverie. "Incidentally, my mother is a devout Catholic and I'm pretty certain she will prefer that you attend a parochial high school. Will that bother you?"

Gaia thought back to the orphanage where she had felt constricted by the heavy religious atmosphere, the endless rules and regulations—and her own seemingly interminable loneliness. Her heart sank. "No," she said.

The car glided to a halt on a tree-lined street. A light went on. They mounted several steps and trod across the porch of the large, old-fashioned, comfortable frame house. Gaia was led inside a bright clean kitchen, and given a large glass of milk. Dom embraced his mother and said good-bye to Gaia, who sat blinking stupidly in the bright light, and drinking thirstily, her head heavy. She was taken upstairs to a pleasant bedroom, given pajamas, a toothbrush, towels, and a comb. But she would skip the preliminaries tonight. She slipped out of her clothes and fell into bed.

She was asleep instantly. Her dreams were brightly lit that night.

Mrs. Perrini was considerably shorter than she. Her thin figure was clothed in the traditional mourning garments assumed by older bereft immigrant women who keep Italian traditions. She was a widow and Dominic, she told Gaia the next morning at breakfast, was her sole living son. Following that remark, she lapsed into inaudibility, and seeing naked agony in her eyes, Gaia wasn't about to ask her to repeat herself.

Yet there remained a hunger for joy within Mrs. Perrini. She was openly delighted to receive such a youthful and lovely houseguest. "*Ahime!*" she sighed, thinking of how she had lived lonely and nearly hermitlike in the immaculately clean house. In recent years she hadn't been much given to small talk, succoring her memories to her breast, nor did she ask questions of her youngest son. Dom had his own apartment somewhere in Manhattan, where she had never been invited or asked to be taken. All her life she adhered to the inviolate dictum: Privacy was the right of a grown man; questions were not to be asked. It was a law rigidly enforced by her deceased husband.

"Mariuccia," Antonucci Perrini addressed her when she was his young bride, "there is this that you must remember above all else. Never ask me anything about my work. And if the Holy Father in heaven will give me the power to plant male seeds in your womb, our sons will belong to you in their babyhood, but when they grow older I shall claim their fealty, and you must no more question them than you would me."

Gaia's presence within her home had opened the gates of remembrance. She thanked God that in the waning years of her life she'd received the gift, the blessing she craved all throughout her childbearing years: a daughter to belong to her alone.

Gaia addressed her as "Signora."

Despite the stiffness of her joints and the wrinkling of her skin, a zest for life stirred anew within Mariuccia. She vowed to guide and mold her charge with unspoken love and acts of kindness, as she would her own daughter. How wonderful it felt to talk to someone eager to listen! Gaia sat across from her, drinking the coffee she'd quickly grown to love—although Signora limited her to one cup per day—listening to her lilting, heavy-accented voice as she told of long-ago events.

It was all right, thought Mariuccia, to tell the girl a little— as long as she was careful to leave certain facts out. Gaia was so full of questions about Dom; the ones Signora freely replied to concerned his childhood.

Dominic, her youngest-born, followed a sequence of stillbirths; he was twelve years younger than his next-eldest brother. By then the Perrinis were already living in Brooklyn, having moved there from the cramped Italian ghetto on the Lower East Side.

"He was always handsome, greatly resembling his father, who was a good-looking man. Would you believe that it isn't simply a mother's pride speaking, but there was sensitivity in Dominic that Antonucci never had. In some ways he was more my son than his father's. I'm afraid it made it difficult for him to be born into this family."

She related many, many stories, some of them inconsequential, about Dom's babyhood, his sturdiness in walking early, the beginning years in school, his prowess in ball games with neighboring children. But she would say nothing about his ninth year or beyond, the back of one hand drawn to her mouth as if to block further words. Gaia, who had been intrigued, petitioned her to continue. Signora's eyes rolled from one side to the other. After pausing she went on in a curiously cracked voice. "Dominic used to say I worked too hard. When he came home from school, before even smearing jelly on bread and taking an apple, he used to ask what he could do to help me. Well, one afternoon he was on his knees washing down the kitchen linoleum, and his father unexpectedly entered. He yanked him up by his shoulders and struck me across my cheek. 'No sissy work for my son!' he shouted. After that, Dominic was given tasks by his father . . . he ran errands."

For a while she sat with her shoulders hunched, her head sinking to her chest. Gaia placed her arms around her and Signora reached up and patted her face. As if it were necessary for her to purge herself, she unleashed other stories—of how, when the American immigration inspector questioned Antonucci concerning his prospects in the land of opportunity, he stated in Sicilian-dialect Italian that he was upright, a devoted husband, and a potential family man. He gestured toward Mariuccia's swollen belly and she recalled that she had blushed. He assured the inspector that his sole purpose in traveling to America was to *fabbricare* a better life with his sinew and hands. The official was impressed and the Perrinis were admitted to the United States.

"Did your husband easily find work?" Gaia asked in halting Italian, recently learned.

Signora nodded, her eyes filling with tears. Again, conversation ended as the painful scenes intruded. She wasn't a stupid woman and knew more than she had let on to Antonucci, because she heard neighborhood gossip about his dark deeds. Usually she was removed from this aspect of his life. From time to time, like bilge water escaping a drain, it eventually seeped through. She shuddered, even now, thinking of the time when Signora Bregna, the woman with the pitifully deformed, lopsided face, came to her pleading. "You are the *don's* wife. Being a woman you can sympathize with me. My maiden name was Salinari—I am of good stock—but because of my appearance I had no choice except to marry beneath me. My man was a braggart, but he was a fool. He hadn't the sense to see that when your husband gave him his own candy store that nothing coming free is of value. He was gunned down in the store, shot dead. I am left with children . . . there is no income."

She timidly broached the topic of the Bregna family's survival to Antonucci. He scolded her, "I warned you to never interfere in my business." Later on, she heard from neighbors that the widow had been resettled in the Bronx. She felt justified in having intervened.

Oddly, it seemed to her, she was looked up to by other women with what amounted to envy. She was married to a powerful man. Her husband had found a means to speedily prosper, to feed his family with the finest provisions . . . by feeding off of other immigrants. Beginning in the teeming environs of Mulberry Street and, when they moved to Brooklyn, expanding to more sophisticated rackets, Perrini was as a king in his new land. Mariuccia cringed at the whispers: "prostitution . . . loan sharking . . . hijacking . . . murder by contract." As Antonucci had attested to the immigration inspector, his sinew and hands were the essential means of his success: hands he used to garrote with and muscles that brutally enforced La Cosa Nostra punishment. As a young virile man, he easily made *capo*, as she bore sons for him.

When the three older sons, Vito, Guido, and Luigi, grew beyond adolescence into manhood, their father's connections provided them with easy access to the mob. They quickly rose above hoodlum duties and were designated as *capos*. Vito was a specialist in gambling and phony charity scams. Guido's expertise was in rub outs, often on loan at high price to other families. Luigi oversaw the running of brothels and X-rated film production.

Dom graduated from the eighth grade and entered high school.

Antonucci was proud of his sons. He anticipated that Dominic would do as well as his brothers when he came of age. As for himself, he had risen within the ranks and not only was boss of the Perrini mob family, but had been recognized by other top mobsters and was afforded a seat on the inner-circle

council, where laundering of gang money was discussed and
hits ordered. And he was something more. It was he who was
the ultimate strategist for internecine wars, disposing of his
associates while he sat with them and kissed them on both
cheeks. He clasped his arms about their bodies in comradely
embrace before thoughtfully fitting them with cement over-
coats to shelter their dead bodies from the chill waters of New
York harbor. He became the boss of bosses.

Gaia was holding the picture when Dom entered her studio.

"I thought I'd find you here, *cara.*"

She clutched the frame to her breasts, regarding him in
stunned silence because she had never shown Dom the portrait. It was a part of her secret inner world wherein a real
mother existed.

"What have you got there? Let me see." He took the frame
from Gaia and studied the sketch. "This is quite good. The
face holds an openhearted expression, a projection of warmth.
There's only one thing wrong with it."

Her voice was small. "Yes?"

"You've made yourself look too old."

A moment's pause, then relief. He hadn't guessed and she
was unable to bring herself to tell him that this was her
representation of a mother she had never known. She knew
that he believed in realities, that he would think it bizarre for
her to cling to such ethereal comfort. She must try to appear
alert and well-focused, as though she wasn't scared by the
responsibilities she now faced.

"What time is the board meeting?" she asked coolly.

"Within the hour, when the directors arrive."

"Who are they?"

"Men you needn't concern yourself with." He was oddly
curt.

She was amazed, but reacted with instinctive stubbornness.
"What do you mean, Dom? If I'm going to meet them I really
think I should be aware of who they are."

His voice was sharp. "Leave it alone!"

She watched Dom's face assume remoteness as his eyes flashed anger. It was so unfair that he would withdraw from her emotionally when she was fearful and needed him the most. How could he be kind to her one moment and then drastically change? It was as if a cold hollow substance had suddenly landed in the pit of her stomach.

"Listen to me, and hear me well," he continued. "Don't you dare say anything out of line in the boardroom."

"If I choose to speak at the meeting, you can't stop me." What had come over him?

He began shouting. The vaulted ceiling deflected his voice, amplifying it, making it more resonantly penetrating than she had ever heard it. And yet, she blocked out his actual words. She felt a strange dizziness, as if magnetized by the charged atmosphere, drawn into his vortex, fueled by it. But she also felt oddly in control of her own response, conditioned into silence by the imposed discipline of her childhood . . . yet she had to find out, once and for all.

"Forgive me, but I must ask you something. Dom, why did you insist I accept a designer's job at Ferrante when I had a prior offer from Tiffany? And, for that matter, why did you encourage me to study jewelry design in the first place? Did you know all along that this was going to happen . . . who I am?" She could scarcely look at him.

"No. It was pure coincidence. Am I to be *accused* because I encouraged you to develop your natural God-given talent? When have I ever done anything to hurt you? Answer me that?"

She swallowed, feeling worse than before. "You've never intentionally hurt me."

"Whatever that means." Why was he shouting at her? She had the feeling she was being pressed into her old subservient mold. Why was he making her feel guilty? "You've always been so good to me. I never meant to—"

He abruptly cut her off. "Don't worry about that. You haven't."

She was astonished at him, but remained angrier at herself. She had been telling herself that when he yelled at her, it was out of his special feeling. He wanted her to be as shrewd and as smart as he was. Hopelessly loving him, she hadn't minded if he was manipulating her with a fine Italian hand. She glanced furtively at him; his face had reddened and a temple vein protruded. No more, she said to herself. No more secrets from me. Maybe then, she was thinking, you will really open yourself to loving me.

Dom watched Gaia closely. He felt he could tell what she was thinking. So, she hadn't seen that his show of anger was contrived. Good. It was a bad habit of his at those rare moments when he tasted fear to berate the person closest to him when his rage was directed elsewhere.

· 8 ·

The law offices of the firm of Bari & Battaglia occupied the entire twenty-third floor of one of the new prestigious glass-walled buildings lining Park Avenue. Entry to the structure was past sliding doors governed by an electric eye that led into a black and white marble lobby. Inside was an artificially controlled atmosphere that provided heat in the winter and warmer-weather conditioning. Other than filtering city pollution through powerful roof ventilators, the atmosphere was hermetically sealed from the world at large.

Except, of course, for the electronic communications devices within individual offices: computers, telexes and telephones.

Merrill Ross had just hung up from a conversation with Vito Battaglia, the senior partner. Direct contact initiated by the old man—as he was referred to behind his back—was a considerable rarity. So far as he was personally concerned, Ross had never before been so signally honored, if honor it was, he wryly thought. The call was occasioned because Battaglia had himself just completed a conversation with Giuliano Rinzini, the Roman *avvocato*, concerning the Ferrante estate. Rinzini was not merely the legal counsel of the deceased jeweler, but executor of the will.

"Are you handling the matter?" the older man asked.

Christ! Who else did he suppose was in charge? Wasn't he the head of his department? But Ross answered pleasantly: "Yes, sir, I'm on top of it. All is proceeding according to schedule." That should shut him up and make the old man leave him alone instead of sticking his Italian nose in and confusing his work.

"Are you sure?"

"Of course." Would he say so if he weren't? Like every other estate, the details to be taken care of were pro forma. A translated copy of the last will and testament of Ugo Ferrante, il Principe di Corchese, had been retrieved from the safe (the translation had been compiled several years before when the photostat copy of the Italian original was received).

"And does the girl . . . what's her name . . . know she's inherited? Has there been any difficulty there?"

"Gaia Gerald."

"What?"

"Her name."

"Oh."

"She knows."

"Was she accepting?"

"I should say so, although she was upset."

"Go to the store immediately. Calm her down. That's important. If she harbors any suspicions she might be difficult . . . upset the apple cart."

"Do you mean she might refuse the inheritance, sir?"

"Young man, you are presuming."

"That is a lawyer's prerogative, isn't it, sir?"

"I have no intention of continuing this discussion. What I want you to do is to get yourself over to the store at once. Be at her side. Talk to her. Say whatever is necessary to her. Hell, romance her if you must, but keep that girl from interfering if she has a mind to."

"Why would she be likely to? I wouldn't if I inherited millions."

"Attend to it!"

"I will as soon as I contact Mrs. Silvia Wood, the prince's living daughter. She was Silvia Ferrante, onetime Contessa di Malvestiti, and now Mrs. James Wood, of Grosse Pointe, Michigan, wife of the automotive industrialist."

"Humph," Battaglia cleared his throat. "I know who she is. You don't have to bother with that. Signor Rinzini will take care of it."

"Do you know, sir, whether he will inform Mrs. Wood of her niece's existence?"

"I do not. And I think we'd better leave that discovery for when she arrives in Rome. That's Rinzini's headache."

"Fine, sir. It was the reason I hesitated calling her earlier."

"Get over to the store."

Merrill Ross had been employed by Bari & Battaglia for seven years, hired directly upon his graduation with honors from Harvard Law School. Adept at his specialty of wills and estates, he assumed responsibility within the firm. It rankled him that more recent law graduates began their employment at a salary substantially higher than his. When he complained to Vito Battaglia, his request for a raise, profit sharing, and a junior partnership was shrugged off.

"It's the times," Merrill was told. Try as he might to cajole the old man, Vito Battaglia refused to be budged.

Consequently, Merrill evaluated his worth to the firm. He headed a four-person team, consisting of an associate, a female paralegal who was also an accountant, and one secretary. A conservative estimate of the total estate funds administered by Bari & Battaglia amounted to something more than one billion dollars, the greater proportion of which derived from the estates of deceased mafiosi. He recognized the names from newspaper reportage. Merrill Ross, however vicariously, was stimulated by his proximity to great wealth. But he intended to acquire his own.

Merrill considered his chances to butter up the old man. Perhaps he ought to emphasize that, although he bore the surname of his Jewish father, his mother had been Agnes

Mary Brady, and that Marcus Ross had married Agnes in the Church. The rest he would omit: As his father strayed from Judaism, so did his mother from her faith, seeking to please her husband. Together they joined, but did not become active members of, a nondenominational church.

Yes, Merrill would assuredly keep to himself that his parents' attitude toward religion had become agnostic, and that he himself did not believe in a higher order at all. Success was wealth, wealth a God. And by God, he deserved a raise!

Of course, were he married, with a family, he would logically need more income. However, on this point, Merrill wasn't about to alter his life-style.

That he was a bachelor was necessitated by the long hours he kept. He sometimes ruefully contemplated this, but not excessively. He enjoyed being single and took great pride in his attractiveness to the women with whom he had temporary sexual relationships. He placed a greater priority on his personal freedom than on entangling romantic alliances. Why should he bother with all that baggage? He'd seen too many of his peers' marriages either dissolve in divorce or linger bitterly in the acrimony of separate encampments within their households after children were born, making life miserable for all concerned: husband and wife, the friends who vicariously suffered with the combatants, and especially the offspring of the union for whose sake the parents were remaining together.

No, Merrill was scrupulous in his intention of continuing to be emotionally uninvolved. He had decided that a basic selfishness was expressed during courtship, each person calculating what they would derive from the relationship. His most recent girlfriend had incessantly pressed him for matrimony. It was the kiss of death. He was (once again) without a particular woman in his life—although he needn't ever sleep alone.

He attempted sorting out how these divergent facts might be parlayed into a higher income and junior partnership. Merrill was wholly dissatisfied with his current compensation for his legal competency: After all, on the most recent reorder of the firm's engraved stationery, his name was *above* the line of demarcation from the newer law associates. The money couldn't be far behind, could it?

He was eager to meet Gaia Gerald.

· 9 ·

Grosse Pointe

"WOOD RESIDENCE," THE BUTLER ANSWERED THE TELEPHONE. HE sought out Madam's personal maid and instructed her to inform their mistress that an overseas call awaited. She raced up the stairs but garbled her message because she was obliged to interrupt a masseuse's ministrations upon her employer's diet-spare body. She had to repeat herself, all the while anticipating being yelled at.

"From Roma, you say?" Silvia Ferrante di Malvestiti Wood immediately sat up, throwing off the sheet that partially covered her. "What are you waiting for, ninny?" she demanded. "Hand me the phone."

"Yes, ma'am. The gentleman is mostly talking in Italian."

"Does that surprise you? Rome *is* in Italy." She threw back her head and imperiously announced her presence on the wire by reciting her full name.

It was an *avvocato* who informed her in saddest tones that her father had died during the night, but that happily he was executor of the estate.

She was numbed, but not from a sense of grief. Her life had been isolated from her father for so long a time that she felt no rush of loss. No, Silvia was elated; at last, she was the inheritor of Papa's fortune. She abruptly broke off the conversation with the lawyer in Rome. "I shall see you at the funeral," she told him. Silvia hardly needed to have him confirm that she alone had inherited the Appia Antica villa and his international jewelry business.

Fleetingly she remembered the years of her youth. Of her beautiful sister, Angela Maria, long dead . . . killed with her American husband in a highway accident. As Papa's sole survivor she was fantastically rich!

Years after Angela Maria's death, Silvia still felt pervading resentment against her younger, prettier, sister. She recalled the way she had viciously lashed out at Angela Maria, taunting her with the name *omicida*—murderess. She'd never let Angela Maria forget that their mother died upon giving birth.

Silvia's animosity fed upon inconsequential comparisons. Her sister's near-black hair was naturally curly, hers was straight. Angela Maria's complexion was fair, her own skin was olive-tone, an unhappy circumstance with her dull-blond hair. The younger sister was a consistent student with good grades, Silvia had a short attention span for study. Angela Maria seemed always to be complimented, while Silvia was chided for not doing her best. Angela Maria lacked the complication of personal fears that Silvia had to struggle against, as anxiety strove to override the assertiveness that wedged its way unpleasantly into her personality. By the time she reached adulthood, she was hopelessly locked into a personality mold of her own making, thwarting every emotion except anger, stimulating utmost happiness as well as passion. Fulfillment—on every level—grew increasingly elusive until she no longer expected it—including her marriage to Jim Wood.

Her earliest sexual experience was at the age of five, initiated by the trusted acquaintance of her father whom they all called Zio, for "uncle." He induced her to enter a room with him where he indoctrinated her into mysteries. She could no longer recall his face, just the memory of his fat abdomen squashing against her, and how the stench of his sweat corrupted his powerfully scented cologne when his squat penis lengthened into a hard instrument—and one she then truly believed was magic. At first she was timid, but when he assured her that he would "tickle" her with it, she giggled in paroxysms of delight as sensation from his fingers rippled across her skin. She was beyond understanding the beginnings of pleasure within her body, but she obediently removed her panties hoping for more, saddling his thighs in the uncomfortable position he wanted, willing to be rhythmically manipulated as "that thing" relentlessly pressed against her pee pee but failed to extinguish a flame ignited beyond its reach.

Buried in her memory was the day she had unexpectedly come upon her sister alone with Zio. Angela Maria had been crying hysterically, Silvia could see. Zio smiled and approached Angela Maria, who attacked him with flailing fists. Silvia walked over to them and pushed her sister against the wall. Zio picked up Angela Maria in his arms, placed her on his lap, slid his fingers up her dress. Silvia watched as her sister lay quietly crying against the man's shoulder. The man's face contorted as if in pain.

"Zio, Zio!" Angela Maria cried out, but he didn't answer. His fingers were in his mouth, his eyes shut. Spasms racked his body, and he let Angela Maria go. She walked out.

In her early teens, without an adult to censure her, Silvia bleached her hair and began applying cosmetics. The result was a parody: a ludicrous brassy-headed figure wobbling on stilted heels, corns forming from ill-fitting pointed-toe shoes. Her provocatively lacy underwear gapped; she became addicted to padded brassieres that centered attention upon the artificial wads straining the bodice material of her dresses and blouses. Though she adored low frontal necklines, there simply was no cleavage. Silvia peered through heavy fringes of stiff, resolutely upcurled eyelashes and totally failed to see the disharmony of her too-soon adherence to adult fashion.

Her attitude toward the mistresses Ugo Ferrante lustfully bedded in his antique four-poster was that of wrathful disdain, without any moral censure. It was simply that she was contemptuous of the style and manners of the largely uneducated girls he bedded, girls often not much older than she. They didn't belong in opulent surroundings, those little waitresses, occasional shopgirls, and the more frequent out-and-out street prostitutes. Silvia shuddered in suppressed indignation, her small shoulders quivering at the sight of them being led up the curving stairs like timid foals, offering fodder for the stallion's devouring prick.

Their offensive presence prompted Silvia to embark upon elaborate shopping sprees. When the bills arrived for him to pay, Ferrante frequently balked, swearing at her, his great head jutting forward, bloodshot eyes flashing a demonic red, his mouth roaring obscenities in a voice that was like the fearful breaking of thunder. She defiantly persisted in going her own way, and more clothes than she could possibly wear were delivered to the villa. Silvia learned early on to select stark designs with the shaping cut into the pattern to flatter her short-waisted proportions. In later life this style became her signature, and no one in the circles she arrogantly swept through would have speculated that her figure was less than perfect. As a teenager, however, should a *commessa* in any of the fashionable designer shops attempt to guide her toward a less sophisticated wardrobe, she would petulantly mimic her father's explosive temper and threaten to have the woman discharged.

"You dress like a whore," her father muttered one night after they'd been arguing for hours. He pinned her down on his big antique bed. "Let's see if you behave like one."

Ugo Ferrante drunkenly invaded his elder daughter. She never told anyone about it. And she never healed.

From that time, Silvia's existence evolved upon a fragile balance of compensations, although she wasn't naturally introspective enough to understand this. She became almost violently promiscuous, though she was no closer to achieving orgasm than when Zio had pushed against her a dozen years before. She instituted herself among the swirl of gaiety emanating from the late night into early morning in the establishments along the Via Veneto. Here she was accepted on her own terms. The more sexually wild performances Silvia gave, the more she must willingly do the next time, the greater her intent to be increasingly outrageous. One man wasn't enough, she wanted many, all at once.

One day she would be cleansed. *When her father died and she inherited his fortune.*

She must now try to forget that other far-distant world when she was young, when she hated Angela Maria and was suffused by envy of her. She had inherited. She was rich. She was above everything, at last.

What a triumph to have Papa's wealth to spend however she wished. No longer need she wheedle a *stronzolo* husband until he bought her a sable coat. She considered her recent marriage to Jim Wood a disaster. The American self-made millionaire who had seemed so desirable when she stalked him at a Swiss ski resort had reverted to being a thrifty midwesterner on his home turf.

Silvia was bored hearing him boast how his first industry job had been on a Ford assembly line. He advanced to become an engineer for American Motors. Convincing bankers of his vision and expertise, he obtained use of a former General Motors plant and became the first manufacturer to turn out a product with European styling, cost economy, and profitability. Wood Motors was an outstanding success. At the age of fifty he was many times a millionaire. Not that his money did her much good, Silvia thought bitterly.

Hadn't he shown himself for what he was when that *brutto* husband of hers embarrassed her in front of a mere nothing fur salesperson? She had set her heart on acquiring a floor-length chinchilla cape, and Jim had the meanness to demand she return it to the shop. She vowed to never forgive him— and plotted revenge.

Dull, dull, dull, her life in Grosse Pointe! She was expected to lunch, have tea, and play tennis with unworldly unsophisticated women. It made Silvia want to scream, but then she secretly smiled to herself, knowing how she would greatly embarrass Jim Wood—as he had done to her in the fur store.

She organized a charity ball—a masquerade. On the evening of the party, Silvia purposely staged a raging argument with her husband. As she'd intended, he went on ahead to the ball, attired in black-tie evening clothes and a Groucho Marx nose with attached glasses. This was his concession to being costumed. She would have felt contempt for him had she not something else in mind.

Once it was late enough for everyone to be present, Silvia made her costumed entrance. Apparently nude, but actually swathed in diaphanous flesh-hued silk, wearing a long-haired blond wig concealing her breasts, she rode sidesaddle on a white horse directly into the ballroom of the venerable Book Cadillac hotel.

The result was pandemonium and she laughed to see that Jim Wood was red-faced with embarrassment. What she failed to anticipate were his next-day instructions to his lawyers, who filed for a Michigan divorce. Within that state he could call in political favors to assure that the court would award her minimum alimony. Too late aware that she'd overplayed her hand, Silvia petulantly refused to vacate his richly furnished home—until now.

Happily, a new life had opened for her. She was thankful that Angela Maria had died childless. There was no second-generation offspring to claim her sister's share of the estate.

As for her own daughter, Mara Elisa di Malvestiti, born late during the tenure of her first marriage, but not strictly of that union, Silvia determined to provide her with an income despite the fact that she was in her late twenties and should be providing for herself. Papa had probably omitted any bequest to Mara because the girl was illegitimate. What hypocrisy, that her debauched parent, Ugo Ferrante, had turned moralist!

Across the passage of years, Silvia still scorned her first husband, Pietro di Malvestiti, for his inability to service a woman, although her compensation was her title of Contessa. When Mara was born, the di Malvestitis accepted the baby as their own in order to support their pretense about Pietro. They could not face their son's homosexuality and raised his wife's child as a di Malvestiti. Silvia departed to partake of life in her own style.

Now, upon her father's death, she intended to assume a title of higher rank, henceforth to be known as the Principessa di Corchese.

"Hurry and pack my bags," she commanded her maid.

Bolting from the massage table, she dismissed the masseuse and shouted for the butler. He was told to arrange for use of the company jet. Jim would agree to that, glad to have her depart. The marriage was never really a marriage. There would be a stopover at Kennedy, where she would transfer to a commercial flight to Rome. "Be certain to book me first class," she called after him. Following a moment's thought, she summoned him back. "I'll require several hours in New York."

There was a Ferrante store on Fifth Avenue. Who, if not she, had a better right to scoop up the jewelry she desired? Who other than the new owner?

· 10 ·

It had been a furiously busy morning at Ferrante-New York. The plainclothes security officers were deployed to keep an attentive eye on the swelling crowds who relentlessly pressed through the Fifth Avenue entrance. Most who entered were curiosity seekers, intrigued by news flashes on early-morning radio and television, and in the stories carried in newspapers. One enterprising reporter had sifted out the larger story. Sure, Ugo Ferrante was dead. The big news—one of the store's designers had inherited the American business. Not only that—she was young, talented, and absolutely beautiful.

He wrote it up with relish . . . a Cinderella story.

But the reporter hadn't bothered to ferret out the inner story. Gaia didn't know who she truly was.

The Àtrio tallied larger-than-usual sales receipts that day. Additional clerks had to be transferred from other selling departments to perform duty in the alcove. Customers were enthusiastically purchasing the Gaia Star as though it were a talisman. Most of them were reluctant to depart.

"Do you suppose that if I wait, the Gerald girl might come by?"

"Oh, did you hear that she'll be here? What is she like? Really like, I mean."

"What does she *look* like? That's what I want to know."

"I'd adore getting a glimpse of her, maybe her autograph."

"That would be great on a check."

Much laughter.

Several more sophisticated patrons entirely ignored the Àtrio. The focus of their concern was to know whether the store would continue to operate. Some had placed sizable deposits on fine jewelry that was in the process of being custom-created for them. One woman in particular was worried that the store's exclusive china patterns would become irreplaceable. How would she handle future breakage in her dinner set? A few more nervous persons appeared on the premises to claim personally owned jeweled goods that had been left for repair, and that reposed in a section of the massive second-basement vault.

"I assure you, madam, that the vault is burglarproof."

A worried rejoinder: "Is any lock system truly impenetrable?"

A youthful female messenger (bonded, as were all of the store's employees) giggled to the vault clerk as she appeared time and again to transport jewelry to a waiting owner. "It's worse than a run on the banks."

Shortly past noon, workers issued from nearby office buildings, enlarging the crowd already within the store as they passed in on a wave of vociferous excitement. They had absorbed the news now blazoned in three-inch lettered headlines in the *Daily News* and *Post*. This was a fairy tale come true. It might have happened to anyone of them.

From the rear-mezzanine security office, operatives viewed the active main floor on closed-circuit television. The state of affairs demanded utmost caution. A solid block of young women had entirely isolated the Àtrio from the main selling floor as their excited voices projected a carnival atmosphere. It was a condition to which no fine jewelry store had ever been subjected.

Jack Dillon, head of inhouse security, swung his feet from his desk, shrugged on his suit jacket, and bounded from his balcony office down the marble stairs. At the fastest pace he could manage, he pressed through the crowd, considerably alarmed when his hand-held communications unit was swept out of his grasp, smashed to the floor, and rendered inoperable. Dillon swore under his breath, making his way from one plainclothes security guard to another, ordering each one of them to reinforce the command post near the main entrance. From a closetlike patrol station close by the Fifth Avenue door, he telephoned to a security service, reading the number from a slip of paper taken from his jacket pocket. He placed an immediate order for a supplement of hourly-hired outside guards.

This done, Dillon wiped his florid brow with his handkerchief. His jacket was noticeably strained at the seams, testament to a substantial weight gain since he had been forced to retire from his post as detective, New York Police Department. It had been rumored that he'd formed a liaison with one of the major crime families. He was hired immediately by Ferrante-New York, the order emanating directly from the store's board of directors. No public reason was given for their decision.

"There will be five guys coming in," he informed gray-haired Roger Perry, conventionally dignified in his neatly pressed suit, white shirt, and dark silk tie. Perry headed the main-floor security force, and had been passed over for promotion when the ex-detective was brought in. Until then, Perry had assumed that as the senior member of the Ferrante security staff, he would be automatically promoted to the post of chief when the prior head suddenly left his job. This was not to be.

Salinari was unkind and hurtfully direct when he'd summoned him to his office. "A new chief of security has been employed," he told him, "Jack Dillon."

Perry's normally pale complexion blanched further. "Mr. Salinari, I assumed—"

The reply was waspish. "Then you obviously *presumed* too much."

Anguish filtered into Perry's voice. "It isn't fair to be overlooked after all my years of service."

"I can do nothing. The matter is closed."

Roger Perry backed down. He was too company-oriented to inform the union, which, in any event, could have done nothing, since an executive position was in question.

Three things about his new boss especially irritated him. Jack Dillon was surly and officious. His grooming habits left much to be desired. And he hadn't the class appropriate to the store's prestige. Look at him, his hair greasy, beady little eyes, sweating like a fat pig.

"When the guards get here, call me," Dillon ordered.

"I only hope their attire conforms to the unobtrusive image at Ferrante."

"They'll be showing up in uniform."

Perry sighed. "Which agency are they coming from?"

"Bullet Security."

"It isn't on the accredited list of the Retail Jewelers Association," Perry replied, adding, with a curl of his lip, "sir."

"I don't give a shit about that, and don't you make a fuss. Besides, the name was given to me when I took over here. One of the board members has an interest in Bullet Security. That's what I hear, and it's all you gotta know."

The five uniformed guards were stationed on crowd-control duty on the sidewalk *outside* the store. Minicam crews and reporters from the major television networks gathered at the Fifth Avenue entrance; they were extremely vocal about seeking entry to interview Gaia Gerald. Miles Tuchelin came out to reason with them. "Ms. Gerald will not be available to appear on camera. Sorry, guys, but I think you can sympathize with her feelings."

"Sympathy she wants?" someone chortled. "She's a millionaire and she wants sympathy?"

"I have a prepared statement." Miles handed out photocopied pages.

As the reporters swarmed around him, the shorter Tuchelin's bright red hair vanished from sight.

"When will she be available for an interview?"

"Have you at least got some publicity eight-by-tens of her that we can run?"

Miles' voice could be heard. "I've included her photo in the packet."

"Come on, Tuchelin. When can we get her on camera?"

"Sorry, that's impossible at this time."

"When?"

"I can't promise."

Roger Perry, who was manning the inside door, alarmed at the store's overcrowding, was admitting only those individuals known to him. When the door was opened to allow Miles Tuchelin onto the sidewalk, it had to be swiftly shut again in the face of the impatiently pushing crowd seeking to enter.

A dark-bearded young man had methodically elbowed himself near the entrance. He had immediately grasped where the power was, and, recognizing the little redheaded man's authority, said, "I'm Merrill Ross, lawyer for the estate. Do you suppose we can both get inside?"

"If not this way," Miles gasped, "we'll have to make our way through the crowd and use the employees' entrance on the side street."

Merrill gazed down on him. "Are you sure you're not too small to survive the crush?" It was asked with unmistakable condescension.

Miles' eyes narrowed. He checked his anger. "Haven't you heard? Appearances can be deceiving."

Perry maneuvered the plate glass door with its invisible sensors open a crack. Both men sidled inside.

A hired airport limousine drew up to the curb. Silvia Wood observed the scene through a tinted window.

"*Dio santo!*" she exclaimed to the chauffeur. "I can't possibly walk through this mob. Go and find someone to escort me."

Eventually two of the uniformed guards approached, urged on by the chauffeur.

"What is going on?" she demanded after allowing her door to be opened.

"All of these creeps want to see the heiress," one of the guards replied.

Frightened, she tentatively stepped out of the car, clutching her oversize cobra shoulder bag to her body. "They are going to mug me," she squealed. "How did they know I was coming here?"

No one replied as, with one man in the lead and the other behind her, she was alternately tugged forward and pushed through the crowd. "Help!" she shrieked. "Idiot! Stop crushing me." Nevertheless she experienced a thrill being sandwiched between the two burly guards' bodies.

Roger Perry saw her entourage approach as he peered outward through the glass doors. He pushed one of them open just wide enough to admit her.

With nervous fingers she removed her kid gloves, and his eyes widened imperceptibly at her magnificent large-stone rings: a grass-green emerald surrounded with (at an estimate) four carats of superior diamonds, also a pear-cut diamond solitaire that was something close to twenty carats, and a wide *pavé* diamond wedding band that reached to her knuckle.

"I am the Principessa di Corchese," she haughtily announced, "the daughter of Ugo Ferrante."

Roger Perry went pale. He berated himself for dereliction of duty; he *ought* to have recognized the blond, Italian-accented, heavily perfumed woman—even though Mrs. Wood (he believed that was her marital name) had in the past initiated transactions by telephone from Grosse Pointe. The jewelry she ordered was mailed out first class without invoice and uninsured, the safest and most unobtrusive manner of sending jewelry through the mails.

"Dear, oh dear," he heard himself mumble, astonished that she apparently did not know the full story behind the confusion within the store. Assuredly, it wasn't his place to inform her. "I will ask Mr. Salinari, our general manager and president, to speak to you," he said.

Silvia's reply was imperious. "No, I can't be bothered. I am here to select some new jewelry from my store, and I have little time, as I am en route to my father's funeral."

He noted that her lavishly made-up eyes showed no sign of recent weeping. "Madam . . . but . . . Princess," he hesitantly ventured.

"Why do you stare at me?"

"If you will please follow?"

She struck out after him with long strides of her cabretta-clad legs, her sable coat flapping. Several times he glanced back and saw that she was close behind him. He escorted her past a receptionist's ornate desk to chamber number 3, which was furnished with gilded chairs upholstered with fine velvet and a rare antique desk with a framed mirror upon it. It was where customers seeking privacy examined the most expensive jewelry.

Her gaze swept across his face. "Don't keep me waiting," she demanded. "Send a salesperson in. *Subito!*"

"At once." He backed out.

As a security measure, the door automatically locked from the outside. He would summon a salesperson to attend the princess, aware that the clerk's attention would produce no commission. Well, that couldn't be helped. His larger concern was that—as everyone except the woman inside the chamber knew—Ferrante-New York had been inherited by Gaia Gerald.

Another limousine, this one pearl-gray with reinforced steel panels and smoked bulletproof glass, came to a stop as near to the Ferrante entrance as its chauffeur-bodyguard could maneuver in the Fifth Avenue traffic. Many similar armored cars were in daily use on the city streets, so subtly fortified that no one gave them a second glance. It was an accepted fact that wealthy men—and mysterious men with untold secrets—had to be protected from violence.

Three hard-visaged middle-aged men piled out of the rear after the chauffeur held open the door for them. Their custom-made suits efficiently concealed paunches and obscured other figure defects. Despite a chill in the air, they wore no topcoats or hats as they hastened to enter the store, walking swiftly, not because they were cold, but because the milling crowd presented an unpredictable situation. With their eyes apparently focused directly ahead of them, they took in the people to their immediate right and left without altering their line of vision. As if sensing something ominously compelling about them, those persons who were closest to them parted to let the men through. Although there was a murmur of interest among the television crews, no cameras were activated nor did interviewers press forward.

One of the television people was rueful after the heavy glass door admitted them to the store. "Know who those guys were?" he asked.

Another admitted, "There was something familiar about them."

Inside, Roger Perry greeted the men with the quiet respect and attention he knew they demanded and deserved. Sending two of the store security guards ahead as a flying wedge, he insured that their progress to the elevator would be without incident, pleased that the crystal-chandelier-adorned customer cab was waiting at the main floor.

Perry reached his hand into the cab and depressed the button for the fifth floor. He considered himself rewarded when one of them almost imperceptibly acknowledged his service with a flicker of his steel-gray eyes. The double doors closed without a sound. The other guards returned to their posts, but Perry remained standing before the indicator long enough to see that the elevator had ascended to the correct floor. Only then did he turn away, satisfied that he had done his duty.

Of course he knew these men's names, but he always sensed that they preferred never to be addressed upon their entering or leaving.

They were the board members of Ferrante-New York.

· 11 ·

ALONE IN HER STUDIO, GAIA FOUND HERSELF UNABLE TO CONCEN-
trate. She kept averting her gaze from her sketch pad to the
door, and from the door to the telephone. Dom was either
somewhere in the store or he'd left the building without
bidding her good-bye. She felt absolutely crestfallen. He'd
been so angry with her.

Thinking back, she endeavored to work through her emotions to review the reason for his recent outburst of temper
in Salinari's office. How had it begun? What did she do to
cause it? Gaia bent her head forward. Her cold fingers supporting her brow felt refreshing.

Dom had warned her to remain silent at the forthcoming
board meeting. What else could she possibly do, knowing as
little as she did, besides sit quietly observing procedure? And
remembering the imminent meeting, Gaia realized with a
start how deeply immersed she'd become in brooding. She
vigorously shook her head and sat erect. This was certainly
no way to begin her new duties.

If Dom had gone away from the store, he'd shortly return.
He had to. He was one of the board members.

Gaia came to a decision. The concept of her wealth continued to seem unreal. It was her new power that was tangi-
ble. She experienced a wish to order immediate changes of

those things that had irked her as an employee, and she contacted the secretarial office on the intercom. Presently, Etta Spring arrived, she who was Salinari's right hand.

The older woman, shapeless in her unbecoming flowered-print dress, her graying hair set in tight ringlets that unfortunately emphasized her facial pudginess, puffed a cigarette in the partitioned enclosure. She was never without a lit cigarette, in hand or burning nearby.

Concealing her surprise that it was Etta Spring who responded to her call, Gaia offered a nervous little smile.

"I want to work for *you*," Etta said.

Gaia hesitated. She'd always felt intimidated by her, and there had never been any sort of rapport between them. But a wiser voice within her warned that she'd need to lean upon Etta's corporate experience. Why then did she taste a sense of foreboding?

Nevertheless, she agreed. "I'm glad to have you."

She dictated a memo to all personnel. Use of the time clock was immediately abolished. Employee attendance would be more informally noted by department heads. Gaia watched the old-line-conservative secretary's lip curl disapprovingly as she scribbled shorthand symbols on her pad.

The phone rang and Etta Spring bounded up to answer. After listening briefly, she set the receiver in its cradle and informed Gaia, "The board meeting is about to commence. I must go in there now and check out the bar."

Gaia was surprised. "Is there a cocktail-party atmosphere during meetings?"

Etta Spring's expression was disdainful. "Certainly not!" Her eyes flickered as she hesitated in leaving. "A word of advice. The directors are devious men and not to be trusted. Remember, I've warned you. It will be in your best interest to align yourself with Mr. Salinari."

Gaia said quietly, "I prefer to make my own assessment, thank you."

The woman seemed to freeze, but then shrugged and left with Gaia staring after her, disturbed and thoughtful.

It required substantial effort for Gaia to force herself to walk from the design studio into the corridor. She was extremely nervous. When Dom met her to escort her to the boardroom as though nothing had happened between them, Gaia greeted him gratefully.

"Hurry, *cara*," he urged. "You are on your way to becoming a titled lady."

She looked at him in confusion. "What do you mean?"

"There is no confidence in allowing Salinari to continue on the board. You will be the new chairperson and president of Ferrante-New York. How does that sound to you?"

She felt numb.

It was to be her closely guarded secret that she disdained Gaia Gerald. The girl was a *nothing*, fortunate that her jewelry designs had momentarily captured the public fancy, and luckier today by far. As for herself, Etta Spring had never won even so much as a dime in a lottery. She had always worked like a dog for her own money, contending with the ridiculously aristocratic demands of that old plebeian fool Salinari all day. Still, her only power was through him; the girl was an unknown quantity she'd have to learn about.

She vowed that her time for subservience was at an end. From here on she intended to seize whatever opportunity presented itself by manipulating either the old man or the girl. Exactly how, or which, she wasn't yet sure.

But she would find out.

· 12 ·

THE BOARDROOM SPREAD ACROSS THE ENTIRE WIDTH OF
Ferrante's rear building. Salinari had allowed himself free
reign in furnishing it, and there were similarities to his elaborately decorated office. The walls were paneled with imported
twenty-four-karat gold leaf overlaying rosewood. Beneath
were the intricate carvings of master artisans. In the center
of the room was an extraordinarily long refectory table.
Above, hung a tiered crystal chandelier electrified at outrageous expense—the fragile pendants had been specially ordered from the best Venetian glassworks. The table surface
was a sheet of glossy gray-toned marble that assumed a silvery
hue wherever it was branched with thread-thin white veins.
Around the table were six remarkably uncomfortable black
crushed-velvet upholstered chairs. Their ancient structure
often had a tendency to sway as mended joints separated
under the weight of even a very slim person.

Etta Spring had already switched on the more than sixty
miniature flame-shaped chandelier bulbs. Upon the table was
an assortment of packs of American cigarettes, eggshell-den-
sity porcelain ashtrays, sterling silver table lighters, and an
impressive walnut cigar humidor for Dom Perrini's use.
There were none of the note pads or ball-point pens generally
in evidence at meetings, nor was there a recording system to

be voice-activated. All they needed was her ready steno book and sharpened pencils. Water carafes and tumblers were dispensed with in favor of the portable bar she had wheeled into the room after checking to see that it was stocked with a supply of liquors, mixers, and ice in its self-contained refrigeration unit.

At the windows heavy scarlet draperies of velvet blocked out daylight, but more importantly prevented any curious observers from viewing the room's activities from surrounding office buildings. Antique chairs matching those at the table were sporadically placed along the walls beneath woven mythological scenes depicting knights in battle, maidens with roses, and heraldic coats of arms on the Renaissance tapestries. The secretary seated herself stiff-backed on the chair nearest to the bar and waited.

Salinari purposely entered ahead of the directors. He quickly proceeded to the head of the table and assumed the chairman's seat. Etta Spring rose. She poured him his favorite Spanish sherry and placed it before him upon a sterling silver coaster, distressed to observe his hand unaccustomedly shake as he took up the stemmed glass. At that moment she knew irrefutably that she was the stronger of the two—and the more resourceful. How vastly different matters might be if *she* were the one seated in his chair. The shift in ownership was a dangerous threat, but *she* would know how to deal with it.

The directors entered without conversing. In silence they stopped at the bar, accepting without question or thanks the drinks Etta Spring had prepared for each of them, remembering their individual preferences. They were standing with glasses in hand when Dom Perrini came in with Gaia. All eyes scrutinized her. The youngest one of the men appraised her in what seemed to Gaia an openly sexual manner. She wondered whether Dom was aware of it.

"Care for a brandy?" The swarthy man approached her. He reeked of a powerful cologne.

"No thank you." Her eyes sought out Dom.

He introduced the directors. The attentive one was Mr. Smith, who clasped Gaia's hand, holding it so long that she grew embarrassed. Dom led her away from him to meet Mr. Roselli, who made no move to extend his hand to her. A tall man turning corpulent in his fifties, he smiled automatically while his cold eyes remained uninvolved. Mr. Bronf nodded crisply from across the room. The overhead lighting glared on his polished bald plate.

Etta Spring remained standing behind her. Gaia could feel the woman's appraisal, almost her satisfaction, at her new boss's vague discomfort. Gaia tightly crossed her arms beneath her breasts to keep from trembling. She glanced toward Etta, and the older woman hastily lowered her eyes.

By now the board members had seated themselves along the sides of the table. Dom took Gaia to the foot of it, directly opposite Salinari.

"Thank you," she whispered appreciatively as he pushed in her chair.

"I'm going to sit next to you, so you mustn't worry." He slid into the chair at the side of the table to her left. "Look toward me if you have any question. Come on, cheer up. I'll guide you. Don't you know that every actor worth a damn has stage fright before a performance?"

"Except this is real."

He smiled and she managed a faint response.

Salinari called the meeting to order, but his voice was choked with phlegm. He nervously cleared his throat and began to speak, but Roselli interrupted him almost immediately, abruptly raising his left arm above his head in a violent cutting motion. His diamond ring glittered like a sharp piercing searchlight as his arm rose in the air.

Roselli was powerfully built. His bull-like neck bulged from an immaculate shirt collar. The jacket of his navy cashmere and wool suit camouflaged a large stomach. His tie was discreetly proper; the points of a fine linen handkerchief thrust upward from his breast pocket. On his raised wrist he wore a status watch with diamond numerals set onto its opal face. Gaia's impression of him as a dangerous man was reinforced by his manner of speaking: hollow and unemotional.

"You needn't bother with routine," he told Salinari. "We're here. That's sufficient."

Bronf nodded agreement. "I'm sure we all agree that reading the minutes of our last meeting should be dispensed with due to the urgency of our present business: Ugo's death and thus the new ownership."

Gaia found her body tensing and her legs began to tremble. Her chair squeaked so loudly that she forced herself to be still. It was a tremendous effort. Both men's eyes were on her. Roselli's look was seething with displeasure, while Bronf merely accorded Gaia a contemptuous glance.

She was letting them get to her. No . . . she had to be firm, in control. She tried to give Salinari her full attention. Unfortunately, he was still struggling to clear his throat. How weak he is, really, she thought suddenly. When he managed to address the directors, none of them paid him any notice. The air grew heavy with tobacco smoke clouding beneath the chandelier.

Bronf eyed her. "Little lady, what do you have to say for yourself?" His question was unpleasant—a challenge.

She glanced in confusion at Dom. He nodded encouragement and she murmured, "Why . . . I want to do what's best for Ferrante-New York."

"Excellent! You plan to be cooperative. That's very bright of you."

She wasn't sure what cooperation entailed, but she bristled at his condescending manner. She looked down at her unpolished fingernails, whitened from clutching the table edge. She was so unnerved that she began thinking of all her light little speeches to acquaintances about how a creative person only took valuable time from more worthy projects by applying nail polish and waiting for it to dry. Besides, she would add, running her fingers through her hair, it was so artificial, so unnatural.

Smith had taken the chair on Gaia's right, facing Dom. As she was looking down at her hands, he covered them with one of his. Caressingly, he closed his grip. "Such long fingers. An artistic hand, obviously talented. Don't be distressed, dear.

No one expects you to comprehend the complexities of our meetings."

His rank patronizing annoyed her, but her more immediate concern was Dom, worried that he'd notice the fingerplay. He was staring at her, his eyebrows drawn, furrowing his brow. Gaia withdrew her hands to her lap, silently beseeching his attention. Dom looked away from her. At any other time, she would have hoped it was a manifestation of jealousy. At this particular moment, she felt forlorn. Unconsciously biting her lips, she gazed along the length of the table, but, almost at once, she was badly flustered. Roselli was scrutinizing her. Gaia flushed. Had he been aware of this little silent scene?

"The young woman doesn't resemble Ugo," he declared.

She was momentarily puzzled until the implication of his words hit her. Everyone was staring at her.

Dom spoke. "I don't look like my father, do I?"

"However," Roselli continued, "if Dominic vouches that she's Ugo's granddaughter, I am satisfied."

There was a hum of general agreement.

Gaia was appalled. Who were these men? she thought. Why did they frighten her?

Dom said firmly, "There is no reason to question Gaia's legitimacy."

"I accept that," Roselli said. "Now, miss, I want you to listen carefully to what I say. We board members have left other businesses to come over here just to meet you. We want to help you all that we can. The fact is, you're out of your element. Without our assistance, running Ferrante-New York is going to be more than you can handle. You needn't worry, however. You're going to be what's known as a figurehead. It's necessary; you haven't the experience to make decisions. Which brings me to why this meeting was called . . . to give you our pledge that we'll take care of all the business details. Your part is to look the way an heiress should."

Gaia was so astonished that she couldn't summon a quick reply. It seemed incongruous that Roselli offered assistance at the same time as he implied he had serious doubt about her identity. And *look the part, don't interfere in our plans* was what he was saying. She yearned to discuss this with Dom, but how could she with the other men present? She tried to think of how to reply. She wanted to make a statement without disrupting the proceedings. Her voice was considerably louder than she'd intended: "I assure you I am serious about my responsibility to Ferrante-New York." The reply was ambiguous yet truthful, she thought with satisfaction.

He nodded curtly. Her answer was accepted. And quickly passed over.

They think I'm an idiot, she thought.

Roselli motioned to Etta Spring. "Take this down so you don't overlook attending to it. See that Miles Tuchelin sets up her television appearances and interviews. We want to get across a glamour image for her. Tell him he's to coach her. That's important!"

Hearing Miles' name mentioned made Gaia feel a bit more at ease. It was he who'd promoted her Gaia Star. Miles was her friend. Then she recalled how he'd gone before this board—spoken to these men—to gain the directors' permission when Salinari vetoed her Àtrio. It caused her to ponder what Miles' link might be with them.

Salinari spoke up. He was extremely agitated. "The young lady may prove to be undependable. *I* have expertise. Better to leave matters as they were. With me continuing as the visible head, you know there'll be no trouble."

Bronf glowered at him. "We're not expecting trouble."

But Salinari was desperate. "With me at the helm the business will continue operating as before."

Despite the fact that she had never liked him, Gaia couldn't help but empathize with his distress. If Salinari generated no power against these men—and he had long been chairman—what chance did she have?

Smith slightly winked at Gaia. "Since this charming gal has become the store's new owner"—here he slightly paused—"once we find out about the stuff in Italy, we can—"

"You've said enough!" Bronf roared. "Quit chasing women and keep your mind on what's going on here."

Irked, Smith said, "I only meant we'll be able to get hold of it legit—"

"That's enough!" Roselli ordered.

Gaia couldn't follow this exchange at all. "What do you have in mind?" she asked, but no one explained. She resolved to think about it later on. Dom's foot urgently pressed against hers. She looked questioningly at him, but he was engaged in conversation with the others. The room had suddenly filled with an even higher level of tension, and Gaia decided that here was the moment for her to speak.

Her chair scraped harshly against the floor as she halfway rose, leaning into the table. "Gentlemen, please—" Now they were looking at her. "I . . . uh . . . wish to propose—"

"What in hell is she doing?" Roselli asked. It didn't sound like a question but a warning.

For one terrifying moment her heart missed a beat. "I would like to offer a prayer in Ugo Ferrante's memory." She was unable to refer to him as her grandfather.

"Yes, yes," Bronf impatiently retorted. "We prayed before we came here." The tension went out of the room and the board members returned to murmured discussions among themselves, totally ignoring her. She sat down, chagrined. There was no way for her to break into their conversation. It was as if she weren't present.

Dom, too, had joined with the others. This contributed to the greatest part of her dismay. He, to treat her like this! Gaia wanted desperately for him to notice her. She was too agitated to pay attention to the substance of what these men were saying. She drew a deep calming breath. She sensed a deep-seated meanness in them, despite their expensive suits and manicured nails. Their cordiality toward her was wholly sham, a manipulative technique. But when she tried to figure out what was happening and why, her mind seemed entrapped in a maze.

Who precisely were they? Roselli mentioned their other businesses. It was unnecessary, she knew, for a director to have any connection with a corporation other than his or her appointment to the board. From what stratum of society did Ferrante-New York's directors come? What was there about them to give her the impression that if she pressed the wrong button these seemingly sophisticated men might very well turn into snarling animals? And how did Dom fit in with them? She observed that he appeared extremely uncomfortable. She couldn't believe that he was aligned with them. She refused to!

She felt Dom's gaze. "Are you all right?"

"Yes."

"Good. It will be over soon."

"They're ignoring me. I don't want to continue sitting here."

"You must."

"Why?"

"Because of the transfer of stock to you."

"That's impossible. The will hasn't been probated. When I spoke to Merrill Ross, the estate lawyer, he didn't say anything about—"

"I'm telling you."

"But—"

"Mr. Roselli has spoken to Mr. Battaglia. He's Ross' employer."

From the far end of the table, Salinari overheard, and he was eager to project an opportunity for himself. "You must know she's correct," he said. "It could take the better part of a year, maybe longer to settle the estate. I am positive it is illegal to conduct ourselves as if that had already been accomplished. This is why *I* should continue to be board chairman and president."

Roselli snapped at him. "It's not your concern. Bari & Battaglia is handling the estate, and Vito gave his okay to go ahead with what we have to do."

Salinari persisted. "Let's be certain. One of their lawyers was in the building earlier." He looked at Etta Spring. "See if Merrill Ross is still here," he ordered, his outstretched hand conveying urgency.

She jumped to her feet, scattering her steno book and pencils.

"Sit down!" Roselli commanded. "You're not going anywhere."

The secretary nervously retrieved her possessions and resumed her seat.

Gaia looked sympathetically toward her. Etta Spring was an employee, just as she had been. But when Etta's gaze met hers, there was such bare hatred that Gaia quickly averted her eyes.

Bronf yawned. "I'm positive we all have more pressing matters elsewhere. Let's wind this up and get our asses out of here."

"I agree," Roselli said. "I hereby nominate Gaia Gerald chairman of the board and president of Ferrante-New York."

Smith winked at her. "I second it," he said.

Gaia was making restive movements, about to protest, when she felt Dom's increased pressure against her foot.

But Salinari was determined to make his final and most eloquent plea. "Prior to any voting, I wish to make a statement." His delivery was hesitant. The bright lighting emphasized the lines around his eyes. He turned his head toward Etta Spring. "Be certain that you accurately record what I shall say in the minutes."

She held her pencil poised in readiness. "Yes, sir."

He cleared his throat. "Under my aegis, management has been efficient; I may justifiably say, spectacular. So much so, that during the past year the store's profit factor has substantially increased . . ." Here he paused.

Dom's voice overlapped Salinari's. "It is due to the success of Gaia's Àtrio. Percentagewise the moderately priced jewelry sold there outsells the more expensive jewelry."

Salinari's face paled, but he continued valiantly. "Yes. Just so. And Ms. Gerald's Àtrio was installed during my administration."

"A project you rejected until the board overruled you," Dom countered. "Your management has been negligible."

"Yes, but in other ways—where it mattered most—haven't

I always maintained a high social presence, attending the best charity parties of all the—"

"*Shut up!*" This from Roselli. Again, the room was suddenly, almost fervently still, with a tension that could be sensed in the air.

Approaching hysteria, Salinari refused to be silenced. He prattled on about his skills, his social connections, his business acumen, but now he was incoherent, demoralized by his plight.

Gaia attempted to make sense of the little she could understand. It was spoken of in the store that Salinari's marriage was likely one of convenience. They said that were it not for his wife's predilection for social climbing, she would have left him long ago. Gaia recalled seeing her photographed at the opening of the opera on the arm of a far younger man who was described as her "protégé." Gaia had heard that Salinari spent his nights in a rented town house and, having today seen the contents of his office, she could now believe the rumors about the town house's expensive furnishings and magnificent art. She'd heard that the elegant black limousine so much a part of his style and mystique actually was paid for by Ferrante, that his chauffeur and his valet were on the store's payroll. No, she couldn't believe that he was about to give all that up easily.

Etta Spring brought him a glass of water. Salinari sipped it and became relatively composed, sounding more rational. "I project an upper-class image," he was saying.

"You are incoherent!" Bronf declared. "Nothing but a useless fool!"

Salinari ploughed on as if deaf. "I foresee a period of increasing prosperity for Ferrante-New York . . . I refer to the *jewelry business.*"

Gaia caught this and she pondered why he'd emphasized the jewelry business. What other sort of business could he mean?

"We need access to the tool for expansion . . . money for the purchase of rare gems. Buying costly gemstones requires constantly renewed financing. *I* am the man who speaks to the bankers, who socializes with them, who uses social influence to gain certain . . . advantages."

"Meaning loans?" Roselli sneered.

Salinari's chest visibly heaved as he gulped great inhalations of the smoke-laden air. "Precisely," he said.

Gaia watched how the old man drew himself up, foolishly pleased with himself for getting his point across. She could see in his face that he imagined he was gaining back some ground with the board.

But Roselli shattered his illusive euphoria. "Why even bother with banks?" he asked.

Hesitant and less sure of himself, Salinari continued. "It is where the money is."

"Not all of it." There was an implied ominousness in the timbre of his voice.

Salinari's mouth opened to reply, but he promptly snapped it shut. His posture sagged and he crumpled into his chair. His voice cracked and his tone was almost petulant. "Don't push me out. You can't dump me. I warn you, I know too much."

The men exchanged glances.

Roselli's question lashed out. "Are you threatening us?"

Salinari gasped. "No, never! Of course I wouldn't—"

Etta Spring bore down too hard on her pencil and broke its lead point. The sound seemed loud in the charged silence of the room. Somehow it signaled the end of the struggle. Salinari had lost.

"Okay, that being out of the way, we vote," Bronf said decisively. It was clearly but a formality now.

Gaia was thinking only of the question, *Why use banks?* She tried to consider other available sources of cash or credit for the enormous sums needed to purchase quality large-carat gems. She looked around the table at the three directors, Roselli, Bronf, and Smith, without hearing what they were saying. She turned to Dom, who was talking quietly with the others. Suddenly, her jumbled thoughts fell into place as she thought of a single word, a term she often had read in newspapers and heard in B pictures on late-night television.

Laundering.

Quite plainly, Roselli meant rackets money.

Smith's benign smile was intrusive. "Congratulations, my dear." He was bending forward to kiss her. She backed her head away, startled, and turned her face toward Dom, silently questioning him, her eyes expressive.

He whispered into her ear. "Believe me, it isn't what you or even what Salinari wants, but what is necessary. Responsibility is a part of wealth. You must learn that and accept it."

But her thoughts lingered upon what she'd been mulling over. "Damn it, no one is going to bring dirty money into my business." She spoke as if to herself.

A message in his eyes warned her to be cautious. "You and I will discuss it in private."

She felt betrayed by him. It was physically painful and she hugged her stomach. "There's no way I'm going to be a glamorous, silent figurehead, Dom."

"Gaia, just keep quiet."

She was too stunned to retort. Her head was swimming. What the hell was going on and how did he expect her to react?

"Things will work out. Just trust me, *cara.*"

She remembered the first time he'd called her by that loving name was when he took her from Chicago to New York. She was immeasurably saddened.

"Trust me," Dom repeated.

The idea struck her that this was precisely what the board members wished her to do. They were confident she was either too inexperienced or too naïve to object. *If that was so, then Dom was their man.*

Meanwhile, Salinari had left his chair and approached Gaia. He stood by her chair, hunched over her. "Please," he beseeched her, "I need to remain in office." She could smell the sourness of his breath and felt sickened by the change in him, by her own feeling of pity, but she determined to be wary. "Tell me what there is about the store that I don't know?" she asked.

Salinari averted his eyes. "I can't."

"You *must* if you want my help."

"There is nothing you can change."

"Perhaps I can."

"Don't so much as think of trying."

"Why not?"

He shrugged his shoulders in a helpless gesture and she realized he had sunk into the morass of his private worries. "When news of my dismissal gets out I'll be ignored socially . . . I won't be invited anywhere. My position with the store gave me status. Without it . . ."

Gaia would have answered, at least attempted to comfort him, but she was suddenly aware that the directors were beginning to quit the table, easing out of their wobbly antique chairs. She mustn't let them know she was trying to get information from Salinari—both for his sake and her own. Roselli was in the lead, already making his way to the door, preparing to leave. Dom remained seated, talking intently to one of the men. Clearly he wasn't about to do anything to stop them. Gaia felt this wasn't the time to speculate upon why he had cast his vote with them, those men whom she wanted to believe he was totally unlike.

"Please, gentlemen, return to the table," Gaia called out. "I haven't adjourned the meeting." She hoped no one could see her tremulous anxiety.

Roselli turned first, openly hostile, trying to cover his naked hatred in a smile. To Gaia it was an evil grimace, full of ambiguous threat. Nevertheless, she stood her ground.

Bronf and Smith took their cues from Roselli, displaying open amusement at her presumptuousness, mocking her as if she were a child.

Their superciliousness only fueled her indignation and determination, and her voice grew resonant and strongly confident. "You have voted for me to fill an important office. Chairwoman of the board of directors and president." She paused and looked around at their faces—all except Dom's. No, she couldn't look at him until this was over. "I can only presume you did this because I am unqualified."

"You're going to prove it right now, aren't you?" Roselli snarled.

Dom grabbed her arm, yanking her toward him. "What are you doing?"

"Exercising my office." It was odd, Gaia thought, how she could hear herself speaking from afar, as if she were another person to whom she was listening.

"The hell you are!" Roselli nearly shouted.

Gaia felt the color rise to her cheeks.

"Before you say any more," Dom told her, "consider this. There are certain considerations, certain facts you know nothing about . . . Gaia, it would be more than unwise to involve yourself." He reached into an inner jacket pocket and withdrew a folded typewritten paper, spreading it on the marble tabletop directly in front of her. He extended his gold pen for her to take. "Sign this," he whispered. "I'll discuss everything with you later, when we're alone."

Gaia tentatively reached for the pen, then drew away her hand as if scalded.

Roselli came closer. "Sign the paper!" His eyes were blazing.

She looked from him to Dom.

"Sign it, *cara*," Dom said. "Here, next to the penciled *X*."

"What is it?"

Dom answered. "A power of attorney so I can legally represent your interests—so that you needn't go to these meetings anymore."

She slid the page back to him across the smooth marble. "I won't." It was a supreme effort to keep her tone cool and controlled.

Roselli picked up the pen Dom had placed on the table, thrusting it into Gaia's hand. It clattered onto the table, rolling away from them. "You, Dominic, tell her she *has* to sign it."

"It's for your benefit," Dom urged her.

"I can't believe that. Not when you're both pressuring me." She continued backward, away from the table, Dom and Roselli following her.

Dom motioned Roselli to stay back and he led Gaia to a far corner of the heavily draperied room. He stood very close to her, holding both her arms in his powerful hands. He spoke softly, almost caressingly. "Gaia, I am worried for you. You *must* sign."

"I am worried too," she admitted, "but the point is, you seem to be giving me no choice. You spoke of my *responsibility*. Did you mean to uphold the store's reputation, or to yield my allegiance to its directors? My guess is that something strange, maybe even illegal is going on. No, I can't yet put my finger on what it is, but I intend to stay around and find out."

Roselli called out. "What are you whispering about? Is she going to sign or not?"

Dom said, "Gaia is a bit edgy, which is only natural under the circumstances."

"Tell her she'll be very sorry if she doesn't sign. We're getting extremely impatient," he rejoined.

Until now, Gaia had disliked and mistrusted Roselli, but her feelings became even stronger. A furious hatred for him swept over her. She felt physically weak, but tried to hide the fact that she was quaking with nervousness.

The good of the store must be my first consideration, she thought. Her voice gathered strength from her resolve. "As each of you are aware, I am the sole owner of Ferrante-New York. All of the voting shares are mine." Gaia drew a deep breath. "It is my decision that Messrs. Roselli, Smith, and Bronf are hereby dismissed as directors."

Bronf and Smith turned to each other and gasped.

Roselli pounded on the table and began to swear in Italian. Smith was flabbergasted, his eyes rolling in his sockets. "Can she do this?" he asked.

"She's just done it!" Bronf shouted at him.

"When this little bitch realizes her mistake, she won't even be able to regret it," Roselli muttered, leading the other two men to the door. "Come! We're leaving."

Keeping her eyes averted from them, Gaia stated calmly, "Mr. Perrini will continue as a director."

Roselli had the door ajar. "It's up to you to take care of

this," he snarled to Dom. He motioned to Bronf and Smith to follow him. The door slammed shut behind them.

Only Gaia, Dom, Salinari, and Etta Spring remained.

Gaia sank into the nearest chair. She wanted, desperately needed to believe that Dom remained her concerned protector. Yet she knew that his interests had at least heretofore coincided with those of the deposed board directors. She looked at him now, but his calm, strong profile told her nothing. She felt tears spring to her eyes. She suddenly wished that nothing had changed from when she had no responsibilities other than to create jewelry. Possibly it could never again be a way of life for her. She had been told that she'd inherited from a grandfather she never knew. Whether or not she was his rightful heir, she intended to act in a manner that was best for his prestigious jewelry business. How quickly she had changed from being the shy orphan and obedient young employee who didn't dare speak out for fear of punishment.

"Dammit," Dom demanded finally. "Are you so innocent you don't know the kind of people those men are?"

"I don't want them to have anything to do with the store."

"Just like that, huh?"

"They're gone now. What can they possibly do?"

"God forbid that you find out."

"I'll issue instructions to security that they never be allowed in the store."

"And you really suppose that will be sufficient protection?"

"I would think so."

"Well, you're wrong!" He opened the door. "You're incredibly naïve, Gaia. I'm going after them. I'll try to ease the situation."

"You'll try to appease them?"

"You'd better believe it."

There were tears in her eyes. "Don't, Dom. Don't bring them back. Or, Dom, I'll . . . I'll have to remove you, too."

For a moment it appeared that he would reply. Instead, he abruptly turned on his heel and walked out of the room.

Salinari approached her with an unaccustomedly toothy smile. "Dear child, remember that you need me to run the store."

She felt the pity for him vanish. She had disliked him for as long as she'd been an employee. His overbearing manner and conceit had consistently placed him apart from the staff. She'd listened to, even relished the gossip about him, had even been blatantly amused by his posturing, as others were. He was stiff-necked, socially awkward, occasionally glaringly inefficient. And now she'd seen how weak, how fawning he was deep down.

But she entirely lacked experience in management.

"Mr. Salinari, will you continue on at Ferrante?"

Gaia caught Etta Spring's total surprise. The secretary wasn't nearly as astonished as she, herself, at making the offer. Retaining Salinari was the last thing Gaia had expected to do, but she had to be practical. Inefficient though Salinari was, she knew even less. She wouldn't last a week without him, she knew.

In another part of the store, someone was already plotting how to eliminate her. *She won't be around here for long—not long at all!*

· 13 ·

Gaia was alone in the boardroom when Miles Tuchelin strode into the room. "Hon," he told her, "there's a bunch of media people waiting on Fifth Avenue in front of the store, all howling like wolves. I'm afraid they won't go away until you see them."

She said dispiritedly, "I—I don't feel up to giving any interviews."

He looked at her sharply. "I guess the board meeting was tough, huh?"

She sighed. "You don't know how tough." ·

"Sorry to have to put you through another ordeal."

"Can't you make them leave, Miles?"

"Not on your life."

Gaia shook her head, massaging her brow with both hands. She closed her eyes for a moment. This morning, when she'd arrived at work as an employee, seemed years in the past. By midday, she'd coped with the directors, and now Miles expected her to summon additional reserves of strength and submit to indiscriminate questioning because word had somehow leaked out that she was an heiress, a Cinderella. Her emotions were raw. She was wound up, tense, and vulnerable. She sank against the boardroom table, which rocked slightly under her weight.

"I wouldn't insist, except that if you refuse to see them you'll be given bad press." He placed a hand on her shoulder.

Gaia drew a deep breath, trying to clear her head. *Bad press.* . . . That reminded her of something, but she couldn't place what. If she hadn't been overwrought she would have summoned the connection to mind by now.

"Shall I phone security at the door and have them admitted?"

"What? Oh—Miles . . . not just yet." She was endeavoring to remember—and suddenly she did. Roselli had said that he wanted Miles to set up press and television exposure for her. Gaia wondered whether he was already carrying out that directive.

Miles persisted. "You'd better let them in now, Gaia. They've been waiting quite a long time."

What he didn't mention was how he considered that, in many ways, he'd been waiting long enough, too.

They crowded into the boardroom, carrying open notebooks, with pencils poised, holding tape recorders, packing minicams on shoulders. Once the klieg lights were set up it was impossible for Gaia to see her questioners' faces. But she determined that, just as she intended to take charge of her responsibilities to Ferrante and her life, she would do similarly at this session.

Gaia refused to allow herself to be conventionally interviewed; she kept up a constant patter about the traditions of Ferrante-New York. She was worried she would be forced to tell them the fact she must never reveal: that she was an orphan who didn't know her lineage.

Even as she chatted, she was thinking—attempting to reassess Roselli's reasons for wanting the public eye focused upon her. She only knew that he, the former director, had intended for her to supplant Salinari as a figurehead, and that the board meeting was rife with implications that the legitimate business had an underbelly swollen by illicit activities.

These were the facts, but she was no closer to a solution.

* * *

The klieg lights were at last extinguished. The electric cables had been coiled and were carried out by the technicians. The last reporter and cameraman had departed.

Miles saw them to the elevator and returned to Gaia, who was leaving as he approached her in the corridor.

"You were sensational!" he exclaimed.

She observed him closely. "I intend to be. In every part of the store's business." Her voice was almost cold.

He seemed surprised. "All by yourself?"

"If I have to, yes."

"Oh, there's something else you have to do next. How it could have escaped my telling you, I'll never know!" He clapped a hand to his forehead. "It's because of today's excitement. I tell you, I'm so elated for you, hon, that I'm off the wall! There's a woman you have to see. She's in one of the main-floor private customer rooms."

Gaia's nerves were still raw. "Later, Miles, if you don't mind."

"Well, I won't mind, but she will." He was practically giggling.

She faced him. "Okay, who is she?"

"She's Ugo Ferrante's daughter."

· 14 ·

By early afternoon, the street-level sales floor remained overcrowded. Gaia pushed her way through the crowd, her eyes excitedly darting everywhere, taking everything in, despite a fatigue she would not give in to.

Little by little, she inched her way past curiosity seekers who had come in to congregate before the jewelry displays, and blocked the aisles. With some ingenuity, she was able to squeeze through a group of ladies, gently pushing aside some couples, occasionally taking a shortcut by scooting behind several of the sales counters.

She was fired with anticipation at the prospect of meeting Ugo Ferrante's daughter. She hoped against hope that her childhood daydreams of being reunited with lost parents would at last be partially realized, that she was about to find out who she really was—not merely be told she was an heiress, but experience the warm, living embrace of a woman who could be her aunt. Gaia wondered whether Silvia Wood resembled her dead sister, presumably Gaia's mother. She had a fleeting mental image of the sketched imaginary portrait she kept in her studio. And with swiftly moving thoughts, and the highest hopes, she envisioned how she and Silvia would sob at the joy of discovery and the pain of so many lost years.

She approached an exquisite burl desk positioned to bar

entry to the privileged section of the store. The attractive female receptionist-guard greeted her. "Everyone's buzzing with the news about your good fortune. Congratulations."

Gaia came to an abrupt halt, slightly shaking her head, still immersed in her reverie.

"If it couldn't happen to me, I'm glad it's you," the girl continued. She produced a magnetic card from a concealed jacket pocket of her charcoal worsted suit. "I guess you've come to be with the occupant of room number three." She looked at Gaia as though she wanted to say more but was uncertain whether or not she should. "Have you ever met Mrs. Wood?"

Gaia shook her head, too excited to reply.

"In that case . . . " She left it unfinished.

They stood before the room's door, which could not be opened from the inside, so as to prevent theft in a place where hundreds of thousands of dollars' worth of jewelry was casually spread upon black velvet pads for a customer's consideration.

"A salesperson was here earlier with Mrs. Wood," the receptionist confided, "but then Mr. Tuchelin took Mr. Merrill Ross into the room—he said Mr. Ross is your lawyer. I hope it's okay that I admitted him. With Mr. Tuchelin vouching—"

Just then, an Italian-accented feminine voice was heard from within the room, screaming a string of expletives, some in English, but most in her native tongue. Her rage was unmistakable.

"You'd better open the door for me." Gaia made an effort to sound more positive than she suddenly felt.

The woman inserted a sensitized plastic card into a wall slot beside the room's entrance. The door silently swung outward.

Gaia found herself breathing irregularly as she attempted to peer inside, but a man's large solid back blocked any chance of immediately seeing her would-be aunt. Hesitating at first, she then tapped him on the shoulder just as the door shut behind her. He turned around, astonished to see her.

"Hello. I am Merrill Ross. How do you do? But Ms. Gerald, you are the very last person who should be here." There was an element of warning in his tone. "Mrs. Wood is impossible to deal with," he asserted. "I'm not sure whether she misunderstands my English, or pretends to."

"May we be alone?" Gaia asked him. She glanced away from him so quickly that all she really saw was that he was tall and had a close dark beard. Her eyes were fluttering nervously and her legs felt weak.

"I should remain with you."

"No, please leave us." The room's other occupant was staring back at her.

He reluctantly summoned the receptionist to reopen the door.

Left alone with Silvia, she faced the small angry woman who was pacing the room. Seeing Gaia, Silvia stopped quickly. They gazed at each other in silence for what seemed an eternity. Gaia's color was high, her breathing short and rapid. She was too excited, she knew, to readily take in what Silvia Wood looked like. But as she forced herself to study her aunt, Gaia found herself somehow immensely, crushingly disappointed. In no manner did this woman resemble the sketch on Gaia's studio table. She was shorter than Gaia had imagined. Her blondness had a glazed look, and her heavily applied cosmetics emphasized the frighteningly plastic quality of the skin so tautly stretched across her cheekbones and jaw. Sharp unfriendly eyes peered at Gaia from under a suggestion of elevated brows that were not brows at all but sweeps of penciled lines. Gaia assessed the expensiveness of her clothing, shoulder bag, and fur, each item outrageously and flamboyantly designed. Nothing was the way Gaia had expected it to be. She was wholly taken aback.

The air was permeated with a musk-based perfume, making the room seem close and smaller than it was. Gaia watched the woman's interest shift from appraisal of her to her own reflection in a table-stand mirror. One talon-fingered hand played with a necklace of large entwined black and white natural Oriental pearls on the table. She sprung open its multi-carat diamond clasp and fitted the strands at the base of her neck, where Gaia saw that age was less effectively hidden than upon her face.

"So they sent in another *commessa* to serve me. Do you agree that this is suitable for a funeral?"

"I . . . uh—" No words would come.

"Cat got your tongue?" The question was abrasive. "No matter. Why should your opinion interest me? The last sales-clerk disappeared when that presumptuous man who called himself a lawyer interrupted us."

Gaia found her voice. "Aunt Silvia—" She let the name trail off. "I am Gaia."

"What is it you just said?" The carefully drawn eyebrows looped upward. "How dare you presume that we are related? I am Silvia, Principessa di Corchese."

"I'm your niece!" Gaia cried out in desperation. No sooner had she uttered this than she was shocked that she'd said it.

"Ha! You are impertinent as well as an outright liar. The only living relatives my father had are me and my daughter, Mara." She reverted to lusty Italian as her voice expanded in her fury. "So far as I am concerned you are nobody. *Nient'altro!*"

"I hoped we would resemble one another."

The preposterously black-lashed eyes turned full upon her, unblinking, with a concentrated look of hatred. "You are an orphan, as I have been informed, and likely illegitimate. You seek to pass yourself off as my dead sister's daughter. *Strega!* The lawyer told me you have inherited the New York store. We shall see. So far as I am concerned, you have no claim whatsoever on my father's estate."

Gaia's throat was constricted. "Will you tell me," she pleaded, "what your sister looked like? Do I resemble her?"

Silvia averted her face. Her posture was stiff as she sat. A nervousness of movement, a slight shaking of the hand that fondled an assortment of jeweled pieces displayed on black velvet pads atop the table were outward signs of her tension. Abruptly she half rose, bending toward Gaia, her manicured

red-painted nails extending toward her, lashing the space between them.

"*Opportunista!*" she shrieked. "Did you suppose I would
acknowledge you? To me, you are an employee here. One
who will soon be fired when I order it."

Gaia swallowed hard. She wouldn't let herself cry. Hope
had so quickly, so painfully evaporated! Here was no loving
family to compensate for years spent in the orphanage, to
erase the unhappy boarding situations. She'd been so foolish!
She turned away from Silvia's cruel eyes and began to leave.
But suddenly, she thought better of it. Long ago, she had told
herself that nothing good comes easily. She suddenly realized
that she must continue to reach deep within herself for a sense
of pride as a human being. And in this flash of comprehension, she remembered her vows of stewardship of Ferrante-
New York.

It was an inviolable trust.

Upon the table, items of costly jewelry were randomly
strewn about. There was a sumptuous diamond *pavé* collar,
nearly an inch in width, with its perfect stones mounted in
platinum, and a matching pair of boldly designed earrings.
The design was a recognizable Vanderman hallmark. A
golden starfish pin was incredibly formed of cabochon rubies.
A fiery black opal butterfly pendant was strung on an intricate eighteen-karat gold-and-emerald-studded chain. Diamond flowers with turquoise and yellow sapphire leaves were
captured in a bangle bracelet. And there was the rarest jewel
of all: an unset round-cut fifty-two-carat pure white diamond
without blemish and worth more than the remainder of the
combined collection.

"*Presta attenzione!*" Silvia was saying. "Have my selections
packed so I can take them with me. What are you waiting for?
There can be no delay. *Subito! Subito!*" she shouted. "I must
leave for the airport where my plane departs for Roma."

"I am afraid you must leave the jewelry here."

"You defy me? This is my father's shop."

"Not anymore."

"Ah, I see! It is blackmail. If I accept you as my niece, I may have these."

"The jewelry is a part of this store's stock. It is not yours, nor is it mine."

"Your vengefulness will gain you nothing. In Italy I intend exposing you in court and retrieving all of this, and more, from you."

Despite Gaia's determination to protect the store, she was unnerved by this reference to the doubt of her inheritance. "I haven't set myself up as your niece. Until this morning I never suspected—"

"That you inherited half of his estate? Ha! Liar! Imposter!"

"I haven't made it up. It's in the will."

Silvia rapidly spat out a slew of Italian invectives. Then she gathered up her sable coat, while her huge cobra-skin bag yawned open. In a swift movement, she swept jewelry from the table into the wide leather mouth.

Gaia was incredulous. "You can't do that. Stop it!"

"*Caca!*"

Gaia banged on the door for the security guard. "Open up. I need you!"

She quickly explained what had happened to the jewelry. The guard immediately positioned herself within the doorway, blocking Silvia's exit. Gaia hastened past the reception desk, and, looking out toward the larger store, she raised an arm, motioning urgently to the plain-clothes security guards nearby. They took off in her direction, each of them drawing a concealed gun. Some onlookers reacted with enormous shock; one woman screamed. Gaia waited at the desk. She caught a glimpse of Miles Tuchelin's frozen figure and the startled expression on his face. Merrill Ross stood nearby.

There was no time to explain to them. She told the approaching guards, "You can put away your weapons. The situation is under control. There's someone . . . a lady . . . to be escorted to the street."

"No arrest?"

"Just get her out of the store."

"Very well, miss," the nearest man said as he went to assist.

The other guards holstered their guns and returned to their posts, trying to appear innocuous, although their identity had been revealed.

Gaia headed across the main floor in the opposite direction, toward the elevator. She yearned for the privacy of her studio. Work, she needed to work. Her eyes swam with tears and her surroundings blurred. Close by her a man backed away as he cautiously eased his weapon—a long-blade knife—into concealment up his jacket sleeve. Using the store's crowding to his advantage, he had intended to plunge the blade into a vital area of the pretty new owner's body. For now, he felt he'd been stalking her in vain. People were watching. He'd have no chance to escape. When she passed near him, he even smiled pleasantly. But Gaia, deep in thought, paid him no notice.

The man with the knife in his sleeve looked after her. "Next time," he said softly, "I won't miss."

· 15 ·

A HALF HOUR LATER WHEN GAIA WAS BACK IN HER STUDIO, THE telephone rang. Its shrillness made her start, jangling her already buffeted nerves.

It was Dom. Despite her recent suspicions, Gaia experienced the familiar quickening of her pulse.

"We can relax, *cara*. I've persuaded the three directors you booted out that you are remorseful and didn't understand who they are."

"I still don't."

"Gaia, what made you do it?"

"I suppose because if I own the business, I am also responsible for it."

"That's not answering me."

She didn't want to explain that she'd been guided by a sort of intuition, a feeling of their complicity in something wrong. Moreover, she was troubled about his connection with Roselli and the others. For the past several years, Dom could do no wrong in her sight. Was this because she viewed him through eyes blinded by love? Or—it was painful to force herself to consider this—was what she termed love in reality a chimera of her gratitude?

"Surely you must recognize the danger in crossing them."

"You just said you'd fixed it."

He didn't answer. Instead he changed the subject and invited her to have dinner with him that evening.

Ordinarily she would have eagerly accepted, but she was utterly exhausted and had been planning to remain at home, attempting to sort out the events of the day. *Ask me another time. I am in mourning for Ugo Ferrante, whether or not he truly was the grandfather I never knew,* she wanted to say.

But her desire for physical nearness to Dom betrayed her. She didn't want to be alone this evening, after all. . . .

He said he would call for her at her apartment building shortly after seven o'clock. He mentioned the time so she would be ready and waiting for him in the lobby. She couldn't recall that Dom had ever entered her apartment.

It was mid-afternoon. Gaia had eaten no lunch, but wasn't hungry. When Etta Spring inquired whether she might order her something from a nearby coffee shop, Gaia thanked her and refused.

"Etta," she said calmly, "would you please tell Mr. Salinari I'm stopping by to talk to him?"

"He isn't in his office."

"Oh? What time will he return?"

"Not until tomorrow. After the meeting he developed a terrible headache and went home."

So should I! Gaia thought. She leaned forward to her work table, her head on her arms, seeing snatches of the morning before her weary closed eyes.

She tried to concentrate, but too much had happened too fast, and try as she might, Gaia couldn't sort out all that had happened since morning.

She decided she would calm herself by thinking of something pleasant.

Ah . . .

There was the spectacular *Avanti!*

It was an 89.6-carat oval-shaped diamond of a remarkable pink hue. It was extraordinarily rare, internally flawless.

The eye perceived the stone's fiery heart through precisely cut facets, like so many angled windows. Although not yet on

public display, the *Avanti* was already world famous; Miles
Tuchelin's skillful handling of publicity had taken care of
that, even before it was placed on view within the store. A
touch-sensitive electronic case was being built to safeguard it,
and its design and construction consumed as much thought
and time as the cutting of the stone itself.

For Gaia, this rare stone contained the mystique of
gemology, one of her favorite studies in her training for a
design career. Gemology: part science, part history, part superstition. Since the dawn of civilization when the first colored mineral crystal was discovered, gems were admired,
revered, even killed for.

Prisms of naturally faceted translucent stone inspired awe
and were venerated, such as in preColumbian art, where sizable emeralds were objects of sacred worship. Large Burmese
pigeon blood-red rubies shone in the heads of golden idols
installed in ornate Asian temples. Being caught for theft of
these gemstones meant brutal torture until the release of
death.

But gems also had associations with healing and the preservation of life. In Persian, Assyrian, and Babylonian antiquity,
and in a later Egyptian era, colored stones were crudely
carved to be worn as amulets, bestowing upon the wearer
magic against evil spirits. Such was the beginning of jewelry.

Long before Christ, gems were already mined and trade
routes established. Deep-blue lapis from Media and Turke-
stan was imported into Egypt at least several centuries before
Moses' birth. In ancient Rome and Greece, the art of the
cameo was refined with the use of shells, coral, and jet. Their
artisans were familiar with pearls; they mounted opals,
amber, and many hues of quartz in their golden vessels and
for their personal adornment. The Bible is replete with gems.
The twelve tribes of Israel were frequently depicted by a
dozen various-colored gems set into the High Priest's breast-
plate. The apostles of Jesus would have similar gemological
designation. By the Middle Ages, the sapphire was mystically
ascribed divine power and was set into high churchmen's
rings. Many holy chalices bore designs fashioned of gem-

stones. And while the Church frowned on zodiac worshipers, followers of astrology ascribed tremendous and various powers to gems representing each of the astrological signs.

But although other species might be larger or more perfectly formed, of all the gemstones it was and remains the diamond that generates the most excited adulation. South African-mined diamonds were the height of fashion in Paris by the early nineteenth century.

In the twentieth century, diamonds were not mined solely by DeBeers, but it was this well-renowned firm that successfully controlled the output released into the jewelry market. Gaia had often marveled at the spectacular cushion-cut ninety-facet Tiffany diamond, a flawless canary-yellow gem on permanent display in that rival store.

But the *Avanti*, the spectacular large pink diamond, was purchased more recently. Ferrante-New York's agents paid over $2 million for it to an Antwerp wholesale jeweler, and then airmailed it by ordinary postal service to New York. Michael Vanderman felt quite ill before the small unmarked cardboard box arrived in his hands. He unpacked it and held the then unnamed, unpolished stone up to the light. It was still clad in a gray filmlike skin that obscured its potential fire, although not its huge 137-carat weight. What a pity, he thought, that so much of its bulk would be lost in cutting.

Salinari refused to bring in free-lance cutters, and the hair-raising task of cleaving it fell to Peter Lazarus, the store's head diamond cutter. Although by no means a novice, Lazarus was terrified to the point of physical panic when he was told. The most minute miscalculation could render the stone a relatively valueless pile of slivers; a great job would mean its fame as the most famous flawless pink diamond in the world.

As a designer, Gaia was among the privileged employees who were allowed to take turns holding, fingering, and caressing the rough stone. The Belgian dealer had allowed a pinhead-size window of discovery to be cut. Using a loupe, Gaia perceived the most astonishing shimmering pink she had ever seen.

Lazarus cautiously enlarged this opening, patiently chiseling away the gray rock. Months of anguished study followed until he felt himself intimately familiar with the diamond's grain. Gaia would often visit him in his workroom, bringing him an afternoon bottle of soft drink. She saw how he was aging under the strain. Together the old cutter and the young designer would bemoan Salinari's lack of feeling for the romance of the fine-jewelry trade.

"Here, have some cookies. I brought these for you. You need to relax for a bit, Mr. Lazarus."

"Thanks." He took two. "You're right, of course. Except I get so wound up that I live with the diamond twenty-four hours a day. I'm driving my wife crazy, but I don't seem able to control myself. This morning she told me I was talking in my sleep about the stone."

"It's an awesome responsibility," Gaia said. "Did you ever consider telling Salinari that you refuse to cut it?"

"Sure I did," the gray-haired man replied. "I won't though. I'm hooked, Gaia. I've been a cutter for nearly forty years, but I've never had the opportunity to come anywhere near such a stone. You know, I don't just talk in my sleep. I have nightmares, too. Every one of them the same. My mallet brings the blade down on the wrong spot and the stone shatters."

"If you're so worried maybe you shouldn't go on with it."

"I have to. It's become my compulsion. I know I won't destroy the diamond. That's why I'm doing all of these sketches on graph paper, and plaster and lead matrices, making calculations and recalculations. I've accepted the challenge. It's the high point of my life. It's almost like . . ." His voice trailed off, but then he continued softly, "Like an act of faith. Like a power is working inside of me, outside of my thoughts, my emotions, my fears or desires. Soon I'll retire; I can't give up my only and last chance. Do you understand me, Gaia?"

"I most certainly do," she earnestly assured him.

"If I wasn't sure of all of that, I'd quit now."

She nodded, forcing a bright smile. Inwardly she was still worried. Not even so magnificent a mineral specimen as the unpolished but now fully exposed pink diamond was more important than a man's mental state, and she truly feared for Peter Lazarus' health, envisioning a breakdown if anything went wrong.

Time and again Lazarus carried it to the pure north light at the workroom window. There, and under special lamps, he established that there were no internal problems of carbon spots or inclusions too deeply embedded to polish away.

"Once the stone is cleaved, the larger portion suggests a perfect oval shape. Of course, there will be substantial carat loss when it is faceted, girdled, and polished, but that's true for any stone. Even in a declining market, this beauty of ours will be worth far more than its purchase price."

Eventually he announced that he was ready. The air hummed with tension as all the designers silently assembled. Miles Tuchelin arrived with a photographer, who was instructed to keep his distance and not use any flashes. Salinari was accompanied by Etta Spring.

They waited.

Lazarus checked the pink stone secured within a cuplike dop. He inspected the cutting wheel suspended above the diamond. Steadying himself, he mounted a block that raised him above the metal-clad table. Someone stifled a cough. Silence again.

He raised his right hand, testing his grip upon the metal mallet. Then slowly, carefully, he brought his elbow into his body. With a movement of his wrist, the mallet rose and swiftly descended. On the mark! The blade bit into the diamond. Two pieces cleanly separated, one considerably larger than the other.

Soon everyone was talking at once in loud excited voices. Lazarus wiped away the inked-in guideline. The larger piece weighed in at 102 carats. During the faceting process, a considerable proportion of that carat weight would be blown away as diamond dust.

Each person present took his turn holding it. When the glittering stone rested upon Gaia's open palm, her hand involuntarily trembled. She felt as though the diamond was almost pulsating. "A gem so alive, so splendid, and of such fine quality should have a name," she murmured.

"Why don't *you* name it," Lazarus suggested.

"Me?" She glanced nervously toward the head designer. "It wouldn't be proper."

Lazarus' face was glowing with his triumph and he persisted. "You more than anyone in the store besides me—and I count myself out because I was the one who worked with it—have a reverence for this diamond. Day after day you visited, observing its progress. Gaia, more than any person here, you're the one who truly has a feeling for it. You ought to christen it."

"I *have* thought of a name," she admitted. "It's a wonderful one, befitting the stone as well as the store's image." Then she looked around her, embarrassed. "At least, I think it is a wonderful name."

Michael Vanderman's gaze was fixed upon her.

"Let's hear it," Miles Tuchelin said.

"All right, but first, let me explain. I felt that the name of this diamond should be a sort of statement. And because it is owned by Ferrante-New York, I thought the name should be Italian."

"What is it?" Vanderman sounded testy.

All eyes were upon her. She paused dramatically.

"*Avanti,*" she said, speaking clearly. "It means, literally, *forward* in Italian. It signifies this stone, our feeling for it, and the future of our store."

"*Avanti!*" Lazarus shouted. He held up his champagne glass in the air, and the others joined him in the toast.

"*Avanti!*" they cried and emptied their glasses.

It was late afternoon when Gaia roused herself from her reverie. The memory of that day had revived her spirits, but she still felt physically exhausted. Wanting to appear fresh when Dom called for her to take her to dinner, she decided she would leave early for home and take a long potent soak in a sandalwood bath.

On her way to the elevator, she detoured to Etta Spring's desk outside Salinari's office door. The secretary was in the midst of a phone conversation, and Gaia waited patiently for her to finish.

"Just a moment," Etta spoke softly into the telephone, looking furtively toward Gaia. She covered the mouthpiece with a dry-looking hand and looked into Gaia's eyes, scarcely hiding her fury. "I already told you," she said. "He's not here. He will be in the store tomorrow."

"I want to be sure Mr. Salinari will be available to meet with me."

Etta Spring nodded brusquely, still holding the phone receiver in her hand, as though she could scarcely wait to continue her conversation after Gaia was out of hearing range.

Considerably irked, Gaia stood her ground.

With a sideways glance at her, the secretary said into the mouthpiece, "I have to hang up . . . no, I can't talk now. Good-bye."

"Who was that?"

Etta waved a hand at her cluttered desk. Papers were strewn across its top, a ledger book was open on a pull-out extension, and a page was half-typed in her machine. "I have lots of work to attend to."

"The phone call?"

"It's been constantly ringing."

"That doesn't answer my question. Unless, of course, it was a personal call, in which case I wouldn't—"

"It was Mr. Roselli," she said angrily.

Gaia felt her cheeks flush with annoyance. "Why is a former board member calling you? Or did you phone him? You were present at the meeting. Surely you understand that he has no further connection with Ferrante-New York."

Etta Spring's voice sank to near inaudibility. "He called me."

Gaia was furious. "I won't ask what your conversation was about. I will, however, remind you that earlier today you came into my studio and stated that you want to work for me."

"As I told you, Mr. Salinari will be in tomorrow. He's the one to explain."

Gaia was exasperated. "But *you* were speaking to Roselli just now."

"And that's what I told him."

"What?"

"To talk to Mr. Salinari."

Not knowing whether to believe her or not, Gaia affected a cool demeanor and said coldly, "The next time Mr. Roselli calls, you will connect him with me."

"If you say so." She began typing.

Gaia opened her mouth to say something else, but changed her mind. Tonight she was going to be with Dom. A familiar, recognizable thrill of anticipation stirred within her, surpassing any emotion she would feel at Ferrante.

"Good-bye, Etta," she said lightly, and turning on a graceful high heel, she strode out of the room.

Etta Spring stopped typing.

Little Miss Uppity, she thought. The young pretty heiress has no idea what's in store for her. She hadn't heard the ominous threat recently communicated over the phone.

· 16 ·

The midtown streets were already jammed. Cabs were predictably scarce. Passengers struggled to squeeze into buses. It was too lovely a day for the subway. Gaia started for home on foot.

Skyscrapers were already effectively blocking sunlight from the avenues. Only at the east-west cross streets was there a glimmer of brightness. It looked as though tonight there was going to be a spectacular sunset. If she walked at a steady pace, not much delayed by traffic at crossings, she would reach her apartment before then. With every step she knew how glad she was to be going home, and she pressed forward a little faster. On Lexington Avenue, seconds prior to turning into her street, she wondered if reporters would be waiting for her in the lobby of her building. There were none in evidence, and she smiled in relief as she hastened past the doorman *Thank goodness I decided on the unlisted phone,* she thought. They'd have to do a little more digging to find me here.

Jimmy, the doorman, smartly saluted Gaia. She was one of his favorite tenants. Her smile to him broadened. At the elevator, she turned and said, "By the way, Jimmy, Mr. Perrini will be coming by later, around seven. When he asks you to buzz me on the intercom to tell me his car's waiting, can you please say to him that I am expecting him to come up?"

"I'll try, Ms. Gerald," Jimmy said, shaking his head doubtfully, "but you know how he's always in a great hurry."

"This is important, Jimmy." She was embarrassed and felt the need to improvise. "It's his birthday, and I have a gift for him in my apartment."

The doorman's eyes brightened with mischief. "Oh, sure," he said. "In that case, I'll try to convince him you need to see him in your place."

Riding up in the elevator she shook her head in self-accusation. Ordinarily she avoided outright lying. Gaia wondered whether the inheritance was changing her character. By the time she inserted her door key in the lock, she'd determined that it had—irrevocably. She was the guardian of Ferrante-New York, and she would stop at nothing if that meant protecting the store's good reputation—even to ruining her own.

Not that having Dom visit her apartment fell into such a category. These past few years she had entertained several men there. Some of them overnight.

But wasn't that really Dom's fault?

"I hope you'll be all right living here," he'd said when he took her to the apartment for the first time.

Who wouldn't be? Her eyes had widened as she walked into the impressive foyer of the Murray Hill co-op. Dom had obtained it furnished for her, after his mother—whom Gaia deeply, deeply mourned—quietly died of a heart attack in her Brooklyn house. Dom didn't want Gaia to continue living there alone.

Five years later she was still struck by the incredible luxury of the apartment. The living room windows had ceiling-to-floor lattice sliding panels. The walls were a soft robin's egg blue, a shade she hadn't changed when it was time for a subsequent repainting. A curving sectional couch was upholstered in a soft-as-silk Egyptian cotton floral print—large splashy muted flowers on a vivid jade background. Upholstered armchairs in a harmonizing monotone fabric faced it, and in between was an impressive chased-bronze coffee table. Gaia immediately recognized the table as a work of modern art, and wasn't entirely surprised when she chanced to see a similar one in the American Craft Museum. Occasional tables, Waterford lamps, majolica, original prints, and several vivid modern paintings completed the strikingly original decor.

A highly polished marquetry floor covered by occasional area rugs extended into a smaller windowed room that served as the dining area. A black lacquer table was surrounded by four delicate but strong high-back chairs upholstered with such a fine-grade black suede that the leather felt like the skin of a ripe peach. A contemporary-styled iridescent chandelier was above.

Ultramodern kitchen appliances were of deep wine-red. The tile flooring was white with alternate stripings of gold and wine. A door opened to the foyer, and from it a small vestibule led into a dressing area with a handsome shell-pink marble bathroom to one side, and on the other was the sort of feminine bedroom Gaia had admired prototypes of in prestigious glossy magazines. Mother of pearl inserts formed a garland on the headboard of her bed. A bleached-wood bureau, a tall lingerie chest, a chaise longue, and a graceful writing desk didn't diminish the spaciousness of the room. A remote-control television was near the bed. Gaia would never forget the shock of her first night here, when she slid open one of the mirrored closet doors that took up the entire length of the room. Within it was a full-length raccoon coat on a satin padded hanger. It fit her perfectly.

This afternoon she hung up her most recently acquired gift from Dom, the white fitch coat. Even once she'd begun to earn her own way as a jewelry designer, no matter how often she tried, she couldn't persuade Dom to stop giving her presents. In her secret heart, Gaia wasn't sure that she truly wanted him to. But she recognized that his generosity toward her was a substitute: There was something she wanted far more.

Him.

She often lay awake late into the night, wondering who it

was he left her for when he dropped her off at her apartment
building soon after dinner. In the elegant restaurants where
they dined, Gaia was aware of the acquisitive glances beautiful women cast at him as if she weren't present. She would
cringe, feeling somehow inadequate to be his dinner companion.

It was as if she remained a child in his eyes.

She hungered for him sexually, and when she couldn't have
him, Gaia took lovers. The affairs were short-lived. The men
were poor proxies for her image of the way it could be physically loving Dom.

Tonight he would be with her in the apartment. Although
she yearned for it to be otherwise, her reason wasn't a romantic one.

They had much to discuss.

· 17 ·

THE BUILDING'S DELIVERY ENTRANCE, DOWN A FLIGHT OF STEPS from the avenue, was closed and locked from the inside after six P.M. At sidewalk level was a metal gate that also could only be opened from the inner side. A small painted sign hung on the gate: ALL DELIVERIES AFTER SIX P.M. TO LOBBY.

The man wore jeans of the most intensely dyed black. He had on a nondescript black leather jacket; a wide-brimmed, cheap-looking hat obscured his face from the tip of his nose upward. He carried a wrapped floral bouquet and held it prominently so the doorman's eyes would focus on it. He shuffled his feet and kept his face averted, as if innocently glancing about the lobby, empty except for the two of them. He was certain that he would never be accurately described beyond his clothing, which he afterward planned to discard.

She didn't at first hear the insistent buzz. Gaia was stepping out of the bathtub, toweling herself, when it sounded again. Thrusting her damp feet into mules, she headed toward the house phone near the apartment entry when her doorbell sounded. She glanced nervously at the foyer clock—no, Dom wouldn't be this early.

"Who is it?" she called through the door.

A male voice replied. "Florist delivery."

At first she didn't respond. Wasn't that like Dom, she thought, sending her a token of himself, but not appearing.

"Leave it outside my door," she said. "I'm not dressed."

"Sorry, ma'am. I need your signature on my trip sheet."

The house phone buzzed again.

"Yes," she spoke to Jimmy, "it's all right. The man is at my door."

"Excuse me, Ms. Gerald," the doorman apologized. "He moved so quickly . . . was already in the elevator while I rang you."

The man pressed hard on her doorbell.

"Quit that!" She was annoyed.

"I can't leave the flowers if you won't personally sign."

"Take them down to the lobby and Jimmy will sign for them."

"Sorry. This here's perishable goods. They told me I had to deliver to you personally or take it away with me." The voice sounded annoyed, and a little whiny.

Gaia sighed with impatience. "Very well. Just a minute." She padded into her bedroom and put on a pink terry robe that had been lying across her bed. As an afterthought she extracted a couple of dollars from her handbag. She was sure the delivery man wanted a tip more than her signature.

The doorbell chimed again.

"I'll be right there," she said aloud, and under her breath, "Keep your shirt on."

Gaia unlatched the door. She looked up at an unsmiling, craggy-faced man. No delivery service uniform. Somewhere in the back of her mind the thought occurred to her that he was older than the usual delivery boy. He bent down to set the flowers at the side of her door, straightened up, and took a step forward.

"What—"

She endeavored to shut the door against him, but he thrust her sharply backward, pushing his way into the apartment.

"Stop . . . what are you—?" She was shrieking until her outcry was aborted by her own terror.

As she struggled against him, an inner voice was telling her to fight him by using her intelligence; he was so much stronger. Although horror-struck, she attempted to draw him into conversation to delay him, perhaps stop him from whatever he intended to do. At the same time she was trying to convince herself that he was just a thief who would do her no bodily harm. Then she remembered that she was nude beneath her robe. My God . . . what if he raped her? But wasn't that preferable to being killed? She continued speaking to him in a voice that didn't sound in the least like her own.

He made no response. Gaia kept backing away from him, apprehensive, alarmed that he had allowed her to see his face. A criminal bent on theft wouldn't want to be identified later on. Suddenly she grew more frightened than before.

Despite her struggles, they had already progressed from the lighted foyer to halfway into the dark living room as he menacingly pressed forward. Then, suddenly moving around her, he strode toward the sliding window panels. There was a metallic screech as one was torn from its track. Cool evening air rushed into the room.

Her thinking was desperate . . . if she might just reach the side wall switch on pretext . . . then, possibly she could sprint beyond to get to the bedroom and lock the door against him. "I'll turn up the lights so you can see," Gaia said inanely. But he was too fast for her. He grunted and grabbed her wrist, twisting back her arm, dragging her toward the windows. She struggled with all of her might but couldn't free herself. His face was eerily lit from the light of the street. She seemed to see only his mouth, contorted with rage.

No . . . Her mind reeled. *Not the window . . . he's going to push me out* . . . Gaia was positive that she was about to die.

"Please . . . please don't." Her senses swirled and she suffered a strange illusion, as if the dreadful tableau didn't personally involve her. This other girl was kicking, scratching, screaming as he relentlessly dragged her while she attempted to pit her body against his intent. She was struggling, squirming, trying to twist away.

"Why?" Her own voice was deafening. "Why are you killing her?"

Time was rushing by—too fast. Ideas stirred within her near-frozen mind. A few moments more and he would push her out the window. Somehow she must summon up all of her strength and push *him* from the window. No, that was ridiculous. She would tumble out before he did. *No, no, don't look down . . . not down . . . Make a supreme effort to break away from him and run to the front door.*

Nearly losing her balance in the effort, Gaia managed to squirm out of his grip, falling to her knees, then regaining her feet, running. She bumped into a chair, crashed her shin into the bronze coffee table, then recovered her equilibrium and fled as fast as she might. But he was rapidly coming after her. Reaching the foyer, her arm was outstretched, her fingers reaching for the doorknob. Even if she got the door open, he would surely pursue her into the corridor. But there were other apartments . . . she prayed for the tenants to be home and save her. With a last surge of strength, she tugged the door open. And started screaming. And screaming. And screaming.

She collided with a man facing her door.

It was the superintendent, passkey in hand. Behind him, wide-eyed, stood Jimmy with one of the building porters. Gaia stumbled into Jimmy's arms, a strange whirling in her head. The elevator door opened and two policemen emerged. They rushed past her into the apartment, routing out the intruder who was attempting to hide in a closet. He was overpowered, handcuffed, remaining sullen and uncommunicative when he was read his rights. He didn't so much as glance at Gaia as he was led out the door into the corridor by one of the cops.

Gaia was too upset to be interrogated, and the other policemen mentioned that a precinct detective would be by later to get her statement. Then the building superintendent explained that Jimmy had summoned both him and the police.

Gaia looked at Jimmy with embarrassment as—feeling less dizzy—she straightened up, now leaning against the wall.

Jimmy's voice was imploring. "Ms. Gerald, believe me, I never mentioned your apartment number. He must have watched where I inserted the plug when I called you."

"A lousy thief," the superintendent averred.

A murderer, Gaia thought, deciding it was wisest to keep this to herself.

Her death would have been accepted as an accident. No, not that—a suicide . . . the shock of inheritance . . . they would have said that she wasn't able to cope. Her executioner would have escaped into the night.

Who had planned her death? Was it someone at Ferrante? Salinari hated her so much. He hadn't been in his office when she wanted to talk to him. Gone for the day, Etta had said.

And what of Etta Spring? She'd seen hatred in her eyes. Or had she misread what was, after all, merely envy? Was envy sufficient reason to wish her dead?

Michael Vanderman must surely feel put upon that his youngest designer was now his boss. Slim proof, Gaia thought. He was such a decent man—or seemed so.

Could it have been Miles Tuchelin? His talent for promotion had brought enormous success to the Gaia Star—and to Gaia Gerald. What possible advantage would her death bring to him?

She reconstructed a brief memory of the lawyer, Merrill Ross. He was a mystery to her. She suddenly recalled how intensely he had gazed at her this afternoon. Then she had barely noticed him, so overcome with meeting the woman who might be her aunt.

What of Silvia? She, who had spouted words filled with venom? By now she was airborne on her way to Rome. Did that mean she hadn't had the opportunity to make arrangements for Gaia's death before taking off?

She remembered the wrath of the former board members, Roselli, Smith, Bronf. Was she wrong to suspect they had underworld affiliations? How easy to imagine them making one or two phone calls to arrange everything. What had Dom said about how dangerous they were? But somehow she couldn't quite believe any one of them would have ordered her killing in revenge for being dumped from the board. She might be wrong . . . and that could be a deadly mistake. But Gaia suspected these three men wanted her alive, to be manipulated to do their bidding—at least for the present.

Still, someone had contracted for her to be murdered. She tried to comfort herself by believing: The police will find out who wants me to die when they question that dreadful man they arrested in my apartment.

Then I'll know.

Until that time there was no one else to suspect.

Certainly not Dom.

· 18 ·

"SHE WAS NEARLY TAKEN OUT IN HER APARTMENT LATE THIS afternoon," the caller said.

"Nearly? That means she's still alive?"

"Yes."

"Who ordered the hit?"

"I don't know."

"Don't shit me." The voice on the distant end expressed anger.

"I don't have to take that from you."

"Like hell, you don't."

"Okay, okay. Let's quit arguing and get on with it."

"She's to be closely watched. Do you get me?"

"You bet I do."

"No one is to reach her except you."

"I understand."

· 19 ·

"I'LL BE THERE WITHIN HALF AN HOUR," DOM SAID.

Alone in her apartment, Gaia had switched on all of the lights. Several times she retraced her steps to the front door to reassure herself that it remained bolted. Then she telephoned Dom in his office. He was the sole person from whom she thought of seeking comfort.

By the end of their conversation he sounded agitated and alarmed. "Don't open your door to anyone but me," he cautioned her.

Immeasurably relieved that he was on his way to be with her, she pictured him weaving his car through traffic. Jimmy wouldn't have to persuade Dom to come up after all.

Becoming calmer, Gaia realized she was still wearing her terry robe, and decided to change into something more glamorous. It would help her forget. She selected royal-blue velveteen jeans and a black satin blouse. She brushed out her hair, freshened her makeup, chose a pair of sandals, and was fastening a silver chain belt around her waist when the idea of making such deliberate preparations seemed absurd. She recalled how, when Dom had first shown her the apartment, she had flung her arms about him after wandering through its beautifully decorated rooms in ecstatic happiness. "It's perfect!" she'd exulted. "A romantic place where you will be my guest."

He'd smiled, looking embarrassed, and shortly thereafter made apologies about an appointment he must keep. Dom left and never returned.

For more than a year she indulged her hope of becoming his lover. Before Signora's death she would have considered herself wanton to contemplate them having sex. In her own apartment, self-imposed restrictions might be more easily abandoned. Yet Dom remained unattainable. Night after night she yearned for him physically as she lay alone in her bed. And, oh, God, the guilt she suffered after bringing the first man into her home. She was the aggressor as much as he, yet she felt violated. She hoped Dom would somehow find out and be jealous.

Singles bars became open territory for hunting casual sexual alliances. But increasingly, she found her transient sex partners distasteful. It was too scary out there. Lately, she ceased frequenting bars and stayed at home alone. Having an orgasm with the wrong man didn't compensate for not being alone with the one man she desired.

Even before the plane taking her from Chicago had set down its wheels on a LaGuardia runway, Gaia, in the awakening sensualism of a half-child/half-woman, had committed her entire being into his care. She didn't want to admit to herself that his interest in her was that of an adult to a child. Her repressed longing for Dom then was a peculiar entwining of romanticism and animalism. Gaia was confidently saving herself for him.

She had always known there was a deep mystery in Dom's life. Signora's eyes had told her that. She knew he was in the building-construction business in New York, and yet he made frequent unexplained flights to Europe and to the Orient. His gifts to her following each trip were expensive and original. Was it her overactive imagination that projected a darker, ruthless side to his character? Oddly, it only made her more fascinated by him.

One time she'd asked Dom why he'd recently traveled to Rome. His anger at her question was somehow defensive, she thought. As quickly as it flared, it was over.

Although Gaia wasn't much of a drinker, she poured herself a stiff bolt of Napoleon brandy and quaffing it too fast, she coughed, then, sipping more slowly, continued her musing. She remembered when she had lived in Signora's house and had urged his mother to talk about Dom's childhood. But somehow, Signora had left something out, Gaia knew. Her dark guileless eyes would cloud over at having to stop herself from telling Gaia everything. Gaia had too much respect for her to urge her on.

"Il buono figlio," Signora tenderly called her youngest—the good son! Dominic was her change-of-life baby, and although her prayers had been for a daughter, she vowed to instruct at least this one child in the graces of gentleness and decency. There were twelve years between him and Luigi, her next youngest. Because the elder sons absorbed their father's interest, Dominic was her special baby.

As he grew older, it worried her when the lively, strong youngster withdrew from her into a sort of private vacuum where it was hard for her to reach him. She knew that he was unhappy, but he had already grown too manly to bring his hurts to her. She could only guess that in their neighborhood streets, boys his own age were treating him with unwelcome deference because of his family connections.

Dom was fascinated by baseball and sought to try out for the sandlot team. However, the coach took him on without trial.

"What position do you like?" he questioned.

"First base."

Afterward, Dom found out another boy had been bumped so he could play.

Kids volunteered their bikes for him to ride, although he had his own. They presented him with delicacies from their lunch boxes that they would rather have eaten themselves. In class, it was obvious that the teachers—young women from local families—were influenced by his surname, and added percentages to his marks.

Mariuccia spoke to the parochial school's principal.

"Signora Perrini, the sisters are grateful to your husband. He has granted favors to their families and this is their way of repaying him."

Disgusted by the patronage he received because his name was Perrini, Dom took no pleasure in always getting his way, in never knowing the thrill of coming up against a worthy opponent. He wanted a one-on-one relationship with people on his own merit, but was invariably treated as someone to be feared, who could, if he chose, summon the forces of retribution.

So Dom grew to accept that he could never find anyone to present a challenge to him. For him, there were no fistfights. He never went home with a bloody nose. He wasn't to be roughed up. The word had gone out . . . he was the son and brother of important men.

When he was in high school, he confided to his mother that he hoped to be the first in the family to attend college. He wanted to become a lawyer. She went to church and lit candles of thanksgiving. She was adamant in persuading Antonucci not to oppose this. Dom enrolled at Brooklyn College.

It was somehow offensive to his brothers that he was a good student, and she frequently observed the mockery in their eyes. Vito, Guido, and Luigi's chief study was the law of jungle survival in the rackets. Her eyes would fill with tears, and she couldn't repeat to Gaia the scene she overheard of them taunting him and the awful language they had used. She continued to hear it in her mind but still didn't fully understand.

"Hey, shitass, ya busy studying? A real man lets his cock think for him. You ain't never had any, have you?" This was from Vito, the oldest.

"Crap, he ain't never even serviced the house broads," spat Guido, referring to a brothel that was family owned.

"Only a real asshole wouldn't fuck for free. He ain't so smart after all!"

Luigi wheezed in unpleasant laughter.

"Maybe he can't get it up."

"Sure! He's tied to the old lady's apron strings."

"Maybe he ain't a man. Is that it, sissy boy?"

"Nah." Vito chuckled. "He's a motherfucker. That's it, a motherfucker."

Standing undetected in the hall outside the room where they'd interrupted Dom at his studying, Mariuccia was afraid she would faint. With the back of one hand flung across her mouth, she watched from her hidden vantage point, and saw young Dom slowly rise from his chair at the desk. He moved without haste, devoid of outward anger. A strange smile played upon his lips. There was no hint of impending violence. The skin beneath his collar sweated as he faced his brothers, hearing their raucous laughter as they poked one another's sides, and pealed gales of amusement. Suddenly, his fists lashed out. He caught Vito with a blow to his jaw that landed with a cracking sound. He flashed a chop to his neck.

"Chee-rist!" Vito fell backward against a chair, where he made no attempt to stir.

Dom confronted Guido and Luigi. He was beyond caution, ready to take them both on at the same time. Mariuccia knew she mustn't intervene. Then Vito found his voice, speaking while he massaged his aching jaw. The old man was out of town on business and Vito was his deputy in his absence. His chief worry was that he would hear of this fracas. It was his father's dictum that there was to be unity within the family. If he was informed, it wouldn't be by Guido or Luigi. Vito could bear down upon *them*. With his eyes squinted, he speculated about their younger brother, who, until today, had been no more threatening than a baby. If he talked—? How could he assure himself that Dom presented no danger to him?

He thrust forth his hand. "Shake, kid. I want ya t'know I'm not mad. No hard feelings?"

Dom clasped it.

Vito breathed easier. There was no way the old man was

going to find out. "Anything I can do for ya, y'only gotta ask," he said, preparing to depart, pushing Luigi and Guido ahead of him.

Their mother fled up the stairs. In her bedroom, she prayed to the Virgin Mary to protect her younger son, to keep him from harm and temptation. She recalled how Vito had cast aspersions upon Dom's manhood. There was no necessity for prayer on that score. Although she pretended not to notice, she'd seen girls clustering around him.

Within a matter of days, Antonucci summoned Dom to his storefront office. This signaled that their meeting concerned something his wife must not hear.

"Vito tells me you're doing real well in college," he began. "Your brother loves you. He came to me and urged I should do something special for you . . . you know . . . open doors."

Dom was silent. Vito wasn't so dumb either. He'd figured out how to prime the old man for a payoff.

"Next summer, instead of you taking a job as a lifeguard at Brighton Beach and making out with the girlies, I'm gonna fix it so you work in Nick Battaglia's law office. How's that for doing right by my youngest boy?"

"Thanks, Pa, but I've already got a law clerk's job lined up."

"So what? Tell them you won't take it."

"I want this job. It's with a prestigious firm."

Antonucci's face darkened. "Nick is my lawyer. He's the best mouthpiece I ever had. Another kid would bust his gut for such an opportunity."

"It's not for me."

The old man was outraged. "You'll do as I say."

"There's no way I'm going to tie up with a mob lawyer."

He screamed. "You were born into this family. As long as you live, you can never turn your back on its business. One day you'll be *consigliare* to the family."

"To bail hookers out of jail and bribe witnesses? Never! That's not what I want out of life."

"Life, he says. How dare you talk to me that way. Get out before I kill you! I'm ashamed you're my son."

By the time he'd walked home, Dom's mind was made up.

Not even as powerful a man as his father was going to press him into a mold. He sought out his mother to tell her what he planned to do. Despite her protests, including her plea that he was her shining hope to bring respectability to the family, he was adamant. She shouted at him, and this hardened his resolve. In her own way, she was as domineering as his father.

Dom quit Brooklyn College in midsemester. He applied for a scholarship at UCLA, was accepted, and flew out to California, taking one suitcase with him. He intended never to return.

Less than a year later, Antonucci Perrini was fatally hit by a barrage of bullets. His widow, older sons, and their respective families were lamenting partipants at his gangster-style funeral with its plethora of gaudy floral displays and long-faced, dark-clad mourners. FBI cameras secretly recorded the passing of an American success and all those who attended the rite. The Mass was nearly over by the time Dom arrived at the church. His flight from California had been delayed for hours. He stood apart from the others, his eyes revealing nothing.

Rivalry among Vito, Guido, and Luigi ensued almost immediately after their father's death. They were so involved in the internecine struggle that they neglected to protect family interests from outsiders and, rather quickly, other gangs began chipping away at the Perrini operations. Several council bosses had ordered hits on them, and eventually just one Perrini son remained alive and unsplattered by the bloodbath.

He was the youngest, uninvolved in the family business—Dom.

Gaia remained seated in her living room, trying not to think about what had just occurred in this very room. Flashes of the man who tried to kill her passed before her closed eyes—his rough dark hands on her arms, his twisted purple lips, the black of his jeans. The bottle of Napoleon brandy was on the table beside her chair. She poured herself another drink and, holding the brandy snifter with its stem between the third and fourth fingers of her cupped hand, she swirled the amber-colored liquid.

Dom was on his way to her.

In the meantime, she must blot out the horror. Memories of past happiness came to mind and she gratefully surrendered all conscious thought to her reminiscence.

High school graduation. A bright, sticky day. And later, the prom!

Signora had sewn a beautiful white silk organdy gown for her, embroidering it with genuine seed pearls. Gaia had never before owned anything so lovely. And Signora hadn't used a store-bought pattern. "It is like the wedding dress my mama made for me," she said, tears glistening in her eyes. Gaia embraced her but Signora quickly turned away.

"You had better wear one of my aprons to protect it at supper."

Gaia laughed happily. "I guess you can see I don't want to take it off."

Signora nodded. "It wouldn't be practical to change your clothes. The young man escorting you will be coming by shortly after we finish eating."

Signora had taught her to cook flavorful Italian specialties, but this evening Gaia didn't have to work in the kitchen. Besides, she was too excited to do anything. At around eight o'clock, a tall good-looking boy named Peter was coming by to take her to the school prom. Other than on this occasion, outsiders rarely entered the house, for Signora wasn't given to entertaining. She had outlived all her friends, and Gaia was too shy to invite schoolmates to visit her at the house she still couldn't quite believe was her home. She was happy to have her nightly meals alone with Signora, chatting about the day's activities, although her conversation elicited scant reply from her. Yet she was content in the household's peace. She would volunteer to help with household chores, only to find that the floor was already waxed, the silver shined, the heavy tasks done. There was no servant, but, as Signora would often say, "What else to do with my time than keep my house?"

On this evening, Gaia could not stop talking about the prom and her date. She could barely swallow a mouthful of the succulent lasagna with its delicate filling and pungent sauce—Signora's specialty—despite Signora's compelling gaze that silently urged her to eat.

While they sat in the dining room, they heard the front door creak open. Dom entered the house. Gaia's heart leapt. She was wondering how she might immediately remove the protective apron without Signora protesting.

He patted the top of Gaia's head in passing her chair and bent to kiss his mother's cheek. "How many times have I told you to keep the door locked?" he asked.

"No one ever comes here."

"Mama, you are a Perrini. There could still be danger."

"The past is done with."

"Not necessarily."

"I'm not afraid," she said with proud stubbornness.

"You must think of Gaia. Would you want her involved in some leftover horror?"

She crossed herself. "God forbid."

"Will you promise to keep the doors and downstairs windows locked?"

She nodded. "Dominic, let me give you food. There's plenty more in the kitchen."

He pleaded that he wasn't hungry, but accepted a cup of scalding espresso. While waiting for it to reach a drinkable temperature, Dom prepared and lighted a cigar. Gaia went to the parlor for an ashtray, taking the opportunity to discard her apron.

As Gaia reentered the room, looking shyly at him, Dom felt astounded by her loveliness. Her skin glowed against a modest heart-shaped neckline bordered with seed pearls. Puffed sleeves billowed cloudlike on her upper arms. The slim bodice revealed how very womanly she'd become. A white velvet sash emphasized the smallness of her waist, and the skirt flared out in ripples that ended just at her ankles. She stood proudly in white satin pumps, the first moderately high heels she'd owned. But it was her face to which his fascinated gaze returned. Gaia's hair was swept back, a dark shining frame to her fresh beauty. With her lips parted in a happy smile, she was looking to him for approval. How could a sophisticated man tell a young girl that her beauty stunned him, that he thought she was more beautiful than any woman he'd ever known.

"Perfection!" he pronounced, and was relieved that she was pleased with his perfunctory praise. Dom smiled at his black-garbed mother. "You, too, are to be complimented, Mama. I assume you made the gown."

Mariuccia Perrini slightly bobbed her head. She was remembering how, as a young girl, she'd been married in such a dress, on a bright sunny day in an imposing Sicilian church.

When Gaia was again seated at the table, wearing the apron Signora had insisted she put back on, Dom withdrew a long slender package from his pocket. It was wrapped in mauve and silver paper with a bright silver ribbon tied around it. He placed the box on the tablecloth in front of her chair. "I've brought you a graduation present."

With trembling fingers, Gaia removed the wrapping, carefully placing it to the side to be saved. Underneath was a jewelry box with the inscription FERRANTE-NEW YORK. She pulled it open and drew in her breath . . . a string of cultured pearls. Throwing her arms impulsively around his neck, Gaia shut her eyes as she pressed her lips against his cheek.

"Here, *cara*, let me fasten it for you."

"It matches the gown," she said excitedly. "Did you know Signora was making it for me?"

He smiled. "I didn't."

"Anyway, you remembered." She grew serious. "I'll always be grateful."

"It's an important occasion. And now, Gaia, that you have a high school diploma, what would you like to do next?"

"Next can wait." Signora spoke in emphatic Italian.

"Why, Mama?"

She pursed her lips, as if determining whether she ought to voice her opinion. "First she will have the joy of a young girl.

Tonight a boy is calling for her and is taking her to the prom."
She spoke the word "prom" as if it were a gem in her mouth.

Dom's face darkened. "Why did you sanction it?" he demanded.

Gaia looked from one to the other of them in dismay. She had never seen Dom get angry at his mother.

The small woman stood her ground. "Be silent. It is her right to attend."

"Absolutely no!" he shouted. "I forbid it."

Tears glistened in Signora's eyes. "*Figlio* . . ."

He gently embraced her. "*Mama mia*, you are a saint. I know you mean well, but picture what could happen to a young innocent girl, really yet a child in such a crowd."

"Gaia has good values."

"Assuredly she has. You have guided her."

"Then why do you object, my son?"

He hesitated. Gaia had the distinct feeling that what he ultimately said had nothing to do with what he was thinking. "I know nothing about this boy. Is he Italian?"

Gaia responded. "Peter is Polish, I think."

"The date is out of the question."

Gaia knew that Dom wasn't prejudiced. She sensed that he had another reason and was using Peter's Polishness as an excuse.

"But he'll be here in half an hour," Signora protested.

"You will send him away."

Gaia's face fell. She suddenly felt awkward in her gown. Dom's gaze was upon her and she flushed.

"Do you want terribly to go?"

She slightly shrugged.

"Then I'll be your escort."

Her mood lifted with an exquisite joy. "The two of us?"

"Would you like that, *cara?*"

"Yes. Oh, yes."

They were the focus of all eyes as he swept her across the dance floor after handing a fifty-dollar bill to the startled trio who were strumming hard rock on the podium. "Play some-

thing I can dance to," Dom told them. They valiantly attempted "Strangers in the Night"—occasionally off-key.

Gaia floated in Dom's arms as he led her into steps she'd
never danced before. In a blur she saw brightly colored paper
streamers overhead, fastened to the rafters. They moved together across the scratched wood floor of the transformed
gym, and she felt a oneness with him. Dom's powerful presence silenced any criticism that might have otherwise been
forthcoming from the chaperoning nuns and parents, and
envy burst in the hearts of the other girls who pretended they
were as pleased by their pimply and ungainly partners. The
boys silently acquiesced to his authority, the power of his
manliness, in the intuitive bond of respect youths have for
larger-than-life heroes.

Except for Peter. After downing a pint of cheap rye in the
lavatory, he staggered into the gym. By then, Dom had left
the dance floor with Gaia, and rock sounds were again
predominating. Peter shouted his fury at the man and was
ignored as if he were invisible. Earlier, he'd been humiliated
in front of that old Italian woman who wouldn't even let him
in, and laughed at by his friends when he'd arrived at the high
school alone. Who the fuck did this guy think he was? "Asshole . . . asshole," he yelled.

Dom took a firm grip of Gaia's arm and hastened her into
the vestibule and down the school steps to the sidewalk. They
were halfway down when the boy tackled Dom from behind.
Both tumbled to the pavement, throwing Gaia off-balance
against the balustrade. Dom landed on top and twisted Peter's
arm until he winced, but the boy squirmed free, wildly
throwing his fists. An unaimed fist connected and brought
down the man. Dom got to his feet and savagely thrust him
backward. The boy sobered and sought to roll out of his
reach. Dom now stood with his legs apart above his erstwhile
assailant. He reached beneath his jacket to a shoulder holster,
drew out a .38-caliber weapon and pointed it.

"Mother of Mary!" the boy shrieked.

His terrified cries diluted to a city night sound as he got his footing and fled down the dark tree-lined blocks.

Dom replaced his gun and dusted his clothes off with his palms. Gaia timidly inched closer to him.

"No tears?" He inspected her face. "That's good. You will be a strong woman."

He leaned down and brushed her lips with his. Her arms instinctively went around him. He tightened his hold on her. His lips pressed harder as his kiss became increasingly insistent. Her heart quickened as she closed her eyes. This was actually happening—no longer the fantasy she'd often given herself over to. Her lips parted and his tongue penetrated her mouth, to be clasped by hers. She felt his teeth biting into her lips, and just at the point of her submission, he totally withdrew, leaving her shaken and panting. She had been aroused and was left unsatisfied.

Dom kept a small distance away from her. "A man can be bestial," he muttered.

"I wanted to as much as you did."

"Stop it, *cara*! You don't know what you're saying."

"Yes I do."

"Please, child"—he ran his fingers up his forehead—"forgive me."

"I love you," she cried out.

"And I do you . . . as an uncle."

"Not anymore." It was a plea. "I'm grown-up now. You know it."

"This will never happen again."

"I will wait."

"*Dio mio!*"

Leaves from the trees that lined the curb rustled in a breeze and the glow of a streetlight shone through the branches and touched her face. Dom saw her gentle smile, more womanly than childlike.

"Fix your face," he said brusquely. "Your lipstick is smeared."

She wiped it off with a tissue and they began walking in silence. Near the corner, a candy store remained open. It was the same one where Antonucci Perrini's rackets team had operated in the back room, where Just Out Bregna had been shot to death. Renovation had followed; a new manager had been installed. The egg creams improved, and in his own childhood Dom had been a frequent customer.

"Would you like a soda?" he asked.

"Yes, thank you."

He looked relieved. She was a little girl again.

Afterward, he saw her to his mother's door. He had parked his car in front of the house. "I won't come in," he said quietly.

"I'll never forget tonight," she said.

He appeared to be uncomfortable. "In a day or so I'll come back to talk to you with Mama present. We must discuss your future. I think, instead of going to college, you would do well to study jewelry design. You have great artistic ability, and you will learn to work with precious metals and gems. How does that sound to you?"

She considered. "It's exciting. Do you really believe I could become a jewelry designer?"

"I'm positive of it."

She nodded and mounted the wooden porch steps, disappointed that he hadn't kissed her again, but not actually expecting he would.

"One more thing, Gaia."

She turned eagerly.

"I want you to understand . . . I often carry large sums of cash. That's why I have a gun."

"Yes."

She remained at the white painted rail, watching him unlock the car door and start the ignition. She hoped that someday he would invite her out for a drive with him. Her girlish heart floated whenever she imagined it.

The car door opened and Dom leaned his head out. "Don't stand outside. It's getting chilly. Go into the house." Then the door slammed shut and the car pulled out silently, leaving a slight odor of gasoline.

Turning to unlock the front door, Gaia momentarily gazed in the direction Dom had driven. She watched the car until it turned a corner and was out of sight.

She had implicitly believed his explanation about the gun.

· 20 ·

THE SOUND OF THE HOUSE PHONE BUZZING SNAPPED GAIA BACK into reality. It was Jimmy. The doorman's voice was elated. "Mr. Perrini is on his way up," he announced.

Standing behind her locked door, Gaia nervously awaited him. She felt the responses to his arrival: the excitement that made her skin flush, her throat muscles tighten, her pulse throb powerfully enough to sound in her ears. She was aware that, if she hadn't been so lucky, Dom would be arriving to identify her murdered body. The doorbell chimed and, without glancing through the peephole, she unbolted the door.

For moments he stood staring at her, taking in her appearance. When he spoke his manner was carefully light. "Wait a minute! Can this be the same girl who phoned me panicstricken? Why, you look fine, *cara*. Not a hair out of place. Perfection!"

It was strange, she mused. Although she heard him speak, voices from the past were assuming dominance inside her head. "Perfection!" he had said in Signora's dining room as she pranced before him in her prom dress. So, he was guarding himself from her again, just as he'd done so many years ago. She took a deep breath. Her recent shock still disoriented her. She willed herself to return to reality.

Whatever dumb idea had impelled her to doll herself up in

this sexy outfit? She felt a blush creep up her cheeks. She could very well understand Dom's amazement at the way she looked. She certainly didn't appear like a person who'd nearly been thrown from a window. "I'm wearing this to cheer myself up," she said lamely.

He frowned and she assumed it was in disapproval. Then she realized he was looking toward the damaged window, one of its panels teetering crazily. He strode across the living room to remain staring down at the street for what seemed to her to be an extraordinarily long time. He turned and looked at her. "There's no way you would have survived."

He'd put her fear into words, and it triggered her out-of-control response. She started shaking . . . shaking . . . shaking. Unable to stop, she found support by gripping the back of a chair—until Dom rushed over to her and clasped her to him.

"*Cara, cara,*" he murmured, his lips against her hair.

Leaning against him, she grew quieter.

"Hush, darling. You are safe."

She looked up at him, deriving pleasure from his strength. Her hands traced the muscles of his shoulders and she flung her arms around his neck. As she caressed the nape of his neck, she brought her mouth close to his and with increasing frenzy sought to reach his lips. He avoided her, turning his head, at first embarrassed, then halfway laughing, stretching away. Yet he kept holding her tightly to him. Reaching on her toes, she arched her face upward.

"This is wrong," he said huskily. "You are like a daughter to me."

"No," she protested. "And it hasn't been that way for a long time—if it ever was. Dom, admit it!"

Her appetite fed his and his lips crushed hers. His passion further inflamed her. Her breasts were flattened against him, her belly angled into his, his pelvis pushing irresistibly against her. Becoming aware of his hardened, jutting penis, she avidly reached for it. She was throbbing and moist. Gaia's other hand was on his trouser zipper, sliding it down. Dom groaned as he explored her breasts, having already opened her blouse buttons. The pressure between her legs mounted excruciatingly when he urgently began massaging her nipples. His breathing was growing shallow as together they swayed, stroking, kneading, burning. Sensation heightening past the point of return. A delicious agony. Joyous wordless cries. She groped past the slit of his trunks to capture and at last encircle him with her fingers: hot and quivering, strong, thick, lengthy—as she had sensed he would be! His hands pressed against her waist. Gaia trembled. She was frantic for him to be inside of her, and began to unfasten her dark velvet jeans when he stopped. Totally!

Her mouth was open; she pursued while he backed away from her, firmly although gently removing her hands from his crotch. Although she remained silent, there was a potent question in her eyes.

"This should never have started. It is all wrong."

"How could something so wonderful—?"

"I've been afraid of this happening. It's why I always kept away from you."

"I love you, Dom. I want to sleep with you."

She had never seen him look so unhappy "We have a different relationship."

"If you're worried that I'd make demands, honestly, I wouldn't. You could still be free for—for . . . other women . . . oh, Dom—" Her hands reached for him again.

"Stop it!" he shouted.

"But—"

"I don't want you to belittle yourself. Not to a son of a bitch like me, or to anyone else."

"You must be kidding. I'm nearly twenty-seven years old and I have a mind of my own."

"Good! You're showing spirit. I like that."

"Except you don't like me the way I want you to."

"Forgive me, *cara*. I must have a dirty mind, and I can't forgive myself."

He went into the bathroom. When he returned, his clothes were ordered, his manner carefully distant.

Following a hasty glance at herself in the foyer wall mirror and an attempt at smoothing her hair, Gaia seated herself upon the living room couch, her back precisely positioned as she gazed down at her lap.

From the foyer, Dom said, "Did I tell you, I intend arranging for you to be guarded around-the-clock."

She cleared her throat to reply in a conversational tone of voice. "I don't want that. If I hadn't foolishly opened my door, I'd have been safe enough. Believe me, I'll exercise caution."

"You let *me* in."

"I knew you were on your way up. Jimmy called and I heard the elevator open. Then you rang."

"Did you look through your peephole?"

She admitted that she hadn't.

"That proves it. You need to be watched carefully."

"I won't have it, Dom. From now on I'll be more careful."

"And from now on they'll be more cunning."

"They?"

He hesitated. "Whoever ordered the hit."

"He could have been a burglar." She was trying to persuade herself as well.

"I am not convinced that he intended to rob you."

"You are frightening me. Do you know that?"

"Someone evidently hired him to make it look like suicide."

She swallowed. Hearing Dom say it was worse than thinking it herself. She hadn't recognized the intruder and he'd let her see his face. Obviously he was certain she would never be able to identify him. And how could she if she was lying crushed on the sidewalk? "The police have the man in custody. They'll find out who he is, and his motive."

"You are incredibly naïve, Gaia. You don't believe things are that simple."

"If I refuse the inheritance, whoever it is will leave me alone. I'll be safe."

"I thought the store meant something to you. I didn't take you for a quitter." He watched her reaction.

She became furious. "I never once quit in my life."

Dom smiled. He was pleased that he had made his point. "I will arrange for your bodyguards around the clock."

"I told you I don't want that. Anyway, there's no need. If there is any danger to me, it's probably from Roselli and the other two ex-directors. They looked like they could have sent someone to do away with me. A detective is going to contact me, and when he does I intend mentioning them. The police will know how to handle it."

"This minute—now—tonight, you're not being protected by the police."

"Dom, I'm locked in, and you're here with me."

"I have to leave. Another time, when it is safe for you to go out, we'll have our dinner date."

"Yes," she said unhappily, "and you'll want me to meet you in the lobby."

He located a number in his pocket leather-bound directory and picked up the telephone.

"Who are you calling?"

"I already told you. I'm getting you a bodyguard. At least for tonight."

"It will embarrass me to have someone standing outside my door."

"I've already thought of that. It will be best for him to be in the apartment with you." He dialed, gave her name, address, and apartment number into the phone. Afterward he said to Gaia, "This is the only way. With him here, I know you'll be taken care of."

"I'd rather have you with me."

Already unlatching the door, he didn't reply. When he was halfway out, he looked back at her, a long searching inspection as if he wanted to remember the way she looked at this moment. "*Ciao*, Gaia."

"How will I recognize the guard before I open the door?"

"He'll be wearing a uniform."

She bolted the lock and leaned with her forehead on the door until she heard the sound of the elevator closing behind him. She felt dispirited. If he wouldn't take her to dinner in a restaurant, why hadn't he eaten with her in the apartment? She would have prepared a light meal, or had a gourmet dinner delivered. She thought wryly, Passion and food are like oil and water.

She went into the bathroom and splashed cold water on her face. Toweling it dry, she closed her eyes and shivered, thinking of the way she'd felt when her body was pressed against Dom's. Suddenly, something else came to mind. The stiff shape beneath his arm, against his upper torso, something strapped to him for ready use.

A gun!

Déjà vu.

It triggered an awful memory . . . of when Peter had cried out on the gymnasium steps . . . Dom had pointed the gun at him.

What did Dom then tell her? That he needed it for protection. She remembered the hard look on his face as he reached inside his jacket and drew out the gun. She remembered how terrified she'd been.

Now . . . tonight . . . the gun frightened her anew. For what purpose, she wondered, did he carry a weapon? Had she asked, would he have given her the same answer? As a school-girl, she'd believed him implicitly. *Can I believe him now?*

In the bedroom, she threw off her clothes and quickly put on a sweater and a wool suit. She ran a comb through her thick hair and glanced in the mirror. A whimper, like an animal in agony, came from her lips.

She stared her mirrored image for several minutes, especially into her own eyes. What she saw in them was fear. At that instant she *knew*. The last thing she wanted was to have a stranger in the apartment with her. Not even if Dom had sent him. *It's high time I begin looking out for my own safety.*

She slid open her closet and hunched herself into the sleeves of the white fitch coat. She grabbed her handbag, confirming that she had sufficient cash and all her credit cards. She left the lights on just in case anyone might be staring up from the opposite sidewalk. On her way out of the apartment, she closed the door quietly behind her, trying not to make any noise as she double-locked it. It was a strong lock and would, at best, keep someone out or at least slow his entry.

Hastening along the corridor, Gaia paused before the elevators. Suppose she bumped square into the security man on his way up? She fled in the opposite direction.

She took the service stairs, and clattering down the steps, she worried that her heels were making too much noise on the metal treads. When she reached the basement, she rushed past the incinerator, where a porter was stoking the fire with his back to her, oblivious of her passage, and exited cautiously into a small courtyard. Then, she tiptoed up a half-flight of iron stairs to the street level. Worried that she might call attention to herself by hailing a cab, she ran to the next cross street to search for one. At the corner she paused and looked behind her. A station wagon was pulling up in front of her building. When it passed directly beneath a streetlight, she could read the name painted on its side: BULLET SECURITY.

Wasn't that the same guard service called in for occasional duty at the store? On whose orders? Gaia's suspicions arose. Wasn't it common knowledge that there was a connection between the security firm and the board of directors whom she'd just this day fired? Trembling, she pulled her coat closer around her. The fur was Dom's most recent gift.

Dom, she thought.

Then: *Oh, my God.*

· 21 ·

MINUTES EARLIER, THE CONCERNED DOORMAN HAD OPENED THE
street door for Dom Perrini. Jimmy badly wanted to inquire
how Ms. Gerald was, but observing Dom's frown, he reconsidered. As he saw it, Mr. Perrini was a complex man. On the
one hand he was capable of enormous charm, but he could
also turn cold as ice the next instant. There was no way
Jimmy was about to tamper with a hornet. Especially when
a hefty tip could be compromised. Hadn't he been keeping a
watchful eye on Mr. Perrini's illegally parked two-seater 450
SL Mercedes, smack alongside of a hydrant near the entrance?

A ten-dollar bill was palmed into Jimmy's hand.

He tipped his cap. "Thank you mightily, sir."

"A security man from Bullet will be arriving shortly. I
want him to go directly to Ms. Gerald's apartment so she
doesn't have an opportunity to send him away. Have you got
that?"

"Yessir."

"Don't announce him on the house phone. You understand?"

"I do." It was good that Mr. Perrini was looking out for the
Gerald girl's best interests, Jimmy thought.

A gust of cold wind whipped against Dom's face as he
strode out of the lobby to his car. The air carried a hint of

humid saltiness from the East River. His eyes burned from incinerator smoke disgorged by a faulty flue. New Yorkers are so accustomed to inhaling industrial waste that to him it was a tonic. He took deep draughts, filling his lungs before isolating himself behind the locked doors and windows of his iridescent silver car. Dom brooded upon his destination while neglecting to snap on the stereo, as he generally did when driving alone. Proceeding north on Madison Avenue to the East Eighties, he turned left on a street where a light had burned out, creating a pool of darkness mid-block. Here elegant apartment buildings hemmed in a row of several four-story, well-kept Georgian town houses, their red-brick fronts bespeaking respectability behind white-framed windows. He eased into an open space before a particular house that gave no hint of occupancy from its dark windows. But a lantern-shaped lamp illuminated a sleek black paneled door. He mounted several steps, pressed the bell, and was promptly admitted by a man who would have appeared to a passerby to be a butler. Dom didn't live here. His apartment was twenty blocks south, with a view of the East River and the flat sprawl of Queens from its high-storied terrace and windows.

The vestibule of the town house, with its worn carpeted stairs curving upward, fading paint, and dim lighting, projected a gloom of gentility gone to seed. In a room to the right was an intense overhead light beaming down upon several gambling tables. Blackjack, roulette, and craps were each in active play, with high wagers the rule. The gamblers were all men, so engrossed in their bets they were not even aware of his entry. Within these walls none of them felt the need to be on guard.

To the rear was an equally large room overlooking a garden concealed from street view. The room was pulsing with multihued strobe lights, its decor the garish submodernity of a disco. When Dom opened the sound-insulated door, he was hit full force by the swell of a deafening beat blared from the enormous loudspeakers. He barely blinked. A gyrating young woman separated herself from the frenetic bodies and the small dance floor to position herself before him. She was wearing a plunging black sequin halter and satin miniskirt, a seeking expression on her face, her eyes half-closed, her mouth forming an oval from which the tip of her tongue protruded to slowly lick at its perimeter.

The music, the lights, the moving bodies, combined to create a provocative chaos that Dom thought would sweep any memory of Gaia from him. It was why he had come here. To enter the atmosphere of blatant sexual contortions, where several of the beautiful blank-faced young women were naked to the waist and some of the men were trouserless, their flabby stomachs riding against feminine heads with faces pressed against their groins. As he watched, the tempo seemed to intensify. An orange-haired girl beckoned to him, stroking herself wildly. He let her lead him to the tiny dance floor. Closer in, he observed the perspiring men's strained faces as they plunged into the wet mouths, and he was distantly aware of the old joyless look of the young women when they raised their heads from grubby sticks of quickly flaccid penises. Their faces were smeared with lipstick as they danced away, half nude, their breasts bobbing, while the men hastily drew up pants that had fallen crumpled on their shoes. The girls clustered before a mirrored wall, extracting lipsticks from small purses and reapplying the greasy color, while the men straightened their clothes and prepared to leave. What they had come here for had been done to them. There was no need to remain in this room.

Until Dom was recognized.

Face to face with the orange-haired girl, they swayed without touching, their hips, arms, and feet moving with the abandon of an unstructured dance. She slithered into him, flinging her arms about his neck while they continued to dance. She could feel his cock pressing against her, and she maneuvered her gyrating steps, separating her legs so that it jutted into the space between her thighs. She was prepared. She held a secreted packet of coke beneath her tongue. She took it between her teeth and bit it open. Then snakelike, with her tongue, she extended the moistened powder to his nostrils.

Feeling that his hands were oddly disassociated from his

arms, and his arms from his body, Dom saw his fingers glide into the neckline of her halter. One breast was withdrawn as some of the sequins were torn off, showering in falling flashes of brilliant light. The satiny material ripped to expose the other. The girl's head swung in circles as she continued grinding her hip against him.

She spoke breathlessly in the manner of her ancient profession. "Keep going, sweetie. You turn me on."

He was now ringing her breasts as though they were pillows of cloth. Her pained face was ecstatic. As other couples departed from the makeshift dance floor, they continued.

"Make her beg for it."

"Jam your dong into her."

"Nah, he can't. Don't you see he's too spaced out? He had a snort too many."

"A thousand says he can do it within three minutes."

"No way!"

"Ya don't think so? I'll raise it to five grand. Any takers?"

"Piss off! These bitches fake it."

"Okay, ten, if it's genuine."

Suddenly another man's voice issued from close by. It was eerily familiar to Dom, but in his hazy state he couldn't place it. It was a rasping, hollow, emotionless voice. "I'll lay down twenty big ones against."

Dom attempted unsuccessfully to focus his vision, but the room was swirling.

"Twenty-five and you're on!"

The man with the rasp hissed, "I'll cover, sucker. And I'll raise. Fifty thousand says Dominic will screw up."

The waviness within his head shifted as Dom heard. It was difficult to concentrate, but he knew there was just one person alive who still called him Dominic, as his father had in the old days. *Roselli!* He wanted very much to talk, but it was incredibly difficult to form speech, to say the words: "Fifty thousand says I'll fuck her to or . . . orgas . . . sm."

"I accept," Roselli said. "You other guys can make your own wagers. The big one is between Dominic and me."

Side betting livened up. Wagers were offered, argued, and made.

Dom felt stifled as though he was gasping for breath. The girl's too-sweet gardenia perfume sickened him. He fought against vomiting. It wasn't the money riding on his performance that was nauseating him. It seemed as if a stronger inner voice spoke within his mind. Why the hell had he come here to debase himself? It was wrong of him to sacrifice his need for the one woman he admired and desired, whose soft reproachful eyes had told him of her genuine love for him.

"Gaia, Gaia," he moaned.

"My name's Carolee, honey," syruped the girl.

"Whore. Bitch," he growled. My God, was that his voice he heard? It was unrecognizable to him.

The girl's eyes were rolling in their sockets. Oh, he could make her respond all right. He knew he was a wonderful lover. Too many women who meant too little to him had told him so. In his young manhood other guys had been envious of his capacity for excess, but Dom had always made it a habit never to make a bet that he might lose. On the other hand, this tart was an actress who had become jaded from too many performances. And of course he would have to struggle to overcome the effects of cocaine, both in himself and in the girl.

The spectators formed an eager semicircle around the couple. They were chanting in unison. "Fuck! Fuck! Fuck!"

He automatically pressured the girl, his hands moving in concentric circles down the length of her, past her navel, fingers kneading her abdomen. The effort to fight lethargy within his mind seemed excruciating. But then he remembered. A bet had been made. He would win $50,000 if he succeeded, or lose that and more if he failed. It was less the sum of money than a question of pride.

He had never been an exhibitionist. Now he must go on with it. All of his senses fought against the pervasive effect of the coke and the repulsion the moaning whore inspired. Think! He must think! Wasn't there something about a time limit that had been set? A man who had appointed himself timekeeper suddenly called out: Of the three minutes, twenty-five seconds were already gone. Dom was appalled. This meant he was sure to lose. There was insufficient time to build up sexual tension within her until her dam burst and she responded in genuine frenzy.

"Hey, what's going on? His pants aren't even open. How's he gonna make it?"

"Immaculate conception."

There was general guffawing.

Sixty seconds had passed. Even if he banged her roughly up to her womb, it might not produce the result he sought.

Less than two minutes left now as the voice chanted its countdown. He felt dizzy and shook his head. Shouts issued from the sides of the room.

"Take out your schlong."

"What's the matter? Is your dick asleep?"

Goddamn it, he had no intention of exposing himself. Nor was there time for him to. He needed a sure thing. Worse, the girl was writhing, although he still hadn't touched her. No normal sexual approach would achieve orgiastic success. It was said that whores only made it with other whores.

The counting continued downward.

Suddenly he knew what he must do. With his left hand he gripped one of her arms and forced her to the floor. She lay there looking up at him, simulating passion, her legs apart, tight miniskirt drawn up, no panties. A spreading grin mocked him—waiting.

With his right hand he reached inside his jacket to his shoulder holster. The gun he carried had a five-inch barrel. The girl watched him draw it out and screamed. He bent over her, his hand clamped on her shoulder to prevent her from backing away from him on her haunches. Her eyes were wide with terror.

"This is what is going to fuck you," he heard the growling voice that didn't seem to be his say aloud.

She visibly shivered when the cold metal pressed against her vagina.

"Ever hear of Russian roulette?" Dom asked her.

She shrieked in fear, but he kept her pinned to the floor with his knees as he inserted the hard barrel into her. In . . . out . . . in . . . out. She kept shrieking.

"Don't squeeze the trigger," she begged.

"Make love to it with your cunt or I will." Relentlessly he pushed it into her, working it circularly. In. Out. In. She raised her hips and pressed her clit against the barrel. The explosion was hers; she orgasmed helplessly, cascading spasmodic shivers shaking her entire body.

Dom stood up. Momentarily, he shut his eyes. He reached in his jacket for his initialed linen handkerchief, flapped it open, then carefully wiped off the barrel of his gun. Crumpling the handkerchief, he flung it at the feet of the crowd.

He was immune to the congratulations, and the men drifted away to settle payment of their private wagers. A hand came down between his shoulder blades.

"I owe you," Roselli said.

"Whenever." Dom was intent on leaving.

"Stay a while. I want to talk to you."

Dom's head had fully cleared, but he had a throbbing headache now. "Another time. Okay?"

"Have you seen your other girlfriend lately?" Roselli was squinting, awaiting reply.

It was an ominous moment. Was Roselli testing him or asking for information? Did he know of the attempt on Gaia's life? It was a strategic standoff. Neither man cared to reveal his hand.

Dom looked at him, his face carefully blank, and said nothing. He had come here to forget Gaia, and suddenly he saw her soft, pleading face turned up to him. He scowled.

"Go ahead and leave if you want to," Roselli said in a peculiar, strained whisper. "I'm sure you know you can depend on my paying you. In full measure."

As Dom left the room he was unsure whether it was a promise or a threat.

The same man who had admitted him opened the front door. A sizable tip was obligatory. Dom sprinted down the steps and across the sidewalk to his car. The night wind whipped about his face, but the brisk air failed to refresh him. His head was still so full of cobwebs that when he unlocked his car, he accidentally set off the burglar alarm. He laughed bitterly and turned it off, starting the engine with an angry twist of his wrist. He drove away, speeding down the empty streets. He scraped the side panel when he entered his apartment building's garage. It seemed unimportant and he'd forgotten it by the time he stood in the elevator transporting him to his floor. Once inside his apartment, he went directly into the guest bathroom and retched over the open toilet bowl.

But he couldn't vomit.

He decided this was his punishment.

· 22 ·

WITHIN A SOUNDPROOF ROOM SECRETED IN A LOWER MANHATTAN skyscraper, two men sat together. They had just finished listening to a recording picked up by an extraordinarily sensitive microphone that recently had been concealed by a bogus telephone repairman in a certain East Eighties town house.

One of the men depressed a lever to rewind the tape.

"What do you make of it?"

"Interesting."

"That's for sure."

They both grinned.

"Yeah, but aside from the porn, what did we learn?"

"Well, Perrini made himself a big man with the boys, and with Roselli in particular."

"Did he? I wonder. And do you happen to know whether his gun is licensed?"

"I'll check it out."

"Do that. It could be vital. He has"—and here the man snickered slightly—"access to the Gerald girl."

· 23 ·

It was well before 8:00 a.m. when Gaia arrived at the Ferrante employees' entrance. While she waited for the guard on duty to temporarily disengage the alarm system so she might enter, a man emerged from a car parked at the curb and came up behind her.

"Are you Gay Gerald?"

She jumped slightly, frightened until he produced his police shield and identification card.

"Detective Patrick O'Reilly, NYPD," he introduced himself. "Where the hell have you been all night, if you don't mind me inquiring?"

Taken aback, she put off answering, and they entered the building together. Riding up in the elevator, she glanced sideways at the stocky plainclothesman's open, jowly, middle-aged Irish face. A forelock of salt-and-pepper hair was combed across his brow in the style of John F. Kennedy; somehow this affectation imbued him with an aspect of trustworthiness. Detective O'Reilly seemed to her a Rock of Gibraltar after the scary, sleepless night she'd just spent alone in an impersonal hotel room. She led the way to her design studio, indicating that he should take the chair while she perched on the high stool opposite him.

"I asked you where you've been," he reminded her.

"I . . . was nervous about staying in my apartment so I tried to check into the Waldorf-Astoria. They were all booked up because of a convention or whatever, so they referred me to the Lombardy."

"That's a posh hotel. So why do you look like you didn't sleep well?"

She was ready with a feisty answer, but thought better of it.

"I presume you had a good reason for leaving your apartment?"

She felt that he was treating her as though she were a culprit. This irritated her and she didn't reply.

He persevered. "Why did you run from your apartment?"

"I wish I knew." She realized how this must sound to him.

"Hey, it's *me* you're talking to. Someone who's on your side."

Gaia blinked. "I told you. I was nervous."

"We arrested your attacker. Who else are you afraid of?"

"I didn't say I was."

He nodded approvingly. He admired her gutsiness, and was genuinely sorry to have to wear her down until she answered. "Once your assailant was taken away in handcuffs, you had no reason to be afraid . . . I mean nervous. Yet for some reason you left your building by the delivery entrance."

Her head jerked toward him in surprise.

"Oh yes, we know you didn't pass by the doorman. So, I ask you again. What frightened you so much that you decided to leave . . . sneak out, as a matter of fact? Don't hide anything from me. I'm trying to help you, you know."

Gaia bristled defensively. "I was nearly murdered. Wasn't that reason enough?" No, she could not reveal her doubts about Dom to this sincere warm cop, as much as she was growing to like him and his frank open manner.

A backward wave of his hand. "Please be at ease. Why don't you work at whatever it is you designers do while we continue chatting."

She couldn't help but smile. "I like the way you call this chatting."

He grinned. "An occupational peculiarity. I urge you to bear with it. I have a damn good reason for taking this line."

The time had come for her to yield, and she knew it. "I'm sorry."

"No offense taken." His gaze roamed the studio's furnishings and came to rest upon the framed portrait.

"You?" he asked.

"It's my mother." Now what had made her say that? She'd replied too hastily. How could she expect him to believe anything she told him? She sighed and corrected herself. "Because you are a detective and would find out anyway, you may as well know that I am an orphan. I often attempt remembering my mother. That's why this drawing isn't actually her likeness, but—"

He stopped her from continuing. "I get it."

She looked at him with appreciation and relief.

"Along with everyone else on this planet, I'm informed about your inheriting this whole shebang."

Gaia stiffened. "Oh?"

He saw that his designation of the prestigious Ferrante-New York had offended her. "Don't mind me," he said hastily. "I speak in the jargon I've picked up along the path of duty."

Gaia relaxed, and they again smiled at one another.

"May I ask *you* a question?"

"Turnabout is fair play," he said.

"Who is the man who nearly killed me?"

"A hood we've long suspected has been leaving bodies in car trunks. Don't worry about him. He's safely locked up. High bail."

Her heart thumped. "Was he hired by anyone in particular?"

"He's a free-lance contract hit man, if that's what you're angling for."

It wouldn't be easy to find anything out, that was clear. She drew a deep breath, hesitating before plunging ahead. "There are three men I'd like to know more about. I just know their surnames, or what they call themselves. They were directors of the store, and I—"

"Vince Roselli, Walt Smith, and Abe Bronf. They claim to be businessmen."

She was tense. "Are they?"

Again he skirted her question. "What is Dominic Perrini to you?"

Gaia's heart skipped a beat. "My guardian. I mean, he used to be."

"I see."

She had to forcibly push herself to inquire: "Why do you want to know?"

"No reason. I'm a curious guy by nature."

She fidgeted. "Please, won't you tell me?"

"I guess he's important to you, huh?"

She made a pretense of being busily involved with an assortment of jewelers' tools atop the slate-surfaced work table. O'Reilly observed and made no further remark.

"Oh, by the way." She tried to sound casual. "I've heard of a security company by the name of Bullet. Do you happen to know anything about them?"

"I certainly do. Tell me, why do you want information of them?"

"Uh . . . Ferrante is always in need of excellent security services."

But she didn't fool him at all. She could tell by the way he looked at her. "Bullet is mob-connected. We've been tapping their phones," he said calmly.

Gaia blanched. Dom's request for someone to come to her apartment had surely been monitored.

If he noticed her dismay, he gave no sign of it. "Speaking of security," O'Reilly said, "I've got a suggestion for you. You have a man by the name of Jack Dillon heading your in-house security. I'd get rid of him if I were you."

"Why?"

"For one thing, because he was brought into the store by Roselli. There are other reasons I don't care to go into right now."

"Oh, I see . . . I appreciate your telling me."

O'Reilly stood up. "Well, I guess that's all for now." He reached into his hip pocket. "Here's my card if you ever need to reach me quickly. It's the precinct number. Day or night, they'll get a message to me."

She felt clutched by tension. "Please . . . wait—"

Already on his way out, he turned back, studying her with keen eyes. "Yes?"

It proved incredibly difficult to form the words. "Who . . . who contracted for me to die?"

He regarded her almost sadly. "Unfortunately, we real-life detectives aren't nearly so clever as the actors portraying us on television. I don't have interlocking pieces on that one yet."

Minutes after the store opened, Gaia asked one of the switchboard operators to locate Jack Dillon and summon him to her studio.

She was seated on her high stool, eye to eye with him, when he entered. He was surly and apparently suspicious. His glowering expression, the way he thrust his hands into his pockets, his unshined shoes, the shirt that should have been relegated to the laundry, all gave Gaia no compunction about what she must do. His appearance definitely wasn't in keeping with the store's image.

"As you must be aware, I am the new owner of Ferrante's." She looked away from him uncomfortably. "Necessary personnel changes have to be made because of reorganization. I'm afraid I'm going to have to let you go. I'm sorry." Gaia winced. It was much too blunt. She must school herself in how to better handle unpleasant staff situations whenever they arose.

He was mocking. "Just like that?"

She wanted to sound businesslike. "Of course you will receive severance pay."

He stood up to her. "You can't dump me."

For a moment he confounded her. When she next spoke, it

was with more spirit than she felt. "I just discharged you. Will you leave or shall I call security?"

"I *am* security."

"Not anymore." Gaia was beginning to worry. He was clearly a violent man and she was alone with him.

"Shit! I don't report to you or to old man Salinari. My orders come to me from the board of directors."

"*They* have been discharged as well, Mr. Dillon."

He looked at her in surprise.

There was a light rap on the door. "Come in." She raised her voice, thankful at the interruption.

It was Miles Tuchelin. "How ya doing? Oh, sorry. See you're busy."

"No, stay! Mr. Dillon was just leaving."

At first, Dillon hesitated. Then he said, "Sure, I'll go." As he walked out, he said, "It's your funeral!"

Miles stared after him. "What the hell's gotten into him, saying that to you?"

"I just fired him."

"Oh? Then it's just talk and not a threat."

Gaia wished she could be convinced that was so.

"Hey, you're trembling." he said.

"No, no, I'm not, but I'm glad you're here. Miles, you may have heard, there are vacancies on the board of directors. I'd like to have you become a director." She smiled. "What do you say?"

His face was radiant. "Gay, that's incredible!" If he didn't yet own the world, he secretly felt that one day he might.

"Then it's settled? You accept?"

"Count on it. You need to be surrounded by people you can trust. I want you to feel free to confide in me. Will you remember that?"

She nodded her head and he pecked a kiss on her cheek. They talked for a while about some of his plans for future Ferrante publicity. When he left he was humming a sprightly tune.

Alone, Gaia shut her eyes and massaged her temples. She wanted to compose herself and gather her thoughts before proceeding to Salinari's office. But abruptly, she opened her eyes wide.

She was recalling the look on Miles Tuchelin's face yesterday afternoon when she had left Silvia Wood to summon the guards. There they were, running toward her, guns drawn. She glimpsed Miles through the crowd. His expression appeared to be frozen, and he didn't move. She might have been in serious trouble. If he truly was her friend as he professed, why hadn't he rushed to her side? He had a strangely bitter look on his face. Had he kept away out of cowardice? Or was there another reason?

No—she couldn't let this thing destroy her instincts about people. "Gaia Gerald, you are getting decidedly paranoid!" She said it aloud, and, throwing back her shoulders, walked out.

· 24 ·

GAIA WAS EXASPERATED.

Salinari hadn't arrived at the store. Nor was he to be found in his opulent East Sixties town house, or so his British butler informed her each time she telephoned. His accent became more pronounced upon her repetitive inquiries.

At 11:30, when she was about to walk into his office, Etta Spring somewhat indignantly intercepted her at the door. The secretary curtly said that he hadn't as yet come in, and no, she hadn't any idea of where he might be.

The suspicion that she was being lied to formed in Gaia's mind. For the present, she would say nothing about it. Unable to settle down to work in her studio, she wandered through the store's selling areas. It was something to occupy her mind and keep her from dwelling upon the very real danger she'd been in the previous night.

In the second-floor table-service department, she paused to admire an assortment of opalescent bone china. Recognizing Gaia, the buyer told her that the pattern was selling briskly. It was open stock and might be reordered by customers in case of breakage. Across the floor in the silver department, she tested the weight of a magnificent chased candlestick. "Absolutely the highest-grade sterling," a saleswoman assured her. On passing a display of crystal stemware, she couldn't resist the time-honored test of flipping her fingernail against the rim of the gossamer-thin goblet. A pure ring was her reward.

At 12:40, she used a section manager's telephone to reach Etta Spring on the intercom.

"I've just this minute hung up from speaking with Mr. Salinari," the secretary averred. "He called from the club. He's lunching there and will be in the store later."

"Which club is that? I want to speak to him now."

Etta's reply was icy. "I wouldn't know." She hung up.

Containing her annoyance, Gaia resumed her restless pacing. Would she have to fire Etta as well? No, she was far too valuable—for the present at least.

She looked about the packing and shipping department, watching as an ostrich wallet with rounded eighteen-karat-gold corners was gift-wrapped. The customer, an elderly-looking blue-haired lady, beamed. Next to them, a packer was using air-puffed plastic sheeting to insulate an ornate Dresden vase against shipping damage. Placed in a silver and mauve Ferrante box, this was fitted into a cardboard carton. White poly peanuts were poured in to occupy all spaces.

At 1:25, she observed procedure in the busy credit office, where the staff was checking on customers' credit-worthiness. What were the limits to be placed upon an individual's charge account? Would an ex-husband assume payment? Did a letter of credit have authenticity?

At present, a credit scenario was being developed on a man with streaked green and blue frizzed hair who wore an eight-carat diamond fastened in his left nostril. He was a famous pop singer who had selected a $285,000 diamond necklace as a gift for his girlfriend to celebrate her pregnancy. Having offered a credit card as payment and a scribbled check to cover the balance, he awaited approval in one of the private customer rooms. An inquiry was teletyped to the credit bureau. One call was put in to the Jewelers' Credit Protection Association, another was placed to an officer at the bank his check was drawn on. Satisfactory results flowed back. The sale was approved.

One fifty-five found Gaia perched on the stool in her studio, listlessly doodling on her sketch pad. Mona Hof stuck her head in, smiling openly. Previously, the avant-garde designer had always been aloof.

"I'm ordering lunch sent in. Want anything?"

"No thanks." Gaia hadn't any appetite.

"As you say, sweetie. But we must have lunch together soon. Ta ta!" With a wave she was gone, leaving behind the scent of her heavy perfume.

Gaia started involuntarily when her phone rang. It was Dom's habit to call her once during the day at about this time. She approached the phone, apprehensive about discussing her flight from her apartment. "Hello?" A dial tone hummed in her ear. She hung up slowly and began to tremble again. The Bullet guard must have reported to Dom by now. Was it a sign of Dom's guilt that she hadn't heard from him?

After 3:00 P.M. word came from Etta Spring that Salinari was in his office.

When Gaia entered the vast ornamented room, she didn't sit on his uncomfortable "audience" chair, but walked directly to an armchair in front of his desk and sat down. She watched him force a dry little smile.

"I will be delighted to assist you in any way that I can, dear girl."

Why did she feel as if she could read his mind? The little bitch isn't going to make it easy for me, his eyes seemed to say. Maybe it was because of the way he screwed up his face when he looked at her.

"What was your college major?" he asked in his imperious manner.

She regarded him with surprise. Did he intend to issue his own questions to get her off his back? "I didn't attend college. I went to Parsons' four-year art studies program with emphasis upon jewelry design. I also took outside courses in gemology, model-making, and—"

He interrupted in a voice layered with mock concern. "Oh dear, none of those subjects is business-oriented."

Gaia could hardly believe it. She was allowing him to take

the ball away from her. Salinari, no matter what his attitude or his resentment, was her employee.

"I wanted to talk with you because I have many questions I want answered," Gaia said.

He sighed, characteristically rubbing his veiny hands.

"Why don't you discuss such matters with Dom Perrini?"

"Because I am asking you."

Gaia was satisfied that there was no way he could mistake her assumption of authority. She noted that his desk was clear of the reports and papers on which one would customarily expect to find a chief executive officer working. She surmised that the rumor she'd heard was true. Etta Spring handled the important matters that he considered were too mundane for his attention.

Gaia found herself becoming annoyed. He was vain and he was incompetent, concerned only with guarding his position. Whether or not he was privy to the undercurrents she suspected—that the jewelry business was being used as a front for more sinister purposes—he was the key to open Etta Spring's ledger and files. There, she thought, I can find my own answers. She began with an ordinary request.

Gaia asked that he summon the secretary to bring in her files on each of the store's departments. Etta quickly entered and handed Gaia a single sheet of computer paper.

FERRANTE-NEW YORK

1. Jewelry manufacturing (factory): graders, cutters, polishers, setters, goldsmiths, engravers, etc.

2. Sales departments:
   Diamond-set jewelry
   Colored-stone jewelry
   Designer collections
   Pearls
   Gold jewelry, both 14K and 18K
   Silver lighters, key rings, etc.
   Wedding and engagement rings
   Watches and clocks

Tableware: china dinner service and crystal
   Also, table silverware
   Engraved stationery

3. Bridal registry

4. Repair: both jewelry and timepieces

5. Packing and gift wrapping

6. Personal shopping service

7. Credit office

8. Design

9. Sales

10. Cashiers

11. Buyers (of unmounted stones and jewelry findings)

12. Security (including electronic and other devices)

13. Accounting: sales, billing, inventory, payroll

14. Secretarial and general office

15. Management

16. Display

17. Customer relations

18. Estate purchasing (for customer-owned jewelry)

19. Publicity

20. Janitorial and maintenance

21. Window dressing and display

Gaia put the list on the desk, facing Salinari.

"Why do you give it to me?" he asked.

"Because I am familiar with all of that. Besides, it is incomplete."

Confused, Salinari picked up the list, obviously at a loss as he scanned it. "I am sure that you're wrong."

"There is no mention, for instance, of my Àtrio."

"It would be redundant. It is covered under 'Design.' "

She purposely took her time in replying. She was following her instincts and knew she would proceed faster if she could somewhat unsettle him. He would continue trying to pressure her away from her inquiry. By acting somewhat haughty and aloof, she would be besting him at his own ploy. "I want to see records, statistics, whatever memoranda exist with respect to the Àtrio." All shyness had evaporated. Her gaze was steady.

He appeared nonplussed. "Why?"

So she was putting him on the defensive! It made her all the more determined. "Get me that information," she said firmly.

He smiled, his lips straining against the dry taut skin of his cheeks. It was obviously intended to allay any concern she might have. "You haven't had business training, my dear. You wouldn't be able to interpret the figures."

A silent voice within her head exulted; she was most assuredly on the right track. Let him convince himself she was either too stupid or too ignorant to make sense out of a ledger sheet. That way she would more quickly have it before her.

Several minutes later Etta Spring appeared carrying a bulging manila file envelope and a cloth-bound ledger. She plunked these down on the side of Salinari's desk closest to Gaia.

Out of the corner of her eye, Gaia could see Etta looking balefully toward her, but she gave no sign of recognizing this. The moment Etta left the room, she eagerly rose. There was no further need for dissembling—she bent her head with interest as she flipped the large ruled pages over, one by one. She was doing exactly what it was her right to do—exploring facts on her design sales, reading figures she had never been privy to before this moment. Following a period of silent study, she raised her head, her gaze accusingly fixed upon the old man. "There is something missing," she said.

He wrung his hands. "What's that? Oh, I am positive you are wrong."

"The cost printout. It's not here."

He regarded her anxiously. "You heard me ask Miss Spring to bring in everything on the Àtrio."

But Gaia was too engrossed to reply. She was untying the woven cotton string of the file envelope. From it, she withdrew a long computer sheet that unfolded like a paper waterfall as she lifted it.

Salinari perched his glasses on his nose. "Let me have that." He reached out to her. "It will be necessary for me to interpret it for you."

She effected a sweeping motion with one hand to gather the joined pages to her.

He sounded desperate. "Miss Spring brought that in by error. It is highly confidential."

Gaia paused, an index finger marking her place. "From *me*?"

His tongue moistened his drawn lips. "I only meant—"

She ignored him, appalled at what she read. "There are items here I don't understand . . . figures that must be false."

"Where? Let me see?"

She refused to hand it to him. He was nervously searching for his glasses. He needed time to consider how to protect himself.

She read aloud. "Outside brokerage fee, $27,500. Here again, $16,350. And again. There are more. *What brokers?* They aren't named."

Their faces were close together as they raised their heads from the printout—Gaia furious, questioning, already convinced of fraud.

She continued, "And what have brokers been recompensed *for*, when my designs are manufactured and sold to retail trade within this building?"

One of Salinari's hands gripped his expensive tie, bony fingers worrying the silk. He cleared his throat before replying. "You are placing me in a most awkward position."

"I intend to. I've just read notations that disturb me tremendously. I put it to you that these so-called unnamed brokers are nonexistent and that the commissions paid out are pure and simple fraud."

He dug his nails into his sparse hair. "And to think they assumed you'd be easy to manage."

Did *they* include Dom? Her voice was caught in her throat, but she forced herself to ask, "Who is *they*? Who engineered this?"

"The directors." His voice was pitched low.

She let that sink in. *All of them?* She yearned to ask. But she said nothing else.

An hour later, Gaia was still immersed in reading the printouts, examining each almost as fast as Etta Spring could carry the columned sheets to her. Gaia had drawn her chair closer to Salinari's ornate desk, spreading the lists across its surface. His glasses sliding down his nose, he stood behind her scanning the pages.

"I'm not an accountant," she said after a while, "but that doesn't prevent me from recognizing serious omissions. For example, I know that a magnificent emerald *suite*, necklace, bracelet, and brooch—the three pieces imported from Brazil—was recently sold by the store. However, I can find no entry of it either being placed in stock, nor of its sale. How do you explain that?"

He moistened his lips. "Let me ring for Miss Spring to come in. She evidently omitted it by error." Gaia was doubtful of that. As she entered, Salinari frowned at her. "You've been very careless with these records," he scolded.

Her face seemed to grow pudgier as she pressed her chin into her neck, her eyes watchful, regarding him with unconcealed resentment. "I have always handled business matters in the way I was instructed to," she asserted.

"Was it Mr. Salinari who gave you your instructions?" Gaia questioned.

She fidgeted. "At times—"

Salinari interrupted. "Be careful," he warned. "Don't say any more than—"

Enormously nervous, Etta Spring finished for him. "More than you want me to? Is that what you were about to say?" Her voice shook. "Mr. Salinari, I'm surprised at you, attempting to shift blame to me when, all along, I've only followed orders."

"Whose?" Gaia's voice was firm.

Etta looked at Salinari for approval, as though it was hard to break old habits. "Mr. Salinari, I may as well tell her. It's her business now. There's no way we're going to keep it from her."

He made no reply, but shuffled dispiritedly behind his desk and sank into his deep armchair. The life had completely gone out of his face. She was now certain that her suspicions were correct: There was serious fraud going on behind the front of Ferrante. She just had to find out the specifics. Her cheeks were glowing, her eyes searching Etta's face impatiently.

"Look," said Etta, "I was never involved. I mean, I never profited." She added as an afterthought, "Nor did Mr. Salinari profit directly."

Gaia saw his pupils glint through slitted eyes. He had removed his glasses and gave the appearance of a man immersed in thought.

For the moment he was so upset that he couldn't recall her name, this designer girl intruding in his domain. Didn't Roselli expect that she'd ask questions? If he wanted to make her head of the company, she'd have to know. Then, if she wouldn't go along with them . . . Salinari's thoughts were turbulent. There was no mistaking her assumption of authority. At least, he thought, she hadn't physically occupied his chair, symbol of his place of honor. He drew himself erect, smiling softly to himself. In social circles he had a reputation of being a charming man. He had carefully cultivated a flattering and cajoling demeanor. It was the reason he was accepted by those people whom he considered important. Very well, he would charm her . . . Gaia Gerald. That was her name. Yes, he would charm her; he would tempt her . . . he would divert her attention.

"My dear girl, what do you say, let's put aside this discussion. It's getting quite late. You young people are so impatient. You will find that, as you get older, you want to stretch time. Let us relax for a moment. Don't you agree we might pause? Just for a little while."

Despite her anger, he could see a softening in her expression as she gazed at him. Quite obviously, she was seeing him as an old man. So be it. He wouldn't take offense; he would take advantage. He let his hands tremble, his head shake. She was turning her inquisitiveness aside, however temporarily. But how? Ah yes, the *Avanti*. The precious *Avanti*.

"I take great pride in our large pink diamond. How wonderful that you thought of the name for it. Splendid, simply splendid."

Gaia slightly nodded.

He was a bit disappointed. Well, he really couldn't expect her to take the bait so quickly. He continued his ploy.

"It has occurred to me that you are the proper designer to create a mounting for the *Avanti*."

He watched her eyes enlarge. Good! She was biting.

"I couldn't accept the assignment. I respect Michael Vanderman too much. He is head designer and it is, by right, his project." Her voice was firm, but didn't he hear something plaintive in it?

"Then I will speak to him."

"No! As a junior designer, I would never presume to take over from Mr. Vanderman."

"Dear girl, you are responsible to no one. You own the store."

"Which is all the more reason I hold him in respect. His jewelry designs are world famous. Do you suppose I am about to usurp his authority?"

"You are so closely connected with the *Avanti*. I am sure he recognizes your devotion to the gem." He could see by her reaction that the diamond enthralled her. If he could just get her to start talking about it, he felt she'd be so swept up that she'd neglect her prying questions. "Please"—he endeavored to sound sincere—"let me at least hear your ideas for the stone."

"*You* want the *Avanti* to be used in jewelry?" He could discern scornful accusation in her voice.

"I am profit-minded."

"It would be ponderous to wear, a magnet for thieves and, more than likely, would be locked away in the purchaser's vault while a copy was substituted for use. I think that, like Tiffany's large canary diamond, the *Avanti* should be placed on view within the store as a mark of Ferrante excellence."

"I know that. That's what we've always said."

"You were always against it," Gaia reminded him.

He tensely opened and flexed his fingers, resting his wrists upon the desk. He would try flattering her for her intelligence. "My dear, you have a far greater feel for the *Avanti* mystery than I. I admit that I considered the Ferrante silver candlestick motif sufficient recognition for the store." He attempted to conceal his bitterness upon being overruled. He intended to cajole her. "Clearly, I was wrong. Won't you share your knowledge with me?"

She hesitated. "I'd rather continue hearing about the computer list."

"Please . . ." He tried to sound feeble. "I'm not a young man. Sorry, my dear, but I'm very tired." He observed her glance at her watch.

"Will you be here early tomorrow morning?"

"Absolutely."

"Because it's too important to put off."

"I agree." So far, so good! He had bought himself time. This evening he intended telephoning Dom Perrini. Yes, Dom would advise him how to handle it. In the meantime, he intended to appear friendly to Gaia. "Allow me to give you a lift home in my car. My chauffeur will be waiting in front of the store." Salinari confidently anticipated her refusal. She had a tendency to work late.

"Why, thank you."

He was taken aback. Gaia returned to her studio to get her coat. When Salinari stalked past Etta, he was so annoyed that he ignored bidding her good night.

She watched him pass her desk. *Arrogant stuffed shirt!* Etta thought. He was ignoring her as though she didn't exist. How eager he was to attribute blame to her for past irregularities in the store. As though any of this was her fault. She was the secretary who was supposed to shut her eyes while others made their fortunes.

She noted that Gaia Gerald had left before he did. Probably she'd still be in her studio when Etta herself called it a day. She decided that she'd stop in and reiterate her loyalty to the heiress. Salinari proved today that he never appreciated her faithful service.

It was then that she remembered. Oh well, she hadn't mentioned it to him.

Mr. Roselli had telephoned. Nothing to bother Mr. Salinari with, he told her. He was wondering whether he planned on using his limousine when he went home that afternoon.

She told him, "Yes."

He hung up.

Etta shrugged. It was none of her business.

· 25 ·

The limousine was a charred, surreal skeleton. Across the sidewalk, a dented, twisted newspaper stand was an eerie mirror image of the explosive power that had destroyed the car. There was a horrible smell, and singed bits of newspapers and magazines were strewn across the pavement. The newsstand owner, an elderly blind man, had survived. Cowering beside him, his muscular German shepherd continued to whine.

Firemen brought up a hose and sprayed the automobile's heated steel. While one police officer put in a radio call for bomb-squad detectives, the other, with fire department assistance, pried open a rear door with a crowbar. The stench of burned flesh within was nauseating. With a handkerchief held to his nostrils, the cop took a cursory look.

"Dead," he said, to no one in particular.

The other officer by now had his notebook open and was questioning the newsstand man.

"As I told you, my sense of hearing is sharper than most people's. The car—I could tell by the sound of it—was a limo . . ." His voice faded.

"Go on." The officer wanted to get the witness's statement down as quickly as possible.

The blind man had bent to comfort his dog. "There, Max. It's okay. We're alive!"

"If you'd continue telling me—"

"Oh, sure. Where was I?"

"About it being a limo."

"It pulled up to the curb, y'know, and this one guy who must have been the chauffeur comes rushing out."

"Any impressions of him?"

"Mister, I can't see."

"Yes, but—"

"I remember the voice. Yeah, that and the door slamming behind him. Real solid impact. Big car, as I said. So, anyway, I already had my hand on the *Post*, expecting he wanted the final edition. Instead, he whizzes by me yelling, 'Duck yer head under the counter if you wanna live.' "

"Would you recognize his voice if you heard it again?"

"I'll never forget. It had a rough edge . . . nasty . . . know what I mean?"

"Anything else?"

"You bet! I ducked, grabbing my dog. Moments later . . . boom! Loud enough to make me deaf. Last thing I need is another handicap. Know what I mean?"

· 26 ·

MERRILL ROSS SLAMMED DOWN THE PHONE RECEIVER, CONSIDER-
ably annoyed. For the third time since 3:00 P.M. he had attempted telephoning Gaia Gerald at the store. Again the operator had switched his call to Etta Spring's extension. In her
husky smoker's voice, the secretary reiterated that Ms. Gerald
was unable to be reached. She was in conference with Mr.
Salinari. Ross' clipped response was controlled, indicating
that although he was infuriated, he wasn't about to unleash
rage upon a mere employee who was, doubtless, only following a superior's orders. Merrill Ross preferred dealing with
those who had power.

Ambition burned in him like an obsession. He had placed
the phone back in its cradle quietly, but he was seething with
frustration. He sat at his desk doodling tight pyramids, one
overlapping the other, on a yellow ruled legal pad, a habit he
had whenever he became engrossed in deep thought. He was
thinking just then of the fact that he still hadn't achieved
partnership at Bari & Battaglia. There was no doubt in his
mind that soon, very soon, he would be promoted. They had,
after all, just assigned him the Ugo Ferrante last will and
testament.

When he was first assigned the Ferrante estate, working in
concert with the Italian lawyer, Giuliano Rinzini, he pri-

vately considered it incredible that an orphan would material-
ize to inherit the wealth of the American portion of the jewelry store business. She had to be part of some fraud. But
when he met Gaia Gerald, he was impressed by her honesty;
if she was caught up in a conspiracy, she was its unknowing
pawn. He recalled the astonishing green flecks in her hazel
eyes when she turned her beautiful face toward him. Possibly
it was the way the lights were set in the ceiling of the private
viewing rooms, the intensely concentrated spotlights strategically located to spectacularly display the rarest of jewels.

After spending an hour doing battle with that Italian
virago, Gaia's gentle loveliness was overwhelming. He'd
taken in the perfect face, the slim figure with its ripe though
subtle curves. He had felt the familiar tightening of the muscles in his loins, and now he felt himself growing hard again,
remembering the contours of her body. In the small viewing
room at the store, she had merely glanced in his direction,
then looked quickly away. He would change that, he decided,
rubbing the smooth surface of the pencil against his lips.

None of his past romantic relationships had begun with
such initial impact upon him. But he must proceed with con-
summate caution. Overnight, she had become a rich and powerful heiress. He couldn't afford to come on to her like a
caveman.

He glanced at his desk clock. It was a few minutes before
five o'clock. There were the papers he needed her to sign,
already typed and on his desk. Merrill Ross decided he would
personally take them over to the store. He could explain any
questions she might have. He told himself that his being with
her was necessary. After she signed, he would be there to
notarize her signature.

He departed the Park Avenue office building, walking
swiftly uptown. Despite the brightness of the late afternoon
sun, he felt somewhat chilled. Hunching his shoulders
slightly, he walked with the long swift strides of a tall man
until he swung into the ornate Fifth Avenue entrance of
Ferrante-New York.

He found Etta Spring at her desk, but she looked blankly

at him when he demanded to see Ms. Gerald. Her eyes were rimmed with red. Her mouth gaped open. On the desk top a phone receiver lay as if her hand had been too weak to support it.

"Hallo, hallo," a voice issued from it.

Ross bent across the desk and picked it up, listening to the male voice. He answered, "Yes, can I help you?"

"Who the hell is this?" The caller sounded impatient.

"Who are you?"

"Detective O'Reilly, NYPD Homicide."

His throat tightened as he identified himself.

"This concerns Gaia Gerald," the detective said. "Can you come right over to the station? There are some questions about her inheritance I'd like to clear up."

Merrill found it difficult to breathe. "You're from homicide? Did something happen?"

"Yeah, I appreciate your concern but I'm not about to handle this over the phone. How quickly can you make it here?" He gave him the precinct address.

"I'll be right over."

· 27 ·

It fell to Miles Tuchelin to make funeral arrangements.

At first, locating Mrs. Salinari was a problem. Then, after several telephone messages had been left for her at an exclusive women's reducing spa in the Southwest, she returned his call.

"This is unsettling news," she lamented. "No, it's impossible for me to fly back to New York today. Such a shock! I need more than ever to continue with the spa's regimen, to calm me. I am left bereft and I must think of myself . . ." Her voice trailed off, creating a greater distance between them than the geographical one.

"The service and interment are scheduled for Friday," Miles said.

"So little time," she moaned. "What do I need to . . . prepare?"

"Mrs. Salinari, the preparations have already been taken care of."

He listened to her vexed exclamation. "What am I going to take to wear? All I brought is casual wear!" There was a tinge of rising hysteria in her voice.

After she'd hung up, Miles disgustedly slammed down his phone. He didn't suppose for a moment that she was coming apart out of grief for her dead husband. She hadn't actually said it—but he could just hear her thinking that she would go out immediately to shop for a smart black outfit.

Sure, the old man wasn't exactly lovable, but neither was his widow.

Vincent Bregna Salinari's death produced no outpourings of sorrow from anyone in the store. Etta Spring was in shock, of course. But Miles didn't know whether it was from sorrow. Salinari had been generally and intensely disliked by all of the staff.

Miles steeled himself to complete his planning. It was a depressing chore, and for a man not given to introspection, Miles was extraordinarily melancholy. If only he could speak to Gaia of the dark images that flooded his mind. But there was no Gaia. He was anticipating a summons to the morgue to identify her remains.

How greatly he missed her already. He wandered into the empty space of her studio and sadly gazed about the small enclosure as if to conjure up her presence. He fingered her pencils and then took up the framed portrait from her work table. He looked searchingly at it as if seeking some elusive clue. Her possessions were so irrevocably imbued with her personality that he had the odd illusion that, at any moment, she might walk in and discover him fondling her property. Would she have been angry with him? All that Miles could have said in his defense was that at this moment she seemed to him to have been the one woman with whom he felt an emotional involvement. Did this woman seem more real to him than any other because he had been immersed in creating copy about her for the news services—which had already dubbed her the "Cinderella Girl"?

His eyes welled up with tears and he sank into her little chair.

· 28 ·

ACROSS THE ATLANTIC, SILVIA FERRANTE DI MALVESTITI WOOD
had made herself comfortable in her late father's elaborate
villa, situated on a protected estate off the historic Via Appia
Antica. Located several miles south of Rome in rolling green
terrain, the area had more recently become known as the
Beverly Hills of Italy, attracting a number of international as
well as Italian motion picture stars.

She made it known to the servants immediately upon her
arrival that she must henceforth be addressed as Principessa.
It pleased her that her daughter, Mara, had chosen to remain
in her city apartment. Time enough to meet her tomorrow at
the church, where they would be the only mourners from
Ugo's family. Influential and society people would also attend
the Mass, and she reminded herself to insist that Mara be
appropriately dressed in black. She didn't intend to be embarrassed by her. Afterward, when his remains had been placed
in their final repository within the tunneling catacombs on
the estate, then Mara could wear her gaudy clothes, or damn
well nothing at all.

Silvia was in high spirits, but carefully assumed a saddened
demeanor when another condolence call came for her. Her
head cradling the telephone, she glanced down at the pile of
newspapers on the table. The Italian wire services had carried

a graphic description of the car that was blown to bits in New York, and of the two passengers who had been tragically killed in the explosion. She decided that a long hot soak was what she needed, and excusing herself from the caller, she hung up and ran swiftly up the stairs.

B·O·O·K

II

· 29 ·

Rome

Dom Perrini's corner suite on an upper floor of the opulent Hotel Excelsior was situated beneath a dome-shaped turret, integral to the richly embellished architecture of arches, massive stonework entablatures, and ornate balconies of the hotels lining the Via Veneto. Above the active street, strung up on staffs extending from the massive building, several Italian flags were flapping in a brisk breeze, and above the entrance were banners honoring visiting dignitaries. Prominent among these was the American stars and stripes: Dom Perrini was a frequent and honored guest.

Should he step out on either of his balconies, he would overlook *ristoranti* lining the opposite side of the street, their tables spreading onto patches of pavement in such profusion that, with their colorful Cinzano umbrellas, they resembled so many riotous mushrooms sprung up following a spring rain shower. From the other balcony he could look down directly into the walled verdant courtyard of the American embassy, where tallest among all species of trees were the palms. The building, the Palazzo Margherita, was likely older than the United States.

At the open double windows looking outward, he stood transfixed, in his maroon silk robe, scanning the panorama of the city. This was his habit each time he arrived in Rome, and the view never failed to fascinate. Even the cacophonous traffic noises and the *furioso* drivers were a delight when he was this far removed from their endangerment. Out in the distance were rooftops of varying heights, a spectrum of ancient buildings in matte hues of ochre, oxidized red, and tones of brown. Closer in, the colors were subtly altered with washes of more delicate tints distilled by medieval and Renaissance stone: pinks into hints of purple, tans dulled by the dust of history into brownish grays. Churches dotted the landscape. In the piazzas, fountains spurted water sprays among grandiose displays of statuary in otherwise mundane neighborhoods. Ancient cobblestones still paved these areas and were ridged from the wheels of long-ago chariots.

It was wonderful to be in a city with almost three thousand years of history, where the past merged with contemporary life, where serene villas existed in harmony with a neighboring *caffè*, where people sat eating little pizzas or drinking cappuccino. *Ristoranti* exuded the beguiling aroma of garlic-laced olive oil, and everywhere aromatic wines flowered the air. Dom watched the activity at Harry's Bar, noting the enthusiastic handshaking whenever people met and the kissing upon their leavetaking. He turned away from the window, thinking that despite his ancestry, he was as much a *turista Americano* as any other visitor who traveled here for more innocent purposes than he.

The telephone began ringing in short shrill bursts. "*Pronto.*"

It was Giuliano Rinzini. He told Dom of Silvia's insistence that they discuss the estate. "She knows about the limousine disaster in New York," he said, "and she's been absolutely intent on its implications for the inheritance."

"When will you meet with her?" Dom asked.

"Shortly. Before the funeral. She may be with her daughter, Mara."

"Does that matter? From what I've heard of Mara, she'd rather be in someone's bed than fully dressed anywhere, especially in any office."

"I didn't say that her presence would change matters.

Still," Rinzini suggested, "it might be wise for you to be present. Let the girl flirt with you while I draw out the mother."

"I can't. You know very well that I am not alone."

"I forgot about that for a moment."

"I don't know how you could." Dom was testy.

"*Chiedo scusa.*"

"No harm done," Dom said. But he was frowning.

In the adjoining chamber there were sounds of movement. The woman sharing his bed had evidently awakened. He heard water running in the bathroom. He would allow her to freshen herself. He was always a considerate lover, aware of the importance women place on appearance. But he found himself counting the minutes, eager to return to her side.

Gaia had responded ecstatically to their lovemaking. She fully gave herself to him, delighting in his gratification, and responded with her own overwhelming rapture.

When he'd first entered her room in the early evening and looked down upon her lying in the bed, she had slipped the sheet from her bare breasts, her arms extended to him. He'd uttered a gasp and was quickly beside her.

"This is wrong," he remembered saying, and she assured him it wasn't.

At the start, to lie close in embrace, to kiss deeply, gazing into one another's eyes, and soon to explore one another's bodies, to kiss and touch and caress and rub. To experience the sensation of melting and burning at the same moment. To have no shame; whatever they did with one another was right. She adored him with her encompassing tongue, and nearly fainted when he sucked the sweetness of her body, her breasts, her stomach, her groin. He savored the juices between her legs and they were swept on the crest of uncontrollable waves to the heights of passion. His organ thrust deep within her. She twisted as helplessly as a leaf in the wind. It became a gale, unimaginably intense. She screamed at the peak of her delight. He shuddered, groaning. They were lying on the wave-receding beach. Together.

* * *

He had always been a loner, shunning emotional involvement; his life-style made that an inevitability. The act of
fornication was performed with a skilled player equally uninvolved. Because he realized this, he was never fully gratified.
It was never deeply satisfying, only a much-needed release of
physical tension, like a particularly rigorous form of exercise.

When he reentered the bedroom, Dom knew in his heart
that their coming together was a joining of love he could
never again deny himself. Her freely given response to his
lovemaking was not sham any more than was his own emotion. When he had thrust into her, every movement of her
body had caressed him in the sweet natural reply of a loving
partner; and when her warm wet walls had clasped him with
a hunger that intensified his pleasure, it was beyond any
experience he could recall. When he let go at last, it was a
release into the utmost limits of joy. For the first time in his
life, Dom had total concern for the woman who lay beneath
him. Afterward he covered her face, neck, arms, and body
with kisses that were the gratitude of a man awakening into
love.

Now, in the light of morning, her nudity was silhouetted
against sunlight filtering through gossamer curtains. She una-
shamedly turned to him, holding a hairbrush in one hand,
fluffing up her dark hair with the other. He looked appreciatively at her slim body, with its ripe womanly curves. Her
breasts were high and round, her hips sleek and firm. She
gathered her hair on top of her head and held her arms there
so he could keep looking at her that way. He smiled. "So
you're finally awake," he said.

She let her arms fall to her sides and her hair came tumbling down.

"*Cara*, you are so beautiful." He opened his arms and she
came to him. "You must be chilled." He untied the sash and
drew his robe around them both.

She tittered. "How wicked of you and how perfectly delicious."

"Listen here, young lady, no more sex."

"Nevermore?" She playfully poked him in the ribs.

He chuckled at her antics. "Stop that! You know as well as I that we have an appointment we must keep this morning."

Thoughtful and suddenly somber, she replied, "As if I could forget."

He gently released his hold on her.

She shook her head. "I'm not sure that I ought to go."

Dom silently studied her. "You're up to it, aren't you?"

"I can't convince myself that I belong at Ugo Ferrante's funeral. There'll likely be many people present who won't accept me as a relative. Then, too, they will have heard about the car bombing, and"—her voice cracked—"how Gaia Gerald was fatally injured."

She spoke her name as if it were a question. She wanted desperately to explain her fear so that he wouldn't fault her—this man who'd made exquisite love to her throughout the night, who would now certainly turn from her if she failed him. She decided that he was right. And besides, she must accompany him if he thought staying meant she was a coward. "When must we leave?" she asked, keeping her tone even.

"We'll have to hurry. I want to arrive at the church just before the Mass commences. That way there will be no chance of prior contact with anyone—for them to guess about you."

"You mean, to decide whether or not I'm the granddaughter," she said glumly.

Seated beside him in a rental car, she was quiet as he skillfully maneuvered through the erratic traffic. The nearer they got to their destination, the more her stomach churned, and she found herself clenching her hands, absolutely oblivious to the crowded beauty of the streets.

He was watching her out of the corner of his eye. "Are you okay?"

Was it her imagination, or was his manner too glib? Her voice was barely above a whisper. "I can manage to go through with it."

"Good girl."

The church of St. Luigi dei Francesi was built of ochre-tinted stone, and loomed at the far end of a cobbled piazza, now flooded with sun as residents conducted their ordinary businesses—selling fruits, vegetables, and baked food near its central statue-adorned fountain. Close by the church were parked limousines, chauffeurs lounging beside their vehicles to take advantage of the bright morning. Fashionably dressed women, most of them garbed in black, some but not all accompanied by male escorts, were beginning to ascend the steps of the church. Many of these had at one time or another been bedded by the deceased jeweler. They had come not so much to mourn as to observe, with darting inquisitive glances, who else among their social set was present. They were lavishly adorned with Ferrante-Roma jewelry, none of the pieces gifts from il Principe, but sales he had effected by pandering to the women's covetousness as well as their desire to please their bodies.

When the last among the congregants had trailed inside, Dom parked at the foot of the steps. Gaia sat unmoving, and he came around to her side of the automobile to open the door. She hesitated briefly, looking upward at the church.

Who would accept her as the American granddaughter, and who would not?

Everyone thought she was dead.

But it was time to think of another's death. "Gaia, come," said Dom, reaching into the car with a big strong hand. She took it and stepped out of the car, blinking in the bright sunlight.

· 30 ·

SEVERAL REPORTERS AND PHOTOGRAPHERS WERE GROUPED AT THE
base of a short flight of worn stone steps leading to the sixteenth-century church. It would be impossible to enter without passing them. They had earlier pounced on Silvia with
their flashbulbs popping and notebooks open, but she had
waved them away and pressed her daughter to hasten on—
although Mara would have paused. There were occasional
bursts of intense brightness as one or another of the mourners
had their pictures snapped while ascending to the open metal-
girded wooden doors. When they saw Dom Perrini emerge
from the car, they rushed forward eagerly. They were acting
on a tip from one of their wire services, the one that originated in New York. It had intimated that an intriguing correction relating to a prior news item could be revealed by
pressing Perrini for what he knew.

A limousine leased to Ferrante-New York had been
bombed two days ago and word had spread that the heiress,
Gaia Gerald, perished along with Vincent Bregna Salinari,
chairman of the board and president of the jewelry firm. This
had never officially been denied. Detective Patrick O'Reilly,
when interviewed later, stated that the news media had not
deliberately been misinformed, and it was not incumbent
upon the NYPD to correct the media's wrong assumptions.

Dom was tugging Gaia after him as the reporters swirled around them. They were getting nowhere and it became plain that no headway would be made unless she responded to the questions thrust at her, posed in rapid, excited, too loud Italian, not all of which she could understand. She cringed at being the center of attention, but decided not to delay the moment of truth.

She admitted who she was.

"*Si, mi chiamo Gaia Gerald.*"

Two afternoons ago in New York, when Gaia had rushed back to her design studio to grab her coat because Vincent Bregna Salinari had offered her a lift home in his limousine, she was positive that Etta Spring had somehow surmised—at least that was how Gaia interpreted the secretary's frozen look of disapproval. But when she'd sought to find the limousine waiting at the Fifth Avenue curb, it was nowhere visible.

After waiting some ten minutes she'd started looking for a taxi, and running on her high heels down half a block along Fifty-fifth Street, she pursued and hailed one—a triumph in the afternoon rush hour. It was only when she was about to step into the cab that she recognized Salinari's limousine parked in front of the employees' door, farther down the block. Really, did he expect her to use that means of exit from the store, now that she owned Ferrante-New York? Piqued, she drove away in the taxi—and saved her life.

She had first given the cabbie her home address, but changed her mind and redirected him to the Lombardy. He glared at her reflection in his rearview mirror. Taxi cabs made their best money on short hauls. This stupid lady was making him backtrack more than ten blocks.

Not until she was safely inside a pleasant guest room with the door bolted did Gaia begin to feel secure. It was during that evening that she finally admitted to herself Dom Perrini had connections she could speculate upon.

Ravenously hungry, she'd ordered a hamburger from room service, and fifteen minutes later, a knock sounded. She opened the door, her mouth salivating with anticipation, but was startled to see Dom standing before her. She regarded him in astonishment as he swiftly entered, first glancing to either side of the corridor as if he wanted to be certain no one had observed him.

She was suffused by panic. When he made no threatening move toward her, she grew somewhat composed, although remaining wary.

"Lucky that you went into hiding," he said. "Someone is likely seeking your whereabouts right now."

"I'm not very well hidden if you found me," she couldn't resist saying.

"I suppose you heard what happened to Salinari in his car."

"No, what happened?" she asked.

"Do you have a passport?" He ignored her question.

She was bewildered and didn't answer.

Dom was impatient. "Well, do you?"

"No. But why—"

He walked over to the telephone. "I'll contact someone who can do me a favor. You have to be supplied in a rush—it's an emergency. Maybe under a pseudonym. The way things are here, you'll be safest out of the country."

A brief almost cryptic conversation followed. He immediately tapped out another number and said he'd need two first-class accommodations to Rome for late that night. Another rap on the door. "Who is it?" he called out.

"Room service."

"Did you order?" Dom asked her.

"Yes."

"You shouldn't have. That was stupid. Go into the bathroom. Even if it is a waiter, don't come out until he's gone."

She moved slowly, dazed.

"Hurry! We haven't got all night." He gave her a tiny shove. "Lock the door," he hissed once she was inside. "Okay, you can come out now," he called shortly. "Your dinner's here."

"I have no appetite." The food no longer tempted.

"None?"

"No. I couldn't eat. Really."

He lifted the domed silver cover. "It looks great," he said sarcastically, looking at the hamburger underneath.

"I just wanted something simple," she told him. "Why don't we share it? It smells appetizing."

"Can't. I just grabbed a bite."

Somehow, Gaia pictured the way it had been whenever she and Dom were in a restaurant together and beautiful women at nearby tables glanced meaningfully at him despite their escorts. She shook her head and the image dissolved. There was too much to think of that was more immediate. She picked up the hamburger and took a bite.

The phone rang. Dom answered. "Okay, I understand," he said into the mouthpiece. "And thanks. I owe you one." He addressed Gaia. "We'll be leaving here in half an hour. I'll settle your bill."

"I paid in advance . . . no luggage."

"Of course. Have you a scarf you can tuck around your face?"

"Yes, in my coat pocket. Dom, what—"

"Good. I don't want you to be recognized. I'm leaving my car in a garage and we'll taxi out to Kennedy. When I was looking for you, luckily I called the desk clerk here. Next time you decided to vanish, *cara*, don't do it with such an obvious pseudonym. Gale Geraci. Really!"

A chill traversed her body. Dom noticed.

"Are you all right?"

"Fine." Her back turned to him as she reached into the closet for her coat.

"Let me help you on."

The soft bulk of the fur masked her trembling.

When they were seated together in the cab, she remembered her first ride with him to the airport in Chicago. She'd taken nothing with her then, either. Damn, damn, she mustn't think of the past. "Dom, what is going on? Please, tell me."

"First tell me why you did not ride home in Salinari's limo."

"Well"—her voice was low-pitched, hardly above a whisper—"when I left the building from the Fifth Avenue side, I realized his car wasn't anywhere in sight. So I decided he had gone without me. Then on the side street, a cab discharged a passenger, so I ran for it."

"And saved your life," Dom said, looking searchingly at her, as if memorizing her face. He took her hand in his and told her what had happened.

Tears unexpectedly welled in Gaia's eyes. She found it impossible to reply.

He put her arm around her, drawing her close. "I'm going to hurry you through the air terminal; your scarf will shield your face. We have clearance to board immediately, ahead of the other passengers. Someone from the State Department will be at the plane to snap your picture and affix it to your passport, which will then be handed to you. Since this is all happening at the last moment, I'm afraid it will have to be under your name. After that we'll settle into our seats until the plane takes off. We'll arrive in Rome at about ten A.M. Italian time. You'll have some time to rest. The next day you are going to attend your grandfather's funeral." He took her hand.

My grandfather's funeral, she was thinking. *It might have been my own.*

· 31 ·

THE SERVICE WAS APPROPRIATELY SOLEMN. A YOUTHFUL CHOIR
alternated with the liturgic Latin. It was a ceremony befitting
a prince of the realm, however spurious il Principe di Corchese's title claim might be.

In death as well as in life, the bogus prince Ugo Ferrante
had the loyalty of the aristocracy. The Roman and New York
stores were thought of as a single entity, until Ugo's will
revealed otherwise. There was much discussion and whispered speculation on this topic during the ceremony. But no
one in attendance at St. Luigi dei Francesi came close to
guessing the true reason for the stores' separation. Perhaps
this was because none present had ever patronized the original small shop in the medieval Jewish quarter of Rome—or
would both remember and admit to going there. No, the talk
buzzed with comparisons to other international jewelry establishments such as Buccellati, Bulgari, and Van Cleef &
Arpels.

They had come because it was important for them to be
seen; the funeral was as much of a social event as any of the
charity cocktail parties, fashion shows, luncheons, or formal
balls of the season just commencing in October. Even the
Church recognized the significance of the event; two high

Church prelates, both given to frequenting the best functions, were to assume token roles in the service.

Dom led Gaia into the ornate basilica. They were among the last arrivals. She fervently wished that he wouldn't take her down the entire length of the long central aisle to be ogled by the whole crowd. Her cheeks burned, feeling the hard inquisitive gazes as he persevered toward the altar, past a succession of chapels with superb paintings and remarkably preserved frescoes. She caught just a bit of some of the caustic remarks: Her Italian wasn't very good; she might not understand all the words, but the implications were clear.

"Look! It's the American girl."

"Do you suppose this tramp was another of his mistresses?"

"She claims she's his granddaughter."

"Hah!"

"Nice little pussy I bet she's got."

"Shut up, will you?"

"What will Silvia do?"

"Well, knowing her . . . something deadly."

A ripple of laughter. It was the laughter that set off Gaia's nerves.

She forced herself to look straight ahead as they marched up the aisle. Dom selected a front pew directly opposite the one where Silvia sat with a quiet young woman. Perhaps that is my cousin, she thought, with the first glimmer of hope she'd felt all morning.

The jeweler's ornate coffin was a work of art in itself. It was positioned on the altar in such a way that his face could be seen by the mourners. Gaia started in rapt fascination, oblivious to everything but the powerfully contoured dead face. Even with the eyelids drawn shut, his face stiff, Ugo Ferrante in death still projected a brutish vitality. The bushy eyebrows, his large nose, a strong jaw, sensual lips set in an expression of frozen contempt revealed an aura of the man's personality, a stubbornness that survived the flesh. Gaia caught her breath, clenching her fists. Larger than life, she thought spontaneously, and an involuntary sob escaped her, surprising her as much as it did Dom. Inquisitive necks craned, well-coiffed heads turned in her direction, and Gaia instinctively lowered her own face in an attitude of prayer. *He doesn't look like me!* she was thinking.

Dom nudged her as the congregation kneeled. When they raised themselves from the kneelers, she became aware of a disruption in the pew immediately behind them. She craned her neck to see a huge unkempt man forcing his way to an unoccupied place in back of Gaia. The mean look he gave her was so acutely penetrating that she lowered her eyes and quickly turned away. A flush suffused her. Was it her imagination, or did he share one face with the deceased Ugo Ferrante?

The moment the funeral was over she looked back again, intending to scrutinize his face another time, but, oblivious to those he was crushing in his haste to depart, he was already pushing toward a side aisle. She saw only that he wore some sort of mountaineering garb. She and Dom remained, unable to exit quickly in the slow-moving crowd. She remained silent, deciding not to speak of what she'd seen. Besides, wasn't it just her overwrought state that caused the stranger's leonine face to assume characteristics it didn't possess?

Around them, the women were chatting enthusiastically of other topics, frequently eyeing one another's Ferrante signature pieces. The buzz of conversation had already shifted from the deceased. They would not follow the procession in their chauffeur-driven limousines out into the country along the Via Appia Antica to the Corchese estate. It wasn't worth the trip, they agreed, to see where its late owner would be interred—within the catacombs of the villa that lay spread like tree roots beneath the surface property, in twisting, largely unexplored passages shored up with blocks of marble.

In New York, when Gaia had first learned of Ugo Ferrante's death, her first reaction was one of enormous sadness. But here in Rome, she was suffused by indignation and fury toward him. Was he so unfeeling a man as to presume that by conveying half of his fortune to her it made up for the years she believed herself an orphan? By what right had he denied her knowing him while he lived, if indeed he was her grandfather? All of her life Gaia had hoped that someday she would discover her antecedents. Now legally acknowledged, she couldn't convince herself that she belonged.

The bright sunlight was at its glaring noontime peak when Dom and Gaia emerged from the church. Gaia looked for the man she'd glimpsed in church, but in vain, for although she had a view of the entire square from the top of the steps, he was nowhere in sight. Dom whipped out his dark glasses and steadied her as she precariously felt her way down the pitted stone steps on her thin heels. Below, critically observing her descent, stood Silvia. The young woman beside her was slim, extraordinarily pretty, laced with sensuousness. Her eyes were alert, her features intelligent, although, on closer scrutiny, as sharp as a feral animal's. Gaia's heart sunk. This woman would not be a friend, she knew. And, as with Ugo Ferrante, there was no discernible resemblance to her that might prove them to be truly cousins.

Mara di Malvestiti petulantly removed her head scarf and a blond tousled mane sprang unfettered to beneath her shoulders in a sun-glinted shower. She was looking toward Gaia; Silvia was obviously pointing her out. Silvia's countenance underwent an angry change as Mara, attired in a miniskirted black suit, lace hose, and bare high-heel sandals, sprinted toward Gaia, arms held outward in a gesture of welcome.

"Ah, my cousin," Mara exclaimed. "I have been so curious to meet you." She spoke in a clear, if slightly accented English.

Silvia angrily shouted, "Mara, come back here."

Her daughter winked conspiratorially at Gaia. "I think it's fun that you've given my mother the jitters."

"I never intended—"

Mara interrupted. "Don't apologize. I find it positively delicious."

Dom interrupted, at the same time opening the rental car door. "Ladies, another time. We have to be on our way."

But Mara was not to be put off. Her eyes, ringed with kohl,

had the empty shine of someone high on narcotics. "Want to have fun? I'll tell you the hottest places to visit after midnight. Chances are, you'll find me dancing—unless I'm lying on one of the side couches being fucked. For me, that's what life is all about. Sometimes I get laid three, four times a night, and the joke is that it is hardly ever in my own bed." She began to laugh uproariously. "Isn't that funny?" Tears of laughter escaped her eyes and she used the back of one hand to wipe them away, smearing the kohl in a streak almost to her hairline.

Silvia's voice was strident. "*Andiamo*, Mara."

"*Sì, sì, subito!*" she called back. And under her breath, "Fuck you."

Gaia said uncertainly, "It was nice to meet you."

"You understand." Mara leaned toward her in a confidential attitude, "I don't give a shit about your inheritance. I don't live to accumulate money the way she does, the high and mighty bitch! All I want out of life is great cock." She appraised Dom. "I'll bet you've got a wonderful one, *amante appassionato! Eh?*"

"Let's go now, Gaia, shall we?"

She nodded, sliding into the seat alongside his.

Mara watched, and shouted after them, "Why are you running from me?"

Dom started the engine and began slowly easing a path through the crowded piazza to reach one of the streets spoking outward from it. They could hear her through the closed windows. "Don't leave." She shouted, "You have nothing to fear from me. It is Mama who vows she'll murder you."

Gaia turned to Dom. "Do you think Silvia could have been the one who hired that . . . that thug to kill me?"

He shook his head. "I doubt it. After all, she was en route to Rome when you were attacked.

"Yes, but didn't I tell you? She was in the New York store on the previous day. We had a confrontation when she tried to stuff a handbag full of jewelry."

His attitude was attentive and thoughtful. "Really? I didn't know."

"How much she must hate me. Oh, why did you take me to the funeral? What did it prove? Besides, you assured me I would be safe in Rome."

"I had to get you out of New York. You certainly weren't safe there."

"Yes, but why here? Here I am on public display!"

He grew angry. "Goddamn it, because it was your right to be present. But now, I'm taking you back to the Excelsior, where I want you to lock yourself in the suite. No room service. No sightseeing. No shopping. Understand?"

"And that will keep me safe?" she asked bitterly.

"I want you to promise me that you'll remain in the suite while I call on someone."

"Who?" Gaia watched him closely and thought he seemed annoyed at being questioned.

Dom hesitated before replying. "Giuliano Rinzini. He was your grandfather's attorney."

"Was he at the funeral Mass?"

"I saw him there," he admitted.

"Why didn't you introduce us?"

He was silent. What reason could there be for Dom to exclude her from his meeting with the man who was executor of the estate? "I am going with you," she declared.

"I told you what you must do. You will lock yourself in the suite."

"And if I refuse?"

"Then I'll have to hire someone to restrain you. Gaia, don't look at me like that. It's for your own safety."

Her voice was pained. "Such as Bullet Security?"

"Yes, exactly like them."

Gaia heard the echo of Detective O'Reilly's voice: "mob-connected."

· 32 ·

THE TELEPHONE WAS EMITTING SHORT SPASMODIC RINGS AS SHE entered the suite. As the door slammed shut behind her, she raced across the sitting room, hoping to reach it in time.

"Hello! Hello! *Pronto!*"

There was a crackling sound in her ear, somewhat like tissue paper being squeezed into a ball. "Is anyone on the line?" she demanded. A series of clicks followed. Then, distantly, a voice. She couldn't make out its gender.

The hotel operator interrupted, louder and more clearly. "Signorina Gaia Gerald?" she asked.

"*Sì.*"

In Italian the operator explained that an incoming transatlantic call had been disrupted but—she was careful to explain—not by anyone at the hotel switchboard. The signorina must be patient until the connection could be reestablished.

Twenty minutes later the phone again rang. This time Gaia swooped up the receiver on its first ring.

The voice was unmistakably familiar. "How *are* you, Gaia darling? I thought I'd never see you again." It was Miles Tuchelin. "Thank God you're alive. Do you know the police—actually Detective O'Reilly—led us to believe you were in the limo with Salinari?

· 232 ·

"It wasn't until this morning that he told Etta where you might be reached in case it was necessary for any business matters. I guess O'Reilly assumed that if we believed you were dead, I would assist his investigation, and one of us might indict ourselves. As though anyone here would harm a hair of your . . . but no more about your purported demise."

"Somewhat like Mark Twain's," she observed.

"What? Oh, yes. Of course. Very apt. How are things in Rome? Have you met your relatives?"

She certainly didn't intend to indulge in small talk about *that.* "Are things going well in the store?" Gaia glanced at her wristwatch. It was eight o'clock in New York, she calculated. Ferrante's had not yet opened for the day. "You're in awfully early, Miles."

"Yes, I am. Well, first, the scuttlebutt. Mrs. Salinari, our widow lady, is graciously returning to town today, protesting all the way because she was forced to cut short her stay in a spa. Claimed she needed to remain there longer to settle her nerves upon hearing the news. Anyway, his funeral is this afternoon."

Gaia said nothing, thinking, About now Ugo Ferrante's coffin is being entombed in the catacombs. She shivered involuntarily, imagining that eternally dark enclosure.

"Hey! Can you hear me?" Miles was speaking louder.

A pause. "I can. But Miles, tell me about the store."

"One more thing. Salinari's chauffeur is missing."

"Oh? Do the police have a theory?"

"Sure. He planted the bomb. What they want to know is why, where he is, and who he's working for."

Her throat was too dry for her to speak. *So do I. Oh, so do I.*

"Hello," Miles said. "Are you there?"

After a moment, she said, "I'm still on the wire. About the store, is it operating smoothly?"

"Everything is super great."

It was exactly the way she ought to have expected the flamboyant promotion director to respond. "That's wonderful, Miles. I know Ferrante's is in good hands." She gave him instructions for things she wanted him to check on while she was away, then chatted about how beautiful Italy was.

"Well, don't get fat, darling," Miles cooed. "And come back soon."

"I will. Ciao, Miles, and . . . *grazie.*"

"Oh, *prego,* darling, *prego!*"

Gaia once again felt happy that she'd selected Miles for the new board of directors. His fresh outlook, his clear eye for spotting or implementing a style trend, his enormous energy, his openness to new ideas, all would provide good balance to the others she would find, who would make up for Miles' lack of corporate knowledge with superb business acumen. But while it had been diverting to converse with Miles, he had provided no positive information about the store's day-to-day business. She really ought to place a call to Etta Spring. She dallied with the idea, but put it aside. She felt ridiculously intimidated by the stern, accusatory woman, as if the secretary were an authority figure from her childhood.

Her nap was interrupted when Dom returned, cheerful and excited about taking a late lunch. He had returned the rental car, so they took a taxi to a lovely old restaurant on the Piazza Barberini, where tables were placed around a bubbling fountain in a tiled inner courtyard.

"We can't dally as long as is the Roman custom," he told her. "When we finish our meal, I'll drop you off at the Excelsior again. I'll be returning to Giuliano Rinzini's office. We haven't finished our discussion."

"I'm surprised that you didn't bring him with you. I do have a slight interest in whatever you two say together."

He looked quizzically at her. "Grouchy today?"

"Not at all," she replied briskly. "I just can't understand why I am excluded from your meeting with him. Not even to be with both of you at lunch."

"Because Rinzini is a disagreeable man. Hardly conducive to good digestion."

"Fuck digestion!"

"Gaia!" He was plainly shocked, but when he looked at her, he couldn't help smiling. The table shook with laughter.

"I think the *pollo spezzatino*." Dom looked up from the menu, at Gaia. "Have you decided?"

"Whatever you select."

"Good. The chicken is an excellent choice." He glanced at the wine list and opted for a *soave* of excellent vintage.

The steaming plate was set before her, the garlic-seasoned pieces of chicken, livers and mushrooms appealing in a delicious sauce, with a side plate heaped high with linguini. Dom approved the wine, and the attentive young waiter poured. Dom raised his glass in salute. Gaia automatically touched the stem of her glass but did not sip the wine.

"What's the matter?"

"I've lost my appetite."

"Don't say that, *cara*, when I came all the way across Rome to be with you."

"I'm sorry, Dom. But I really do want to accompany you to Rinzini's office."

"So that's it! You're holding your meal hostage."

She was indignant. "I am not playing a game."

"I'll tell you what you must know this evening."

"Oh, and when will you return?"

"That depends on how much there is to discuss."

"I see." Or rather I don't, she thought.

"When you get back to the suite, why don't you have some gowns brought to you for your approval. You came abroad without packing."

"Perhaps."

"Select one for tonight."

She didn't answer.

"You'll have plenty of time. A real Roman dinner doesn't begin until ten o'clock."

Gaia was amazed. "So late at night?"

"When in Rome, do as the Romans do." His voice caressed the platitude, and she felt her anger abate. All right, then, she thought, looking into his worried face. She picked up her fork and began to eat.

Back in the Excelsior suite, Gaia found herself pacing from the sitting room to the bedroom and back again. Then, standing in the doorway, she stopped to stare at the bed. It was the place where her dreams had been fulfilled. There, Dom had been her lover for hours and hours, and she'd been transported upon waves of almost unbearable ecstasy. Joined to him, clasping one another, she'd wished it would never end.

And now she doubted him again.

· 33 ·

THE CLIENT ENTRANCE TO GIULIANO RINZINI'S LAW SUITE WAS
through an inner courtyard with a nonworking fountain
where weeds flourished between slabs of stone paving. The
Renaissance building, a shabby stone palazzo, had been neglected in the years since World War II. The upper stories
had been recently renovated into warrenlike apartments for
Rinzini to rent at high profit. The layout of the lower-floor
rooms occupied by his office were left untouched. From the
outside, the building suggested picturesque decay, but this
was not to enforce historical significance or add aesthetic
value to the palazzo.

"I wouldn't remain a wealthy man for long if I spent
my money foolishly," the parsimonious lawyer told Dom
Perrini.

As a young *avvocato*, Rinzini had made a practice of hanging out of an open window of his office, which at that time
overlooked a dangerous intersection. Several times a day
there were collisions below. The metallic grinding of meshed
fenders and infuriated tempers was like music to his ears. He
would scramble to the street, inflaming the interlocked drivers to the point where he could offer his services to one or the
other—and sometimes, surreptitiously, to both.

He was making a steady living out of such cases on the day when an elderly accident victim returned to Rinzini's office after his case was already settled. The man wanted Rinzini to draw up his will. Seizing the opportunity, Rinzini suggested himself as executor. When the client died, Giuliano Rinzini delightedly discovered that sticky fingers were magnets for great gain. Whatever percentage of assets the heirs received was substantially diminished by his unwarranted "expenses."

He became an affluent man in direct proportion to his growing inventiveness in misappropriating legacies. He acquired accomplices in banks and bribed the favors of petty probate court clerks. One success led to another. And as word of his inventiveness spread throughout Rome, he was sought out by certain mafiosi.

As he prospered he grew in girth, and in conceit. He was proud to give his wife the very best, a good woman who demanded little and bore him seven children, four of them sons. But he was proudest of his affiliation with the stylish slim mistress he maintained in a life-style far more opulent than his wife's. It was worth the money, he admitted to himself begrudgingly.

Dom had known Rinzini for over ten years. Vince Roselli had dispatched him on his first trip to Italy with the purpose of delivering a sealed packet to the lawyer. After Rinzini had studied the contents, he suggested that they repair to a *caffè*. Dom made an excuse not to. He kept refusing on each subsequent trip. Rinzini never gave up extending the invitation because he would have liked to have been seen in public with such a distinguished-looking American man. But they scarcely looked at each other at the Church of St. Luigi dei Francesi. There it would have been unwise to acknowledge their acquaintance.

The two men sat together in Rinzini's cramped book-lined office, smoking the cigars Dom had brought with him.

"Welcome back," the lawyer said. "This morning, before

our lunch break, we went over the particulars. Are they clear to you?"

Dom nodded.

"*Meraviglioso!*" He made a clapping sound with his fleshy hands. "*Prestare attenzione.* I will detail the immediate plan."

· 34 ·

IT TOOK NEARLY HALF AN HOUR FOR HER CALL TO BE PUT THROUGH to Merrill Ross in New York. She could wait. Anger and resentment made the time pass quickly. For too long it had been her habit to accede to the wishes of others . . . in the orphanage . . . in foster homes. Dom had influenced her to accept the Ferrante-New York apprenticeship instead of an offer of employment by Tiffany & Co. Why? And why did she let him manipulate her? Her mind was awhirl with indignation and suspicion.

Could Dom have refused to take her with him to the lawyer because he knew that she understood a fair amount of Italian, and that little could be safely said behind her back? He'd declared he was removing her from danger in New York by bringing her to Rome. If she was safe here, why must she remain locked in the suite? He'd taken her to the church, where she had been as prominently on view as Ugo Ferrante's body in his coffin. The pieces didn't fit.

He'd said that he would explain everything upon his return. She was positive that when it came down to it, he'd find some reason not to.

Suddenly she contemplated what was most hurtful of all. Had their intimacy, which seemed so marvelous to her, been a calculated act? She remembered how he had kept his distance from her in New York. She forced herself to wonder whether Dom had always used her attraction to him as a tool to render her amenable to his decisions: In Rome he'd already used it so skillfully.

"Operator." She jiggled the phone. "Isn't my call to New York ready?"

"I will ring you."

"Yes, thank you."

Again she paced. She stared out of the windows. She nervously settled herself in one chair, then another. She was tempted to cancel the call she'd placed.

A few minutes later, the telephone rang. "I have your party," the operator said.

Gaia began the conversation feeling self-conscious. She would not confide her grave doubts about Rinzini, and she had no intention of voicing suspicion of Dom's motives.

"How good to hear from you. You're in Rome, you say. How's the weather?"

"Warm."

"It's chilly here."

"Oh? Well, of course, Italy is farther south."

"That's true."

"Uh . . . the reason I'm phoning you is—" She paused.

Why *had* she telephoned Merrill Ross? Aside from his being the estate lawyer in New York, and her intention of questioning him about Giuliano Rinzini, she needed to consult with someone. Merrill Ross projected intelligence and dependability. She had read a brief curriculum vitae on him in New York. It was quite impressive. She felt that she could rely upon his counsel, and certainly she'd require legal advice down the line as she administered her business.

"Are you there?" he asked.

"Yes, Mr. Ross." Gaia felt impelled not to waste time by more gradually leading up to it. "I wanted to let you know that I'm considering appointing you to a directorship of Ferrante-New York. In addition to the title and duty, there would be a substantial remuneration."

"Why, Ms. Gerald, that's wonderful . . . except that there

could be a conflict of interest because I'm the lawyer for the estate." He was thinking that this would be his ticket to quit Bari & Battaglia.

"We'll discuss it further when I return. In the meantime, the other reason I'm calling is . . . " She found it hard to continue.

"Are you in some kind of trouble? Is that why you're calling me? While I'm delighted you're considering me for a directorship, I have a feeling you need help and that's why you called. Please trust me. Let me help."

Gaia perceived a warmth in his voice, but it was hard for her to come straight out and ask the question uppermost in her mind. "Did you ever meet the lawyer, Rinzini?" There! It was spoken.

"No, I never did. Actually, my contact with him is through Mr. Battaglia, since I don't speak Italian."

"I was hoping you could give me an assessment of him."

"Only by inference."

"In what way?"

"Well, I'd be wary of him if I were you. Perhaps I shouldn't say this because he's a fellow lawyer, but my impression of him is that he isn't above cutting corners where it suits him."

Gaia appreciated this open expression of his thoughts, his honesty. Wasn't it more than Dom had accorded her? She was beginning to feel extremely comfortable talking with Merrill Ross. The question that motivated her call no longer seemed silly or awkward to ask.

"Mr. Ross . . . Merrill, do you have concrete proof that I am Ugo Ferrante's granddaughter?"

"Let's say I have no reason to doubt it."

She was disappointed that he affirmed nothing more positive.

"You're upset, aren't you? But, Ms. Gerald, you're in the right place to discover that for yourself."

"How?" It would be too embarrassing to tell him that Dom was preventing her from meeting Rinzini.

"Isn't there a family villa?"

"Oh, I couldn't go there. It belongs to Silvia Wood. I've heard she calls herself la Principessa now."

They chuckled together, sharing their impressions of Silvia, and Gaia felt closer to him.

"Look, why don't you take advantage of your proximity to the villa? I really think you should."

"I'm positive I wouldn't be welcome."

"I didn't suggest that you should be a guest."

"Sneak in? That advice from a lawyer? I couldn't."

"I deny I said to sneak. I'm sure you'll gain entry in some manner. It's in that building where you're likely to discover the key to your identity."

Or lack of it, Gaia thought.

· 35 ·

GAIA STRODE WITH PURPOSE ACROSS THE EXCELSIOR LOBBY, OBLIV-
ious to admiring glances. With her fur coat over her arm, she
wore the same outfit she had flown the Atlantic in, a dark-
gray wool suit with touches of black velvet—a couturier creation she had purchased on sale at Lord & Taylor. Her jacket
was open and a silken-knit silvery gray sweater appealingly
emphasized her breasts. She wore pearl earrings set in gold
of her own design, and around her neck was a twenty-two-
inch heavy gold chain with the Gaia Star suspended from it.
Noticing the light clothes the people in the lobby were wearing, she stopped at the desk and asked whether she might
check her fitch coat.

She stuck the check stub into her wallet and headed for the
entrance. Because she was looking down, intent on closing
her shoulder bag, she was too late to avoid colliding with a
noisy group of American men approaching from the opposite
direction. They were literally reeling in from the Via Veneto,
obviously reveling in the excesses of vino.

"Hey, will ya look at this cutie?" one of them said.

"Going our way, gorgeous?"

One of them spread wide his arms. "What's your name,
honey?"

"Hey, asshole, she doesn't speak English."

"So? Pussy is an international language."

There was general guffawing.

Gaia remained silent, trying to avoid them, looking for a way around them. Their deep tans and pastel and white clothes proclaimed them Hollywood types. A man loomed up large, blocking her path, positioning himself directly in front of her. His sport shirt was open and the largest-size Gaia Star pendant rested on a hairy expanse of skin—obviously for him a macho statement. There was sexual invitation in his unmistakably meaningful glance.

Almost reflexively, she hastily buttoned her jacket, concealing the mate to his. She appreciated the customer as much as she might detest the man. She found herself grinning—he was wearing *her* jewelry—and sidestepped him, securing the doorman's attention.

"I want to hire a car and driver." She spoke in Italian.

A man with a dark mustache began urgently motioning to her. He left his dusty red Fiat, sweeping off his cap from a tangle of curly hair. "I am a great guide."

She looked him over.

He pressed his case. "Call me Joe. I speak English very good."

Gaia's eyes questioned the doorman. "I notice all the other cabs are painted yellow," she said.

Before he might reply, Joe answered, "Recent rains washed off the yellow paint." His dark eyes expressed honesty as he blatantly lied. "I am the best taxi driver in all Rome." He bobbed ahead of her, glancing back.

"I want to go to the Via Appia Antica."

"Leave it to Joe." He nodded. "Joe knows Rome. Not only the Appian Way." He was eager to show off his English. "I will point out all the sights as we pass them." He was delighted to have lucked out with this rich American lady. She hadn't asked him his charges, leaving him an opportunity to make more than he otherwise might.

Gaia expected him to open the rear door of his small car for her. When he didn't, she started to do it herself.

"Wouldn't la signorina prefer the front seat? It is much more comfortable."

"The back will do fine."

"The springs aren't broke in the front."

She agreed with his logic, and after she was settled, he ran around the car to his side. He burst out of the hotel driveway into the active Via Veneto traffic at top speed. Gaia's knuckles whitened as she clutched the sides of her seat.

"I lived in Chicago for two years," he volunteered.

"Oh?" She turned her head toward the side window as he swung wide to avert what could have been a sure collision. She had no intention of telling him that she had once lived there, too.

"I take detour," he announced. "We stop off at *Foro Romano* . . . the Roman Forum to you Americans."

"No. I want to make no stops."

"We won't stay long. You will see the ancient temples, the columns, the arches. Septimius Severus to the left and the Arch of Titus at the far end of the Via Sacra. Also, for two hundred lire extra, I will sell you a guidebook."

"No."

"No?"

"Straight to the Via Appia Antica."

He shrugged. "Perhaps a side trip so you can walk down the Spanish Steps? Below, past the piazza is the famous Via Condotti, where fine ladies like you shop."

Gaia half-smiled. "Flattery will get you nowhere."

"You want me to take you to the Via Appia Antica?"

"Yes." Ferrante-Roma was situated on the Via Condotti. She wouldn't visit that store after Silvia's imperial invasion of the New York Ferrante's. She could hardly believe that she actually intended gaining entry to the villa.

They rounded the impressive Colosseum. "*Il centro di Roma*," Joe said. "Pollution and vibration from traffic cause it to crumble," he said. Immediately, his cheerfulness returned. "The *cuore* of Rome is the Vatican. Perhaps, you would like—"

"No side trip," Gaia said emphatically. "Drive to the Via Appia Antica."

He grew silent. She suppressed a chuckle, knowing he was probably annoyed with her single-mindedness. Her smile departed as they bore down the Via delle Terme, dangerously negotiating the Piazza Numa Pompilio on screeching wheels, scattering produce vendors, their customers, and a flock of pigeons. This confrontation obviously restored his good spirits. He happily hummed when he drove the length of the Via di Porta Santo Sebastiano and continued beyond its historic gate to the beginning of the Via Appia Antica. The Fiat bounced along its original lava stone roadway. Traffic had considerably thinned out and Gaia focused on what lay ahead for her.

"This was a military road built by Emperor Appius Claudius. Will you want me to stop at the ancient monuments and tombs? No?" He sighed. "See, there is the Church of Domine Quo Vadis. It is built on the spot where Santo Pietro had a vision of Jesus. He asked Him, 'Domine, quo vadis?' Jesus replied, 'To Roma, to be crucified anew.' Pietro also turned back to the city, later to be crucified by Nero."

Gaia had learned this from the nuns. So many things in Rome seemed to remind her of her early years. Possibly this journey wasn't such a good idea. But deep within, a stubborn voice insisted she continue, and she commanded Joe to drive faster past the shrines of antiquity into her own future.

· 36 ·

Across the rear of the pink travertine marble villa was a wide terrace, an addition to the house during Ugo Ferrante's ownership. From it, a flight of steps descended to a Renaissance garden spreading its patterned design across the gently sloping terrain. At intervals along its perimeters were topiary shapes of animals and fanciful towers—hedges trained to grow over twigs and chicken wire. Gravel paths led to a central fountain where water gracefully spurted from hidden jets. The terrace, with its mosaic stone flooring and garden-style floral-chintz-cushioned chairs of wrought iron, carried out in bolder colors the delicate trace of stones underfoot. Close to the building, plants were lined up in terra-cotta pots, and near the coping were several large earthenware jugs with spoutlike appurtenances resembling water faucets. These were meant for springtime blooming when geraniums poured out of every hole. Although the weather remained mild in autumn, a sense of imminent seasonal change pervaded. Even so, it was a pleasant place to sit in the late afternoon, soaking up the warmth of the sinking sun reflected against the villa windows.

It was here on the terrace where Silvia confronted her daughter. Mara di Malvestiti lay on a chaise, partially clothed.

Her arms and legs were wound about a slight, unsavory-looking Roman youth whose unhealthy complexion in the direct sunlight marked him as one of her night companions from the *mezzatinta* world of discos, bars, and God knows what other establishments that flourished in certain quarters of the city.

To Silvia, the boy was as unsavory as the rodents that sometimes ventured from fretwork in the stones beneath the terrace. In her childhood, before the terrace was built, there had been a patio elevated from ground level by those stones. Then she had been petrified of the voracious mammals—some as large as cats—and had screamed loudly whenever she observed them scoot out into the open. She remembered how differently Angela Maria had reacted. Her younger sister would take off a shoe, bang it on the railing, and set up such a clamor that the rats would scurry back into their recesses.

"What are you afraid of? They don't want you."

"If you're not scared of them then you're a rat, too."

She put her shoe back on: *"This was their home before it was ours."*

Silvia could never forgive her. Never mind that Angela Maria loved all living creatures.

Her hatred for her sister would manifest itself in acts of vicious revenge. She stole Angela Maria's favorite silver comb and hurled it from an upper window into the shrubbery. With a rock she hopelessly scratched the little mirror above Angela Maria's dressing table. Her sister didn't say a word. Without requesting permission, Silvia would wear her sister's best dresses, purposely spilling messes of food down their bodices and skirts. She dipped a blouse sleeve in blue ink, resulting in a permanent stain. Emboldened, Silvia grew taunting when Angela Maria would never cry or complain. Her silence was clearly a sign of weakness, Silvia thought.

But one night, as she slipped between the freshly laundered, lavender-scented sheets of her bed, anticipating snuggling beneath the down comforter, she could swear that she felt *something* under her body. She sat up, wild-eyed. Her screaming became quivering hysteria, for sprawled across the bottom sheet, inches below the pillow where she had been lying, were two huge dead rats.

Silvia was enormously annoyed with herself. Why did she have to recall that now? She involuntarily shuddered. Memories were bound to surface because Papa had died. It was logical to think of her deceased sister; that stupid American girl was being presented as Papa's heir to the New York store, calling herself Angela Maria's daughter. And there was her own daughter, wearing a tight T-shirt and opened blue jeans, coiled around this horrible young man. Mara seemed on the verge of orgasm, using the boy's scrawny body to get off.

The spastic movements of Mara's body diminished and she lay back contentedly, her eyes closed against the sun, stretching in sexual satisfaction, one knee out against her lover. "All right, Luigi, you've made your score. Get the hell out of here. Go back to Rome."

On his feet, he looked down at her. "Are you coming?"

Her reply was slow and insolent. "I just did, sweetie."

Silvia testily interrupted. "Mara, you and I need to talk."

The girl regarded her mother through slit eyes. "Want to tell me about the birds and the bees when I already know where to get black-market contraceptives? You're a bit late with your maternal instincts, aren't you?"

"Shut up!"

Mara smiled slyly. "I knew that you were watching. Is that how you get your kicks? I suppose it's the reason you insisted I leave my *appartamento* and stay with you until after the funeral."

"You are disgusting."

"No more than you. What sort of a woman parks her child with her husband's family and takes off? Do you realize that the di Malvestitis never spoke ill of you? Nor did my father, gentle and confused man that he was."

"Well then, you knew how he was. Why would you have expected *me* to stay with him?"

"I surmise he wasn't actually my father."

"Does it matter?"

Mara answered in a singsong voice: "Nothing matters. It's why I'm always high on one drug or another . . . but never on life." She laughed and ran her fingers through her matted hair.

Silvia gave her a disgusted look. "That's your problem." She stoked her anger to fever pitch. She wasn't about to let this girl—really a stranger—goad her into an admission of guilt. Besides, Mara seemed to have her loyalties all wrong. Instead of willingly joining in the fight against that American bastard, Mara seemed utterly indifferent, offering no cooperation or support whatsoever. All her brains are in her crotch, Silvia thought. Infuriated, she screamed at Mara: "Why is your little stud standing around here? This is family business."

The boy scurried into the house. Crazy women! After a necessary visit to the *gabinetto*, he'd happily leave them to their quarrel and tool his Ferrari toward the city.

Mara jumped to her feet. "Jealous old cow, now look what you've done. It's your fault he's run out on me."

"*You* told him to go."

Silvia found herself outyelling her. "Lower your voice."

"Why should I? So you can have the last word, *mama mia?*"

"Because you and I are the genuine heirs of your grandfather's estate, and together we must forge a plan to keep that American bitch from taking the Fifth Avenue store away from us."

"How?"

"That is what we need to discuss . . . why we must talk . . . as allies."

The red Fiat drove through the hilly estate section, passing homes that Joe, rattling off famous names, pointed out as residences of international screen luminaries. He wasn't strictly correct in associating a given mansion with an individual, but so what? The signorina wouldn't know any better. For her own part, Gaia was scanning the nameplates affixed to entrance portals and gateways. Eventually, to the left side of the roadway she read CORCHESE.

"Wait! Stop here. On the road," she directed.

"You come so far and don't want to go in?" Joe was perplexed. Besides, he was anxious to enter the estate grounds. Until today he had only driven past these bastions of glamour and wealth. He eased the car forward in low gear.

Gaia's breathing had become shallow. She felt light-headed, the way she felt when she was interviewed on "The Today Show" for the first time to publicize her creation of the Gaia Star. It was Miles Tuchelin's calm persuasion that then rid her of her jitters. "Breathe deeply," she could remember him saying. "Take long slow breaths." The strategy worked, and she had charmed Jane Pauley—and the millions who'd seen her on television. Now she inhaled the sweet late-afternoon country air and hoped her heart would slow down.

She had rolled open her window. The crunching sound of the tires on the gravel driveway was pleasing to the ear. Trills of bird song sounded from the bordering trees in the mild interlude before autumnal change: elms still verdant, rows of cypress, hollylike leaf-bearing evergreens, holm oaks, and pines. Beyond was a vineyard gone to seed, allowed to become a tangled underbrush.

As they slowly proceeded toward the villa, they passed monolithic marble and stone relics, tall standing pieces of columns and capitals. Closer to the house, on the opposite side of the road, was a swimming pool, and near it both tennis and bocce courts. A lawn stretched forward from the villa. There the driveway curved to meet three broad stone steps with pedestals at their sides. Inset in the pink marble at either side of the door were ancient friezes depicting allegorical scenes of battle. Installed within a niche was a bust of an unknown nobleman. The door was fashioned of bronze panels set into wood and an electric bell had been added in more recent times.

"Park here for a while," she told Joe. "I need to think."

Overcome by wonder at the splendid view on all sides, he began singing aloud with the *robustezza* of an Italian male. Gaia leaned away from him to avoid being unintentionally struck. Fingering the handle, she opened the door. She made up her mind. This had been her grandfather's house! At least, she might call him that until proven differently. She shifted her body, preparing to step out of the car onto the grass.

Joe realized he was about to lose his passenger. "No, no, I must drive you." He was perturbed. "It wouldn't be proper for you to walk."

But she was already striding across an expanse of grass, intending to save her shoes from the gravel. Suddenly, the ground began sinking under her. It was like a bad dream: She started falling, her arms and legs flying up as she plopped down on her behind.

Joe jumped out of the car and ran to where she sat, awkwardly positioned in a depression of earth. "Signorina, are you hurt?" He looked as though he was about to weep as he helped her up. His arm crept around her waist, his fingers inching toward her breast.

"I think I'm all right," she said, extricating herself from his arms. She glanced back to the spot where she had gone down. "The ground gave way under me. I don't understand it."

He shook his head importantly, holding aloft one hand to signal the wisdom of his assessment. "It is a catacomb," he pronounced. "The ground sinks as old tunnel supports give way. You are very lucky. You might have fallen all the way though."

"Into the tomb?"

"It is so. Much of Rome is built on the catacombs. There are also very many around here. The living exist with the dead."

It must be so, she thought, thinking of Ugo Ferrante, buried just this morning in the catacomb. "Please stop talking about it." She dusted her clothes with her palms.

He persisted. "Some of these old villas have partially collapsed into the catacombs running beneath their foundations."

"Enough!" Gaia demanded.

Offended, he grew silent. *Americani!* he thought as Gaia strode toward the entrance.

She had mounted the steps when the bronze door opened

and a pale young man nearly missed bumping into her as he made a hasty exit.

"*Scusi, scusi,*" he apologized profusely.

He had left the heavy door ajar behind him. Gaia stood before it pondering and peering through the crack. Momentarily she considered ringing the bell. She decided not to, and pushing the door open wider, quietly entered to find herself in a cool marble vestibule.

"Hello!" She intended to call out, but her voice was a whisper. "Is anybody here?"

She was met with hollow silence until, from somewhere in the rear of the villa—possibly outdoors—she heard a woman's angry voice battling with another in loud argument. There was something familiar to it. Gaia abruptly recalled her unpleasantness with Silvia in Ferrante-New York and her rudeness at Ugo's funeral. With no wish to encounter her, and impelled as much by impulse as by curiosity more persuasive than the morality of uninvited exploration, she swiftly darted up the same staircase that Ugo Ferrante had mounted on a long-ago day when he first came to the di Corchese villa to purchase a carved bedstead at auction, and found himself a wife.

· 37 ·

She tiptoed along the lengthy and lavishly ornamented second-story corridor, uncomfortably aware that she was committing a criminal act and equally alarmed at the prospect of confronting Silvia, who would be livid with rage to find her there. Yet she had a compulsion to continue on, peering into those rooms where the doors were open. She was unable to shake off a light, ethereal feeling, a presentiment of other-worldliness. *Angela Maria,* she thought, *guide me to whatever it is that I must find.*

And whether through a sixth sense or an overactive imagination, it came to her that there were few happy memories here. The echoes of the past persisted in the ornate furnishings, the incredibly delicate frescoes on the bedchamber ceilings, the crystal chandeliers, and the elaborate silken bedsteads. She had traversed the entire corridor. In the last and, by far, the largest of the rooms was a massive four-poster canopied bed with an elaborately carved headboard. Why, it's practically obscene, she thought, staring at the carved figures with wide eyes. She spent moments gazing upon it while she stood in the doorway. Then she turned away and retraced her steps.

About halfway down the length of the passage, she discovered that a door she had believed to be shut was actually unlatched, swinging gently on its hinges as if beckoning her. She pressed the door farther open with her palms, fingers outspread, and stepped inside the room.

A pastel-painted bed with a floral-stenciled headboard, a similarly painted bureau, an upholstered chair, and a small settee next to a low table—all situated before a white marble-faced fireplace looked as if their occupant had left them in readiness for her return.

Gaia walked to the window. Underneath, fitted into a corner, there was a low clothes cabinet. Should she search the bureau drawers? What exactly was she looking for?

Out of the corner of her eye, she sensed movement and caught her breath until she realized she had glimpsed her own triple reflection in the sectional mirror that rested on a pale pink tulle-skirted dressing table. She walked toward it, floating, as if in a dream. Resting on the mirrored surface of the girlish table was a single perfume bottle reflected three times in the sectional mirror above. Alternately mauve and frosted, the glass bottle had been sculpted into a many-layered design that reminded Gaia of a flower's petals. Its cylindrical crystal stopper rose to a height twice that of the small bottle. A section of the glass was relatively flattened and smooth; a dull mark remained where a label had once been pasted on.

Gaia's senses quickened. Too, too many times had she made forays in vain to perfumeries and the counters in department stores, sampling products, hoping to rediscover an elusive wafting memory of a fragrance—a fragrance she fancied was worn by a woman who had held her in her arms, who had bent over her crib in the night to whisper lovingly as she had tucked a blanket about her.

She reached with fascination toward the bottle. As her fingers closed upon the smooth cold glass, her breathing grew shallow and rapid. A moment more and she would know whether the contents, when exposed to the air, would release the familiar perfume.

"It's *you!*"

The voice was unmistakably guttural. "*Intrudesi!* What are you doing here? How did you enter?"

Silvia stood between her and the doorway. Escape was out of the question. Her wisest course was to be truthful.

"I came to see my grandfather's home. A young man admitted me as he left."

"And so, too, are you leaving. *Immediatamente!* You are not welcome here!"

"I only wanted to see—"

"Don't tell me stories. Get out!"

Silvia came toward her with her hands outstretched, but Gaia skirted around her.

Her fury increased. "Giorgio!" she shouted. "Where is that old fool! *Stupido!* Never around when he's needed."

"Don't worry. I'm not staying."

"You'd better not. You don't belong here."

"My mother—"

"*Sua madre!* Ha! Angela Maria died childless."

Gaia experienced a sudden, absolute hopelessness. "Is that true?"

"You wouldn't believe me. There is a *fortuna* at stake."

Gaia walked over to the door. From the far end of the corridor, there was the sound of high-heeled shoes tapping against the marble floor, a rhythm growing louder, coming closer. Presently, Mara appeared in the doorway. She had a wide foolish smile on her face as she linked arms with her mother.

Gaia felt a tightness in her throat and tears welling behind her eyes. She pushed past Mara and ran down the corridor, her footsteps echoing crazily against her head. At the top of the stairs, she was overcome by a wave of dizziness. She gripped the banister to steady herself and momentarily closed her eyes. When she opened them, she saw a round elderly man ascending the steps. He labored, puffing, and as he came nearer to her, Gaia perceived that the color of his face was almost as pale as his silvery hair. She saw, also, that his eyes were rheumy. By then she had begun slowly walking down. When they drew level with one another, he looked at her, shock apparent in his face. She instinctively reached toward him, grabbing hold of his hands to steady him and keep him from tumbling. He opened his mouth, his jowls shaking, his eyes wide.

His voice, when he spoke, was thin and reedy. "*Signorina! Signorina! Da quanto tempo è qui?*"

How long had she been here? The question puzzled her, and she shook her head. She was leaving. What was the point of talking?

The old man had straightened up and seemed more vital. Or was that her imagination? "Will you be all right?" He said nothing, but nodded and continued staring into her face. Perhaps he is a trifle mad, she thought.

"*Dove abita?*" he questioned.

Where did she live? Really, was that any of his business to ask? Nevertheless, she heard herself answering, "*Gli Stati Uniti* . . . New York."

She released his hands and proceeded down the stairs. Upon reaching the mosaic reception foyer, she gazed back up at him. As she had sensed, he was looking after her, smiling broadly, exposing unevenly spaced discolored teeth. "*Angela Maria,*" he whispered.

Had he actually articulated the name she wanted to hear— or was it her imagination playing tricks on her again? She was running up the steps toward the old man when Silvia appeared at the head of the stairs, her air imperious, her arms crossed. Her voice was harsh. "I expected you to have left."

The old man remained standing where she left him. He was looking down on her, smiling, his countenance lit with recognition.

No, Gaia sternly addressed herself, *he is an old man with extremely poor eyesight and a muddled brain. That's the explanation. It can be nothing more.*

Angela Maria died childless . . .

She ran from the house.

· 38 ·

AT THE VERY SAME MOMENT THAT GAIA ENTERED THE HOTEL Excelsior lobby, Dom Perrini was on the telephone upstairs in their suite.

"I've already given you her description," he fumed. "Why can't you simply answer whether or not you have any report of Signorina Gerald's whereabouts?"

The Italian policeman with whom he was in conversation effusively professed apologies. Then he stated, "No female body has been found fitting this likeness." Amazingly, he continued apologizing. "I am very, very sorry."

Asshole! Dom thought in exasperation. "I didn't imply that she is dead," he shouted into the mouthpiece. "I told you she is missing. There is a difference!"

"No report here. *Niente affatto.* I trust that you will soon be reunited with her. *Buona fortuna.*"

The connection was broken off. Dom was left standing with the dead receiver in his hand, wondering what he ought to do next. Staring out of the window in despair, he determined that he would call the American Embassy when, behind him, he heard the corridor door open. He turned to see Gaia enter. His chest expanded with the enormity of his relief. "Where the hell have you been?" he shouted. "I've just had the police on the line; they were ready to write you off as a murder victim."

Her mouth dropped open with incredulity; then she smiled at him—a warm inviting smile.

"It's not funny!"

"I'm not laughing," she declared indignantly. "Besides, *you* assured me that I'd be safe in Rome." She turned away.

"Safe? Of course you are," he replied briskly. "It's that when I returned and you weren't here, well . . . At any rate, here you are, and that's what is important. Did you go shopping, *cara?* No. I see no packages. I suppose it was the lure of sightseeing that drew you out. I would have preferred that you remain in the suite. Do you remember me telling you that before I left?"

Yes, she thought. To visit Giuliano Rinzini, where you refused to take me.

"Where were you?"

She was on the verge of replying when a swift-flowing perverseness, some kind of preservation instinct, caused her to clamp her lips shut. After all, what right did Dom have to interrogate her? Shouldn't he be detailing to her everything that took place at his meeting with Rinzini? Her suspicions mounted. "Wait a minute," she said, "first you tell me what you and the lawyer spoke to one another about."

"That doesn't concern you."

"I think it does."

"What I mean is that you needn't concern yourself about it."

"But, Dom, I do."

"I assumed that you trusted me to guard your interests." It was all that he would say.

"It's unbelievable . . . not telling me. Don't I have the right to know?"

He made no reply. Oh, how well she knew his skill at being closemouthed. This was a facet of his complexity that when she was a teenager invariably had heightened her physical desire for him. Now it infuriated her.

She walked into the bedroom and stood before the bed in

which they had made rapturous love the night before. She felt her anger abate, but it was replaced by a deep, dry sorrow. The unbridled joy of that night was as abruptly diminished as if she had switched off a light. She sat on the bed and stared straight ahead of her, unseeing. She was unaware of her surroundings, of the distant sounds of the horns from the street, of the light as it grew dimmer around her.

Later, when she emerged, Dom put aside his Italian newspaper and rose.

"We must decide where to dine," he said. How formal and proper, she found herself thinking. It wasn't so much his words but the dull tone of his voice, as if he were talking from a vacuum, that made her feel this way.

"I'll describe several restaurants to you, and you can decide."

"If you don't mind, I'll skip dinner."

"Why?"

"I have no appetite."

"Oh? Is that all? Wait until you smell the air in some of these places. They—"

She turned her lower lip inward, biting on it before she spoke. "Not tonight." Her pulse raced. "Besides, I'm sure I'll have something to eat on the plane."

He stared blankly at her. "What plane?" Dom demanded.

"I'm flying back to New York tonight. I made my reservation from the bedroom phone."

"*Cara!*"

Gaia took a deep breath as she turned back to the bedroom. She had hurt him; that was obvious. And yet it didn't make her happy.

"Have you forgotten the attempt on your life in New York?"

"No." She was angry at him, but she still owed him some sort of explanation. "Dom, I discovered, today in Rome, that I *don't* belong. I'm sure that I am not a Ferrante. If I was, somebody . . . would have recognized a resemblance and acknowledged me. That certainly didn't happen." Gaia shook her head. "Then, because you've kept me from meeting Rinzini, I feel it proves I am right." Now she spoke more rapidly, as if wanting to get past the unpleasant truth as quickly as possible. "For some reason I don't yet understand, I've been established as the sole owner of Ferrante-New York. Very well, so be it! I intend to stop being afraid and administer the business for as long as it is mine. I'm not going to be accountable to anyone. Not to serve your interests, Dom, nor anyone else's. That's because I revere that store and its reputation. And I intend to protect it."

"I never took you for a fool, Gaia."

She turned her face toward him.

"Until now."

She was settled in a first-class window seat. Upon boarding she had asked the stewardess for something to settle queasiness, and the drug had caused her to fall asleep.

She woke up several hours later, feeling stiff and hungry. She squirmed in her chair, stretching out her long legs and flexing the muscles of her arms. It didn't quite do the trick. She got up, excused herself going past her seat mate, a kind-looking middle-aged woman, and made her way along the aisle to the lavatory. She caught sight of her weary face in the mirror. Am I really this pale, this exhausted? she wondered. She bent down and splashed her cheeks with cold water. Rome hadn't met her expectations. What had begun in a thrilling relationship with Dom, away from her fears in New York City, away from everything, for that matter, had come to this.

No wonder she looked fatigued. Had she been overly hasty in her decision to leave Dom? Well, it was too late to have a change of heart now. At least she could rely upon makeup to brighten her outward appearance. She groped the depths of her shoulder bag, searching for her cosmetic kit, and her fingers closed upon a cool unfamiliar object. She drew it out curiously. In her hand was the frosted crystal and mauve perfume bottle. She hadn't realized until this moment that she'd slipped the bottle into her bag when Silvia had discovered her in the villa bedroom.

Gaia felt her hands shake as she tried to twist open the pointed glass stopper, but it refused to give.

Someone rapped on the lavatory door. "In a few minutes," she called.

She desperately attempted to worry the stopper free. It still wouldn't give. She ran the bottle under hot water; the tap was marked *Hot,* but the water was tepid. The stopper refused to budge. As stubborn as I am, she thought irrationally.

Out of the corner of her eye she spied a book of matches on the small countertop. Her hands still trembling, she struck a match and touched the flame to the bottle's neck. Another try of the stopper. Nothing! She lit another match, and this time immersed the neck of the bottle deep into the flame. The stopper was hot to the touch; she counted to ten and pulled. It lifted easily. The scent that had been protected by its airtight seal for so many years—longer than she had been alive— wafted into her nostrils.

Her head swam from the heady floral perfume. It was delicious, oh so deliciously familiar, so beautiful. But was it really the same as the one she remembered? She shut her eyes and breathed in the elixir escaping like a spirit from its bottle. Her fingers were scented with it. She held them against her nostrils and deeply inhaled, overcome by emotion. It *was* the perfume . . . it was *hers* . . . ah, if only she might see her mother's face . . . .

The rapping on the door sounded again. She closed the bottle, carefully put it in her bag, and opened the door, murmuring her apologies. When she returned to her seat, the lady beside her twisted toward her.

"What is that lovely perfume you're wearing?" she asked. "For a moment I thought it was Joy, but it isn't. The scent is totally unfamiliar."

Not to me! her heart sang. Oh, not to me!

· 39 ·

NEW YORK WAS UNREALISTICALLY PRISTINE FROM THE SKY. GAIA gazed out the window at the city below. The sky was a clear bright blue; sunlight gleamed upon the rows of tall buildings and shone back in jewel-like rays from skyscraper windows. She was weary but exhilarated. This is the New World, she thought, and for me a new beginning. At last her impatience was relieved when the Kennedy tower permitted their descent from a stacked holding pattern. Passing through Customs was easy—she had nothing to declare. The cab ride into Manhattan was almost miraculously swift, and she blinked as if startled awake when they emerged from the Midtown Tunnel into the crowded lively streets of Murray Hill, with their flower shops and fruit stands, idling businesspeople, honking commuter buses, and tiny beautiful restaurants. Her eyes opened wider; she breathed more quickly as if taking in all of New York with her senses.

By coincidence, the taxi drove past her building. Probably it was safe to return to her apartment, but she was tremendously eager to reach the store. There was so much to do.

She entered Ferrante by the Fifth Avenue door. Instinct told her that she needed to get to her office the quickest way. Ordinarily, she would have stopped in her Àtrio, but not today. She made a beeline for the customer elevator, nodding politely at the various salespeople who turned to greet her.

Emerging from the ornate chandeliered cab at the fifth floor, she passed Etta Spring and exchanged a few words of greeting. Etta actually seemed glad to see her. She'd find out why soon enough. She pushed open Salinari's office . . . no, she had jet lag! The office was hers now. She had headed for it as such without even thinking. Gaia made her way across the Oriental carpet toward the desk and slumped happily into the great chair without taking off her coat. She would just rest her eyes for a moment. She quickly fell sound asleep. It was a restful slumber, but it wasn't nearly enough. She woke up after half an hour, determined to accomplish what she had come to the store to do. The staff must be made aware that she had taken charge, that she was forcefully at the helm of her business.

Gaia picked up the desk phone and instructed Etta Spring to notify each of the people with whom she wished to confer. They were to join her in the boardroom in an hour's time. "Miles Tuchelin," she said, "the various department heads, including Michael Vanderman, Roger Perry as new head of security, and, of course, you."

Only then did Gaia shrug off her coat. She tightly squeezed her eyes shut and, alternately, widely opened them. She willed herself to fend off this pervading weariness. Wasn't there someone else whom she wanted to be present? she asked herself.

Merrill Ross!

She decided to call him herself; it would be better to begin with him on a more personal level. While looking up his number in Salinari's small sleek Rolodex, she stifled another yawn. Damn it! Her body was functioning on European time.

"How wonderful to hear from you. I'm delighted you are back in New York."

The warm robust quality in his voice was unmistakable. The impression that he cared made Gaia once again feel comfortable talking to him.

"Thank you. It's good to be missed."

"Did Dom Perrini return with you?"

Fighting off a surge of sleepiness, she wondered why he was asking that. "I left him in Rome."

His hesitation was barely perceptible. "I'd like to come right over to the store to see you. Is that all right?"

She yawned again and excused herself. "I slept on the plane. I shouldn't be this tired."

"May I come over?"

"Didn't I ask you to?" She sounded bewildered. "I've called a meeting and I want you to be present."

The phone seemed unnecessarily jarring to Gaia when it rang. Etta Spring confirmed that all of the persons she'd named would be assembled in the boardroom in thirty-five minutes. Gaia glanced at her watch. Had nearly an hour passed this quickly? If she could just get some rest before the meeting convened, she felt she'd be alert.

Twenty minutes later, Gaia started, raising her nodding head to glance disorientedly about her. She'd been awakened by the ringing telephone. "Mr. Ross is on his way in," Etta Spring said.

Before she'd hung up, the door opened and he rapidly approached her. Her sleepy eyes were enmeshed in his strong gaze. She had seen him before but had never truly *looked* at him. How on earth did one forget a tall, handsome, dark-bearded man? His smile was charming; she smiled, too. His beard was shaped close to his jaw and the lower portion of his cheeks. A spreading mustache gave him a swashbuckling appearance, Gaia thought. His body was rugged, a muscular overlay on a sturdy frame. But it was his eyes to which her gaze returned. An astonishing steel gray, they were commanding, intelligent, almost fierce. His hand was outstretched to clasp hers.

"I'm Merrill Ross."

"I remember." She was surprised at how very attracted she felt to him. Her hand felt good in his strong warm clasp.

"I'm glad you waited for me so I can escort you in."

"In where?" she asked, momentarily confused. "Oh, you mean to the meeting."

He looked sharply at her. "Are you all right?"

"Certainly . . . I am."

"Oh, you must still be a little groggy from your long trip home."

"I'll be all right."

"You mustn't fight your body. Sleepiness is normal. You passed through several time zones on your flight."

"Does it show?" She was dismayed.

"Gaia—may I call you that?"

She nodded. "Yes, Merrill."

"You are definitely not up to conducting a meeting."

"But I've summoned all the heads of departments."

"You have ten minutes to call it off."

"I don't want to appear indecisive."

"Better to change your mind now than show yourself to be vague during the meeting."

She looked at his remarkable eyes. "Yes, you're right. I believed I was alert, but I admit I'm not."

"Shall I have your secretary call it off?" he asked, already starting toward the door.

"Let me notify her." Gaia smiled ruefully. "I guess I want to prove to myself I'm capable of that much." She picked up the phone receiver. "Etta, will you please reach everyone you've notified about the meeting. Tell them it's been canceled. I'll . . . uh . . . reschedule it. Say I'll get back to them."

"Good! You did the right thing." His eyes were locked on her face.

"I've made a fool of myself."

"Nonsense. You're plainly exhausted, and no one can fault you for a human reaction. Tell you what, I'm going to get you into a cab and drop you off at your apartment."

At her building, he insisted on accompanying her past the doorman and into the elevator. "I'm seeing you straight to your apartment."

She inserted her key in the lock but had trouble turning the tumblers.

"Let me," Merrill said, reaching around her and opening the door. "There's an envelope on the floor." He picked it up.

"Thank you," she mumbled. The sight of her familiar apartment seemed only to intensify her yearning to sleep.

"Aren't you going to open it and read it?"

"Later on, when I wake up. It was kind of you to bring me home."

"Perhaps the message is important," Merrill persisted. "Shall I read it to you?" he suggested.

"Sure." She sank onto a foyer bench.

He tore open the envelope. A short message was typed on a matching sheet of paper. He stared at it without speaking. After a moment, he said, "Gaia, I don't think you'd better remain here. Let me help you pack a few things."

"No." Her voice was almost petulant. "I've got to lie down."

He shut the door and entered the apartment. Squatting on his haunches to be at eye level with her, he held her hands. "Listen to me. Try to understand. You will be in danger if you stay. The note . . . it threatens you."

Her eyes flew open. "What does it say?" she whispered.

"Let me handle it."

"Read it to me," she insisted.

"Where do you keep a suitcase?" He started to rise.

"Let me see!" She yanked the sheet of paper from him.

"Don't read it! Give it back to me." He sought to grapple it away from her. But Gaia had already scanned it.

Bitch,
No matter that you missed attending Salinari's funeral. There will be another one soon. Yours!

It was unsigned.

· 40 ·

ON A HIGH FLOOR WITHIN WORLD TRADE TOWER 2, THERE WAS a particular soundproof office with no designation on its entrance door other than the suite number and beneath it, in discreet gilt lettering, the single word: PRIVATE.

Within the locked premises was an array of equipment geared to both communication with and interception of satellite and ground units. There was a scrambler for transmittal of messages and a decoder, which untangled received information into understandable language. These were the most advanced components deployed anywhere in the world. The most obscure telephone call or radio transmission could be isolated and monitored.

This was a secret operation of the United States government, subscribed to by various security agencies: the FBI, CIA, and other less publicly recognizable operations.

Contained in its own room was a microwave broadcasting studio—one that had the capacity to receive as well as transmit on the highest-frequency wavelength. Built-in jamming devices rendered absolute security from foreign interception.

Not all communications concerned foreign policy, however; some were strictly internal criminal matters involving Interpol.

A voice was presently being filtered through an unscrambling device and recorded on tape.

"The Gerald girl made an appearance at the Fifth Avenue store, where she set up an interdepartmental meeting and subsequently canceled it."

"Affirmative. We've planted a bug on her phone."

"Then you know she's tough . . . but her inexperience shows."

"She has no specific knowledge that Ferrante-New York is something more than a Fifth Avenue jeweler."

"No. And we can't have her messing up matters any further. She has already gotten rid of the board members, which makes it all the more ticklish for us to nail the really big score they've been planning.

"The one they've set her up for."

"It's too important for us to chance losing. Smuggling cocaine in the false bottoms of jewelry boxes is minuscule compared with this thing."

"As is trafficking in stolen jewelry, transporting it from continent to continent."

"If they pull this next planned caper off, it could well be the single biggest theft in history."

"Certainly one of the most dramatic."

"The girl could ruin everything we've been sitting in wait for."

· 41 ·

THE BEDSIDE CLOCK SHOWED 9:26. GAIA PASSED A HAND ACROSS her eyes. *Was it morning or evening?* Darkness seeped through the cracks of the venetian blinds. Definitely P.M. She'd been dreaming again. *Where was she?* Gaia sat up and the mattress wooshed beneath her. She had been sleeping on a water bed. *A hotel room?* Unlikely. The water splashed beneath her weight as she rubbed her eyes. Yes. Merrill Ross. He insisted on taking her home with him. She stood up and turned on the light.

It all came back to her then: the jet lag that had overcome her; the danger implied by the message left at her door; Merrill's offer of his apartment to serve as her refuge, where she might sleep unafraid.

How kind of him.

Nevertheless, she felt jarred by the boldly designed black, silver, and white decor of the bedroom and its furnishings. She caught sight of herself in a mirror. A slim figure with tousled hair, wearing only bra and panties. She experienced a rush of vulnerability, and went into the bathroom to put on her clothes.

With the door locked, she hung her garments upon a Lucite and silver metal hook. The stark masculine theme was continued in metallic wallpaper with a harmonizing striped shower curtain, Lucite and black fixtures, and black velour towels. She showered quickly, avoiding her reflection in the many large gleaming mirrors, and, with a thick cotton towel wrapped turban-style around her curly wet hair, she applied her makeup. It was to prepare for a performance or to protect her, more than to enhance her looks. Color had returned to her cheeks and her eyes danced and sparkled.

She was mentally redesigning the bedroom as she put on her clothes, but suddenly she felt ashamed. Hadn't Merrill offered her safety in his home?

When she ventured into the living room, she found him seated on a deep orange leather chair, his feet extended onto a companion hassock. He was absorbed in a news broadcast.

"Hey, you're awake!" He motioned with a wave of one hand that she join him. "You look great!"

Gaia settled somewhat uncomfortably on a royal-blue leather couch that was separated from his chair by a large square chrome-and-glass coffee table. Without concentrating on the television, she darted quick glances about the room, so alien to her personal taste. Near the window was an enormously overgrown plant scraping the ceiling; side-wall track lights focused on color-splashed acrylic paintings; a standing bar was an intense shade of yellow, while across the room, a glossy white desk of spare design was paired with a high-back, poison-green office-style chair. Much of the wall behind the desk bore raw steel shelving on which there seemed to be mostly law books, with an occasional paperback. The natural-wood floor extended into a tiny dining area furnished in similar stark design, and a brightly lit, ultramodern kitchen that looked suspiciously pristine.

Gaia became aware of being intensely hungry, but was too shy to simply help herself to something to eat. Since Merrill was engrossed in the television news, she determined that she would watch with him. There followed scenes of the aftermath of a devastating earthquake in Chile, wreckage of two small planes in midair collision over Florida, and in local

news there were rumblings of a threatened garbage strike. At
last, the commercial break.

"Is there something I can eat? Cheese, or a cracker to nibble
on?"

"Wait until the 10 P.M. newscast is over and I'll fix you a
drink."

"I'm really very hungry," she said in a low murmur.

He turned his face to her with shining eyes and a look of
elation. "I'm waiting to hear the stock market closings. I
watch my holdings rather closely because I've promised myself that I'll become wealthy before I'm much older. Not all
of us get rich quick the easy way, like you."

She was startled. *It certainly hasn't been easy, so far*, she
wanted to say.

He obviously was completely absorbed.

Gaia decided that she would try not to think he was
thoughtless. This was the same man who'd given his bed to
her with no ulterior motive.

"Today in New York City," the commentator was saying,
"there was a surprise roundup of alleged crime figures. Working in close cooperation with city detectives, special FBI
agents arrested three men reputed to be principals in an international jewelry scam."

There was a shot of the handcuffed prisoners being led
away by their somber-looking captors. The men were unrecognizable, their jackets concealing their faces from the
minicams. The camera shifted, focusing on the eager young
face of the reporter.

"Reputed rackets boss Vincent Roselli and *capos* Walter
Smith and Abraham Bronf were taken into custody following
indictment by a federal grand jury on two sealed counts.
However, the word on the street is that the indictments concern extensive worldwide jewelry theft, freely shipped both
out of and into the United States in a complex money-laun-
dering scheme. Ferrante, the exclusive Fifth Avenue retail
jeweler, has not been named, but speculation—"

"Oh my God!" Gaia exclaimed, jumping out of her seat.

"Later!" Merrill silenced her, intently watching the screen.

"There he is!" he hooted. "The sanctimonious old bastard. I might have known—"

The reporter pushed his mike before an unsmiling, hard-eyed elderly man whom Gaia thought looked remarkably like an English bulldog. "Mr. Battaglia, is it true that you represent the three accused?"

"I certainly do," he bellowed, "and I tell you that these are innocent men being hounded by a D.A. greedy for front-page fame and political power."

"That's a strong statement. Mightn't you be accused of defamation of character?"

The attorney spread his hands in an attitude of deprecation. "I am an honest man. I speak only the truth. How can I be accused of anything?"

"And are your clients honest?"

"Absolutely! I am at present arranging bail for these gentlemen. I assure you that none of them will have to spend a day behind bars unjustly." His voice rose. "They are being framed by one man." He raised his finger. "One man I will not now name, who masterminded everything. Someone who has been out of this country, in Italy . . . Rome, specifically."

"Dom!" Gaia whispered.

"What about the rumor that a prestigious jewelry store is involved?" asked the reporter.

"All will be exposed," he said, pausing dramatically, "in due time." And as he turned his back to the camera and strode away, Gaia leaned forward instinctively to see the man who had been partially hidden by Battaglia's bulky figure.

It was NYPD Detective Patrick O'Reilly.

"But you said before that you were hungry," Merrill remonstrated.

"That was *before* . . . before the newscast."

"You still have to eat. Listen, I can call up and have Chinese delivered."

"No thank you." She shook her head. She would keep her suspicions about Dom to herself. She would share her fear with no one.

Merrill was talking. " . . . and above all else, Ferrante's reputation must be protected. It is *your* inheritance, and you weren't party to anything that went before."

She didn't answer, knowing she must somehow think things through. She was increasingly aware of feeling out of place in his high-style masculine apartment, and wished she were home among the familiar beautiful objects that Dom had given to her.

"I'm grateful that you brought me here," Gaia said, then added wistfully, "except I'd really like to go home now."

"You can't!" He sounded appalled.

"Roselli and his crowd are in jail."

"Didn't you listen to Battaglia? They won't be for long. Your personal danger hasn't diminished."

She sighed. "Then, may I use your phone?"

"Who are you going to call?"

"Merrill," she remonstrated, "you're treating me like a prisoner."

He spoke more softly. "I want to protect you. It's why I brought you here, or did you forget?"

"I'm grateful. Truly. It's only that—"

"—that you're being foolish."

She wasn't about to tell him that she'd intended to try to reach Dom at his Brooklyn number, in case he was back in the city. Could she trust Merrill? A worried expression played upon her features.

"I'm getting to know you pretty well," he said. "What's troubling you?"

"It's your closeness to Vito Battaglia," she blurted out.

"I'm not close to him."

"How can you tell me that when you work for him? He's representing those crooks I kicked off the board of directors. Battaglia is what you call . . . oh, I'm so upset I can't think of the term."

"A mouthpiece for the mob."

"Exactly! And he's your boss."

"It frightens you, doesn't it?"

"Why shouldn't it?"

"I'm not like him. Believe me, I have no connection with that end of his practice. I am an estate lawyer, and that's it. Period!"

"If you work for his firm, there has to be some—"

"Will you listen to me?" he asked, not unkindly.

She remained silent, watching him. Merrill seemed so eager to explain himself to her. She would give him the chance.

"You wonder why I'm associated with Vito Battaglia's law firm. When I graduated from law school, Battaglia came up with the best monetary offer. It's as simple as that. As you know, my specialty there is estates. It's only after their clients are dead that I administer to their interests." Merrill allowed himself a small smile. He came over and stood very near. "You don't trust me now, is that it?"

She was disconcerted. "I'm sorry. I mean, I would like to but—"

"Would you prefer me to give up my job?"

"Yes, I would."

"Then would you trust me?"

"I didn't exactly say I don't—"

"But if I stopped working for him, it would put you at ease, wouldn't it?"

"Yes."

"Make me an offer."

She was taken aback. "What sort of offer do you have in mind?"

"In-house counsel for the store, and what you told me when you were in Rome—the board of directors. What you don't know, Gaia, is that for some time I've wanted to leave my job. I detest what Battaglia stands for. It's been a matter of waiting for the right job offer to come along."

"Only, I made no offer."

"Okay, admittedly I've made the overture to you. Is that wrong?"

She was thinking. "And you'll break all ties with him?"

"Absolutely. With the exception of the Ferrante estate."

She turned her head away from him.

"That's for your protection," he explained hurriedly.

"What's more important to me is, do you believe I'm trustworthy?" He looked directly into her eyes.

Gaia fidgeted, inclined to stand up and walk away, but she was fascinated by his amazing gray eyes. She reasoned that a guilty man would have kept his gaze averted. His clear light eyes radiated truthfulness. She needed competent legal representation. There was an advantage, she thought, for him to have worked for Vito Battaglia. He would know how to circumvent any of the older lawyer's schemes. Yes, Merrill Ross could help her guide Ferrante-New York.

"The job is yours," she said. "I don't know what remuneration to offer you. Let's say that whatever you are making now, the store will pay you appreciably more."

He smiled as he reached for her hand. "How do you know that is farsighted business procedure?"

Gaia felt a wave of shyness and stood up, facing him. "Because you've been good to me and . . . I trust you."

"I'm so glad, Gaia—incredibly glad." He put his arms around her, holding her lightly. She was aware of their closeness, but their bodies were not pressing. She felt a flow of incredible warmth, an almost unbearable desire to melt into him and have him sweep her up. But he was embracing her to reassure her; he sensed she was endeavoring to be brave. For a moment Gaia found herself wondering what it would be like if he bent his lips to hers and kissed her. He offered her protection; she wanted him to protect her. At that moment she was unsure whether, if he had urged her, she would have made love with him.

She was angry with herself. She was still in love with Dom, wasn't she? What was wrong with her, that her emotions were so easily swayed by a man's physical contact? She wanted Merrill to hold her safe from fear, that was all. There was just that and there would be nothing more between them. No, she would go to no man out of weakness. She was vulnerable because she was frightened.

He pulled away, looking searchingly at her. "Are you all right? I never meant to—"

She wouldn't let him finish. "I'm fine. It's good to know that we're friends," she said firmly.

"It certainly is. You can depend on me, Gaia."

"I'm sure I can." She wondered whether he sensed, somehow, the fantasy she had just sternly canceled from her brain. It doesn't mean anything, she told herself. It was simply that events in her life were rushing by so swiftly that she was unprepared for her reactions.

"Well, let's see about getting you something to eat."

She nodded. "Yes. I'm famished," she said liltingly, following him into the brightly lit kitchen.

· 42 ·

Two husky men sat in an unmarked car assigned to Interpol from the NYPD vehicle pool. They were in civilian clothes, sipping coffee that had absorbed the flavor of Styrofoam, their gaze fixed upon the entrance to a high-rise apartment building on the east side of Broadway, just slightly north of the massive buildings of Lincoln Center.

For Emil Natov, the bushy-browed multilingual agent, summoning up the requisite amount of patience on surveillance duty had become a nerve-splitting necessity of his trade. Finishing his coffee, he set the empty container on the car floor. "I'm getting too old for this. It's the sitting that gets to me." He didn't say he thought the work utterly demeaning.

"I agree," the man behind the wheel said. "Being in action is what gets the vital juices flowing."

Their dispatch to New York had been alerted through roundabout channels, originally with NYPD, through the FBI, fed to the CIA, and thence transmitted to Interpol working out of Rome. Gaia Gerald had been shadowed while she was in Italy. Natov's orders were to follow her to New York.

The glass panes of the building's revolving door suddenly flashed as it whirled on its axis. Natov's heart rate quickened as a man stepped out onto the sidewalk, one arm raised to hail a taxi.

"That's the man whose apartment she's staying in."

"Merrill Ross?"

"Yes." Natov was already getting out of the car. "She's alone. It's my opportunity to speak to her."

"Perhaps I should trail him."

"No. Wait for me to come back down."

The Interpol agent flashed his identification and walked past the doorman grimly. He scarcely seemed to notice his surroundings; he headed straight to the elevator, which closed silently behind him.

The doorbell buzzed. Gaia stood motionless by the door, listening, hoping that the person outside would leave, presuming the apartment to be unoccupied. Several more buzzes echoed demandingly through the apartment; the sound seemed to pierce her chest.

"Gaia Gerald!" a deep foreign-accented masculine voice called.

She peered through the peephole; an Interpol identity card was raised before it. Printed on it was: NATOV, EMIL.

"Let me see your face," she called out.

A round serious face stared back at her from beneath heavy eyebrows.

"If you don't leave, I'll—I'll call the police."

"Ask for Detective Patrick O'Reilly."

Halfway convinced of his genuineness, she still hesitated.

"It's for your benefit to admit me."

"How can I tell?"

"I can offer you explanations."

He sounded legitimate; he had I.D.—but it was her gut feeling that prompted her to admit him. She slid the chain from its sheath, unlocked the door, and stood in wary silence as the large solid man walked past her into the bright-hued room.

Settling himself exactly where Merrill had sat the previous evening, he regarded her assessingly. "There are matters concerning the past . . . " He allowed the sentence to trail off.

She looked across at him, waiting. But her question burned

for a reply, and she blurted out breathlessly, "Will what you tell me prove who I am?"

"You are Gaia Gerald. That is irrefutable."

"Yes, but . . . I meant regarding my ancestry. Am I truly Ugo Ferrante's granddaughter?"

Natov shook his head regretfully. He found himself admiring the young woman's tightly controlled attitude, but his instructions were to reveal only just so much to her. "What you ask isn't within my province to judge," he said. "What I am about to tell you is the history of the Ferrante family. And about someone else. You'll hear it all in good time. Sit back. Listen. Then perhaps you can decide for yourself."

B·O·O·K
III

· 43 ·

Late Summer, 1924

At an auction held in the largest drawing room of the Villa Corchese, anyone with even a hint of imagination could see that multiple extravagances had impoverished a once-powerful family. Relatively few choice possessions remained within the rose-hued marble building, a sprawling seventeenth-century mansion situated on verdant rolling hills. The property was protected by an edict issued by Benito Mussolini. Artifacts—archaeologically significant statuary, or pieces of these; portions of ruined ancient structures; fluted and round columns, often with their capitals beheaded and resting on the earth—and underlying catacombs were to remain in their original state, sold together: villa, land, and artifacts.

Ugo Ferrante, peasant-born in a Dolomite village, hadn't an innate interest in either antiquity or art, but had chanced to find an illustrated catalogue, left behind by a customer in the jewelry shop where he was employed, in which a black and white photograph of a massive bedstead had caught his eye. The dimensions of the bed weren't stated, but it was obvious that it could well accommodate two people. It had a sturdy rounded headboard covered by intricate carvings of men and women joined in sexual union. Four stout posts stood at the bed's corners. A canopy stretched across the whole; silk draperies flowed to the floor. A caption was printed beneath the photograph:

> Roman beds of this type are extremely rare. This well-pre-
> served specimen is a tribute to its maker's talent and is truly
> a work of art and of museum quality. Unfortunately, the name
> of the artisan-carpenter is lost, though we know the bed was
> built of unblemished walnut on commission for il Principe di
> Corchese. Minutest details of carving are rendered on the head-
> board and upon its wide-girth posts, executed with a strong
> hand and an impressively delicate touch in a sensuous motif.

The catalogue writer discreetly omitted that the carvings were pornographic. He didn't need to state it. The photograph said more than he ever could.

Ugo Ferrante had studied the picture closely. This is a bed to fuck in! he thought, smiling broadly. He spoke to his employer and was guaranteed an advance on his salary.

The bidding had been unusually lively. The successful purchaser made no pretense at hiding his glee from the slender, well-dressed curator who had been outbid. Such a pity, the curator mused, that the bed was now the possession of this crude person.

It was a hot humid day, and although the thick stone walls of the villa provided insulation against the afternoon's oppressive humidity, Ugo Ferrante visibly sweated when he made out his check in payment. So many thousands of lire, far more than he had ever spent for any single purchase. He bent his leonine head; beneath the undisciplined growth of his dark hair, and in the rivulets of the furrows of his brow, beads of perspiration formed. When he raised his head to shoot a triumphant glance toward the curator, his large heavily-fringed eyes seemed black and menacing. His head was too large for his muscular short body, broad of shoulder and sinewy. In the heat of the bidding, he had loosened his collar and tie, and a growth of hair was visible under the shirt. His large powerful hands lay sprawled on the table before him. On the little finger of his left hand, he wore a remarkable diamond, set in gold, that he had borrowed from stock. The ring was designed to be worn by a gentleman. Ugo Ferrante was not that. His clothes were somberly correct, but he exuded an earthier heritage. All of the men present looked down their long Roman noses at him. But their women, had they been in attendance, would have been excited by his tremendous virility. In the proper circumstances, he would have no difficulty seducing them.

He had a peasant shrewdness, a quick, fierce intelligence that became pointedly brash the more uncomfortable he was with a situation. He sometimes argued rather violently with his employer, Leo Unger, quick to forget all that he owed the Jew who had befriended him when no one else would have seen potential in him. His humor was crude, but he could suppress it when he wished to. He harbored a fundamental scorn for the rich who were born to wealth, and sometimes mimicked them at Leo Unger's shop—after, of course, they had made their purchases. And now, he had bested them . . . the wealthy European collectors who had commissioned art-oriented advisers to attend this auction. That made the fact that this exquisite bed was his all the more sweet.

Saliva freely gushed into his mouth as he thought of how he would perform in his bed. How he would humble their women, and thus strip these men of their carefully preserved social mores. He was becoming sexually excited and his penis was jutting against the broadcloth of his pants. But he hadn't thought his objective through. The bed couldn't possibly fit into the smallish bedroom of his *appartamento,* not even if it extended onto the narrow terrace above the Via Gramsci, where he sometimes pensively gazed toward the treetops in the hilly Parioli district.

He capped the gold fountain pen—also borrowed from the store's stock—and looked down at the order of purchase. He felt proud. Ownership of the bed befitted the man he intended to be. He had stormed the portals, as it were, of a world where Leo Unger would never be admitted—the rarified, affluent, and virulently prejudiced atmosphere of the European aristocracy. He harbored no gratitude toward his illiterate mother, who had insisted he apply himself to such schooling as was available in their high Dolomite village. He resolutely shut off all memory of the long red-roofed houses, the lush green fields in spring, the cold mysterious look of the land in the frigid winters. He allowed himself to imagine but one vision of the village, a particular view from a high craggy peak.

In winter, it was from this vantage point that he determined he would run away. He had to elude a girl.

Ugo had traveled once again up the ice-slick trail to the overhung cave at the base of the sheer cliffs. The cave was stocked with food, warm blankets, and a lantern. Outside of the cave, sheltered by the rock face from the snow and wind, was a sizable patch of bare, still-green grass. It was here that Ugo brought his family's small herd of goats, tending them, collecting their milk for cheese making.

He had built a warming fire near the mouth of the cave, but on this day the wind blew the smoke into the hollowed area and he had to smother the flames. The girl had arrived a short time before, carrying provisions for him. Her cheeks were still reddened from the cold, enhancing the brightness of her expressive brown eyes. Warming herself at the fire, she had removed the outer layer of her weather-insulating garments. Ugo's busy hands were now assisting her to divest herself of the rest. Her mouth was parted and wet, her eyes closed with willing surrender. Suddenly, smoke filled the cave and Ugo got up and extinguished the fire; Maria started to shiver. But talking soothingly to her, Ugo drew her deeper into the cave, opened his leather pants, and filled her with his organ, burying his mouth in her neck. She clung to him. She felt incredibly warm. She gazed dreamily at him, seeking to kiss him. He pulled away and came.

Satiated, he urged her to return down the mountainside while it was still light enough for her to safely return to the village. There was an ingenuousness about her that caused her to prattle happily.

"How greatly I shall miss you as the winter deepens. The

path will be too difficult for me to climb, my delicious Ugo."

He occupied himself rebuilding the fire, carrying kindling wood to a more sheltered location. There was no more substantive answer than a grunt.

She bent across his back, flinging her arms around his neck. He jutted his elbow against her. "Get off of me," he shouted. "Do you want to sprain my back so I'll lie here paralyzed and the wolves will eat me?"

Her eyes grew wide with concern. "Did I hurt you? Tell me, did I?"

"It's plain you're a woman already. Always nagging."

"Are you all right? Just answer that."

"Well enough," he said grudgingly. Then irritably, "Are you going to stand there making cow's eyes, or are you leaving?"

"I'm going." But she didn't move. Her tone of voice took on a wistfulness. "In the early spring we can post our banns. Say you will, Ugo."

Turned away from her, he muttered, "We'll see."

She giggled. "Except you may not recognize me. I'll seem a different girl."

He stared at her as though she was crazy. "Get going," he insisted.

She remained standing, a secret dancing upon her tongue, bubbling for release. "I wasn't going to tell you . . . " She kicked at a stone with her foot, scraping the leather of her heavy shoe and not seeming to notice.

Ugo couldn't contain his irritation. "Say it and be off."

"Well . . . " She hung her head, drawing courage. Then the words tumbled out, slamming against his eardrums. "When I change my name from Maria Volpe to *Signora* Ugo Ferrante, it won't be just me you'll be getting. By then my belly will be big and round."

He stared at her in speechless horror. A turmoil roared within his mind. Should he push her off a cliff? If he picked up the rock she had idly kicked at, he could smash it against her eyes, her face. He might pretend he was about to kiss her and clasp his strong fingers around her throat to squeeze the life out of her.

When it was apparent throughout the village that she was pregnant, and when in her foolish way she babbled his name as her lover, there would be no escaping matrimony. He had no intention of marrying her. Simple Maria, the villagers called her. It was whispered that there was an erratic strain in the Volpe family—a madness that left its mark on every member. His son or daughter carrying the genes of insanity—never! Never while he lived.

His mind worked feverishly. If he killed her, he would be safe only as long as snow blanketed the grave he would dig for her. By spring her remains would be discovered. It had happened before. Although he'd been a small boy then, he remembered how a murderer was routed from his house and beaten to death before a *poliziotto di montagne* could intervene.

Ugo calmly bade her good-bye, urging her to take care on the trip down the mountain. She turned around several times, waving her arms, smiling happily. He forced himself to wave back.

"Until the snow thaws," she shouted back up to him.

He waved again.

That evening he didn't bother to milk the goats. Through the night he heard their cries of agony. By dawn he was stirring within the cave. He wrapped up in a cloth sack only what was absolutely necessary, and slinging his pack over one shoulder, he emerged to look down upon his village for the last time. Plumes of smoke rose from the chimneys, gray wisps coiling upward. Snow melted near the chimneys, exposing the glazed red roofing tiles. He gazed down in silence, frowning. Then he moved, descending by a different, more arduous route than she had taken. It led him southward, toward Venice. From there, ever southward. When he was a small boy, his mother had once told him a story about an adventurous cat named Puss in Boots.

"Why did the cat wear boots?" he'd asked. "Where was he going?"

"To Rome," she said. "All roads go to Rome, they say, *piccolo* Ugo."

Gaia was fascinated. Ugo Ferrante's life was like a fairy tale, and she sat listening like a little child. But she wondered, What on earth does it have to do with me?

· 44 ·

Agent Emil Natov continued his rendition of the Ferrante history. His voice was gruff and almost harsh. Gaia felt charged with excitement.

Ugo Ferrante refused to allow the bed he had just bought to be dismantled and crated. There was shouting and arguing from all sides, much to the amusement of some and the impatience of others. He was looking through a jeweler's loupe affixed to one alert brown eye. Squinting the other one and lowering a bushy dark eyebrow, he examined the detail of the erotic carving, a primer of sexual positions for the uninitiated. He decided he would overlay the wood with twenty-four-karat gold leaf. He could obtain this at wholesale cost. Although he was an earthy man and enjoyed a bawdy joke as much as anyone, he thought the contorted paired couples on the bas-relief disgusting. There was but *one* best position for a man with a woman: on top of her.

"Is he a jeweler?" someone asked.

"My wife would know. She's always buying the stuff!"

"A pity she isn't here."

A man who overheard the interchange said, "I've seen him in the Unger shop . . . the one that used to be a silversmith's, but now sells jewelry."

"In the Jewish section?" The questioner's voice rose incredulously.

"Recently the store moved to the Via Condotti. So much more convenient. Before, it was hard to find . . . really, it was so insignificant you might easily pass it by."

"Is he a partner, do you suppose?"

"With a *Jew?*"

When the youth Ugo Ferrante traveled toward Rome from the north, he had no idea where in the city he ought to head. He just knew he had to be there: Roma. To pay for occasional lodging, a dinner, and breakfast, he had offered his services every few kilometers. He helped repair a farmer's fence. He minded a pair of Doberman pinschers while their owner supped, and was nearly the dogs' meal when they attacked him. He serviced a woman old enough to be his mother in the back of her automobile, and she gave him one hundred lire. This was enough to allow him to hail and board a bus. When his money ran out, he was as hungry as before. There were many kilometers to be covered on foot before he might enter Rome.

It was night when he arrived and, dead tired, he dozed for a bit on the bank of the river Tiber. He wakened, startled by an official-sounding voice calling to him. He didn't wait to find out who it was and scurried across one of the graceful low bridges spanning the river. His eyes were closing as he stumbled along cobbled streets, weaving like a drunk. At last, unable to take another step, he tripped and sank down where he'd fallen in the doorway of some sort of shop. It wasn't until the dawn began to break that he opened his eyes and noted the empty display case and the painted wooden sign nailed to the building alongside the door: GIOIELLIERE.

He was too weak to stand and lay helpless, huddled in the shop entrance, moaning, feverish, his eyes glazing over. Presently the door opened from within. The ascetic-looking jeweler noticed the dirty exhausted figure as he walked to the front of his store to place platinum diamond-set earrings in the glass display case. Leo Unger was frail in appearance, with a long thin face, a drooping graying beard, and two tightly curled ropes of hair swinging past his ears. He stopped still at the sight of the crumpled boy, then bent to inspect him. The jeweler's lean body was surprisingly sinewy. Lifting the heavy youth by gripping him under the arms, he dragged him backward inside where he managed to get him on his feet. Then, guiding him, he bore his weight through the front shop, past the rear workroom, and into a small living space. He propped him on a chair before an oil-cloth-covered table and patiently fed him spoonful after spoonful of hot oat cereal, pausing from time to time to urge him to sip a little of the half milk, half coffee in a cup that he held tilted to his lips.

He saved his life.

Leo Unger was a kind man, but his new apprentice was undeniably clumsy. After months of tutelage, he still couldn't trust him to properly handle any of the delicate procedures in the workroom. Tweezers, seemingly, weren't made to be held by his broad peasant's hands that were used to rougher outdoors work. Once he had let fall a paper packet full of diamond chips. The two of them dropped to their hands and knees, moistening their fingertips to retrieve the minute stones. Unger, who was crawling along the floor, scooping them into the purposely long nail on his left-hand little finger, saw but pretended not to notice that Ferrante was slipping an occasional diamond chip into one of his pockets. It isn't such a great loss, the jeweler consoled himself. Each small stone by itself had no carat value and was fairly worthless. It was the boy's connivance at theft that distressed him. Still, he didn't want to put him out on the streets again, so he thought of how he might continue to employ him and benefit them both. Obviously any further work involving unset stones was to be ruled out.

Leo Unger made a withdrawal from his cash strongbox. "Do you understand anything about buying quality clothes?" he asked.

Ugo stared at him without comprehending.

"For you!" Leo poked him in his now well-fleshed ribs.

Ugo gaped.

"I see you don't get my meaning, and how could I expect you to? Myself, I am no example of elegance in my black clothes. So here is what we will do . . . "

Ugo Ferrante swiveled on the heels of his new highly polished shoes to admire views of himself in his navy blue pin-striped suit. A salesman instructed him how to knot his narrow tie and, after several bad starts, he had gotten the knack. He wore a white jacquard cotton shirt, and two others were packaged for him to take with him. The salesman asserted that he looked like a gentleman, and he felt transformed into one. A few lire were coming to him in change. He transferred the diamond chips from his old clothes and carefully folded a lira note about them. It made him feel affluent. Neither the stones nor the lire would be returned.

Leo Unger clasped his hands in admiration and shooed Ugo out of the workroom. From now on his apprentice would tend the shop. The jeweler kept a strict inventory of his finished pieces so there would be no opportunity for theft. Besides, he would pay Ugo Ferrante a commission on each piece of jewelry that he sold.

The customers came—women from upper social strata, drawn by the incredibly artistic unique designs. They were waited on by the handsome new clerk, and when he stared boldly into their eyes, they flirted with him. Several of the women urged Leo Unger to allow him to deliver purchases— during the day, of course, when their husbands were away from home.

The business prospered.

"Someday," Unger said, "I suppose I will make you my partner. It will be a small percentage of the net profit at first." He shrugged. "Later on, who knows?"

That time was close at hand.

Ugo Ferrante had, at last, put away his loupe and stalked out of the auction room. He passed through a loggia whose mosaic floor was a succession of pictorial designs. The empty

silken-covered walls revealed the outlines of missing paintings presently under the gavel. Opposite, a bank of windows
and an open door looked out onto a garden that, despite lack
of care, was still randomly in bloom. Evergreens, myrtles,
and lofty cypresses crowded its perimeters. A gravel path
rounded a stone fountain adorned with statuary. Momentarily, he stared, overwhelmed. Then he strode into the vestibule, his attention drawn to the great staircase ascending to
a second level. With no thought of seeking permission, he
unhesitatingly mounted it three steps at a time. He wandered
unembarrassed along the bedroom corridor, glancing into the
many unoccupied chambers, most of them bare of furnishings. He moved along, never pausing to admire the rococo
architectural appointments nor the many allegorical ceiling
frescoes: scenes and garlands of flowers that were so well
preserved they were almost as brightly colored as when the
paints had been applied to moist lime plaster centuries before.

At the far end of the corridor, he looked into the largest of
the rooms. Its windows, which were open, overlooked the
garden. The scent of flowers hung in the air. A slim figure of
a girl was silhouetted against the window, sitting in an attitude of hopelessness as she gazed forlornly out. Sunlight glistened on her shiny dark hair like a golden vermeil. She sensed
his presence and turned toward him. He saw that she was
older than he had at first supposed. Delicate fingers nervously
flicked away any dust that might have lodged in her hair from
pressing her head against the window frame. Her neck was
slender and her dark curls rested in ringlets on narrow shoulders—a charming effect that somewhat mitigated the boni-
ness of her chest. She wore a simple black dress, no jewelry,
as though she was in mourning. She regarded him inquir-
ingly.

"If you are here for the auction"—her words were cool and
measured—"it is in progress downstairs."

"I've already bought a bed," he bluntly stated. "Now I'm
looking over the house."

It amazed her that this intruder offered no apology for
standing face to face with her in her bedroom, as though he

had the same right of occupancy as she. She was also aware that he seemed to have no realization of acting improperly. He appalled her. But what could she do about it. Gisele Silvia Angela Maria di Corchese was helplessly trapped in a world in which women had no effective legal status. Despite her protests, her older brother—her sole immediate living relative—was actively selling off their estate. As a woman she had no say.

She looked at him steadily, and noticed that his clothes were well-tailored, his heavy watch of real gold, his gem-set ring unique and most likely very expensive.

"Do you like what you've seen in the villa?" she asked him, smiling.

"Uh huh." His reply was insolent as his gaze swept over her figure.

Ah, yes, he was obviously taken with her. She stood, rigid with nervousness, as he moved close to her. He extended a large powerful hand to her face and tilted her chin upward, appraising her as she had seen dogs judged. At that moment, she realized if there was any chance to remain as mistress of the villa that bore her family name, she had no other course but to seize it.

When he kissed her on the lips, she made no protest and pretended to be unoffended, and more, to reciprocate. Her budding materialism would have shocked the holy sisters who had been her finishing-school teachers. She had been a near-charity pupil, doubly orphaned, with just her good name to sustain her. When Ugo Ferrante more boldly fondled her, she prayed to God for forgiveness and broached what was on her mind. As she expected, this oaf was elated at the prospect she suggested.

The contracts were duly drawn, both property and marital.

Gisele pitied herself from what she thought of as the depths of her own degradation. She had married beneath her, but she had kept the villa. What she didn't know was that it had been purchased with Leo Unger's money.

When Ugo approached him asking for the loan, Leo recognized a great opportunity: This was a clever business move.

If Ugo Ferrante was set up as a real gentleman, it could go far to increase the store's business. On the Via Condotti, Leo had encountered substantially higher operating expenses; he had to enlarge the trade. It was who you knew. Leo Unger had already gone as far as he dared, but it wasn't enough. He'd cut off his *payiss,* shaved off his beard, adopted Western attire, but still, he was *different;* he was a Jew.

His gift to the groom was a ten-percent partnership; to the bride, her rings. For these, he received no thanks.

Gisele visited the shop but once. Her driver dropped her near the Via Condotti, a street closed to cars. She strolled among other pedestrians, pausing to admire the *vero cuoio* shoes on display in one shop, an array of marvelous silks, laces, and velvets in another show window. Passing Bulgari, she wondered at heavy-weight jeweled chains, an identifiable hallmark of their design. When she eventually approached Leo Unger's much smaller establishment at the far end of the street, she swept in imperiously, holding her delicate head up high. The shop was at the wrong end of the Condotti, she told them haughtily; it was difficult to locate; why was the sole designation above its entrance GIOIELLIERE? No wonder there was no one in the store.

She avoided her husband when he came from behind the counter to greet her. "Hasn't your shop got a better name?" she said sharply.

Leo Unger appeared from inside the workroom. He'd assumed a bent position, intending to press his lips to her gloved hand, when she smartly snatched her fingers from his grasp. He straightened up, eye to eye with her. "I suppose the full business name is 'Leo Unger, *Gioielliere,*' " he said.

Giselle sniffed disdainfully. "You're idiots. Both of you."

Ugo, on the verge of shouting, stepped toward her, but Unger waved aloft both his hands, signaling that he remain quiet.

She turned, enraged, on Leo Unger. "Let me assure you that your being a . . . *Hebrew* hurts the business.

"*I* nevertheless own it," Unger said quietly.

"Not all of it," she snapped.

"Shut up, you stupid *ficcanaso*!" Ferrante was furious.

"Liar! You don't care about money, do you?" she yelled at him. "Well, I do! Why else would I marry a boor like you?"

How he hated her. The *ficcanaso*'s temper was liable to ruin his sweet deal. The Jew had already given him ten percent of the jewelry business, supplied the cash to purchase the estate, and bought him an Alfa Romeo. A few months more and he was sure he could talk him into replacing it with a more expensive car—a Lamborghini, perhaps. He had no intention of repaying his debt for the Via Appia Antica estate; he doubted that Unger would ever invoke the mortgage terms. Still, he had to be careful.

Gisele's rosebud mouth tightened. She tossed her newly bobbed head. "At the very least you should change your name from Unger to Ungaro," she said. "Make it more Italian. Next you ought to place a splendid gold-lettered sign above the shop and in foil stencil upon your window: UNGARO." A small smile played upon her lips. "Better yet, UNGARO E FERRANTE. Eh?"

Leo looked at her for a long time, but he wasn't seeing her long blouse and short pleated flapper skirt. He wasn't aware of her rouged lips, nor of her shingled hair and deep cloche. He was mulling over in his mind what she had suggested. Her reasons didn't matter. After a while he answered, "Why not?"

He slid open a showcase and removed an 18-karat bangle. He opened its hinged lock and snapped it upon her wrist.

She hardly glanced at it. "*Grazie,*" she murmured, and swished out of the shop.

He began calling himself Leo Ungaro. He was grateful to her, although he well knew she hadn't suggested this for his benefit. Possibly her bigotry was no less than that of the Black Shirts who were gaining in power. Sooner or later, he told himself, restrictions against the Jews would prevail. With a Gentile partner, a prudent name, and extreme caution, he might escape their harsh attention.

The sign, UNGARO E FERRANTE, was cast in gilt metal and affixed to the building facade. When a store next door was vacated, the shop was enlarged. Leo was content to remain in the background. It was Ugo who made appearances at social events with Gisele accompanying him. Leo willingly selected jewelry from the store safe—special pieces to complement a new ball gown: pigeon-blood rubies to wear with pink satin, emeralds for white lace.

The business prospered.

And frequently on the morning following some function or other, individual pieces Gisele had worn were sold, sometimes an entire set: tiara, necklace, earrings, bracelet, and rings were delivered to some other woman who had admired them on her.

Then, suddenly, her brother died in a drunken automobile accident. Gisele took another trip into Rome and made another suggestion. Ugo Ferrante assumed his deceased brother-in-law's titled name. They were il Principe and la Principessa di Corchese. Leo was very, very pleased.

Her husband, however, remained a peasant.

During the early years of their marriage, Gisele could not say that she found Ugo mean, although she always assumed a posture of superiority that would have infuriated any man. But she had other worries. She dreaded sleeping with him in the large four-poster bed. Until she fell asleep, she lay still in frigid watchful apprehension, her long neck stiff on the pillow, her eyes open and suspicious in the darkened room, her arms crossed over her small breasts as if to shield her womanliness.

Confused and more than a little awed by her, at first Ugo was gentle with her, persuading her to submit rather than roughly taking her as had always been his way with other women.

"I'm sleepy. Please don't!" Gisele's protests were in vain.

He buried his lips in her thick dark hair, compulsively pursuing when she averted her face. Pinning her down with his body, he compressed his lips on hers, forcing them open, probing with his tongue, sometimes drawing blood when she tried to reject him.

He was stronger than she was. Her face smarted from the

roughness of his late-evening beard. The nights were his to command. Only in the morning might she exercise control by refusing to eat her breakfast until he had departed for the store. During the night she was helpless. His hands rolled back the sheet, lifted her nightgown. She lay in shock, rubbed sore as he rocked on her. Sometimes she would close her eyes and wonder if her breath came too rapidly in spasms.

One night, after they had been married for a month, Ugo got into bed and lifted her nightgown as usual, but sat astride her, peering angrily into the pale fearful face. He lifted a heavy hand and slapped her.

"You're a bigger slut than any whore in Rome," Ugo shouted. "They, at least, give a man what they're paid for. You are my wife and you won't let me treat you like a woman." He heaved deep grunts of anguish and, to her surprise, began to sob. She made no attempt to soothe him.

So Ugo Ferrante began to take random mistresses within the city. He was limitlessly sensual and still returned to Gisele demanding his marital rights. He would stagger in at night, angry and drunk, twist her about as if she were a rag doll with a vagina. Her unfettered shrieks thrilled him as he invaded her over and over. It didn't seem to give him pleasure, but impelled by his raw need, he demanded that sensation be fulfilled.

No longer rigid in his embrace, she struggled against him, slashing at him with her nails, one time purposely biting his penis. He was enraged and violated her in ways he had never handled a prostitute.

Gisele became pregnant and delivered a daughter. She selected one of her own names, Silvia. Then she announced she would have no further relations with Ugo. While he was away during the day, she had a locksmith fit their bedroom door with a new key. Ugo returned home hours later to discover the room barred to him. He went wild and thrust his powerful shoulders and large head against it like a battering ram until its hinges snapped. Inside, he made straight for the bed, where she cowered.

"*Puttana,* I'll fuck you until you give me a son. After that you can go to hell."

The midwife was exceedingly worried. "La Principessa is too tense. She is fighting this birthing," she whispered to a maid in attendance, out of the patient's hearing.

In Gisele's social set of faded nobility, it was the ultimate snobbism to spurn hospital delivery rooms. She would deliver in no other place than the four-poster bed in her villa. This, she was adamant about. Now she was in agonizing labor, sometimes out of her head, then fleetingly restored to reality. Hour following hour, the ordeal continued.

The midwife sponged her face and spoke of having her removed to a hospital while it was still early and there was time.

Gisele came to momentarily and was obdurate. "My son will be born in this bed."

Her condition worsened and the distressed midwife dispatched the maid to locate il Principe. He rushed in, sweat pouring down his pale tightly drawn face.

"What of my son?"

"The child could die, too."

"I'll carry her to my car and take her to a hospital."

"No! Not at this stage. The Via Appia Antica is unevenly paved. Mother and child will die for sure. Telephone for an ambulance. It will be staffed with a doctor."

"Yes, of course." He rushed into his study to place the call.

But it was too late.

In the lying-in chamber, Gisele gasped in the course of emitting an excruciating scream. Although the baby's head was now visible, it wouldn't budge any further. The midwife was cautious. She was afraid of crushing the skull. Then ... movement ... slow ... too slowly. When the infant's torso appeared, the mother hemorrhaged and blood seeped onto the sheet. The midwife urgently wiped it away from the child's nostrils, so engrossed in what she was doing that she ignored the mother's moans.

Gisele reached out, seeking to hold onto one of the gilded

bedposts. She was too weak and her hand fell away from it with gold leaf embedded beneath her nails. She was dead.

The infant girl survived and was named Angela Maria.

Emil Natov paused. "Are there any questions?" he asked.

"No," said Gaia. Was Angela Maria my mother? she thought, but said nothing.

· 45 ·

Agent Natov drew an ashtray toward him. "Will it bother you if I smoke?" he asked *after* he'd lit his cigarette.

Gaia indicated by a sweep of her head that it wouldn't.

Wisps of smoke curled from his lips. "Now I am going to skip to the time of World War II," he said.

On the evening before liberation day, Angela Maria Ferrante was betrayed.

Marksmen's bullets sprayed staccato rounds. Explosives rocked the foundations of ancient buildings. Rome, the Eternal City, was overrun by Nazis. It was a time of tenaciousness and disease, a total lack of freedom, and a fierce idealism.

Victims were trapped in flash searches of buildings from cellars to rooftop terraces. Patriots were tortured in the dreaded SS-administered Via Tasso Prison. Building walls were covered with the conqueror's edicts printed on pink paper—always pink paper. Males were to be conscripted. All those between sixteen and sixty must report for deportation to Germany as forced laborers. Men went into hiding. Men and women were forced into trucks to be driven up to the same stone wall built centuries before to *protect* Roman inhabitants. They were forced to dig trenches and were shot while they labored. The trucks kept rolling up, disgorging their human loads. With German efficiency, people were forced to climb atop those who previously had been killed. It simplified the disposal of the bodies.

Rome awaited salvation. There was the real threat that the Germans would mine the interlacing catacombs beneath the city, and that in one master burst of maniacal rage they would literally blow Rome apart, a strategy to offset their retreat.

To the south, the rumbling of battle could already be heard as the liberating troops fought . . . closer and closer to the city. Silent Romans apprehensively viewed the German armored exodus northward. Their divisions assembled in the Piazza Venezia. Mussolini had once exhorted the populace from a balcony overlooking it.

American, French, and English tanks were already surging from rolling terrain onto Highway 7, otherwise known as the Via Appia Antica. Their advance was disorganized. Units vied for position, each seeking to reach Rome first.

General Mark Clark summoned several news correspondents to ride with him in his jeep. Among them was Hugh Timothy Gerald, out of Chicago for a national American news syndicate. The general explained to the reporters that he hoped to enter Rome without firing upon it. Surveillance information indicated that there might be pockets of rearguard action by the Germans. Consequently, the Allied troops under his command would postpone entry until dawn.

At first light the divisions of troops surged forward. Without major incident, General Clark drove through the Porta Maggiore. But soon, he lost his sense of direction and ordered the jeep to stop. He asked a priest how to reach the center of Rome.

It was liberation day, 8 A.M., June 5, 1944.

They had sought refuge within a shabby building, bounding up the stairs to the top floor. There in an unfurnished room with peeling walls and ugly rust-colored ceiling stains of past leaks, they waited. Angela Maria wanted to appear brave, but her knees were weak. This place had specifically been selected for such an emergency because it overlooked the street, narrow, cobbled, and at the moment, deserted.

Angela Maria was a member of an underground group headed by the British agent Peter Lawden. His aide was Rinaldo Munni, an Italian Partisan. Lawden was a staunch capitalist, Munni a zealous leftist, and she an idealist. They would never have met in ordinary times. She watched the men pace when one or the other of them wasn't peering through the eyehole. We are like caged animals, she thought.

The night before, they had completed their final assignment, posting black-lettered messages on rough oat-hued stock, the only paper obtainable in a time of shortages. They had carried them from a hidden press, the ink not yet dry.

> THE ALLIED ARMIES ARE AT OUR GATES. Do not initiate terrorism against the departing Germans. Let them pass in silence and forestall further bloodshed. SALVATION IS AT HAND.

They slapped them over the hated official pink notices of German decrees with pride and a fierce joyful revenge.

Bruno Volpe, powerful, unkempt, and almost a wild man, had recently joined the group and fought vigorously against the hated Germans. Unlike everyone else on the team, except for Peter Lawden, whose mission was to organize the Resistance and to personally transmit shortwave communications to a central intelligence office whose location even he did not know, Volpe wasn't a citizen of Rome. His attire was that of a mountain man. He wore his heavy boots in all seasons, even when it turned warm. Despite his hulking size, he was agile and could scale walls that left others breathless. He could outrun any one of them. It was his brute strength that made him valuable—that, and the fact that he never showed any fear. He was capable of moving swiftly and noiselessly. A man without small talk, who pretty much kept to himself, he'd made the Partisans uncomfortable in his presence whenever they rested together between assignments, until they got used to him.

But Angela Maria invariably still experienced a chilling shiver whenever she was in his company; and she managed to keep her distance from him. Yet his eyes were generally turned on her. There was never lechery in his unsmiling appraisal of her. She saw something worse.

It was a gaze of unmitigated hatred.

And now, at the last moment of the Nazi occupation, Lawden had been warned by a street fighter that someone had denounced them to Kommandant Mueller, a high-ranking SS officer. The safe place closest at hand had been this room. It was only after they were locked within it that he had gotten another message . . . Volpe, the Fox, as he'd wanted to be called, had betrayed them. And Volpe would know exactly where they'd be.

"Damn it all!" Lawden exclaimed. "He's got us confined here like bloody ants in a trap."

Munni fumed. "I used to think there was something strange about that *coglione*, but I shrugged it off. He was fighting on our side. That was all that mattered."

"No, the blame is mine. I ought to have been more wary of the bastard when he wouldn't take orders and did things on his own. Successfully, I admit. But the man was a horror. Did you ever see the maniacal glee . . . it's the best way to describe it . . . that suffused him when he made a kill? Pulling his goddamn bloodied knife out of some sonofabitch Nazi's back, or his throat, and then holding the blade aloft."

Lawden slapped his palm with the empty bowl of a pipe he always carried, although he never could find the tobacco to tamp in it. "No, I can't forgive myself. Events are foretold with tall shadows, and I must have had blinders on." He tilted his head like a tall molted bird. "It hurts me though that our sweet Angel should come to this. For us, Rinaldo, it's a way of life."

"*Oppure la morte*," he replied slowly. "She is the bravest one of us. Does she weep like any other woman would?"

Angela Maria looked toward Rinaldo Munni, embarrassed by his praise. He had dark curly hair, olive skin, incredibly white teeth, and although she could not imagine where he obtained garlic—scarce as it was in wartime—he invariably had a pungent aroma wafting about him. Her thoughts drifted to another time. If I can't escape and I am killed in this room, at least let me be thinking of happier times. The best of those moments she associated with the aroma of her favorite perfume. Not for her the famous ones that Silvia used, hers was formulated for her in a small perfumerie shop since demolished in an Allied bombing. She'd hidden the tightly stoppered lovely purple flacon in one of her vanity table's deep drawers. Someday, after this terrible war—should the perfumerie shop reopen—she'd be able to purchase the lovely scent again.

"I'm not brave. I'm so frightened that I am already chilled as if I were dead."

Sounds of movement were heard in the street. Lawden squinted through the smeared windowpane. He turned back to them. "It's all right. People are heading toward the piazza."

Angela Maria's heart was beating hard. "Could we mingle with them?" she asked.

"We might have, but they've already passed by."

Her voice rose in desperation. "We must take to the roof."

"No," Rinaldo Munni objected. "That way leads to the gate of heaven. I've checked it out. The rooftops are constructed in such a manner that there is no possibility of us leaping in safety from one roof to another."

"Then there remains no way except to attempt running for it."

"Not now. Most likely someone watches the street door."

"Peter just said that there's no one remaining in view."

"Ah, but *viewing!* That's another story. Quite likely the Fox is hidden within a nearby doorway waiting for the Krauts, just as we are."

Lawden, who had remained crouched at the window, spoke urgently. "I see a couple of German uniforms headed this way. One of them is hauling a large sack, probably filled with loot. Uh, uh, this is it! They've entered this building."

Munni crossed himself. "May Bruno Volpe burn in hell."

As he moved across the room closer to the door, Lawden whispered to him. "You're a mixed-up prayerful sort of Commie, old chap," he said. Both men briefly smiled. The Englishman then put his hand to his mouth to signal silence.

Nearing footsteps sounded on the worn creaking stairs.

"Quickly!" He yanked Angela Maria. "Flatten yourself against the wall beside the door so it will shield you from their sight."

Both men drew their pistols.

"When they enter, we'll try to shoot first. You must immediately run out of the flat—"

There were tears in her eyes. "We've worked too long together. I want to remain."

There was a staccato rapping on the door.

"*Ja?*" Lawden answered in German.

The reply came in Italian. "*E molto importante. Si puo entrare?*"

As Munni recognized the voices, relief showed on his face. "It's okay," he told Lawden. After the door was unbolted, one of the men entered while the other stood guard outside.

He was dressed in an ill-fitting German uniform that had seen better days. He was on the verge of opening the sack when he noticed Angela Maria. His eyes widened and he swept off his peaked cap.

Munni tugged at his sleeve. "Is there a way out?"

"*Sì.* There are uniforms in the bag. You will put them on." He kept staring at her. "We thought there were just two of you."

Lawden spoke up. "They are for Angela and Rinaldo. I'll take my chances."

Munni objected: "You British with your chivalrous code make us Italians laugh. Ever look at her figure? Anyone could tell she's a woman." He was already drawing up the trousers of one of the captured German uniforms. When he shrugged into the tunic, he lamented, "*Madre di Dio*, it's caked with dried blood."

"How do you suppose we got them?" the Partisan asked as he motioned to Lawden to dress himself. "Let's get out of here."

They scrambled down the stairs.

"We'll keep our Angel between us," Lawden decided, "as if she's our prisoner."

From the vestibule, they peered into the street. No one was visible and they ventured forth stiff-legged, imitating the Germanic military gait. "*Achtung!*" he commanded as they set off toward the piazza.

Just then, from the far end of the street behind them, came the sound of heavy trucks rumbling across the uneven pavement.

"Hurry!"

Abandoning the gait, they ran, the two Partisans bringing up the rear. Lawden and Munni each held one of Angela Maria's arms. Once, because she glanced back, she nearly lost her footing. A German staff car and three personnel-carrying trucks had halted in front of the building from which they'd come.

"*Nummer drei.*" The kommandant had a deep voice that carried well. "You!" he selected a corporal. "Get in there and machine-gun the door. Execute them on the spot."

The corporal smartly saluted and, with his rifle ready, he ran up the stairs ahead of a contingent of soldiers. He burst through the open doorway. From further down the stairwell, the others heard the riveting burst of bullets.

He came out directly. He was sweating profusely. "It is done," he cried out, hastening down. The men on the lower steps quickly turned toward the street. None of them wished to tarry. The Allies were already in Rome.

The corporal held a thumb up, barely pausing as he sprinted past the staff car, to be hoisted into the back of the nearest truck, which was already revving up its motor. It would be wise for him to never tell anyone that the prisoners had escaped, lest the kommandant's wrath be turned against him. Possibly, far worse, would be the enmity of the one called Volpe . . . *the Fox.* Who could guess where he might turn up next? Most German soldiers feared him and memorized his description.

Astonishingly, he had seen him the day before when the Fox appeared out of nowhere and engaged in conversation with the kommandant. He watched them shake hands, hardly believing what he saw . . . the fastidious officer and the ragged

Partisan. A deal had been struck. Of course, now he knew
what that was—betrayal of Peter Lawden, who was a thorn
in the side of the Nazi command.

The corporal sat in the rear of the truck remembering how
the Italian had disappeared as quickly as he'd come. He had
twisted away from the kommandant, bolting in the corporal's
direction, passing by him so close at hand, his head tilted, sly
like a fox. The specter of his eyes burned into him. They were
almost inhumanly cruel—rapacious.

· 46 ·

Bruno Volpe HAD BECOME A NEAR LEGEND, ERODED BY THE COLD sweat of his victims into a monument of fear. He was spoken of in whispers, lest he suddenly appear and take vengeance upon those who discussed him. His dialect, like himself, was as rugged as the high mountain range where he was born. He slashed out at whomever he saw as his enemy, slaughtering Fascist or Nazi, patriot or Partisan. He was driven by a raging inner fury that no one understood because his violence was incredible to them. After slashing a man's throat from ear to ear, twisting the blade of his knife into another's entrails and reaching into the bloody gore with one hand, holding his knife high in the other, he would roar triumphantly, his face upraised with an expression of sheer joy. Then he would wipe the blade on the dead man's clothes, sheathe and pocket it. His moment of elation had passed. His face assumed its customary guarded watchful look. He was a man who waited, his eyes darting as if he was seeking a personal enemy.

Peter Lawden's first impression of the Fox was that he would be useful to him. He scoffed at the warnings that the Fox was a madman, that he had a hidden motive for his lust for killing. The Englishman was sufficiently convinced that his own superior intellect could keep the essentially stupid mountain man in control. After all, wasn't he a trained intelligence officer? Despite the difficulty posed by the German occupation of Italy in the north, Lawden obtained facts and wasn't surprised by the Fox's treachery. Once he began to unravel the truth about him, he'd been wary of such a possibility. Except that it came sooner than he'd expected. Lawden had been counting on liberation day beating Volpe to the punch. This was an error of judgment and it rankled that he was to blame.

Munni and Angela Maria believed that Volpe's betrayal was prompted by madness.

Peter Lawden knew better. He knew that he and Munni weren't the prime targets. As the three of them ran, he decided that he must explain to Angela Maria.

She had literally run into Lawden five months before as he was rounding the corner from the Via Lucullo into the Via Sallustiana. She had knocked the wind out of him and it took a moment for him to recognize that she was in a state of shock. "Can I help you, signorina?"

Her lips moved but no words were formed. It was her wide-open eyes that spoke eloquently of some horror that had rendered her temporarily speechless. Lawden saw that she was young, probably no more than sixteen. Her face seemed wan and extraordinarily pale against her dark hair, especially when a soft breeze bobbed curled wisps against her forehead and cheeks.

He couldn't leave her to wander about, but he couldn't afford to draw attention to himself, so he began walking with her, actually guiding her steps. When they reached a *caffè*, he led her to an inside table, ordering espresso for them both. In a time of shortages, it was predictably weak but nevertheless bracingly hot. At first she sat staring at her cup. Then when she took a sip of the boiling coffee, this startled her and her eyes took on a less staring expression. As he watched, her mind and her tongue became unfrozen.

Her voice was so low-pitched that he had to strain to hear. "They've . . . they've taken him away—the dearest, kindest man. He was the only person to give me affection." She wiped her eyes with the back of one hand. "I should have been with him. He needed me."

"Did the Nazis arrest your father?" he questioned gently.

"No." She burst into heaving sobs.

Breathing deeply, she fought to control herself. She looked at Peter Lawden's sympathetic and typically British face with its aquiline nose and bone-prominent cheeks. She decided she could trust him. Besides, she had to talk to someone; she was suddenly entirely alone in the city. She had no thought of returning home. She began to relate her story.

Her father's lust had, for as long as she could remember, provided him with ever-changing mistresses, a number of whom took up temporary residence in the villa. None of them were motherly. Angela Maria had been a lonely little girl who retreated into shyness when confronted by strangers, especially those among her father's houseguests. Not so her sister. Silvia was her opposite, a natural flirt. She was coquettish even with Mussolini when he had visited some years earlier. Il Duce's pomposity had brought Italy into an uneasy alliance with Hitler, and it was the Germans who were currently entertained at the villa. Like the titled Italians he imitated, Ugo Ferrante had previously opened his home to higher-echelon *Fascisti*. Now he courted Nazi officers. He desired to save his estate and personal property above his wish to save his country. The prevailing uniforms, like turning leaves, had changed in a new season to German brown.

When Giorgio, the butler, was conscripted despite his being overage for military duty, Angela Maria was bereft in the villa. From childhood, he had been her sole friend there. How many times she had sat near him in the pantry while he polished heavy chased silver, often sipping a glass of milk and nibbling on cookies as she poured out small confidences she could never tell her father. "If you need a friend," he told her, "go to Signor Ungaro. He is a kind gentleman."

That meant traveling to Rome, hitching a ride whenever she could, other times using a rickety bus service. The better-functioning buses, like Giorgio, had been taken away. Leo Ungaro had seldom been a guest at the Via Appia Antica villa in the past and now that was impossible. He was a Jew, and it fascinated her that he looked no different from other men except for the yellow star he wore affixed to his left sleeve. At the beginning, she visited him at the Via Condotti store, where recently the trade had been largely with German officers demanding and receiving huge discounts. Soon increasingly severe restrictions were placed against Jews. Many had already been rounded up and transported by cattle cars to concentration camps. Ungaro had been spared until then because Ugo was his partner.

"Don't come here anymore," he had said. "They have ways of finding out that my name was originally Unger. Your affection is precious to me, child. But I want you safe."

Angela Maria frowned and vehemently refused. Over the next several weeks she appointed herself his protector, watching over him as he worked in the store, watching everyone who came into contact with him. To cover her daily trips into Rome, she pretended to Ugo that she was meeting girlfriends in the city—until a day they'd each anticipated with dread, when he whispered to her in a corner of the shop, lest they be overheard, that he had made his plans and wouldn't be in the Via Condotti store anymore.

To all intents, Leo Unger had disappeared from Rome. Only Angela Maria knew that he had sequestered himself in a concealed inner room within his smallish palazzo on the Via Sallustiana. He boarded up the once-magnificent windows to create an aspect of disuse about the building. His sole visitor was Angela Maria, who brought him foodstuffs filched from the villa's storeroom.

He could no longer be seen in the public areas of Rome. The Germans were deporting Jews to the concentration camps, to Auschwitz and Belsen. Innocent people were rounded up after the Nazi officers extorted their wealth and jewels in ransom, and they were forced into cattle cars.

When she returned to her father's villa, she was exceptionally withdrawn. She knew that Leo Unger's life was in her safekeeping.

Her silence didn't pass unnoticed by her sister. "Cat got your tongue?" she taunted. The saving grace was that, in the evenings when the brown Nazi uniforms filled the villa, Silvia's attention turned to them. Frequently tipsy, she giggled as they groped her and she willingly accompanied them to her bedroom. Several times she offered unwelcome advice to Angela Maria. "When are you going to be clever like me and consort with the officers who visit? It is the Germans who have the wealth now. Perhaps," she tittered, "you can get one of them to give you some pretty trinket they've taken from the Jews."

"Never!" Angela Maria turned away.

Ugo overheard, and gave them both an angry look.

Nearby, Silvia's voice erupted in petulant disagreement with a Nazi officer. He thrust her away from him, addressing Ugo. "Your elder daughter is mooing like a miserable cow," he said insultingly. "Tonight I shall bed your other daughter. The virginal one."

Angela Maria looked frantically about her for a means of escape. Her admirer, a Gestapo general, allowed her to move about at will as he consulted with one of his recently arrived lieutenants. Easing slowly backward, she tried to be inconspicuous. Once she had reached a corner of the room where she was able to withdraw to the far side of a gilded grand piano with miniature classical scenes painted on it, she felt relatively safe. A door just behind her opened onto a side terrace.

It was too late for the bus run, and she could hardly afford to be overtaken as she walked toward Rome on the Via Appia Antica. She peered into the German staff cars. When she found one of them with a key left inserted in the ignition, she hastily slipped behind the wheel. After barely avoiding flooding the engine, she drove haltingly, fearful of pursuit. Arriving safely in the city, she abandoned the vehicle on an unlit street several miles from the Via Sallustiana. Not until then did it occur to her that she had never before driven.

"Now I am an escaped person like you," she announced to Leo Ungaro.

"My hiding place shall also be your refuge. Is that what you wish?"

She said it was. They would share this, just as he had entrusted her with his secret about the fortune in jewels.

"Impossible! I am a Jew. Should we ever be found together, you would be in as grave danger as I."

"I have kept your secret. No one suspects that you are here."

"I suppose you are right," he said.

They were both wrong.

He settled himself on a couch and gave her his bed. He insisted, over her protests, that this was the only way he would allow her to stay. While she slept, he sat on the couch writing throughout the remainder of the night. When he had finished, he sealed the several sheets of paper in a thick envelope, hoarded from prewar times. As morning broke, he asked Angela Maria if she would undertake to deliver the envelope. "I wouldn't ask it of you, but there is no one else," he said. "It is my last will and testament. I want you to take it to this man." With his finger, he underscored the name he had written on the envelope. "He is a lawyer . . . not one I especially trust, but I believe he will do what I ask for payment." He handed her a stack of lira notes. "Instruct him to place this envelope unopened in my safe-deposit box. Here is the key, and here on this paper a power of attorney."

She read the name on the envelope. "Giuliano Rinzini. Why can't it be hidden here in your house?"

"The Nazis could search and find it at any time."

"You're safe here, aren't you?" she asked anxiously.

"For the moment . . . but in case I have to leave—" Leo saw her distress and he extended his arms. "Come, give this old man a kiss good-bye."

"Please leave the palazzo with me," she begged him.

"No, child. Even if I must remain locked in one room, this is my home. I wish to remain here for as long . . . " His voice trailed off.

Angela Maria sensed that she must leave him imprisoned with the beautiful art treasures he had crowded into his refuge. When she turned back to him at an ingenious false wall—perfectly balanced on an axis so that it swung open and shut noiselessly—he raised a hand to wave her on. His fingers clutched a Fabergé egg.

It was the last time she saw him alive.

When she hastened back to the Via Sallustiana, the boards were ripped off the lower windows and from the main entrance. Men in brown German uniforms were piling paintings and statuary into a khaki-painted truck.

With both of her hands clapped to her mouth so that she wouldn't scream, she backed into a doorway on the opposite side of the street from where she watched undetected. Two soldiers emerged from the palazzo carrying a body bag. One end of it was torn. Before her horrified gaze, Leo Ungaro's head poked through, dangling backward, bumping against the pavement until they heaved him high and swung him into a makeshift hearse.

Angela Maria stopped speaking and looked up, glassy-eyed, at Peter Lawden.

He wanted to touch her hair comfortingly as one does a child's, to hold her to him in order to diminish her living nightmare, but she was as terrorized as a small animal at bay. She was an innocent, and he wasn't about to add to her trauma.

"Well now, little lady, I can't leave you here by yourself." He intended to convey hearty optimism for her benefit. "You'll need looking after, such as we can give you under the circumstances. Don't be afraid. Come along with me. At least you'll have shelter, a bit of food, and you'll be with friends, I promise you."

She nodded, and her emotions shook her. She was silently crying.

"We can't remain here any longer." He left coins on the table for their coffee. "When we leave, take my arm as though we're strolling. We don't want to call attention to ourselves.

She did as he told her, accommodating her pace to his. And as they walked, words formed to convey her sorrow.

"I loved Leo as though he were my father. I often wished he was. I want to kill those Nazis who murdered him."

Some one hundred feet from the piazza, they continued to run hard. Rinaldo Munni, having glanced back, whooped joyfully when he saw that the German unit was pulling out of the narrow street in the opposite direction. Peter Lawden nevertheless urged them to keep up their pace. Although he didn't say it to the others, he was alert to the possibility of their being trailed. All around him people were smiling, tears streaming down their faces, embracing one another, shouting happily.

And suddenly, Lawden knew it was urgent for him to speak to Angela Maria alone.

He drew her away from Munni. "Before we disperse," he said to her, "there is something of importance you should know. It affects you personally."

She turned to him puzzled; her mouth open to ask him a question, but Munni interrupted, spreading his arms to enfold them. "This is the way we part. Eh, *amico*? He addressed Lawden, wetly kissing him on both cheeks. As usual, he was scented with garlic. "After the war is over, will you return to London and carry a furled umbrella as an English gentleman does? Stick it up your ass!" he said affectionately. The men cuffed each other like small boys and shrugged the Nazi uniform jackets from their shoulders. Then Munni turned toward Angela Maria. Despite his leftist leanings, Munni was a middle-class man, always imbued with a sense of rank. He kissed her hand. It was she who embraced him.

"God go with you," he told her, and he disappeared into the crowded piazza.

Finally, Lawden stood alone with Angela Maria. "I hope you will return to your father's villa," he said. "While you

were with us, I managed to protect you from the men who
. . . their interests in you were . . . Well, I kept you out of their
way the best I could."

"I was aware of it, Peter, and I am grateful."

"My word, if I didn't have more than twenty years on you,
I might have—"

She smiled. "Thank you."

"You're not offended? I meant it respectfully, you know."

She shook her head. "Knowing you, I'm honored."

"You're not the sort of girl who should be on her own. This
city is going to be rough . . . chocolate bars and nylon hose
in return for favors to the troops. Do you understand my
drift? . . . Yes? . . . Well, *good!*" He paused, and his face took
on a more serious expression. "There is something more I
must tell you. I've been mulling it over in my mind and I've
decided it is your right to know."

Angela Maria could sense that whatever he had to say mer-
ited her close attention. She recognized the guarded undertone in his voice, akin to the whispered warnings he had given
whenever he'd allowed her to play a small role in their mis-
sions: to pretend to flirt with a Nazi soldier; to scoot across
a street and divert attention from some covert activity; to act
as a lookout while they stole weapons, rifled files, planted
explosive charges.

They were jostled by excited people into the center of the
square, where a sort of mass intoxication spread and intensified. Everywhere around the piazza banners were being un-
furled from overhead windows, bed sheets with slogans of
victory inked on. There was singing; others were tearfully
joyous. There was the constant sound of raised human voices.

"Please tell me quickly," Angela begged him, growing apprehensive about what his information might be.

"Of course you know it was the Fox who betrayed us. I
believe that he gave our location to the Nazis because of his
maniacal desire for revenge."

She said emotionally, "He had to be insane to have turned
on us."

Peter Lawden fixed his watery blue eyes on her face. "Not on us, m'dear. I am convinced he was after *you.* "

She stopped walking and stared at him.

It was impossible to talk; everyone was moving in a different direction, and they were swept along in the human current.

He pulled her toward him, putting his arm about her shoulder to keep them together. "I possibly should have told you before, but God knows, you've been through enough these past months, and until today I've kept his identity secret because the last thing I ever wished was to alarm you. I believe that Volpe also gave away your jeweler friend's hiding place. That wouldn't have been because he was after Leo Ungaro or Unger, however you wish to call him, but because he assumed it was your father you were surreptitiously visiting."

"My father? But . . ."

The crowd kept pressing them forward, compelling them to move with its tide. Momentarily she was pulled away from Lawden. He reached toward her, and she felt him clasp her hand to keep them from being separated. "Listen to me," he shouted to her, "and you will understand. Bruno Volpe, the Fox, is—" He emitted a loud cry. His hand gripped hers tighter for an instant. Then it dropped away.

She lost sight of him for a moment and then realized he had fallen. She tried to protect him from being trampled. She was bending over him. "Peter, what is it? Let me help you up."

He lay sprawled, face forward, and didn't answer.

She shrieked.

A knife handle extended from his back. Blood was pouring from the wound and soaking through his jacket.

"He's dead," someone said.

She bent over further, intending to pull out the knife, but she shuddered and backed away. Strangers lifted her to her feet. "I am convinced he was after *you,*" Peter had said. Had

Volpe done this, too? Whoever had killed Lawden might still be close by—ready to kill her, too.

But she still didn't know why.

Gaia shuddered. She was thinking of threats upon her own life.

· 47 ·

AFTER ENTERING ROME AS ONE OF THE AMERICAN NEWSMEN
selected to ride with General Mark Clark, Hugh Thomas
Gerald, whose byline was familiar to the newspaper readers
of his syndicated column as H. T. Gerald, decided to roam the
city on foot. He was impressed to see that the city's newspapers, *Il Tempo, Avanti!,* and *Il Giornale d'Italia,* now free of
Nazi-imposed censorship, had already hit the streets with
banner headlines announcing the liberation. On inner pages
there was more somber factual reportage of SS cell doors at
the Via Tasso and Regina Coeli prisons being flung open by
Allied liberating soldiers. Those who could still walk had
emerged into the sunlight of a free Rome, their eyes shocked
into squinting at the unaccustomed brightness. Many were
hobbling, their muscles wasted from long incarceration. Others were evacuated on stretchers by medics. These filthy,
malnourished, pale, and physically wasted survivors were the
fortunate few among the prisoners. For others, rescue had
come too late.

Everything that Gerald saw, he made mental note of. It was
all so vivid that there was no need to scribble in his notebook.
When he randomly interviewed passersby in his makeshift
Italian, their descriptions of loss and privation sent pain
through his body. He felt personally involved as he continued

wandering through the bustling streets. He had heard of the famous Via Veneto and inquired how to get there. By chance he was passing the Palazzo Margherita at the moment the Stars and Stripes were being hoisted on a tall flagpole before the reclaimed American Embassy. He stood watching from across the street, cap in hand, his right hand at salute, swallowing hard and experiencing enormous pride. Behind him, people who were ensconced at sidewalk tables began cheering and waving their arms.

"Viva! Urrà! Bravo!"

Presently he found himself being hugged by many of them and kissed on the cheeks. Just as vigorously, he returned their embraces. He accepted a sip of a robust red wine, then, slapping down money on one of the tables, instructed a smiling waiter to treat everyone on him. They urged him to remain, but he pulled away. The story he would file had taken form in his mind. He would begin by relating this experience.

"Telefono?" he inquired, cupping an ear with his fist.

They pointed him across the street to the Hotel Excelsior.

In the lobby, he dodged cleaning crews determinedly eradicating all evidence of German occupation. A large photograph of Hitler had been spread on the floor for all to walk upon. Gerald ground his heel on the Führer's face, and was greeted with broad smiles and shouts. The ordinary decorum of the establishment was in abeyance on this day.

Soon seated within a *cabina telefonica*, he was speaking to the operator. With patience and a measure of good luck, he hoped to establish a transatlantic connection, calling in his column to the IP news bureau editorial office in Chicago.

At last Giuliano Rinzini might openly emerge from his office. Throughout the German occupation he had confined himself here, never using electricity lest he call attention to his presence. Only at night had he ventured into the streets to scrounge for scraps of food, then to scurry rodentlike back to his hiding place.

This morning, as usual, he had crept to the window, carefully positioning himself to the side of it, peering out without being seen. Instantly, he perceived that the atmosphere had dramatically changed. There were no German uniformed men in view, no ominous armored vehicles rumbling through the streets with the swastika emblem hoisted. Amazingly, he was watching a line of flower-bedecked tanks wending their way past cheering crowds. *Dio sacro!* It was now once again safe for him to be openly seen on the streets, to mingle with the celebrants, perhaps to boast of *his* heroism. How would they know that he had secreted himself in order to avoid conscription? *Fools!* He was contemptuous of those who had allowed themselves to be inducted. But he had little patience to think about them. He was jubilant. He would have his telephone reconnected, the electricity turned back on.

One of the few people who had known of his presence was the building janitor, whom he'd bribed for his silence. Even so, Rinzini had negotiated the amount to a smaller sum than the man requested. He was shrewd and conniving, and he was vain about this, confident he would someday be a rich man.

His worst moment and greatest alarm had been on the day when there was an insistent rapping on the law office's door. Panic-stricken, he had cowered beneath his desk, crouching there without moving, barely breathing, petrified of being discovered. Eventually, after a final rattling of the doorknob, the caller had departed.

An envelope had been pushed across the sill beneath the locked door. Tiptoeing across the room, he had picked it up and read his name in bold old-fashioned script. When he slit open the heavy watermarked envelope, he found tucked into it a hastily written power of attorney and several more thoughtfully written pages. A will! A smaller envelope contained a bank vault key.

Since he was never free to go about the city during business hours, there had been no opportunity to carry out Leo Ungaro's wishes. Today when he took to the streets, the envelope was in his inner jacket pocket—not that he expected the banks would be open. During his isolation he had thought almost constantly about what had been delivered into his hands. He determined that there were two possible courses of action, the second of which would benefit *him*.

His first act must be to learn whether Leo Ungaro was still living. This he would discover easily enough by visiting the Via Condotti shop.

He hadn't allowed a day to pass without praying for the hunted Jew to have been dealt with by the Nazis . . . not merely for him to have been captured but for him to be dead. As Giuliano Rinzini walked past merrymakers, he told himself that it wasn't as though *he* would have killed him. Later on, he would stop into a church and light a candle for him.

He took no part in the celebrations as he pressed onward through the active streets. He was a man with a mission and contemptuous of the populace's emotional outpouring. Let them behave as mindless fools. He was a man about to take advantage of his greatest opportunity. And wasn't he deserving of good fortune? He prided himself on his shrewdness. Hadn't it been clever of him to purposely seek out an office overlooking a busy intersection where he might lean from the open window whenever he heard automobiles collide, and then hasten down the stairs and into the fray, positioning himself between the angry drivers, to whom he announced himself as an *avvocato?*

"Not merely a lawyer," he pronounced, "but one who also happens to be a witness."

Upon occasion, he connived to represent both litigants in an immediate settlement. Naturally, he received double fees. And so it was that when Ugo Ferrante, il Principe di Corchese, managed to hit two cars almost at once, Rinzini found a way to pander to his client's proclivity for female flesh. In this manner he worked his way into handling minor legal matters for the prestigious jewelry firm. He was aware that this connection was likely the reason why his name had come to Leo Ungaro's mind when he required the services of one who was unquestionably trustworthy . . . a lawyer.

Giuliano Rinzini's small eyes glistened with the prospect of eventual untold wealth as he continued pressing through the crowds, chuckling to himself with his thick lips tightly closed. If anyone noticed him, they would have thought he was chortling at Rome's salvation. Then he was confronted with the imposing facade of the Banco Nazionale Del Lavoro with its doors wide open. An Italian flag was displayed in each of its windows.

Rinzini instinctively laced tightly crossed arms over his chest. He could feel the outlines of the packet in his breast pocket. The bank's being open for business was a sign that he should no longer continue toward the Via Condotti. It was less important to know whether his divine entreaty for Leo Ungaro's fate had been realized. He made his decision. He would enter the bank, present the power of attorney, and attain access to the Jew's safe-deposit box. True, his name and signature would be placed on file. That might later prove incriminating, but a clever man such as he was would work out that detail.

A sly smile wreathed his pudgy face. He began whistling off-key, walking much faster and more confidently. There was a chance for him to become a giant among men in the postwar world . . . if he bided his time . . . and was clever.

. Of course, much depended on Angela Maria.

· 48 ·

AM I BEING TOLD THIS STORY BECAUSE I AM SUPPOSED TO BELIEVE
that Hugh Thomas Gerald and Angela Maria Ferrante were
my parents? Gaia wondered.

Why? And how might she be certain this was the truth?

When Hugh Thomas Gerald first spotted the girl, it was
after he had phoned in his column and decided to take in the
sights of Rome. "Lucky stiff!" the Chicago rewrite man had
blurted out, obviously envious of him. "Nothing for you to
do but go sightseeing . . . and those *Eye*-talian gals should be
mighty grateful to us Yanks."

Gerald was too full of excitement and pride to let the distant voice bother him. He headed for the Vatican. The majestic dome of St. Peter's had coexisted with and finally survived
a harsh invader. The Pope had received the Nazi commanders
in his antechamber, where he pitted the Church's influence
against them. Roman monasteries, convents, and churches
were declared by papal order to be places of refuge for the
city's Jews after approximately one-eighth of the Jewish population had been gassed at Auschwitz. Additionally, there
were priests who worked with the Resistance, slipping
through the Vatican gates, relying only upon their clerical
garb for a measure of protection.

Gerald stood before those gates now, feeling his eyes mist over. He wiped at them impatiently.

Suddenly a dark smiling man grabbed him, wanting to spread a rumor that was passing from tongue to tongue. Everyone was excited over it.

"Il Duce stole out of Rome during the night with his mistress."

Another man shouted, "Good riddance, but he should have cracked his skull falling off the balcony."

"I heard he was so despondent that he was unshaven."

"*Buono!* She will not wish to kiss him."

This was greeted with much laughter.

Hugh was swept along in the celebrations. Everywhere, people perched on heroic-size sculptures for the best viewing advantage. Some were comically positioned on a triton having a man's torso and a fish's tail. He pushed on. In another *piazza*, boys had climbed onto Moses holding the Ten Commandments, while others balanced upon a duo of angels and sat upon four lions. Everywhere the ubiquitous pigeons were displaced.

Gerald committed himself to the human flow as he inched from place to place. Along with happy shouting Romans, he found himself cheering American-made Sherman tanks as they rolled by. He was totally exhilarated, immersing himself in a city throwing off its frustrations. When he paused in the Piazza Colonna, it was to observe water newly gushing from spouts concealed within sixteen powerfully wrought lions' heads in the sixteenth-century fountain. Hats were being tossed into the air. People were screaming themselves hoarse. It wasn't until he was ready to leave that he saw the incredibly beautiful girl. Although she held her head high, he was aware that abject sorrow seemed to cling to her. And yet there was such a strength and courage implied by her determined stride and erect carriage that he began to follow her, not as a man on the make, but as one instinctively wishing to oversee her safety. Yes, to protect her!

Her dark curly head was bobbing ahead of him now as she proceeded southward, and he realized that she was totally unaware of him being near her. He continued to trail her. They were leaving the more crowded center of the city. As he admired the graceful way in which she walked, he neither analyzed nor comprehended his actions, careful to always keep his distance from her. It was almost as if she were some pretty bird that would take alarmed flight upon being flushed from its ground sanctuary. She was moving more swiftly. He kept pace, sometimes behind, occasionally far to her side, and he began creating a scenario for her. She was, he decided, returning to a home in which she had been unhappy. It was a wild guess. He couldn't know at the time how accurate his observation of her was.

He noticed the deserted jeep.

Without giving thought to any possible consequences, he leapt into it, seated himself behind the flat steering wheel, and nosed into the vehicular stream, relatively thin in the direction she was traveling, toward the Via Appia Antica. Then, when she noticeably tired, he determined he would offer her a lift. He would have done this sooner except that he was positive her pride would have made her refuse.

He came to a stop ahead of her and waited for her to catch up to the jeep. He called out, "Would you like a ride?" It was later on that he realized he'd spoken in English.

She understood. English had been a second language in her school. As though shaken from some reverie, she seemed startled for the moment, until she looked at him and saw who he was. She smiled shyly and shook her head negatively. But she continued to stand, appraising him. What she saw was a square-figured, handsome Irish-American. His dark eyes bore into her. Angela Maria was positive that he knew exactly what she was thinking: I've never met a man who resembled this one! He had the air of someone sure of himself. Italian men, though they might try to pinch her behind, were more devious. He embodied the image she had long secretly envisioned. It was *his* face, *his* voice that she had seen and heard in romantic daydreams ever since she was a small girl. A smile flooded her features. "You don't intend to do me harm, do you?"

He, who was as fascinated as she, assured her in a voice made husky by emotion, "I would never hurt you."

"I know that." She looked directly into his eyes.

Love at first sight can be called an accident of fate, a happenstance meeting of separate personalities that bind as complementary elements in nature's laboratory. Any sensitive lover will affirm that the moment of truth, of seeing an entire lifetime in another's eyes, is as much déjà vu as it is precognition. The soul is stirred to remember past shared lives, to be certain of happiness in this one, and to be assured of jointly shared eternity. True love *is* exceedingly rare.

He drove back to the Excelsior. They spent the next forty-eight hours together in a room with a balcony onto which they never ventured. When they first faced one another naked, she was unashamed.

He felt the light touch of her fingers and her lips as she traced the muscular contours of his broad shoulders. When he clasped her to him, he loved her for the faint sigh that she emitted. She laid her head against his chest, and he could tell that she was darting glances toward his penis, slightly gasping as it rose its head in erection. He kissed her, parting her lips, delighted by her response. He sucked her nipples, and listened as she voiced little sounds, half sigh, half awakening passion. When he guided her hands to touch him, she complied with an explorer's eagerness, fiercely clasping his hardness, instinctively reacting, gyrating her hips.

"I want you inside of me," she said, moaning.

She was too tight for entry. "My darling," he said, "you're a virgin." And he covered her face with kisses.

Angela Maria was too ashamed to tell him how, as a small child, she had once been violated in her father's house.

During their two days and nights together, they told one another everything else about themselves. His father had been killed in an industrial accident when he was twelve. His mother, who hadn't remarried, had died just a year ago. He had wangled a bucket seat in an army aircraft to fly to her funeral in Chicago. "It was important for me to be there," he said. "There are no close relatives. Aside from her friends, she would have been alone."

Angela Maria then told him of her father and sister.

"We must be each other's lovers, and family, as well," he declared gravely.

She spoke painfully of Leo Ungaro's death, and how Peter Lawden had befriended her after the Jew's murder. She described her alliance with the Resistance, and how Lawden tried to keep her separate from its more dangerous elements. Then tears filled her eyes and her body shook when she related how the Englishman had been fatally stabbed in the back. "Peter suspected that the Fox betrayed us to the Nazis. His name really is Bruno Volpe, and he worked in our unit. I remember how he would seem to be watching me. When I'd look up, feeling his stare, he never glanced away, but continued fixing me with those hard cold eyes of his." She shuddered slightly.

Hugh Gerald wrapped a sheet around her, holding her close to him. "You must try to forget, harsh as that sounds. Blot out the memory. It's the only way we can survive living through war."

"But you don't understand. That isn't all. Immediately before . . . before Peter was killed, he was at the point of telling me something concerning Volpe. It involved *me!* Peter was an intelligence officer, and he claimed that he'd discovered a hidden connection between the Fox and me. He was about to reveal—"

"Hush," he tried to soothe her. "It's more painful when you remember."

"Remember *what?*" she asked bitterly. "That's when he was assassinated—undoubtedly by Bruno Volpe, who will forever be an unsolved mystery.

On their third morning together, he took her with him to seek special permission from the American military command so that they might marry. Only, Hugh Gerald had approached the wrong authority. He was a civilian and Italian law would apply. Roman officials were sympathetic and willing to expedite their wedding but, *ahimè!*, the bride-to-be was still a minor. There was absolutely no way the ceremony could take place unless her father's signature was on the marriage application.

He worried that when the Allied armies pushed northward, he would be compelled to leave her. Angela Maria needed the protection of his name. Together they drove to the Via Appia Antica estate and approached Ugo Ferrante, whom they found alone on the patio in the rear of the villa.

"So, you've returned," he grunted, hardly looking up.

"Hello, Papa."

"*Pronto!* Just like that, eh? You left home in the midst of a party and return months later. For all that time I didn't know whether you were alive or dead."

She spoke slowly in Italian, watching him. "If the Germans had murdered poor Leo Ungaro a half hour or so earlier . . . if they had invaded his palazzo then, I would have been trapped with him."

He stared at her, his eyes burning wild, his mouth agape, his arms extended toward her with both hands trembling.

Angela Maria took a step backward. One hand flew to her mouth.

He hoisted himself half out of the chair. "*Dio, Dio!* I never suspected that you were with him." He sank back upon the cushioned seat as though he was devoid of strength.

"*Ah! Adesso capisco!*" she barely whispered. "I understand! I didn't suppose . . . now it's been proven. You always did take advantage of an opportunity, Papa. It must have been too easy for you to pass up betraying him to your Nazi friends."

"What friends?" he asked bitterly. "They've gone and I am left to worry that the Partisans may decide to come after me the way I hear they are hunting down Fascists and executing them."

"You never were a Fascist, Papa. You weren't even a Nazi sympathizer. Your allegiance was always to yourself. You surrounded yourself with those who had the power. I am sure you will again. Besides, you are a much richer man than when Leo Ungaro lived."

"I didn't denounce him. I told them where he was hiding to . . . protect him."

"Hah!"

Ugo Ferrante stood up. "Who have you brought with you?" he asked in English as he eyed Gerald. "I can tell he is an American. Are *you* denouncing me?"

Hugh Gerald broke in. "I resent your speaking to Angela in that way."

He shrugged. "If I am the opportunist my daughter claims me to be, I must be a good host. Can I offer you some wine?"

"I don't want any wine." Gerald decided to be blunt. "What we want is your signature."

"A confession?" He was suspicious.

"We wish to marry."

He turned his unshaven face toward Angela Maria. "So? I cannot refuse or you would turn me in."

"I don't play your game, Papa," she retorted furiously. "Hugh and I are in love."

"You refused to fuck a German officer. Is it more purifying with a Yank?"

Gerald flexed his right fist, thumping it against the palm of his other hand.

"Don't hit him," she screamed, rushing between them.

"Come away." He gripped her arm, drawing back from her father. "I'll forge his signature on the application. Knowing what I've heard here, he won't dare cause any trouble."

"No! Hugh, give me your pen. Where's the form?"

He removed both from a pocket. She snatched them up.

"Papa, *scrivame!*" She placed pen and paper upon a table.

Ugo Ferrante bent his head, hunching his shoulders as he complied. He attempted to embrace her as she drew near him. Angela Maria instantly stepped away. "*Buono!*" She read aloud, "Ugo, il Principe di Corchese. The title is a lie that suits my father, but it is accepted in law." She turned toward Gerald. "Please take me back to Rome."

"Not so soon," her father protested, reverting to Italian.

"Why, you haven't yet seen your sister. She is to be married, too. Into the di Malvestiti family. The prospective groom is likely a *finocchio*, soft and useless to a woman . . . not even conscripted, that one! *Chi se ne frega?* Who gives a shit? What is important is that she quickly become respectable in the public eye. I've told her she must marry him so the Communists and the new power echelon will forgive that she played around with the Nazis.

"As for me . . . I will be excused, also. After all, as the sole owner of the jewelry business, I'm in a position to offer the choicest stones as bribes. Even Communists can be corrupted." He half laughed. But there was no humor in his sad eyes fixed upon her.

Later, again alone on the patio, he sat staring at the garden and seeing nothing. After a while, sighing heavily, he rose and walked inside. He could still hear the undertone in her voice when she bade him good-bye. He would never be welcome in his youngest daughter's home, wherever she would live with her American—so far away.

She hadn't let him tell her how much he loved her and that he would miss her. Had she wanted to hear of his worry over her when she was missing? What did she know of a parent's agony? How might he have guessed that she was very nearly trapped with Leo? Yet she wouldn't listen to his explanation. Eliminating the Jew was a matter of business. He had nothing against him personally. Why wouldn't she understand?

Now he must punish her; he would disinherit her. Perhaps, if she became fed up with her American, she might return home again. Then he would forgive her and reinstate her in his will. He picked up the telephone and dialed Rome.

"*Pronto*," said Giuliano Rinzini.

"It's me. Ugo. I have something I want you to do."

· 49 ·

"WHAT EXACTLY WAS IN THE ENVELOPE LEO UNGER REQUESTED Angela Maria to deliver to Giuliano Rinzini?" Gaia asked Emil Natov.

His response was curt. "I have told you the full story of the Ferrantes."

Gaia looked over at him. "Not entirely," she asserted. "The story had too many holes."

"I have no further information."

She leaned back in her chair, thoughtful. "Whatever documents were enclosed might have had something to do with the New York store. Surely if you know about the envelope's existence, you must also know what it contained."

"Ah, you are intrigued by a mystery. Unfortunately, if the original papers are preserved, they are privately held."

She stared at him, incredulous. "This is unbelievable. It's as though you or your superiors don't want me to find out. Why did you come here and tell me all this, but not tell me everything? Don't you realize it's my right to discover all that I can about my business . . . especially why the New York store and the Roman one are separate entities, connected by no other tie than the Ferrante name they share. And if your story is true, then it seems Ugo Ferrante actually stole the business from Leo Unger."

"Is that what you believe?"

"Don't you?"

Things were progressing as he intended them to. She'd taken the bait. Aloud, he said, "Isn't it enough to have heard about Angela Maria? You should be proud to be her daughter."

"You haven't given me any proof that I am."

"That is something you must either believe or disbelieve. It is your choice."

"If you can't supply the proof, then why did you bother to tell me her story?"

Natov kept his expression carefully remote. In order to further elicit Gaia Gerald's curiosity, hopefully to fan it into heat, he must play his cards with seeming uncaring.

"What else do you know about Leo Unger?"

He shrugged while alertly watching her.

"That gallant, tragic old man who founded the business . . . it is he with whom I most empathize. As owner of Ferrante-New York, I want to learn as much about him as I can. I've often wondered how a Ferrante store came to be founded in New York City. If he'd been here in 1943, his life would have been spared."

"Well now, there is another mystery for you. Obviously, his life wasn't what was most important to him."

"What do you mean?"

"He did travel to New York in the 1930s. As an Italian with no command of English, he tended to stay in a community where Italian was spoken. Naturally, when he secured funding for the Fifth Avenue store, it was from these people."

"Was it Roselli who provided the backing?"

"It was before his time. Antonucci Perrini was the one."

"So that's how they got to be on the board of directors?"

He slightly smiled approval, regarding her with a grudging admiration. It was his experience that beautiful women generally lacked in other departments. This lovely young woman was the antithesis of his philosophy.

"What is the other mystery you alluded to?"

"It concerns the *reason* for your store's existence."

"Profit."

"Try philanthropy."

"Come on! You're not trying to tell me that valuable jewelry was sold below cost."

"Hardly. But what if there was a fortune in jewelry awaiting transport from Rome with faked manifests?"

"Oh, no! You'll never make me believe he was a thief."

"Perhaps not. If the shipment was legitimate, and none of the pieces ever arrived in New York, where would you suppose they are today?"

"It doesn't concern today. That was many years ago."

"Correct. If it was not a mere rumor, none of the jewelry could have been taken from where it was hidden because by then the Nazis had occupied Rome; and for it to surface would have meant German appropriation."

"Why even discuss it when you called it a rumor?"

"Did I?"

For Gaia, a more potent visualization was the specter of Leo Unger's body being dragged to a German hearse. She couldn't get it out of her mind.

Emil Natov stood up. The seed had been implanted. "I must take leave of you," he said. "Other, more pressing matters await me."

Gaia walked with him to the door. She supposed she should thank him but somehow she couldn't bring herself to do it. He bent down, bowing, to kiss her hand, and Gaia was left in the doorway staring wonderingly after him.

B·O·O·K
IV

· 50 ·

Gaia had assured Merrill that she would remain in his apartment throughout the day.

"For your safety," he'd said. "I have to be at Bari and Battaglia all day, but that's on your account, so I can work on the estate. I'll be home about eight tonight."

Now her promise seemed to have been obliterated by what Emil Natov had related to her. Or rather, what he *hadn't!* The more she pondered upon what the missing information might be, the more it became a compulsion. She determined to act on her own—no matter what the consequences.

When Detective Patrick O'Reilly answered his desk phone, he wasn't at all surprised to hear Gaia's voice. He figured she would try to elicit further facts from him subsequent to the Interpol operative's visit to her. O'Reilly pridefully believed the NYPD's investigation technique was more ground-level effective than that of the international police agency. He particularly resented their interference into what he considered to be *his* case. FBI intervention had already been activated and was tolerable. The federal and city units were accustomed to cooperating. Except, it rankled him that the FBI had insisted he should keep his hands off of Dom Perrini, who was just about then landing at Kennedy after a flight from Rome. He itched to bring him in for interrogation, but the FBI insisted that they would take charge of the Mafia chieftain's son and heir.

"You told me that you were going to be my sole police contact," Gaia complained.

"And so I am. Anything on your mind?" He decided to play it as if he didn't know she'd been visited by Interpol.

"What can you tell me about Leo Unger?"

"Who?"

She repeated the name while her pulse began racing its pounding warning.

"I never heard of him. Who is he?"

She was flabbergasted. "Are you kidding me?"

"Not on your life." O'Reilly strove to keep his voice even. He was infuriated at Interpol for keeping him uninformed.

"Well, if you don't know—"

He brusquely interrupted her. "Had you heard that Roselli, Bronf, and Smith were arraigned?"

"Yes. At least they're imprisoned where they can't hurt me."

"Really? What makes you think so?"

He clearly heard her gasp. "Aren't they in jail?"

"They're on the streets. Haven't you heard of bail?"

"But you know where they are, don't you?"

"Sometimes. Occasionally we lose their tail."

"I . . . I glimpsed you on television last night," she said.

"When you were watching with Merrill Ross?" he asked.

She was taken aback. "How did you know?"

"How did the Interpol guy find you, do you suppose? You're an easier subject when it comes to tailing."

She rapidly considered. So the detective knew about Emil Natov. And if the police and Interpol could so easily track her, someone else could also find her. *If they hadn't already!* As they spoke, she heard the sound of the apartment door being unlocked. "Someone is coming in!" she whispered in sheer panic. Saying this, she slammed the receiver onto the phone. Running into the bedroom, she shrugged herself into her white fitch coat, which rested across a chair. Snatching up her bag, she secreted herself behind the half-open bedroom door. *A weapon!* She frantically glanced wild-eyed about the room.

"Mr. Ross, is that you?" A woman's voice projected from the foyer.

Gaia remained silent, perspiration beads raising on her forehead.

Presently the door she hid behind creaked, and between the opening of the door and its frame, a frightened dark-skinned face peered at her.

"Oh, it's a girl!" A look of knowing filled the wise eyes. "Why didn't ya call out? Scared me near silly, you did. Lissen, I seen Mr. Ross' girlfriends before." She tittered.

A sign on the Madison Avenue building read: HAIR GOODS, ONE FLIGHT UP.

Steep shallow stair treads led to a floor-through suite in a converted brownstone town house that had many years earlier been given over to commercial enterprise. Mme. Ponselle came forward with an eager welcoming smile. Short, dumpy, with clouds of false blond hair piled on her head, she modeled her wares.

"I want to purchase a wig," Gaia said.

"Sit down." She indicated an old-fashioned barber's chair, at the same time casting an appreciative sideways glance at the coat Gaia discarded onto a straight-backed chair. The smile she favored Gaia with also cast an inner glow. Judging by her prospective customer's expensive fur, it augured well for the price she might charge.

The small woman stood on tiptoe to closely inspect Gaia's curly dark hair. As she fingered the texture, she protested in an exaggerated French accent, "Not a full wig, surely." Her hands fluttered. "Mademoiselle more correctly wishes a piece for evening glamour. Such beautiful hair must be expertly matched, and no one on earth can do this better than Mme. Ponselle. Naturally, I will place an order for the finest European hair in your shade of darkest brown. Nothing tinted, you *comprenez?* I won't sell you Asian hair as most other shops would. How fortunate that you've come to me."

"I want a full blond wig," Gaia persisted.

"*Vous? Une blonde?*" Her voice squealed at a high pitch. Then, all business, she recovered herself. Profit was profit, even when so beautiful a girl as this one proved foolish. "*Oui,* madame."

Presently she stared at the face reflected back at her from the mirror. It was surrounded by a mass of shoulder-length pale-blond hair.

"*Regardez cette couleur.* It is pure, without red tones, not brassy. If you wish to become a blonde, it best suits your complexion. Once I have expertly cut and styled it, you will be pleased."

"Let it be frizzy and keep it long. I want to look entirely different."

As Mme. Ponselle scissored, Gaia felt sure that, with the application of appropriate makeup, she would be entirely unrecognizable.

· 51 ·

When Gaia emerged from a taxi and dashed past a franks and soda vendor into Saks Fifth Avenue, she was extremely self-conscious of her newly blond voluminous hair—especially when a young man who was passing her turned abruptly on his heel and followed her along the central aisle traversing the floor. His hand reached for her arm.

"Pretty gal, I want to have a relationship with you," he declared.

Edgy, Gaia involuntarily gasped, emitting a startled little cry. He immediately backed away.

"Nut! You're a nut!" he scornfully proclaimed, and stomped away.

Gaia shook her head and walked over to the Chanel counter, where she made a hasty selection of products that would suit her as a blonde. That day, a special promotion at the counter was a complimentary makeover. Gaia was so tensely wound up, she unconsciously grimaced as the beautician worked on her face.

"It will look much nicer if you stop frowning," the Chanel representative asserted. "Why would anyone as pretty as you look so worried?"

Never suspecting until then that her apprehension showed, Gaia thanked him, and rushed off to the fur department, where she placed her fitch coat in storage. The clerk regarded her with astonishment. Other customers were taking their furs *out* of storage at the chilly hints of winter to come. But the coat was a one-of-a-kind design; it would have instantly identified her to anyone who had ever seen her wearing it— and that included just about the entire staff of Ferrante-New York.

In the misses' designer department, she selected a shell-pink silk coat fully lined in pale dyed sheared nutria; a butterscotch-color worsted suit; a pastel silk blouse; flesh-toned pantyhose; and—? Of course! Beige kid pumps; a matching leather shoulderbag; harmonizing gloves.

Gaia used her charge card, although it meant signing her name. No one would think to check on her purchases. By the time the statement arrived in next month's mail, there would be no further need for deception.

Standing in a dressing room, Gaia critically studied her appearance in a triple full-length mirror. She had the impression of staring at a total stranger. She willed herself to be confident, gearing herself to do what she must. Moroseness was the precursor of failure, she reminded herself, and Gaia was intent on saving more than just herself.

There was Ferrante-New York to consider. It was a New York institution, and she wasn't about to allow its spectacular reputation to be destroyed.

Making her way out of Saks, Gaia passed a bank of wall telephones. She fumbled in her bag for change, experiencing a desperate urge to call Dom, to confide in him as she had done in the past. Her heart beat faster, anticipating the excitement of hearing his voice. Oh, how much she wanted to lean upon him for advice.

But caution stopped her. A moment's joy might jeopardize all that she was planning. Gaia knew herself only too well. She would never be able to keep a secret from Dom. Loving him was her weakness. In her heart she trusted him. It was her mind that dictated otherwise. The heart is a foolish little organ, she thought, and threw the coin back in her bag. Good work, she said to herself.

· 52 ·

As Gaia rode upward in the ornate customer elevator, she drew a deep calming breath. Its effect was momentary. Emerging at the fifth floor, she forced herself to walk calmly and briskly down the long corridor toward the Fifth Avenue side of the building. Her heels clicked against the vinyl of the floor. She'd gotten this far without anyone noticing—recognizing—her behind the blond wig and new clothes. Having passed the rear flight of electronically guarded steps leading to the workrooms and factory, she was nearing the shut door of the conference room, approaching Salinari's old office— now hers. With her face averted, she rushed by the open general offices.

Abruptly, a feminine voice stayed her. "Miss . . . say, hold up there, miss. Can I help you?"

Without turning her head, she attempted to change her voice. "Mr. Perry sent me up. I'm on my way to see Miss Spring."

"I'll show you where she sits."

"Uh—he told me where to find her. Thanks anyway." Gaia hastened forward.

The next couple of seconds would bring her to the open archway leading to the secretarial area outside of the chief executive office.

Etta Spring sat before a computer keyboard, her hips cushioning out from the swivel chair, a half-smoked cigarette protruding from her lips. Although she persisted in her work, from a slight movement of her head, Gaia was positive that the secretary was aware of her standing just inside of the entry.

Gaia cleared her throat with emphasis.

When Etta Spring eventually looked up, the cigarette ash had grown a trifle longer. She didn't bother to flick it away as she squinted her eyes. "So, it's you!" Her flat tone of voice held no semblance of cordiality.

Gaia found herself struggling with disbelief. Was she crumbling before the woman's recognition? Her disguise had worked brilliantly in other parts of the store. "I am . . . Jane Ponselle," she said as the name came into her mind.

"Ms. Gerald, let's not play games. Maybe you can fool others around here, but never Etta. I suppose you're pleased as an Egyptian cat because you made your way up here undetected. Guess my recognizing you threw you. Sorry about that."

Her dislike of Etta Spring intensified. But there was no getting around that she needed her. "Do you recall when you said that you wanted to work for me?" she asked.

"Don't make me out to be an idiot. I told you that last week in your studio, while Mr. Salinari was still around."

Gaia paled beneath her pastel makeup. God, the woman was heartless! But it was too late to turn back. "Absolutely no one is to know that I'm here. Is that understood?"

Etta slightly shrugged.

"You'll be paid a bonus in appreciation for your help."

If this is a bribe, so be it, thought Gaia.

"I'll want payment in cash. There'll be no tax for me, and I can bury the transaction in the computer so there'll be no record of it."

Gaia was genuinely curious. "Can you do that?"

"Are you kidding?" Her voice held a sneer. "I assumed you want our arrangement to be kept confidential."

But Gaia wasn't about to allow this woman to dominate

her, and, to effect a change, she pushed open the heavy door to the large office, noting with satisfaction that on this occasion the secretary hadn't attempted to stop her from entering.

There was a faint hum of air conditioning, necessary to protect the more fragile of the many art objects crowding the room. As she walked across an Oriental carpet toward the ornately carved desk, she visualized Salinari as he had looked when he sat behind it and informed her that she was an heiress—just last week. It seemed years ago.

Gaia squared her shoulders and shook off the memory. From this moment on she would be practical during every single waking moment. Although she very much would have preferred to settle herself in the familiar surroundings of her design studio, that was out of the question. There she would be recognized, and she had too much to do.

"If anyone questions who I am, say I am Jane Ponselle, a decorator. The first thing I want you to do is call Sotheby Parke Bernet. Everything in here is to be catalogued and sold at auction."

The secretary, holding her pencil aloft, sputtered, "But these antiques, these paintings—"

Gaia cut her off. "Use this desk phone. Now!"

When Etta told her that an appointment for the inspection of the art works had been set, Gaia carefully positioned her hands on the tooled-leather desk top, lacing her fingers so as not to betray her excitement. It was so good to be back, to be working again.

"About our arrangement, something you said earlier intrigues me. It concerned 'burying' an entry in the computer."

"It would be a sore thumb if a sizable cash payment to me surfaced."

"Precisely, and I want to know about other fake entries."

"What makes you think there are any?" The secretary reached into a pocket, withdrew a cigarette, and lit it.

Gaia recognized a delaying tactic. "Come now, I already know about the Àtrio."

"Honestly, Ms. Gerald, I had no part in that."

"The name is Ponselle," she corrected. "I don't want you

to make a slip about my identity outside of this room. And concerning the Àtrio, if I was accusing you, you'd have known it. I don't presume your guilt, but that doesn't mean you are unaware of what's been happening."

Etta Spring drew deeply upon her cigarette, expelling smoke through her nostrils. It cast an overlay of gray upon her already-sallow complexion. "Let it be," she urged.

"Either you give me insight into what's been going on or you are fired on the spot, and you can forget about your bonus and any other perks you have coming to you."

"It was a scam that was operated by the board of directors," she said reluctantly. "They thought it was hidden, but I picked up on it."

"Jewel theft?" Gaia asked. She was breathing heavily.

"Yes, but not of our stock of gems or finished jewelry. That would have been difficult to cover up on a massive scale. These were important pieces transported from continent to continent for resale. None of them suspected I knew about it, except that I'm not exactly dumb."

So it is this store! Gaia felt crushed. While she had no personal responsibility for past operations, the onus of it would certainly carry forward. She wondered which would be the more horrible: to have the publicly good reputation of Ferrante-New York tarnished or to be shut down by law-enforcement authorities. She wasn't certain whether the latter could take place. Gaia made a mental note to discuss such a possibility with Merrill.

"And that's not all!" Etta Spring broke into her thoughts.

"What else?" She jumped slightly.

"One afternoon when I went to Mr. Salinari's desk after he'd left for the day . . . you see, it was my routine to pick up his signed mail for stamping . . . there was a brown leather jewelry case on top of the desk, unopened. I could see it wasn't ours; we don't use that color leather. So—"

"Yes, and I suppose it was stolen jewelry," Gaia interrupted. Her throat was tight and her voice sounded unfamiliar in her own ears.

"That, and something more."

"Go on, tell me!"

"The case was unlocked and I opened it. Inside was a fabulous necklace of diamonds, robin's-egg-size fiery opals, each ringed with emeralds, but I saw that the beige velvet padding to which the necklace was fastened was lifting at the edges where it should have set firmly into the bottom. So I tried to tamp it down. It wouldn't budge, like there was too much filling underneath. Then I noticed that my fingernails had shoveled up a white powder. I quickly shut the case and snapped the fastener shut. I blew on the desk in case there was evidence of powder on it. Back at my own desk, I carefully shook the grains under my nails into a small envelope. I took it to a druggist in my neighborhood who's known me for years. He told me it was cocaine."

Gaia could hear the throbbing of her pulse. "Where," she asked, "did the necklace come from?"

"South America. Rio de Janeiro, I believe. Anyway, I placed the case in a safe upstairs in the factory where they store loose gems. Next morning, I made sure to come in extra early so I could remove it before anyone got curious and looked inside the box. Then I replaced it on his desk. The old man was already getting somewhat addled, so he didn't ask any questions about whether I had noticed it."

"When was this?"

"Eight . . . no, nine months ago."

Gaia recalled that Dom had traveled to South America around that time. As usual, he'd brought back something for her. It was a huge magenta silk shawl, exquisitely trimmed with inserts of handmade lace and delicately rendered embroidery. And a pair of small robin's-egg-shaped opal earrings.

· 53 ·

ETTA SPRING PROVED TO BE THE IDEAL TUTOR FOR GAIA. AS Salinari's right hand, she had dealt with many affairs beyond her duties . . . details that he had neither concept of, nor interest in. He was the figurehead and hers was the intelligence that kept him functioning. Through the years, Etta had grown embittered and cynical. And now, she, who knew more about running the store than anyone, was again called upon to play second fiddle, this time to an inexperienced young woman, a pretty-faced usurper. Life was markedly unfair.

Gaia's questions were intelligent and voiced with a persistence that demanded answers. Seated behind Salinari's desk, she read printouts of sales figures until her eyes grew weary. To keep them from being interrupted, Etta had all telephone calls routed to an assistant secretary. Late in the afternoon she inquired who had called. Two of the messages interested Gaia.

Miles Tuchelin had stopped by to ask whether anyone had heard from her. The other was a telephone call from Dom Perrini.

When Etta briefly returned to the outer office, Gaia's hand reached toward the desk telephone, almost of its own volition. She thought of her night in Rome with Dom, and tears glistened in her eyes. Then she abruptly clenched her fist. If Roselli, Bronf, and Smith were implicated in plotting against her, then it followed that Dom was, too. Hadn't O'Reilly hinted at this?

No, she couldn't chance telephoning him.

Miles Tuchelin bounded into the ornate office within three minutes of her summoning him. He involuntarily snickered as he contemplated her changed appearance.

"I'm sure I look ridiculous," Gaia offered apologetically.

He studied her for a moment longer. "Not so," he answered. "Beautiful is the way I'd describe you, but why'd you do it? You were sensational as a brunette."

"Detective O'Reilly recommended that I stay undercover."

"So you go about fixed up for a masquerade?"

She was having second thoughts about having let him see her.

"I tried phoning you at your apartment."

"I'm not staying there."

"Where can I reach you?" He could see her reluctance to reply. "In case I need to get in touch," he said.

She hesitated. "I'd better not say. It's not that I don't trust you. Otherwise, would I have asked you to come to this office?"

Miles turned his head away, and Gaia felt ashamed. He had been her staunchest ally in the store. He created a success for her jewelry designs; he made her into a recognizable personality. And now she looked—and acted—like someone else. Gaia felt foolish and sad.

"Miles, I'm sorry. I'm also afraid. But I refuse to allow the attempts on my life to stop me from assuming control of this business."

"What if you get yourself killed? Remember, the store will be here with or without you."

"No, it too can be destroyed," she said stubbornly. "It's my responsibility not to let that happen."

"Okay, let's be rational about this. Do you have any idea who is out to get you?"

She shook her head. "Not the slightest." She felt she'd already said too much.

"For all you know it could be me."

Gaia flinched.

"My goodness, we are getting paranoid," he said. "Well, as for me, I'd put my money on Roselli and his cohorts. My guess is that they planned to set you up so they could raid the store's assets or stage something so illegal that it couldn't be hushed up. You're the new chairman of the board and president. It's you who'd be facing charges. But once you kicked them off the board, you became a liability."

"Please go back about your normal work," Gaia said nervously. "And please don't tell anyone that I'm in the store."

He seemed insulted. "Of course I won't. How could you suggest that I'd betray your confidence? Oh, by the way," he asked as afterthought, "what about Dom Perrini?"

"What about him?" she questioned sharply.

"I was just asking—"

"He's my . . . friend."

"Okay," he said, his hand on the doorknob. "No harm meant."

· 54 ·

Shortly before 6:00 p.m., Etta Spring stuck her head into the large office. "Store closing time," she said.

Gaia glanced at her watch. In the past, she had many times continued after hours, relishing the quiet of being alone in her studio when she could work uninterrupted. And she was assuredly safe. The store, its offices, and workrooms were protected twenty-four hours a day.

"I believe I'll remain here for a while," she replied. "On your way out, be sure to alert the guard that Jane Ponselle, the new interior decorator, is working and isn't to be disturbed." This would give her an opportunity to wander about the fifth floor at will, primarily to visit her own design studio once that area was vacated.

She grew impatient, waiting until past 7:00, when any stragglers among the staff would have departed. She continued poring over the books, but became restless, and leaned back in her chair, admiring the works of art on haphazard display in the room. A pity they would be sold, but it was for the best, she thought.

Just when she was about to leave the sanctuary of the office, the telephone abruptly rang. Gaia stood stock-still, her heart pounding rapidly. Hesitating, she finally decided it would be stupid not to answer. Probably the security guard at the employees' entrance was checking on how long Jane Ponselle intended to remain—a normal-enough procedure. Should she not answer the phone, it would arouse his curiosity. She would shortly find herself confronted by the guard, face to face, instead of later being able to easily slip past him, unrecognized, into the side street.

"Hello?"

"Gaia." Dom's deep masculine voice was agonizingly familiar.

She was so nervous that she could barely speak.

"All day long I've been trying to reach you. How are you, *cara?* Why did you run away from me in Rome? You were safe with me. Here in New York, you're in terrible danger."

She swallowed hard. "I—I'm in hiding," she said lamely.

"None too successfully, when I can reach you by phone at the store."

"I've made myself look different," she blurted out. Immediately, Gaia worried. Why hadn't she kept that a secret from Dom?

"I've tried calling you at your apartment any number of times but, of course, you haven't been there. Where are you staying?"

She grasped the receiver, as unable to answer as if her vocal cords were paralyzed. She couldn't possibly reveal that she'd been in Merrill's apartment. Aside from anything else, how would that look to Dom? Would he ever believe that she'd slept alone?

"Gaia? *Cara,* are you there?"

Her voice was a whisper. "Yes."

"I don't want to frighten you, but you must know that you're a walking target. Where in the store are you? Tell me exactly."

She hesitated briefly. "In old man Salinari's office." How strange, her mind ruminated on another level, it is my office now.

"Listen to me. Stay right where you are. Don't move about, and don't answer the phone again, because I won't be calling you. I'm coming over to get you. Do you understand?"

She was numbed and said nothing.

"Gaia!" His voice was sharp. "Are you listening to me?"

"I heard."

"Very well then. Remain where you are. I'm leaving Brooklyn now. It will take me half an hour to reach you."

Gaia, her heart pounding in her throat, walked to the windows facing Fifth Avenue. The traffic at this hour was sparse. An overhead streetlamp at the corner of Fifty-sixth Street was dark and only the passing automobile headlights supplied temporary illumination. She felt trapped. She had to get out of this room quickly. Half an hour, Dom had said. There was time enough to stop off in her studio, where she could make some sketches. It would calm her while she waited for Dom to pick her up. And she had an idea for a design.

She hastened down the corridor, relieved to find that all of the lights inside the studio had been turned off. This was familiar territory where she had no fear. In the semidarkness, with only the hall light shining in, she made her way to her workspace. Here she switched on a small lamp above her easel on which was a ready drawing pad. Gaia's pencil flew across the page. She sketched the fluid outline of a woman with uplifted bound hair, clothed loosely in a flowing dress. She paused and began to draw a male companion piece. It was a beginning, offering something positive on which to work. Later, after many more sketches, when the drawings were greatly simplified and precisely rendered on graph paper, they would be ready to be cast in gold. She envisioned them as matching pendants—male and female—a new entry in the Gaia Collection.

She tore off the sheet from the pad, folding it into a smallish square that she could fit into the purse she'd bought that morning. She was relaxed, almost smiling now, thinking of the way Miles might market her new design. The figures were sensuous.

Her knuckles brushed against an object she had transferred from her large handbag to this smaller purse. It was smooth and cold . . . the mauve perfume bottle she had carried back from Italy! She set it on the table in front of the framed portrait she pretended was her mother's likeness. Only then did she glance at her watch. Twenty-two minutes had gone by. Dom would be coming any minute. She stared at the perfume bottle intently, as if it held a message inside it, and then she stood up abruptly.

She decided to be gone from the premises before Dom arrived. It was foolish to trust him; why could she never resist the power of his caressing voice? No—she needed time to think it through. She walked to the brightly lit hallway, hastening toward the employee elevator. She thought she heard the low hum of the rising customer elevator. The service car was far larger and weightier; its cables made more noise than those of the smaller, more elegant customer car, and something about the humming made her sense the customer car was drawing close. She darted into the ladies' room, its door whooshing shut behind her.

A quick glance showed that the room and its toilet cubicles were empty. She stood waiting, breathing hard and staring into the mirror lining the wall above the sinks. Her blondness made her seem a stranger to herself. She looked pale, sweat beading on her forehead. She felt sick inside.

Suddenly the lights were extinguished. She heard a steady drip from a leaking sink. *Calm! Stay calm!* Something compelled her to leave the room—it was too close, too dark to stay and wait. She was sufficiently familiar with the layout to enable her to reach the door. But when she opened it, she saw the lights were turned off everywhere.

Sheer terror washed over Gaia until she forced herself to consider her location in relation to the employee elevator. It surely wasn't more than a few steps beyond. From behind her, she listened in dismay to the whooshing sound of the lavatory door closing. The sound would give her position away. She had to hurry. She moved blindly out into the corridor, toward the side where the elevator was. Her hands, flailing, came unexpectedly against the wall, her fingernails making a scratching sound on the surface. She groped her way along the wall.

After what seemed an eternity, her fingers pressed against the painted metal door. It slid open under slight pressure. Why, it was going to be all right! The car must have been at this floor all along. Intent on escaping, it didn't strike her as unusual that the elevator also was unlit. She stepped forward.

Space.

Gaia shrieked, her arms thrusting out, seeking to grasp the sides of the door frame, attempting to pull herself back. In that split second she sensed there was someone standing close behind her, reaching toward her.

Her screams penetrated the length of the shaft to its base.

She felt herself begin to fall.

· 55 ·

O'REILLY SIFTED THROUGH THE ELEVATOR MAINTENANCE REPORTS
for the Ferrante-New York elevators. It was the day following the "malfunction," which he refused to label accidental.
The experts he had summoned were checking out the car, its
mechanism, the cables, shaft, and particularly the fifth-floor-
landing door. He didn't have to wait long. It was as he expected. They reported that there had been *no* mechanical
failure.

Earlier, he had requested to be shown the master fuse box.
The building supervisor informed him that, as a safety pre-
caution required by Ferrante's insurer, each floor had a separate system. O'Reilly inspected the box on the fifth floor. At
least two of the four fuses had probably been loosened in their
sockets. It was unlikely that this could have occurred without
human assistance.

It had already been established that there was no car at the
fifth floor when the victim, Gaia Gerald, had assumed the
elevator was in position for her safe entry. The opening of the
door to the shaft was entirely independent of the cable operation that governed the rising and lowering of the cab. In fact,
small but significant marks on the door indicated that someone had pried it open, perhaps with a crowbar. Gaia thought

the door slid open under the pressure of her hand; in reality, it had been ajar, with a gaping void below.

What had happened was not, by any means, an accident. *It was a premeditated attempt at murder.*

O'Reilly considered the various suspects.

Dom Perrini had arrived at the store, as noted upon entry in the guard's records, some five minutes prior to the accident.

Miles Tuchelin, advertising and promotion manager, declared he had been working in his own office midway along that same corridor.

Etta Spring, head secretary, claimed to have noticed upon reaching the Columbus Circle subway station that she'd evidently left her wallet on her desk and so had to return to the store to get it; or so she'd said in her statement.

The security guard apparently was above suspicion, having been employed by the store for over eleven years. Roger Perry, chief of the in-house protective service, absolutely vouched for his reliability and honesty.

What if there was someone unauthorized who had been afoot in the premises? In a building so electronically protected that just a single guard needed to be on duty at night, this seemed unlikely.

About Perrini: Several days ago O'Reilly had asked headquarters whether there was a yellow sheet on Dominic Perrini, son of a deceased and prominent don. He was disappointed, and surprised, when the answer came back in the negative. However, that didn't eliminate him as a suspect. Perrini operated along gray, undefined lines. O'Reilly intended to learn how his fortune had been accumulated, particularly what his present business deals involved. There was no way he intended letting him off the hook.

Miles Tuchelin's sincerity somehow ticked him off. Okay, so he wasn't crazy about effeminate men like Tuchelin, but it wasn't prejudice that caused his dislike. There was something in Tuchelin's eyes when he voiced his concern . . . fear, perhaps? And behind the man's slight frame was a wiry musculature, a strength that lay hidden under the soft acquiescent mannerisms.

But he couldn't pin down anything at this point. Dammit. His mouth tasted awful; his head pounded.

The sole other means of possibly gaining a vital clue was from the victim herself. It was a fucking miracle that she was alive. For the second time the Gerald girl had survived a murder attempt. Furrowing his brow as he considered this, O'Reilly made a clicking sound with his tongue.

Wasn't it said that events occurred in threes?

· 56 ·

Sunlight streamed across the hospital bed. The nurse moved to adjust the blinds, and the patient asked her not to. Gaia had a persistent headache but she wanted to see and feel the sun. The muscles of her body were terribly sore and felt lifeless. Yet she was alive. She was alive!

She had total recall of everything that had happened the evening before.

With horrified fascination she recalled her screams reverberating through the elevator shaft . . . the certainty that she was about to fall . . . the sensation of falling through the dark air of the shaft . . . a man shouting . . . the wrenching pain shooting through her body and the tightness around her ankles.

She was hanging upside down, swaying. Behind her she could feel rough unsurfaced brick.

Then there were the excited voices issuing from up on the landing. She could make out the words but was too far in shock to recognize who was speaking.

"Oh, my God! What happened?"

"Let me help you pull her up."

A deeper voice, like a growl. "Watch it! You bumped into me and I nearly let go of her. *I'm* bringing her up."

"You can't do it alone."

"Get away!"

Gaia's eyes were wide open. The blond wig had fallen from her head and her scalp felt cool. She made no sound. A bright light illuminated the shaft, and she began crying, emitting small whimpers.

"Okay, I've hoisted her up higher. Now take hold!" Other hands gripped her. She was swiftly yanked up and placed flat on the floor. Overhead lighting was restored as Dom's face loomed above hers.

She attempted to sit up. "You?" she asked Dom.

"Don't try to talk."

Although she protested that she was able to walk, he carried her in his arms. The customer elevator took them to the main floor. From there, down a flight of stairs and around a twisting hallway, up a shorter flight, and they were on the sidewalk. She was conscious. Dom still carried her. Miles hovered to one side. She heard the security guard call out to them, "I can't leave the building."

Dom spoke to Miles. "In my right outer jacket pocket, you'll find my car keys. I'm taking her to the nearest hospital."

Then darkness.

Lying in bed the following morning, her recollection focused upon the expression in Dom's eyes as he'd looked at her. It was such a piercing intense gaze, she shut her lids tight as if seeking to block out the memory.

Was it love? Horror? Or enormous surprise and fear at being nearly caught in the act of murder?

After telephoning Merrill Ross, Gaia checked herself out of the hospital that afternoon—against the doctor's orders.

"I've been pacing the floor worrying about you all night long," he'd scolded. "Where the hell are you? Why did you leave the apartment?"

"It's too involved a story to tell you over the phone."

"When am I going to see you? Where are you now? Are you coming back?"

"Oh, yes. I want to very much . . . that is, if you'll have me."
"You bet I will." His voice was hearty.
"Will you take a cab and call for me?"
She told him where she was.
"Jesus!"

· 57 ·

The voices were being recorded while the men spoke.

"Gaia Gerald was discharged from Lenox Hill Hospital early this morning. When Perrini came by later, she had already left."

"Where did she go?"

"Unknown. We weren't expecting her to leave, so we weren't covering."

"Was the store checked?"

"She isn't there."

"Did she leave the hospital alone or with someone?"

"There were no nurses around who knew. She left during a change of shift."

"You checked her apartment?"

"No. Not there. We have a man out watching it."

"That police detective—O'Reilly—does he have a lead on her whereabouts?"

"If he does, we can't say. What we do know is that he pulled in Perrini and Roselli last night for questioning."

"Were either of them booked or held on charges?"

"No. Both men are back on the streets."

"Any idea of who attempted to push her to kingdom come?"

"Not unless O'Reilly has come up with a lead."

"Are you waiting for an invite? Ask him."

"That's the point. He's not in the city."

"Wha-at?"

"He flew to Chicago around seven A.M."

"That doesn't figure. Why would he go there?"

"Can't say."

"Let's have someone on him right away. It may be the only way to find our woman. After the way she dashed out of Ross' place yesterday, I doubt she'll go back there again."

· 58 ·

Patrick O'Reilly was proud of his name, his heritage, and his profession. From the start, it had fascinated him that Gaia Gerald, an orphan with an Irish surname, was the heiress to Ugo Ferrante's prime Fifth Avenue jewelry store. But it wasn't for sentimental reasons that he'd flown to O'Hare Airport and was presently on his way into Chicago proper.

Sure, he still suspected Dom Perrini and Vince Roselli, although he'd let them both walk. Of course, Roselli was already bound over on the larceny charges involving improprieties connected with Ferrante-New York.

As for the first attempt upon the girl, the punk who'd been hauled out of her apartment was already free on bail. He had a solid alibi for this one; he'd stand trial for one count only. The victim's testimony that he tried to push her out of her window would be countered by his defense that he was there to burglarize. The little crook would probably win. He'd seen it all too often, how too many juries tended to give credence to the criminal.

But what struck O'Reilly was that both attempts on Gaia's life—in the apartment and at the store—were essentially alike. In each instance, a fall from a great height was intended.

The more he dug into this case, the greater his conviction that there was a single missing piece, so long overlooked that it was believed not to exist, but a piece of evidence, a fact of some kind that was so key that answers would flow from it to cement the rest of his case together. It could mean that all along he'd been looking in the wrong places. What he was searching for might well be buried in forgotten archives somewhere in Chicago. He convinced his captain that it was worth a try.

He presented himself to a Chicago police liaison officer and was given carte blanche. Dusty birth rolls, lists of mortgages, tax records, all were accessible to him. He perused microfilm printouts on display screens until his eyeballs felt as though they were being pushed to the back of his head.

Nothing. No clue emanating from the surname Gerald.

He turned to the Catholic diocese, where he consulted with a youthful priest who could offer him nothing but access to the orphanage files. Again, O'Reilly found no clues. Discouraged, he thanked the young priest for his efforts and was about to leave when the young man urged him to wait. "Perhaps Father Burney can be of help," he suggested.

Presently, a thin, erect old man appeared in the office. He nodded and stood waiting, his hands clasped, drawing Patrick O'Reilly's gaze to the bulging purplish-blue veins beneath such thin, papery skin that O'Reilly had the impression of the elderly priest's life-force ebbing right before his eyes. But when the old man spoke, his voice was robust. "Ah, yes," he said, nodding his head, "that would be the Children's Home of Little Flowers.

"If she was an orphan, that was the orphanage supported by Catholic charities where she would have been sheltered. Alas, it no longer exists—abandoned in 1969 due to expensive repairs we would have had to make. It stood empty for years, except of course for the homeless who used it for shelter in the winter. But then there was the terrible fire . . ." His voice trailed off for a moment, and next he added, almost dramatically, "The once-grand mansion was almost destroyed."

O'Reilly grew immeasurably excited. "Where are the orphanage records?"

"Father Chazanoff will, no doubt, find some dusty file cabinets in the basement of this building." He extended his right hand to the detective. "Now, if you will excuse a tired old man, I must attend to my devotions."

"Follow me," said the younger priest quietly. "My work has never taken me down there, but let's see what we can find."

And in a file folder under the initial *G*, O'Reilly come upon the few facts about Gaia Gerald. These consisted of the mimeographed pages that were once under discussion in a State Street law office when a conference on Gaia Gerald was initiated by two social workers. Included in the material was a handwritten notation that James Farraday was legal counsel to the orphanage.

O'Reilly felt optimistic for the first time in hours. He asked Father Chazanoff for a telephone directory, and made note of the address and phone number of Farraday, James, Esq. To telephone would be wasting time. He'd just be put off.

O'Reilly strode into the State Street office but was stopped by a imperious young woman at the front desk. "The initial consultation fee is a hundred and fifty dollars," she informed, "and I just may be able to fit you in for—let's see—a week from Wednesday at three-fifteen."

That was when O'Reilly flashed his badge, which he was always reluctant to display out of New York. He was quickly ushered into the inner office.

Farraday rose from behind his desk. "Sorry about that little misunderstanding," he said. He smiled, but his eyes darted around the room nervously.

It was the posturing of some sort of guilt, O'Reilly decided. He knew the outward signs—a too-pronounced cordiality toward a police officer. *If this was my territory!* he thought.

"What did you say the girl's name is?"

He repeated it.

"It is vaguely familiar. An unusual blending of Italian and Irish, is it not?" The lawyer studied the mimeographed sheets. "Well, of course, here it is. Gerald. She was released from the home to the care of foster parents."

"I read, too," O'Reilly said. "Quite well."

"Well, there's nothing else."

"Think hard. The names of her real mother and father. Can you recall them?" His stare was commanding.

The lawyer reddened. "Their names don't come to mind if, indeed, I ever heard them."

"Come on! Project yourself back to that meeting again. There were you, the two social workers—"

"Why don't you speak to them and not bother me?" he interrupted irritably.

"Because I am here. Unless you'd rather I put in a call to your police headquarters and have you brought in for questioning."

"Okay." He was furious. "I'm thinking." After a few moments, he said, "What was the nun's name?"

"Sister Mary Agnes. She represented the home at the meeting."

"Yes, I do seem to recall something. *Yes!* I asked her what had happened to the full file. From what she answered, I gathered it had been lifted or destroyed . . ." He drew a hand across his eyes. "There was a woman . . . a volunteer in the orphanage who had typed and mimeoed the file. Her name . . . it was . . . I forget. I seem to recall reading in a newspaper that she was the girlfriend of a . . . of a mob guy, if you can believe that."

"A mob . . . well, what happened to her? Where is she now?"

"She was murdered. It was a burglary, I seem to remem—"

"Murdered! Before or after Gaia Gerald's file disappeared?"

"After, I think. I can't be sure. No, that's right! It was *after.*"

In O'Reilly's mind an instant picture formed, like a Polaroid developing. The face he saw was that of Vince Roselli.

Stopping by a coffee shop, O'Reilly ate a sandwich and slowly drank a Pepsi. There was no sense in trying to find the two social workers. He didn't have the time to track them down, and from the mimeographed pages, it was evident they had asked questions of Sister Mary Agnes, not unlike what he'd been trying to elicit today—and came up with nothing.

But he thought of one other way to go. It would be a long shot. But no one gets anywhere in this business without taking a risk, he thought. He headed for the *Chicago Times* editorial office.

It was there that his winding trail turned into a path of gold.

"Sure, I remember a fella by the name of Gerald. Hugh, but he wrote a column as H. T. Gerald. He had a daughter? I seem to recall his wife's name was Angel. At least, he called her that. I suppose it was really Angela. She was Italian-born."

"Angela Maria," O'Reilly said.

"You knew them?" the reporter asked, interested.

"No, but I'd like to hear whatever you can tell me." He showed his identification to the man.

O'Reilly listened as the story unfolded.

Hugh Gerald was briefly assigned by his news syndicate to New York, then Los Angeles. After a year in New Orleans digging into the machinations of Southern politics, he went to Detroit for an automotive union investigation. A long burning summer in Phoenix lengthened into fall and winter. Six or seven years married, he was dispatched back to Chicago, where he reported on mob politics. Hugh tried to protect Angel by never relating details of the stories he worked on until they were in print, when the danger became somewhat nullified. Then she became pregnant.

With the baby on the way, the investigative assignments he specialized in were too fraught with peril. Hugh Gerald informed his editor that he intended to make a change in his career. An agreement was struck. He would complete his present assignment because he was already familiar with the ins and outs of mob corruption that he was then investigating.

But when Gaia was a year old, her father was still involved in the investigation that had brought them to Chicago. By her second birthday, he was too fascinated to stop.

For, when Gaia was nearly three, he uncovered the most shocking involvement of all.

He had been studying the activity of a foundling home and had discovered that the nuns who ran it were being duped by gang interests. There was a growing market for healthy babies, and, after they made their generous contributions, the wealthy could persuade the innocent nuns to hand the children over. It was a delicate operation but so very lucrative.

The story was winding down and Hugh would be given an entirely different type of writing assignment . . . one more relatively uncontroversial . . .

It was not to be.

On a brilliant warm Sunday afternoon, he collected Angel and the baby. They were going for a drive into the countryside. He'd had so little time lately for his wife and child, but soon all that would change.

Husband and wife shared the car's front seat, and the baby was already toying with the straps of her raised seat in the back, gurgling happily to herself, when the steering wheel went out of control. They were on an active highway. It was a miracle that when the automobile careened across a white line, oncoming traffic escaped being struck. A crash against a tree trunk. An explosion beneath the front seat.

Someone had taken no chances at missing. The bomb went off just as planned. But as the force of the explosion shook the car, the rear door burst open. The baby was thrown. She landed in a growth of green hedge that cushioned the shock of impact.

No one came forward to claim the surviving baby girl. And so, on the day when little Gaia Gerald was discharged from a hospital, she was placed in the care of the sisters at the Children's Home of Little Flowers.

It was the same orphanage her father had been investigating.

· 59 ·

Merrill Ross prided himself on the fact that he was selective of his female companions. Invariably they tended to be very tall, and thin to a degree just short of self-induced starvation, with rib cages prominently outlined, collarbones that protruded, and hips so sinewy that there was no soft cushion of fat layered beneath the skin. It elated him to be recognized as a man seen exclusively in the company of high-fashion models; it excited him to sleep with the creatures who people the fantasies of other men.

For three nights Gaia had shared his apartment, sleeping on his waterbed while he adjusted his lanky frame to the living room couch.

When he offered Gaia refuge, it was with no thought of her sexual companionship. Of course he was attracted to her. He was, from the moment he'd first seen her. But now she needed help; she feared for her life. His reasoning was as simple as that. But when Gaia failed to return to his apartment after leaving it when he'd specifically told her she *must* remain concealed, he uneasily speculated upon where she might have gone. He found himself fervently hoping that she would shortly appear at his door, and he promised himself that he wouldn't scold her for leaving because he would be so overjoyed to welcome her back.

The morning after he had brought her back from the hospital, he called his office and told them he wouldn't be in. From this day forward, he would devote himself to her. He found himself becoming stirred by her presence. Her full-breasted figure, her dark curly hair could never approximate his rangy blond ideal. He observed her closely as she moved delicately about the small rooms, occasionally stretching her torso to alleviate the pinch of a sprain, or extending a long leg to stretch a muscle. Her movements were incredibly sensuous. Still, he held off. If he approached her now, wouldn't she naturally presume he was after her money? This was why he was determined to proceed slowly in his courtship of her. *Courtship!* How absurd. And yet, it defined the manner in which he intended pursuing Gaia's affections (with certain modern creative twists). And while he remained aloof, polite, deferential, and caring, he increasingly took to speculating how she might respond in bed.

Of particular importance to him was that she so obviously appreciated his hospitality as a place of refuge. He knew that she felt guilty because she was dislodging him from his bedroom—that was good! He wanted Gaia to consider herself in his debt. It was Merrill's philosophy that a man should never surrender power to a woman . . . not to any woman . . . not even if she happened to be an heiress. Of course, that was good, too!

And while it was a tantalizing game that he was playing, his nerves were ready to snap. Having her for a houseguest made it impossible for him to go out to the places where he'd made an almost religious practice of being visible. He couldn't leave her alone, and he couldn't take her with him because she'd likely be recognized.

So they watched television together. Although Gaia's attention remained focused upon the screen, his appraising, increasingly bold gaze roved over her relaxed body. He found himself greedily staring at the curved rise of her breasts, her lean waist, and the long shapely legs thrust out across the polished floor. *How badly I want to touch you! I want to fuck you*

. . . Imagining became obsessive. Her inaccessibility made Gaia the most desirable woman in the world for him.

One night, as she rose to enter the bedroom, Merrill followed her to the door and lightly enclosed her in his arms. When she questioningly tilted her head upward, looking directly into his eyes, he bent his face to hers and kissed her. At first gently, soon insistently. Her mouth was warm and soft. He parted her lips with his probing tongue, and her mouth opened invitingly to him.

He would not caress her body. If his analysis of Gaia was correct—and he prided himself upon his skill as a lover—by holding off, he was telling her that he considered her a *lady*. This would inevitably induce her to feel loved.

He would wait for her to initiate a lead for him to follow.

The next night, as she stood by the doorway next to him, she pulled him into her arms. He led her to the bed. She was pressing her hips against him in a frenzy of abandonment. He undressed her. She clung to him with wild pleasure. She was still rotating her hips when he entered her. The warm wet walls sucked in his organ. He could feel her coming again and again and again.

"No more, I can't stand it. I . . ." She gasped. "I'm going out of my mind."

"Good," he said. "So good. The way it's supposed to be. You're getting the best . . ." He climaxed.

They lay together, quiet and exhausted. When he left her to go into the bathroom, he returned to find her lying face down, sobbing into a pillow. For several moments he stood watching. Then he bent over her to stroke her tangled curls.

With her head cradled by his arm, they fell asleep.

Toward morning, as approaching daylight filtered through the blinds to gray the objects in the room, Merrill wakened while Gaia still slept. Raising his head, he studied her. Never had he anticipated that she would be such a sensational lay. He'd expected shyness and restraint, but her response had been unbridled, intensifying his pleasure.

An hour later when she began to move, fluttering her eyelids, his hands gently moved across her body. She shifted her head until she was face-to-face with him, lying so close that they inhaled each other's breath. Feeling the heightening crescendo of her excitement, he rolled her onto her back, and raising himself above her at arm's length, he looked down at her. Her arms were raised up to him, and the yearning expression on her face told him all that he wanted to know. He locked her hands in his so that she couldn't move them. Speaking quietly and distinctly, he asked her to marry him.

What the hell, he thought. Who needs courtship?

· 60 ·

"You look feverish," Merrill observed. "Are you feeling ill?"

"I'm fine." She attempted a smile. Every part of her body still tantalizingly throbbed from their lovemaking. If he touched her again now, she would again lose all control. It was a pulsating unguarded sensation. So why was she thinking of Dom?

He had sought to murder her. He was so near as she fell into the shaft . . . Dom had urged her to trust him. But what trust could survive fear?

Trust was a word Merrill had also used. Why shouldn't she trust him? He'd taken her into his apartment and hidden her. He'd been unfailingly kind and concerned. His ardor was joyous because he made her feel safe and beautiful. His protective arms shielded her from danger. He was consistently kind and caring.

"Our falling in love was nothing either of us ever expected would happen," he declared. "It's a laugh, but when we first met I thought you weren't my type of woman. Sweetheart, I can tell you're not the sort who would openly live with a man. I respect that. It's why we should get married. As your husband, I'll be with you day and night. The days to safeguard you, the nights to make love."

She looked at him fondly, reaching out her hands. With hers enclosed in his, she could feel a calm suffusing through her. He was bestowing strength and courage upon her, she thought. The past must be put behind her where nothing in it could intrude upon her present happiness. Dom Perrini, as she had wanted him to be, was unreal. The Dom she thought she knew so well had been concocted in her own imagination. That was the truth of it. Whatever she pretended about him was as unrealistic as making believe to herself that the framed portrait in her studio was truly her mother.

"I want to be your wife."

Merrill's sole remaining connection with Bari & Battaglia was that he would continue to handle the Ferrante estate through probate. The only time he left his new wife alone was when he went to the law office. He carried back legal papers requiring her signature for the Italian court. Gaia Gerald Ross.

"Your handwriting is beautiful. The name reads clear as a bell, sweetheart—just like you."

She basked in his approval, as if her husband's praise was the sun's warmth.

Never, until now, had Gaia felt so safe.

· 61 ·

Ferrante-New York operated as usual.

It was Merrill's suggestion that they postpone a honeymoon, but Gaia, too, was secretly pleased, although she wasn't about to hurt her new husband by saying so. Her feeling for the store and her desire to work were so intense as to be an almost spiritual need.

Days had passed without hearing from Dom, and she often wondered whether he knew of her marriage. She tried not to think about it; keeping busy was her best therapy. Although still awed by her responsibilities, Gaia was gaining familiarity with the details of managing the store—cash flow, profit and loss, assets, inventory, interest due on outstanding loans, negotiations. Gaia hated to have to pretend confidence in dealing with bankers. How grateful she was to depend upon Merrill at these meetings. She knew she could count on his support. She remained outwardly assured, of course, but privately she was overwhelmed.

Her husband, however, proved to be somewhat of a surprise in a totally different arena. Their sex was still wild and unregulated, but there were times when she felt almost brutalized. Perhaps that wasn't fair of her, she decided; it wasn't Merrill who had changed, but she! She still experienced shivers of ecstasy when he touched her and induced her to satisfy him, but she found that her orgasms had slackened off. She couldn't understand why. Merrill either never noticed or failed to comment on it. Gaia kept her silence and tried to figure it out herself. After all, it was more than likely just a result of the tension she felt in the store, new at her duties, although she now had Merrill to lean on.

It puzzled her that he sprinkled his ordinary conversations with "darling," "dear," "sweetheart," but never when they were alone, as if the endearments were for show. At the moment before their intimacy, his words were vulgar, not tender; rough, not caressing.

Gaia retained a horrific memory of how the Wikowskys shouted at one another when she boarded with them in Chicago. It prevented her from bringing up any matter that might provoke dissent. Their sole disagreement concerned where they should live. Gaia missed her beautifully furnished Murray Hill apartment and urged him to move in there with her.

"Have you forgotten you were nearly murdered there?" he asked. "If you want to go on living with me, it will have to be in my place," he'd said.

"You know that I do."

He grinned. "Of course you do. I'm too good a fuck for you to do without—"

Gaia was appalled. "Do you have to talk like that? It's . . . it's—"

"Just kidding, Gaia. You need to lighten up."

What he kept to himself was that he had contacted a Connecticut real estate broker to seek out a suitable estate. Gaia would have to be eased into it, but with her fortune it was ridiculous not to put the money to good use.

One morning about a week after they were married, Merrill began urging Gaia to return to her jewelry designing full-time. "Darling, it hurts me to see you neglecting your talent. Such a waste for you to ignore it." Etta Spring, who was present, voiced agreement.

Gaia sighed. "As much as I'd love to design more Àtrio

pieces, there's never going to be enough time for me to devote entire days to it. The larger responsibilities of Ferrante's won't permit me to—"

"There would be if you'd allow me to lift the burden from your shoulders." Merrill interrupted. "However, it's your decision, Gaia. I was only trying to help you because I happen to care for you."

"That's never been in doubt." She smiled at her husband.

Merrill sat at his desk near the window of the newly painted front office—formerly Salinari's. Gaia had been surprised when he'd chosen the preferred location for himself.

"I . . . I'd wanted to sit there," she demurred.

He remonstrated, "You're not thinking clearly, darling." He had one eye toward Etta Spring for her approval. "Gaia, see the building opposite . . . Well, suppose someone aimed a rifle at you from one of those windows? Not that I want to worry you, but we must be careful."

Etta nodded, while Gaia fought to maintain outward calm. Inwardly her stomach churned. Was there still someone out there who wanted to kill her?

· 62 ·

CHIEF DETECTIVE RALPH HIMMEL SLAMMED DOWN HIS TELE-phone, unleashing a stream of obscenities. He opened a desk drawer and found his roll of Tums, popped three in his mouth, and punched out a number on the office intercom. "Get your ass in here," he bellowed.

If there was one place O'Reilly disliked, it was the pea-green office of his superior. It always meant bad news. Himmel was staring at him now with that horrible frog face of his. I'm in for it, he thought.

"I've been told to kick you off the Ferrante case," Himmel said bluntly.

"What?" O'Reilly could feel the heat of indignation rising from his back to his shirt collar. "But the case is still—"

"There's this fed agent—John Davis, he said his name was—who claims you're involving yourself in matters that are better handled by the FBI than by NYPD."

O'Reilly pummeled a fist into the palm of his other hand. "It proves that I'm onto something. And they're not."

"Yeah? Tell me about it."

"How about a fortune in jewelry hoarded during World War Two, and worth somewhere in the hundreds of millions? That's bucks, good old American greenbacks."

"Any idea where it's stashed?"

"I'll come to that. Let me tell you from the beginning?"

Himmel regarded him through a cloud of smoke. "Go ahead," he said.

"It goes back in time. I asked myself why an orphan suddenly inherited an estate of great value from a grandfather to whom she never suspected she was related. In Chicago it struck me as peculiar that there was no existing birth certificate for her when she was supposed to have been born there. Not in church records that relate to the orphanage; not on microfilm lists of Chicago births. Gaia Gerald could be a genuine heiress. Most likely she's been set up. I began to question the coincidence that she was working as a designer for the very store she subsequently inherited. Coincidence always makes me curious.

"Since I reached a dead end, so to speak, with her background, I decided to dig into the store's history in New York. Seems there was an Italian Jew, name of Leo Unger, later changed to Ungaro, who opened the Fifth Avenue store in the 1930s when Mussolini first began bearing down on the Jews.

"This guy Unger-Ungaro, actually founded the store many years earlier in Rome. Ferrante came into the business later on and worked for him at first. Mussolini played cozy with Hitler, and pretty soon the SS was busy shipping Jews out of Rome to German concentration camps. That's precisely when the New York store's name was changed from Ungaro to Ferrante. Oh . . . and another *coincidence*. The Germans captured and killed Leo Unger. Changing his name to Ungaro didn't save him. He was unmarried—with no family. Ferrante took all.

"Unger had used the two stores—the one in Rome and the one in this city—as an escape route to funnel Jewish money as long as he was able to operate. Possessions were converted into expensive jewelry that was supposedly consigned to the New York establishment. Actually, when the shipments arrived here, they were administered by an American Jewish trust, to be held for distribution when the war ended and surviving claimants came forward. There's a list of hundreds of Italian-Jewish names. I saw the list."

"Was distribution ever made?"

"In small part. The largest portion of jewelry remains in Italy. Hidden to this day."

"Any idea where it is?"

"Dom Perrini may know. He travels back and forth to Rome pretty often. He's still a board member of Ferrante-New York; *he's been on the board of directors all along.*"

"Then you're implying that the girl was brought in as an heiress because they intended for the fortune in jewelry to surface. They'd grab it for themselves and the so-called heiress would take the blame for the theft."

"That's it."

"Bronf, Roselli, and Smith sure as hell aren't going to enlighten us. Pull in Perrini for interrogation."

"I can't. He's skipped to Rome. I request department permission to go after him."

"You have no authority in Italy."

"I'll work through the Rome police. I walked a beat in Little Italy; I learned enough Italian to get along. What I want is to tail Perrini. I'm convinced he will lead us to the cache."

"O'Reilly, if all this is true, why do you suppose there were attempts on the girl's life?"

"I'm not sure. I'm calling it stupid mob vengeance. She did, after all, oust the three directors from the board."

"Yeah, but if they snuff her, she's obviously not going to be around to take the fall when the jewels surface. How does that follow?"

"I don't think they knew what they were getting when they picked her. She's feisty, and they know damn well she isn't going to cooperate."

"Do you suppose that now they're going to set up Perrini?"

"Sacrificing one of their own? Could be, but I strongly doubt that. He may be planning on dumping them and going after the loot solo. Anyway, all the answers are somewhere in Rome with him."

"You're convinced of that?"

"Absolutely."

"Okay, O'Reilly. I'm ready to go to bat for you upstairs. I'll get you some traveling money. Only, for God's sake, try to keep your expenses low. You've got your passport?"

"Sure I do. Remember, I went to Ireland last year on vacation."

"O'Reilly, you're soon gonna be the best-looking mick in Rome!"

· 63 ·

The elderly's woman's murder went unreported in the city's newspapers, neither did any television or radio reporter make mention of her slaying.

It happened in a cramped dark apartment two flights above a courtyard. A horrified superintendent had reported it to the police.

Homicide detectives foraged through tightly packed bureau drawers, sifting through mementos of a happier existence. There were mostly faded photos of family groupings taken years ago. In some of the pictures, Roman landmarks were evident in the background; and since the deceased woman had an Italian surname, this was logical.

Whatever past affluence was indicated by the photographs, this household was obviously lacking the amenities money could provide. The furnishings were shabby, likely to be dumped on the sidewalk for sanitation department pickup. The small closets held nothing of value.

All of which made it odd that the murder weapon was the heavy antique silver candlestick now lying on the floor beside her. Blood had congealed on its polished surface; blackish-red blood matted the woman's gray hair. Rigor mortis had stiffened her body into the crumpled position of her fall.

The door bore no evidence of break-in; the windows hadn't

been tampered with. It was obvious that the victim had admitted her final visitor a couple of days earlier, according to a coroner's report.

The report also stated that this was by no means a crime of sexual violence. The single bed in the narrow bedroom was neatly made up; the body, save for the blows to the back of the head, was untouched. There was no indication that robbery had taken place.

A telephone placed on a table next to the bed had been dusted for fingerprints; there were none except the victim's. One of the detectives flipped through the pages of a personal directory of names and numbers. In prominent proportion were listings of Jewish philanthropic organizations. Individual names were occasionally crossed out with the Italian word *morto* penned alongside. On the page bearing an *F* was a single entry: the name and telephone of Ferrante-New York.

"Odd!" the detective muttered. "This lady wasn't likely to be a customer. Poor old soul probably lived in a fantasy world. There're sure no signs of wealth around here."

The candlestick was carefully picked up and sheathed in plastic. The killer had made an effort to wipe it clean of fingerprints, but there was evidence that this was done swiftly. A check would automatically be made of the remaining smudged prints.

It hadn't seemed relevant to note the maker's name and the style number engraved on the candlestick base.

FERRANTE-ROMA
MODELLO 1933-A65

Two detectives sat in their unmarked car, double-parked in front of the dingy apartment building. Afternoon shadows slanted into the side street. To the west the sky was a bright blue.

"Let me check it out before we drive away." In a terse dry tone, the younger of the two noted a few items, reading from his pad. "Victim DOA. Name: Celeste Shapira. Motive unknown. Apparently, not robbery. We have weapon. Prints are blurry but there's a chance they can be matched . . ."

"Anything else?"

"Oh, the naturalization papers. She was a naturalized American citizen, born in Rome, Italy. Oh, yeah, there's this." He held out the telephone bill. "It's the same number as on the phone upstairs, but the bill isn't addressed to her; it's to the Committee for the Preservation of Italian-Jewish Assets. Assets! Did you see any?"

"Nothing except that candlestick someone bopped her with."

In both men's minds it was clear that this was another murder that wasn't ever going to be solved.

"Let's stop for coffee."

"Good idea."

· 64 ·

"THERE ARE NINE SPECIFIC FRAGRANCE CATEGORIES," THE
chemist for the rare-essence manufacturer was saying. "*Oriental* is sultry. *Modern* is synthetic. *Spicy* is pungent. *Woodsy-mossy* is oak moss combined with wood scents. *Citrus* is
self-explanatory. *Green* is a melange of grasses and leaves.
Fruity says what it is. *Solitary floral* is one flower. *Floral bouquet*
is the most popular. That's what your perfume is. I detect
jasmine, a touch of rose, the delicacy of iris with an undertone
of Oriental sandalwood—an exquisite balance. Naturally, the
correct proportions must be ascertained. Not a difficult procedure since we have the basic formula."

Gaia was seated on a gold and white upholstered chair in
an elegant little consultation room. She had been unaware of
how tightly she was clenching her hands until now. She kept
seeing in snapshot flashes the villa bedchamber where she'd
discovered the mauve perfume bottle. But in reality she was
in an old West Side factory loft building, where Fragrance
Specialists Inc., commissioned by most of the New York cosmetic houses to formulate and manufacture perfume, maintained an office and lab.

Miles Tuchelin, who had accompanied her, leaned forward.
"I told you Dr. Wilton was the person to whom to take this."
He was ebullient. "He's known throughout the perfume

trade as a *nose*. It is the highest accolade for anyone in the business."

Gaia was delighted. "I'm so grateful," she said. "Dr. Wilton, you can't believe how long I've been going from one perfume counter to another sniffing the samples."

"And never finding what you were seeking?" He waved a glass testing wand in front of her. "This was worthy of your perseverance. It is, indeed, lovely."

"Will you be able to make up a small amount for me?"

"As a sample?"

"For my personal use."

Miles was astonished. "Gaia, I thought the reason for our coming here was because you intended to market the perfume."

"Miles—" If it weren't for Miles, she wouldn't be here. When she had first confided in him, it was out of frustration at her inability to match the perfume. He immediately researched which was the most competent laboratory, and escorted her when her husband refused to.

Merrill had been enraged. "I won't assume responsibility for your safety if you leave the store without me." He'd vented his disapproval. "I have no time for such nonsense."

She had just begun to feel safe again, and it was due to Merrill's caring presence. But why couldn't he understand?

"Merrill, I've explained how important this perfume is to me."

"It's old junk."

His words stung as though she'd been slapped. "How can you say that when you know it was Angela Maria's?"

He looked startled, as if realizing he'd been unnecessarily vehement. Merrill smiled slightly. "If it means that much to you—go play with your perfume. But if anything happens to you, I'm not to blame."

There were times—whenever he was crossed, she noticed—that Merrill tended to be caustic. This husband of hers, who had avowed himself her protector, was a very difficult man. She imagined him as having porcupine quills on his psyche. By way of apology, he would often explain that his annoyance with her was due to the enormous tension incurred because he was guarding her safety.

"I'm never really out of sorts with you," he said.

She wanted to believe him. Simply because she had strong feelings about something was no reason to hope for his agreement. Merrill was a here-and-now man, a realist. And she had to accept that.

He was especially adamant in his ideas of how the store should be operated. Many times, she found herself in disagreement with him. But she would invariably convince herself that he had far more practical knowledge than she did, and she'd back down. This wasn't the same as accepting Merrill's opinion for the sake of peace, but that of recognizing (she told herself) his business acumen.

When she looked across the office and saw him working at his window desk, she was reminded of how ambitious he was. She would feel happy, then. His drive was strong and advantageous.

One afternoon she went to stand beside him, gazing over his shoulder at what he was working on. She impulsively leaned down and, placing her arms about his neck, kissed him on the spot where his cheek emerged from its blanket of dark beard, which she admired.

"Stop it, Gaia! What are you doing?"

"I was only . . . showing you how I feel," she murmured, hurt but trying to keep her voice light.

Then his tone grew softer. "I want you as my private woman, not for an office affair. Be a good girl. Go back to what you were doing."

"I can't believe you don't intend to market the perfume under the Ferrante label," Miles declared when they sat together in a taxi on their way back. It was 4:30, and, as usual, traffic was blocked curb to curb on the crosstown street. "How can I convince you that a perfume will make a statement for the store? Imagine the publicity!"

"I'm not sure," Gaia said.

"Not sure? You've heard of First de Van Cleef and Arpels, Le Must de Cartier, Tiffany's hand-carved rock-crystal flacon containing Elsa Peretti's signature perfume. If our competitors sell perfume—"

"I know, and I would agree, except—"

"Except what? Gaia, talk to me. This is your old friend Miles. Have I ever led you wrong?"

"I'm concerned whether Merrill will approve."

"Merrill? What's *he* got to do with making creative decisions? He is the firm's legal counsel."

"And my husband."

Miles Tuchelin fell silent. After a moment, he couldn't hold back. "Are you happy, Gaia?"

Startled, she attempted to smile. "Why on earth wouldn't I be?"

"Doesn't the idea of having a Ferrante perfume excite you?"

"Of course, it does. You mean I should make my own decisions, don't you?"

"You're the one who said it."

"Yes, yes, you're right." Her face lit up. "What do you say to naming it Angela Maria?"

"Not much. I'm afraid the name is meaningless to anyone other than you."

"We could use just the initials . . . A.M."

"No good. It sounds like morning. Remember that it's P.M. that counts. A perfume must impart mystery, imply sensuous night activity."

"Shall we use the store's name? Our most expensive jewelry is worn by our customers at night . . . to the theatre, restaurants, charity balls."

"Worn at night, yes, but not in bed," he archly corrected her.

"You're making perfume sound pornographic," she protested.

"Isn't it supposed to be? Haven't you seen perfume ads lately?" Then Miles whooped. "I've got it! Are you ready for this? Our in-house perfume will be marketed under an initial, but not what you suggested." Being a showman, he significantly paused. Reaching in his pocket, he withdrew an envelope. On the blank back of it, he drew:

She studied it, creasing her brow. "I can understand the *F* stands for *Ferrante*, but . . . oh, Miles, can we do this?"

"Of course!" He was elated. "There's nothing like the word *fuck*—implied of course—to make things sell. And I suggest we ticket it at three hundred dollars an ounce. At that price, vulgar becomes chic."

"I'm not sure."

"Because you're shocked?"

"Yes. I'll ask Merrill."

"Gaia—"

"Yes, all right, I'll think about it. I'll make the decision."

"Fair enough. Let's talk about something else. I'm preparing an ad campaign for the Roman pendants. I'll show you proofs when we get back in the store." He glanced ahead through the cab windshield. "That is, if the traffic ever moves." He sighed. Then he said, "Oh, by the way, is there any truth to the rumor going around the store that the *Avanti* will be sold?"

She was dumbfounded. There wasn't a person on the staff who didn't know that an electronically protective glass column was presently being constructed at great expense to place the flawless pink diamond on permanent display within the store. "It's unbelievable that anyone would say—" she sputtered.

"All I can tell you is that word's going around that the *Avanti* has already been offered to European brokers for over fifteen million U.S. dollars."

"Impossible!"

"It's what I hear."

"I would never sanction it."

"Someone evidently did."

"There you go again, accepting gossip as truth. You should know better."

"What I *know* is who plans to sell it."

She stared at him, having to clear her throat before she could continue. "Who does?"

"On second thought, maybe you're right and it is nothing but gossip."

"Tell me who."

"I'd rather not say, in case I'm wrong."

"It's my right to know. I'll find out whether you tell me or not."

"If the story has no substance, I wouldn't want to implicate an innocent person."

"Miles!"

"Forget I said anything."

"How can I?"

· 65 ·

AN ELDERLY MAN HOBBLED ACROSS THE HOTEL EXCELSIOR LOBBY.
Entering one of the elevators, he ascended to the uppermost
floor. His name had been announced to the occupant of a suite
that he unhappily discovered to be at the far end of a long
corridor. He was gravely ill; walking was an exertion. Time
had not dealt kindly with the former Partisan Rinaldo
Munni.

A knock upon the suite door and it was promptly opened.
He peered into the American's unsmiling face, recognizing
him from a newspaper picture taken with the heiress Gaia
Gerald the day of il Principe's funeral, snapped in the piazza
in front of the church where the Mass was held.

Dom Perrini's gaze was penetrating. "Come in."

Munni shuffled to the nearest armchair and sank into it
with a sigh. Looking at Perrini, he made an assessment. *He
is shrewd. Buono!* He will quickly understand what I have to
tell him.

For his part, Dom Perrini appraised his visitor. He was
annoyed at being in Rome. Yesterday, he'd been told he was
to leave for Italy on the first available flight out of Kennedy.
His immediate mission was to confer with this feeble man.

"Why me?" he'd bitterly complained. "And why, for God's
sake, not you?"

"You know very well we're not in a position to function outside of the United States. *You* have to go." The speaker was peremptory—cold. "We'll take care of *her.*" Dom sensed that he might never be free of the grip in which he was held. Negotiating proved futile. He was forced to comply, furious though he was.

During the traffic-clogged taxi ride into Rome, he was immersed in bleak thoughts, oblivious to the city, which, until now, had never failed to overwhelm him with its magnificence.

Munni coughed. "*Signore,*" he prompted.

Dom regarded him, trying to mask his annoyance. "What have you to give me?"

The Italian awkwardly reached into an inner jacket pocket, obviously enduring considerable pain. His hand trembled as he held forth a folded newspaper clipping. "It is from *Il Giornale.*"

"This photo of Signorina Gerald and myself is what you got me to come to Rome for?"

"Look closer."

The picture was blurred from too-frequent handling.

"Do you see the man standing in the background?"

Several steps behind Gaia and slightly to the side of her was a figure in rough mountain-style attire that had better purpose out of doors than among the well-dressed attendees.

"Who is he?"

Munni grew agitated, drawing short breaths. "It is the Fox! His name is Bruno Volpe. I recognized him at once. He hasn't changed much over the years."

"Then you knew him before?"

Munni was remembering with a pang of loss. "I tried to warn Peter Lawden. Oh yes, I did try." His voice faded into a lengthy silence.

Dom seated himself on a chair directly opposite, drawing it closer. "Tell me about it."

Munni seemed to stare at him from a place far away. With adroit questioning and greater patience than he'd imagined he possessed, Dom drew Munni's memories from him.

* * *

Liberation day. The German troops were pulling out of Rome as the Allied armies poured through the city gates. The Partisans under Peter Lawden's command were disbanding. Munni had decided, after emotionally bidding Lawden goodbye, that he preferred to remain with the British agent for a while longer. After all they'd been through together, parting was painful. Hastening to overtake him and the girl, Angela Maria, he was having difficulty making his way through the surging groups of celebrants. Like a man fighting ocean waves, he made headway only to be thrust back.

As he managed to maneuver closer, he was appalled to see Bruno Volpe. The Fox was right behind Lawden and the girl. He was stalking them!

"*Pronto! Pronto!* Look behind you!" he kept screaming. But his voice went unheard.

A glint of sunlight flashed upon the blade of a knife. The Fox held it in his raised hand, poised to strike Angela Maria in her back. Munni's mind was working furiously. Time seemed to slow down. Why should the Fox want to kill her? Munni felt utterly helpless. The crowd shifted and he saw Volpe's knife bearing down toward Angela Maria. But Peter Lawden, walking behind the girl, suddenly pulled her next to him, steadying her so she could continue ahead of him.

The knife plunged into Lawden's back instead.

Confusion. Screams. Bruno Volpe made his escape, pushing past the shocked rigid circle around the twitching body. Munni desperately tried to catch up with him, but the crowd was surging in the opposite direction, toward the victim. Munni watched, tears streaming down his face, as Volpe escaped down a narrow street and, leaping to a lower level, circumvented a flight of stone steps. When Munni finally pushed his way to that spot, there was no sight of him.

Dom picked up the clipping from a table and carried it to the window. He was alone now. He shrugged, shaking his head. He had flown the Atlantic to hear the babblings of an old man. What danger could this so-called Fox pose for Gaia?

The photograph told him nothing. Although the man in the photo was standing fairly close to Gaia, he didn't look threatening. No, Gaia's real enemies were in New York. He knew that better than anyone.

· 66 ·

GAIA HAD SCHEDULED THE MEETING FOR EARLY AFTERNOON. Merrill didn't show up and Dom Perrini was in Rome. Under discussion was the new marketing campaign for $\mathcal{F}$ ... As the meeting progressed, Gaia found herself glancing again and again toward the door, expecting Merrill to come in at any moment.

The conference had gone on for three and a half hours. All present were enthusiastic about the ads—they were fresh, provocative, daring even. The faces at the table, on the other hand, were pale and tired. Gaia asked for a motion that the meeting be adjourned.

"Before we leave, there's another matter of importance," Michael Vanderman said. "For several days there's been a rumor throughout the store that the *Avanti* is about to be sold. I attributed it to just that . . . a rumor—"

Gaia interrupted. "I assure you, a rumor without merit."

"So I thought until late this morning before I broke for lunch. I've been designing a commissioned necklace and was positioning large-carat rubies and diamonds into wax. Not about to leave it out, I opened the workroom safe. What I did next, I can't explain, except that it was on impulse. I had an urge to admire the *Avanti*, so I removed its leather case from the safe and carried it to the northern light at the window.

When I put my finger on the catch, the lid swung up but the gem was missing from the molded depression in the suede lining." He glanced worriedly at Gaia. "Until a moment ago, when you declared it was only a rumor about the sale, I thought you knew about the *Avanti* being gone. I assume there is a reasonable explanation . . ." His voice trailed off.

She sat there, numb, temporarily incapable of reply.

Vanderman worriedly apologized. "I would have mentioned sooner about it being missing if I hadn't supposed you sold it," he said to her.

She shook her head, her eyes focused upon the tabletop. Then she looked across to Miles Tuchelin. "Tell me that name," she demanded.

He was too agitated to think clearly. "What name?"

"The person you refused to name that afternoon when we were in the taxi."

He swallowed hard. "You must realize that I was merely repeating gossip. Even now, there's no proof implicating him." He twisted his mouth to one side of his face in indecision.

Him! Gaia immediately thought of Dom . . . had he taken the gem with him to Europe?

Tuchelin exclaimed, "I'm going to call the cops and, Gaia, you'd better file an insurance claim."

Etta Spring interjected, "That's precisely what *mustn't* be done. Confidentiality is paramount. Should it become general knowledge that we lost the *Avanti,* how do you suppose the bankers will react when we request loan extensions or any new loans? Ferrante-New York might as well shut its doors."

Just then the corridor door opened and Merrill stood observing them. "Did I wander into a wake?" he quipped.

Gaia asked, "Merrill, where were you?"

"Sweetheart!" he chided her. "My bride is turning into a nagging wife," he said jokingly to the others.

No one laughed.

"The *Avanti* is missing," Michael Vanderman said simply.

Gaia watched Merrill's face closely. His eyes revealed nothing; he looked amazingly calm and in control. Slowly, he reached into a pocket of his overcoat and withdrew a balled-up handkerchief. Corner by corner, he unwound the linen. She believed she'd stopped breathing when, on the palm of his hand, she saw the largest known flawless pink diamond in the world.

Vanderman took the gem from him, reverently examining it, holding it aloft between his open forefinger and thumb for the rest of them to admire. Etta, Miles, Michael—all stared, open-mouthed, at the gleaming stone.

Except for Gaia. She was staring at Merrill.

He smiled, wanting to change her grim expression as he came closer and whispered in her ear. "What I need to say has to be told to you in private, darling. Then you will understand. I took the *Avanti* because it was the only way I could safeguard you."

· 67 ·

THE INDIVIDUAL MAKING THE REPORT IDENTIFIED HIMSELF AS FBI.

"No satisfactory response from informal request to NYPD that they withdraw from the Ferrante matter. In any event, they claim we wouldn't have full jurisdiction because Interpol is likewise investigating."

"Is information being shared three ways?"

"In New York, yes. I can't vouchsafe the same for Rome. Over there, it's become a competition as to who's going to locate the treasure trove first. At 18:45 EST today, Patrick O'Reilly of NYPD enplaned from Kennedy for Rome on Pan Am flight number 110."

"Are you requesting permission to follow?"

"No sir. Not at this time. We already have a man in place there. I await his report."

· 68 ·

AFTER HIS MARRIAGE, MERRILL ROSS CHANGED HIS LOOK. THESE days he chose to wear hand-tailored conservative business suits, expensive silk ties, and understated shirts that individually cost as much or more than did his former "law firm suits." Back then, his money had been spent on designer jeans, bold sports clothes, imitation Gucci loafers. All of these had been discarded. In the days of Bari & Battaglia, it was his habit to return after work to his apartment, hurriedly change his clothes, stop in at a bar, pick up a girl, and go to his bed or hers. Now, he found himself working with Gaia more and more closely, for far-longer hours.

Leaving the store together several hours after closing, they would share a late dinner in a quiet restaurant and afterward invariably returned to the apartment.

Gaia was secretly ashamed that she had come to think of it as her prison, where she must be locked in by her keeper until morning. Not that she was unaware of Merrill's powerful animal attraction for her . . . it was precisely this that intensified her difficulty. As their sex became increasingly routine, she couldn't help but wonder whether her unfettered ecstatic response at the outset of their relationship had been solely in her imagination—the novelty of a new partner. She sometimes wondered whether he was having an affair on his lunchtime breaks, when he left her alone in their office, sometimes for hours.

Several times, on the verge of painfully asking him out-right, she changed her mind, saying nothing.

Merrill seemed unaware of Gaia's growing confidence in her business ability; she'd rapidly evolved into an adept exec-utive who was subtly repositioning Ferrante-New York. For instance, in the past, Salinari had allowed trayfuls of multimillion-dollar gems to be kept on hand for the occa-sional customer who could afford to select such an extrava-gant bauble—a screen star, a corrupt politician, a rock favorite, an oil-rich Arab—and walk out that day with his or her purchase.

Gaia decided to diminish the inventory of large stones.

"Upon a customer's request, from now on we'll cull the wholesale market to come up with an appropriate stone. We still won't lose the customer."

What she said was practical and made good sense. Etta Spring silently approved.

But selling off excess stock to obtain working capital was not to be compared with selling the *Avanti*. The spectacular pink diamond was to be the store's symbol, an adjunct to its silver-candlestick motif. She had copied the oval cut of the *Avanti* in her design for the perfume bottle, and had arranged with Dr. Wilton to tint *F* . . . pink.

"I can bet you're popping to know why I took the *Avanti*," Merrill said.

She answered carefully, seeking to control her rage. "I was surprised to find you were casually carrying it around with you."

"It was the safest way to conceal it."

"The *only* secure place for the *Avanti* is when it is locked in the vault. How dare you have taken it? You know how valuable that diamond is."

"Which is why I had it."

Gaia threw out her tightly clenched hands in exasperation. "Enough! Don't play games with me, and don't suppose I'm ignorant of the ruse you employed in order to take it. If it was anyone but you, they'd be fired—no, not fired—turned over to the police for theft."

"My, my, we're overly excited. Stop jumping to the wrong conclusions. I took that stone because I look out for your interests. Not that you apparently appreciate it, my love."

As angry as she was, in a corner of Gaia's mind, it registered that he was addressing her with endearments. *And they were alone!* She drew a deep breath before continuing. "I have been informed of the way you misrepresented your authority when you took the *Avanti.*"

"I did not! Baby, that's hurtful. You no longer trust me, I see. *I* admit how I obtained the stone. I wish to emphasize that I did it for you."

Confused, she lowered her eyes, trying not to allow him to capture her gaze in his, where she would be locked in what she always thought of as a powerful visual embrace. Nevertheless, her accusation must be spoken.

"You forged my signature to a typewritten note stating I authorized you to remove it from safekeeping. Don't deny it. I've seen the paper."

"Did you denounce it as a forgery?"

"I was too embarrassed—no, make that *ashamed*—that my husband would deceive me."

"Okay, I've heard enough. Now *you* listen. I said I took the stone on your behalf, and that's what I did! I may have gone behind your back to obtain it. I did that for you, too! Gaia, I avoided telling you this sooner, but your suspicions leave me no choice. So here goes: You have been saddled with running the store when, ultimately, there's every likelihood you are going to be victimized."

Her eyes widened in alarm. "Has there been another attempt on my life that I'm unaware of?"

"Nothing like that. It's your presumed Aunt Silvia. She's commenced legal proceedings in Italy to deprive you of your share in her father's estate. I want to liquidate some of Ferrante-New York's assets—while you still have control. Sure, I wanted to sell the *Avanti.*"

About to reply, she changed her mind, swallowing hard. Looking at him for his answer, she remarked, "You assured me that my inheritance was valid."

"Yes, of course it is."

"If that's true, why should I worry about her suit?"

"Because one can never tell which way a case may go. Selling the stone would be insurance."

"No. Absolutely not."

"It's your smartest move."

"Merrill, I said no!"

He studied her determination as she stood with fists clenched. "You'd better think differently before it's too late."

"Late or early, this isn't open for discussion."

"Not even if you wind up as just another Ferrante-New York employee waiting to be sacked?"

Gaia studied him for a few moments, and then turned her head away from him, speaking slowly and softly, as if to herself. "All my life I yearned to find my family. The perfume was important to me because I fantasized it had been my mother's. I wanted so desperately to belong somewhere—to have a heritage. If Hugh and Angela Maria weren't my parents, then I belong nowhere again."

"You do belong . . . to me. Sweetheart, it's up to me to take care of you—to look out for your interests."

"Will you file countersuit?"

"That would be expensive. It's another reason we have to take everything out of the business that we can get our hands on."

"I don't think so—and I won't do that as long as I am Ferrante-New York's owner."

"That's stupid!"

She turned on him. "If you consider me stupid, did you marry me for the not-so-stupid money?"

"You're upset. Don't—"

"You bet I'm upset." She was amazed to find herself openly,

uncontrollably crying. "Merrill, I want to move back into my old apartment."

"If that's what will comfort you, okay. I'll come with you."

"You always refused to."

"Right now I can see how distressed you are, and you need me with you."

"I need to be alone."

"Honey, I can't let you go. You're my wife and I happen to love you very much."

She was emboldened. "How many other women do you love at lunchtime?"

"Is that what you think? You're wrong, terribly wrong. Gaia, I love *you*."

"Maybe you do, Merrill."

"Is that the way it is? Just maybe?"

He was standing closer to her, and she could feel the heat of his body, see how much broader he was than she, and she remembered how much she had come to depend on him— Merrill, her husband, who had appointed himself her protector. She had grown to care about him despite the cruel and often condescending way he sometimes treated her. He had her best interests at heart, even if he often acted wrongly. No, it was too soon to give up on the marriage. But she must make him understand that all she required was time by herself to think things through.

· 69 ·

"HI! YOU'RE AMERICAN?" A BARREL-CHESTED RUDDY-FACED MAN addressed O'Reilly from where he sat at a marble side table in a small *tavola calda* near the Piazza del Popolo.

"I used to be." O'Reilly was feeling dispirited. He'd gotten lost twice since his arrival in Rome a few hours ago, and was just beginning to feel the effects of jet lag. He needed a drink badly.

"Join me. I'm getting out of here this afternoon. Back to St. Louis."

O'Reilly sat down opposite him. "Can I get a beer here?"

"Probably German, but what the hell, we gotta adapt."

Two Bavarian brews later, he was smartened up.

"I gather you're here on business. Let me initiate you."

O'Reilly raised an eyebrow, "They've got rules?" he asked.

"Sort of. Businesses close for lunch from one to four. Then again, don't ever call on a guy much after six-thirty. He may already have left for the day."

"I'd call that sort of late to find an office open."

"You don't follow what I'm saying . . . here businesses remain open until seven. If it's imperative you meet with him—I mean, you're not going to be in Rome forever—you invite him to dinner—never before nine P.M. Don't ask him to bring his wife. You'd be considered rude because she's in his personal department. His mistress might come.

"Suggest a drink before the meal and you've made a gaffe. Order an aperitif or wine. Again, you'll be uncouth if you pay the bill at the table. Any display of money is considered vulgar."

O'Reilly laughed heartily.

"Sad but true. You've heard the old saying: 'When in Rome . . .' but believe me, it ain't easy."

O'Reilly had the feeling it wasn't going to be.

Displaying her usual flagrant contempt for vehicular courtesy, Silvia proved herself more than equal to the onslaught of Rome's traffic. She had driven into the city from the Via Appia Antica estate and, after a sequence of near crashes that didn't raise a hair of her perfect coiffure, her scarlet Lamborghini shuddered to a halt on the narrow street in front of her daughter's *appartamento*. Her plan was for the two of them to visit Giuliano Rinzini's office in the smallish palazzo she remembered as once belonging to Leo Ungaro, her father's long-deceased partner.

The idea of confronting the executor of Ugo Ferrante's estate was not hers. A meeting of the factions had been arranged by Napoleone Chirco, the *avvocato* she'd recently retained to break the will's provisions and deny Gaia Gerald's ownership of Ferrante-New York. Chirco wished to avoid a lengthy legal procedure that would tie up the estate's assets until a future court battle was waged. Today he intended to bargain trade-offs with the corrupt Rinzini.

Silvia preferred to be accompanied by an involved witness. Mara was her logical choice, although the girl seemed to have no real interest in material wealth, unlike her mother. Probably because she's grown up with two generations of money behind her, she thought. Sitting in her car, she tooted the horn angrily. There was no response from her daughter's terrace, where, typical of many old Roman buildings, greenery extended past the roof coping.

There was no choice other than to climb the four rickety

flights. She entered the building, sniffing with displeasure at stale cooking aromas wafting through the stairwell. On the uppermost level, she paused before her daughter's badly scratched wooden door. She would wait until her ragged breathing became even. Silvia wasn't about to have Mara see her less than perfectly poised.

She knocked.

Again no response. Abruptly, she stepped to the side as two young men rushed out, each with a night's growth of beard, one of them closing his pants, the other hunching on a shirt as they scampered down the steps.

"*Entra,*" Mara's voice sang out.

"Your taste in men is identical to a sewer rat's," Silvia called out disgustedly while walking gingerly over the creaking floorboards.

An open sofa bed with its rumpled bedding implied recent active use. A small table was stained with spilled foods from previous meals. Its two unmatched chairs were laden with clothes. One of the wardrobe's doors was missing an upper hinge. An overstuffed chair, backed into a corner, sagged in the seat where its springs had fallen. The water closet and bathtub were somewhere along the public corridor, and in the room a small sink served all other purposes. Silvia gazed about with disgust. There wasn't a place to sit down.

At the door leading to the roof terrace, Mara stretched, extending her lithe full-breasted body in a backward arc, both arms extended, her tangled blond hair reaching past her shoulders. "*Dio,* I am tired!" she exclaimed. "I need to rest, Mama. I'm not going with you to Rinzini's."

Silvia, who was sorting clothes strewn across one of the chairs, waspishly said, "Try sleeping in bed for a change."

Mara burst into laughter. "You and I are both cats on the prowl."

"With one exception. The men in my life are moneyed." She was irritated at having to explain herself. She'd adopted the title of Principessa and returned to European society, bouncing from country to country, indulging in extravagant entertainments with spurious nobility. She was in her milieu.

She rejected any thought of herself as a greedy avaricious woman. James Wood, the husband she'd recently discarded in Grosse Pointe, had rejoiced in his freedom and obtained a quick divorce. Alimony checks from him arrived with clockwork precision. She wanted more.

The enmity of her girlhood relationship with Angela Maria would follow her all her life. And right now, she would prove Gaia Gerald a fraudulent heiress. Silvia wanted nothing less than her late father's entire estate. To that end, she required Mara's backing.

She ingratiatingly smiled at her daughter. "*Carissima*, what will you wear? Whatever you choose will be agreeable to me. Have your sleep later, my darling. It is important for you to accompany me to Giuliano Rinzini's office. Surely, you must know it is your interest in the estate that I fight to preserve."

"*Vai in mona*," Mara insultingly said.

Silvia's smile remained fixed. She wasn't going to deviate from exhibiting persuasive sweetness. "A bit cruder than I would put it, but we are alike under the skin. As you say, both cats on the prowl."

At that, Mara embraced her mother. "Very well," she said, "if it is that important to you, I'll come along."

Bruno Volpe set forth toward his destination. He made his way on foot, rudely pushing and jostling slower walkers. He'd learned his way about the city during the German occupation, finding the layout of its thoroughfares and *piazze* unchanged since then.

Locating Giuliano Rinzini's palazzo office was easy. Approaching the building, he noted its present shabbiness, remembering that it had once been home to Ugo Ferrante's Jewish partner. And Volpe recalled, too, how Ugo Ferrante had put out the word that it was Volpe who revealed the Jew's hiding place to the Nazis. He'd used the Fox's reputation as a killer to justify the claim. Volpe had been enraged. Having a Jew clubbed to death by the SS was not his style.

He was master of the blade.

· 70 ·

THE PRIVATE DETECTIVE EMPLOYED BY GIULIANO RINZINI
presented his report in the lawyer's office, a once-beautiful
room. Its elegantly carved walls were now hidden behind
floor-to-ceiling bookcases crammed with unused law volumes,
their discolored fraying bindings deteriorating beneath layers
of dust. Overhead, paint flaked from pastel renditions of angels cavorting in puffs of clouds.

Rinzini's instructions had been to obtain all available information concerning Bruno Volpe, the rough-looking man who
had created a stir of interest by appearing at il Principe's
funeral Mass. His nearly illegible signature was in the guest
book. His face was the spitting image of the deceased's.

The detective's findings were concisely stated.

Bruno Volpe was a wanted man in Rome since World War
II. There was an outstanding murder warrant. One Rinaldo
Munni had sworn to an eyewitness accusation against him for
the street killing of an Englishman by the name of Peter
Lawden.

The detective had traced Volpe to Auronzo, the Dolomite
mountain village of his birth. He'd dressed and acted like a
mountain peasant from the region and was thus able to freely
question the villagers. There he'd heard the secret repeated.

When Ugo Ferrante ran off to Rome, leaving behind the

pregnant girl he'd falsely promised to marry, he put behind him the fact that he'd fathered a child. There was no doubt that Bruno Volpe was his illegitimate son. As such, he was the natural heir to a substantial portion of his father's estate.

Giuliano Rinzini's eyes brightened. A cunning smile spread across his face, creasing into his jowls. He was positive that Volpe could easily be bought off with payment of an insignificant sum.

Silvia's greed was threatening to upset his patiently nurtured plan to subvert the valuable American asset of Ferrante-New York. He would dangle the existence of Bruno Volpe as a potent threat, thereby restraining her. The payment he'd give Volpe would be well worth it.

Nothing could keep him from control of the estate. Hadn't he years and years ago made a contract with the Mafia chief, Roselli, who'd sent Dom Perrini to transport Gaia Gerald from Chicago and guide her until the time was ripe for Ugo Ferrante to die? Hadn't he made sure that she was declared heiress-owner of Ferrante-New York? And now Roselli and two of his top aides were under indictment for improprieties concerning the New York store.

Rinzini chuckled. Things couldn't be working out better. He intended to drop his bomb on Silvia at their upcoming meeting. She would, predictably, be so upset at the possibility of Bruno Volpe, an unsuspected half brother, making a claim upon the estate that Rinzini, the clever manipulator, would effect a trade-off. Volpe would be kept in check if Silvia dropped her suit—a simple solution.

Again, he chuckled. He saw himself as a waiting spider. The web had taken him years to weave, but now it was strong as iron.

The rape of Ferrante-New York was a crime with which he would never be associated in the eyes of the law. He was a respected Italian *avvocato*. He had never been in the United States. He was beyond its jurisdiction.

Through the legatee, Gaia Gerald, Ferrante-New York would shortly be his to control.

· 71 ·

New York

"Messrs. Roselli, Smith, and Bronf are here for their appointment with Mr. Battaglia," the receptionist said into the intercom phone.

A secretary promptly appeared to escort them into Mr. Battaglia's office. Only those who paid the largest retainers and legal fees received that privilege.

Vito Battaglia barely glanced toward the men being ushered into his large corner office. The stamp of age showed in his lined pasty-faced complexion. His bald-as-an-egg scalp was concealed beneath a hairpiece that hugged his head like sculpted clay. Without rising to greet his visitors, he said, "I summoned you here because there are a few things I want to personally tell you . . . to set you straight on . . . matters that can't be discussed over the phone since, as we all are aware, wires are tapped."

Roselli asked, "What about the trial date?"

"It's been scheduled for the fourteenth of next month—"

"Postpone it."

"Do you imagine you're talking to a novice?" Battaglia's temper flared. "That's already been taken care of. And the next time it comes up, I'll postpone again."

Vince Roselli spoke from the comfortable leather chair into

which he'd settled himself. "Why should any of us worry when you're exorbitantly paid to take care of us? Vito, what was your purpose in getting us here? We're busy men."

The lawyer didn't answer immediately. As he paused, sunlight slanting through the blinds was reflected against his eyeglass lenses, giving the impression of balls of glaring light beaming from his eye sockets. Aware of the powerful psychological effect this always had on visitors at this time of day, he played it out. When the sun shifted, he again spoke. "Busy men are you? That's precisely why I want to talk to you. None of you is to be *too* busy."

"Meaning what?" Smith asked.

"Meaning leave the girl alone. If anything bad happens to her, you'll bring the wrath of the law down on yourselves, and there'll be no more trial postponements. Is that clear?" he demanded.

"Her detective watchdog is out of the country," Roselli asserted.

"His departure didn't exactly depopulate NYPD," the lawyer barked. "Let me suggest you also keep quiet for a moment. I'm an old man and you're giving me a headache. If my head hurts, I can't think."

The men grew silent. It was a question of respect.

There wasn't a prominent criminal in the country who hadn't, at one time or another, sought the counsel of the great Vito Battaglia. They spewed their secrets into his ears, and he was never repulsed by what he heard, nor did he pass judgment on the morality of their crimes. It was a game for him. They confided in him because they knew he was smarter and shrewder than they. And they handsomely paid him for the privilege. He was a programming machine with unerring accuracy. If he liked the action, he would assign himself a cut. No one had ever protested. When Vito Battaglia spoke, only a total idiot would ignore his advice.

Following a span of some minutes, like a man bestirring himself from a trance, he regarded the three waiting men. "You may continue."

Roselli spoke up. "As I've told you, I placed an open contract on the girl. It happens she's been lucky so far . . ."

"It's you who's been lucky. Haven't I already warned you?"

"As I say, the trouble will be calling it off, but I've got an idea. It's about this guy she married who worked for you."

"Merrill Ross?"

"That's him!"

"Whatever you're thinking, forget it."

"But with his help we could make it seem that she'd died of natural causes. One of our doctors could certify the cause as a heart attack."

"At her age, with no prior history of heart disease? Absolutely not! Ross was an estate lawyer here, and that was it. Period."

Bronf turned this over in his mind. Something smelled wrong to him. "If he's been protecting her, why would he do her in?"

Roselli explained. "I was just thinking out loud."

Battaglia removed his glasses and wiped his eyes. He chuckled. "Ross fell in love with his rich wife."

A rustling of laughter.

"If I don't hit her, I swear I'm going to place a contract directly on Giuliano Rinzini in Rome," Roselli asserted.

Smith said, "Dom Perrini is over there. Tell him to handle it."

"I don't see him as a man of respect like his father was," Battaglia said solemnly. "Use him or not as you wish, but beware."

Roselli was adamant. "Rinzini is as good as dead. If there's any truth to the rumors about a jewelry hoard, I don't want him getting a piece of it. His idea to groom the girl to inherit was a fiasco. She booted us from the board. We don't need Rinzini any longer."

"Agreed," Battaglia said. "By the way, I'm taking over his cut."

"I'd better phone Dom in Rome."

"Not from here, you don't."

"I've got a safe phone stashed away that I'm positive the cops aren't on to. Oh, and about the girl . . . I'll try to cancel the hit. As I already said, I might not be able to stop it in time."

· 72 ·

O'REILLY BECAME THE BUTT OF GOOD-NATURED AMUSEMENT
among the Roman police with whom he had contact. While
they were able to comprehend the New York street Italian he
mouthed in Sicilian dialect, his unconsciously funny gram-
matical mistakes and his atrocious accent occasionally sent
them into howls of laughter. And yet they cooperated with
him. As a law enforcement officer tracking down leads on a
case, he was one of them.

They'd even let him type the list of names into their computer himself: Ugo Ferrante a.k.a. Principe di Corchese (deceased); Leo Unger a.k.a. Leo Ungaro (deceased); Silvia
Ferrante di Malvestiti Wood a.k.a. Principessa di Corchese;
Mara di Malvestiti; Giuliano Rinzini.

He stared at the screen, mulling over the list in his mind.
He decided to tack on a single other name.

Dominic Perrini.

When his requested information was handed to him on a
printout, Detective O'Reilly carried it to the United States
Embassy on the Via Vittorio Veneto. There he called on a
prearranged contact. Before he handed over the printout to
a clerk, he inked in at the head of it: "To: Captain Ralph
Himmel, Chief of Detectives, NYPD. From: Lt. Detective

Patrick O'Reilly." This would be transmitted over FBI access channels via satellite, coded to assure secrecy. Upon receipt, it would require translation from the Italian.

At the same time that O'Reilly's information was being sent to NYPD, a message transmitted from New York was being received in the American Embassy in Rome and automatically decoded.

It was addressed to a civilian secretly operating in Rome on behalf of the FBI.

A runner promptly carried it one block's distance to the Hotel Excelsior. Instructions were that the dispatch was not, under any circumstances, to be left at the concierge desk.

A telephone call from the lobby confirmed that the person was in, and the courier rode in the elevator to the top floor, where he loped along the corridor observing the room and suite numbers as he ran.

A knock and a door was opened.

"This is for you, Mr. Perrini," the courier said.

· 73 ·

New York

WHEN THE BEDSIDE PHONE RANG AT 6:05 IN THE MORNING, GAIA was jarred into wakefulness as she reached for the receiver. Before she could even say hello, an unfamiliar voice sounded in her ear. "Mrs. Ross?"

She felt her body beginning to tense. The receiver seemed heavier in her hand. "Who is this?"

"I'm Sergeant Jackson, NYPD."

"Has something happened to—"

He cut her off. "Mrs. Ross, we have some important information for you. We've intercepted a telephone conversation that partially pertained to you. It appears that certain parties have made an attempt to cancel an order relating to you. But it's my duty to tell you—"

"An order? What are you talking about? I don't understand."

"I'm referring to the recent attempts on your life. Ma'am, we have just intercepted a call in which the caller was attempting to cancel a—a—hit on you, ma'am."

She took in a gulp of air. "I suppose if it's been canceled, I'm all right. Wait a minute. Is this a joke? Who is this?"

"Ma'am, this is Sergeant Jackson, NYPD. And this is certainly not a joke. I'd proceed with extreme caution. The caller was unable to reach the individual he sought." The officer's tone was cool, professional.

His words echoed in her head. Gaia panicked. She was alone in her apartment. It was where a previous attempt on her life had been made. *She wasn't safe here!* But was this man really from the police? Would the police have handled this information in such a—"

"Are you still on the phone, Mrs. Ross? Mrs. Ross—"

"I—I'm here."

"We're assigning a female plainclothes detective to you. She will arrive in ten minutes. She'll accompany you throughout the day. And, Mrs. Ross . . . I must ask you a question. Are you separated from your husband? I tried reaching you there first."

Furious, Gaia slammed down the receiver. She bolted from the bed, turning around in the room like an animal in pursuit of its tail. Then an inner voice instructed: Calm! Be calm. She settled on the edge of the mattress, staring at the telephone.

"Hello?"

"It's me."

"Gaia, what in hell is going on? I had this alarming call from a police sergeant—"

"I know."

"Honey, none of this would be happening if you hadn't left me. You were safe with me." Merrill's voice was soft and worried.

"Why didn't you warn me?" she whimpered. "I'm so scared!"

"I tried to. Your line was busy."

"Merrill, I want to come back."

"That's what I want, too. I was getting dressed when you called. Sweetie, ready yourself to leave. I should be at your place in ten to fifteen minutes, depending on how quickly I find a cab."

"They're sending over a policewoman."

"How do you know?"

"What?"

"Just because that guy told you he's a police sergeant, does that make it so? Wait for me, darling. I love you. You know I'll protect you."

Another voice sounded on the line. It seemed to be in the background, although Gaia distinctly heard the words: "Aren't you coming back to bed?"

"Who's that?" Gaia demanded.

"No one." Her husband's voice was innocent.

"I distinctly heard—"

"Must be from the television. Trust me. I have no woman here."

She felt choked, as though she was about to throw up. He denied what was obvious. She put the phone down, pressing it into the sheets of her bed.

Merrill shouted: "Don't hang up! Gaia! Gaia, are you there?"

Softly, she said, "I'm here."

"Sweetheart, I'm a passionate man. I fly into rages. I act on impulse. I do bad things and afterward I'm sorry. I'll change myself for you. Forgive me."

She said nothing.

"Gaia, listen to me! You're in terrible danger. That's what must concern you now. I'm hanging up. I'll be over as quickly as I can. I love you."

· 74 ·

Rome

It was 9:30 in the morning. Bruno Volpe appeared at the crest of the hill and he paused, gazing downward. The street was quiet and nearly deserted. He propped himself against the shallow doorway of a building opposite the sixteenth-century palazzo in which Giuliano Rinzini had his offices, and feigned boredom as he stared at the high frieze-adorned doorway. He was observing a middle-aged woman standing at the entrance, searching through her handbag for the door key. On cat-soft feet he padded across the narrow empty street and stood behind her. She glanced over her shoulder at him. She felt a shimmer of fear; he loomed above her, his clothes were rough and worn. "Can I help you?" she asked nervously.

"Dottore Rinzini summoned me to come."

"Oh? Your name?"

"My name is my business."

"If you don't tell me who you are I'm afraid I cannot admit you."

"The *avvocato* sent for me."

"Yes, but who are you?" Her head was starting to hurt. She recognized the signs. It was the onset of a major headache. "Signor Rinzini is seldom in so early," she added, feeling foolish.

She opened the door and he followed her inside. She

couldn't think of any way to keep him out. She proceeded
directly into the anteroom where her desk was. He stood
watching her as she grappled in a drawer for an aspirin bottle.
She popped two into her mouth, managing to swallow them
dry because she didn't want to leave him alone while she went
for water.

She was so shaken up that, until now, she hadn't realized
all the office lights were turned on when she came in. Perhaps
Rinzini had carelessly forgotten to switch them off when he
left the office after she'd gone home the previous night. But
this was unlikely. Her employer was a notably parsimonious
man. And it was odd that the inner door leading to his office
was shut. This was always left open whenever the suite was
empty. Could Rinzini be in this early?

She tiptoed to the closed door, pressing an ear to the wood.
"I don't hear anyone speaking inside," she worriedly half-
whispered. "I do hope nothing is wrong."

"Open the door and see," Volpe said.

"Signor Rinzini would be unforgiving. I could lose my
job."

Grunting in annoyance, he thrust her aside. She excitedly
grasped his strong wrist, experiencing a strange and powerful
thrill upon their physical contact.

"No, no! You mustn't open it."

He pushed open the door without knocking. His huge body
blocked her view of the room and he held her in a viselike grip
to prevent her from entering.

"Your boss is dead," he said gruffly.

She dumbly stared at him while he continued to restrain
her. He saw Rinzini's rigid body, frozen in a kneeling position, his hands tied behind him, a bullet hole clearly visible
in his forehead. There was a lot of blood, he observed.

The secretary became hysterical, attempting to force her
way past him. He held her back. Screaming, she beat at him
with her fists. He smacked her face with the back of his hand,
bending her head to one side with the force of his blow. "You
murdered him. You murdered him. You—" He hit her again,
and she was overwhelmed by fear. She felt blinded by it.

Then the fear was supplanted. "Don't kill me also," she pleaded.

Cursing her, he made for the street door. There was nothing he wanted more than to distance himself from this violent sloppy death. That was not his way. He'd recognized a Mafia assassination and he had no intention of becoming involved with *them*.

As he fled the palazzo, bounding down the three steps with a leap, she was sputtering into the telephone, summoning the police. In the narrow street, he cast the quick furtive appraisal of an animal at prey toward the crest of the hill and down below. At the moment, nothing was in sight in either direction. He would make faster time running down the hill. Taking off at a loping gate, he darted diagonally across the street.

"If you're going to continue in that mood, you shouldn't have come with me," Silvia said in annoyance. Mara was sulking next to her, her feet up on the dashboard.

"I come with *you*? How conveniently you forget that you practically kidnapped me to get me to accompany you on this mission to the lawyer."

"That's a foul lie, and typical of you."

Mara reached toward the wheel. "I've had enough of your shit. Stop the car at the corner and let me out."

"Like hell I will." Silvia was glaring at her daughter and missed the sign depicting a car in a circle with a line slashed through it. She pressed down hard on the gas and sped up the smooth, time-worn cobblestones of a very steep hill. Suddenly a man loomed in front of the windshield; the tires couldn't make the car slow down and it spun into a violent skid. Looking in fright in the rearview mirror, Silvia saw the face of a man in pain. She gasped. Mara cranked her head to see what had happened and opened her mouth to scream. But no sound came out.

The man's face was one with Ugo Ferrante.

Bruno Volpe tried to fight the searing pain in his left leg, but he lost his balance and fell to the curb as the car passed him and then halted with a screeching of the emergency brake.

He tried to stand up. His left foot was useless. It was impossible to continue running. Limping, he was confronted by two approaching police cars. Further up the hill from the direction of the palazzo, the secretary was shouting hysterically.

"He is the murderer. Arrest him. With my own eyes I saw him enter Signor Rinzini's office. He killed him. Murderer! Arrest him! Arrest him!"

It is over, thought Volpe. The Fox is trapped. And this is for something he did not do. He smiled as if recognizing a justice only he could comprehend.

B·O·O·K

· 75 ·

GAIA CHECKED HER WRISTWATCH. 10 P.M. SHE BLINKED HER EYES
in disbelief. Hours earlier she'd advanced the hands to Rome
time. Having fitfully dozed during the Alitalia flight, she felt
groggy and yawned openly, unable to stop herself, although
she was embarrassed in front of her seat mate.

The woman next to her smiled and sympathetically said,
"Jet lag is a bore."

She smiled back, stifling yet another yawn. The seat belt
sign went on as they prepared to land at Leonardo da Vinci.

That morning, while waiting to board her flight at
Kennedy, Gaia had made last-minute telephone calls.

To Etta Spring. "I'll call you from Rome," she said. "While
I'm away keep the *Avanti* safe. Under no circumstances is it
to be removed."

"Is Mr. Ross in agreement?"

Gaia thought before replying. She hadn't left any note for
Merrill at her apartment. "My—my husband isn't aware I'm
going away. What I mean is . . . would you—?"

Etta Spring's voice was matter-of-fact. "I'll tell him."

"And about the *Avanti*, you'd better have it removed from
the workroom safe and placed in the basement vault. And
Etta—thanks."

When she phoned Miles, he was curious about her sudden decision to leave New York. She didn't want to tell him the truth, that a hired killer was stalking her and she was too afraid to stay. After speaking to Merrill earlier in the morning, she was terrified, unable to judge whether the woman en route to her apartment was a police detective or her potential murderer. As much as she'd grown to rely on him, she had too much pride to tell him that she was deeply wounded by his infidelity, and she needed time away to figure out what to do. No, she couldn't confide either of her reasons for departing the city and reassigning her responsibilities.

"I'll promote your Roman pendants for the Àtrio. Of course, I'll have to cancel your personal appearances." He seemed aggrieved.

"I can always make them later on."

"You're naïve if you believe that. It isn't easy to secure national television exposure. However, if you must go—" His voice was almost petulant.

"Yes, I must. Oh—and Miles, will you please watch over the progress of $\mathcal{F}$ . . . ?"

"As if you were on the scene," he assured her in clipped speech. "Well, *ciao!* Have a great trip and keep in touch."

"Thanks. I will."

She had tried, unsuccessfully, to inject a note of gaiety. If she was escaping her dangers and worries, why then did she feel so miserable? Why had she instinctively chosen to go to Rome? Why go back to the painful memories of her happiness with Dom? But it was more than that.

The truth or denial of her new identity lay somewhere within that city. More precisely, in Ugo Ferrante's Via Appia Antica villa. Somehow she must gain entry to it. Once and for all, she needed to know whether her $\mathcal{F}$ . . . was really Angela Maria's perfume.

If no Ferrante blood coursed through her veins, it was better to find out—one way or another.

· 76 ·

In New York, Gaia was frequently recognized on the street as the Cinderella Girl. On the cover of the *Daily News;* in a piece on her in *People;* in a montage in *W;* and of course in the tabloids, Gaia was drooled over: young, beautiful, and an heiress! She also happened to be a talented designer, and after her inheritance, her Àtrio jewelry became even more desired.

In Rome, she walked in happy anonymity on the nighttime Via Veneto. Her Italian was adequate; she seemed to blend into the wealthy crowd and tried to ignore the ogling stares of men pressing close. A couple of times her behind was pinched and amatory suggestions were breathed into her ear. She'd revert to the indignant American. "Lay off!" "Get your hands off me!" "Leave me alone!" Her tone and emphasis transcended language. The men usually laughed.

She'd checked into the Hotel Excelsior because it was familiar to her, and immediately ventured out into Rome. The day had started out warm and sunny; she'd walked for hours, and feeling chilly, she retraced her steps back to the hotel. She felt lonely and depressed—all of her energy gone. Perhaps a night's sleep would put matters into focus.

As usual, the stylish lobby was crowded, and she felt

cheered by the activity as she made her way past elegant
rococo furnishings, walking toward the elevator bank beneath a chain of chandeliers.

The door opened and she stood aside, allowing the passengers to exit. Two extraordinarily tall men emerged, engaged
in animated French conversation. Behind them, taking his
time, came a stout German man, tugging his blond *Fräu*,
muttering, "*Schnell, schnell!*" A split second later she found
herself looking directly into Dom Perrini's face. Her heart
jumped into her throat.

"Gaia! When did you arrive? What are you doing here?"

"I . . . I just got in."

He glanced to the side of her. "Alone?"

She was distinctly uncomfortable. Her lips felt stiff. "Merrill is back in New York."

"Oh yes, your husband! I never did get around to extending
my best wishes on your marriage."

His dry terse tone intensified the drama of their chance
meeting.

She remembered her past suspicion that Dom was somehow involved in attempts against her life. He was the last
person she'd hoped to run into, but a perverse voice within
herself questioned, If that's so, why did you check into the
Excelsior? Suddenly she remembered how Dom had kept her
from accompanying him to Giuliano Rinzini's office on her
prior visit to Rome.

"By the way, I'm going to see the lawyer tomorrow," she
said.

"Rinzini?"

"That's right."

"You can't!"

"Dom, the time of your preventing me from doing what I
want is over."

His eyes filled with an expression that she couldn't de-
cipher. "You're too late," he told her. "Giuliano Rinzini died
this morning."

She stared at him in horror and could think of nothing to
say.

"Gaia, as I recall, we never did have our Roman dinner when we were last here together. How about tonight? I could make a late-supper reservation for us at the Hostaria Dell'Orso." His voice was warm, persuasive.

"Sorry, I need my sleep."

His hands were on her arms, detaining her.

"Don't, I—want to go to my room."

"A word of caution, *cara*. Giuliano Rinzini was *murdered*. If you speak to the police, they'll tell you they've arrested his killer, but they're holding the wrong man. I know it to be a fact. I want you to be certain to lock your door and tilt a chair under the knob."

"Once you assured me I'd be safe in Rome." She struggled to keep sudden tears from her eyes.

"I was wrong. Shall I escort you to your room?"

Gaia averted her face. "No thanks."

"Then I'll be on my way."

From the elevator, until the operator shut the door, she gazed after Dom as he strode toward the Veneto entrance. Gaia experienced a pang of remorse. Where could he be off to?

Damn it! Why couldn't she stop caring?

And why had he made her afraid?

· 77 ·

DURING PAST TRIPS TO ROME, DOM HAD VISITED A PARTICULAR ornate seventeenth-century villa close to the Borghese Gardens. His mission invariably was to deliver or receive messages of importance that he subsequently carried back to Roselli in his Brooklyn office. As the son of Antonucci Perrini, he was a trusted courier.

When he was a very young man, his idealism came into conflict with the code of his elders. It was pointedly explained to him that he was his father's sole surviving son. As such, he owed unswerving allegiance. Otherwise, he could well end up as his brothers—dead! A deal was struck. He would not assume the active role of *capo,* but he would be readily available for high-level messenger assignments.

Thus, he was dispatched to Chicago to take Gaia Gerald to New York, and was instructed to win her confidence. Accordingly, sometime before Ugo Ferrante's death, he was made a board director of Ferrante-New York.

His reward was the absence of labor strikes in his lucrative building-construction business, whereby he was the largest supplier of interior "dry" walls and cabinetry in Manhattan's high-rise residential, office, and hotel structures. Dom became an exceedingly wealthy man in an industry where it can be difficult to operate without mob acquiescence.

A private man, he rarely joined his Mafia bosses in their entertainments. This was readily accepted by them. His value to the *consiglio* was in his low profile. What they failed to suspect about him was his other secret liaison.

With the FBI.

He had walked into Manhattan headquarters as a young man. He was directed to an agent by the name of Quigg who supervised the corps of informants.

"The only honor you'll receive will be in your heart—for good citizenry. Your mission will be strictly secret. We won't pay you for your services, but you will be entitled to what we call apple-pie money."

"What is that?" the young Dom questioned.

"Out-of-pocket expenses for a cup of coffee and pie, also your carfare. You may list such items in a voucher attached to your written reports, which we will expect to receive from you on a regular basis."

"I'll absorb any expenses," Dom said. "I'm doing this because *they* demand my loyalty. I despise them. I will do anything I can to destroy them."

"Young man," said Quigg, "be satisfied if we bring down a small wedge of the Mafia. You must develop patience. Your surveillance of them could go on for years, and never once during that time can you reveal yourself. To all purposes, you will be their man. You must confide in no one, and that may prove to be the hardest part of all if ever someone you care for misjudges you."

"I'm willing."

"In the end you will likely have your vindication and also your exposure. If they are ultimately brought to trial, you will be our star witness. It may take many years of a double life for you before that happens. You must realize that if you are found out, you may be killed by them. And no one here will ever acknowledge you if you reveal yourself. You are alone; do you understand me?"

"Alone," he said. "Yes."

On the surface, the villa housed an eminent gentlemen's club. Its style and pretenses imitated the most lavishly superior fraternities in Rome. Italy has more clubs per capita than any other European country, they say. The roster of the membership of this club was comprised of far and away the wealthiest men in the world.

Dom Perrini declined the courtesy of having a club limousine call for him at the Hotel Excelsior, preferring the safety of randomly selecting a taxi. As he drove past the ornate iron gates, he wondered just how badly he was about to be punished.

Continuing along the night-illuminated gravel path, he rode past bordering pomegranate bushes, cypress trees, and innumerable statues of ancient Roman heroes. At the entrance, liveried footmen attired in ice-blue velvet tailcoats and magenta satin breeches awaited. They stood beneath a portico that was nearly as high as the twenty-foot gold-leaf-encrusted reception-hall ceiling. Inside, he was escorted with utmost decorum into a great chamber where the walls bore gigantic coats of arms representing noble families, far more honorable than the men who regularly met here. Beyond was an imposing marble staircase having a balustrade rumored to be fashioned of pure gold. A vaulted ceiling was painted with scenes of chariot races, gladiators in battle, and fanciful dragons. Illumination was provided by an electrified multitier antique crystal chandelier.

With the footman leading the way, they continued further across the inlaid marble floor to an antiquated creaking elevator walled with gold-framed mirrors. On an upper story, he was ushered into a broad corridor where they trod on rare Persian carpets. The servant paused before a shut, intricately carved double set of doors, hung ceiling to floor. At this point, he bowed and departed. Dom refrained from offering the man a tip. It was against the rules. He had been summoned, ostensibly as the guest of a member.

The paunchy man who sat in a high-back leather tufted chair, watching him enter, observed him through squinted eyes. He made no pleasantry or suggestion that Dom be seated in a matching chair placed opposite his beside a roaring fireplace. Just as it was protocol for him not to tip the footman, it was more important that he remain standing. To sit down without permission would mean that he was flaunting his disrespect, a dangerous thing to do.

The Mediterranean-complexioned man spoke in rapid Italian. "You disobeyed an order. Worthless, with no spine, no courage! That's what you second-generation American *capos* are."

"I was never made *capo.*"

"You are as much one of us as your father was. It is a creed that you may not disinherit. Vince Roselli instructed you to hit the lawyer, Giuliano Rinzini. You refused."

"I am not an eliminator."

The Italian spat on the carpet, emphasizing his disgust. "You are a fucking coward. I had to dispatch one of my own men to do it. I hear the lawyer died like a violated woman, pleading to be saved."

Dom swallowed. "I am not required to kill," he maintained.

A beringed forefinger was wagged at him. "You are required to do whatever you are told!" The man glared at him before he continued, almost smiling now. Dom felt himself breathing easier. "It amuses me, however, that the police have arrested the wrong man. Did you know they are charging Bruno Volpe with killing Rinzini?" He chuckled. "It gets funnier. Silvia, Ferrante's daughter, has retained a lawyer, Napoleone Chirco, to handle his defense. We have tapped both of their phone lines, and overheard him inform her that Volpe is her illegitimate half brother, and bound to inherit a portion of the estate."

"How could Chirco have known Bruno Volpe is Ferrante's son?" Dom asked.

"Simple . . . because *we* knew and arranged for Chirco to discover this during the course of his extensive search for the Fox."

"Why? I don't see why the Organization had any interest in Bruno Volpe."

"Because after the war, we sought to conscript him to work for us."

"And he refused?"

"Precisely. It was lack of respect . . . Our vengeance has a long arm. This foolish woman's wishes to assure Volpe's conviction. She wants Chirco to mismanage his defense. Once her half brother has been legally executed, she contemplates both Ferrante stores will be wholly hers."

"How can that be? Gaia Gerald inherited the New York Ferrante's."

"There is no solid proof that she's a Ferrante. Silvia must know that. It's all hearsay, something that *we* connived. When Giuliano Rinzini first conceived that scheme to select an orphan, destroy her birth certificate and identity, then set her up as Ugo Ferrante's long-lost granddaughter, he came to see me in this room. He was a crook, but this scheme was his one brilliant idea. He needed our international connections to make it work."

"Then I was sent to Chicago to take her to New York."

"Exactly! According to plan."

"Why was a contract put out on her if she can't inherit?"

"That was Roselli's wish for revenge for her kicking him off the board of directors. For your information, he is aware that you saved her life in the elevator shaft. Roselli is a dangerous man to cross."

"I'm not afraid of him."

The Italian shrugged. "As you say."

Dom knew that the moment had come to play out his hand. "We are family. As my father's son, I belong. A far-richer prize than Ferrante-New York is the hidden fortune in jewelry. Do you have a clue as to where it is?"

The reply was sarcastic. "If we did, we'd have it in hand, wouldn't we?"

"The story of Leo Ungaro converting Jewish fortunes into jewelry is probably just a fable," Dom said casually.

A glint shone in the Italian's eyes, and his face registered a subtle change of expression he tried to hide. Dom felt he had received an unwitting verification of the treasure's reality.

"Let's just say that the issue of whether or not it exists is a business problem that doesn't concern you."

Dom persisted. "Perhaps killing Giuliano Rinzini was tan-

tamount to slaying the goose that lays golden eggs. He probably knew where the hoard is hidden."

"But he didn't! I recall him sitting in this room, describing
how he'd searched the palazzo where his office was. It was the
reason he'd moved into the Jew's former home. He found
nothing. I think he practically tore the place apart."

Dom kept his eyes on the other man's face. "My profound
respects to you," he said. "I mustn't take up any more of your
valuable time."

The Italian barely nodded his head.

"Ciao," he said from the doorway, neither expecting or
receiving a reply.

· 78 ·

Napoleone Chirco was a wistful-looking man. His slight build gave the impression of weakness. There was nothing about him to make him seem remarkable. His complexion was pale, and his light-plastic eyeglass frames further diminished his facial features. His voice was rather high and lacked power. Altogether, he gave an impression of a kind little person within a vacuum, isolated from reality.

This was a far cry from the truth.

Chirco seethed with a secret inner hatred that fueled him every day of his life. He never allowed this to be apparent to those whom he loved. His wife and children knew only his gentleness. Clients found him to be meticulous and caring.

He suffered from an acute pain, thus far incurable, yet he wasn't physically ill. His salvation would come only if he could turn himself into an avenging instrument against a man whom he considered demonic—a man who had slaughtered indiscriminately, lusting for blood; a man whose murderous crimes were covered beneath the turbulence of war. It was ironic that, unknowingly, Volpe was partial heir to a great fortune.

Among the many acts of bloodshed were the deaths of Chirco's parents. The Fox had smashed his way into Chirco's parents' home seeking temporary refuge. They'd hidden him overnight, and in the morning they were dead. The killings were so brutal that their murderer had left his signature as clearly as if he'd written his name in their blood.

The investigating police immediately spoke his name.

Thereafter, Napoleone Chirco had made tracking him down his lifelong obsession. His parents were quiet, unimportant people. But they deserved to have their deaths avenged. The subhuman monster would pay for what he'd done.

Chirco had discovered that his parents' deaths immediately followed the assassination of a British agent named Peter Lawden. There was a key. Lawden's murder—a prominent foreign official killed in a crowd of people—was more easily provable then the senseless killing of his parents.

Over the span of years, as a lawyer, he had monitored the outstanding warrant for Volpe's arrest to assure that it would never be abandoned. Maneuvering the Italian bureaucracy was easy compared to finding the culprit. Then, the envelope from an untraceable sender was delivered to his office identifying his quarry's blood father. He filed it away.

Napoleone Chirco had long awaited his opportunity.

One day, it came to him unexpectedly. It began when an avaricious woman engaged him to invalidate the bequest in her deceased father's will to an American girl by the name of Gaia Gerald. Chirco perceived that Ugo Ferrante's will was poorly drawn, with only vague intent, neither naming nor identifying a long-lost daughter's progeny. He could probably succeed.

Then, once he'd informed his client that Bruno Volpe was her illegitimate half brother, her intent was for him to defend Volpe badly, to lose the case. He would be handsomely paid.

He didn't care about the money, he told her, although he knew it would make his wife happy. He didn't explain his motives, and she didn't seem to care. "As long as he's absolutely discredited and behind bars," she hissed.

And more, thought Chirco, much more. Funny, he mused, that Volpe is innocent this time, and now it will take an act of dishonesty to bring justice back into my life.

* * *

On the following afternoon Gaia was in her room when the telephone rang in shrill short spurts.

"*Pronto,*" she answered.

"Darling, it's me."

Merrill's voice sounded so close that she instantly visualized his face.

"Where are you?" she asked.

"New York. I'm in our office at the store, staring at your empty chair and missing you very much. When you take off in anger, you certainly travel a distance."

"How did you find me?"

"If you weren't so far away, you'd have heard me wheedling Etta Spring to make her tell me where you'd gone. She told me she's come to respect you and that she wouldn't break a confidence."

"Then, how—?"

"I laid it on her that if she didn't let me in on where you were, you wouldn't be her boss at Ferrante-New York much longer."

"Merrill, I'm not up to game playing."

"What makes you think I am playing? There's a Roman lawyer by the name of Napoleone Chirco who's pretty damn confident he can nullify your bequest. He's already phoned here. Has he contacted you?"

"No, but a newspaper was delivered to my room this morning. He's the same man who's defending Giuliano Rinzini's murder suspect. I suppose you've heard Rinzini was killed?"

"Yes, I know about that, and I'm worried for your safety."

"I'm all right." She wondered whether she sounded more confident than she felt.

"Gaia, listen to me. I don't want to alarm you, but I'm really concerned. Stay locked in your room. Whatever you do, don't leave it. Have the chambermaid and anyone else identify themselves before you admit them or even open the door."

"Merrill, stop it! You're frightening me."

"I mean to. You may not believe me, sweetheart, but you're *the* important person in my life."

"Let's not talk about that now."

"Right. We'll save it until I'm with you. Be sure to stay in your room. Wait for me. I'm flying over."

"No," she began, but realized she was talking into a phone gone dead. He had hung up.

· 79 ·

"Any developments?" Chief Detective Himmel barked. O'Reilly had to hold the receiver a distance from his ear when he answered the call from New York.

"There's been a murder that may have relevance."

"*May* have?" Himmel's temper exploded. "You're not in Rome for 'may haves,' or are you turning it into a fucking vacation?"

"Hardly, Captain. I'm running down leads."

"Come up with something or I'm yanking you out of there," he yelled. Then calming down, he asked, "Okay, who got killed?"

"The executor of the Ferrante estate. They've arrested a guy, a sort of a peasant type."

"Did you get to speak to the executor before he was iced?"

"There was no chance."

The wire crackled as the two men thought their separate thoughts. "O'Reilly," Himmel mused, "did you ever hear of the Committee for the Preservation of Italian-Jewish Assets?"

"You mean in Rome?"

"No, no, New York City."

"Actually, yes. The Committee is a desk and phone outfit. They're not listed in the phone book, but I got to them when

I was in New York. It's operated by a—" O'Reilly sorted his memory. "I've got it! By a Mrs. Celeste Shapira."

"She was murdered. It didn't strike me at the time that it could be a tie-in to your case."

"Got a candidate for the killer?"

"Not so far. She was struck on the head by a silver candlestick. Prints on it are smudged, except for one that's halfway decent. No computer match in law-enforcement files. The FBI has nothing on it. We've just put in an identity request with the Pentagon."

"Check out the make of the murder weapon, Himmel. I'm willing to bet it'll be familiar."

"What are you talking about, O'Reilly? You've been getting too much sun over there—or is it the vino?"

"Himmel, just check out that candlestick and let me know."

"O'Reilly—"

"Ferrante, Chief. I'm willing to bet you it's a Ferrante."

The palazzo lock was easy to snap. There was no one in sight, nor were any curious onlookers visible in nearby windows. The man entered quickly and shut the door behind him. A musty aroma hung heavily in the deserted rooms. Instinctively treading softly, he walked into Rinzini's law suite. He removed his suit jacket, folding it on a chair.

File drawer after file drawer was opened, the case names on folders noted, some discarded, the contents of others scanned. The Ugo Ferrante file was thick, and he sat at a table after spilling out the contents across its surface. There was a carbon copy of Ferrante's last will and testament. Numerous papers concerning business transactions and pieces of correspondence of a business nature were set aside. The final item was a ledgerlike book that read like a combination diary and appointment schedule. In the first pages were initials, sometimes just one. Continuing on the same line on the facing page were descriptions of the physical attributes of women: "Beautiful hands"; "Breasts like udders"; "Protruding stomach." About another, it was written, "Will suck." On one line were the words, *"coitus per anus."* On the same page were scrawled comments in Ugo Ferrante's bold childish handwriting. "Dry. Don't repeat." A woman who was favored received an exclamation point after the remark, "Raunchy wild one, set up for weeklies!"

For a couple of months prior to Ugo Ferrante's death, there was just this one set of initials successively entered. The comment side was bare. Day after day over a matter of weeks, the initials were repeated. On the date of his death, they appeared for a final time.

The intruder speculated upon whether Ugo Ferrante had died in bed during a sex act.

Intrigued about the unidentified woman, he searched the files. There was no name that was compatible with the initials.

Turning away from the filing cabinets, he roamed through the entire suite, seeking a safe, such as most lawyers had in their offices. None was apparent. Just as well, he decided, because he wasn't in the least confident he'd be able to open it. A further look around, and he hunted through Giuliano Rinzini's desk. It revealed nothing in the nature of what he sought.

Then he glanced at the walls of the room where book shelves were packed with law volumes. There were no library stairs, so he drew a sturdy wooden chair over beside one of the stacks. Starting at the uppermost shelf, and sneezing from the infusion of dust, he began opening each book, holding it at arm's length so as not to inhale the dust he was unsettling. He scrutinized book after book by flattening their spines and widely spreading their covers to cause the pages to fan high. Finally, a volume placed at eye level attracted his attention, although he couldn't immediately say why.

When he fingered this book, it felt smooth. Its binding was so faded that no title was decipherable on its cracked worn spine. Exhausted by the grimy routine of his labor, he blinked his eyes while examining his hands, realizing how splotched with gray coating they were. His fingers felt gritty from handling the books. And it suddenly came to him why this one shabby volume was different from all the rest.

It only *seemed* dusty.

He spread open the binding. A breeze of sorts was created as he flipped through the pages, but missing was the accustomed flurry of released dust. Upon closer examination, he let out a whoop of triumph. The center pages were hollowed out, forming a cache, with the outer edges left intact. Placed within, carefully folded, was a small airmail-weight paper. With his breath suspended, he read the message on it scrawled in a handwriting he had come to recognize as Rinzini's. In Italian were the words:

Left-corner floorboard. Ungaro's room.

He looked about. Which was the left corner? Noting where the doorway was situated, he proceeded to the left-hand corner of the room nearest to the door. The flooring appeared solid. He rapped the boards with his knuckles and fingered them. Aside from receiving a splinter beneath his nail, it was uneventful. Sitting on his haunches, he then realized that there was a corridor on the other side of the abutting wall.

He proceeded to the left corner further into Rinzini's office. Stooping, he knocked on the floorboards. One of them conveyed a hollow sound, and he jumped slightly as it swung out on a concealed hinge. The entire wall behind it, bookcases and all, jolted. Books tumbled from shelves, and with a low rumbling the wall opened out, much like a door.

He slowly rose to his feet, feeling a catch in his throat as he peered in upon the pathetic evidence of past cell-like habitation—a narrow bed, a chair, a small table with a delicate vase on it. A chill ran through him. He had heard the story of Leo Ungaro's death—how he was found hiding within his home by the Nazi SS. This was Ungaro's final refuge. The man sweated, trying to control the sound of his own loud raspy breathing.

But behind him, he heard something . . . a rustle of movement.

Dom Perrini turned his head. The man approaching him was O'Reilly, the detective who'd interrogated him in New York.

· 80 ·

STANDING IN THE ILLUMINATED PORTE COCHÈRE LOOKING OUT TO the Via Veneto, Gaia spoke in Italian to the doorman. "Will it be difficult to find a taxi at this hour to take me beyond the city limits, out on the Via Appia Antica?" A clock affixed to the building beside the entrance read half past eight. Dusk was quickly giving way to night.

"Nothing is ever difficult in Rome, signorina," he replied as he depressed a wall button to activate a lighted signal seen on the street.

Presently, a taxi rolled to the loading curb. As the doorman held open the cab door for her to enter, she tipped him. Aware that he was scrutinizing her face, Gaia flushed, never suspecting he was wondering whether the beautiful American might be a Hollywood star. While her Italian was serviceable, her shoes gave her away. They were elegant, but not Italian; he could tell.

Another taxi was just then drawing up behind Gaia's. Dom Perrini emerged from it just in time to catch sight of her. He rushed forward, but the doorman had already slammed her door shut. The taxi made a quick start and merged with street traffic.

Dom ran back to the cab he'd just gotten out of, but a man and woman were already settled in the rear seat. Frantic at losing his chance of following her, he clutched the doorman's arm. "The lady who just drove off—" he burst out. "Did she give you an address?"

The doorman's attitude conveyed shock that it might be assumed he could be persuaded to discuss a lady. To himself, he mused, So, she wasn't an actress, after all. She must be the wife of this agitated man.

"It is extremely important that I know." Dom pressed several 10,000-lire notes into the man's willing hand.

The doorman lowered his voice to a conspiratorial whisper. "La signora was headed somewhere along the Via Appia Antica. It is all she told me."

A taxi pulled up in front of a waiting British couple, but Dom brushed past them and leapt into the cab ahead.

"Well, I never—!" the Englishman was saying as the car pulled out with a screech.

An airport limousine was just then arriving. A male passenger seated next to the driver recognized Dom and opened his window, calling after him. Too late!

"*Ciao, amico.*" The newcomer buttonholed the doorman. "That guy just leaving is my friend. Can you tell me where he went?" As he spoke, he fished a twenty-dollar bill from his wallet.

The doorman hesitated while an additional bill was piled on.

He told him as much as he knew.

· 81 ·

At Rome's Interpol headquarters, a high-priority cable awaited Emil Natov's arrival. It had preceded him across the Atlantic when he flew in the same Boeing 747 as the Gerald-Ross girl. Unknown to her, he'd sat to the rear of the economy section, while she traveled with a first-class ticket.

Natov studied the cable: "Fingerprint, found on candlestick used as a lethal weapon in the murder of C. Shapira, New York City, has been identified in U.S. Army records." The suspect, who had put in seven months' duty as a draftee, with the rank of private, had not as yet been apprehended by the New York City police.

When, following his query, he received a follow-up cable, it read: "Subject presently is in or about environs of Rome, Italy."

At the *commissariato di polizia*, similarly worded cables were delivered to Detective Patrick O'Reilly.

The American Embassy received the information on coded electronic equipment.

Detective O'Reilly knew by instinct that there was no further time left to run down leads. Other law-enforcement agencies were likely as well informed as he, and he'd been working on the Ferrante case for too long to stand by and give someone else the opportunity of discovering the jewelry cache.

Lucky, he thought, that he'd rented a small Fiat. It allowed him the freedom to make his investigation without the Rome police looking over his shoulder. Use of this car had enabled him to reach Giuliano Rinzini's office in time to enter Leo Ungaro's hidden room with Dom Perrini . . . and what a surprise for Perrini his visit had been!

O'Reilly's immediate problem, as he saw it, was that Roman traffic jams made Manhattan seem placid. O'Reilly's first stop was the Hotel Excelsior; the doorman refused to allow him to park *until* he flashed his badge. He'd walked past him angrily into the lobby. No, the clerk told him, Signora Ross had gone out.

O'Reilly tried politeness as he questioned the doorman in his awkward Italian, but the man pretended not to understand. Money, he wants! O'Reilly thought. His voice became a growl, and recalling the badge he'd been shown, the doorman provided answers to the questions put to him.

He'd have to hurry. He ran to his car, started the engine, and pulled out quickly. A horn sounded behind him, and he heard cursing. He laughed and extended his left arm from his open window, expressively cocking the third finger of his hand.

· 82 ·

THE TAXI'S HEADLIGHTS SWUNG IN AN ARC FROM THE VIA APPIA
Antica as the cab maneuvered a turn onto a private gravel
roadway. The further away from Rome he drove, the more
apprehensive the driver became. He'd heard of ghosts rising
from the ancient tombs bordering the Antica, and as they
progressed through the dark hilly terrain, he closed his door
lock, visibly shivering when passing the sepulchers of St.
Callisto, St. Sebastiano, and St. Cecilia. When they reached
the Corchese estate grounds, the moon disappeared behind a
cloud and the trees seemed to menace the tiny car. He un-
clenched his right hand from the steering wheel to make the
sign of the cross.

Seated in the rear, Gaia's mind was focused upon other
matters. During the drive, no matter how many times she'd
rehearsed what she would say should Silvia confront her, she
remained unprepared. Thinking this, she leaned forward.

"Driver, do you suppose you could dim your headlights? I'd
rather not signal our approach to the villa."

"God forbid!" he shouted. "I might easily drive off the path
onto soft ground collapsing into catacombs. Those old tunnels are numerous on estates in this area."

"You're absolutely right. Keep the lights on." Gaia recalled how, the last time she'd come here, she very nearly tumbled into a recessed section of earth.

At last, they'd arrived at the steps leading to the villa. He half turned his face to her. "*Signorina,* can we go back now?"

Gaia opened the cab door. "Wait for me," she told the driver, whose face looked rigid with fear.

A part of her desperately wanted to return to the taxi and leave. But she hadn't driven this far to scurry back into the night. Mounting the broad steps, she forced herself to grope for a bell button, trembling slightly when her fingers touched the chilled stone of the villa. When she located it and pressed, a hollow-sounding peal reverberated somewhere within.

She made an effort to calm herself, concentrating on the softness of the night air filled with sweet country scents, the rustling of breeze-blown leaves, chirping crickets, and a faint whispering impression of gauzy-winged insects. Then, she heard a motor being revved; the taxi had taken off. She hadn't even paid him. He must have been truly afraid, thought Gaia. And so am I.

Suddenly, bright illumination shone down from an ornate bronze overhanging outdoor lantern. While Gaia instinctively held her breath, the door opened. Silhouetted in the frame was the elderly butler, whose hunched figure she could never forget.

"*Chi è?*" he called out.

As Gaia slowly stepped forward, an expression of incredible happiness suffused his wrinkled face. Tears were evident in his rheumy eyes as his arms stretched outward in welcome.

"I knew you would come! I have prayed to my saints that I would see you once again before I die." He began to speak much too rapidly in a dialect she could barely understand. It was evident that he was beckoning her inside, indicating that she rest upon a settee.

"Angela Maria," he said. "*Bellissima,* Angela Maria!"

"*Quale? Dove Silvia? Silvia è qui?*"

"Angela Maria," he repeated.

Gaia sank limply onto the settee's cushioned seat. She felt as though she were living in a dream.

Then, speaking more slowly at her behest, he beseeched her to wait for him to return with something he had been saving to give her.

When he returned, it was apparent that he walked in the painful contortion of extreme arthritis. She asked him to sit beside her, and he offered her a small age-discolored notebook.

It had fallen from its hiding place behind the drawer of a vanity table in the upstairs bedroom Angela Maria once occupied, he explained. "It is a blessing to see you again, Angela Maria," he said. "You look exactly as I remember you."

Gaia's heart missed a beat. The vanity table of which he spoke had to be the same one where she discovered the mauve perfume flacon containing the essence that was to be Ferrante-New York's house fragrance. Perhaps she had dislodged the book.

She glanced at Giorgio. He believed beyond a doubt that she was Angela Maria returned. He frequently dabbed at his eyes, which, upon her closer examination, appeared cataract-clouded. This meant that, so far as identifying her, he could be wholly mistaken, living in his memories. Nevertheless, Gaia felt a thrill course through her. *What if . . . ?*

She carefully opened the notebook, her hands shaking with tension. The script was extremely small and feminine, the writing in Italian. If it was hidden in the vanity, Gaia's mind raced on, it could only have been penned by Angela Maria! She gingerly held it, too numbed to commence.

"You must read," Giorgio said.

Gaia found her voice. "What does it say?"

"Don't you remember when you learned to read as a little girl, you asked me why I couldn't? I am illiterate, but I saved this for you because it is yours. I hoped you would come back." He took the notebook and opened it to a page near the end. "Read." He was insistent.

Swallowing hard, Gaia commenced reading out loud. She spoke slowly because of the emotion she was experiencing.

I try to protect him by sneaking food from our pantry to take
to him in his palazzo where he hides in a tiny room behind a
false wall. Sadly, it has not helped for him to assume the name
of Ungaro. To the Nazis he will always be Leo Unger. He has
told me it is far worse in Il Duce's Jewish restrictions that he
tried to change his name.

I am frightened for him, and for myself because I go to him
and I might well be trapped with him. That is why I write this.
I must write it down, and yet I know it will be necessary to
elude my sister and father. I hide this book in fear it will be
found. I pray none of my father's German guests are asleep in
my old room.

Leo Unger, whom I love more than my father, has converted
Jewish fortunes into precious jewelry. It was to ship it out of
the country that he established a jewelry store in New York.
With the Nazis occupying Rome, no further shipment can be
made. Before he went into hiding, he removed the bulk of the
jewelry from his shop's vault. He hid it where he is confident
no one would think to search for it.

It is underground on my father's estate. In the catacomb
running beneath the soil.

Gaia sat silent. Then she turned to Giorgio. "Did you know
about this?"

"Don't you recall, Angela Maria? I am illiterate."

Her pulse throbbed. Only she knew! It was her secret now.

The entry she'd just read was the last in the journal, but on
the page facing it was a map, crudely drawn. It was in a
different ink than the diary, and seemed drawn by a different
hand. Giorgio bent closer to examine it.

"Yes," he said excitedly. "I was once in the catacomb. This
is how it was. I remember the passage turning exactly the way
this shows it to be."

"Can you lead me through it?"

He gazed sorrowfully at her. "Alas, no. I am too stiff-
jointed to manage walking underground, but I will show you
the entrance."

"And Silvia?"

"La Principessa is in Rome," he said.

"It is important that I go into the catacombs. The fortune hidden there belongs to many people.

He shook his head. "Skeletons, only skeletons."

She involuntarily shuddered. "I have a feeling that there's no time to lose. Let me just ask you once more . . . you did recognize the way the map is drawn, didn't you?"

He nodded. "I remember."

"Then bring a flashlight or some kind of lantern—something with a strong beam that will last. I'm going to go tonight."

"No, Angela Maria. You could lose your way."

"I have the map. You'll wait at the entrance. We'll call to one another. The way it is drawn, it doesn't seem to be placed far inside the tunnel." She continued talking, more to herself to buoy up her courage. "That's all it is . . . a tunnel. I'll be out again in a short while."

The old man seemed convinced by her courage. "Very well. I will get you a lantern." He hobbled across the vestibule into a large drawing room, switching on electricity as he entered. "We keep one in most of the rooms," he said. "Sometimes the power fails."

Curious to see what promised to be a magnificent interior, Gaia followed him into the room. It was beautiful, if a little overdone, in warm colors, busy groupings of antique furniture, an ivory-colored grand piano with embossed cameos on its sides, and a huge marble fireplace. But it was none of these that riveted her attention.

A painting was hung above the mantel. It depicted two children, one of them fair, the other dark-haired. They were posed as sisters might be. Gaia stared at the brunette child's smiling face.

It was a likeness of herself.

Angela Maria. She truly was her daughter.

Now, in her hand she held a notebook that contained the private thoughts of her mother—and one powerful secret that needed her immediate attention. It was a trust from one generation to the next.

She was obligated to search in the catacomb for the fortune, and she wouldn't be afraid. For the first time in her life, Gaia knew who she was. She felt strong, graced by her mother's beauty, and full of power.

· 83 ·

THE MOON SLID IN AND OUT OF CLOUDS, AND MYRIAD STARS INTER-
mittently glittered overhead. It almost seemed as if she and
Giorgio were viewed by a larger eye, giving them the dimensions of a pair of insects moving upon the terrain as they
walked at his slow pace from the villa on a path leading
beyond the grape arbor to where ancient stone steps descended to an ironbound weatherworn wood door.

Gaia tried to remember anything she had ever heard about,
or knew of catacombs. Each was a series of tunneled burial
chambers, usually with wall niches that were carved into the
bowels of the earth. Despite her newly found strength, she
admitted to herself that it was the last place she really wanted
to be.

By now they were passing a garden sheltered by evergreens, myrtles, and cypresses. Already behind them was the
extensive grape arbor. The heavy-duty battery-powered lantern's steady ray was comforting as it lighted the path ahead.
They soon approached a more open area where retrieved
artifacts—jaggedly broken columns, portions of chipped statuary—stood in relief upon the landscape.

Just then, *something*—she wasn't sure what—made Gaia
nervously glance over her shoulder, looking back toward the
grape trellises. Had she seen a light through them?

"Just the lights of a car on the Via Appia Antica," Giorgio assured her.

She was unconvinced. The light had appeared closer, even though she only glimpsed it out of the corner of her eye.

· 84 ·

The secret communications center in downtown Manhattan was currently processing under emergency access a message from Rome. It was immediately transmitted to Chief Inspector Himmel, NYPD.

"Permission sought to apprehend killer of Celeste Shapira without further surveillance. Delay will endanger Gaia Gerald Ross."

A reply was shortly forwarded to Detective O'Reilly: "Permission granted. Effect apprehension soonest."

· 85 ·

DRAWING A DEEP BREATH, GAIA GINGERLY SOUGHT FIRM FOOTING as she began descending the shallow slanting steps. At the level landing, a door loomed large before her.

"Perhaps you'd better wait until daylight."

"The sun will never shine in there," Gaia said firmly. "How do I open this?"

"Do you scc a metal ring?"

"Yes."

"Just pull it. The door will open easily."

Gaia searched about the ground for a heavy stone and, obtaining one, she momentarily set the lantern down while she carried the stone in both arms to the door. She would use it to prop the door open so that it would not close behind her once she entered. Her heart was beating harder now. Giorgio seemed to sense her nervousness, for he touched her gently on the arm and said, "I'll sit here on the top step, waiting for you. You'll be safe."

The door opened outward with surprising ease. She wedged the rock against it, retrieved the lantern, and peered inside. More steps led downward. Giorgio hadn't mentioned them, but in his great age he could be expected to be forgetful. While every instinct of self-preservation cried out for her to flee, an inner voice told her she mustn't turn her back on this mission.

She hesitantly took one step downward. Her nostrils filled with the scent of damp earth. Perhaps she should return in daylight with the police. It was they who should explore the catacomb, wasn't it? Increasingly, she felt gripped by the presentiment that some ethereal hand would reach out to touch her if she proceeded any further.

Just as she had finally decided to turn around, the heel of her right shoe grazed against a loosened stone in the crumbling mortar of the step rise behind her and it plummeted downward. A moment later, she lost her balance, falling, crying out in terror as her feet missed contact with the steps. Her outflung hands grasped the stone walls; her flesh was scraped raw. She felt the lantern drop from her hand as she vainly sought to break her fall. At the bottom, she landed in a heap on a slab of marble, the breath knocked out of her.

No more than several seconds could have passed, but in her panic, it seemed far longer before the shock of her fall subsided. She could feel the blood on her hands, but she was otherwise unhurt. Wiping her hands on her skirt, she started crawling—unwilling to stand as yet—toward the still-functioning lantern, which had come to rest a few yards further into the cavernous tunnel, its light fortunately beamed toward her. Sitting hunched before it, she gathered it into her lap, and began to sob softly.

"*Aieee!*" The cry broke the tomb's silence. It had issued from above, past the door into the night. It was unmistakably Giorgio.

There was a deadly silence, then the sound of feet steadily plodding down the outer steps.

No, it wasn't the dead that Gaia had cause to fear.

· 86 ·

DOM PERRINI'S TAXI WAS HOPELESSLY BOGGED DOWN IN A JUMBLE of traffic. Horns blared, drivers exchanged unpleasantries, sporadically bounding from behind their wheels to argue wildly with one another.

All color had drained from Dom's face. "Try to work around this mess," he said impatiently. Gaia's cab was already so far ahead that it was more than likely past the St. Sebastiano gate, proceeding on the Via Appia Antica.

His youngish driver turned to him with a wide stupid grin and shrugged. He seemed to be enjoying the turmoil as a spectator.

"Look over there. If you maneuver around, run along the sidewalk as those cars are doing, you could drive down that street and then cut back up ahead."

No answer. The driver's attention was focused on a knock-down, drag-out fight between two enraged drivers. Leaning out his window, he was thumping his door in high glee.

Dom bent forward, yanking him in, securing him in a hammerlock. "You damn fool! Didn't I tell you to get moving?"

Although shaken, the driver was obstinate. "I could be arrested if I drive on the sidewalk," he said, smiling foolishly.

From a distance, growing closer, sirens wailed.

"If you don't do it," Dom growled, "I'm liable to kill you with my bare hands."

· 87 ·

THERE WAS NO WAY TO ESCAPE FROM THE CATACOMB WITH THE intruder behind her. Gaia made a headlong and desperate flight into the labyrinthlike interior.

Forgotten was the map in the notebook that she carried in her skirt pocket as she frantically sought to find a hiding place. She was trying not to make a sound, but her own panting seemed almost deafening in her ears. She fled past sarcophagi positioned within niches, thankful that the lids of the carved stone coffins were intact. Smaller recesses contained statuary, busts that had long ago been sculpted to resemble the deceased. She slowed as she turned one corner, pausing to listen intently for any noises, and fell over a sprawled, partially dismembered skeleton. She let out a little cry of shock, and instantly worried that her silly fear might have given away her location.

Hearing nothing more, she continued pressing further on. Several winding turns later, her lantern shone on several rats as large as cats, which, stunned by the bright glare, scampered into crevices along the walls.

It was only with the most concentrated effort that Gaia could force herself to continue walking. She was becoming concerned that the light she carried might be giving away her location. Chilled to the bone more from fright than due to the low temperature underground, she snapped the control switch to the *off* position and stood trembling in the total blackness, lowering herself behind a sarcophagus, pressing herself against the damp wall behind it.

She had to keep herself from shaking. What had she done as a little girl? She began counting slowly, by threes . . . nine, twelve, fifteen . . . sixty-three, when a faltering light infiltrated her area of the catacomb. Gaia pressed the back of one hand to her mouth to keep from screaming. The light, which had almost faded, was now momentarily brighter as the person carrying it came closer. She wondered whether she might faint and, at the same time, wished she would.

Someone had paused directly on the opposite side of the sarcophagus behind which she was hiding.

The voice was familiar when he spoke in English. "I know you're hiding from me, Gaia. Aren't you being foolish? I can see your foot protruding." Merrill! How had he found her here?

Breathing hard, she recalled that she had never been afraid of him. "Did you come to help me?" she asked, her voice as high as a child's. She stood up, bending her head beneath the lower alcove ceiling as she eased her way around the cold stone coffin. Just then, his faltering light flickered and died.

"Do you have a lantern?" he asked. "Answer me!" he demanded when she remained silent.

"Yes." Her voice was hoarse.

"What are you waiting for? Turn it on and hand it to me."

When he saw her strained pale face in the restored light, he spoke to her in a reassuringly gentle tone. "Darling, I've been searching for you so I could rescue you."

"Weren't you behind me? I heard a cry—"

"I think I must have been ahead of you; I doubled back—"

"Merrill, Merrill." She began to sob. "Thank God it's you," she said through her tears.

He took her into his arms. "We're together, and that's what matters," he said.

· 88 ·

THE RENTED FIAT'S ENGINE STRAINED TO ITS MAXIMUM CAPACITY as the car swerved at great speed from the Via Appia Antica onto the private roadway leading into the estate.

A man saw the car approach and stooped behind a row of shrubbery to conceal his presence. He slipped his gun from its ankle holster as he watched the automobile draw up to the villa entrance near where his own car was parked. Raising an infrared magnifying viewer to his eye, he was able to recognize Patrick O'Reilly, the American detective. "Flatfoot!" he scornfully murmured to himself. What possessed the NYPD to send one of their detectives to pursue a case that he, Emil Natov, had been processing for Interpol? Evidently, New York City didn't care how extravagantly it spent its taxpayers' dollars.

Natov was convinced that his search for the jewelry was almost ended: His stomach was upset, and that was how he always felt when a case was winding down to an end. Such confirmation of his instincts, the fact that O'Reilly was on hand, and sighting the other two men briskly walking, each in his turn, toward the catacomb entrance was clear proof.

Of course, Natov reminded himself, he had known of the catacomb's existence all along. He was likewise certain of its vast length, probably connecting at some point with other catacombs burrowing through these hills, unless cave-ins had blocked them. He had never intended to explore the passageways himself. Even if a treasure in jewels was hidden somewhere along its tunnels, he might never locate it. There were too many niches, perhaps false walls, and the jewelry might have been buried beneath the walkway. This was why he had primed Gaia. She would lead him to the exact spot.

Her curiosity to learn her identity had, as he'd expected it would, brought her to the villa. Unobserved, he'd watched her welcome at the door from old Giorgio, and then saw them start off in the direction of the catacomb.

He was elated. At last his patient surveillance of the Corchese estate would pay off. Now, he judged, would be the right moment for him to follow the other two men along the pathway leading to the underground entrance.

The first of them he'd recognized as the young woman's husband. He allowed him to proceed freely. She would be sorely in need of his comfort when the couple had the jewelry expropriated. In making this decision, Emil Natov thought of himself as a kindly person.

The second man was also known to him. Dom Perrini was most likely involving himself for his personal enrichment. He didn't know what to make of the insiders' rumor that Perrini was working for the FBI.

He made his way toward the catacomb entrance but decided that he would hang back and observe the proceedings. At a small distance, a tumbled early-Roman pedestal offered him the combination of a resting place and surveillance post. For the time being, he would venture no closer. As audience, he might observe the action until it played out.

Natov had no desire to make off with the treasure for himself. Money didn't really interest him; he had enough. Waiting on the pedestal, he visualized the unassuming manner in which he planned to acknowledge his accomplishment.

O'Reilly came loping along the path, gun drawn. He had no time to admire the shifting silvery glow on the monumental relics as the full moon shone brightly through a lacy cloud pattern, revealing the stone steps leading downward to the tombs. And as the moon broke through the clouds, he saw a body slumped below the upper level. Just then, the moon was again invisible, and he turned on the small flashlight he always carried in his pocket. He felt for the aged man's pulse but sensed that he was dead. He studied him more closely. A bloody skull and a darkly stained rock told the story of a murderous blow. For some reason it was familiar . . . the blow to the head, the victim's age. But he had no time to think.

He beamed his flashlight down to the yawning catacomb entrance, and saw the outline of a man. O'Reilly couldn't figure out whether he had emerged from the labyrinth or was on the verge of entering. "There is a gun to your back. Stop right there!" he shouted. The man froze in his tracks. And O'Reilly, studying him, recognized the figure of Dominic Perrini.

Dom raised his hands, unable to place the voice, which was certainly American. Warnings coursed through his mind. It could be a hired killer sent by Roselli or his Italian cohorts— someone imported to waste him because they'd found out he was working for the Bureau all along.

He sought to turn and face the man, who remained on an upper step. "Keep the mitts steady," the detective warned. "Stay as you are. I'm coming down."

Dom bided his time, but when he sensed the man had negotiated all of the steps, he whirled around and leaped on him. The two tussled on the rough stone stairs; the weapon flew out of the detective's hand, out of reach of both men.

Suddenly, the opponents froze as a woman's scream echoed through the underground passageways. Seconds later, from deep within the catacomb, there issued a mighty roar, a crescendo of rumbling that caused the earth beneath them to vibrate.

Startled, they separated. Getting to his feet, Dom found his cigar lighter in his jacket pocket and snapped on its flame. The realization of who his opponent was became a matter of no importance, for he could see that the entrance to the tunnel was now totally blocked. Large chunks of stone, sheared-off pieces of marble, were wedged into a solid bank of earth.

"Cave-in," the detective said dully.

"Bastard! If you hadn't stopped me, I would have found her and been with her." His voice was filled with raw pain. "They're in there together . . . she and Merrill."

"And if you were in there, you'd be dead, too!" It was all that the detective could think to say.

· 89 ·

<small>FIVE HOURS UNTIL DAWN.</small>

The catacomb entrance was beginning to look like a movie set. Earth-moving machinery, hauled by trailer trucks to the estate, was being set in place under blindingly bright battery-powered lamps. Munitions and explosives experts were shouting incomprehensible instructions to one another as they examined the rock crevices.

Inside the villa the police had taken over the largest drawing room as a coordinating post. The head housekeeper had been awakened and had sleepily told them that la Principessa was in Rome at a party, and that they must go away before she returned. They had entered anyway, and settled in for the long haul. Laborers' boots trod flecks of earth and stone into the fine silken-wool carpeting. They sat on the delicately patterned damask upholstery. Cigar and cigarette smoke clouded the air, and ashtrays weren't generally used. Snuffed-out butts were ground into the windowsills.

A heated discussion had been in progress for several hours: whether to dynamite or to dig. Emil Natov, in from his outdoor perch, attempted to chair it in his irritatingly self-important manner, but was unable to maintain any order. Excavation contractors and demolition experts shouted one another down. The police were in the dining room, where

Giorgio's body had been brought from the ancient carved steps. He was officially pronounced dead. Whoever had dealt the blow did so with brutal force, but the rough-faced death weapon would yield no fingerprints.

O'Reilly stood near the old man's body, and suddenly it came to him. Celeste Shapira! She, too, had died from a blow to the head. He remembered that they'd been able to partially identify the thumbprint on the silver candlestick that had been used to kill her. But there was no point in pursuing this now; the immediate problem was how to clear entry to the catacomb.

"The chance of them being found alive is a slim one at best," the excavation foreman was saying.

"Don't even *think* that!" Dom raged at him. "Haven't you ever heard of air pockets? Miners have been rescued long after being trapped underground—sometimes as much as a couple of weeks later."

"Not in this terrain," the demolition contractor objected. "The ground is a mix of soil and stone. It shifts. It already has."

"As I already told you, they'll probably be found suffocated," said the excavation man.

Dom exploded. "No! No! She's alive, I tell you!"

O'Reilly rose and went to him. "Come sit down. If you're to help, you must compose yourself."

He shrugged him off. "What the hell is everyone doing in here? We've got to get out there and free her."

Natov spoke up. "We're making important decisions."

"Detonation caps should not be placed to blast an opening," someone said. "The charge would set off a landslide, and the bodies will be crushed."

Dom felt the room begin to spin. He clutched a chair back for support. "Stop saying *bodies*," he implored. "Gaia is alive. She has to be. I'm going back out there."

He started for the room door, but before he reached it, Silvia arrived to block his path. Attired in a décolleté silver bead-encrusted gown under an open chinchilla coat, she flashed her heavily made-up eyes in disbelief as her gaze swept across the room. "*Merda!* What's going on in here? Get your filthy asses out of here!" she shrieked at them.

Much to the ranking police lieutenant's annoyance, Emil Natov approached her. "Principessa, there has been a cave-in," he said dramatically.

"Is the villa sinking?" she anxiously questioned. "Oh, *Dio!* Each year it settles more. Windows on this level are becoming flush with the ground in places. Masonry beneath the terrace in back of the house crumbles." Her eyes narrowed upon Dom Perrini. "You!" She beckoned to him. "Make them go outside and begin shoring up the foundation.

Dom pushed past her, paying no attention.

"How dare you ignore me?" she shouted at him. "Come back here."

Dom turned to face her, rage and exhaustion etching his face. "Sit down or go upstairs, as you wish," he said, tight-lipped. "Just stay out of our way."

Silvia's mouth gaped open in disbelief. A laborer talking to her like this? "Giorgio, get in here," she shouted. "Worthless old fool! You can consider yourself fired for letting these filthy workmen in the villa."

"Your butler is dead, Principessa," Natov said, a sorrowful expression on his face.

"He was murdered . . . found outside the catacomb," the police lieutenant informed her.

"How convenient! It won't be too far to carry him for burial."

Dom was glaring at her.

Silvia noticed. "Are you still here?" she complained.

"Go to hell," he muttered as he left the building. Day had begun working its way into the eastern sky.

· 90 ·

Gaia was dreaming. The excruciating soreness of her bruises was lessening as she felt more and more chilled to the bone. Gradually this, too, ceased to discomfort her.

Had there been a voice persistently calling her name? So far off . . .

Gaia was no longer listening. She didn't respond.

The workers who had waited helplessly during the night were ready for the moment when a way into the catacomb could be cleared. A triumphant shout! Men climbed down, banking the sides and supporting the ceiling with upright wooden planks. A secure entrance was forged into the catacomb.

But when they peered inside, there was no sign of life.

Disconsolately wandering away, Dom hoped to find some clue . . . anything that might have been overlooked. He recalled talk in the villa about depressions where the earth's surface appeared soft and yielding due to collapse of an underground vault. He paused, surveying the immediate terrain. That precise condition seemed evident here. As he had done during the night, once again he called out Gaia's name.

No response.

He sank to his knees, patting the earth, testing where it appeared most giving. Something drove him, and he began scooping it up in handfuls.

O'Reilly had been keeping a close watch on Dom Perrini, but during the excitement of effecting entry he'd lost track of him. Now, he urgently set off to search.

Silvia looked out from an upstairs window and watched with satisfaction as the machinery was loaded back onto flatbed trucks to be hauled off of the estate.

After several minutes, she was about to turn away when a movement caught her eye. A man whom she had never seen before appeared to be spying on the activity. Keeping a distance away from the laborers, he padded beyond them to where the catacombs extended toward hills.

Should she send her maid outside to inform the police? She decided against this. It was none of her affair. Just so long as she was safely within the house.

It didn't concern her.

· 91 ·

Gaia stirred.

The dream continued.

She was in Merrill's arms. How greatly she needed to feel protected. It was a miracle to find him with her in the catacomb. It proved how much he loved her. Would he ever forgive her from running away from him in New York? Yet he had followed her here. If he loved her that much, it was all that mattered.

"To think that, of all people, I was running from you," she was saying. "Only, Merrill, we may be lost in here. I didn't notice the many turns I took. Do you have any idea how we can retrace our steps?"

"Leave now?" he asked. "Oh no, we're staying. Gaia, where is it?"

She looked at him, her brows constricted upward in puzzlement. "What are you talking about?"

"Don't attempt insulting my intelligence. I know why you're down here." The expression in his eyes was menacing. The way he held her suddenly seemed to have become less protective.

I'm wrong, Gaia told herself. *This is my imagination.*

"Tell me where to look for it."

"You're hurting me." She attempted to wrest away from him.

His eyes bore into hers. "If you hadn't thwarted my selling the *Avanti*, we wouldn't have come to this. I'd have been satisfied."

"But that stone isn't ever going to be sold."

"So you decreed," he cut her off. "So I began to do some research. My father was Jewish, and I vaguely remembered him talking about a treasure in jewels belonging to victims of the Nazis in Rome. Until I began to think about it, it had seemed ridiculous. But I kept wondering whether it might not be true, and I began fitting pieces together, tracking down leads. I located an old woman who had a list of the original contributors. We had a terrible argument. I was afraid she'd scream . . ." His eyes clouded. Soon he resumed speaking. "An old fool was what she was! Living like a pauper." He paused. "Like that other old fool sitting on the steps. He said *I* couldn't enter . . . well, as you see, he didn't stop me."

"Giorgio! You didn't hurt him, did you?"

"Hurt . . . ?" His voice trailed off. "I followed you to Rome . . . to see where you'd lead me. And here I am." His fingers pressed against the sides of her face, and she could feel the cold metal barrel of his flashlight angled across her ear.

She unsuccessfully attempted pulling away. She began speaking with his hands still on her face. "Merrill, I do know about the jewels. They belong to Jewish people who've suffered. Leo Unger converted their money into jewelry, intending to return it to them. But the Germans killed him. That's why, you see, it is up to us to find them and then to give them to the people they belong to."

He didn't speak. His face, so close to hers, held a mocking expression. And suddenly, he began to shout at the top of his lungs, although she was standing close beside him. "I asked you where the jewels are. Where the fuck are they, Gaia?"

He shook her violently, and she could see the madness in his eyes. "Gaia," he screamed, "I'm warning you. Don't enrage me. I won't be able to stop myself."

She groped in her pocket. She would give him the notebook

with the map. He'd believe that she trusted him, and she might be able to get away. "Here it is," she said softly, and held it out to him.

He snatched it from her, opening the small book on the stone lid of the sarcophagus that had given Gaia abortive shelter. He poured over the sketched diagram, but continued to look up; he was too aware of her presence for her to try to leave.

"Okay, I've got it pegged," he eventually said. He started forward, tugging her along behind him. "Give me the lantern," he said, grabbing it away from her. She tripped over a stray stone. He yanked her along behind him, swearing all the while that she was purposely slowing him down.

Abruptly, he made a turn to the right into a small chamber. Here, a low shelf was built into the marble-faced wall decorated with faded friezes. An especially ornate carved marble sarcophagus occupied the central portion of the shelf.

"You're going to have to help me slide the lid open."

"Please, no!" She panicked. "There'll be a skeleton inside."

Enraged, he thrust her forward. "Give it some strength. Bear down with your weight."

Her already-bruised palms were rubbed raw. Slowly, the top budged, stone scraping against stone.

Gaia's arms ached and Merrill grunted from the physical effort. By now, the top was sufficiently open for him to be able to reach inside with both arms. "Take the lantern and hold it above me so I can see what I'm doing."

He lifted out a large old-fashioned doctor's-type satchel and what looked like a portion of a cracked rib.

Merrill hooted in a wild burst of irrational laughter. "Can you believe it, a treasure on top of a skeleton? Doesn't it tickle you?"

He poked Gaia hard with the sharp edge of the bone and, off balance, she fell backward against a wall where the fresco had peeled to reveal raw brick.

Intent upon the cracked leather bag, his laughter ceased as he sank to his knees trying to worry the rusted lock open. He cursed, then felt in his pockets and withdrew a metal nail file.

Working in a frenzy of continuous motion, he repeatedly stabbed it into a portion of the deteriorated leather. Forcing a hole, he widened it until he could reach in. Piece by piece, he extracted items of precious jewelry. There were diamond rings with glittering large-carat stones, a ruby-and-diamond bracelet, gem-set lavalieres, old-fashioned brooches, a tiara . . .

Gaia began cautiously backing away. At the last possible moment, she intended to pick up the lantern. If she recalled the diagram correctly and moved quickly, she had a chance to find her way out of the catacomb. She reached for the light and it tilted slightly.

Merrill looked up.

"Where the hell are you going—" he began, but she was already running; sweat poured down her back. She didn't get far.

He caught up with her in seconds, and furiously slammed her against a wall, throwing her against it with such impact that small stones and wads of earth became dislodged, falling to the tunnel floor.

He picked up the lantern in one hand and, with the other, he dragged her back to the place where he'd left the jewels. He began tossing them back into the satchel. "Sorry, sweetheart, if I hurt you," he said. "It was your own fault, but that doesn't matter. The point is, you're expendable now. There's no one who knows I'm in here with you."

"Please!" She begged for her life. "I'll sign everything I own over to you. Let me go, and I'll—"

"You own nothing!" He grew angry. "Your Aunt Silvia is seeing to that."

"I'll never bother you. You won't see me again."

This struck him as being enormously funny. Insane, high-pitched peals of laughter echoed in the small chamber. "My darling, you're right about that. I'm going to have to put you in with the skeleton where I found the jewels. I suppose I'll have to find something hard enough to clobber you with." He twisted her head to him. "First, kiss me, sweetheart. A romantic ending, don't you agree?"

She gathered spittle and splattered his face. He was crazy, totally, utterly out of his mind. How could she never have suspected? But he'd always seemed so controlled, so positive that his way must prevail. There must have been signs of his insanity she'd overlooked.

He dropped his hold on her to wipe his face, blotting himself with his handkerchief. In that instant, she fled headlong into the darkness, her arms extended toward the side walls to guide herself in running away from him in the total darkness. Was it her own heavy breathing she was listening to, or did she hear the relentless padding of his feet coming behind her? Was she breathing increasingly loud, or was he drawing closer? Gaia kept on running, straining to move faster.

At first, a glimmer of light. She kept running. A hand clamped her shoulder. She fought him, and tried to get away, to keep running. He dropped the light and grabbed her with both hands, pinning her against a wall. She scratched at his face, and he furiously sank his teeth into her fingers. The pain was excruciating; she swayed in agony. Then, the instinctive age-old defense of womankind occurred to her. She jammed her knee smartly into his groin. He doubled over with pain, and her arms were freed!

But just as she began to run again, a louder, deafening sound issued from somewhere in the tunnel. The beginnings of her scream were muffled by stone crashing, snapping, rolling with the momentum of an avalanche.

With her arms protectively crossed before her breasts, she fell toward the side, escaping the hailstorm of jagged pieces of stone that fell upon Merrill. He lay unmoving beneath them. Flung a distance away, partially covered with rock, the lantern remained lit.

With tears flowing down her cheeks, Gaia found herself crying out, "*I'm alive . . . I'm alive . . .*" until she comprehended that she was walled in, hopelessly trapped. Eventually the lantern bulb would flicker out.

There was no way she would ever get out.

· 92 ·

Excavation had reached a depth of almost five feet when a cry went up from a workman. His blade had uncovered an ancient brick wall. Dom, who had been wielding a shovel alongside of the laborers, broke his rhythmic digging. Once again, he called out Gaia's name. No answer was forthcoming. Wearily leaning upon the handle, he wiped his brow with the back of a dirt-smudged hand.

O'Reilly stood watching him from the excavation rim. He twisted his mouth in compassion and had to turn away. The sight of Dom's despair—and of his perseverant hope—was too much for him.

The laborers began chiseling away mortar binding the bricks. They asked Dom to stand away as they worked. O'Reilly walked over and squatted at eye level with him.

"If it helps you any," O'Reilly told him, "I know how much you loved her. I'd always assumed you were Vince Roselli's man, doing his bidding. I'm ashamed to say I thought you were manipulating her."

Dom was silent for a while, staring blankly into the detective's face. "No," he said finally, "I tried to protect her—from the time Roselli told me to take her away from the Wikowskys' in Chicago. Before I took her to my mother's house, I knew nothing of her existence."

"I was looking to book you for pushing her into the elevator shaft when, actually, you arrived just in time to prevent her from falling to her death. I was fucking wrong, and you were a hero."

"No way a hero," Dom protested. In an agony of grief, he kept thinking of Gaia's face, the warmth of her body, her voice, the lilt of her laugh. A terrible vision of her dead body clouded his mind. Perhaps she was lying crumpled with Merrill Ross' arms about her. Pained, he muttered, as if to himself, "That bastard Ross shouldn't have been the only one she could turn to for comfort—the murderer of the Shapira woman in New York—"

O'Reilly was flabbergasted. "How do you know that?" he interrupted.

"I received a communiqué, just as you must have. The fingerprints on the candlestick were identified as his. I've been aligned with the FBI ever since my father and brothers were murdered by the mob. Oh, it wasn't in vengeance for their deaths. I hated what they were. It was when the new *don*—Roselli—claimed my allegiance that I began my work with the Bureau. When he and his *capos*, Bronf and Smith, come up for trial, I'll be the star witness testifying against them."

"What I'd like to know is how the Mafia first became involved with Ferrante-New York."

"That was before my time. It happened when Leo Unger went to New York to found a Fifth Avenue store. He wanted it to be a conduit to save the wealth of Nazi victims. He needed backing, and not speaking English, he was introduced to the wrong people in the Italian-American community.

"Enter Giuliani Rinzini, Roman *avoccato*. He had borrowed from the mob in Italy and couldn't pay them back. So he had to tell them of his scheme involving Gaia Gerald. It's my guess he did away with Ugo Ferrante before his time, even though he was an old man. I have to tell you, his death took me by surprise. I had no chance to properly prepare Gaia. But you know, I'm unsure whether Rinzini knew that she was the true heiress. I think he did. It was some obscure, skewed view of the universe that made him choose her. That's my guess. A desire to toy with fate, or justice in the crooked world? But we may never know. We do know, though, what he and the Mafia needed was an orphan girl of the right age. It happened the mob had their fingers on that Chicago orphanage. Gaia was perfect, Rinzini knew. And, possibly, he alone knew just how perfect."

"And they refused to allow her to be legally adopted," O'Reilly said.

"That's right. They destroyed her birth records; then, later on, when they decided to knock off Rinzini, they supposed they would have found out where the jewels were hidden. It was the right time to have Gaia inherit. She was set in place to be the owner of Ferrante-New York and, as such, to take responsibility for the theft of the jewels that don't belong to the store now, and never did."

"She screwed it up for them, so they were out to kill her," O'Reilly said. "They never anticipated she'd fire them from the board of directors." He ruefully shook his head. "She was one damn brave girl."

"Don't say *was!*" Dom was too distraught to talk any further. He was thinking that if only he hadn't stopped off at the Ferrante villa when he arrived at the estate, he wouldn't have trailed Merrill Ross to the catacomb. Giorgio would still be alive.

And Gaia . . . ?

In a fearful sense of urgency, he returned to the wall. Thrusting aside workers, he began lifting out individual bricks from the disintegrating mortar. He kept at it until he made an opening large enough to pass through. Someone clamped a hard hat on his head. Another man pressed a powerful flashlight into his hand. Shouts of encouragement followed him as he disappeared into a damp cavernous tunnel.

· 93 ·

THE ROCK-EMBEDDED LANTERN FLICKERED AS ITS BATTERY FAILED, and was finally extinguished. Blackness was thick and touchable, with a thousand hidden horrors. Gaia blinked open her eyes as consciousness returned. She'd remembered how Merrill had attempted murdering her. Was he alive? Had he freed himself from the pile of stones? Was he waiting to grab her again? Moisture dripped onto her neck from the rock overhead, sliding across her skin in icy, tickling rivulets.

Gasping with every breath that she drew, Gaia managed to raise herself to her knees. She must try to save herself, but were the walls crumbling, was the way blocked? And should she begin to walk, testing each step with her eyes seeking out invisible ghosts, would she ever be able to find her way out of here?

You are not going to faint, she sternly told herself. With any luck, you will survive. No obstacle was insurmountable as she began clawing her way forward, scraping her hands and knees as she frequently fell.

But even as she thought there is nothing to fear, she felt the touch of a hand upon her skin where her sleeve was torn.

· 94 ·

ACROSS AN EXPANSE OF LAWN RISING FROM THE EXCAVATION, A telescopic rifle extended from behind a tree trunk, its barrel glinting in the sun and ready for use whenever Dom should emerge from the catacomb bearing the treasure. The marksman's plan was to shoot, then reach in and grab the jewels while the unarmed workmen reeled from shock and confusion.

He tensed, watching several laborers crouch at the opening in the brickwork, ready to receive something being handed to them. They were blocking him from seeing what it was. Nevertheless, he readied himself and, stepping into the open, · took aim, preparing to squeeze the trigger. *Uno, due, tre* . . .

A bullet whined.

The marksman spun to the side. Staggering toward the tree, he fell.

Hastening toward him, Emil Natov ran, his handgun still drawn. At the tree he stooped to feel the man's neck. There was no pulse.

The sun beat down with the warmth of a mild autumn day, but Gaia shivered convulsively as she lay on the grass with her eyes shut. O'Reilly had taken her from Dom's arms when he came staggering up from the pit. The detective removed his jacket to cover her. Then as O'Reilly raised his head, he noticed Natov urgently motioning to him from higher up on the hill. He hesitated until Dom hoisted himself from the digging before he ran toward the Interpol agent.

Gaia knew nothing of how she had come out of the cold and darkness. She felt the air on her face and the warmth of the sun . . . and that something was being done to her, rhythmically pressing inward beneath her ribcage. She became aware of men's voices speaking in Italian. There was another voice, much closer. Her eyelids fluttered open and she tried to see what was happening. Lips were pressed to hers, blowing warm, living breath into her mouth. She opened her eyes wider and stared into Dom's familiar dark eyes, seeing intermingled in them tears, anguish, and hope.

Most of all, what she saw was love.

· 95 ·

Napoleone Chirco had a new lilt in his voice, but not because he had excellent news to report to Silvia. He was telling her how the court had, moments earlier, issued its ruling. Gaia Gerald would not inherit under the last will and testament of Ugo Ferrante, il Principe di Corchese. There was silence on the other end of the telephone.

"Principessa, you don't reply. I'm sure I can understand that you are stunned by happiness. I must tell you, I hadn't expected a favorable decision to be made this quickly."

"*Idiota!*"

"Didn't you hear me, Principessa? You alone have inherited your father's estate."

"There is no estate," she screamed into the mouthpiece.

"I assure you, I am holding the court papers in my hand."

"Papers? I'll tell you about papers. Leo Ungaro's will was found in a secret room of his old palazzo where Giuliano Rinzini kept his office. Rinzini evidently retained the will and placed it as a souvenir in the hidden room. Who's to ask him why—the man is dead. What's important is that my father barely had an estate."

"How does Ungaro's will affect—"

"Ungaro owned ninety percent of Ferrante-Roma. He was the sole owner of the New York store. This villa and acreage belonged to him. He held the mortgage and my father left the debt unpaid."

"*Dio!* Who inherits under the Ungaro will?"

"Gaia Gerald—through my late sister, Angela Maria."

"What will you do?"

"I am buying the villa from her out of my alimony."

"Possibly you will be lucky and locate the satchel with the jewels that a second cave-in has left buried."

"Not likely. She is retaining rights to the catacomb until they are found. Already, law-enforcement people are searching. She intends to locate the original owners or their heirs and donate the rest to some charity or another."

"What bad luck."

"It is for you, Signor Chirco. You will not be paid."

Stupid shallow woman, he thought. I've gotten more than enough from you. Thanks to you I could play my tricks on Bruno Volpe. The brutal Fox is behind bars, convicted of a murder he did not commit, paying for the killings years ago that could never be proven.

Oh, I have been paid, he thought, smiling wryly. The Fox is vanquished.

My parents can rest in their graves.

EPILOGUE

New York

REPORTERS SWARMED OUTSIDE FERRANTE-NEW YORK. WITHIN the store, microphones were thrust forward, klieg lights cast their bright glare, and flashbulbs burst as camera lenses focused on the chest-high, slender, four-sided glass vitrine.

Inside was the astonishing pink diamond.

The *Avanti* was at last on display, gleaming brightly in the precise center of the store's main selling floor. The concentrated lighting seemed only to intensify the extraordinary color of the stone.

"High-quality colored diamonds are far more uncommon than the finest-grade whites. The scarcest color is pink," the beautiful dark-haired woman was saying into a group of microphones. Moments before, she had pulled upon a silvered cord, and with a dramatic sweep of revelation, the mauve velvet cover that had been spread across the vitrine was swept high toward the ceiling. The *Avanti* glistened in its electronic case, bonded to the floor and protected by invisible sensors. The gemstone was exhibited in a Lucite cradle. It appeared to hover in air, visible from all angles.

The television at the foot of the comfortable bed in the darkened room was tuned to the 11 P.M. news, where the screen was filled with an enlarged shot of the *Avanti*.

The man and woman had moments earlier been kissing passionately, their bodies in the slow, warm contact of a post-lovemaking embrace.

However, when the news came on, they separated slightly, intently watching the coverage of the *Avanti* as it was placed on exhibition.

"Isn't it breathtaking?" the woman asked huskily.

"Beautiful," he replied.

The camera drew back, and Gaia was viewed on the screen. Slim and graceful, her pale-pink dress brought out the color in her cheeks—and complemented the deeper pink of the stone. Extraordinary happiness was evident in her buoyant manner, her ready smile, and the aliveness of her flashing eyes as she spoke to the reporters around her.

The man in the bed entwined his fingers in the woman's soft dark curls. "Beautiful," he said again.

"The *Avanti* is exceptional," she replied.

"I meant that *you* are."

She drew in a shuddering breath. "Oh, darling." Her voice was throaty.

He withdrew his long fingers from her hair to switch off the television by its remote control. The room was in total darkness.

His arms promptly went about her body. Hers circled his neck. They resumed their deep probing kisses, their mouths unleashing a heightening ardor of sensations that coursed throughout their bodies. She cried out joyously as her body arched, then vibrated in a crescendo of quivering pulsation.

When she was again able to speak, she whispered to him, "You make me come without even entering me."

"It was never like this for me with any woman but you, *cara*. When I give you such pleasure, it elates me in a way I've never known."

"But now I want to satisfy you, my darling."

"We have all night."

"All of our lives," she said. "For just now I will kiss you and love you with my tongue."

He sighed, savoring the succession of thrills she led him

into, until the increasing momentum of his response caused him to hold her away from him.

"Enough!" he panted protestingly as he raised her. When her head was beside his on the pillow, he rolled over atop her. It seemed to them that their bodies were melting into one another.

Then he elevated himself, his hands crossing over, holding hers. There was a sound of metal contacting metal.

"Our wedding bands touched," she marveled.

"I know, darling."

"Dom!" she exulted.

"I love you, Gaia."